Praise for R. J. Ellory

'Ellory is a powerful talent, and this, his fourth novel, seems set to launch him into the stratosphere of crime writers' *Independent on Sunday*

'*A Quiet Belief in Angels* is a beautiful and haunting book. This is a tour de force from R. J. Ellory' Michael Connelly

'Ellory writes taut, muscular prose that at its best is almost poetic . . . *City of Lies* is a tense and pacy thriller taking the reader into a world of secrets, betrayal and revenge' *Yorkshire Post*

'A sprawling masterpiece covering 50 years of the American dream gone sour . . . [A] striking novel that brings to mind the best of James Ellroy' *Good Book Guide*

'Genuinely heartbreaking . . . an extremely vivid, moving picture of the human condition, *Ghostheart* is a superb tale of tragedy and revenge' *Big Issue*

'An ambitious first novel . . . incisive, often beautiful writing' *The Times*

'You know you're on to something from the opening line . . . compelling, insightful, moving and extremely powerful' *Sydney Morning Herald*

'Another fine book from Ellory, with an unpredictable conclusion' *Daily Telegraph*

R. J. Ellory is the author of five previous novels: *Candle-moth*, *Ghostheart*, *A Quiet Vendetta*, *City of Lies* and *A Quiet Belief in Angels*, which was a Richard & Judy Book Club Selection for 2008. Twice shortlisted for the Crime Writers' Association Steel Dagger for Best Thriller, and also for the Barry Award for Best British Crime Novel 2008, Ellory's books have been translated into nineteen languages. Having originally studied graphics and photography, he intended to pursue a career in photojournalism, but for many reasons this never came to fruition. He started writing more than ten years ago and hasn't stopped since. He is married with one son, and currently resides in England. Visit his website at www.rjellory.com.

By R. J. Ellory

Candlemoth
Ghostheart
A Quiet Vendetta
City of Lies
A Quiet Belief in Angels
A Simple Act of Violence

A Simple Act of Violence

R. J. ELLORY

An Orion paperback

First published in Great Britain in 2008
by Orion
This paperback edition published in 2009
by Orion Books Ltd,
Orion House, 5 Upper St Martin's Lane,
London WC2H 9EA

An Hachette UK company

3 5 7 9 10 8 6 4 2

Copyright © R. J. Ellory Publications Ltd 2008

A CIP catalogue record for this book
is available from the British Library.

ISBN 978-1-4091-0266-3

Typeset at The Spartan Press Ltd,
Lymington, Hants

Printed and bound in Great Britain by
Clays Ltd, St Ives plc

The Orion Publishing Group's policy is to use papers that
are natural, renewable and recyclable products and made
from wood grown in sustainable forests. The logging
and manufacturing processes are expected to conform to
the environmental regulations of the country of origin.

www.orionbooks.co.uk

For my wife, Vicky, and my son, Ryan,
who tolerate my idiosyncrasies,
and understand that I love them without limit.

ACKNOWLEDGEMENTS

Though authored by one, a novel is not the achievement of a single individual.

A number of people have contributed in different and generous ways to this work and, while a simple acknowledgement cannot do them justice, they should know that this novel could not have been fully achieved without them. Though I have come to know them through our work together, they have now become part of my family. Those that are not mentioned by name will, I hope, forgive me – they know who they are.

I owe a special debt to my agent, Euan Thorneycroft, a man of endless patience and unmatched standards; Jon Wood is the very best editor an author could wish for, and I thank, too, his wife Ellie for her friendship, and for making Jon a better man; my friends at Orion – too many to mention – have made this past year truly memorable. Robyn Karney, who makes such difficult work so easy has, with her keen eye and commitment, made all my books that much better. I would like to acknowledge the huge support and encouragement of Amanda Ross, Gareth, Duncan, John, and all those at Cactus TV; my thanks also to my brother Guy, who reads with a sharp eye and challenges so ferociously.

Last, but far from least, my gratitude to all at the Richard & Judy Book Club, 2008, for the tremendous endorsement and promotion afforded to *A Quiet Belief In Angels*.

R. J. Ellory, 2008

ACKNOWLEDGEMENTS

Assassination has never changed the history of the world

Benjamin Disraeli

PROLOGUE

She stands in the kitchen, and for a moment she holds her breath.

A little after five in the afternoon. Already dark outside, and though she can remember standing in the same spot a thousand times before – ahead of her the sink, to her right the counter-top, to her left the doorway to the hall – there is something different.

Extraordinarily so.

Air is the same, but seems harder to breathe. Light above her the same, but somehow harsh and invasive. Even her skin, something never noticed, appears to feel tighter. Her scalp itches as she starts to sweat, she feels the pressure of her clothes, the weight of her arms, the tension created by the rings on her fingers and the watch on her wrist; feels her underwear, her shoes, her necklace, her blouse.

This is it, she thinks.

My name is Catherine. I am forty-nine years old, and this is it.

Fuck.

Moves to the right. Reaches out her hand and touches the cool surface of the sink-edge. She grips it and, using it as leverage, turns slowly towards the door.

She wonders whether he's inside the house already.

She wonders if she should stand still and wait, or if she should move.

She wonders what he expects her to do.

It is quite some time before she makes a decision, and when she makes that decision she goes with it.

Walks right across the kitchen and into the front room of the house – businesslike, straightforward; takes a DVD from the bookcase against the wall and, with the remote in her hand, she opens the player, puts the disc inside, closes

1

the player, pushes buttons, and waits for sound . . . and then the picture comes and she hesitates.

Music.

She ups the volume.

Music by Dimitri Tiomkin.

It's A Wonderful Life.

Remembers the first time she saw this movie. Remembers every time she's seen this movie. Whole sections by heart, word-for-word. Verbatim. Like she was cramming for a test. Remembers the people she was with, what they said, the ones that cried and the ones that didn't. Remembers things like that at a time like this. Figured that she'd remember the important things.

Hell, maybe these *are* the important things.

Heart is big in her chest. Heart the size of a clenched fist? Apparently not. Not in her case. Heart the size of two fists together, or the size of a football. The size of—

What? she thinks.

The size of what exactly?

Looks at the TV screen. Hears the sound of the tolling bell, and then the playful strings-section melody. The sign that reads YOU ARE NOW IN BEDFORD FALLS. A picture post-card street, snow falling . . .

Catherine Sheridan starts to feel the emotion then. It isn't fear, because she's long since passed the point of being afraid. It's nothing immediately definable – something like loss, perhaps something like nostalgia; something like anger and resentment, or bitterness that it had to end this way.

'I owe everything to George Bailey,' the voice from the TV says. 'Help him dear Father. Joseph, Jesus and Mary . . . help my friend Mr Bailey . . .'

A woman's voice: 'Help my son George tonight.'

The camera pans away, up into the sky, away from the house and into space.

It's everything and nothing all at once. Catherine Sheridan sees the whole of her life collapsed like a concertina, and then drawn out again until every fraction and fragment can be clearly identified.

She closes her eyes, opens them again, sees children sledding on shovels, the scene where George saves Harry from the icy water. And that's how George got the virus in his ear, and that's how he lost his hearing . . .

It is then that Catherine hears something. She thinks to turn, but doesn't dare. A sudden rush of something in the base of her gut. *Wants* to turn now. Wants so desperately to turn around and look him square in the face, but knows that if she does this she will break down, she will scream and cry and plead for this to happen some other way, and it's too late now, too late to go back . . . too late after everything that's happened, everything that they've done, everything they've learned and what it all meant . . .

And Catherine thinking: *What the fuck were* we *thinking? Who the fuck did* we *think we were? Who the fuck gave* us *the right to do what we did?*

Thinks: *We gave ourselves the right. We gave ourselves a right that should only have been granted by God. And where the fuck was He? Where the fuck was God when those people were dying, huh?*

And now I have to die.

Die like this.

Die right now in my own house.

What goes around comes around.

That's what Robey would have said: 'What goes around comes around, Catherine.'

And she would have smiled, and said: 'You were always such a fucking Buddhist. The job you do, the things you've seen, and you think you can quote me some sort of self-serving, zero-responsibility platitude. Fuck you, John Robey . . . you ever listen to yourself?'

And he would have said: 'No . . . no, I never listen to myself, Catherine. I don't dare.'

And she would have known *exactly* what he meant.

After a while you don't dare face what you did. You just close your eyes and grit your teeth and clench your fists and make believe everything will come out right.

That's what you do.

Until a moment like now.

Standing in your own front room, Jimmy Stewart on the TV, and you know *he* is behind you. You know he is right behind you. You have some kind of an idea of what he's going to do 'cause you've read it in the newspapers . . .

3

Catherine looks at the TV.

George is at the bank.

'Avast there, captain . . . where ya headin'?'

'Gotta see Poppa, Uncle Billy.'

'Some other time, George.'

'It's important.'

'There's a squall in there, it's shapin' up into a storm.'

And Catherine senses *him* behind her, right there behind her . . . could reach her hand behind her back and touch him. Can imagine what's going on inside his heart, his head, the rush of emotion that will be almost overwhelming. Or maybe not. *Maybe he's tougher than me. Much tougher than I believed.* But then she hears the slight hitch in his throat as he inhales. Hears that slight hitch and knows – just *knows* – that he feels this thing as much as she does.

Closes her eyes.

'It's a good face,' the voice from the TV says. 'I like it. I like George Bailey. Tell me . . . did he ever tell anyone about the pills?'

'Not a soul.'

'Did he ever marry the girl? Did he ever go exploring?'

'Well . . . wait and see . . .'

Catherine Sheridan closes her eyes and grits her teeth and clenches her fists, and wonders if she needs to fight back. If it would make sense to try and fight back. If anything will ever make sense again.

God I hope we're right, she thinks. *I hope that everything—*

Feels his hand on her shoulder. She's rigid now, every muscle, every nerve and sinew, every atom of her being is tensed up and taut.

Sorts of leans back toward him as she feels his hands close around the back of her neck. Feels the strength in his grip as it tightens, and knows that it is taking every ounce of his will and self-discipline to do this thing. Knows that this will hurt him more – much, much more – than it will hurt her.

Catherine tries to turn slightly, and even as she does so she knows she is only contributing to the swiftness with which this thing will be done. Perhaps that's *why* she turns. Feels the pressure of his fingertips, feels the pressure change as he moves to the right, as he maintains his grip on her throat, as

4

he changes pace, builds pressure, eases back, uses his forearm to tilt her head to the left . . . and her eyes sting as tears fill her lower lids, but she's not even crying. This is some kind of involuntary reaction, and the tension rises in her chest as her lungs begin to resist the absence of oxygen . . . and she starts to feel dizzy, and when her eyelids flutter she can see deep rushes of unidentifiable colors . . .

Sound erupts from the middle of her chest. A red-raw thundering fuck of a sound. Rushes up through the middle of her chest and stops dead at the base of her throat.

Oh my God, she's thinking. *Oh my God . . . Oh my God . . . Oh my God . . .*

Feels the full weight of her own body as it starts to drop, feels the way he struggles to hold her upright, and though she knows it will soon be over there is something inside her – something genetic, something basic, an instinct threaded through and around her being – that still fights for life even though she knows it's no goddamned use now . . .

Now her eyes feel full of blood, they see nothing but red. Great smashing swathes of burgundy and rose and scarlet and crimson and claret . . .

Oh my God . . .

Feels the weight of her head as it lolls forward.

Knows that even if he stopped right now, even if he released his grip and let her go, even if paramedics arrived and bound her to a stretcher and pushed a mask over her face and told her to *Breathe goddammit woman, breathe!* . . . even if that oxygen was pure and untainted, and they raced the ambulance to Columbia Hospital or the University Medical Center . . . even if they did these things there would be no way she would survive . . .

In her last moment she strains to open her eyes, and there she sees George Bailey's face light up at the dance, sees Mary look back at him, and it's one of those moments, one of those stop-dead-in-your-tracks, love-at-first-sight moments that only ever happen to the best of people, and only ever happen once. And if you don't go with that moment, if you don't go with that rush of spontaneous magic that fills your heart, your mind, fills every little bit of everything you are . . . if you don't just go with it you'll remember it for the rest of your life as the one thing you should have done, the only thing you *really* should have done, the thing that might have made your whole life different, might have made it worthwhile, made it really mean something more than what you ended up with . . .

And Jimmy Stewart says: 'Well, hello.'

Catherine Sheridan can't fight any more. Doesn't want to. Her spirit is broken. Everything that was something now counts for nothing at all. Lets it go. Feels herself slide to the floor, and feels him release her, and thinks: *I'm not the one who has to go on living with the knowledge of what we did . . .*

Thank God for small mercies.

By the time he started doing things to Catherine Sheridan she was long since dead.

ONE

Washington D.C. was not the center of the world, though a significant percentage of Washingtonians would've had you believe it.

Detective Robert Miller was not one of them.

Capital of the continental United States, the seat of federal government, a history stretching back hundreds of years, and yet despite such depth of history, despite the art and architecture, the tree-lined streets, the galleries, the museums, despite one of the most efficient metro systems of any American city, Washington still possessed its shadows, its sharp corners, its blunt edges. People were still murdered there each and every day.

November 11th was cold and unwelcoming, a day of mourning and remembrance for many reasons. Darkness dropped like a stone at five, the temperature below zero by six, and the streetlights running parallel lines as far as the eye could see seemed little more than invitations to follow them and leave. Detective Robert Miller had very recently thought of leaving, of taking another job in another city, and he had his own specific and personal reasons for considering such an option. The reasons were numerous – and they were bad – and he'd spent many weeks trying to forget them. At that moment, however, he stood in the back lot of the Sheridan house on Columbia Street NW. The cherry-blue bars of parked squad cars were reflected in the windows, the hubbub and commotion of too many people with too many agendas – attendant uniforms, forensics, crime scene photographers, neighbors with kids and dogs and questions that would never be answered, the hissing and static of handhelds and squad-car radios . . . The end of the street was a carnival of noise and confusion, and through all this Miller felt nothing but the change of pace he'd known would come. It

7

quickened his pulse. He could feel his heart in his chest and the nerves in the base of his stomach. Three months' suspension – the first month at home, the second and third months behind a desk – and now he was here. No more than a week of active duty and the world had already found him. He had walked from the daylight, directly toward the shadowed underbelly of Washington, and he had been welcomed like long-lost family. And to show its appreciation for his return it had left a beaten corpse in an upper bedroom overlooking Columbia Street North West.

Miller had already been inside, had seen what he wanted to see, a great deal he didn't. The victim's furniture, the pictures on the walls, all a reminder of a life that once was. And now that life had gone, extinguished in a heartbeat. He had left by the back kitchen door, wanted a breath of air, a change of tempo. Forensics were in there, businesslike and unemotional, and Miller needed a little distance. It was so bitterly cold, and though he wore an overcoat and a scarf, though he buried his hands in his pockets, he felt a sense of something altogether more chilling than the weather. He stood silently in the featureless back-lot and watched the madness unfold around him. He listened to the seemingly nonchalant voices of men who were somehow inured to such things. He had believed himself unreachable, but he had been reached, reached with ease, and it frightened him.

Robert Miller – a man of unremarkable appearance, perhaps no different from many other men – waited for his partner, Detective Albert Roth. Miller had worked with Roth for the better part of two years. They couldn't have been less alike, but Al Roth was neverthless an anchor, a fastidiously professional man, abiding by protocol and regulation, thinking for both of them when required.

Miller had persisted in Homicide, but recent events had overwhelmed and buried whatever sense of purpose he'd originally felt. The things he'd learned seemed to possess as much use as dry sticks and fresh air. He'd made tentative enquiries to Vice and Narcotics, even to Administration, but remained undecided. August had been a bad month, September worse, and even now – still reeling from all that had taken place, feeling as if he'd somehow survived an ugly car crash – he did not truly understand what had happened. He and Roth did not speak of the past three months, it was something sensed, and though Miller felt it would perhaps have been better to speak he never started the conversation.

That evening Miller had been at the Second Precinct when the report came in. Al Roth had been called out to Columbia NW from his home, and when he arrived he and Miller stood in silence in the dead woman's yard. Just for a few moments, a sign of respect perhaps.

They went in through the rear kitchen door. Men crowded the downstairs hallway; there were people on the stairs, and the hubbub of voices and the intermittent flash of cameras was backed by the sound of orchestral music. They stood without speaking for a time, and then Roth asked 'What the hell is that?'

Miller nodded toward the front room. 'DVD playing . . . *It's A Wonderful Life* of all things.'

'Very fitting,' Roth replied. 'She upstairs?'

'Yes, bedroom to the right.'

'What did you say her name was?'

'Sheridan,' Miller replied. 'Catherine Sheridan.'

'I'm going up there.'

'Mind the pizza,' Miller said.

Roth frowned. 'Pizza?'

'Delivery guy dropped it on the hallway carpet. Came over here to bring an order and found the front door unlocked. Says he heard the TV in the front—'

'What? And he came in the house?'

'Says they have strict policy not to leave without payment. God knows what he was thinking, Al. He thought he heard someone upstairs, figured that they couldn't hear him because of the TV so he went up there. He found her in the bedroom just as she is now.' Miller seemed to look right through Roth as he was speaking, then he got it together, his thoughts and words coinciding. 'There's forensic people all over the place. They're gonna kick us out in a moment, but you go on up there and take a look.'

Roth paused for a moment. 'You okay?' he asked.

Miller could feel the substance and darkness of his own thoughts. He saw it in his reflection, the lines around his eyes, the shadows beneath. 'I'm okay,' he said, but there was something indefinite and subdued in his voice.

'You ready for this?'

'As I'll ever be,' Miller said, his tone one of philosophical resignation.

Roth stepped past Miller, walked across the front hallway and started up the stairs. Miller followed him, the two of them edging their way along the corridor to the dead woman's bedroom. A huddle of three or four men were gathered around the doorway. One of them – a face Miller recognized from some other moment, some other dark quarter of their collective past – nodded in acknowledgement. They knew who Miller was. They knew what had happened to him, the way his life had been opened up for the newspapers and shared with the world. They all wanted to ask the same question, but they never did.

As Miller entered the room the other officers seemed to step back and fade from his line of sight. He slowed up for a moment.

There was nothing like dead people.

Nothing in the world.

People alive and people dead were not even close. Even now, despite the number of bodies he'd seen, there was always that moment when Miller believed the victim's eyes would open, that there would be a sudden intake of breath, perhaps a grimace of pain, a faint smile, something that said, 'Here I am . . . back again . . . sorry, I was elsewhere for a moment.'

There was a first time, of course. But there was something about the first time that had stayed with Miller for every other time. It stopped his heart – just for a second, less than a second – and said, 'Here's what people are capable of doing to people. Here's another example of the way life can smash someone to pieces.'

Now, the first thing was the irregularity of her position. Catherine Sheridan was on her knees, arms stretched out to her sides, head on the mattress, but turned so her cheek touched the sheet beneath her. A second sheet had been carelessly draped around her waist and obscured much of her legs. She seemed to be looking back along the length of

10

her body towards the door. It was a sexual position, but there was no longer anything sexual about her.

The second thing was the expression on her face. He could not describe it. He knelt on the floor and looked right back at her, right up close, saw his own features reflected in the glassy stillness of her eyes. It was almost impossible to describe the feeling her expression had given him. Acceptance. Resignation. Acquiescence perhaps? It contrasted with the vicious lividity of the bruising that covered her shoulders and arms. From the neck down, what little he could see of her waist and thighs, it appeared she had been beaten mercilessly, relentlessly, in a manner so unforgiving it would have been impossible to survive. Already the blood had laked, the swelling had become accentuated as fluids thickened and clotted. The pain must have gone on and on and on, and then suddenly – a welcome silence after some interminable noise – it had ended.

Miller had wanted to reach out and touch her, to close her eyes, to whisper something reassuring, to tell her the horror had ended, peace had come . . . but he could not.

It had taken some while for the blood to stop thundering through his veins, for his heart to stop skipping beats. With each new victim, the old ones came too. Like ghosts. Each of them perhaps desiring some greater understanding of what had happened.

Catherine Sheridan had been dead for two or three hours. Assistant coroner later confirmed that she'd died between four forty-five and six, afternoon of Saturday, November 11th. Pizza had been ordered at five-forty. Delivery guy arrived at five after six, found her body within a matter of minutes. Miller had been called from the Second just after six-thirty, had arrived at six fifty-four. Roth had joined him ten minutes later, and by the time they both stood looking at Catherine Sheridan's awkward pose from the upper hallway of her house it was close to seven-fifteen. She looked cold, but the skin had not yet turned completely.

'Same as the others,' Roth said. 'Pretty much the same anyway. Smell that?'

Miller nodded. 'Lavender.'

'And the tag?'

11

Miller walked alongside the edge of the mattress and looked down at Catherine Sheridan. He pointed to her neck, the thin ribbon upon which was tied a standard manila-colored luggage tag. The tag was blank, almost as if a Jane Doe had been delivered to the morgue, nameless, without identity, unimportant perhaps. 'Ribbon is white this time,' he said as Roth appeared on the other side of the bed.

From where he stood Miller could see Catherine Sheridan's face very clearly. She had been an attractive woman, slightly-built, petite almost, with brunette shoulder-length hair and an olive complexion. Her throat was bruised and the same bruises were present on her shoulders, her upper arms, her torso, her thighs, some of them so brutal that the skin had been broken. Her face, however, was unmarked.

'See her face,' Miller said.

Roth came around the foot of the bed, stood beside Miller, said nothing for a while and then slowly shook his head.

'Four,' Miller said.

'Four,' Roth echoed.

A voice from behind them. 'You from Homicide?' Miller and Roth turned in unison. One of the CSAs stood there, field kit in his hand, latex gloves, behind him a man with a camera. 'I'm sorry, but I need you guys out of here now.'

Miller looked once more at the almost placid expression on Catherine Sheridan's face, then made his way carefully out of the room, Roth behind him, neither of them saying anything until they were once again downstairs.

Miller stopped in the doorway of the front room. The credits were rolling on *It's A Wonderful Life*.

'So?' Roth asked.

Miller shrugged.

'You think—'

'I'm not thinking anything,' Miller interjected. 'I'm not thinking anything until I know exactly what happened to her.'

'What have we got?'

Miller took out his notepad, scanned the few lines he'd scribbled when he'd arrived. 'No sign of forced entry to the property. Seems he came in through the front door because the back door was still locked when I got here. I had forensics

12

take pictures before we unlocked it. No sign of a struggle, nothing broken, nothing obviously out of place.'

'Percentage of attacks committed by someone known to the victim is what? Forty, fifty percent?'

'More I think,' Miller replied. 'Pizza delivery guy found her. Large pizza, custom order. Suggests that it was ordered for two. If the guy who did this was already here then it suggests it was someone she knew.'

'And then she may not have known him at all. Maybe she just liked pizza.'

'There's also the known identity,' Miller replied, referring to the many cases of entry made to houses by people dressed as police officers, gas and telephone engineers, other such things. The familiarity of the uniform made people drop their guard. The perp entered uninhibited, the crime was committed, and even if the individual was seen it was ordinarily little more than the uniform that was remembered. 'If there was no break-in, no struggle, no apparent resistance, then we're more than likely dealing with someone she knew, or someone she felt she could trust.'

'You want to start around the neighborhood now?' Roth asked.

Miller glanced at his watch. He felt weary, like emotional bruising. 'The papers get word of this there's gonna be shit flying every which way.'

Roth smiled knowingly. 'As if you hadn't had enough of your name in the papers.'

Miller's expression told Roth that such a comment wasn't appreciated.

They walked away from the back of Catherine Sheridan's house, came up along the hedgerow that divided her plot from the neighbor's and stood for a while on the sidewalk.

'You wouldn't think it, would you?' Miller said. 'If you didn't know that someone was dead in this house . . .'

'Most of the world is oblivious to the rest of the world,' Roth said.

Miller smiled. 'What the hell is that? Yiddish philosophy?'

Roth didn't reply. He nodded toward the house on the right. 'Let's take that one first.'

13

There was no response at either of the adjacent properties. The house facing the Sheridan lot was dark and silent.

Over the street and two down they found someone at home – an elderly man, white hair protruding in clumps from above his ears, a thin face, eyes set too far back behind heavy spectacles.

Miller introduced himself, showed his ID.

'You're wanting to know what I saw, right?' the old man said. He instinctively looked toward the Sheridan house, the light-bars flashing in reflection on the lenses of his horn-rims, the firework display of activity that was so instantly recognizable as bad news. 'It was about four, maybe four-thirty.'

Miller frowned. 'What was?'

'When she came home . . . about four-thirty.'

'How are you sure?' Miller asked.

'Had on the TV. Was watching a gameshow. Pretty girls, you know? Watch it most every day. Comes on at four, runs for half an hour.'

'So if you were watching TV how do you know that Ms Sheridan came home?'

It was cold, bitterly so, there on the old man's doorstep. Roth's hands were gloved but still he massaged them together as if he was choking something small. He gritted his teeth, glanced at the road like he was waiting for something else to happen.

'How do I know? Come inside a minute.'

Miller glanced at Roth. Roth nodded. They stepped inside. Place was neat but could have done with a clean.

The old man waved them into the front, showed them his chair, the TV, how it was positioned.

'If I'm here I can see the house.' He pointed. Miller leaned down to sitting height. Through the window he could see Catherine Sheridan's front door.

'You knew her?'

'Some.'

'How well?'

'Hell, I don't know. How well does anyone know anyone these days? Ain't like how it used to be. We were polite. Said

14

hi every once in a while. She never came for dinner if that's what you mean.'

'And you saw her go inside the house?'

The old man nodded.

'And then?'

'Some kid with thick glasses won three thousand bucks and darn near pissed himself.'

Miller frowned.

'On the game show.'

'Right . . . on the game show.'

'And you didn't see anything else?'

'What else was there to see?'

'Someone approaching the house?'

'The guy that killed her?'

'Anyone . . . anyone at all.'

'I didn't see anyone.'

Miller handed him a card. 'You remember anything else you give me a call, okay?'

'Sure.'

Miller turned, looked at Roth. Roth shook his head; he had no further questions.

The old man inhaled slowly, exhaled once more. 'Hard to believe,' he said quietly.

'What is?'

'That he went and killed my neighbor. I mean, what the hell did she do to deserve that?'

Miller shrugged. 'God knows. What did any of them do?'

Roth and Miller moved on. They spoke with neighbors in three houses further down but came back none the wiser. No-one had seen a thing. No-one remembered anything.

'Like I said,' Roth repeated, 'most of the world is oblivious.'

They returned to the Sheridan place to check on the forensics unit. Miller stayed downstairs, surveyed the scene before him, tried to imprint every detail on his mind for later reference. He thought of the movie that had been playing. It was something to watch with family at Christmas, not something to watch as you died.

Roth came down and waited with him as forensics went through Catherine Sheridan's kitchen, her bathroom, through drawers and cupboards, fingertip-searching her belongings, perhaps believing that they would find something to help explain what had taken place. They knew they were just looking for a single clue, a hint, a suggestion, a lead . . . the *one thing* that would let them catch this creature by the tail and haul it to the curb.

It would come. Sure as Christmas. But not when they expected, nor how, nor why.

Before Miller left he asked after the lead CSA, waited while one of the analysts brought him from upstairs.

'You're the chief on this?' the CSA asked.

'First one here, that's all,' Miller replied.

'Greg Reid,' the CSA said. 'Would shake hands but . . .' He held up his latex-gloved hands, smears and spots of blood visible on them.

'I'll leave my card on the table here,' Miller said. 'Just wanted you to know who I am, my number if you needed me.'

'Have to give us the time we need,' Reid said. 'A day or two . . . I got a whole house to process. You speak to whoever you have to speak to and then come back, okay?'

Miller nodded. 'Anything immediate shows up, call me?'

'Do have something,' Reid said. He nodded toward the telephone table near the front door. 'Bag there has her passport and a library card in it. She went to the library today, looks like she returned some books. The passport is the only picture I can find of her right now. You'll need a picture for your walkabout. Maybe have one of your people clean it up, make her look like a human being.'

'Appreciated,' Miller said. 'Let me know if there's anything else.'

Reid smiled sardonically. 'What? Like we find the guy left his name and address?'

Miller didn't respond. He was tired. A CSA's relationship ended with the crime scene; Homicide would live with this until it was done.

Roth and Miller left by the rear door, paused once again in the lot and looked at the back of the house. Lights burned. Shadows up against the windows from the men working inside. Miller stood there until he felt the cold getting to

16

him, Roth beside him, neither of them speaking until Miller told Roth to take the car.

'You're sure?' Roth asked.

'I'm going to walk. I could use the exercise.'

Roth looked at Miller askance. 'You feel like everyone you meet wants to ask you questions, don't you?'

Miller shrugged.

'You heard from Marie?'

'Not a word.'

'She didn't come get her things from your place?'

'I think she's gone away for a while.' Miller shook his head. 'Fuck, who am I kidding? I think she's gone for good.'

'Amanda didn't like her,' Roth said. 'She said that she wasn't down-to-earth enough for you.'

'Tell Amanda that I appreciate her concern, but it was simply a fuck-up. We all know that.'

'You figured out what you're gonna do yet?'

Miller appeared momentarily irritated. 'Go home, would you?'

Roth glanced back at the Sheridan house. 'This is the last thing you want, right?'

Miller looked down at the sidewalk, didn't answer the question.

Roth smiled understandingly. 'I'll go home now,' he said, and started away towards the car.

Miller stayed for ten or fifteen minutes, his attention focused on the lights in the Sheridan house, and then he buried his hands in his pockets and started walking. It was close to ten by the time he reached his apartment over Harriet's Delicatessen on Church Street. Harriet, ancient and wise, would be out back, drinking warm milk with her husband Zalman, talking about things only they could remember. Miller took the rear stairwell up to his apartment instead of his usual route through the deli itself. Such moments as this, wonderful people though they were, Harriet and Zalman Shamir would keep him up for an hour, insisting he eat chicken liver sandwiches and honey cake. Most other nights yes, but tonight? No, not tonight. Tonight belonged to Catherine Sheridan, to finding the reason for her death.

Miller let himself in, kicked off his shoes, spent an hour

17

outlining his initial observations on a yellow legal pad. He watched TV for a little while before fatigue started to take him.

Eleven, perhaps later, Harriet and Zalman locked up and went home. Harriet called him goodnight from the stairs, and Miller called goodnight in return.

He did not sleep. He lay awake with his eyes closed and thought of Catherine Sheridan. Who she was. Why she had died. Who had killed her. He thought of these things and he longed for morning, for morning would bring daylight, and daylight would give distance between himself and his ghosts.

*U*se a knife. Knife killings are personal. Almost invariably personal. Multiple stab-wounds to chest, stomach, throat – some shallow, glancing off the ribs, others deep, sufficient to leave oval bruises where the blade ends and the shaft begins. Suggest uncontrollable rage, the fury of hatred or vengeance. Such things to confuse, to muddy the waters and cloud issues of forensic pathology, criminal psychology, profiling. Everything needs to appear as if something else.

Did you know that less than half of all rapes are actually resolved by the police? And this despite the fact that in the vast majority of cases the perpetrator is someone well-known to the victim? That less than ten percent make it to the Crime Lab? In only six percent of those cases is DNA recovered and tested. With the total tests running at something in the region of a quarter of a million cases per year, do you realize only fifteen thousand victims will ever find justice?

There are people who know this stuff. You can find it on the internet. It ain't rocket science. On the almighty world wide web you can find a hundred different ways to cover up the crime. Household bleach will remove fingerprints, saliva, semen, DNA. Wear gloves for God's sake, and not leather ones with a grain. Wear latex gloves like a doctor, a surgeon, an orthodontist. They're not hard to find. Cost next to nothing. Don't wear your own shoes. Buy new sneakers. Cheap ones. Don't go out killing folks in three hundred dollar Nikes, for with all physical objects you have two basic characteristic: class and individual. A cheap sneaker has class characteristics. It's a mass-produced item. There are millions of them in circulation, and to all intents and purposes they are absolutely identical. The more expensive the sneaker the more unusual the tread, and the fewer the people who have them. And before you go out, check those treads yourself. Treads pick things up. Carpet fibers, bits of crap from the street, from your own

19

apartment. Like I said, it ain't rocket science. Some objects, car tires for example, have both class and individual characteristics. The class is the basic shape of the tire, the indents and grooves and patterns. Then you have different elements and angles of wear dependent upon the type of vehicle and the kind of terrain it has traversed. These factors can sometimes create a uniqueness that can be attributed to one car, and thus one driver. That's your individual. Watch those guys on TV – CSI, you know? – and it looks like they have all this stuff down cold. Do they, fuck. You just have to be careful. Use your common sense. Think the thing through. Don't get complex. The more complex you get the more things can go wrong. Trick is to look at it from the end back to the beginning. Get what I mean? Look at the aftermath, the scene as someone else will find it, and more than likely you'll remember the cigarette you smoked at the end of the street, the butt you flicked into the shrubbery, the gum wrapper, the foil that's smooth and shiny and great for prints . . . You getting the drift now? You understand where I'm coming from?

And if you don't want blood, then strangle them. Choke them to death. No weapon better than your own hands. Then disappear. Disappear fast, 'cause if they can't find you they can't find the weapon.

Could run a seminar. How about that, friends and neighbors? Run a seminar at George Washington University. Mayhem and Murder 101.

Bitch of a thing.

TWO

Life is so much tougher when you know you should be dead.

It was like a line from a song. There was a cadence and a rhythm to it that made it difficult to forget. It started somewhere in Miller's mind, and once it had started it just seemed to keep on going. Like the flat-nose .22s the Mafia used. Sufficient punch to get it through the skull, insufficient to make its way out again, and that dime's-worth of lead just battered and ricocheted around inside, banging off the internal walls of some poor sucker's head until their brain was chicken soup. The thought went like that, and he wanted it to stop. He thought of the girl who had died, the girl who had left him, the IAD investigation, the newspapers. He thought of these things, just as he had thought of them for the past three months, and he tried to make them inconsequential and irrelevant. He sat in the office of Washington Second Precinct Captain Frank Lassiter. He focused on what he'd seen at the Sheridan house the night before; he waited patiently for what he knew was coming.

Lassiter came through the door like a raid. He banged it shut behind him, dropped into his chair. He shook his head and scowled, and when he opened his mouth he hesitated for a second. Perhaps he'd planned to say something else, and then changed his mind.

'You know what this is, right?' was the question he asked.

'The serial, or this woman specifically?' Miller replied.

Lassiter frowned, shook his head. 'This is the proverbial worst case scenario, that's what it is.'

'We're presuming that the MO is the same as—'

Lassiter cut him short. 'We're presuming nothing. I don't have anything from forensics yet. I don't have a coroner's report. I have a murdered woman, second in this precinct's jurisdiction, and because the other two were out of precinct,

21

because this whole system is a jigsaw puzzle of bullshit and bureaucracy, I don't have anything to hang anything on. All I know is that the chief of police called me at seven this morning and told me that the whole thing was now my problem, that I better put some good people on it, that it better be sorted out . . . you know the speech by now, right?'

Miller smiled sardonically.

'So here we are,' Lassiter said.

'Here we are,' Miller echoed

'So what the hell is this crap about transferring out of Homicide?'

'I don't know, captain, some crap about transferring out of Homicide.'

'Sarcasm I don't need, detective. So you're gonna leave us then?'

'I don't know. Perhaps I believed . . .'

Lassiter laughed suddenly. 'Believed what? It's dead people, that's what it is. That's why it's called Homicide.' He placed his hands on the arms of his chair as if to stand. For a moment he looked closely at Miller. 'You don't look so good,' he said.

'Just tired.'

'Still in pain?'

Miller shook his head. 'It was just bruising, a dislocated shoulder, nothing serious.'

'You get some physio?'

'More than enough.'

Lassiter nodded his head slowly.

Miller felt the inescapable tension of what was coming.

'So you ran the gauntlet, eh? You know how many times my name's been in the papers?'

Miller shook his head.

'I don't either, but it's a lot. A fucking lot. They're buzzards. That's all they are. They fly around corpses and pick stuff off of them.' Lassiter shook his head. 'To hell with it. This isn't a conversation we're having right now.' He got up from his chair and walked to the window. 'I'm pissed with the pair of you by the way,' he said. 'For leaving last night. I read your report. How long were you out there? Half an hour?'

'Forensics,' Miller replied. 'It was a new crime scene, we were just in the way. We started round the adjacent houses but no-one had anything important to say.' He paused for a moment. 'And no, we were not out there for half an hour, we were out there nearly three hours.'

'Three houses, Robert. Three fucking houses? Give me a break. Only thing that pisses me off is a lack of professionalism. Can tolerate all the moaning and whining about the hours, the low pay, the overtime, the fact that no-one ever gets to see their wives and kids and cats and dogs and mistresses, but when it comes to a lack of care—'

'Understood,' Miller interjected.

'You heard that speech before too, right?' Lassiter said.

'I did, yes,' Miller said. 'Couple of times.'

'So what the fuck are you gonna do? You're gonna quit? Or you gonna put in for a transfer?'

'I don't know. I figured I'd look at it at the end of the month, maybe after Christmas.'

'So I need you to do this one.'

Miller said nothing.

'Chief wants the whole case transferred here. All four killings. Right now we have nothing that tells us it's the same perp. From your report it appears that they could be, but apparencies I don't need and can't use. The strangulation, the beating, the ribbon with the name tag thing, all that stuff. Seems to be the same MO, right?'

'It does, yes.'

'What was the name of the first one . . . Mosley?'

'Yes, Margaret Mosley, back in March.'

'Was that your case?'

'No, not really. I was the first one out there, simply because I was on shift,' Miller explained. 'I think Metz took it in the end.'

'No . . . I remember what happened now. Metz was going to take it and didn't. It wound up being handled by the Third.'

'This thing is all over the place isn't it?'

Lassiter smiled wryly. 'You have no fucking idea.'

'So why us? Why the Second?'

Lassiter shrugged. 'First one was in our precinct, second in the Fourth, third one in the Sixth, now this fourth one is back in the Second. We have two of them. The chief loves us, hates us maybe. Jesus, I don't know. He wants us to handle it, be the central point for all four investigations. It's become an issue. He needs it dealt with as one case. Makes sense. To date it's been dealt with – *not* dealt with actually – by three different precincts. Newspapers have gone crazy for it, as we all knew they would, and maybe he thinks that after all the crap that you stirred up we can repair our reputation by making this mess go away.'

'This is such horseshit—'

Lassiter raised his hand. 'Politics and protocol is what it is, nothing more nor less than that. It feels personal, but it isn't.'

'And did the chief suggest I do this because of what happened?'

'Not exactly . . .'

'Meaning?'

Lassiter walked from the window and sat down again. 'Thing you have to understand here is that there's always going to be some social-conscience bullshit liberal that assumes we do nothing but kick the crap out of innocent civilians for fun.'

Miller smiled sarcastically. 'I know about police department politics. I don't need a lesson—'

'Fine, so I don't need to explain myself. If you're here then you're on duty. If you're on duty then you have an obligation to accept the cases I assign to you. I'm assigning this thing to you, and short of handing in your resignation right here and now there's very fucking little that you can do about it.'

'Love you too, captain,' Miller said.

'So go and talk to the FBI.'

Miller frowned. 'The what? The FBI?'

'I'm afraid so . . . chief has asked for help from the FBI. They've sent someone to teach us how to do this shit.'

'This isn't federal . . . what in God's name do they have to do with this?'

'It's a helping hand, Robert, and I sure as shit could do with one. The chief spoke to Judge Thorne . . . gotta remember we have our election party coming in the New Year. No-one's gonna be losing their job over this, let me assure you. I need someone to head this thing up, and you're the man. Afraid that's the way it's gotta be. Maybe it'll give you something to get your teeth into, eh? Maybe it'll remind you why you worked so hard to be a detective in the first place.'

'I have a choice?' Miller asked.

'Fuck no,' Lassiter replied. 'When the hell did any one of us have a choice about this kind of thing? You had three months' vacation from this shit. You've been back a week. I need you to go make nice to the FBI, and then you and Roth pull all the files together, go through them, get this thing moving. We have four dead women, I have the chief all over me like a rash. There are more column inches about this than Veterans Day, and I need you to be a fucking hero and save the day, alright?'

Miller rose from his chair. He felt the weight already. He felt the sense of impending pressure that would bring the delicately balanced house of cards that was his life crashing down around his ears. It would fall silently. There would be no warning. He would just wake up one morning incapable of stringing a sentence together or making a cup of coffee. He did not need a serial killer. He did not need to be responsible for a headlining multiple homicide case, but even as he considered this he wondered if he hadn't created his own justice. Perhaps it was a way out of his indecision. It could be the end of him, or perhaps his salvation. He looked at Lassiter, opened his mouth to speak, but Lassiter raised his hand.

'You asked if you had a choice. You got your answer. Go see the FBI and make some sense of this bullshit would you?'

Miller started toward the door.

'One other thing,' Lassiter said.

Miller raised his eyebrows.

'Marilyn Hemmings is the coroner on this. You will have to deal with her. The press will get wind of this for sure. After that picture in the *Globe* I don't need to tell you—'

'I get it,' Miller said. He opened the office door.

'If I had someone better . . .' he heard Lassiter call after him as he closed the door gently behind him.

Know the feeling, Miller thought to himself, and made his way towards the stairs.

Several miles away, the outskirts of Washington, a young woman named Natasha Joyce stood in the doorway of her kitchen. She was black, late twenties perhaps, and there was something on the TV that caught her attention. She backed up from where she'd been washing crockery in the kitchen. She had a plate in her hand, a drying towel, and she tilted her head and squinted at the screen through the doorway while the anchorwoman spoke.

A face appeared on the screen.

A moment's hesitation, perhaps something close to disbelief, and then the plate slipped from Natasha's fingers, and even as she stared at the face on the tube she was aware of the plate falling in slow motion toward the floor.

Her daughter, a pretty nine-year-old named Chloe who was playing on one side of the room, turned around to see her mother standing in the doorway, her eyes wide, her mouth open.

Everything went slow. Everything felt insubstantial. Everything that should have taken a second took a minute or more.

The plate reached the ground. It too seemed to hesitate for a heartbeat, and then it exploded into twenty or thirty pieces. Natasha screamed in surprise, and because she screamed her daughter screamed, and for a moment Natasha was puzzled because she knew she'd dropped the plate, she knew it would reach the ground and break, but nevertheless the sound still came out of left field like something unexpected.

'Mom?' Chloe said, getting up from the rug, turning and walking toward her. 'Mom . . . what happened?'

Natasha Joyce stood motionless, surprise evident on her face, and it was all she could do to hold back her tears.

THREE

Ten minutes later Miller stood by the window in a third-floor office. Neutral-colored split-level paint job, beige topped by lighter beige. Beat-to-shit furniture. Radiators that groaned and creaked in some vague attempt to get warm, emitting a smell of rust and stagnant water. To Miller's right and down through the window he could see the corner of New York and Fifth. Behind him on the desk was a copy of the *Washington Post*. From where he stood he could read the banner headline reflected in the glass. He felt cold and quiet inside.

Fourth Victim of Suspected Serial Murderer

There was a history behind such a statement. The French named it the *monstre sacré*: that thing we created that we wished we had not.

Washington possessed its own variation. They named him the Ribbon Killer. His story preceded the death of Catherine Sheridan by eight months and three other killings. The ribbon he'd left behind had not been the same in these previous cases. The first was blue, the second pink, the third yellow. Pale baby blue, cotton candy pink, spring sunshine yellow. In each case a blank manila luggage tag, much the same as tags tied to the toes of corpses in the morgue, had been attached to those ribbons. Catherine Sheridan's ribbon was white, she was the fourth victim, and Washington's Second Precinct under Captain Frank Lassiter had taken the news of her killing like a head-shot. The ribbon and tag was a small fact, the signature perhaps, and had the Homicide detectives assigned to the first murder foreseen a series they would have withheld that detail. The first was a thirty-seven-year-old city librarian named Margaret Mosley, beaten and choked to death, her body discovered in her own apartment

27

on Monday, March 6th. The second did not occur until Wednesday, July 19th. Her name was Ann Rayner, forty years old, a legal secretary with Youngman, Baxter and Harrison, once again found beaten and choked to death in the basement of her house. The third was Barbara Lee, a twenty-nine-year-old florist; pale birthmark beneath her left ear, hailed originally from Baltimore. Same MO. Found on Wednesday, August 2nd, in her house on Morgan and Jersey. And then there was Catherine Sheridan.

The women were neither abducted nor tortured it seemed. There were no signs of sexual abuse or rape. Nothing appeared to have been taken from the properties, and thus robbery was also eliminated as a motive. From all indications, all four were home when the intruder entered the premises, perhaps held them at gunpoint, spoke to them, told them what he wanted . . . for there were no signs of a struggle, no broken furniture. Each of them was beaten, and the beating was swift, relentless, unabated. The beatings were confident, nothing restrained about them. And then, after the killer had strangled them, he tied a ribbon and a blank name tag around their necks – blue, pink, yellow – and now one in white. The police had let slip the detail; the media had run with the detail; the populace of Washington took the detail and made it their own. Ribbon Killer.

Miller had read books, seen movies. It was simple in fiction. Four women were dead, and a man – a criminalist, perhaps a man with personal flaws and a difficult reputation – would look into the circumstances of these deaths and find the common connection. There would be something unique and special, and he would shine the light on this unique and special thing and say 'See? Here we are. Here is the thing that will tell us who he is.' And he would be right, and they would find the perpetrator, and the denouement would make it all as clear as daylight.

Not so in life. With the initial case, that of Margaret Mosley in March of that year, Miller and Roth had walked the streets around Bates, around Patterson and Morgan and Jersey Avenue for little more than a day. They'd asked questions, waited for answers, listened carefully as those answers never came. Other detectives had then taken their place, and meetings were held to discuss the fact that they'd learned nothing of any great value. Then the case had been reassigned out of precinct, Miller had forgotten about it, had heard about the second killing several weeks after its occurrence. By that time he was already waist-deep in all that had happened, in the IAD investigation, the coroner's inquiry, in the slow, painful death of a fourteen-month relationship with a girl named Marie McArthur, and thus – understandably – had given it no great deal of attention.

Between the first killing in March, the second in July and the death of Barbara Lee in August, right through September and into the first week of November, Miller knew there was nothing of any significance that had shone a light on the truth. Had there been he would have heard from Roth or one of the other detectives. The Second Precinct was a close community; they lived out of one another's pockets. The case was a nightmare, and though the newspapers turned to other stories, though the sports page and the mid-terms became once again the focus of attention for the vast majority of Washingtonians, the nightmare had evidently continued to walk and talk and breathe the same air as everyone else. Somebody had killed four women. He had killed them swiftly, violently, without clear reason or rationale, and the burden of investigation, identification, discovery and proof had now arrived with Robert Miller.

Miller told Roth about the FBI when he arrived. Roth sneered sarcastically, but he did not challenge Lassiter's authority.

On loan to the Washington Police Department by the Behavioral Sciences Unit, FBI Headquarters, Quantico, Virginia, their visitor was in his mid-fifties, his manner perhaps that of a college professor. He wore a flannel jacket with cotton pants, the knees dusty and worn as if he spent much of his life kneeling awkwardly, peering into darkness, making cryptic notes. His name was James Killarney. He did not look like a married man. He did not look like someone's father. He greeted each entrant with a half-smile, a nod; he knew his presence was somehow unwelcome – nothing personal, simply a matter of territorial and jurisdictional issues long-ingrained in the system. He seemed at ease, unhurried, as if such events were a matter of course.

It was a little after nine in the morning as seven detectives took seats in that closed-door session on the second floor of Washington's Second Precinct building. Amongst that group were people such as Chris Metz, Carl Oliver, Dan Riehl and Vince Feshbach – veterans of homicide, men that Miller would have considered more suited to heading up such a case. One for one they all carried the same look. *I have seen everything. There is nothing the world can bring me that I cannot face. Soon, perhaps sooner than I think, I will have seen it all.* Theirs was a look that Miller had hoped he would never assume, that it would be different for him, that he would never look that way. But he did. He knew that now. He believed he wore it better than all of them.

The tension was evident in glances, shifting expressions, in the way each man present looked at the man beside him, the man adjacent, and back to Killarney at the front. This was Washington, such things could not be permitted to go on, but nevertheless the feeling of unexpressed resentment was tangible. Miller himself was caught between this and his curiosity about what the visitor from Arlington could tell them about their case.

Killarney smiled. He stood for a moment at the front of the room. And then he backed up and perched on the edge of the desk. Like the teacher, the college lecturer. All that seemed absent was a blackboard.

'My name is James Killarney,' he said. His voice was quiet, the voice of a patient and compassionate man. 'I am here to talk with you about the situation, for I have some experience with such things, but before we begin I wanted to share with you some points of interest.'

Killarney paused as if waiting for questions, and then he smiled again and continued talking.

'At Berkeley they give seminars on criminal psychology. They deal with every variation of physical abuse from un-provoked and spontaneous attacks on women, through pre-meditated violence, all the way to kidnapping, torture, sexual abuse and rape and, finally, murder itself. They go into the whole maternal deprivation thing, you know?' Killarney waved his right hand nonchalantly, tucked his left hand into the pocket of his pants. 'How the superego is the part of a person's personality that deals with moral and ethical issues, and if a person is deprived of maternal care at an early age then the superego will be underdeveloped.' Another smile, the smile of a grandfather. 'Basically, a stream of nonsense issuing from the mouths of people who have nothing better to do with their time than make up fairytales about how people think.'

A consensus of murmurs, brief laughter.

'There is one point however, and it has to do with the method and motivation of those who commit acts of violence and murder.' He paused a moment, looked at his audience. 'From observation, from experience, there appear to be two types of perpetrator. We call them marauders and commuters. Marauders are those who stay in one location, usually bringing a victim back to a single point to commit the crime. The commuters are the ones who travel out to different locations. The attacks are again divided four different ways. Power-reassurance, power-assertive, anger-retaliatory and anger-excitement. Each of them possess different motivations and therefore manifest themselves in different ways.'

A shuffle of papers, homicide detectives reaching into jackets for pens.

Killarney frowned. 'What are you doing? Taking notes?' He shook his head. 'No need to take notes. I am here merely to orient you as to where you should go with your investigation, to keep track of your progress. These are simply categories, and should be viewed as such. The first we call power-reassurance. This is all about the need to reduce doubts about sexuality. A man who's concerned he might have homosexual tendencies attacks women to prove to himself that he possesses a desire for women. He uses less force than other types of attackers. He plans carefully. He tends to attack in the same location and keep souvenirs.' Killarney withdrew his hand from his pocket and folded his arms across his chest.

'The power-assertive is what's known as the "acquaintance-type". These people come across as friendly

31

and non-threatening. They become threatening later, usually when a sexual advance has been rejected. They become frightened. They feel invalidated, intimidated, weakened. Sexual tension becomes physical tension which swiftly becomes anger, rage, hatred. They switch to expressing their motive through violence. If they can't have the victim, then no-one else can.'

Killarney surveyed the faces before him, ensuring that he held their attention.

'Third we have anger-retaliatory. Just as it sounds, this is all about anger and hostility toward women. The victim is symbolic. The anger-retaliatory will humiliate the victim in some way. Their attacks are often unplanned and violent. And the last one, anger-excitement, comes out of a sadistic need to terrify the victim, to cause as much suffering as possible. Attacks are like military operations. Locations, weapons, methods, all of these things are selected carefully and often rehearsed. They use extreme violence, sometimes torturing the victim, often killing them. The victim is ordinarily a stranger, and the perpetrator tends to keep records of the attacks.'

'And how does this relate to the victims we have?' Miller asked, something of a challenge in his tone. Though the FBI's invasion of Washington PD territory was not Miller's doing, he believed that a failure to act aggressively would be considered a failure to lead. He had been assigned the case, and from this moment forward he would have to demonstrate his willingness to take the first step.

'We have a marauder,' Killarney said. 'But we have no clear indication of which of the four categories our friend falls into. Closest is anger-excitement, but there appears to be no sadism, no desire to terrify the victim. In this last case he even restrained himself, did not beat her face as he did the first three. But there are anomalies. He does not torture. There is no extreme violence.'

'What about the beating?' Miller asked.

Killarney smiled knowingly, patiently. 'The beating? The beating he gave them was just a beating. When I say extreme violence I mean *extreme* violence. The beating these women received was quite restrained in comparison to much of what I have seen.'

Silence.

'So?' Miller prompted.

Killarney looked around and then returned his attention to Miller.

'What's your name?'

'Miller . . . Robert Miller.'

Killarney nodded. 'Miller,' he said, as if to himself, and then he looked up, eyes wide. 'I understand that you are now heading up this investigation.'

'So I've just been informed,' Miller said, and then realized the real source of his provocation. He had been cornered. He had been given something he did not wish to own. Killarney was perhaps there to help, nothing more nor less than that, but regardless he represented not only the removal of Miller's power of choice, but also the implication that Miller – now given complete responsibility for the investigation – was not capable of handling it without assistance. Such was the nature of high-profile cases: the chief of police had to trust his captains, they in turn had to trust their deputies and lieutenants, but always the sense of uncertainty, the recognition that as the chain of command stretched further so the liabilities increased.

'So tell us what you think, Miller . . . tell us what you think about the Ribbon Killer.'

Miller was suddenly self-conscious. He felt Killarney was putting him on the spot because he'd interrupted him mid-flight, some desire to re-assert his control over the proceedings.

'I was there at the first one,' Miller said. 'Margaret Mosley.' He looked around the room. The other detectives were watching him. 'I went in there and found her . . . didn't find her, you know? I mean I was the first detective there. There were uniforms there when I arrived. Coroner was already on her way. I went in there . . . into her bedroom, saw the victim there on the bed.' Miller looked down, shook his head slowly.

'What was your first impression, Detective Miller?' Killarney asked.

Miller looked up. 'First impression?'

33

'The first thing you felt.'

'First thing I felt was like someone had punched me in the chest.' He raised his fist and thumped a point in the middle of his ribcage. 'Like someone hit me with a baseball bat. That's what I felt.'

'And did you move through the scene, or did you survey the scene from a stationary point?'

'Stationary . . . like we were taught. Always survey the scene from a stationary point . . . look for anomalies, things out of place. Look for the obvious before anything else.'

'And?'

'The ribbon, of course.'

Killarney nodded. 'Yes . . . the ribbon, the tag. And then?'

'The smell of lavender.'

'No doubt?'

'No, it was lavender . . . same as the other two.'

'You were at the other two?' Killarney asked.

'No,' Miller said. 'I just happened to be on duty when the first one occurred. I wasn't officially assigned to this case. I did see the preliminary file on the third however, and then last night, this most recent one . . .'

'Who was present at the second?' Killarney asked.

'Second one came under the Fourth Precinct,' Miller said. 'None of us dealt with that one.'

'And the third . . .' Killarney glanced at the pages on the desk beside him. 'Barbara Lee . . . any of you present at that one?'

Carl Oliver, seated to Miller's right, raised his hand. 'Me and my partner, Chris Metz.'

Metz also raised his hand to identify himself, and added, 'That, officially, fell under the Sixth's jurisdiction, but they didn't have anyone free so we were called in.'

'Which explains one of the primary reasons that this serial has continued unchecked for eight months,' Killarney said, 'and also explains why your chief of police has assigned it to one precinct, one lead detective . . . right, Mr Miller?'

Miller nodded.

Killarney turned back to Carl Oliver. 'So tell us about the third one, Detective Oliver.'

'Same,' Oliver said. 'Lavender.'

'So we have our signature perhaps. The ribbon in the second case . . . Miss Ann Rayner, was—'

'Pink,' Al Roth interjected.

'And then we have the blank name tag. A luggage tag? A John Doe tag? A lost property tag? This we don't know, can only begin to guess at.'

Killarney nodded slowly, unfolded his arms, put his hands in his pockets. 'Margaret Mosley, Ann Rayner, Barbara Lee, Catherine Sheridan. Thirty-seven, forty, twenty-nine and forty-nine years of age respectively. Ribbons in blue, pink, yellow and white. The same perfume at each crime scene. Perhaps our friend doused the body, the bed and the curtains with lavender water in order to obscure the smell of decay. Possibly he believed he could delay discovery of the body.' Killarney tilted his head to one side, sort of squinted at Miller, then looked at Roth. 'Or perhaps not. Regardless, it did not work in this last instance because pizza had been ordered.'

'Perhaps both the name tag and the lavender mean nothing at all,' Miller suggested.

'Indeed, Mr Miller. Oh what tangled webs we weave when first we practice to deceive, eh?' Killarney smiled knowingly. 'Personally I blame the television.'

Miller frowned.

'And the internet,' Killarney added.

'I don't understand—'

'You know how many tricks of the trade you can find on TV and the internet?' Killarney asked.

Miller opened his mouth to speak.

'A rhetorical question, Mr Miller. Point I'm making is that pretty much anything you might want to know about what we're looking for at a crime scene can be learnt on the internet. If you know what criminalistics and forensics are looking for you can hide it, or, indeed, you can give them something to find that means nothing at all.'

'You think he'll kill again?' Miller asked.

Killarney smiled. 'Kill again? Our friend? Oh yes, Mr Miller . . . I can pretty much guarantee that.'

Glances were exchanged between the detectives present – awkward, uncertain.

'So now you want to know how you're going to find this

guy, right?' Killarney asked. 'You want to know what I know. You want to hear the magic words that will throw the light of truth and reason into this darkest of places, isn't that so?'

His audience waited, silent and expectant.

'Well, there are no magic words, and there is no light of truth and reason,' he said quietly. 'You will find this man with persistence . . . nothing but unrelenting persistence. This is not luck. This is not guesswork.' Killarney smiled. 'I know I am telling you something you already know, but sometimes all of us need to be reminded about the simple truths of investigatory work. And if you want a reason, a rationale . . .' He shook his head. 'Well, I'll tell you this, gentlemen, you cannot rationalize an irrationality. The only person who understands precisely why this Ribbon Killer does what he does is—'

'The man himself,' Miller finished for him.

'Very good, Detective Miller. You win the Kewpie doll.'

My name is John Robey, and I know everything you could ever wish to know about Catherine Sheridan.

I know the street where she lives, the view from the back yard. I know what she likes to eat and where she buys her groceries. I know the perfume she wears, and which colors she feels will suit her. I know her age, her place of birth, the way she feels about many little things, and why . . .

But I know other things as well. The important things. The things that frightened her. The things that caused her to wonder if she'd made the right decisions. What she believed would happen if she got those decisions wrong.

I know the mundane, but also the complex, the simple as well as the elaborate.

I know the shadows that follow as well as those that wait.

And I have my own shadows, my own fears, my own small secrets. Such as my name, for my name wasn't always John Robey . . .

But such details do not matter now. Such details we will speak of when there is time.

For these brief moments I shall remain John Robey, and I will tell you what I know.

I know about love and disappointment, about heartbreak and disillusionment. I understand that time serves to dull the razor's edge of loss until memories no longer cut so deep, they merely bruise with the repetition of trying to forget.

I know about promises kept and promises broken.

I know about Catherine Sheridan and Darryl King and Natasha Joyce. I know of Natasha's daughter, Chloe.

I know about Margaret Mosley; I know her apartment on Bates and First. I know the bay window with the sunny aspect that looks out towards Florida Avenue.

I know Ann Rayner, the basement of her house off of Patterson Street NE.

I know Barbara Lee, her corner house on Morgan and Jersey, no more than five blocks south east of where I now stand.

I know that I am a tired man. Not because I have not slept. These days I sleep too much. No, it is not that kind of tired.

I am exhausted from carrying these things.

There is The Quiet Half. We all possess a Quiet Half. Here are our sins and transgressions, our crimes and iniquities, our lapses of reason and faith and honesty, our vices and misdeeds and every time we fell from grace . . .

The Quiet Half haunts; it follows like those proverbial shadows, and then it waits with unsurpassed patience and fortitude. What do they say? Ultimately everyone dies from wrongdoings and shortness of breath.

I carry enough for one man. Truth? I carry enough for three or five or seven.

Caught up with me I suppose, and when I turn to look at my own Quiet Half I realize that there is only one way this thing can be exorcised.

By telling the truth. By carrying the light of truth into the very darkest places, and not caring who or what is illuminated on the way.

In that moment it will all come to an end.

Only one thing I can do . . . between now and then I can carry the light. Expose the shadows. Show the world what's there.

They don't want to see it – never have, never will.

Too late. They're going to see it anyway.

FOUR

Miller and Roth began work that afternoon, Miller already feeling a sense of urgency regarding what lay ahead. Killarney had finished his briefing, answered questions, and then Lassiter hammered them about results. Killarney would be tracking with them, he would not interfere, but he would be kept apprised of their progress.

Miller's initial thought – that he did not wish to become embroiled in some lengthy, high-profile murder case – had been replaced with a feeling that this was perhaps the best thing he could do. Already it had begun to pull his attention away from recent events.

The words Killarney had uttered were still clear in Miller's mind as he and Roth left the Second and made their way toward Columbia Street. Roth had with him the picture of Catherine Sheridan. The image, taken from her passport and digitally-enhanced to improve the contrast and color as Reid had suggested, had been reproduced in a postcard format. Miller had stared at the image, tried to see the woman. There was something about her features, something individual and striking, but he could not determine what it was. She looked as if she had lived with as much drama as had characterized the nature of her death.

The previous day, Saturday the 11th, had been Veterans Day. Unusually chill, for sunshine varied little in Washington, and November temperatures rarely dropped below the high forties. A small thermometer on the veranda of the Sheridan house would have given the temperature as thirty-five Fahrenheit. Being Veterans Day, processions and remembrance marches would have been the focus of attention for the majority of Washingtonians; Arlington Cemetery, children dwarfed by the stainless steel statues representing America's loss in Korea. A day of remembrance, of mourning, of the

World War II Memorial inscription: 'Today the guns are silent . . . The skies no longer rain death – the seas bear only commerce – men everywhere walk upright in the sunlight. The entire world is quietly at peace.' There would have been the sound of brass bands in the distance, Sousa marches challenging the hum and rumble of the city's morning traffic. Respectful people, glancing back toward the sound as they remembered what Veterans Day meant to so many. A father lost, perhaps a son, a brother, a neighbor, a childhood sweetheart. People who stopped for a moment, closed their eyes, breathed deeply, nodded as if in prayer, and then moved along the sidewalk. Memories were left hanging in the crisp atmosphere, and as people passed by it was as if they could feel the sorrow, the nostalgia, the haunt of warmth as they walked right through them. For a single day Washington had become a city of memories, a city of forgetting.

'Library after the house,' Miller said as he and Roth pulled away from the sidewalk and drove toward Columbia. 'That's if the library is actually open today.'

Roth didn't reply, merely nodded.

Greg Reid was in Catherine Sheridan's kitchen when Roth and Miller arrived. He smiled, raised his hand in acknowledgement. In daylight he looked like William Hurt, his features receptive to life, to others, perhaps a man who gave more than he took. 'So you're on this job then?' he asked.

'We are,' Miller said. 'How's it looking?'

'I sent her away to the morgue,' Reid said. 'Did my preliminaries, took prints, pictures, all the usual. Have a few things for you.' He nodded toward the kitchen table. 'You've got the library card, right? There's also some food from a deli in the kitchen, some bread, butter, stuff like that. It's organic bread, you know? French. No preservatives. Date-stamped yesterday.'

'Which deli?' Roth asked.

'Address is on the wrapper,' Reid said.

Miller took his notepad from his pocket. 'Any messages on the answerphone?'

Reid shook his head. 'No answerphone.'

'Computer?'

Reid shook his head. 'No desktop, no laptop that I could find.' He smiled awkwardly.

'What?' Miller asked.

'Never seen anything like this place,' Reid said.

'Like what?'

'This house.'

'How d'you mean?' Miller asked.

'Take a look around. It's very clean, almost too clean.'

'Perp more than likely cleaned everything,' Roth said. 'They have this shit down cold now. God bless *CSI*, right?'

Reid shook his head. 'I don't mean that kind of clean. I mean it's like no-one really lived here. Like a hotel, you know? There's none of the usual kind of mess you get with normal people. Washing basket in the bathroom is empty. There's combs and cosmetics, toothpaste, all that kind of thing, but it seems like there's too little of it.'

'Did you cover any of the previous crime scenes?' Miller asked.

'I did the one in July over on Patterson.'

'Ann Rayner,' Roth said.

'Same guy you figure?' Miller asked.

'Seems that way from all appearances.' Reid paused for a moment. 'Made a note for the coroner to check, but there may be something else . . . can't be completely sure on basic examination.'

'Which was?'

'This one, Catherine Sheridan . . . she had someone with her yesterday.'

'With her?'

'Looks like she had sex with someone.'

'You're not certain?'

'Certain as I can be from cursory examination. She had spermicidal lubricant in the vaginal area. Nonoxynol-9. Check with the coroner to be sure, she can do an internal.'

'But no signs of rape?'

Reid shook his head. 'Nothing outward to suggest it, no.'

'And time of death is confirmed?' Roth asked.

'Best we can place it, liver temp, temp of the environment, somewhere between four forty-five and six p.m. yesterday. Coroner can maybe give you something more accurate.'

'Did you check last number redial?' Roth asked.

Reid shook his head. 'Had my hands full with the lady herself, figured you could do that.'

Roth walked through to the front of the house. He put on latex gloves, lifted the receiver and hit the redial button.

Miller could hear him share a few words with whoever was on the other end of the line, and then he hung up and walked back through to the kitchen. 'Pizza company,' Roth said. 'Have their name and address.'

'Good enough,' Miller said. 'We're gonna check the houses around here, the library, the deli, then the pizza place. How long before you're done here?'

Reid shrugged. 'I haven't done the upstairs fully yet. Did her body, packed it up for the coroner . . . have a whole floor to cover yet. Gonna be a while.'

'We'll come back later,' Miller said.

'Figure you could give me the rest of the day,' Reid said. 'I'm here on my own now.'

Reid left them in the kitchen, headed back upstairs. Roth found the bag from the deli: French bread, a half pound of Normandy brie, a pat of unsalted butter, all untouched. The bread was dated the 11th, just as Reid had said. *Baked fresh each day. No preservatives. Tomorrow this will be a baseball bat!* the label read. Made Miller smile, Roth too, and then Miller remembered how Catherine Sheridan had been found, the way she'd been positioned, the color of her face, the rigored awkwardness of everything . . . Such a sight was sufficient to kill a smile. Kill it for several days.

Roth made a note of the deli address, and together they left by the back kitchen door and crossed the lot to the sidewalk.

Catherine Sheridan's thoughts were something Miller could only guess at. For the time being he had to be content with little more than where she went that Saturday morning, perhaps a little of why. He and Roth walked up and down the street. They spoke with a handful of people who had not been home the night before. No-one else had anything to say. The house on the right of the Sheridan lot was now demonstrably empty. They had not been able to tell the night before, but Roth walked around the back, cupped his hands against the window and peered into the lower floor.

Furniture shrouded in dust-sheets, rooms of stillness and silence. The left-side neighbor was still not home. Miller and Roth drove away from Columbia Street, headed toward the Carnegie Library.

'We're not usually open on a Sunday,' the librarian told them. Her name was Julia Gibb, and she looked like a librarian; sounded like one too. She spoke in hushed tones. She peered at them over half-rimmed spectacles. 'Today we're open because of Veterans Day. Yesterday we were only open until noon, and today we're open until noon again to make up for it.'

There was a moment's hesitation, and then she said, 'It's about Miss Sheridan, isn't it?' She reached beneath the counter and withdrew a copy of the *Post*. 'I don't know what to say. It's a terrible, terrible thing . . .'

Miller asked questions; Roth took notes. Julia Gibb did not know Catherine Sheridan, no more than any other customer. She'd noticed nothing out of the ordinary in her behavior, save the fact that she had returned books but withdrawn none.

'I keep trying to remember if I said anything to her,' Julia Gibb told them. 'Yesterday? Yesterday I don't think I said a word.'

'Which books did she return?' Miller asked.

'I made a note of them,' Julia Gibb said. 'I know it's nothing important, but seeing as how she was here yesterday I imagined that someone might want to know.' She slid a piece of paper across the counter toward Miller. Roth picked it up, glanced over the titles – Steinbeck's *Of Mice and Men* and *East of Eden*, *Beast* by Joyce Carol Oates, a couple of others he didn't recognize.

'And what time was it when she left?'

'Quite early . . . perhaps a quarter of ten, something like that. I know we hadn't been open long.'

'Did you see her when she left again?'

'Well, I was with another customer, and I heard the door close to. I looked up, didn't see who it was, but could only assume it was Miss Sheridan because when the customer I was dealing with had gone I realized I was alone.'

Miller nodded, looked at Roth. Roth shook his head; he had no more questions.

'We're done for now,' Miller said. 'Thank you for your help, Miss Gibb.'

'You're welcome,' she said. 'Such a tragedy isn't it? Such a terrible thing to happen to a woman like that.'

'It is,' Miller replied matter-of-factly, and then glanced once again at the slip of paper upon which she'd written the titles before tucking it safely into his overcoat pocket.

As they drove away from the library Miller realized the effect such brief moments created. They served to remind him about people. Catherine Sheridan was a person – somewhere back of her death was a life. Just like Julia Gibb's. Regular people watched as the lives of others exploded around them. Collisions of humanity. Moments of horror. No-one understood them, and often no-one cared to understand. Now, in his pocket, he had a list of the most recent books she'd read. Would her choices have been different had she known they would be the last things she would ever read, he wondered? A strange thought, but in light of what had happened one that further demonstrated the fragility and unpredictability of life.

It was the same when they reached the delicatessen on the junction of L Street and Tenth. Owner's name was Lewis Roarke, something Irish in his accent, in the dark rush of hair, the blue washed-out eyes. He didn't remember Catherine Sheridan, even when Roth showed him the enhanced picture. Busy day. It was early. Folks coming in to buy polony, chorizo, milano salami, string bags of select cheeses for hampers, subs. Folks with kids, grandparents in tow. Food on the go. This kind of thing. No, he didn't remember Catherine Sheridan, but then why should he have done? From her picture she seemed like a regular kind of lady. World was full of regular kinds of ladies. Nose piercing, streak of blue hair, something such as that, maybe then he would have remembered, but a regular lady? Smiled, shook his head, apologized despite having nothing to apologize for.

Roarke took the card that Miller passed over the high glass counter, waited until Miller and Roth were across the street and then tossed it in the trash. Hadn't remembered anything now, what's to say he'd remember anything tomorrow, the next day? There were customers ahead of him. *Yes, how can I help you?*

Miller and Roth sat in the car down the block from the deli.

'So she goes to the library,' Roth said. 'She returns her books but withdraws none. She goes to the deli, presumably all of this on foot. She buys bread, butter, cheese, but then she doesn't return to the house until about four-thirty.'

'Because she went somewhere and had sex with someone,' Miller said, matter-of-fact.

'Maybe, maybe not. You want to see the coroner or go to the pizza place?'

'The pizza place,' Miller said. 'Want to speak to everyone she made contact with.'

Roth started the engine.

'Truth is,' Miller added, 'that if she hadn't ordered the pizza, we might not even know she was dead.'

FIVE

A distance away from Washington's Second Precinct, the kind of distance measured in class and culture and color, Natasha Joyce stood in the corridor outside her daughter's Sunday school classroom and waited for eleven o'clock. Annexed to a run-down community hall, the Sunday School building had retained something of its character beneath the outward display of graffiti. The front door carried more deadbolts and padlock hasps than Natasha could count, and along the internal walls, those places where childrens' pictures and activity posters were displayed, you could still see the rough surface of the concrete blocks, the makeshift paint job, the chips and scars that came from neglect and lack of funding. It was a quietly desperate place, a sad reflection of Washington's unknown quarters.

From where Natasha stood she could see through the frosted window, could see the hazy blurs of color as children ran back and forth within, could hear the rush and collision of voices, the catcalls and laughter. The bell sounded, and Natasha Joyce stepped inside the room. She smiled an acknowledgement to Chloe's school teacher, Miss Antrobus. Nice enough lady, but uptight. She was mulatto, like a mixed-race, half and half. Couple of generations back one of the white folks did a black man, something such as this. Now Miss Antrobus didn't belong to anyone. Not to the blacks, not to the scared whites out of Georgetown. Perhaps she found her anchor in Jesus. Perhaps she was just pretending.

Miss Antrobus looked at her again, smiled, and then made her way through the throng of kids to where Natasha stood by the door.

'Might be nothing,' Miss Antrobus said. Her eyes kind of went this way, that way. Appeared she was looking for something that wasn't there.

'I had a copy of the *Post* on my desk,' she went on. 'Article about that terrible thing . . . the woman that was murdered.'

Natasha Joyce froze quietly. She was aware of the tension in her face but tried to show nothing.

Chloe was by the door, itching to leave, like there was pepper under her skin.

'Chloe saw the woman's picture . . . said that she knew her.' Miss Antrobus smiled nervously. 'I knew it couldn't be true . . . must have mistaken her for someone else.'

'She *does* have an imagination,' Natasha replied, and glanced at Chloe.

'Did you hear about it?'

Natasha frowned. 'I'm not sure I understand . . .'

'There was a woman murdered on Saturday. Her picture was in the *Post.* Chloe said she recognized her. She didn't . . . *you* didn't know her did you, Miss Joyce?'

Natasha shook her head. 'No. I can't imagine who she thinks we might know,' she replied, and she heard the edge of anxiety in her own voice. She tried to smile but it came out strained and artificial. She walked to the door, reached for the handle. With her left hand she waved a 'come on' to Chloe.

Chloe was suddenly beside her, bright-eyed, attentive. 'Mom,' she piped up. 'That lady . . . you remember? She came down with that man when they were looking for Daddy, that man who gave you the money . . . you remember when he gave you that money and we bought Polly Petal . . .'

Natasha had the door open. She was hustling Chloe out and down the corridor, looking at Miss Antrobus and smiling as best she could.

'She was in the paper today . . . that nice lady—'

Natasha glanced back at Miss Antrobus. She was watching her, watching Chloe. Expression on her face like she was ready to start calling someone.

'Someone else,' Natasha told Chloe, loud enough for Miss Antrobus to hear, and felt confused and upset. She didn't understand what was happening, but she knew she was lying to her daughter.

Three blocks from the school Natasha Joyce bought the

Post. She looked at the picture of Catherine Sheridan; she read the first two or three paragraphs of the article.

'It's her, isn't it, Mom?' Chloe said.

Natasha shook her head. 'Don't know, sweetie . . . looks like her. Maybe it's just someone that looks like her.' She hoped to God that she was right. She hoped to God that the monochrome face that looked back at her was the face of someone else entirely. Now she'd seen it twice – once on the TV, once in the paper. She was afraid. More than afraid.

'I think it's her, Mom . . . she has the same look in her eyes.'

'What look is that, darling?'

Chloe shrugged. 'Don't know . . . maybe like she knew someone was going to get her.'

Natasha laughed nervously. She remembered standing in the cold breeze with those two people. A woman and a man. How long had it been? Five years. Jesus, it really was all of five years ago. The woman's name was not Catherine Sheridan. And the man. Chewing gum, twitching a little, like nervous was his middle name. Like he was watching for someone, someone he believed might see them.

They'd asked after her boyfriend, Chloe's father. His name was Darryl King, and Natasha remembered thinking, who are these people? How the hell would people like this know Darryl?

Chloe looked up; wide-eyed sweetness and light, innocent as snow. 'Who d'you think might have killed her?'

Natasha laughed again. 'It's not the same lady,' she said. 'I'm sure it's not the same lady.' She folded the paper and tucked it under her arm. She took Chloe's hand and started walking.

Didn't say a word all the way home, and when they arrived Natasha sat in the frontroom for a while. Like she was waiting for something she knew would come. Could hear Chloe playing in her room. Natasha wondered how much Chloe had figured out. She seemed cool, seemed like nothing in the world could bother her. That was the way Natasha had always wanted Chloe to feel, like nothing in the world could ever reach her. Mom could run interference between Chloe and the world. Natasha had done it with Darryl, and though

Chloe had only been four when he'd died, she knew that kids were perceptive, and sometimes the youngest were the smartest of all. It had been a thing. A real thing. A full-time kind of thing. Keeping Darryl's world out of the line of sight, out of earshot, out of Chloe's life. Hard, almost impossible, but Chloe seemed to have survived, seemed to be okay, seemed to have remained untouched by everything . . . until the newspaper.

She glanced at the paper again, at the face that looked back at her. She tried to remember when she'd last seen the woman. A couple of weeks before Darryl died – before Darryl King got himself killed for getting involved in things he never should have been involved in. And regardless of whether it was the same woman or not, this thing hurt Natasha. It made Natasha realize that Chloe *had* seen what was going on, that she *had* been paying attention, that she could remember all the way back to when her father died. Back to when that woman had come looking for Darryl. And the man with her, the fact that he'd taken such an interest in Chloe, like he felt guilty or something . . . Gave her twenty bucks. Just pulled twenty bucks right out of his pocket and gave it to her. And they bought that doll, the doll that took pride of place in amongst everything else for so long. Polly Petal. Stupid fucking Polly Petal doll. And now, five years on, she'd seen this woman's face in the paper . . .

Natasha shuddered. She felt giddy, almost frightened. She didn't want to think about such things. She didn't want to remember the past. She wanted the past to stay right where she'd left it.

After a little while she walked out of the kitchen and stood in the hallway. She watched her daughter through the half-open doorway of her room. Shuddered when she saw that doll sitting right in front of her, as if the two of them were watching TV together.

All smashed to hell, isn't it? Natasha thought, and in thinking this she remembered how her life had been with Darryl King all those years before. How much she had loved him. How much she had believed that he was the one, the only one, the single most important thing that had ever happened to her. And then later, when he became someone

49

else. She remembered his attitude, his arrogance, the way his life had started coming apart at the seams.

This is the Big H baby! This is the junk, you know? This is my skag, my horse, my thunder . . . I do this shit, or it does me. Who the fuck cares?

I'm not doin' no crack here, sugar. I got my 24-7, my bad rock, my candy, my chemical . . . I got fat bags, french fries, some gravel and hardball . . . I got hotcakes, jelly beans, prime time, rockstar, sleet, sugarblock and tornado . . .

I got the whole fucking world in my pocket, baby. Should try this shit, you know? This shit gon' make you hot!

And how he would kick off sometimes, his world-has-done-me-wrong thing.

Tell you what the world thinks about people like us? People like us don't give a damn what it takes. We take what we need. Rob everyone blind. Steal from our own grandmothers. Fuck you mo'fucker. Fuck you! That's who they think we are, and that's who we're gonna be!

How many times had Natasha thought about giving up that life? She'd thought about it all the time . . . especially when Chloe told her that someone had called her a crack whore.

What's a crack whore, Mommy?

No-one should be called a crack whore when they're five years old.

The truth? Ultimately Darryl King had not been the truth. However much Natasha might have loved him, and however misguided that love might have been, she knew that his vision of the world was not how it was. She did not live like an animal. She did not live in filth and shit, in squalid rooms piled high with stolen TVs and PS2s and greasy takeout cartons. Not everywhere was damp; not everywhere smelled like urine and baby puke and people dying. The corridors of her project building did not echo with the phlegm-spittle hacking rasp of tuberculoid grandfathers, the cries of un-wanted newborns with colic. Perhaps, because she came from here, she was loathed and despised and undesirable, just as Darryl would have had her believe. But she did not believe it. Not all the time.

She had a nine-year-old daughter. Her name was Chloe.

50

She was not unwashed or unwanted. She was not named Delicia or Lakeisha or Shenayné-LeQuanda . . .

Chloe's father was dead. His name was Darryl King. He was crazy, but Natasha had loved him – desperately, unconditionally at first, and then when it all went bad she had continued to love him for the hope that it could somehow become what it had once been. Natasha Joyce had loved Darryl King enough to give him a child and then, later, when it all turned bad, to sit with him through the blood pressure, the sweating, the nausea and hyperventilation, the hypersensitivity, the tactile hallucinations, the images of bugs burrowing under his skin, the euphoria, the paranoia, the depression and exultation, the panic, the psychosis, the seizures . . .

Loved him enough to try everything she could to stop him taking drugs.

But the power of his addiction had been far greater than any love or loyalty he had possessed. He'd taken everything they had, everything they didn't.

One time Darryl left them; hadn't come back for two days.

Natasha had known that one day he would leave and never return.

Natasha Joyce knew that life was just a matter of escaping what you did not want, trying to hold on to what you did. You kept trying, or you accepted what people thought you were and decided you could not change.

Darryl had done that: he'd become what other people thought he should be. A loser. A lowlife. A crackhead nigger.

This had brought it all back to her. A face had looked right back at her from the front page of the *Post*. Natasha didn't want it to be the same woman who'd come looking for Darryl, smartly dressed, ever-so-polite, beside her the nervous sidekick – chewing gum, saying nothing, giving her twenty bucks for Chloe when he left. Natasha had figured them for cops, but they were not. The woman had done all the talking. Seemed decent. Scared though. She'd said her name. Natasha could not now recall what it was, but she knew for sure that it hadn't been Catherine Sheridan. And now some crazy guy, a guy they named the Ribbon Killer, had murdered her. They said it was his fourth victim. One thing Natasha Joyce knew for sure. Knew that crazy guy was going to be white.

And that's if they were the same people. Looked like her. *Like*. That was all. Lots of people looked *like* other people.

It was intuition that told her. Intuition, a gut feeling, whatever the hell it was called . . .

Chloe had seen the face in the paper and hadn't hesitated.

Natasha looked at her daughter, and she thought *Gotta get you out of here, girl. Gotta get you outta here whatever it costs. You're not gonna have the life I've had. Not my life, nor Darryl's, nor the life those scared white folks in Georgetown think you deserve. Gonna do whatever has to be done.*

Something like that. Kind of thought she'd had before, but this time she felt it with a sense of certainty, a sense of urgency, a sense of importance.

Thought of Darryl again; thought *Darryl – whoever the fuck you were, whatever the hell you were into, whoever the hell you might or might not have known . . . your daughter, our daughter, deserves better than this . . . What d'you reckon, Darryl, you fucked-up, smashed-to-pieces, crackhead loser black asshole motherfucker? Oh God, Darryl, I don't know that I could have loved you more. Tried everything. Gave everything I had to give while I watched you fall apart. And afterwards I made believe I could forget it all. Didn't want to know what happened. Pretended that all this shit was behind us, but it wasn't, and it isn't now, and it's true that all the things you never faced will somehow find you . . .*

And then she glanced once more at the *Post*, and thought *Damn bitch. Why d'you have to go get yourself murdered by some crazy motherfucker.*

Natasha felt she couldn't wait to see if scared Miss Antrobus called the cops and told tales. She figured that Miss Mulatto-What a friend we have in Jesus-interfering-bitch was just that kind of woman, and thus Natasha knew she would have to make the call herself. Tell them that maybe she knew something.

Natasha Joyce was twenty-nine years old. Chloe's father had been dead for a little more than five years. What little life he'd had she'd watched disappear effortlessly through a hypodermic needle. Now the police would come again. If

Miss Antrobus made the call then they would come over and see her. They would want to know how Chloe had known the woman's face in the newspaper. Natasha had never been able to lie. She would tell them that someone had come down to the projects to speak with Darryl King. Then they would want to know what Darryl King had been involved in, how he'd known this dead woman. Natasha would say that she wasn't sure it was the same woman. They would see it in her eyes, how afraid she was of becoming involved in this. Natasha hadn't wanted to know then, and she didn't want to know now. But something inside told her that understanding any part of what had happened back then would make her feel better. Not because it would be good news, because after Darryl started doing heroin nothing had ever been good news, but because it might bring a degree of closure. It had been a fucked-up time, a really fucked-up time, but it had been part of her life. Part of her life that had given her Chloe, and for no other reason it made sense to understand. Why? Because then she might be able to tell Chloe the truth. When Chloe was old enough to understand, she might be able to look her in the eye and tell her that her father wasn't a complete waste of life. That he was *somebody*. That he did at least one good thing. Maybe these people had been good people. Maybe they'd been trying to help Darryl. Or maybe he'd been helping them. Maybe he was even trying to get out of the life and these people had been doing something that could make it happen.

Or maybe it was all shit.

Maybe they were nothing but smart-suit bigshot smack dealers from Capitol Hill come down to slum it with the niggers. And then the woman had gotten herself killed. This Catherine Sheridan. And if it was the same woman who'd come looking for Darryl, then maybe the guy that came with her had murdered her. Maybe they'd argued about some deal and he'd beaten the shit out of her and choked her. Maybe he'd murdered the other three first, or he'd murdered her like the first three to make everyone think it was this Ribbon Killer . . .

That would have been a smart move, Natasha thought.

She knew she would have to call the cops, have to tell

them who she was and where she lived, that the dead woman in the newspaper had come to see Darryl King five years before, that there might be a connection . . .

Have to tell them that Darryl King went missing and wound up dead, and even now she still did not know what happened.

Natasha took the newspaper. She tore the front page off and dropped it in the sink. She took a lighter and set it on fire, watched it curl up into a black fall-leaf.

It burned from the edges inward – slowly, patiently, the smell of smoke bitter in her nostrils.

Last thing to go was the woman's face, and the last part of her face was the cold and lifeless eyes, eyes that looked back at Natasha Joyce as if Natasha was somehow responsible for her death.

SIX

Robert Miller and Al Roth stood in a pizza parlor near the junction of M Street and Eleventh. Miller believed that Roth's time would have been better spent recovering all files and reports from the previous three murders, but house calls and interviews always had to be conducted by two detectives. A corroborative system had to be established and maintained regardless.

The manager was young, no more than twenty-three or four. Pleasant face, honest-looking, fair hair cut neat. 'Hey,' he said, and smiled.

'You're Sam?' Miller asked.

'Yeah, I'm Sam.' He looked at each of them in turn. 'You called earlier, yes?'

Miller showed his badge. 'An order was made yesterday evening, somewhere around five forty-five, delivered to a house on Columbia around six.'

'The dead woman, I know. I don't know what to tell you. Delivery guy . . . Jesus, I don't even know how you'd deal with something like that.'

'You took the order yourself?' Miller asked.

'I did.'

'And how did she sound to you?'

Sam frowned, shook his head. 'She? No, it wasn't a woman who placed the order. It was a man.'

Miller looked at Roth. 'A man?'

'Yes, definitely a man. No question about it. I took the details – stuffed crust, extra monterey jack, double mushroom, you know? I'm writing down the order. I ask the guy for his number, he gives me the number. I ask his name, he says "Catherine". I say "What?" He laughs. He says "That's who the pizza's for. Catherine". I say "Okay, for Catherine". I read him back the order. He then repeats it back to me real slow. Made the conversation stick in my head, you know?'

'Like he wanted you to remember the conversation?'

'That's what I'm thinking now. He wanted me to remember him.'

Miller looked at Roth. Everything that needed to be said was right there in Roth's expression. Catherine Sheridan's killer had called and ordered pizza. He had wanted her to be found immediately.

'How did he sound?' Miller asked Sam.

'Sounded like Washington, you know? Nothing special. Just sounded like a regular guy. Maybe if I'd known I was gonna be asked about him I would have paid more attention.'

'It's okay, you did good. You kept the number he gave you?'

'It's on the order slip.'

'You have that?'

Sam shuffled through things behind the counter, looked in two places, came back with a yellow paper the size of a playing card. 'Here,' he said, and handed it to Miller.

'Can I keep this?'

'Sure you can.'

Miller took the slip, glanced at it. 'Three-one-five area code,' he said. 'We have a three-one-five area code in Washington?'

Sam shrugged. 'I don't know. I'm not sure. Tell you the truth I didn't even think about it when I wrote the number down. Saturday we're so busy—'

'It's fine,' Miller said. 'We'll check it out.' He handed Sam one of his cards. 'You think of anything else—'

'Then I'll call you,' Sam interjected, smiling again like he was glad to be helpful.

'Thanks,' Miller said, and shook Sam's hand.

'No problem.'

Miller reached the door and paused. 'One other question. About payment. Don't you take card details over the phone?'

'Sure, sometimes we do, but most of the deliveries are cash.'

'And this was a cash order?'

'Sure yes. It was just a regular order. Only thing about it was when he gave the woman's name. Apart from that it was no different from any other call.'

'Okay,' Miller said. 'Thanks for your time.' He held up the yellow order slip. 'And for this.'

Neither Miller nor Roth spoke during the brief walk back to the car.

Miller felt a quiet sense of certainty that anything resembling a normal life would now cease for the foreseeable future. Cease until they had someone, and only begin again if that someone was *the* someone. Always the way these things went.

Once they were in the car, he looked at the number printed across the top of the order slip. 'I really don't think this is a Washington area code,' he said. 'I think this is something else.'

'Question I have is who the fuck orders pizza for a dead woman?' Roth asked.

'He wanted her found,' Miller replied matter-of-factly. 'He wanted everyone to know what he'd done. Previous three were found almost by accident, by chance, something usual. This one? This one's different.'

He shook his head. Almost everything had been the same – the lack of forced entry, the beating, the ribbon and tag, even the smell of lavender. Everything the same, except Catherine Sheridan's face had been left unmarked, and now this. Killarney would have said that the killer had reached his embellishment phase. Modifications, minor changes, knowing that with each aspect of his work he would garner further attention.

'This is what he wants,' Miller said quietly. 'He wants people to see what he has done.'

At the precinct Miller tried the number. He got nothing but a continuous tone. He taped the small yellow slip on the wall beside his desk. He did not want to forget it amidst the madness of paperwork he knew was coming. He and Roth then made the necessary requests to have files relating to Mosley, Rayner and Lee brought to the Second. Miller spoke with Lassiter, asked for whatever help he could get putting the records into some sense of order. Lassiter gave him Metz and Oliver and a couple of uniforms from admin. By two o'clock there were six of them crowded into the second-floor office.

'I need phone records,' Miller said. 'Landline and cell phone. I want bank records, any computers and laptops from the respective houses. I need employment histories, details of club memberships, libraries, gyms, trade associations, magazines they subscribed to, anything like that. We need to look at this like a fingertip search, go back inch-by-inch through everything . . . see if there's any common denominator, anything that connects these women to one place, one person, especially to each other.'

Miller then called the coroner's office, was told that the Sheridan autopsy had not been completed, that assistant coroner Hemmings would not be able to see them until the following day. Miller had not seen Hemmings since the coroner's inquiry on November the 2nd, the testimony that had exonerated him from civil and criminal action. It had been a mess. At one point the police department believed that it could be contained, but no, it had been shared with the world. A routine murder investigation, a visit to question a hooker called Jennifer Anne Irving as a potential witness, the interruption of an act of violence, and Miller had wound up with a lengthy IAD investigation and three months' suspension.

Following that had come public appearances, statements from Lassiter and the chief of police, the entire circus cavalcade that followed such things. Outside the courtroom after the final evidence had been submitted, down along the cloisters that separated the main public thoroughfare from the respective judges' chambers, Miller had shared a few words with Hemmings. Away from the bright lights of intrusive reportage, he had taken a moment to thank her, and as they parted he had hugged her – nothing more complicated than a wish to express his gratitude. It was that moment that had been caught by an alert and eager *Globe* photographer. The implications of that picture did not need to be spelled out. Nine days had passed since that moment. The death of Catherine Sheridan had intervened. Now he would have to speak with Marilyn Hemmings again. It would be awkward, Miller knew. He was not looking forward to it.

That Sunday afternoon Roth and Miller buried themselves in the case files. The day would end with more questions than answers. Miller felt the tremendous pressure of the thing, felt the weight of it bearing down on him. He read reports that did not make sense. He isolated areas where questions could have been asked and were not. All the way back to Margaret Mosley in March there were lines of investigation that could have been followed, but now – as in all cases – whatever might have been there would have disappeared. People moved. People forgot things. People touched the edges of such tragedies and did their utmost not to think of them again.

At six the uniforms left. Metz and Oliver stayed until eight to complete the wallboards that would hold all the relevant maps and photos for each of the four murders. By nine Miller's head ached relentlessly, and no amount of coffee seemed to relieve it. There were things that did not add up with each of the victims, predominantly questions relating to their identification. Dates of birth did not tally with hospitals or registry departments. The previous investigations had been slipshod. There was a great deal of work to do, and Miller – already feeling the rush and punch of the investigation – nevertheless did not relish the time and attention that such work would entail.

Roth got ready to leave at quarter of ten, stood in the doorway of the office and asked Miller if he wanted to come over and stay.

Miller smiled and shook his head. 'I don't need to be a fifth wheel anywhere.'

'Go home then,' Roth said. 'Get a shower, some sleep. This ain't going anywhere overnight.'

'I won't be long,' Miller said. 'Go see your kids . . . take whatever chances you can get.'

Roth didn't say anything else, merely raised his hand and left the room.

Miller got up from his desk and walked to the window, waited until he saw the lights of Roth's car pass along the street below. Miller knew Amanda Roth, his partner's wife;

little more than social contact, but he liked her. He had met the Roth children, three of them, fourteen, eleven and seven. Amanda's folks had helped their daughter and son-in-law buy a three-storey brownstone walk-up when Al was on a nothing salary. Al and Amanda had waited patiently while the MCI Center, now the Verizon, started to attract people back into the area. Waited on through the promises of regeneration money, saw the promises broken, a change of mayor, the promise reinstated, sat back and laughed when the figures started improving, and now the five Roths sat in a house worth the better part of four hundred thousand dollars, all of it paid for, a receipt to prove it. Albert and Amanda Roth were Washington through and through. Anything they had they'd earned, and what they'd earned they deserved. People like the Roths, holding onto their Jewish heritage by their fingernails, were the kind of people Miller's mother had wished him to be, the kind of people he would never become.

From the car pool Miller took a nondescript sedan. He drove home, seeing nothing but text before his eyes, the close print of interview notes, the incident reports, the missing details that jumped out at him and reminded him of how hasty and superficial the preliminary crime scene analyses had been. Such was the case with Margaret Mosley, with Ann Rayner, with Barbara Lee. It would not be the case with Catherine Sheridan – she of the library books, the delicatessen lunch she did not eat, the unknown sexual partner somewhere between ten-thirty in the morning and four in the afternoon.

The lights were with him all the way and Miller parked the car at the top of Church Street just before eleven. The deli was closed, but there were lights in back. He knocked on the door and Zalman came through to let him in. Standing no taller than Miller's shoulder, thinning hair, his face a maze of wrinkles, Zalman Shamir was everything an elderly Jewish man should have been. His manner belied his depth, and though he let his wife run the delicatessen Miller knew that there would not have been a delicatessen without Zalman's tireless work.

'Ach, she is pissed with you,' he told Miller. 'You leave

without eating this morning. Last night we are here when you come and you have nothing to say.'

'Hey, Zalman,' Miller said.

'Hey Zalman you,' he replied. 'You get yourself in back there and explain yourself. Enough of this headache I'm getting already.'

Miller walked past the two or three tables along the right-hand side of the delicatessen, the handful of chairs for the old friends who came down and played chess on Mondays and Thursdays. To his left was the cool counter, the glass shelving upon which Harriet set potato latkes, matzoh balls, gefilte fish . . .

Harriet and Zalman Shamir were good people. They did everything slow, the way it was done in 1956 when they took over the diner on the corner of Church Street. They used to live in the apartment above. Their son was successful, bought them a three-storey brownstone, and they'd moved there eleven years before. Miller took the apartment when he'd made detective, and since then he'd seen the Shamirs nearly every day. Harriet made food, too much food; sometimes she figured Miller wasn't eating enough and let herself into the apartment to put things in his refrigerator. Most nights, most mornings, he would stop and talk with them. She'd always make breakfast for three, had started making it for four when Marie McArthur had stayed over. And sometimes in the evening, when he returned to find the deli still open, they would sit together in the back kitchen and she would ask him about his life, about the things she read in the paper. Zalman would say nothing, there in the background slicing chicken or bagels, squeezing orange juice or some-such. And Miller would talk to them, these strange old Jewish folk, like surrogate parents, like some small brief respite from the darkness of his life beyond those walls. Harriet would ask about cases, about murders, in her eyes a glint of fascination, and Miller would smile and tell her what he could.

'You soften these things up so,' she would say, and press her hand over his reassuringly. 'Zalman and I, we were children at the end of the Second World War. We saw what people could do to each other. We saw the ones that came back from the camps.'

But Miller, regardless, did not feel it was right to drag the details of his day into their life, and so he did not. He would smile at her, he would hold her hand, he would hug her when he left the deli and made his way upstairs. She would call after him, tell him to get a new girl – *a nice one this time mind you!'* – and Miller would hear Zalman Shamir tell his wife to stop interfering, and she would tell him, Ssshhh, such things *were* her business.

That evening Miller heard her call his name from in back of the store.

'Hey, Harriet,' he called back, and he started to smile.

'I hear you,' she said. 'I hear you laughing at me.'

'I'm not laughing at you.'

Harriet appeared in the doorway, her hair tied up with a net, her hands covered in flour. A handful of inches shorter than her husband, a housecoat beneath her apron, a kitchen towel over her shoulder. She always looked the same – old, but never growing older. 'Look at this business,' she said disapprovingly. 'Two days I make breakfast and where are you, eh?'

'I had to leave early, I'm sorry.'

'Sorry is as sorry does. You look like hamburgers and soda pop. You have eaten hamburgers and soda pop, am I right or am I right?'

Miller shrugged.

'Come in the kitchen. Come and eat something sensible for once in your life.'

'Harriet – I'm not hungry.' Miller turned and looked at Zalman. 'Zalman . . . tell her will you?'

Zalman held up his hands, a gesture of surrender. 'I say nothing. I cannot help you with this, Robert.' He shrugged, walked through into the back and made busy with his preparations for the following day.

'So come have some coffee and honey cake, eh?'

'Just one piece . . . a small piece, okay?'

'Ach, so foolish,' Harriet replied, and led him by the arm to the kitchen table.

'So you are on some big business, yes?' she asked, as she sliced honey cake, poured coffee.

Miller nodded. 'Big business, yes.'

'So what is such big business you cannot say hello in the morning?'

Miller smiled knowingly. 'We're not going there again, Harriet. I'll tell you about it when it's done.'

'And what's with Marie now? She has gone for good?'

'I think so . . . I think she's gone for good.'

Harriet shook her head. 'This is a stupid business. Young people without any persistence. One little fight and it's all finished, yes?'

Miller didn't reply. He glanced at Zalman. Zalman shook his head. *I am not involved*, that gesture said, *and don't you dare get me involved.*

'So eat,' Harriet said. 'Eat before you collapse from starvation.'

Miller picked up the honey cake. He sat there in silence for a little while – there in his small oasis, a narrow window through which he could slip unnoticed and leave everything behind.

The world and all its darkness would wait for him 'til morning. Monday the 13th would be a day of autopsy details, returning to the Sheridan house, collating and cross-referencing every detail they could glean from the earlier case files. The prospect both frightened and excited Miller. He felt some sense of purpose. He had not thought of his ex-girlfriend, Marie McArthur, for a good half a dozen hours, and was only reminded by Harriet, then by the presence of boxes in the hallway near his bathroom. Boxes containing the last of her things, the remnants of the months they had shared. Perhaps this – amidst all things – was some small saving grace.

He saw Harriet and Zalman away a little before midnight, and shortly after one – having showered and heaped a pile of clothes into the washing machine – Robert Miller lay down on his bed, the sound of the city through the inched-open window, and closed his eyes.

He did not sleep immediately, however. He lay awake and

considered the one thing. The *one thing* that would speak to him quietly when no-one else was listening.

Eventually, close to two in the morning, he slept, but his sleep was fractured and restless.

*B*ack, a long time back, before I became John Robey . . . there was my father.

Big Joe. Big Joe the carpenter.

He would stand silently, sometimes for minutes at a time. And I would know at times like that that the worst thing to do would be to disturb him. Could hear my mother talking to him, mumbling words that became more and more incoherent as time went on, and he would listen, the soul of patience, and then he would sit on the edge of the bed with his needle, his vial, his patience, his heartbreak, and he would help her overcome the pain.

'Morphine,' he told me. 'Comes from poppies . . . bright red poppies. Blood red they are. Fields of them somewhere as far as the eye can see. Produces opium, and from opium they make morphine, and it helps her, you know? Takes away the pain . . . just for a little while . . .'

Tears in his eyes.

Turns away from me as I back up and stand in the hallway outside their bedroom door.

Looks perpetually exhausted. Sort of man who would wear himself out with thinking. Like no matter when he left, no matter how well prepared, for my father it was always dark before the journey home. I think one time he lost his way. Looked for it ever since, and still didn't find it.

That was my introduction to morphine, to opium, to heroin . . .

Heroin. Comes from the Greek 'heros'. Means hero . . . the warrior . . . half god, half man . . .

Means a great deal of things depending on which side of the thing you're looking at.

Me? I've looked at it from both sides.

I know my father, the carpenter. Big Joe. I know why he did what he did, and how much it cost us all.

65

I remember him standing in the hallway. Had on a hat. 'Come on,' he said. 'We're going out.'

'Where?' I asked. Plaintive child, no more than six or eight or ten.

'Surprise,' he said.

'Give me a clue,' I said.

'Out to the highway and then some.' Smiled cryptically. 'There and back, just to see how far it is—'

'Aw, Dad . . .'

Big Joe would've understood what happened. Why it happened. The reasons for it all.

Big Joe would have understood that, and he would have looked down at me – the plaintive child of six or eight or ten – and he would've said something.

'No matter what they dream up . . . I guarantee you I've endured far worse for far longer.'

Something like that. Something that would prove he understood.

SEVEN

Miller arrived at the Second a little after eight on Monday morning, Roth fifteen minutes later. The disarray of files greeted them, the heap of discarded coffee cups and Coke cans, along with the smell of stale cigarette smoke.

Miller cleared a space on one of the desks and dragged a telephone toward him. He took the yellow slip he'd taped to the wall and dialled the number again. He hoped against hope, but he knew even before he tried. There had been no fault in the exchange the day before. It wasn't a phone number. Miller dialled it three times, got the same uninterrupted tone of an invalid number.

He called the operator, had them check the number through the phone companies' system. It came back negative – not only was it not a current or disconnected number, it had never been a number in the first place.

Miller sat at his desk staring at the small yellow slip. *315 3477*.

'Hey,' he called to Roth. 'Phone number here. Not recognized. What else has seven numbers?'

The telephone rang and he picked it up. 'Miller,' he said. He nodded, took a pencil from the desk tidy, cleared a space for a sheet of paper. 'Sure . . . put her through.'

Miller listened for a while, and then leaned forward in his chair, intent expression on his face. 'Sure,' he said. 'Of course we'll check it out.'

Paused for a moment, listening once more.

'No, of course not. All such things are treated with confidence, but we will check into it. Did you leave your phone number with the desk? . . . Okay, good . . . and spell your name for me.'

The line went dead.

'Fuck,' he said and hung up. He lifted the receiver again,

asked the desk if the last caller had actually left a number. She had not.

''S up?' Roth asked.

'Some woman . . . something about a kid at her Sunday School who says she recognized the Sheridan woman. Hung up when I asked her name. No number either.'

'A kid? What kid?'

'Gave her name, Chloe Joyce. Lives out in the projects. Says she saw a newspaper photograph of the Sheridan woman yesterday and made some comment about it.'

Roth turned his mouth down at the corners.

'Jesus Christ, Al, you know how this is. We get something, we make a report, and then if we don't follow it up . . .'

Roth raised his hand and Miller fell silent. He smiled resignedly as he reached forward and switched on the computer. 'How many of these phone calls we gonna get, you figure?' Roth asked.

Miller smiled. 'I should think a hundred thousand and then some.'

'Standard spelling . . . J-O-Y-C-E?'

Miller nodded. 'Think so.'

'Any idea of which projects?'

'Not a clue . . . try them all.'

Roth typed on the keyboard. Miller waited patiently, found his thoughts turning once again to the hours between ten-thirty and four-thirty on the 11th, the six hours of Catherine Sheridan's life they couldn't account for. The library, the deli, and then returning home to be seen by the old neighbor who liked to watch pretty girls on the tube. Who had she spent those last hours of her life with?

Remembered the last conversation with Captain Lassiter after Killarney had left the day before. Lassiter's eyes like a car crash, carrying everything – the death of his wife, his sister's suicide three years before, the frustration and negation, the all-too-familiar sense of certainty that everything was fucked, and if not now then soon. Eyes like that? They've seen everything, absorbed it, carried it like a professional.

While Roth searched the system Miller called the coroner's office. He spoke with Tom Alexander, Hemmings' assistant.

'Give us a couple more hours,' he told Miller. 'Give us until after lunch can you?'

Miller told him he could, and then asked if Marilyn Hemmings was there.

'She's here,' Tom said. 'Up to her elbows in guts, but she's here.'

Miller thanked him, hung up the phone.

'Got something here,' Roth said. 'Out between Landover Hills and Glenarden, have a woman named Natasha Joyce with a daughter named Chloe.'

'That'll do,' Miller said. 'Let's go pay her a visit.'

Roth drove. Miller asked him to. He wanted to think about what he was going to say to this Natasha Joyce woman. An anonymous call, a little girl's name, that was all there was. But in the absence of anything else it was something.

The roads were clear; they made good time, and before Miller had really figured out what he was going to do they had arrived.

Roth parked up at the edge of the slip road that ran down into the projects complex. He knew well enough that to leave it within the perimeter was to ask for its swift disappearance.

They walked down there together, and near their destination Miller paused. For a little while he stood with his hands buried in his overcoat pockets. He could see his breath. He could see the smashed-to-fuck aspects of life represented by this place. He could see the graffiti, the garbage, the overturned dumpsters, the empty glass bottles, their brown paper skins holding out against the elements; he could see the stairwell that led up to frustration and desperation and a sense of shame and humiliation for so many of these people, and he wondered why.

'Up there,' Roth said, and pointed.

Miller followed him, out between the hunkering cinder block sheds that served as home for people that deserved so much better.

This is the shit we don't want to consider part of our national capital, he thought.

'Eighteen,' Roth said. 'Apartment eighteen, second floor.'

They walked up there amidst too many shadows. It was early morning, but there was something about this place that felt like dusk all the time. And there was the smell of ammonia, of piss and shit and blood and garbage and damp newspaper, of old mattresses and burned-out homemade braziers, of make-believe and wishes that it was something different. But it wasn't.

This is so fucked.

Roth knocked on the door, stepped to the side. Miller on the right, Roth on the left. Roth had his hand on his gun. Still holstered, but the press-stud was open so he could pull the thing in a heartbeat.

Too fucked by half.

Sound of someone inside.

Chains, bolts, deadlocks – a wish to keep the desirable in, everything else out.

'Who is it?' the voice from within asked.

'Police, ma'am.'

Silence.

Roth looked at Miller.

Miller said 'Open the door, ma'am . . . it's the police.'

'Heard you the first damned time,' Natasha Joyce said, and then she turned the key.

Door opened. Miller went first, Roth behind him, already securing the press-stud on his holster. Hallway was bright, freshly painted, the carpet on the floor worn in places but clean. House smelled okay, nothing like the stairwell outside. Small oasis of something there, small oasis fighting against the desert beyond the walls.

Miller held out his badge.

'I know who you are,' Natasha Joyce said.

'You are Miss Natasha Joyce?' Miller asked. 'You have a daughter named Chloe?'

Natasha smiled weakly. 'The teacher, right? She called you?'

Miller frowned.

'That's what you're here about isn't it? The woman in the paper. The one that got herself killed on Saturday.'

70

'Yes,' Miller said. He glanced over his shoulder at Roth. 'You were expecting us?'

Natasha shook her head resignedly. 'Hell, people like us are always expecting people like you, isn't that right?'

And then – standing in the clean, freshly-painted hallway of Natasha Joyce's home, waiting for her to direct them through to the kitchen – Miller seemed caught in some hiatus of near-silence, and all he could hear was the faint sound of cartoons playing somewhere.

'My daughter's in her room watching TV,' Natasha Joyce said. 'Wanted her home with me today, you know? One day out of school ain't gonna hurt her. We can talk in here.'

It was then that Natasha walked Roth and Miller through to the narrow kitchen, showed them chairs on either side of a narrower table, and she herself stood with her back to the sink, her hands gripping the chrome edge, knuckles tight like she was expecting something bad. She looked away and cleared her throat, and then she turned back to Miller because he'd been the first one through the front door, been the first to speak. And even though he was younger than Roth there was something in his face that said he'd lived an awful lot more life. Natasha Joyce had elected Robert Miller the leader of this gang, had decided if she was going to speak, then she was going to speak to him. 'So watchu wanna know?' she asked.

'We got a call,' Miller said. He watched Natasha Joyce closely. Something about her said that life, regardless of what happened, would always leave behind a sense of disappointment. She was a pretty girl, her hair corn-rowed on one side, the other side worn long and pinned back with a barette. But there was something in her eyes. Miller was reminded of another girl, a girl he'd tried to help.

Natasha seemed distracted, ill-at-ease. Through her tee-shirt she had sweated a great deal. On the counter were rubber gloves, the smell of disinfectant in the air. She'd been housework-busy.

'From Chloe's Sunday school teacher, right? Miss Antrobus?'

Miller shook his head. 'She didn't give her name.'

'It was her alright. She spoke to me yesterday when I went

to collect my daughter. I figured she'd call you.' Natasha Joyce sort of half-smiled and then laughed. 'I was gonna call you myself. Fuck it man, I should have called you myself. Now this is gonna look some way that it ain't.'

'What is, Miss Joyce?' Miller asked.

Natasha seemed not to hear the question. She shook her head and went on talking. 'She is one scared bitch man, one scared little bitch. Me? I think it comes from the fact she's a mixblood, half and half, you know? She ain't black, she ain't white . . . hell, no-one wants her. That must be one helluva thing.'

'She didn't give her name,' Miller repeated, 'and there was no complaint about you or your daughter or anything else, Miss Joyce. I think the caller was merely concerned that you might know something about Catherine Sheridan, the woman who was murdered on Saturday—'

'Wasn't her name,' Natasha cut in defensively, like here was where she could get a one-up on these white asshole cops. 'Wasn't her name, and I don't think it was the same woman . . . but she came down here and a couple of weeks later Darryl was dead.'

Miller frowned. 'I'm sorry, I'm a little lost here. You said it wasn't her name?'

'Sheridan. Catherine Sheridan. That wasn't her name when she and that other freak came down to speak with Darryl.'

'Darryl?'

'Chloe's father. Darryl King. He was my boyfriend . . . my man, you know? He was Chloe's father.'

'And he's dead now?'

'Yeah, he died back in 2001.'

'Sorry to hear that,' Miller said understandingly, and then he was straight back to business. 'And this woman, the one who was murdered . . . she came to see Darryl with someone else?'

'God, I don't know. I don't know what the hell to think. There was a woman who came down here to speak with Darryl. She looked like that woman in the paper. She came with another man, a few times as far as I could tell. They spoke to me only once even though I saw them a couple or three times. Said they were looking for him, did I know where he was? Hell, by that time he was heading south . . . real south, know what I mean? He was doing I don't know how much of the stuff.'

'Stuff?'

'Heroin. Darryl was a junkie, mister, a real honest-to-God, professional status junkie . . . so you might be down here asking me about this woman, and I might've seen her a couple of times like five years ago, and that's if it was even the same woman . . . but why she would have anything to do with Darryl King, and why Darryl King would have anything to do with the likes of her, fuck only knows. I don't know that I can help you. Only reason I'm talking to you – and I would have called you even if that interferin' bitch hadn't done so first – is because I started to think that maybe these people had something to do with what happened to Darryl, you know?'

Miller glanced at Roth. His disappointment was evident in his expression. This was old information, all of five years old, and it seemed like something had become nothing in a second.

'The man that was with her,' Miller asked. 'What was he like?'

Natasha pointed at Roth. 'Like him.'

'Like me?' Roth said, and for a second felt awkward.

'Yeah, like you, you know? Shirt, tie, suit, overcoat, dark hair, a little grey at the sides . . . nervous though. He seemed nervous. Hell, I don't know, maybe not nervous, more like he was vigilant, like watching out for something, right?'

'And how did he look, his face, you know? Was there anything particular about how he looked?'

Natasha shrugged. 'God knows. Not that I can remember. It was a long time ago. I wasn't paying particular attention. The woman did the talking. He didn't say nothing. Maybe I'd recognize him if I saw him again, I don't know.' She paused.

'Something else?'

'Nothing really,' Natasha replied. 'He gave me twenty bucks . . . told me to buy something nice for Chloe. Bought her a doll. She loves that doll, still has it. Only reason she would've remembered those people.'

'And they just said they wanted to speak to Darryl, that was all?'

Natasha nodded.

'And is there anything else you can tell us about this man? Distinguishing marks? Anything unusual about the way he appeared? Tattoos, scars, birthmarks maybe?'

Natasha shook her head. 'No, there wasn't nothing else.'

'Sure, sure, of course,' Miller said. 'Anything else you can think of, Miss Joyce?'

'I don't know what Darryl was involved in. Hell, I don't know . . . could be that lady came down here to get some candy for herself and that freak she was with. I saw her maybe twice or three times.'

'You remember exactly when it was?'

'About two weeks before Darryl died.'

'Which was?'

'October 7th, 2001.'

Roth was making notes in his pocketbook.

'And you can't think of anything else that might link Darryl King with this woman?'

'If I could I'd tell you.'

Miller was silent for a moment. 'What do you think, Miss Joyce?' he asked, and there was something compassionate and understanding in his tone.

'About what? What do I think about what?'

'About this woman? You think it was the same woman?'

Natasha shook her head. 'I don't know . . . I can't be sure. They look similar, hell they could've been sisters, right?' She laughed suddenly, nervously. 'I don't know . . . I really don't know.'

'Chloe seemed certain, didn't she?'

'Don't you bring her into this. Jesus Christ, whaddya want from us? Some woman came to see my dead boyfriend five years ago. I can't tell you how they knew him or what they wanted. She might have been the same—'

'Was she the same woman, Miss Joyce?' Miller said, and from his inside jacket pocket he took the digitally enhanced passport photograph of Catherine Sheridan, and the picture was color, and it was a damned sight clearer than the one in the paper, and when he held it up he noticed the sudden

74

change in Natasha's expression, the way her eyes widened, the way she seemed silently to inhale, as if in surprise, as if in shock, perhaps in fear.

'I think maybe . . . maybe yes . . . I can't be sure . . .'

Miller held the picture steady.

Tears welled in Natasha's eyes.

'Miss Joyce?' Miller prompted.

'Ye-yes,' she stammered. 'I think it's her . . . she's the one who came . . .'

Miller put the picture back in his jacket pocket. He looked at Roth.

'I don't want to get involved,' Natasha said. 'This woman has nothing to do with me.'

'I understand that, Miss Joyce, but she came down here to see Darryl, and—'

'Jesus man, that was five years ago, you know? Darryl's dead. Now this woman's dead as well. For God's sake, I have a kid.' She stopped suddenly, looked at Miller closely. 'You have children?'

Miller shook his head.

Natasha turned to Roth. 'You have kids . . . you look like you have kids.'

'Three,' Roth said.

Natasha turned back to Miller. 'He understands. Ask him. He knows what it's like when you have kids. I don't know what the fuck this woman got herself into, and I sure as hell don't know why she came down here looking for Darryl, but this is not the kind of shit I want round my daughter. I spent God knows how long keeping her safe from all the bullshit that Darryl brought home with him.' She breathed deeply, tried to gather herself together. 'We survived it, you know? We fucking survived all of it. God, sometimes I thought we wouldn't, but we did. Now it's over, you understand? I told you what I know . . . I don't have nothing else to tell you. You go ahead and find whoever did this thing but leave us the hell out of it, okay?'

There was silence in the kitchen for quite a while, and then Miller rose from his chair and handed Natasha Joyce a card. 'If you do remember anything else . . .'

Natasha took the card, looked at it, turned it over. She

wiped her eyes with the back of her hand, pushed herself away from the edge of the sink and started toward the kitchen door.

Miller and Roth got up, followed her to the front.

Miller paused in the half-open doorway. 'I understand,' he said quietly. 'I might not have kids, but I understand.'

Natasha nodded, tried to smile though there were tears in her eyes. There was a moment of gratitude in her expression, and then it was gone.

Miller and Roth made their way out toward the stairwell. Natasha watched them go – all the way down the steps and out of sight.

Chloe appeared in her bedroom doorway as she locked the front door.

'Who was that, Mommy?'

Natasha fingertipped away her tears. 'No-one sweetie . . . just no-one at all . . .'

Chloe shrugged, turned, disappeared.

Natasha Joyce stood there for a while, her heart heavy, a sense of coolness around her, and realized that she knew almost nothing of what had ultimately happened to Darryl King, father of her child.

EIGHT

They stopped to get coffee on the way back to the Second. Miller knew they were killing time until lunch. He wanted to see Marilyn Hemmings. He wanted the autopsy results. He wanted to pursue the fact that Natasha Joyce had seen Catherine Sheridan five years before.

Back at the precinct he stood motionless at the window of the office. Roth was down the corridor fetching a soda. Right hand wall now carried two corkboards – large things, maybe six by four – and on them were pinned photos of all four victims, their respective houses and apartments, a map of the area covering the crime scenes, notes and re-minders and the yellow delivery order bearing the number 315 3477.

Roth came in, handed a can to Miller.

'The fucking number,' Miller said. 'I can't think . . .'

Roth stood for a moment. He sipped Sprite noisily. Kind of tilted his head sideways. 'Seven numbers,' he said. 'Coordi-nates for something?'

'What do you know about coordinates?'

Roth shrugged. 'Nothing.'

'Same here.'

'What about backwards . . . 7743513?'

Miller frowned, thinking. 'Stick a zero before it and you've got a case number,' he said. 'The 077 prefix . . . they're all three-three-two sequences with the same prefix, right? Try it on the system.'

Roth set his can down on the edge of the desk, fired up the computer. They waited, anticipatory like kids at Christmas. Punched in the number. Waited some more. CPU whirred furiously.

Miller was at the window. The sky was white and feature-less. Fleeting thoughts through his mind: *Kind of a life is this, for God's sake? Chasing people who do this kind of shit to other people.*

'Fuckin'-A,' Roth said.

'What you got?' Miller asked.

'Our friend again . . . our very interesting friend. Darryl Eric King, born June 14th, 1974, arrested Thursday, August 9th, 2001 for possession of cocaine. Case number 077-435-13.'

'You're fuckin' kidding!'

Roth shook his head. 'Serious as it gets. Look . . . Darryl King . . .' He shifted back so Miller could see the screen more clearly. 'Case number 077-435-13. Darryl Eric King.'

Miller was silent for a moment, his words lost amidst his disbelief. 'This I cannot get my head around,' he said quietly. 'This is too much altogether.' Again he paused for a moment, shaking his head, scanning the screen trying to comprehend the significance of what he was looking at. 'Where was it?' he eventually asked.

'Seventh Precinct.'

'Who arrested him?'

'Arresting Officer was one Sergeant Michael McCullough . . . you know him?'

Miller shook his head. 'What happened?'

Roth clicked pages. 'Released the same day, eight hours later. No formal charge.'

Miller frowned. 'How can there have been no formal charge? He was arrested with . . . how much?'

'Three grams . . . three and a half actually.'

'He has to have been an informant, either that or he turned something over for this McCullough guy. Maybe he gave up the dealer or something.'

'If he was a CI there'd be a flag on the file,' Roth said, feeling that this was so very hard to believe. Frowned, leaned forward, peered at the small print on the screen.

Miller smiled knowingly. 'And we have the most up-to-date and organized file system in the world, right?'

'So we go ask McCullough.'

'Check him out . . . he still at the Seventh?'

Roth closed down the King file, opened up other things, typed McCullough's name, waited a while. Turned and looked at Miller who was standing at the window with his back to the room. 'He's gone.'

Miller turned. 'Gone? Dead gone?'

'No, out of the department. Quit in March 2003.'

'How many years did he do?'

'Let's see . . . 1987. That's sixteen years?'

Miller nodded. 'Lost his twenty-year pension. Who the hell quits four years from a twenty-year pension? You can burn out and do four years behind a desk on disability, for God's sake. That's one helluva lot of money to throw away after sixteen years on the job.'

'Unless he *had* to quit,' Roth suggested.

Miller shrugged. 'Who the fuck knows. Not important right now. What *is* important is that we find him. We need to speak to him. This is a direct link between Catherine Sheridan's murder and a previous arrest.' He looked toward the window and shook his head. 'Jesus,' he said, more an expression of surprise than anything else. 'We have to find this McCullough . . . need to get Metz onto it, anyone who isn't onto something else more important.' Miller walked across the room and sat down at the desk. 'So what do we have? Chloe Joyce says she recognizes the Sheridan woman. We find out that Catherine Sheridan went down to the projects to speak with Darryl King five years ago. We can't speak to him because he's dead. However, he was arrested about two months before he died by this Sergeant McCullough from the Seventh. And King's case number corresponds to the number left with the pizza company by Sheridan's killer—'

'Could it be that McCullough was the one who went to the projects with Sheridan?'

Miller shook his head. 'I'm not going that far. I'm wondering *why* Catherine Sheridan went to see Darryl King in the first place, not just once but twice, maybe three times. And those are just the times she didn't find him and ended up seeing this Natasha Joyce woman.'

'You figure Catherine Sheridan had a habit?'

'Coroner will know,' Miller said, taking his jacket from the back of his chair. He found it hard to comprehend what had happened. He had left Natasha Joyce's apartment annoyed and frustrated. He had walked away with the name of a dead guy, and the dead guy had come back to life in a five-year-old case. The pizza number was not a phone number, it was a case number, it was a lead, it was a great deal more than anything else they had, and it unnerved him.

Less than a mile away, there beneath the county coroner's office complex, assistant coroner Marilyn Hemmings stood over the body of Catherine Sheridan and showed her assistant, Tom Alexander, what she'd found.

'You see it?' she asked.

Marilyn Hemmings was in her early thirties, young for the job perhaps, but had dealt with sufficient questions regarding her capability for such a position to warrant an edge of cynicism and hardness. Nevertheless she was an attractive woman, but the attraction came more from the air of independence she exuded. Washington's city coroner was officially on sabbatical until January, and Marilyn had stepped into his shoes with certainty. Today that certainty was evident as she peered into the well of Catherine Sheridan's chest.

'A question,' Tom Alexander said.

'Which is?'

Alexander shrugged. 'Just curious I s'pose. How long she would have taken anyway?'

'No way of telling. Different people respond different ways. Depends on a number of things. You find out who her physician was yet?'

'Still no success on that.'

'She's not on the county medical database?'

Alexander shook his head.

Hemmings frowned. 'So what do we have here? Still no tie-in on the social security number. Her dentals, her fingerprints, her DNA . . . none of it flags anywhere. And now she's not even on the county medical database.'

'Well, she won't appear on any of our systems unless she was arrested sometime . . . even then they only take prints and they get lost like you wouldn't believe.'

'Don't get me started,' Hemmings replied.

'So what do we do?'

'Finish the thing. Do the usual. Then call whoever's on this, tell them to come down here and get the report.'

'I spoke to them. They're on the way down. It's Robert Miller.' Alexander paused, looked at Hemmings as if waiting for a response.

She half-smiled. 'What?'

'Nothing . . . nothing at all.'

'Bullshit, Tom. You're trying to get a rise out of me.'

'No . . . no, I'm not—'

'You shouldn't believe what you read in the papers—' Hemmings started, but was cut short by the telephone on the desk.

Alexander picked it up, acknowledged someone, thanked them, hung up again.

'They're here,' he said.

'I'll see them,' Hemmings replied. 'Finish up the report, and then you can start hosing the gurneys.'

Hemmings walked from the autopsy theater to her office. She removed her lab coat and took the corridor left to the main entrance. When she arrived she found Miller and Roth already waiting.

She smiled when she saw Miller. He smiled back, awkwardness evident in his expression.

'Robert,' she said warmly.

Miller shook her hand. 'Marilyn,' he said quietly, and then nodded at Roth. 'You know my partner, Al Roth?'

'Detective Roth,' she said. 'Yes, we've collided a few times.'

'Good to see you,' Roth said. He broke the tension between them by adding: 'So, you're through the worst of this newspaper bullshit, right?'

Hemmings smiled. 'Water off a duck's back.'

'You're done on the Sheridan autopsy?' Miller asked.

'Just now,' she said. 'Come to the office.'

Miller was glad to have Roth beside him as they followed her down the corridor. There had been nothing between Miller and Hemmings, and then the newspapers madebelieve there was. It was a difficult thing to experience, would have been easier had they perhaps known one another a little better. Now it was just tension and glances, Miller wondering if she felt as embarrassed as he did, if that embarrassment came from wanting to talk about what had happened, or wanting to pretend it had never occurred.

'Interesting thing about this one,' Marilyn Hemmings said, sitting down behind her desk. 'Close enough to the previous three, but different as well.'

She indicated a chair by the door, another against the wall. Roth and Miller sat down.

'Either of you study forensics . . . pathology perhaps?' she asked.

Miller shook his head, Roth as well.

Hemmings nodded understandingly. 'So a body is found somewhere,' she said. 'A dead body, and there are only four classifications of death as far as we are concerned. Those four are accidental, suicide, murder or natural causes. A man cleaning his gun shoots himself in the chest. It opens his aorta and enough blood floods his chest to compress his heart and kill him. The same man could take the same gun, press it against his chest and pull the trigger. The appearance and damage, the cause of death would be the same, but the motivation in that case would be intentional. He meant to kill himself and he did so. His wife, pissed off at him for cheating on her, shoots him in the chest at close range and kills him. Same cause, same appearance, different motive. Lastly we have the guy who smokes too much, drinks too much beer, gets a puncture in a tire while he's on the highway. He's stressed, angry, tries to change the wheel by himself, and an inherited weakness in the aorta collapses and his chest is flooded with blood and he dies. What we do in all cases is the same. We determine identity of the subject where we can, we determine the cause of death, the manner, the mechanism or mode, and finally we try our best to work out exactly when the person died. That's all possible when you have a complete body upon which an autopsy can be performed.'

Hemmings looked first at Roth, then Miller. 'We did the first three here. We did tests on the ribbons, the tags, fibers, hairs, the lot. There was nothing of any significance . . . nothing at all.'

Miller nodded. 'You said that Sheridan was close enough to the previous three, but different?'

Hemmings smiled. 'I did, yes.'

'How? Different how?' Roth asked.

'That's why I told you about the four different types of death . . . there's no question in my mind that she was murdered, more a question of *how* she was murdered. The mode and the mechanism. They differ from the first three victims.'

'In what way?' Roth asked.

'First three were beaten and then strangled, the ribbon tied around the neck post mortem. This one, the Sheridan woman . . . she was strangled beforehand.'

'Beforehand? What d'you mean beforehand?' Miller asked.

'There is a very specific type of bruising that occurs when a person is alive. It is quite different from the bruising that occurs after a person is dead.'

'And what do we have here?'

Marilyn Hemmings kind of half-smiled. 'We have something that even I don't fully understand, unless I look at it from an entirely different perspective. The subcutaneous bruising – a lot of subcutaneous bruising – and the way those bruises have discolored, it appears that the injuries were sustained post mortem.'

'I don't get it,' Miller said. 'You're saying that in the previous three cases the beatings took place before they were strangled, and in this case the beating took place afterwards.'

'Yes, that would appear to be the case.'

'And the strangulation . . . she still died as a result of the strangulation?'

'Yes, strangulation was definitely the cause of death. In the second one it was difficult to tell. Ann Rayner, the legal secretary. The beating was so relentless she could have died moments before she was strangled. There was haemorrhaging in the brain, in the optical cavities, at the base of the neck. It was a very, very brutal assault, and though there were clear signs of asphyxiation I think she would have died regardless.'

'So what do you see here?' Miller asked.

'I see a very similar death but a different sequence to the attack. I see a woman strangled, and *then* beaten violently, but unlike the others her face wasn't marked.'

'And your intuition? Your feeling on this thing?'

'What do I think? I don't think I could answer that question, Robert.'

Miller shot her a look at the sound of his name. The way she said it. There was no denying the fact that he felt in some way beholden to her. Her evidence had exonerated him from something that could have been the end of his career. She had saved him from something. Was it simply gratitude that he felt, or was he experiencing some other unexpected emotion?

'You don't have to write it down,' he said. 'You can deny you ever said anything. I'm just interested in what you think might have occurred.'

Hemmings glanced at Roth. Roth nodded as if to reassure her.

'I think someone . . . I think someone wanted this to look like the first three. Really wanted it to look like the first three.'

'But it wasn't the same person?'

Hemmings hesitated. 'Opinion, nothing more than that?'

'Nothing more than that.'

'It was someone else, Detective . . . I think it was a copycat.'

Miller looked at Roth; neither spoke.

'There's three other things,' she said. 'First and foremost, there's the fact that we have not been able to formally identify her—'

Miller started to say something but Hemmings cut him short.

'Her passport? Yes, we have that. We even have her driving license, but there is no vehicle registered with DMV.'

'That's not so unusual,' Roth said. 'There's many people who have a license but don't own a car.'

'I know, but that wasn't all,' Hemmings said. 'So far her social security number doesn't tally with her name. Gives me the name of some Spanish woman or something. I wrote it down over there.'

Miller shook his head. 'Sorry,' he said. 'I don't understand . . .'

'What I said,' Hemmings replied. 'I have her social security number, at least what is supposed to be her number, and when I put it through the system I come up with someone else entirely.'

'This is like the others,' Miller said.

Hemmings looked up.

'There are identification issues on the others,' Miller said.

'Victim identification is the first thing we try and do,' Hemmings went on, 'and in this case nothing has panned out. No DNA, no fingerprints, no dentals, and when her social security number came up with a different name—' She shook her head. 'I also had a reason to check for her in the county medical database.'

Miller frowned. 'She was ill?'

'She was more than ill . . . she was dying of cancer.'

The expression on Miller's face said everything. A sense of disorientation, as if he was being given too much information to process. 'How serious?' Miller asked.

'In her chest . . . well, in her lung specifically. Right lung. Significantly advanced, but more importantly she wasn't registered on the CMD, and that means she wasn't seeing a registered practitioner.'

'Significantly advanced?' Roth interjected. 'What does that mean?'

'It's difficult to say,' Hemmings replied. 'Cancer is a strange thing. The phenomenon of cells randomly reproducing themselves, rogue cells we call them, and when there's enough of them going at it fast enough you have a tumor. The body's equipped to fight some of them, and some tumors grow and they're never anything but benign. With Catherine Sheridan it was malignant, very much so, and I don't think she would have lived much longer.'

'Was she taking any medication or undergoing any treatment?'

'There was no evidence of anything in her system. No painkillers, nothing. And like I said, I couldn't find a record of her registration with anyone. There are some alternative clinics, quite a few of them in fact, but the legal ones still have to carry licenses, still have to record patients' details and report who comes to them for treatment.'

'But there are places where people can get medical care that don't record patients' details?' Roth asked.

'Sure there are,' Hemmings replied. 'Backstreet abortionists, veterinarians that do minor operations, illegal cosmetic surgeons—'

'But people who treat cancer?'

Hemmings shrugged. 'Who the hell knows. I've heard about homeopaths using Vitamin K to treat cancer, but generally they fall foul of the FDA and run to Mexico.'

'Why?'

'Why Mexico, or why do they get kicked in the head by the FDA?'

'Why do they get kicked?'

'Because Vitamin K is supposed to work a helluva lot better than most things . . . because it's cheap, because you don't really need any kind of extensive medical experience to administer it perhaps? I'm only guessing, but my experience with the FDA is that they get a real bug up their ass if someone is doing something that looks like it's going to make people better.'

Miller smiled wryly. Marilyn Hemmings carried too much cynicism for a woman of her age.

'So is there any way of proving that the first three were killed by someone other than the one who killed Catherine Sheridan?' Roth asked.

'Anything I tell you could be argued in court,' Hemmings said. 'Way the D.A.'s office runs these days, you've got to pretty much bring the guy in with his signed confession and some video footage of him doing the thing before you even get a warrant to search his garbage.'

'That's a very wide streak of cynicism you have there,' Miller said, once again surprised by Hemmings' tone.

'Cynical? Realistic more like. I see what these assholes do to people every single day, Detective. You do too, I'm sure, but I see it up close and personal. How many murders have you been present at this year?'

'Hell, I don't know . . . ten, twenty perhaps.'

'You cover the zone of one precinct, right?'

'Right.'

'And there are other detectives who cover homicides?'

'Yes, there's anywhere between six and ten of us.'

'Well, right now, with the coroner away, you've got me and Tom Alexander, a couple of others on a different shift. We cover eleven police precincts, fifteen if you count the overflow we share with Annapolis and Arlington. I have a facility that can cope with four hundred bodies at a time, and then a freezer that can take another one hundred and fifty if needs be. We cycle over six hundred a month, sixty-eight percent of those are murders, manslaughters, hit and runs, drownings and suicides. Of those a good two hundred and seventy-five are unlawful killings, and some of the things . . . well, hell, I don't need to tell you what people are capable of doing to each other, do I, detective?'

'I get your drift,' Miller said. 'You said there were three things . . . CSA at the scene said there was a possibility she had sex with someone on the day she died.'

'That was the third thing, yes.'

'Can you tell us anything about the person she had sex with?' Miller asked.

'I can't tell you anything, except they had protected sex. He wore a condom. There's a spermicidal agent called Nonoxynol-9, very common, you find it on dozens of brands. Can't give you anything there.'

'No other pubic hairs around the vagina?'

'No, and nothing beneath her nails, and nothing in her hair, and nothing about the marks on her neck that help me tell you anything about him. Right-handed I think, that's all I can get. Pressure marks on her left are a little deeper. Thumbs centered her neck. He knew exactly where to press, but that could have been good luck. He stood behind her, and then he came around and stood in front of her, and he was standing in front of her when she died. That's as much as I can tell you.'

'We'll sort out this thing with the identification,' Miller said, something in his tone that sounded like he was trying to reassure himself.

'I'll tell you something, Robert . . . there is something seriously awry when you cannot ID someone correctly on any system.'

87

'Give me the name you got on her social security number,' Roth said.

Hemmings took a slip of paper from the desk and handed it over.

'Isabella Cordillera,' Roth said. 'That's all you got?'

'That's all there was. You track her number back and that's the name the system gives you.'

'There's glitches,' Miller said. 'There'll be an explanation. We'll find out what happened on this, okay?'

'And let me know, would you? I'm interested in this one.'

'I'll let you know what I can,' Miller replied. 'And I really appreciate your help.'

Marilyn Hemmings shrugged her shoulders. 'You asked for my opinion, that's all. So there was a different sequence, or a different way he did the same things. Can I stand up in a court of law, put my hand on a Bible and swear that the guy who killed the first three was not the guy who killed Catherine Sheridan? No, I can't. Can I answer your question about what my intuition tells me? Yes, I can do that, and my intuition tells me that it was someone else.'

'And that someone else would have had to have access to the confidential case records in order to have made the killing and the positioning of the body that similar,' Roth said.

'Sure he would have. As far as I understand, the newspapers haven't detailed the position in which they were found, and they haven't said anything about the lavender,' Hemmings replied.

'They haven't, no,' Miller said.

'Which means we are dealing with someone inside the police department, forensics perhaps, the medical crew that attended any of the crime scenes . . . or someone inside the county coroner's office.'

'Or someone,' Roth added, 'that has access to our systems.'

There was silence for a moment as each of them absorbed the implications of what was said, and then Hemmings rose from her chair and extended her hand. Miller shook it, Roth too, and then she showed them down the corridor to the exit.

As Miller reached the end of the walkway he glanced back,

saw Marilyn Hemmings watching him through the porthole window in the door. Hemmings nodded once, smiled awkwardly, and then she disappeared.

You wanna know about the real world?

I'll tell you about the real world.

This is the world where I learned to hate like a professional.

A world where I forgot how to talk to real people, and when I say real people I mean people like you – good people, kind people, people who had an interest in helping just because you were another human being. No better reason than that. You were just another fellow human being and that was good enough.

A world where I forgot how to be kind and compassionate. Forgot how to make telephone calls. Forgot how to order food in a restaurant. Forgot how to say what I meant, to question what I believed in; forgot how to give my word, to keep my promises, and later forgot my own name. I ceased to be the child who went to school, who sat while his father explained woods and grains and densities, and the cycle of nature that made everything possible in an impossible kind of way. Forgot how to look at people and see anything other than what I was told to see.

We talked about these things, Catherine and I. Everything we'd talked about before. And then we spoke about how she would die, and when, and what I would do afterwards, and I told her a story about my father, Big Joe the carpenter, and at the end of it she laughed, and she cried, and we held hands for a long time and said nothing much at all.

It was not the first time we'd talked, but we believed it would be the last.

'This is the real world, isn't it, John?' I remember her saying. And then she smiled. 'You know something? Doesn't take an awful long time to get to that other place, does it?' She sighed, reached out and touched my hand. 'But coming back? Hell,' she whispered. 'I don't know if I've got enough time for that journey.'

NINE

Washington – embroiled in the mid-terms that had raged for months. Vicious Republican advertising, slander and libel and worse. Democrats coming back with everything they possessed. Millions of dollars spent on ensuring Bush's stranglehold on Congress was maintained. No-one wanted to read about serial killers and brutal murders. No-one wanted to take their eyes away from the battle that was occurring right there in their own arena. Miller and Roth were insignificant in the face of this, but for Miller there was nothing that compared to the sense of urgency he felt when confronted with the Sheridan autopsy report. It brought it all home with a crash.

It was after four. Roth and Miller sat at adjacent desks in their office. As Miller finished reading each page of Catherine Sheridan's autopsy report he passed it along. With each new detail he could see every aspect of the crime scene – the way she'd been positioned on the bed, the ribbon around her neck, the neat bow, the blank name tag, could smell the heady intoxication of lavender, beneath that the smell of something dead.

Principally it was the same MO as the first three. The ribbon and the luggage tag were generic brands. Fingerprints and epithelials on neither. No hairs, no fibers. Confirmation that the victim had engaged in sexual intercourse at some point earlier on the Saturday. No signs of rape. No internal bruising or lesions. Presence of Nonoxynol-9 correspondent with use of a condom. No internal secretion to determine DNA of the sexual partner. Presence of soap residue in the pubis and between the victim's toes suggested that she had showered or bathed post-coitus.

'You okay?' Roth asked.

'I'm okay,' Miller replied.

'So she was going to die anyway, it seems.'

'Everyone's gonna die anyway,' Miller said. 'Doesn't change the fact that someone killed her, and we have nothing new but the fact that she had sex with someone . . . and that she doesn't really exist, of course.'

Roth did not reply.

'I need to see the house,' Miller said. 'I need to see it properly. Crime scene and forensics people look at the environment, they don't look at the characters around it.'

'You really think there'll be something that could point us toward the guy?'

'The one she had sex with, or the one that killed her?'

'Either, both . . . could be the same person.'

'I hope to God there'll be something on the guy.'

'And if there isn't?'

'Then we're no further forward or back than where we are now. There's nothing to lose.'

Miller handed the autopsy report to Roth as he rose from the desk, almost as if the feel of the pages disturbed him.

Greg Reid's car was still parked outside the house. It was nearly six. The day had darkened already, the cold had settled in, and standing there on the driveway – the old neighbor's house in view, the crime scene tape still adhered to the frame of Catherine Sheridan's front door – Miller felt a sense of disquiet and unease. The lights and noise and confusion of Saturday night had gone, but the feeling was still the same.

There is something else here, he thought. *I have been here before. A place like this. A place where one thing appeared to be something else.*

Who was she with? Miller asked himself again. Between the library, the delicatessen and home, where was she before the old man looked up from the gameshow girls and saw her entering her house for the very last time?

Where did you go, Catherine Sheridan . . . where in God's name did you go?

'Robert?'

Miller started nervously.

'You coming in?' Roth asked. He was standing right by the

front door, had peeled away the crime scene tape from one side of the jamb and was holding it up.

'Sure,' Miller said, and followed Roth inside.

Natasha Joyce dialled the number she'd found and waited patiently. She was placed on hold, asked to select a department, and then she waited again.

Finally she found someone who seemed interested enough to listen to her, and once she'd detailed her request he said, 'And your relationship to the deceased, ma'am?'

'Relationship? He was my fiancé.'

'No legal relationship then,' the man interjected matter-of-factly.

'He was the father of my daughter. That counts for something, right?'

Natasha could tell the man was trying to be sympathetic, trying to be understanding and compassionate to this poor black bitch on the phone. 'The truth, ma'am? Not really, no. I know it seems unfair, but as far as accessing legal records is concerned, as far as actually getting the police or whoever to open a case file . . . I'm sorry, but it can't be done.'

'I just want to know where he was found. He was the father of my child, for God's sake. He died somewhere and I don't even know *where* he died . . .'

'Give me his full name, ma'am.'

'King . . . Darryl Eric King.'

'Date of birth?'

'June 14th, 1974.'

'And the date of his death?'

October 7th, 2001.'

'Oh . . . 2001, did you say?'

'Yes . . . October 7th, 2001.'

'Well, I'm sorry, ma'am, then I really cannot help you.'

'What?'

'Public records database is archived after five years. Any information I might have here at the public records office was archived last month and then the systems were cleaned of that information completely.'

Natasha Joyce was silent for a moment. 'You can't be

serious,' she said, her voice flat and monotone and disbelieving.

'Yes, I'm sorry, ma'am, that is most definitely the case.'

'So if I wanted to find out which police precinct dealt with it?'

The man hesitated. 'I don't know, ma'am . . . seems like a needle in a haystack to me. You'd probably have to call every precinct house in the city . . . or maybe you could call the police department administration unit at the mayor's office. They might be able to help you.'

'Do you have the number?'

'Sorry no, you'll have to call Information for that.'

'Okay . . . the police department administration unit.'

'Yes, ma'am.'

'Thank you.'

'You're very welcome . . . you have a nice day now.'

The line went dead.

Natasha Joyce stood there for a moment, the receiver burring in her ear.

'Mom?'

She turned suddenly.

Bleary-eyed and tousle-haired, Chloe stood in the hallway, her hand on the door handle, her head tilted to one side.

'Mommy . . . I'm hungry.'

Natasha smiled. 'Okay, sweetie . . . I'm making dinner. Be ready soon, okay?'

Chloe smiled. 'Okay.'

Natasha lowered the receiver into its cradle. She stood there for a moment with a cold sense of unease in the lower half of her gut.

The same sense of unease that Robert Miller felt, standing in the kitchen of the Columbia Street house.

Somewhere upstairs he could hear Al Roth talking to Greg Reid.

Miller felt a strange sense of familiarity. Only once had he stood within these walls, and then for nothing more than an hour, but he felt as if the place had found its way inside him.

He looked at Catherine Sheridan's cupboards, her oven, the refrigerator. He took from his pocket a thin latex glove, slipped it over his right hand, and opened the door of the refrigerator. He found cold cuts, a bowl of chilli covered with Saran wrap, a plastic container of milk in the door compartment, its expiry date two days past. A half bottle of Chardonnay, the cork wedged firmly in the neck. All of it sufficient for one person.

He turned around, tried to see everything and nothing, tried to identify anything at all that appeared out of place. He paused by the back door and looked out through the glass window into the narrow yard. He tried the handle but it had been locked.

He remembered how she looked when he came over here. Catherine Sheridan was an attractive woman. From what he'd seen of her clothes she dressed well. Miller imagined her as self-confident and assured. And then someone did this thing to her – this violation, this sickening act of degradation – and left her for the world to see, there on the bed positioned on all fours, as if he'd wanted her to watch him as he walked away. And then there was the ribbon. A thin white ribbon tied neatly with a small bow at the nape of her neck. The name tag with no name. And the smell of lavender, overpowering and sickly-sweet.

Miller tried to blanche his mind of the image. He believed he would recall it clearly for the rest of his life.

He heard Roth and Reid making their way down the stairs, went out into the hall to meet them.

'Mr Reid,' Miller said.

'Detective,' Reid replied.

'I hope that you've been home since we last saw you.'

Reid smiled, said nothing.

'You have anything for us?'

Reid held out a plastic baggie, inside it a thin slip of newspaper. Miller took it, turned it toward the light.

'Looks like it's from the *Post*,' Reid said as Miller inspected it.

'Where was it?'

'Beneath the mattress in the back bedroom.'

'Caught there, or did it look like it had been placed there?'

95

'Like it had been placed. It was flat, like it was placed on top of the wooden slat and then the mattress was lowered down onto it.'

Miller peered closely at the small shred of newsprint. 'Unofficial results show he has a clear lead over his four rivals,' he read. 'Supporters took to the streets yesterday signing his campaign anthem, "Give Peace A Chance" by John Lennon. A victory would give Venezuelan president, Hugo Chavez, a strong ally in the region but the U.S. administration has already cast serious doubt on the transparency of the—' Miller looked up. 'Of the?'

Reid shrugged. 'Any clue?'

Miller shook his head. 'No idea. Some South American election thing.'

'I think it's the *Post* . . . looks like their typeface,' Reid said again, and then added, 'Have something else for you.'

He backed up, headed toward the front door and leaned down to take something from a case. When he returned he had another baggie, within it a plain manila envelope.

'You have gloves?' he asked Miller.

Miller took a second glove from his inside jacket pocket and put it on.

Reid opened the baggie, lifted the envelope, and slid out some photographs, no more than six by four. There were three of them, two in color, one in monochrome.

Catherine Sheridan – going back fifteen, maybe twenty years, and in each picture she stood beside the same man. He was taller than her by a good six or seven inches. Miller held them by their edges, laid each one out carefully on the kitchen counter.

'Where were these?' Miller asked.

'Under the bedroom carpet. Right underneath the bed where she was found.'

Roth looked closely at each picture in turn. 'How tall was she?' he asked.

'Five three?' Miller said. 'Maybe five four. She wasn't that tall.'

'So the guy here is maybe five ten or thereabouts.'

Miller smiled sardonically. 'Average height, average build,

medium to dark brown hair, clean shaven, no evident distinguishing marks . . . why do these people always have to look like ten million other people?'

'Hey, be grateful you don't work in Tokyo,' Roth said.

'There's something on the back of this one,' Reid said. He handed one of the black-and-whites to Roth who peered at it closely.

'Christmas '82,' Roth said. 'That's helpful.' He looked at the image again. 'What the hell is this here . . . looks like a forest or what? Jungle maybe?'

'Whatever it is, I'm thinking that maybe this is the guy that went down to see Darryl King with our mystery lady.'

Roth smiled. 'As if it could be that simple.'

'Well, maybe it is, Al, but it sure as shit don't make it simple. Who the fuck is he? We've got nothing. No name, nothing that makes him really stand out from anyone else . . .'

'Let's go see Natasha Joyce,' Roth said. 'Let's go see if she recognizes the guy.'

'You can't take them,' Reid said. 'I have to lab report them, check for prints, all that stuff.'

'How soon?' Miller asked.

'I'm not done here,' Reid said. 'Come see me tomorrow morning. I can get you copies. Call me and check they're ready, okay? I'm sorry, but that's the best I can do.'

'And the news clipping?' Roth asked.

'That you can take. I have pictures of that. But bring it back to me in the morning.'

Miller thanked him. Roth headed toward the front door.

'One other thing,' Reid said.

Miller turned back.

'If she had sex with someone . . .'

'She did,' Miller replied. 'Coroner confirmed what you said.'

'So she had sex with someone, but right now there are no traces of semen in the bed.' Reid smiled knowingly. 'That doesn't mean a great deal, but . . .'

'Makes sense,' Miller replied. 'Coroner's report said she showered afterwards as well, which would explain why there are no other pubic hairs.'

'So there's the possibility that she was at someone else's house.'

'Or a hotel,' Miller said. 'But like you say, that's not something we can prove or disprove.'

'Over to you guys then,' Reid said.

Miller hesitated for a moment, standing there in the brightly lit kitchen that only three days before had seen Catherine Sheridan preparing a meal, perhaps drinking a glass of Chardonnay, listening to the radio.

And then someone came to visit. Someone who'd done this thing three times before.

Eight months. Four dead. Not a word.

'Sorry,' Miller said. 'I forgot to ask you . . . the DVD that was playing, any fingerprints on it?'

'Only hers,' Reid said. 'Sorry.'

Miller sighed. He thanked Reid and followed Roth out.

A while back Catherine and I went down to the projects. We drove along the John Hanson Highway that runs between Landover Hills and Glenarden. We went to find a man named Darryl King, a young black heroin addict with a daughter named Chloe. We did not find Darryl, but we found Chloe's mother, Natasha Joyce. Chloe was with her. Sweet girl, couldn't have been more than four or five. Reminded me of other children, other times. Catherine did most of the talking. I watched the car. I watched the road. I chewed gum and craved a cigarette. Natasha Joyce could not tell us where Darryl King was. I could see the fear in her eyes. I wanted her to be unafraid, but I could say nothing. I gave her twenty bucks. 'For your daughter,' I said. 'Buy her something nice, eh?' I think they were the only words I uttered.

We left empty-handed. I knew then that Darryl had lost his grip on things, that he'd become what he'd most feared.

I thought of my father as we drove away, an expression he wore that appeared more and more frequently and eventually seemed permanent. That anything good was transient, short-lived, too easily forgotten. The belief that there was always something worse around the corner.

I thought of Natasha Joyce, looking so much older than her years. Too much life too quickly. All sharp corners and rough edges. A decade of living collapsed between grades nine and twelve. I thought of the four noble truths of Buddhism: that all life is subject to suffering, that the desire to live is the cause of repeated existences, that only the annihilation of desire can give release, that the way of escape is the elimination of selfishness. I thought of how stupid I had become. The old joke: I know a guy who's so dumb he got fired from a job he didn't have.

I thought of these things as we drove back toward Washington, out beyond Chinatown, to the small apartment on the corner of New Jersey Avenue and Q Street. Catherine dropped me off a

*couple of blocks away. A habit we'd gotten into months before. She
didn't say goodbye. Neither did I. Another habit. I raised my hand
and smiled. She did the same. I walked home. She drove away.*

*It would be a while before Catherine Sheridan died, but we both
knew it was coming.*

*Back a long time – before I knew Catherine Sheridan, even
before I became John Robey – there was a history.*

Some of that history was about my father.

*Everyone knew him as Big Joe. Big Joe the carpenter. Hence I
became Little Joe, even though my name was something else
entirely. I stayed Little Joe until my father died, and then everyone
disappeared quietly, effortlessly, and I became myself.*

*'Center of the tree is the heartwood,' he told me. 'The spine, the
backbone, the skeleton.' He lifted a piece of timber, turned it
between his hands, showed me the cross-section, the whorls, the
way it grew lighter toward the edges. 'The sapwood is the flesh.
The flesh is weak, prone to the ravages of time and nature.'*

He smiled, set the wood down, turned back to his bench.

'If you want something to last, build it from the heart.'

*Sometimes I would watch the wood turn in the lathe, or lie still
as the chisel or router scored its flesh. The wood was alive. Still
and silent, but nevertheless alive. My father worked the wood as if
merely helping it become what it had always wished to be. The
grain was symbolic of dreams. White cedar dreamed of shingles,
boats, canoes and cabinets; cottonwood dreamed in loose whirls,
perhaps of veranda posts and rocking chairs; hickory was hard, a
relentless wood, its thoughts of floors and shelving; tupelo gum
soft, remembering days of brilliant foliage, yet now considering the
patient hands of old men, whittling through their final years.
Black walnut was dense, almost unintelligible. I believed that
walnut dreamed of walking canes and caskets.*

*'Your mother will never be what she once was,' he said. I could
smell the oil on his hands, the varnish, the glue. He smiled. 'This
is something I don't know how to explain to you,' he added,
'because I don't understand it myself.*

*'Your mother is going to die,' he went on quietly, and he laid
the palm of his hand against my cheek, and I could smell the
wood, the sap, the varnish, the amber, could sense the grain, the
density . . . could feel the tree itself, aching with the weight of*

fruit, the way the leaves would turn towards the sun as the day progressed.

Believed I could. Wanted to believe I could.

Child with an imagination.

Only later – so many years later – would I understand the danger of imagination, but by then it was too late.

'She will leave us,' he whispered, and then he closed his eyes for a moment and breathed deeply. 'And then it'll be just you and me, kiddo . . . just you and me.'

I find it ironic, so utterly ironic.

I've been watching the news these past few days. Right here in Washington, no more than a hop, skip and a jump away from the White House, and with the mid-term results now in I can see where this thing is going to go.

Catherine is dead, and I know what she would have thought, what she would have said.

'This has been my life. This has been the only one I'll remember for now.'

She would have looked right at me, looked right through me the way only Catherine Sheridan could, and said, 'Way this thing is rigged . . . the world, you know? The way the world is rigged – the media, the propaganda, the whole mindset they create with TV and movies and advertising and all this stuff . . . they want you to believe you're nothing. Haven't met an adult yet who still believes in happiness. Happiness is a kid's thing. Get kicked enough times before the eighth grade and you're already beginning to wonder what the goddamned point is. I've seen all of it. Seen things the like of which I would never wish on another human being. It's been a beautiful story of terrible things, as American as napalm.'

Or maybe not.

Perhaps she would have just said goodbye.

Or perhaps not goodbye, for goodbye was too final, and Catherine believed in the ultimate circularity of all things.

Perhaps 'Au revoir . . .'.

But hell! I am bitter and tired. I have seen and heard the worst of it for so long, and it has colored my judgement. Maybe it's not all that bad. Maybe we really didn't do the things that I saw. Maybe I was mistaken. My vision got blurred. I saw things and imagined they were something else. That's what happened.

Except for one thing. The thing that started all of this. The thing that Catherine Sheridan and me figured we could do something about.

And so we did. We've done it now. Now it's too late to go back.

And while the world does what it does, while the American people wonder whether the situation will change now the Republicans have lost their stranglehold on Congress, I go to work, I do my job, and I wait for the police to arrive at my door and tell me what I've been expecting to hear.

Sometimes I catch myself holding my breath in anticipation.

TEN

Seated in the car, Roth pre-empted Miller by saying, 'What do you think?'

'Think?' Miller said, a rhetorical tone in his voice. 'I don't know that I have any clearer idea of what happened than when we started.'

'About the fact that this woman doesn't seem to exist I mean.'

Miller kind of laughed. 'No-one doesn't exist, Al. Believe me, there's a glitch in the system somewhere. She has a social security number, she has dental records, she has fingerprints and DNA and God only knows what else.'

Roth didn't reply, didn't challenge Miller. He simply asked, 'So where to now?'

'The *Washington Post*.'

'You got the address?'

'Eleven-fifty, Fifteenth Street – it's about three blocks east of Farragut North Metro.'

Roth reached forward and started the engine. Miller glanced at his watch.

Miller was used to people knowing who they were by how they looked. He took it for granted. The *Washington Post* receptionist – pretty girl, late twenties, hair cut in a shoulder-length bob – smiled an acknowledgement, and when they reached the desk she said 'Gentlemen?' like she knew there was going to be trouble of some sort.

Miller took out his pocketbook, showed his badge. The girl didn't give it a second thought.

Miller glanced at her lapel tag: Carly Newman.

From the inner pocket of his jacket Miller took the plastic baggie. 'I give you some text from an article, can you tell me which article it was?'

'We have the whole paper online, you know?' she said, something slightly superior in her tone. 'Washingtonpost dot com. Go there, type in half a dozen or so words, and it can search every copy of the *Post* that's in the system. Goes back I don't know how many years.'

'You can do it for us?' Miller asked. He wanted to tell Carly – sweet girl though she was – that they'd just come from the coroner's office. He wanted to tell her about a smart, attractive woman that someone had taken it upon themselves to strangle, to beat relentlessly, to leave in a very undignified pose, despite the fact that she was dying of cancer. He wanted to tell Carly Newman this before she said something else condescending.

'Of course I can, officer,' Carly said, and she smiled like she'd had second thoughts about what she'd planned to say.

Miller handed her the baggie. She typed a few words from the article and waited a moment.

'Article is entitled "Ortega Set To Landslide Nicaragua Election". Byline is Richard Grantham.' Carly looked up. 'He's one of our staff writers, not a freelance. Political section.'

'Can you print that for me?' Miller asked.

'Sure I can,' she replied. Clicked, scrolled, clicked. Something whirred beneath her desk. She reached down, retrieved it, handed the single page to Miller.

Miller scanned it. 'Election,' he said to Roth.

Roth frowned.

'The word that was missing at the end, remember? "A victory would give Venezualan president, Hugo Chavez, a strong ally in the region but the U.S. administration has already cast serious doubt on the transparency of the . . . election." That was the word missing off the end of the clipping.'

'What's the date?' Roth asked.

'The tenth.'

'Day before she was killed.'

'Someone was killed?' Carly Newman asked, and Miller looked at her and saw the expression he'd seen so many times before. Something real had touched her life. Something dark and awkward, something that would give her pause for thought several times before she forgot it . . . and then tomorrow, perhaps the day after, perhaps next week, someone would say or do something, someone would use the word 'election' or she would meet another person named Miller, and all of a sudden it would remind her of the vague and insubstantial transience of it all.

. 'Yes,' Miller said. 'Someone was killed.' He looked at Roth. Roth held out his hand for the clipping. Miller asked if Richard Grantham would be available should they need to speak with him.

'Not now,' she said. 'Most of the day staff are gone. We just have the night staff here now,' she said. 'But he's here most of the time.' She smiled. 'Richard is a legend around here, you know?'

'A legend?'

'He's about seven hundred years old,' Carly said. 'He looks *so* amazing for his age. He was here when Woodward and Bernstein went after Nixon.'

'Is that so?' Miller said.

'Sure is,' she said. 'Richard did the copy-editing on their articles before they went to the typesetter. He has some stories, real interesting stories.'

Miller thanked her again, and as they turned to leave Carly said, 'The person that was killed? Did that have anything to do with the paper?'

Miller smiled reassuringly. 'About as far from the paper as you could imagine,' he told her, and he could sense the small relief she felt. Perhaps, after all, she wouldn't think about it again. Perhaps she deserved never to think of such things at all. Some people chose this life. Some people just shouldn't be subjected to it.

Outside, now close to eight, Roth and Miller stood silently, their breath visible, the sky clear.

'You take the car,' Miller said. 'I'm about seven blocks north. Say hi to Amanda for me, okay?'

'Sure I will . . . see you in the morning.'

Robert Miller stood for a while longer, hands buried in his overcoat pockets. He exhaled and watched his breath disperse. Winter had set in. What did *The Keener's Manual* say?

'Minutes trudge, Hours run, Years fly, Decades stun. Spring seduces, Summer thrills, Autumn sates, Winter kills.'

He started walking, trying to think of nothing but the sound of his footsteps on the sidewalk. When he reached his apartment he went up the back stairwell. He turned on the central heating, kicked off his shoes, stood before the open drapes and looked through the window toward the lights of Corcoran and New Hampshire Avenue. *This*, he thought, *is my life. This is the world I have created for myself. Is this what I really wanted?*

Remembered standing on the stairs as a child, overhearing a conversation between his parents.

'He'll be a lonely man,' his father had said. 'He doesn't make friends easily. I worry about him.'

'He's independent, that's all,' his mother had replied.

'It's not independence, it's a lack of social interaction. He should join some clubs, go out, meet other kids.'

'He's happy by himself.'

'Happy? What the hell is that when it's at home? The kid's not happy. Jesus, look at him. Has to stretch his face sideways to break a smile.'

'Leave him be, he'll be fine. So he doesn't mix well. He's smarter than most kids, you ever think of that?'

Evidently not, for Ed Miller had chided his son until the day he died.

You don't go out enough. What's up? You don't have a prom date? Jesus Christ, Bobby . . . what the hell is the matter with you? You just don't like people, is that it?

Miller had joined the Washington Police Department at twenty-four. Wondered if such a decision had contributed to the coronary that ultimately killed his father.

What the hell did you go join the police for? What the hell's gotten into you?

Nothing further was said. Ed Miller acted as if his son was someone else entirely, but this attitude did not last. Robert was there when his father collapsed. Used his police training – mouth-to-mouth, cardio-pulmonary resuscitation – but the coronary was bigger than the man and it crushed him effortlessly.

Miller's mom hung in there a couple years more. Saw him

graduate, watched him rise rapidly within his department, saw him grow serious and intense and spend too much time with books instead of girls and friends and social situations. Worried some, like now Ed was gone she'd taken on the job, but things didn't change. Her son stayed the same. Excelled as a cop. Had she hung in there a while longer she would have seen him promoted to detective, youngest to date in Washington's history. Proud smile, discreet tear, a wish that Ed could have been there beside her to see what his son had made of himself. But no, not to be. Both of them dead long before Robert Miller stood on the podium and shook hands with the Washington chief of police, took his badge, turned to face the snapping, flashing camera. It had been important, a moment of significance, but all of it was now behind him, a series of fractured memories, meaningless in the face of these recent months.

From his pants pocket Miller took the baggie with the shred of newspaper inside. A clipping from a *Washington Post* article about a South American election. A murdered woman with cancer who appeared not to have registered with a doctor, appeared not to be taking any medication at all. A coroner whose hunch and intuition told him that the first three killings had been perpetrated by a different man . . . if this was so, there was someone within the police, the emergency services, even the coroner's office who'd copied a brutal killing for their very own particular reasons. And still he and Roth had not really confronted the fact that there was almost nothing to be known about Catherine Sheridan's life. They had not found out where she worked or where her income originated; they did not have the names of her friends, her parents or brothers or sisters . . .

And even her own name became someone else's when they looked beneath the surface.

Evening of Monday November the 13th. Eight months since the first killing. No solid leads.

He figured this was the kind of thing that fucked up a performance review.

The kind of thing that made some people resign.

*

Robert Miller longed to sleep; knew he wouldn't.

He was exhausted. His eyes were heavy, his head hurt, but still he sat there for a while, something haunting the back of his mind, something he knew bore some significance.

James Stewart, Miller thought. *I keep thinking about James Stewart, the film that was playing . . . the music I could hear when we were upstairs . . .*

There had been no fingerprints on the DVD other than those of the victim herself. The killer would not have been so foolish as to leave prints behind, but Miller had hoped there would be a smudge, a rubber smear from his latex gloves, something that told him that the killer had put the DVD in the machine and set it to play. Why? Because it would have been something else to consider about their perpetrator, something that could have shone a light toward the truth. He had put on a movie and ordered pizza. Put on a movie and ordered pizza . . .

Some time close to midnight Miller finally rose from the chair and made his way through to the bedroom.

Despite once again passing the boxes in the hallway, the last reminder of a wasted fourteen months, it was not Marie McArthur that occupied Miller's thoughts. He did not think of the final slow demise of their relationship, the seemingly endless nature of its death, like falling from a cliff, walking toward it in slow-motion, believing perhaps that the edge would never come . . .

No, it was not these things that consumed his thoughts, for he now believed he had expended more than adequate energy trying to understand all that had happened.

His final thought – the one that closed his eyes – was of Marilyn Hemmings. The way she'd looked through the port-hole in the door as he'd reached the end of the corridor. The slight nod, the awkward smile. He remembered how she felt when he hugged her after the coroner's inquiry, the moment before the camera flash, before they realized how it would look – as though something was going on between them, that she had conspired to fabricate evidence to exonerate him from manslaughter . . .

He recalled the image of them together in the *Globe*. The caption beneath had said nothing significant. Nothing significant needed to be said. The world believed what it wanted to believe.

Robert Miller slept at last but he did not dream. And though he woke in the early hours of the morning and replayed everything that had occurred, he reached no better understanding of its meaning. He felt invaded.

That was the only way he could describe it: invaded.

Middle-aged man in a dark grey pinstripe suit. Stood in the hallway of his house. Held a newspaper, a copy of the *Washington Post*. Stared at the grainy photograph of Catherine Sheridan. She looked back at him, expression on her face like she was waiting for him to say something.

The man walked down the hallway and into his study, and despite the late hour he lifted the receiver and dialled a number.

Paused, patient expression on his face.

Line connected.

'You've seen Sunday's *Post*?'

Nodded, then a slight frown.

'She was one of ours? Did we do this?'

Shook his head.

'I thought we put a stop to that bullshit with the luggage tags—'

Frowned intensely. 'I don't care if it is or not. This is getting attention now. Last thing in the world we want is press, for God's sake.'

Listened, shook his head.

'No, *you* listen to me,' he retorted, his voice louder, the tight edge of anger approaching. 'Bullshit theatrics I can do without. This isn't some made-for-TV movie. I give you a job and I trust you to use the right people, not some burned-out psycho who thinks he's playing games.'

Clenching his fist, trying so hard to be patient.

'No,' he snapped. 'Evidently that is not the case. I don't care *what* the fuck happened to him. Right now I have a newspaper story in front of me that says this shit is still going on. Find out where it came from. Put a stop to it. There isn't anything—'

Interrupted, he listened, started nodding.

'So deal with it. Fucking well deal with it. This is the last I want to hear about this shit, you understand?'

Nodded.

'Good, make sure it is.'

He hung up, looked once more at the face of Catherine Sheridan, and then tossed the newspaper onto the desk to his right.

'Fucking assholes,' he whispered through clenched teeth, and then turned and left the room.

'*A*nchor to windward, son,' my father used to say. 'Anchor to windward.'

One time I asked him what that meant.

'Ship comes into port and ties up to the jetty. Wind is blowing inland, will drive the ship against the jetty, so the captain puts the anchor down on the other side to stop the ship moving. Means you think about everything both ways. You make your preparations. You take your security measures.' Held up a thin layer of wood, varnished smooth as glass. 'Veneer,' he said. 'Gonna make a pattern with black walnut and abalone shell and mother-of-pearl. Gonna be the most beautiful thing you ever saw . . . and you can help me son, you can help me do this thing.'

Wouldn't tell me what it was. Asked him ten times if I asked him once, but still he wouldn't say.

All of it anchor to windward.

I helped my father make his preparations without any understanding of what he was planning to do. Would I have refused to help him had I known?

I would sometimes go up there to see her. Fifteen years old. Walking up those stairs, listening to treads creak beneath my feet. Feeling my heart in my chest, wondering how she would be, if she'd be awake and crazy, or asleep, as good as dead, the sound of phlegm rattling in her chest as she breathed.

She scared me. I was a teenager – stuffed with hormones, thinking about girls, about football, about all manner of things I should have been thinking about – and my own mother scared me. Other kids didn't have to deal with this. Other kids had normal parents, normal lives, their greatest concern whether they had dollars and a date for the weekend.

Stood on the landing for quite some time, my hands sweating. And then I approached her door and stood silently for just a moment – a moment to steel myself, to gather my nerves. I felt

111

*the handle slip between my fingers and I had to wipe my palm on
my tee-shirt to gain purchase.*

Pushed the door open gently. Couldn't see through the curtain
my dad had rigged above the bed. Could hear her breathing, raspy
and deep. She was sleeping, and for this I was grateful.

Her skin was pale and transparent. Skin like tissue, like mother-
of-pearl – and like the skin of a drum, taut across her face, the
tension was visible as she murmured and sighed. Fingers thin,
incapable of grasping anything with more than a featherweight
touch, her body beneath the covers like a scarecrow. Nothing to
her. Eaten away from inside, that's how she looked, and she'd
been this way for as long as I could recall. This was not who I
wished my mother to be. This was someone – or something – else,
and I watched her silently, not daring to breathe, not to make a
sound, for if she woke she would start screaming or crying or
talking crazy, and I'd heard that too many times to deal with it
any more . . .

I didn't know what my father was going to do, but Big Joe
always had an answer, always had a solution to the problem.

'Son,' he said, 'your mom has an illness. She has an illness that
doesn't really have a cure.'

I felt breathless and dizzy, tears welling against my lower lids. I
didn't want to cry. I never wanted to cry again.

'There's nothing wrong with crying,' Big Joe said, and he
reached out his hand and held it against my cheek. 'Cry if you
want to.'

'Is it going to help?' I asked.

He smiled, shook his head. 'Some people think it does.'

'And you? What do you think?'

'Don't see how it can.'

'Then I ain't gonna do it.'

There was silence for a little while longer, and then I closed my
eyes and asked, 'How long?'

'Before she goes? I don't know son, I just don't know.'

'Does anyone?'

He didn't say anything.

'So what do we do then?'

'Do? I don't know that there's anything we can do except wait.'

'Then that's what we'll do,' I said. 'We'll wait.'

*

Such memories from an age ago, and now it is Monday evening, the 13th of November, and Catherine is gone. Just like my mother. That, more than anything else, turned out to be the greatest irony of all.

Classes are done. I am packing books into my bag and brushing chalk from the cuffs of my jacket.

I turn and look at the board, and there – right across it – I have written a very famous quote.

'Injustice anywhere is a threat to justice everywhere.'

I think we killed the man who said that.

What was I telling them today? What was I feeding hand-over-fist into their impressionable minds? The ethics of literature. The responsibility of the author to maintain honesty, integrity, to present the reader with as accurate a representation of the issues as can be managed.

'But according to whose perspective?' one student asked. 'Surely truth is relative. Surely truth is perceived very differently from one person to the next.'

'Yes,' I said. 'Truth is relative. Truth is personal, it is individual.'

'So where do we draw the line?' the student asked. 'Where does one individual's perception of what he considers to be the truth become a lie?'

I laugh. I do my very best Jack Nicholson and say, 'Truth? You want the truth? You can't handle the truth . . .'

The bell goes. Class dismissed. The student looks at me as he leaves and I see suspicion and accusation in his eyes. The question was never answered.

And I think: I was like you. A long time ago I was like you.

And then we found the line that divided the truth and the lies. We crossed it so many times it became obscured and faded and eventually disappeared altogether.

Perhaps the worst lies were those we told for the best.

Perhaps the worst lies were those we told ourselves.

ELEVEN

Tuesday morning, sky the color of a dirty bandage, struggling with the idea of rain. Natasha Joyce was home after the school run, seated on the lowest step of the stairwell. Phone receiver pressed against her ear, expression absent-minded, a little vacant. She'd been on hold for minutes, had maintained her patience while the mayor's office treated her to elevator music. White folks' elevator music. Chloe would be away for several hours. The house was clean and she was alone. Kept thinking about the older of the two detectives, that he'd seemed so similar to the man that had come with the Sheridan woman. The woman who had not been named Sheridan. They had not looked physically similar, but there was something *about* them. Maybe the first one had been a cop too . . .

'Ma'am?'

'Yes, I'm here,' Natasha said.

'I'm sorry, ma'am, we seem to be having some sort of difficulty with our computer system. You said King, right? Darryl Eric King?'

'Yes, that's right.'

'Registered date of death was October 7th, 2001.'

'Yes, that's correct.'

A moment's hesitation. 'It should be here, ma'am, there's no question about it.'

'Maybe the delay in sending the records over . . . I spoke to someone before and they told me that after five years the records all go into archives, and maybe there's a delay or something?'

'It's done electronically, ma'am,' the woman at the other end of the line said. She was black, no doubt about it. Seemed like she wanted to help Natasha Joyce get her question answered. 'They just shoot that stuff right over here and it uploads onto our system directly. If the record exists it should be here.'

'So what does that mean?' Natasha asked. She felt nervous, agitated. Something else now didn't make sense.

'What does it mean?' the woman asked. 'It means that someone somewhere has f-u-c-k-e-d up, that's what it means.'

'So what do I do?'

'You give me your number, Miss Joyce, and when I get a chance I'll e-mail the IT people and see what they have to say about this, okay?'

'And you'll call me back?'

'You have internet?'

Natasha smiled. As if. 'No, I don't have internet.'

'Then I'll call you back, yes. Bear with me though. It may take a little while to get an answer from these fellas.'

'Okay, thank you,' Natasha said, and then she gave the woman her number.

'I'll do what I can, alright?'

'Thank you.'

'No problem . . . you have a nice day now.'

'Yes, thank you . . . you have a nice day too.' Started to put the phone down, and then suddenly, an afterthought. 'Miss?' she said. 'Miss?'

Meant to ask the woman's name, but the line was dead.

Natasha Joyce hesitated for a moment, and then she lowered the receiver into the cradle and got up from the stair.

For some unknown reason she thought she might not hear back from the Police Department Administration Unit.

For some other reason she felt afraid.

Miller logged onto imdb.com, looked up *It's A Wonderful Life*. Two hours ten for the feature. Called Tom Alexander at the coroner's office and got a breakdown of the timeframe within which they had to work. Looked at the notes he'd made in the car. Already he'd been up for the better part of three hours, in the office for most of two. What he'd found unsettled him greatly. If what it implied was true . . .

Alexander was saying that Catherine Sheridan had been murdered between four forty-five and six, afternoon of Saturday, November 11th. The old guy next door had seen her coming into the house around four-thirty. Pizza had been ordered at five-forty, this confirmed by the telephone records from the Sheridan number. Delivery guy had arrived around five after six. Had taken maybe two or three minutes to find the body. Miller took the call from the Second just after six-thirty, had arrived at six fifty-four. Roth had appeared in the yard about ten minutes later. The two of them went upstairs, and by the time they entered her room it must have been seven-fifteen. Spent no more than a few minutes up there, came down again, and by this time the credits were playing on the TV. Say it had been seven-thirty, then the movie must have been started at about five-twenty. Maybe the guy killed her and then put the movie on. Miller scratched his head, rose from his seat and walked to the window. Something about the movie. Something about this stupid goddamned movie.

Door opened behind him and Roth appeared. Face red like it was cold outside. Miller hadn't noticed. Had barely noticed anything on the drive over. Attention focused, channelled right into Catherine Sheridan's universe, the world she'd occupied during that last handful of hours. The world that Miller seemed unable to enter.

'So where we at?' Roth asked. 'You had coffee?'

Miller nodded toward a Starbucks cup on on his desk. It was just after nine; he'd been awake since six or thereabouts.

'You didn't sleep so good,' Roth said, rhetorical.

Miller shrugged.

'Amanda says hi . . . asked what you were doing for Thanksgiving.'

'Invitation or being polite?'

'Being polite I figure,' Roth said.

'Be a pain in the ass if I showed up, right? You got family over?'

'Isn't a family. Jews don't do families. We do dynasties.'

'Tell her I'm fixed. Tell her my girlfriend's folks invited me.'

'You don't have a fucking girlfriend.'

'It'll stop your wife worrying about me.'

'I'm not telling her that, for God's sake. I'll get the third fucking degree until I finally confess you're bullshitting.'

'Tell her whatever's gonna work, Al. I'm not gonna come over there and be a fifth wheel at your fucking Thanksgiving Dinner.'

Roth waved his hand nonchalantly. 'I'll tell her something.'

'So, we gotta find out who this Sheridan woman is.'

'What we got?'

'Nada, don't even know what she did for a living. You know what she did for a living?'

Roth shook his head.

'What is it *we* do for a living?' Miller asked sarcastically. He reached for the Sheridan file, pushed aside the stack of files relating to Mosley, Rayner and Lee. 'Went through this earlier . . . there's nothing about her job. Checked the social security number on our system and it comes up with a Puerto Rican woman named Isabella Cordillera like Marilyn said. You put Isabella Cordillera through the system and learn that she died in a car accident in June 2003. You try and access the details of the car accident and it comes up blank.'

Roth reached for the file, leafed through it as if there might have been something overlooked by Miller.

'That's not the only surprise waiting for us in this lot,' Miller said. 'There are social security numbers for the other three, and they look fine on the surface. They check out alright until you start to go back a little further.'

Roth frowned, tossed the Sheridan file onto the desk and leaned forward. 'Those files were made up before,' he said. 'Those files carry the better part of eight months of investigation reports.'

'The investigation reports are fine. I don't have a problem with the reports, Al, I have a problem with the women themselves.'

'Sorry, I'm missing something on this.'

'They were looking for common denominators amongst these women, right? The previous detectives . . . that's what they were doing.'

'Yes, of course. Sure. That's what I would have done.'

'Same here,' Miller said. 'But I started to look at it from a different angle. We're looking for common denominators

117

between them as murder victims, when we should be looking for common denominators between them as people.'

'Like what?'

'First of all they're all single. Secondly, they had few friends . . . I mean, really no close friends at all that we've found. All the statements come from neighbors, work colleagues, but there's nothing in there from the boyfriend, the best girlfriend, the one they went shopping with, went to the gym with, that kind of stuff. Like Amanda, right? She has girlfriends, doesn't she? The ones she spends God knows how long on the phone to every other day.'

'Sure she does.'

'But not this lot,' Miller said. 'None of them have a single report from someone who claimed to be a *close* friend.'

'That can't be right. Everyone has—'

'Apparently not,' Miller interjected. 'Apparently not everyone does.'

'So where from here?' asked Roth.

'So they're all single. They have few friends. I've got Metz and Oliver chasing up everything they can find out about their homes . . . lease and mortgage details, where their personal effects went, that kind of thing.'

'I figure he selects loners . . . watches them, follows them . . .'

'Not realistic,' Miller said. 'He'd have to know them all to one degree or another or it would be the most remarkably random job. Find a woman, start following her, learn her movements, find out something about her work, who she hangs out with, and the moment she looks like she has some kind of personal life you drop her and go find someone else who seems a better candidate. Doesn't work for me.'

'You said something about their social security numbers—'

'Yes, the first three. On the face of it all fine, no problem at all. Any kind of routine and cursory check, no more or less than we would ordinarily do, and everything holds together. If Catherine Sheridan's number checked out the same way I would never have looked further.'

'But it didn't, right?'

'Right. So I start to dig. I go back five years, start to look at drivers' licenses, traffic citations, club and organization memberships, bank account details, anything I can think of, and I see a pattern.'

'Kinda pattern?' Roth asked, leaning, forward, intent.

'There's something about every one of them that doesn't hang together.' Miller stood up, reached for a yellow legal pad on his desk, and sat down beside Roth. He used his pen to point at lines he'd written on the page. 'Margaret Mosley, thirty-seven years old, date of birth on her driver's license is June 1969. Go back to June 1969 and there is no record with the city of anyone named Margaret Mosley registered in Births.'

'So she wasn't born here,' Roth said.

'Social Security file gives her place of birth as Washington.'

'So there's an error somewhere.'

Miller smiled knowingly. 'You ain't seen nothing yet, my friend. Second one, Ann Rayner, forty years old, date of birth given as January 3rd, 1966. Social security file gives no place of birth so we can't even find out if her birth was recorded.'

'Social security file *has* to register her place of birth.'

Miller nodded. 'Just like every healthcare practitioner and medical facility has to register a patient who comes for treatment, right?'

'And the third one?'

'Third one looks an awful lot better,' Miller said. 'Barbara Lee, twenty-nine years old. Date of birth is February 24th, 1977. Social security file gives her place of birth as Washington, D.C. Records at the city registry confirm that there was a Barbara Caroline Lee born in Washington on the 24th of February 1977, but Deaths records that the same Barbara Caroline Lee died on February 27th of the same year.'

'Three days?' Roth asked.

'Place of death is University Hospital. Whoever Barbara Lee was she never made it out of maternity ICU, let alone to twenty-nine years old and working in a florist's.'

'You've been busy this morning . . . God, I wished I'd stayed home.'

'It's all bullshit,' Miller said. He rose from the chair and once again walked back to the window. 'The common denominator isn't in these people as victims, it's with them as *people*. And you wanna know what I think?'

Roth raised his eyebrows.

'I think that we need to find out what the Sheridan woman did for a living, who she knew, if she knew anyone at all. I want to look into what happened to this Darryl King guy, and then we need to find out who went with Catherine Sheridan to see him.'

'You want to find out the deal with this cop McCullough as well?' Roth asked.

'All of them,' Miller said. 'I want to find out who they all are.'

'I'll have someone check all the McCulloughs in Washington,' Roth said.

'So right now we go get these pictures from Reid, and then back to the Sheridan place,' Miller said. 'We go through everything until we find out who she was.'

Roth rose from his chair. 'And the first three? What about them?'

'This one I want to know about first . . . we'll start on the other three when we get some of this information from Metz and Oliver,' Miller replied. He reached for his jacket. 'The guy phoned for pizza. Appears he used the Darryl King case number. We know for sure that McCullough would have had that number. Maybe it's a cop we're looking for. A retired one sure, but a cop all the same. And then there's the newspaper clipping, the photographs beneath the bed . . . maybe something, maybe not, but there's more here than with the first three. I think he's telling us to find him, Al . . . I think he *wants* us to find him.'

Downstairs at the desk Roth left a request with the sergeant to run a trace on Michael McCullough.

'Where you off to?' the sergeant asked. 'Just in case Lassiter asks.'

'Forensics division,' Roth said. 'Got some pictures to collect.'

I was born in July 1959 in Salem Hill, Virginia, on the day that Castro assumed the presidency of Cuba. Salem Hill sits in the fork between U.S. 301 and 360 near Ashland. Our town was nothing more than a wide part in the road. My mother died when I was twenty years old. Thursday, September 13th, 1979. My father died the following day. When I was twenty-one I met Catherine Sheridan, and now she is also dead. Seems to me I know a lot of dead people. More than those who are still alive.

Tuesday morning I want to call in sick.

Makes me laugh to think of it. Had I known how this life would go, hell, I would've called in sick before I got started.

These past few days I've thought more and more about my father. The kind of man he must have been to do what he did. How that influenced me, 'cause though I thought it, it is only now that I'm really beginning to grasp the import and significance of what happened.

What kind of person could do something like that? A man of violence or a man of compassion? A man of selfishness, or a man of such profound generosity I could never hope to comprehend it? I am forty-seven years old, and still I don't fully understand.

My life has two parts, that much I see. Before. And After.

The Before:

'Stand here,' he said. He gave me a piece of wood, thin like the blade of a knife. 'This is mahogany,' he said. 'Hold it up to the light. Look at the grain there.'

I held it up. I saw the grain.

'Grain in wood is like the fingerprint of time. The grain in a cross-section tells us about weather, about disease, about cycles of growth, about years of drought and humidity, about the passage of seasons, all manner of things. The grain shows us what

121

happened . . . the life that existed in the world around the tree, you understand?'

I nodded, smiled. I understood.

He gave me a cloth, a tin of wax. The cloth was soft like down, yellow and smooth.

'Apply the wax in a circular motion,' he said, 'a little at a time. Layer after layer. It will take five, six layers, sometimes more.'

He showed me how I should fold the cloth double, place it over my index finger.

'Smooth your finger along the surface of the wax. Stroke it, don't dig at it. Dig at it and you'll take up too much. You want a fine smear on the cloth. Then you work it into the wood, circular, round and round like I said. When the wax is worked into the wood you leave it overnight, and then you come back to it and you do the same thing, a smear of wax, working it into the surface of the wood round and round.'

He made me show him.

'Slower,' he said. 'Slower than that.'

I circled slower, watched the wood absorb the wax.

'Good,' he said. He handed me another sliver of wood, six inches long, an inch and a half wide. 'Now this one,' he said. 'And when you're done with that one there are more over there.'

'What are they for?' I asked.

He smiled. Stood over me, the smell of wood and wax and tobacco around him like a mist, and he smiled.

'Wait and see,' he said. 'You have to wait and see.'

I did what he asked. I waited. I saw. Had I known, I never would have believed him.

And The After:

I find myself standing in a field, and all of a sudden I realize that everything they told me was a lie, and the lie goes so deep and so far, and the lie went back for so many years that even the liars have started to believe in its profound and unquestionable truth.

So I am standing in a field. No more than a few years beyond my teens, and I figure I am the most important fucking person in the whole world . . . man, I've got a hard-on for how fucking important I am, and I've been here no more than a handful of weeks, and suddenly I realize that I'm going to have to start lying to myself mighty fast and mighty thoroughly to keep on doing this thing.

'I hate the way they look at you,' someone says.

'Who?' I ask. I look at the man's face; his skin is like sun-baked leather.

'The kids . . . the kids whose parents you just killed.'

'Killed?' I say, naïvely.

He looks at me askance. 'Shit, kid, how long you been here?'

'Came in last month.'

A knowing smile, a nod, a wink. 'You'll get the drift soon enough, don't worry. First time for everything, eh? 'Cept here there ain't no foreplay before they fuck you.'

Laughing then. Laughing and walking away.

And I'm left standing in a field in the middle of some god-forsaken shithole on the other side of the world, wondering whether anything they'd told me was the truth.

Selective blindness. Selective deafness.

Would wake up the next day. The cold, hard fist of morning . . .

Welcome to the real world, motherfucker.

In the years to come, hindsight coloring our memories, Catherine and I talked for a long while. We spoke about the Caribbean and the Pacific. The Mosquito Coast and Bluefields. The volcanoes. The forests. The earthquakes and landslides, the hurricanes, the soil erosion and water pollution, the infant mortality rate, the Alliance for the Republic, the Central American Unionists, the Christian Alternatives, the Independent Liberals . . .

And us.

We spoke about us. And what we did. And why we did it.

Anchor to windward. I would remember that. .22 caliber AR7 rifles. Small caliber bullets that distorted easily upon impact making them difficult to identify. Turning the ankles so the joints popped before you entered a silent house. Dry clean procedure to determine the presence of enemy surveillance equipment. Fumigation to remove it. The forger's bridge, a simple technique of employing the fingers of one hand to steady the other so as to enable smooth handwriting. Honey traps. Jack-in-the-box dummies to deceive surveillance about how many passengers were in vehicles. Mail covers and music boxes and nightcrawlers and orchestras . . .

We talked about men of legend, places like Algeria and Salvador, moments of history where political systems that had taken decades to establish were overthrown in an hour. All because oil was found, or gas reserves, or the northernmost corner of one landlocked African state became the safest route to somewhere more significant.

And the cocktail parties where the most revered seemed to drink the most and leave the earliest. A company of fellows seen as if through some distorted funhouse mirror. They saw themselves as they once were – filled to bursting with certainty and patriotism, that self-righteous ardor – and now knew all too well that such things were lost in some quiet corner of decimated jungle, in the eyes of an orphaned child, in the embers of a burned village.

They were all there. Watch any of them for long enough and you could tell who was lying to who just by who they were avoiding.

In most of those places we got it wrong. Months of preparation and we got it so wrong. Intel gave us a schoolhouse, a meeting of important figures. Thirteen incendiary devices – the type and variety favored by Baader-Meinhof and the Red Brigade, the type we taught them to make – and we succeeded in killing eleven schoolkids. Hell, we didn't so much as kill them as detonate them wholesale into the hereafter. Wounded another thirty. Retaliation against us was swift and decisive. They left twenty-two decapitated heads on the steps of the church in Esteli. Two for each child. We came out of there with our tails between our legs, our hearts in our mouths. Of the eight members of our team six had children.

We talked about one of the hemisphere's poorest countries, the external debt, the uprisings, the revolutions, the six hundred and seventy million dollars of reserves against the four and a half billion debt . . .

About the most successful and profitable trans-shipment point for U.S. cocaine and arms-for-drugs dealing in Central America. At least since the early '80s – when we got involved. At least since then.

We talked about the real world.

Me and Catherine . . . God knows how many times we spoke of these things, and they never got easier. We spent so many years running away from such shadows, only to realize that they were our own.

But now it has changed, changed so much there's no going back.

Now it's only a matter of time.

TWELVE

Eleven a.m. and Natasha Joyce leaves her apartment and heads out of the projects on foot. She catches a bus that will take her along Martin Luther King into Fairmont Heights. East Capitol Street metro station, a half dozen stops, and she walks up to the corner of A Street North East and Sixth. Imposing building, marble and granite all over it. Has on an overcoat, but the day is cold, bitter, a blustery wind that causes her eyes to water. Makes her way up the steps and into the foyer, the grand reception of this almighty Police Department Administrations Unit, staffed by people who don't call you back. Homage to the white man. All so much bullshit and bravado.

Man at the desk, pinched face, like someone gave him a good smack just five minutes before. Superior tone of voice – 'Can I help you, Miss?'

'Looking for someone . . . called earlier, was told I was gonna get a call back. Haven't heard nothin'.'

'And who was it that you spoke to, Miss—?'

'Joyce. Name's Natasha Joyce. Didn't take the name of the woman I was dealing with, but she was in the records department.'

The man smiled understandingly. 'I think at the last count we had something in the region of two hundred and forty people working in the records department, Miss Joyce. Perhaps if you can give me a few details relating to your inquiry I might be able to check it on our system.'

'Was after someone named Darryl King. Died back in October 2001. Reason I'm checking up on it here is that he was found by the police back then. They came and told me he was dead. Wanted to find out who found him, you know? Wanted to find out what happened.'

The man seemed puzzled, opened his mouth as if to ask a

126

question and then decided against it. He tapped on the keyboard, he waited, he shook his head and tapped some more.

He smiled as if now pleased with himself.

'Your call at eight forty-eight this morning, yes. Call was taken by operator number five . . . and here we have it, yes. Darryl Eric King. A note on the system to say that there were no records here, and it seems that operator five has forwarded a request to our I.T. department—'

'I know all that,' Natasha said impatiently. 'That was more than two hours ago. She said she was gonna call me back. She hasn't called me back. That's why I'm here.'

The man smiled sympathetically. Expression on his face was one of patience, like now he was dealing with a child, a young child, perhaps a child slightly backward for their age. Everything slowly, everything twice. 'Miss Joyce,' he said. He took his hands from the keyboard, placed them together like prayer time. 'Sometimes it takes a little time to sort these things out. These records are very old—'

'Woman I spoke to said they shoot them on over here electronically. They're here in a flash, a second or two, that's what she said. She didn't say nothin' about records being old . . . like they're old and they gotta walk over here by theirselves or something. That what you're saying?' Her tone of voice was indignant, irritable. White man, pinched face; looked like he was going to get another slap before the day was out. 'What I'm asking can't be that hard, now can it?' She shook her head from side to side. She was ready to start wagging her finger at the little white man. *You tell me what I want to hear, little man, or yo' gon' get a faceful of thunder and no sunshine.* Hands on her hips maybe. Enough now. Four hundred years of oppression stops right here and now motherfucker.

'Miss Joyce. I understand your position completely—'

She was wound up good, and then some besides. 'Understand? Understand what? What you understand and what I understand ain't even in the same fuckin' street, Mister—'

'Miss Joyce.' His voice was stern now. Now he was upset, started to rise from his chair. 'There is absolutely no need for this kind of language. If you don't behave in a civil manner

127

I'm going to have to call security and have you ejected from the building . . . and believe me, Miss Joyce, you do not intimidate me in any way, shape or form. I am trying my best to assist you with your enquiry, and I have not treated you with disrespect or—'

Natasha Joyce backed up and lowered her head. 'I apologize,' she said. She knew she was going to get nowhere fast if she blasted the poor white son-of-a-bitch. 'I'm a little upset, sir,' she said. 'I'm a little upset, and there have been recent events that have reminded me of things that I believed I could forget, and all I'm trying to do is get some help here . . .' She took a Kleenex from her pocket. She had the little-girl-lost thing going on, the half smile, the pitiful expression. Whatever it took, right?

The pinched-face white asshole smiled. He raised his hands in a conciliatory fashion. *All water under the bridge*, he was thinking. *We're starting over again. We're backing up, rewinding this little piece of our lives, and starting all over, okay?*

'Okay,' he said. 'Apology accepted. We are going to do what we can to help you, Miss Joyce, but you have to understand that sometimes these things take a little more time than we want. You have to appreciate our position here, dealing with the records for countless police precincts and however many thousands of officers, active, retired, even deceased . . .' His voice trailed away. Tapping the keyboard. Reading the screen, nodding.

'Wait here,' he said, and he smiled, and rose from his chair.

He was gone for no more than a handful of minutes. Natasha waited patiently, and when he returned he was not alone.

Amanda called as they drove toward forensics.

'Yes, of course I did,' Al Roth was telling her. 'I'll speak to you when I get back tonight . . . yes, sweetheart, of course. I love you too.'

'Trouble?' Miller asked.

Roth shook his head, put his cell away. 'Left here,' he said. 'First right at the end, it's faster.'

Miller followed Roth's directions, pulled up fifty yards or so from the Forensics Division building.

Once inside they identified themselves. The receptionist seemed to have been expecting them.

'From Greg Reid,' the guy said, and slid an unmarked envelope across the counter. 'He's not here. He's out on something else. He said you'd have something for him?'

Miller nodded, handed over the plastic baggie with the newspaper clipping inside.

'You see him, you tell him thanks,' Miller said, and he and Roth left the building and returned to the car.

Reid had copied the photographs, all three of them, and put them through some digital process that made them clearer than the originals.

'He look like a serial killer to you?' Roth asked as he squinted at the man's face.

Miller smiled. 'What the fuck does a serial killer look like?'

Roth handed the picture back to Miller and started the car. 'Christ almighty knows,' he said. 'Anyway, Columbia Street is next.'

It was just before ten by the time they reached Catherine Sheridan's house. Roth pulled up at the curb, turned off the ignition, and the pair of them were silent for a moment. The engine clicked as it cooled.

'We're waiting for what exactly?' Roth asked.

'She walked back down this way,' Miller said. 'Three days ago.' He closed his eyes, frowning tightly, deep furrows in his brow. 'I want to know where the hell she went between the delicatessen and here.'

'We could do a news thing,' Roth suggested. 'Ask Washington if they saw her.'

'No, I don't think so. Lassiter has maybe another two days, maybe 'til the end of the week, and then the chief will want a task force. They don't want it on the news, believe me. Hell, you know the way these things go.'

Roth was silent. He knew when to say nothing.

'What did she do between leaving the deli and arriving home? Was he already in the house by the time she returned? Did she put the DVD on and then he came up behind her?' Miller turned to look at Roth. 'I thought about that . . . about what I do when someone comes to visit, or when the phone rings and I'm in the middle of watching a movie . . .'

'You pause it, right?'

Miller nodded. 'Right. And she didn't pause the movie, and what that tells me is that she was watching it and this guy was already in the house, or the other thing . . .'

'That he did her and then *he* put it on.'

'Right.'

'That'd be fucking weird.'

'I agree,' Miller said. 'That would be very fucking weird.'

'So we're going back in the house?' Roth asked.

'Yep,' Miller replied. He reached for the door lever. 'And we don't come out until we know who the fuck Catherine Sheridan really was.'

I wonder what my father would have said had he known what would become of me. Minnesota gets a Muslim Congressman, connected to Louis Farrakhan, leader of the Nation of Islam.

Officials in Virginia told ABC News that the FBI were investigating claims of voter intimidation.

And only last week, November 7th, the most beautiful irony of all. A former Marxist revolutionary, a man I knew all too well for too many years, wins back the presidency. The current U.S. administration issued veiled threats that they would impose punitive measures.

November of 1980, Reagan and Bush won the election. The war went on for another four years, the Americans busily selling arms to the Iranians and then using the money to support it. The second poorest Western Hemisphere nation, right there behind Haiti, and Reagan wanted so much to hold it against the communist infiltration he believed would make its way up through Honduras, Guatemala and right into Mexico. Gautemala. Hell, we were there too. Still are there, interfering and bullshitting everyone. Five thousand unlawful killings a year.

It's all a thin line. A thin line from Mexico to Colombia through the Panama Canal. The coke. The heroin. The guns. The money. Jesus, what were we thinking? Communist infiltration through the South American pipelines. How many years was I down there? How many real communists did I find?

Such bittersweet irony. Could almost be funny if it wasn't for the number of people who died.

And now Bush Junior is watching the empire fall apart.

June of '86 the United States was found guilty of violating international law by supporting the rebels. The International Court of Justice ruling stated that the U.S. should pay compensation but Reagan boycotted the whole thing and ignored the verdict.

'You are in breach of your obligations under customary

international law not to use force against another state, not to intervene in its affairs, not to violate its sovereignty and not to interrupt peaceful maritime commerce.'

That's what the International Court said.

'You have been found guilty of training, arming and funding paramilitary forces, including laying mines in foreign waters . . .'

'Fuck you, your mommy, your daddy too . . . and fuck the horse you rode in on,' said Reagan.

Through 1987 and '88 we sat on our thumbs while they held talks, and then finally a peace agreement was signed.

Six years later we pulled another mighty stunt. A U.S.-backed rebellion fronted by the National Opposition Union forced the government out again. We persisted with our refusal to pay compensation for the damage we had done, and in 1991 the National Opposition Union, a government we had put in power by force, announced that the proceedings for American compensation would be dropped.

And now the prodigal son has returned. Tough bastard, I'll give him that much. Using Congressional immunity to avoid the rape allegations from his stepdaughter, and he takes the president's seat yet again.

Venezuela is busting its sides with laughter. What did Chavez say? *'We will unite as never before to construct a socialist future. Latin America is ceasing to be – and forever – a backyard of U.S. imperialism. Yankee, go home!'*

Bush's administration calls the election 'transparent'.

I say *'Hey George Dubya . . . remember Florida?'*

So now we're in Washington again, and the Democrats have regained control of the House of Representatives for the first time since 1994.

Four days ago the U.S. administration conceded defeat in the mid-terms. They even lost Virginia, staunch Republican strong-hold that it once was. Out came the non-denial denials, the non-affirmative affirmations, but whichever way you look at it it seems they are now experiencing their own 'extraordinary rendition.'

Watergate . . . hell, that was nothing.

The ramifications head further south than you can even imagine.

Rumsfeld retires. Jesus, the guy is seventy-four years of age. Bush says we need a fresh perspective in Iraq, so who do they wheel out? Robert M. Gates, Bush Snr's CIA director. For God's sake, Gates was CIA director from 1991 to 1993. He held the position of Deputy Director for Central Intelligence under William Casey. CIA director before that from '86 to '89. What goes around comes around. Seems that way.

Oh fuck, I hear someone saying. We're gonna get our asses kicked for the next two years.

Oh I don't think so . . . way these people work they'll have something all figured out by the end of next week. Just you wait and see, friends, just you wait and see.

I watch these things unfold and I am struck by the utter insanity of what we are doing with our country, with our lives. I think of the countries we've bombed since the end of the Second World War. I can list them right now. China, Korea, Guatemala, Indonesia, Cuba, the Congo, Peru, Laos, Vietnam, Cambodia, Grenada, Libya, El Salvador, Panama, Iraq, the Sudan, Afghanistan and Yugoslavia. And those are the ones we told you about.

And we were there alongside every single one, in the underground, the preliminary expeditions, the aftermath. I saw a couple of them, and a couple of them were quite enough for me. For Catherine too. We were there – fulfilling our role, doing our duty, due representation of the Chief Executive of the Federal Government, the Administrative Head of the Executive Department, the Commander-in-Chief of the Armed Forces. Like they say . . . you know what the CIA is doing, then you know what the president wants done.

We held court for far too long. I know what happened there. I also know what happened in Afghanistan, in Colombia, in too many places to name.

And the shit I've seen? The things I know about . . . ?

We have to pay for what we did.

But believe me, this time, some other people are going to pay too.

Sometimes I can't even bear to think about it.

I wonder what my father would have thought had he lived.

But he didn't. He died. And maybe a little of me died with him.

133

THIRTEEN

It was only later – an hour, perhaps two – that Natasha Joyce felt a sense of disquiet and unease. Insidious, almost intangible, it was not what had been said, not what she'd been asked, but the *way* it had been asked.

The Police Department Administrations Unit receptionist had returned with a white woman – smartly dressed, late forties, her manner sympathetic, understanding. She'd shown Natasha to a private office. Natasha followed her, asked no questions, and once inside the plain and undecorated room they sat in silence for a moment. Natasha felt she was being observed, examined, and then the woman laid a thin manila file on the desk, a number of sheets of lined paper, a pen.

'My name is Frances Gray,' the woman said. 'I work for the Washington Police Department's public liaison office. Our function here is to act as a bridge between the public and the people who manage police affairs.' Ms Gray smiled. 'Do you have any questions before we start?'

'Start what?' Natasha asked.

'The interview.'

'Interview?'

'About your request this morning.'

'You're dealing with that now?'

Frances Gray nodded. 'I am.'

Natasha leaned back, folded her arms across her chest. 'Well, I do have one question Ms Gray—'

'Call me Frances. This isn't a formal interview.'

'Frances? Okay, if that's what you want. So . . . so my question is this. How come I all of a sudden get a private office and a person like you when all I've made is one phone call?'

'Standard procedure in such a case, Ms Joyce.'

134

'You're telling me this is standard procedure for anyone who asks a question about someone who died?'

'No, of course not . . . not for anyone who inquires about a regular death—' Frances Gray caught herself, laughed a little stiffly. 'That sounds so cold, so unsympathetic,' she said. 'I don't mean to sound so unfeeling, but the death of your fiancé—'

'I didn't tell you he was my fiancé,' Natasha interjected.

'No, you didn't, but you did mention it to one of the staff at the public records office when you called them yesterday.'

'I did?' Natasha asked.

Frances smiled. 'Yes . . . you called that office yesterday, and apparently they told you that all records were archived after five years, and that you should perhaps try here.'

'You have that conversation on record?'

'Yes, we do. We like to consider ourselves efficient when it comes to dealing with important requests.'

Natasha shook her head. 'This don't make sense, Frances . . . this sure as shit don't make no sense to me.'

Frances frowned, tilted her head to one side. 'Doesn't make sense? What doesn't make sense, Natasha?'

'That you people would go to all this trouble over someone like Darryl. I mean, for God's sake, he might have been the father of my girl, but he wasn't anyone important. Hell, he was nothing more than a two-bit bullshit thief and a heroin addict.'

Frances was silent for quite some time, and then she shook her head slowly. 'You were not told anything, were you?' she asked quietly.

'Told what?' Natasha asked. 'About what?'

'About Darryl King . . . about what happened when he died?'

'Jesus, there can't be that much to know can there? He got himself shot. Some cop found him, that's what I heard. I wanted to see if the cop was still around so I could ask him what happened.'

Frances was nodding slowly. 'Okay . . . okay Natasha. And could I ask you why, after all these years, you wanted to find out what happened?'

'For my daughter,' Natasha said. 'I have a nine-year-old

135

daughter. Name is Chloe. I started to figure I should know something about what happened. Wanted to find out if there was anything more than what I heard. She's getting older, she's gonna start asking questions, and one time she's gonna ask about who he was and what happened to him, and to tell you the truth . . .' Natasha paused and smiled. 'Tell you the truth, Frances, I ain't such a good liar when it comes to kids, you know?'

Frances' expression said everything that needed to be said; she seemed to understand exactly what Natasha was talking about. 'Tell me what you know,' she said. 'You tell me what you know about what happened back then, and then I'll tell you everything else, okay?'

Natasha sighed deeply. She leaned back and closed her eyes for a moment. When she looked up Frances was waiting patiently, ready to hear everything Natasha had to say.

Miller stood for a long while looking at Catherine Sheridan's front room.

In daylight the complete absence of character was clearly visible. There were no flowers, no ornaments, no pictures on the walls. He and Roth had been through the kitchen and found the basics – cutlery, pans, a skillet, a wok. There were the usual cleaning products and cloths, a box with brown and black shoe cream preparations, an applicator, a buffer. There was no pizza wheel, no chopsticks, no pot plants, no spice rack or yolk separator. They went through the cupboards and drawers. They found everything one would need in a kitchen sufficient to cater to the most simple and pedestrian of tastes, but what they did not find – at least from Miller's perspective – was anything personal.

He stood silently surveying the accoutrements and utensils spread across the counter-top.

'It's not right,' he told Roth. 'Something about this place is just not right.'

'How long was she here?' Roth asked.

'According to the file, three, three and a half years, something like that.'

Roth looked toward the window, seemed distracted for a moment. 'You know what this reminds me of?' he eventually said. 'Reminds me of a film I saw one time . . . guy was found dead in Central Park, fully clothed, shoes, suit, tie, shirt, the whole works, even had on an overcoat, but every label had been removed. I mean everything that would give some kind of indication of where he might have come from, where he lived . . . everything was removed. No wallet, no pocket-book, no keys, no driver's license, even no labels inside his jacket.'

'Like someone's cleaned the place,' Miller said. 'Like some-one went through this place and took away everything that would tell us who she was.'

'Did you see any of the other places?' Roth asked.

Miller shook his head. 'You?'

'I only saw the Rayner woman. That was back in July. I visited the scene once. It was nighttime. I didn't see a great deal. I could have gone back there the next day but I didn't. Couple of uniforms went over there with the forensics people, that was all.'

'This hasn't really become something until now, has it?'

'Something?' Roth asked. 'Like how d'you mean *some-thing*?'

'First one, Margaret Mosley . . . that was just a murder. I say *just* a murder, but it was an isolated incident. Looks like a sex crime. Shit happens, you know? Second one, the one you saw, that was a coincidence, right? Like the old saying, first time is happenstance, second time coincidence, third time you have a conspiracy. So the third one comes along, Barbara Lee, and now we have a pattern. Fourth one and we're right in serial territory. This is how it reads to the suits in the mayor's office. Now we've got something to worry about. Now word gets around, people forget about the elections, they remember that there was something there at the back of their minds. They start writing letters to the *Post*, the press is all over the place wanting to know what we're doing about this murder epidemic.'

'And this one is the important one, isn't it,' Roth said, more a statement than a question.

'This one's different,' Miller replied. He walked to the table and sat down facing his partner. 'Way I feel . . . God, I don't know what I feel. I feel like it isn't the same. There's

137

something about it that feels like a copycat, but it can't be –
unless someone within the department did it, you know?
Anyway, regardless of who might or might not have done
this, there's something different about it. I don't just mean
the pizza guy, the fact that our guy killed her and then called
someone over here to find her. Besides that, there's something about the way this *feels* that tells me . . .' Miller shook
his head. 'Fuck Al, I don't know. The pizza thing and this
Joyce woman, and the case number on Darryl King being
the same as the phone number, you know? The news clipping under the mattress . . . maybe that's something, maybe
it isn't.'

'Did have a thought,' Roth said. 'That it could be a copycat
not because the guy had access to any files or records or
anything, but because he knows the original killer.'

'What? Like there's two of them?'

'It's just another explanation for the similarity.'

'Hell, that's even more horrifying than if he's a cop or
something.'

'Okay, so now we need something that tells us who she
was. Right now she's no-one. Right now her social security
number belongs to someone named Isabella Cordillera, and
as far as we can tell there is no-one alive named Isabella
Cordillera.'

'Which language is that?' Miller asked.

Roth shook his head. 'Spanish, Portuguese maybe?'

'We need to check it out, maybe there's something there.'

'So what now? You ready to go through this place with
me?'

Miller rose from the chair and removed his jacket. 'Upstairs,' he said. 'We start upstairs and move down.'

Roth followed, draped his jacket over the back of the chair,
started toward the stairwell.

'A what?' Natasha asked.

'An informant,' Frances Gray said. 'Darryl was working
with the police at the time of his death. He gave them a
significant amount of very valuable information regarding
the drug supply lines running through that part of the city.
As a result of the investigation—'

'He died,' Natasha interjected.

Frances Gray nodded. 'Yes, he did die, but he helped put a number of key suppliers in prison.'

Natasha Joyce felt tears break surface tension and roll down her cheeks. She did not know what to say. She was surprised, very much so, but in some way she was also relieved. Relieved that Darryl had tried to do something to repair the damage he'd done . . .

'Wait up,' she said. 'He was busted or what?'

Frances Gray frowned, didn't answer.

'He was informing on these guys because the police had him on something and he was making a deal to get off of a charge?'

'No, not according to the file we have. According to the file we have on this case it appears that he came forward voluntarily.'

'And he died *how* exactly?'

'You know he was shot?'

'Sure, I know he was shot, but who shot him?'

Frances Gray shook her head. 'That we don't know. Not exactly. We know that it was one of the men inside the warehouse that was raided—'

'He was on a warehouse raid? You're shittin' me! What the hell were the police doing taking some junkie informant on a warehouse raid?'

Frances Gray shook her head. 'I am not familiar with all the specifics,' she said. 'All I know is that there was a police officer contact of Darryl's who was also shot. He retired from the department, but I understand that Darryl worked with him for some time before this warehouse raid . . . I don't know precisely and exactly what occurred. I only have a very few details regarding the actual case itself, you understand? I'd like to be able to answer all your questions, Natasha, but I'm not in a position to do so . . . not because I don't want to, and not because the police department would have a problem with this, but because the records no longer exist—'

'*What?*'

'There was a flooding incident at the previous records facility. This was two or three years ago, and a great deal of the files that existed were damaged beyond repair. The paperwork just doesn't exist any more, Natasha, and so I can only tell you what we know from the brief notes made by the officer after he was released from hospital.'

'And who was that? This officer . . . who was that?'

'His name?' Frances Gray asked.

'Sure his name . . . what was his name?'

'I'm sorry, I can't give you that information. I can't identify a police officer—'

'You just said he was retired, right? If he's retired then he ain't a police officer no more.'

Frances Gray smiled patiently. 'I'm sorry . . . there's still a degree of confidentiality attached to these matters. The people that were arrested and jailed are still in jail, you see—'

'Ah Jesus Christ, we had this the first time round. Nobody ever wants to answer a question in a straight fucking line. What the hell d'you think I'm gonna do, huh? I told you why I wanted to know what had happened. My daughter was four years old when her father was killed. All we were ever told was that he was shot. I never even identified his body. His mother went down and did that, you know? Saw her own son lying there with a bullethole in his chest. Only child she had. Lost her husband years before . . . saw her son killed as a junkie, right? You know what happened to her? I'll tell you what happened to her . . . she died of a broken heart, old woman like that. She just gave up the will to live. Dead within six months. Now there's just me. Me and Darryl's daughter. And we want to know what happened, and when I ask you a simple question—'

'Enough,' Frances Gray said. Her voice cut Natasha dead. 'You don't seem to understand the position we are in—'

'The position you are in? Don't give me that bullshit, Ms Gray. Jesus, the position *you* are in. What the fuck kind of position do you think Darryl King's mother was in? I'll fucking tell you something right here and now. You think how that woman might have felt if you'd told her her son was assisting the police in cleaning up some drug areas of Washington. You wonder how she might have felt about her son being dead if she'd been told that?'

'Miss Joyce . . . seriously, I'm trying to appreciate your

situation here. I'm trying to be as helpful as I can, and right now your attitude and manner isn't helping any.'

'Lord, you should listen to yourself, girl. I'm the one who came down here 'cause you people never called me back. You came down and got me from the desk . . . you wanted to talk to me, you wanted to help me understand what happened, and I ask you for one thing—'

'Which I do not have the authority to tell you,' Frances Gray stated flatly.

'So what the fuck do we do now then? We wait for someone to come down here who *does* have the authority? That what we gonna do?'

Frances Gray smiled, but there was something ingratiating and insincere about it. 'We're going to conclude this interview, Miss Joyce, and I'm going to make some enquiries as to whether this information can be made available to you. That's what I'm going to do.'

'And I'm never gonna hear another word from you people, right? That's the way it's gonna go. Tell me I'm wrong.'

Frances Gray shook her head. She gathered up her file, her paper, her pen; she stood up, straightened her jacket and started toward the door. Once in the corridor she waited patiently until Natasha followed her out.

'I'll walk you back to the desk,' Frances Gray said coldly, and already, even as she was being shown down to reception, Natasha Joyce was cursing her hot head, cursing her impatience, her flick-knife temper.

Attitude. That's what Darryl used to say. *There's attitude, girl, and attitude is the same wherever, but sometimes attitude is gonna help you and sometimes it's gonna get you all of nothing.*

Frances Gray told Natasha Joyce she'd be in touch as soon as she could. She wished her a good day, turned on her heel and click-clacked away across the marble floor into echoes and then silence.

The man at the reception desk smiled. 'Hope we were helpful,' he said pleasantly.

Natasha smiled awkwardly. 'Very,' she said, her tone almost apologetic, and then she hurried out of the building into the late morning rainfall that had started in her absence.

Richard Helms, acting Director of the Central Intelligence Agency in an address to the National Press Club, once said, 'You've just got to trust us. We are honorable men.'

Captain George Hunter White, reminiscing about his CIA service, said, 'I toiled wholeheartedly in the vineyards because it was fun, fun, fun. Where else could a red-blooded American boy lie, kill, cheat, steal, rape and pillage with the sanction and blessing of the all-highest?'

These were some of the things from The After . . .

After the thing with my mother, and what my father did, and how he engineered my assistance . . .

Before that:

Patience personified. Standing there at the workbench, a tin canister of wax to my right, a line of wooden veneer strips to my left. One at a time. Smooth as glass. Smooth as jewellers' rouge and mercury.

'They are thin,' my father said. 'Bend them and they will snap like crackers. Take care to polish them until you can see your face reflected.'

'What are they for?' I asked again.

Smiled, shook his head. 'See that board over there?' He pointed with his dye-stained finger. 'That board has to be cut and shaped. When it's sanded smooth I'm going to draw a pattern in it, and then I'll cut indents and depressions in the pattern, and then the pieces of veneer you're polishing will fit together to form a design.'

'Inlay,' I said.

He nodded. 'Right. Inlay.'

'What's the board for?'

'What's it for?' he echoed. 'What's anything for? It's for its own purpose, you know? Everything has a purpose, and when you understand that purpose—'

'Seriously . . . what's it for?' I asked again.

He reached out and gripped my shoulder. 'I'll tell you when we're done.'

I watched him working. He didn't say a word.

Later, looking back, I was reminded of Catherine in some strange way.

Even in her silences she had more to say than anyone I'd ever known.

And again, from The After:

We realized that Reagan was a cocksucker.

Chief Executive Officer of the Federal Government, Administrative Head of the Executive Department, Commander-in-Chief of the Armed Forces. Supposed to be answerable to no-one.

Three divisions of the United States government – Legislative, Executive and Judicial. Forget the Legislative – nothing but lawyers and penpushers, bureaucrats, faceless minions. Judicial covers the Supreme Court, has authority over all U.S. courts, deals with 'interpretation of the Constitution' whatever the fuck that means, but even there we're talking about the chief justice and eight associate justices, and they're appointed by whom? That's right, friends, the almighty cocksucker himself.

So we come to the Executive, and man, if this isn't a beast of the most extraordinary dimensions. State, Treasury, Defense, the Federal Bureau of Investigation, the Departments of the Interior, the Office of the White House, the National Security Council . . .

It goes on and on and on.

And the Central Intelligence Agency, in and of itself a magnificent oxymoron – we find these guys right there at the very top of the executive branch. Who are they? Let's be honest with one another. They are the intelligence and covert operations and covert execution and wetworks and disestablishment and assassination and coup d'état and undermining whatever the fuck is out there that in any way opposes 'The Great American Way of Life' unit of the President of the United States. A personal fucking army. The dog soldiers.

Some of the people in the Central Intelligence Agency were good people.

But they were not good for long.

It's a fallacy. You cannot have a corrupt and self-serving

143

organization populated by people who are there for the very best reasons. People wind up in the CIA, and they either get with the program, or they understand what the program is and get the fuck out of there as fast as they can. And sometimes, as we all know, they are taken out by force, the real definition of 'extraordinary rendition'.

And then you have people like me.

Started way back when, after the thing with my mom and dad. Way back when I was a kid and I didn't know what the goddamn hell I was going to do with my life.

They saw something, the shepherds. That's what they call them. The guys that go out and gather up the new flock for recruitment and indoctrination and training and all the things you go through, all the steps that whittle down the many into the few. The shepherds.

So they saw something in me. The loner. The loser. The one who didn't fit. They were good. Man, were they good. Subtle, smart, insidious. Working on me. Finding my loyalties, my interests, the things I believed in, the things I didn't. They ingratiated themselves into the very fabric of the university campus. They'd been there for ever. Lawrence Matthews. Professor of Philosophy, Virginia State University in Richmond. I'd been there little more than a year. My parents had been dead no more than eight or ten weeks. Changed my major. Caused a noise. Lawrence Matthews was patient, understanding, a good man. He understood that engineering had been my father's choice, that math and physics and whatever was just not where I lived. English and Philosophy. That's where I belonged, and after my father's death that's where I went.

Professor Lawrence Matthews was there to receive me, and receive me he did. Long discussions. Politics. Life. Death. The Hereafter. God as an icon, God as an identity. All so much horseshit and nonsense. Lawrence Matthews loved that shit. Man, he could talk you round in circles and make you disappear up your own ass. That was his business. Think they trained him as an interrogator, and when he burned out or got a conscience they posted him right there in Virginia State to keep an eye out for the future of the Company. He was a reader. He read people, and when he read something that made sense he would tell the shepherd. The shepherd would come, and he was a friend of Professor

144

Matthews. And Professor Matthews' friend was a good guy, a regular guy, and he could drink a beer and watch co-eds swing by and smoke cigarettes with the best of them.

My shepherd was named Don Carvalho, and I never did find out if that was his real name, and in all honesty it didn't matter what the fuck his name was. He was there to do a job, and he did that job pretty much as good as anyone could ever do a job. Don Carvalho was a master of his own destiny, at least that was the way it seemed to me. He knew everything. Hell, he couldn't have been much more than twenty-eight or nine, but it seemed to me that he knew everything there was to know about anything that counted. Don was a magician, a wizard, a spokesman for the oppressed minorities, a politician, a rebel, an insurgent, a spiritual terrorist for the aesthetes. Don was there to discuss Camus and Dostoyevsky, Solzhenitsyn and Soloviev, Descartes, Kerouac, Ken Kesey, Raymond Chandler, and the films of Edward G. Robinson. His father was a lawyer in Hollywood. His father knew people. His grandfather knew even more people, could tell stories about Cary Grant's work for British intelligence, uncovering Nazi affiliations and sympathizers in the movie industry during the Second World War. Don Carvalho knew people who had worked under Joe McCarthy. His mother was Israeli, came from Tel Aviv, an early 1950s background intrinsically bound up in the formation of something named Mossad ha-Mossad le-Modiin ule-Tafkidim Meyuhadim. The Institute for Intelligence and Special Tasks. The Institute.

'They have The Institute,' Don Carvalho told me. 'And we have The Company.'

'The Company?'

'Central Intelligence Agency.'

'Right,' I said. 'The CIA. I know about them.'

And Don smiled, and shook his head, and placed his hand on my shoulder and said, 'Oh no you don't, my friend, oh no you don't.'

And then changed the subject.

That was how they worked. Give you a taste. Let you ask a question and don't answer it. Fucking good. Catch-as-catch-can. Always testing, always watching, always trying to sound out your principles, your limitations, the extremes to which you'd be prepared to go to get your point across. They were after certainty, after

145

an unquestioning belief in the Right Way To Do Things. Apparently. Or apparently not.

From the point I met Don Carvalho at Lawrence Matthews' New Year's Eve Party at the end of 1979 to my first Langley visit it was six months. Doesn't seem like a long time now. Later Don told me that my 'courtship' was one of the fastest he'd done.

It would be another year before I went into the field, and the things that intervened were some of the most important events of my life. At least that's how I felt at the time. Now I know they were insignificant, all except one. The most important thing happened in December 1980. I was living in an apartment on the outskirts of Richmond. That's when everything changed. That's when everything I saw was colored with a different light.

That, very simply, was the end of who I was and the beginning of who I became.

And to think, it all started because of a girl in a turquoise hat.

FOURTEEN

By quarter after one Robert Miller believed that he'd grasped some small understanding of who he was looking at.

Catherine Sheridan was an enigma.

He was looking at a singularly unique and inescapably *created* identity. This was what he felt as he went through her bookcases, her paperwork, her correspondence, her diary. He studied her passport, her driver's license, her bank cards, credit cards, checkbooks; he found photographs of places she'd apparently visited, people she knew, postcards that had been sent to her from someone who simply signed themselves as *J*.

Having called Reid to verify that CSU and forensics were through, that they were cleared for unlimited access to the house and its contents, Robert Miller and Albert Roth arranged the artifacts and aspects of Catherine Sheridan's life in several ordered sections. They laid stuff out along the upper hallway carpet, and when there was insufficient space to cope with what they were doing they moved everything through into her bedroom. They pushed the bed against the wall and put the dresser and chair in the adjoining bathroom. Clothes, shoes, purses, such things as these were set over to the right. Across the middle of the floor they arranged several piles of paperwork – anything that related to finance, anything that connected to her identity, vacations and visits, personal correspondence (of which there was almost nothing), documents that related to the house and utilities. And when they were done they were once again aware of the fact that nothing seemed even to indicate her occupation. Miller went through her bank statements and, sure enough, at the end of each month, an amount of money was deposited. The better part of four thousand dollars arrived from something called United Trust on the last Friday of every month, and those deposits went back all the way to June of 2003.

'Didn't she come here three and a half years ago?' Roth asked.

'Far as I can gather, yes.'

'So she arrives here in June 2003. There's nothing pre-dating that. Every banking record only goes back that far, nothing earlier.'

'Go through everything again,' Miller said.

'I figured you were gonna say that.'

Twenty past two, Miller looked up, shook his head. 'That's it. Everything stops in June 2003. There's nothing earlier. Looks like she didn't exist before three and a half years ago.'

'Which is when the Spanish woman died in the car crash . . . the Cordillera woman, right?'

'Right.'

'So we have Catherine Sheridan assuming a dead person's social security number but not their name, she comes to this house from wherever, and whatever records might have existed about her prior to that point stay behind.'

'Fucking crazy shit,' Miller said. 'This is—' He shook his head. 'I just don't know what the fuck this is . . .'

Roth arched his back and stretched his arms above his head.

'Witness protection, maybe . . . ?' Miller asked, more a comment than a question.

Roth smiled sardonically. 'Didn't do so fucking good protecting her then, did they?'

The rain had eased off, and Natasha Joyce hesitated beneath the awning of a convenience store before she hurried across the street and up the steps of Carnegie Library. At the desk was a woman, badge on her lapel said Julia Gibb.

'Newspaper section,' Natasha said.

The woman smiled warmly. She leaned towards Natasha. 'Current or archives?'

'Five years ago?' Natasha asked.

'That will be archives . . . second floor, turn right at the top of the stairs, keep going, and through a door at the end

148

you'll find politics, then history, and then beyond that we have media archives, okay?'

'Thank you,' Natasha said, and made her way towards the stairs.

It was a small piece, really nothing to speak of, but she found it. *Washington Post* of October 8th, 2001, page five: *Drug Raid Leaves One Dead.* Natasha scanned the article, barely reading it, barely paying any attention to what the police had to say, what the mayor's office had to say, what any of these assholes—

And then she found him.

Michael McCullough.

Sergeant Michael McCullough, wounded in the warehouse raid. Natasha took a pen and a bus timetable from her purse and wrote down the man's name. *Michael McCullough.* Was this the man that Darryl had been working with, the one who had taken him on the raid, the one who – indirectly, at least – had gotten him killed? Why the fuck did they take Darryl King on a drugs raid?

Natasha closed up the newspaper files, nodded her thanks to Julia Gibb as she left, and then made her way down the street towards the nearest police precinct.

'McCullough,' the desk sergeant at the Washington Fourth Police Precinct said to himself. 'M, small c, big C, u-l-l-o-u-g-h, right?'

'Right,' Natasha said. 'McCullough.'

'And you wanna know what?'

'What precinct . . . if that's possible. He was on a case about five years ago and I need his help with something.'

'And you say he's retired now?'

'Yes, that's right.'

Sergeant Ronald Gerrity, face like a sack of walnuts, small dark eyes like holes in snow, smiled and said, 'If he exists he'll be in the system somewhere.'

Natasha waited, trying to be patient, trying to will the old guy to type faster, to read faster.

'Here we are,' he said.

Natasha's heart leapt.

'Oh shit, no . . . sorry, we got a Mark McCullough here. They related maybe?'

Natasha shook her head. 'I don't know . . . I don't know anyone but Michael.'

The sergeant continued reading, scrolling, reading, and then he paused. 'Jackpot. Michael McCullough. Sergeant. Retired from the Seventh Precinct in March 2003.'

Natasha had her bus timetable out. Scribbling. 'Thank you,' she said. 'I really appreciate your help.'

'That's not a problem, ma'am . . . that all you wanted?'

'Unless you have an address or something?' she asked hopefully.

Gerrity smiled, shook his head. 'That we don't have here . . . don't know how you'd find that. They retire and they become regular joes like everyone else. We don't keep track of them here.'

'It's okay . . . thank you. This really helps.'

'Good 'nough,' Gerrity said. He turned back to his computer, typing slowly, methodically.

Natasha Joyce left the Fourth and made her way back to the bus depot. She had a name, a precinct, a date of retirement. It might be nothing, but then again it might be something. Had she enough time, had Chloe been with her instead of at school, she would have stayed in the city to find out more information regarding this retired police sergeant, but it was getting on and she had to hurry back to collect her daughter.

Something was moving. Something was happening. Her conversation with Frances Gray had been awkward, disconcerting, but at least she had taken something from it. Something that might give her something else. All she wanted to do was find out what happened. Darryl had been trying to do something, trying to make a difference. It made her feel better, it gave her some sense of hope that at least one of the decisions she'd made had not been completely irresponsible. Darryl King had been a good man. She had to believe that. She had to believe that so she could look her daughter in the eye and tell her the truth.

That was all she wanted. The truth. The truth about Darryl King and what happened in October 2001. And if she knew that she could rest easy. She could let go of the past and maybe look toward the future, and that – if nothing else – would be a world apart from what she'd been used to.

They figured it out.

What did I tell you?

Didn't even take as long as I thought it would.

The Democrat's tentative control of the U.S. Senate is now in danger. Democrats hold a 51-49 majority in the chamber. Democrat senator has a stroke. If he doesn't make it, if for any reason he does not return to resume his seat when the Senate reconvenes on January 4th, then the Republican representative will have to choose his successor. Go figure. Who will he choose? That's right friends and neighbors . . . he'll choose someone of his own color. 50-50 Democrat to Republican. A tie? Not so fast . . . Vice-President Cheney has the tie-breaking vote, and he's right in there with George Jnr, as Republican as they come. As simple as that. Take one Democratic senator, move him quietly to the side, have his Republican contemporary select a Republican successor, give the vote to the vice-president and the job's done. The Republicans are back in control. They don't have a lame duck president for another two years.

Democrat senator's doctor was quoted as saying, 'The stroke was not immediately life-threatening. A successful surgical procedure has evacuated the blood and stabilized the malformation. He is recovering without complication in the critical care unit and we expect him to make a complete and fully satisfactory recovery.' His wife was 'encouraged and optimistic'.

You asking the same as me? Would they? Could they? You know, give a guy a stroke in order to wrest back control of the most powerful government body in the world?

I'll say this much: I am not encouraged and optimistic.

It is now Tuesday the 14th. Catherine has been dead for three days. Her house is off-limits. I took the morning off work and went over there. Parked up two hundred yards down the street and saw two detectives arrive. One of them is named Robert Miller. He looks serious, dedicated, the kind of man who has committed himself to a life of asking questions and waiting for answers. The other one is a little older, a family man for sure. Wears a wedding ring, has that tone-on-tone, matching-shirt-and-tie appearance of someone who is taken care of at home. I like the way they look – Miller and his partner. I learned Miller's name from a newspaper article. Mentioned that he was heading the Ribbon Killer investigation. Gave the thing a name. Got to give it a name. Something ain't something unless it has a name, know what I mean? Anyway, Miller is there, and the article said he was involved in the investigation of the killing of Margaret Mosley back in March. They're no further forward now than they were eight months ago. And until I walk right in there and hand them something on a plate they will never get where this thing came from or where it's headed. And then again, maybe they will. Perhaps I should credit them with greater intelligence.

So I watched them arrive and I waited a little longer. I left before they did. Had to make it to work for the afternoon periods.

I'm thinking a day, maybe two or three. Thinking that they'll start to get lucky when they get back to Natasha Joyce with the photos I put under the carpet. She'll tell them what they want to hear, and then it will be down to Miller and his partner to make of it what they can.

I'll be ready for them.

Been ready for a long time.

Things I've had to do . . . hell, those are things that teach you to wait like a professional.

FIFTEEN

Miller stood patiently at the door of Natasha Joyce's apartment. He could see his breath, could feel the chill aching at his bones. Wanted to be home. Wanted to be pretty much anywhere else.

'Not in,' Roth said unnecessarily.

Miller raised his fist again and pounded on the edge of the door frame.

'Seriously, Robert, she ain't in. Let's go back to the car.'

Miller conceded defeat, headed back to the car, but once inside they decided to wait in the hope that Natasha Joyce might return. Thirty-five minutes, that was all, and Miller nudged Roth, who looked to his left and saw Natasha and the little girl make their way down the cracked section of sidewalk and around the edge of the chickenwire fence.

'Hell kind of place is this for a little kid,' Roth said, and reached for the door lever.

Miller put his hand on Roth's shoulder. 'Wait up,' he said. 'Leave them be for a little while. Let her get inside, get her coat off. I don't want to talk to her outside in the cold with the little girl in tow.'

Roth leaned back, said nothing, waited a good eight or nine minutes, and then they made their way back up to the apartment.

'Figured I was gonna call you people,' Natasha Joyce said when she opened the door and let them into the hallway.

'Call us?' Miller asked.

Natasha nodded, walked through to the kitchen. Miller and Roth followed her, the question he'd asked remaining unanswered until they once again sat at the narrow kitchen table.

'Found out some things,' Natasha said.

Miller looked at her. She seemed less nervous. It had been

154

only twenty-four hours since they'd been there. Felt like a month.

'What things?' Al Roth asked.

'Little about what happened to Darryl,' she said. 'I called the police administrations people at the mayor's office—'

'You did what?'

Natasha frowned. 'You make it sound like I did something criminal.' She laughed then, almost naturally, and Miller recognized in her something of the girl she must have been before Darryl King tore through her life with his addiction and all its attendant horror.

'There's an administration unit at the mayor's office,' she went on. 'They have information up there about everything to do with the police. Called them. They said they'd call me back but they never did, so I went up there and spoke to some woman. She told me that Darryl was a police informer.'

Miller glanced at Roth. A moment of recognition between them that harked back to the August 2001 cocaine charge that never materialized. The case file. The pizza delivery number.

'And the man he worked with, the cop he was working with, I found his name. Michael McCullough. Seventh precinct, here in Washington. Retired back in March 2003.'

'This woman, what was her name?'

'Gray, Frances Gray.'

'She told you this? That Darryl worked with a cop named McCullough?'

Natasha shook her head, and then she smiled, pleased with herself. 'She let slip that Darryl had been on some kind of warehouse drugs raid thing when he was shot. Went to the library and checked out the newspapers, found the police guy's name. So I went over to the Fourth precinct and got someone there to check him out on the computer. Guy there told me this McCullough retired back in March of 2003.'

Miller leaned forward, his expression intense. 'And now you have his name, Natasha . . . now you have his name what are you going to do about it?'

'Gonna track the motherfucker down, ain't I?'

Miller raised his hand. 'Under no circumstances, Natasha.'

155

He shook his head, his expression intense. 'Seriously, you cannot do this—'

'Do what the damn hell I like,' Natasha retorted. 'Gonna track him down and find out what happened to Darryl. I want to know what happened so I can tell Chloe when she's a little older. You don't see how much difference this makes to the whole thing?'

'Difference to what?' Miller asked.

'To what that girl is gonna think about her father when she gets old enough to understand. He was shot. He was shot while he was helping the cops do something about the drug dealing in this neighborhood. You don't see what kind of difference that makes about who he was?'

Miller opened his mouth to speak but Natasha kept on talking.

'His mother had to go down there and identify his body. She didn't last more than six months. That old woman died of fucking shame about what her son had become. If they'd told her the truth I guarantee you that old woman would still be alive today.'

Roth raised his head. 'Excuse me,' he said. 'Could I just ask you where your daughter is now?'

'She's down the hall. Old lady named Esme. She likes to go see her every once in a while, keep her company for a coupla hours. They just watch TV together, make some hot chocolate and marshmallows, whatever they like.'

'She's a good kid, isn't she?' Miller said.

Natasha Joyce smiled, and for a moment it seemed as though she was unable to speak.

Miller reached out his hand and closed it over hers. She did not flinch. She did not withdraw.

'Gonna ask you something,' Miller said, knowing now that he had to tread carefully. 'Gonna ask you to look at some pictures for me, and if you do, I'll find Michael McCullough for you. It's gonna be an awful lot easier for me to find him than it is for you. They'll have his forwarding details somewhere within the system and I can locate him.'

'Pictures?' Natasha asked. 'What pictures?'

'We just want you to look at some pictures of a guy and tell us if you recognize him, okay?'

'What guy?'

'We don't know. Could be no-one, and if we tell you who we think it is before we show them to you it could be construed as influencing your judgement. We just need you to look at them with a completely unbiased viewpoint, alright?'

'Bring it on, whatever . . . sure. But I ain't gonna let up on this McCullough. I do this, then you gotta help me find him like you say.'

Roth took the photographs from his inside jacket pocket and passed them to Miller, who turned them face down on the table. He then slid the first one towards Natasha.

Miller felt his heart skip a beat when she turned it over. She looked at it for no more than a split second and said, 'It's him.'

'Who?' Roth asked. 'Who is it?'

'The guy who came down here with the dead woman.'

'You're absolutely certain?'

Natasha took the other photos, rapidly scanned each one. 'Same guy. Same guy in the photos as came down here with her and asked after Darryl. He's younger here, but no question about it.'

Miller looked at Roth. Roth smiled warily. They had something now, but *what* exactly . . .

'So now you gotta find this dude. That what you gon' do?'

'That's what we're gonna do,' Miller said. He rose from the chair and gathered up the pictures. He handed them back to Roth and started towards the door. 'We'll speak soon, okay?'

Natasha Joyce looked at him directly. There was something cold and determined in her expression.

'I'll do what I promised,' Miller said. 'I'll track McCullough down and find out where he went to. I understand you want closure on this thing. You've helped us out here, Natasha, and I *will* come back to you on this guy, alright?'

Natasha looked at Roth.

'He does what he says,' Roth told her.

'You go find whoever you gotta find,' she said. 'Don't forget you promised me on this thing.'

Miller smiled, reached out and took Natasha's hand. 'You take care, okay?'

'We do what we can,' she replied, and then she opened the front door and let them out.

'Fucking thing comes together like jigsaw pieces,' Roth said when they reached the car.

'You see any of the picture yet?' Miller asked.

Roth shook his head. 'You?'

'Something . . . hell, I don't know, maybe something, maybe not. Don't like it though.' He paused for a moment, looked back towards Natasha Joyce's apartment. 'Whatever the fuck is going on here, I don't like it at all.'

*L*ate *afternoon. Class dismissed. Sitting in my room, heels on the desk. Feel something like a sense of nothing, a hollowness, a vacuum inside. Thinking back to when I was a student and they talked to me – Lawrence Matthews and Don Carvalho.*

Thinking about the hat. The damned hat she wore. Stupid damned turquoise beret she wore that day in December when I saw her in a coffee shop in Richmond.

December of 1980, the 10th, a Wednesday. Cold day. Remember that much. That and the damned hat.

It was five weeks after Reagan and Bush stormed into office with a better than ten million-vote lead over Carter and Mondale. Carter had suffered with the energy crisis, the gas station lines, most of the Tehran hostage nightmare. The Republicans were in the House, they were going to clean up everything the Democrats had aborted and bastardized, and I listened to Don Carvalho as he explained that it made no great difference who was in office, that the company he worked for served as a non-biased and unprejudiced force for order and stability regardless of which political persuasion was flavor of the month.

'It's not a matter of politics anymore,' he said. We were seated in an Italian-styled delicatessen on the corner of Klein and Fourth, the two of us in a window seat, Don with his knee raised, his foot on the edge of the seat, the ever-present unfiltered cigarette parked in the corner of his mouth.

'Not a matter of politics?' I asked, more rhetoric than anything else. 'Of course it's a matter of politics.'

Don lowered his foot to the ground, leaned forward smiling. 'See, that's where you're wrong, my friend. Politics is an apparency here.' He waved his hand in the direction of Langley. We never mentioned Langley by name. It was always 'There' or 'Our place' or 'The Hotel'. He went on talking. 'Over there they don't give a fuck about who's in the House. They want to know that the basic

159

and fundamental necessities of democracy and international sta-
bility are being maintained. It's a matter of control, that's all, not
politics. They couldn't give a rat's ass about who's in power where,
which tinpot dictator might have ousted which other tinpot dic-
tator. Coup d'états, all this kind of shit . . .' Don shook his head
and laughed. 'Global ownership is not the issue, John, never has
been. We're not trying to own the world. We're just trying to
maintain the status quo sufficiently to enable decent people to get
what they want and keep it once they have it.'

'You can't expect me to believe that, Don,' I said, and Don just
smiled, same way he always did, and then he changed the subject.

I could see right through him, him and so many others like him.
I had been to Langley numerous times. I was being indoctrinated
into the 'think'. Already I was turning towards the beliefs and
attitudes that were prevalent in our introductory meetings.

'Up there it's like Control Freaks Anonymous,' Don had said.
'Don't listen to the ones that propound and pontificate. Listen to
the ones that state an opinion and label it as such. Some guy says
he knows the way things work, you can pretty much guarantee
he doesn't. Some other guy thinks he has an idea, he's not sure,
he's willing to look at it different ways, that's the guy who we're
interested in . . . that's the guy who can think on his feet, you
know? That's why you're here, my friend, because the man-
agement of this country . . . hell, what am I saying? It's no longer
anything to do with the management of this country, it's every-
thing to do with the management of the whole fucking world . . .
anyway, that job is going to be carried on the backs of a few men
who can think for themselves, not a herd of fucking sheep, and
certainly not a handful of pretentious assholes who can't see
beyond their own ingrained dogmas.'

That was how Don worked. He told me I was good. He told me I
was independent. He told me that every thought that ever walked
from one side of my head to the other could never be anything
other than a perfectly self-reliant and autonomous thought, other-
wise why would I have thought it?

Looking back I can see how insidious it all was. The initial
meetings, the sense of openness in the discussion forums. We
would meet two, sometimes three times a day. Coffee, cigarettes,
comfortable chairs, eight or ten or twelve of us in a room, Don
usually present, another guy named Paul Travers who I guessed

160

was also a shepherd. And they would shoot the shit, talk around in circles, and all the while there were people watching us, people looking at us through one-way windows on the right-hand side of the room. Next meeting another subject, next meeting yet another. Through December, talking about the murder of John Lennon, the American nuns killed in Salvador, the return of Jose Napoleon Duarte and the four-man junta. We talked about Reagan, Carter, Bush Snr., the hunger strikes in Ulster, the assassination of Anastasio Somoza Debayle, his Mercedes ambushed in Asuncion in Paraguay by a small group of men with automatic weapons and a bazooka. Asuncion police reported the arrest of several men whose rebuttal of the accusation was backed up by the ruling junta who merely expressed 'joy at the death of an evil man'. The debate lasted several days. I began to think that this was the direction Carvalho and Travers had been steering us in. Don always had more to say than anyone else. He always knew more of the history and background of the issues we discussed. The days went on. New people arrived. Others seemed to disappear quietly.

'Not the best material for what we need,' Don explained to me when I asked about those people.

'Not the best material?' I asked, surprised at the expression.

'Not free thinkers. Open-minded. What we like to refer to as simultaneous perspective. Able to look at a situation from both sides, from all three or four sides if it's a more complex situation, you know? That's the kind of people we need, my friend . . . more people like you,' and he smiled, reached out his hand and gripped my shoulder, and once again made me feel as though I had been chosen because of some inherent ability I possessed that was a little more of something than everyone else.

And she was the same. Saw her that day – December 10th – walking right by the window of the delicatessen where Don and I were seated, and then she came through the door, a floor-length camel-colored overcoat and the turquoise beret, and she went to the counter and ordered coffee to go, and stood there patiently without turning around until they brought her order.

As she left she glanced in my direction. Don said it was like someone had switched a light bulb on inside my head. Saw a caricature of myself, something out of Hanna Barbera, tongue rolled out and touching the floor, hair standing on end, smoke out of my ears. You know the routine. That was the first time I saw

Catherine Sheridan, though at the time that was not her name. That was when I saw her, and that was when I decided I had to know who she was: know her name, her job, her ideas and thoughts and beliefs and ideology.

Don Carvalho watched me watching her, and he smiled to himself.

I stared at her as she made her way out of the deli and started down the street. I think he perceived my intention to get up and follow her. He reached out and gripped my arm. He made it easy, as he had so many times, as he would so many times again.

'Don't sweat it, John,' he said, his voice almost a whisper. 'She's in the discussion group tomorrow.'

SIXTEEN

'We check out this Isabella Cordillera now,' Roth said, as Miller started the car and pulled away from the edge of the curb.

'And speak to Lassiter,' Miller said. 'We need to keep him in the loop.'

Roth glanced at his watch. 'It's a little after four . . . Lassiter will be there until five, five-thirty maybe.'

Miller smiled.

'What?'

Miller shook his head. 'Think our schedule is gonna stretch at both ends until we're done.'

'I told Amanda it'd be this way for a while.'

'She's okay?'

'Sure she's okay,' Roth said. 'You know Amanda, she's always okay.'

'Figure she's the best thing about you, you know?'

Roth laughed. 'Join the fucking club Miller, join the fucking club.'

Desk sergeant was still there when they arrived back at the Second. 'We don't have a Michael,' he said. 'Not one within the correct age range. Found you a seven-year-old and a sixty-one-year-old. Those are the only Michael McCulloughs in the city.'

Miller shrugged. 'So he moved out after he retired.'

'Go wider,' Roth said. 'See what you can find.'

'We're on it already,' the desk sergeant said.

'Can you call Lassiter for me?' Roth asked. 'Tell him we're back, on our way up.'

'Sure thing.'

The sergeant lifted the receiver and dialled Lassiter's office as Miller and Roth crossed to the stairs.

*

Natasha looked out of the kitchen window and down into the encroaching wilderness, out across the trash and debris that spilled from alleyways and doorways and gantries. She stood quietly and breathed deeply and wondered why Darryl never spoke with her. Not to her, not at her, but *with* her. Why he didn't take her aside and sit her down, and put his arm around her shoulders, pull her close for just a moment, say what he must have wanted to say for so very long. *This is the way it is. This is who I am and what I am doing. This is the way I am trying to rectify the damage that's been done.*

Natasha closed her eyes, a tight fist of something invading her chest, and she thought of Chloe down the hallway, of Esme, of the two of them watching TV together, misunderstanding one another, and how it didn't matter because they were more than happy to do nothing but share one another's company . . . and Natasha wished so hard that Darryl King could have been there. That he could have seen the kind of girl his daughter had become. That he could have been some part of the thing he had created. But he was dead. Shot by someone unnamed for reasons unknown. And Michael McCullough, retired and disappeared, and this man Robert Miller and his partner, and the promise made to find McCullough and ask him what in God's name he thought he was doing taking Darryl on a police raid . . .

This is the life I have now, she thought. *Make the most of it, or get the fuck out.*

She smiled to herself, turned away from the window, and her breath stopped dead in her chest.

Miller switched on his computer, waited for the thing to load up and then typed Isabella Cordillera into the search window. Waited a heartbeat, and then looked up at Roth.

'Take a look,' he said, and he smiled, shook his head, sort of half-frowned and then watched Roth's expression change as he read the first entry on the search page.

'Cordillera Isabella,' Roth said. 'Predominant land mass and mountain range extending approximately three hundred and sixty kilometers from Chinandega on the western coastline to the Honduran border at Montañas de Colón, Cordillera Isabella rivals Costa Rica's Cordillera de Talamanca as one of the most extensive mountain ranges on the South American peninsula . . . et cetera et cetera . . .' Roth looked at Miller and shook his head. 'A newspaper clipping about the election and now this?'

'Think someone is trying to tell us—' Miller began, but was cut short by the telephone ringing on his desk.

Eyes. Eyes dark enough to be barely visible.

That's the first thing she saw, perhaps the only thing she saw, because there was something about the way he looked at her that made her cold and awkward and silent. The way he looked right through her that made her feel as if she was really nothing at all.

She started to breathe, and then he shook his head and raised his finger to his lips, and there was something about the way he looked that told her she should say and do nothing, that something was going on here that was an awful lot bigger than her, and if she challenged it it might just swallow her whole, so the best thing to do was just to stand there silently, and breathe as shallowly as possible, and wait and see what the man had to say for himself.

And what he said was, 'Natasha.'

And when he said her name she sort of unravelled inside and felt weak at the knees, and she had to put her hand out behind her to find the edge of the counter-top, to balance herself, to steady herself, to give herself some kind of support and ensure that she didn't faint right then and there . . .

'Natasha Joyce,' the man said matter-of-factly.

And Natasha – despite her best judgement, despite some inner voice screaming at her that this was something she wanted no part of – nodded, and then kind of half-smiled awkwardly, and she said, 'Yes . . . I'm Natasha . . .'

'Good,' he said. 'That's very good.'

And then he took a single step forward, and even though she wanted to ask him who he was and what he was doing, why he was in her apartment, and before that *how* he'd gotten into her apartment in the first place, it didn't matter, didn't matter at all, because she kind of knew in her gut that whatever he said would be pretty much the last thing she heard, pretty much the last thing that happened in her life, because that single step he took, just a simple matter of eight or ten inches, possessed such a sense of finality, and there was nothing in the world that had ever felt like that . . . even when she was screaming blue murder through labor pains, even when they sent down a woman police officer to tell her that Darryl King was dead from a gunshot to the chest . . . even then . . . even then . . .

Sound of something escaped her lips, and she felt the weight of her own body resisting gravity, but gravity was like heavy water, and the tension that usually supported her, tension she never gave a second thought to, seemed to ease out from beneath her, and though she gripped the edge of the counter-top as hard as she could, though she held on for dear life . . . though she closed her eyes and said some kind of prayer to a God she had long since stopped believing in, she knew that all of it didn't matter any more . . .

She felt her knees like elastic, like something pliable, something with plenty of give . . .

And they gave.

Gave right under her.

And the man with greying hair and dark eyes was there to catch her, and she knew that these would be the last hands she ever felt, that his expression – something understanding, patient, almost sympathetic, almost compassionate – would be the very last way that anyone ever looked at her . . .

Thought of Chloe down the hall.

Thought of the very last thing she'd ever said to the father of her only child . . . a child that would now be raised an orphan, a child that would skip down the hallway in less than an hour from this moment, skip down the hall from Esme's place, and knock on the door, and finding it locked would go right back to Esme, and Esme would come herself, and she would feel that strange intuition that tells you that something's wrong, and you don't know what, couldn't possibly imagine . . . But something about the human mind, about the very way we are, tells you automatically, without even thinking for a second, that whatever has happened is *bad* . . .

That kind of something.

And Esme would turn the handle and feel it resist her, and

she'd beat on the door with her frail fist, and getting nothing at all, not a single solitary sound, she would back up, turn to her left, and go down the hall to Mr and Mrs Ducatto's place. And Mr Ducatto, overweight, Italian, a good guy in his heart but a mouth like a railway tunnel, loud and dirty, would smile with some sense of understanding, trying his damnedest to be patient for the sake of the little black girl Esme had in tow, and he would go back with them and try the door, and suggest they call the supervisor, and Esme would tell him that the supervisor was out for a little while and he would just have to open the door himself, and yes, she would take complete responsibility for any damage that might be done to the door, and that he should charge right at it because there was something wrong, something awful wrong . . .

Broke the door in he did.

Bust that son-of-a-bitch door wide open with his broad shoulder, and it fell inward as the jamb snapped like kindling. Told the old woman and the kid to stay right where they were, and he went in there, and he checked the place out, and he figured he'd come right back and tell them that everything was fine, that Natasha Joyce had fallen asleep . . .

But she wasn't sleeping.

She was in bed alright, no question about it, or not so much *in* bed as on top of the bed, and she was on her back, her arms wide, her head to one side as if waiting for her lover; as if she'd been expecting someone to come right on through that bedroom door and find her . . .

Natasha Joyce was strangled and beaten and covered in bruises, and there were burst blood vessels in her eyes that made her look like something out of some L.A. straight-to-video sex-killer slasher movie, and the way her shoulder was twisted made it seem as if her arm had been wrenched out of its socket, which it had, and when Marilyn Hemmings snapped on her latex gloves at approximately two-fifteen, afternoon of Wednesday the 15th of November – realizing then that it had only been four days since she'd delved into the corpse of Catherine Sheridan – there was a certain sense of *finality* to the way in which Natasha Joyce had been beaten and strangled.

'It is what it is,' she would tell Robert Miller.

But that was Wednesday.

That was later.

In the moment that Natasha Joyce felt everything inside her give way, as she felt the weight of her entire body making its way slowly to the floor of the kitchen, there was really only one thought she had, one simple question – the answer to which would now evade her for ever – *What happened to Darryl?*

And the presence of that question was such that she even voiced it – her words faint, almost unintelligible, as the man with the greying hair and the soft-soled sneakers reached down and pressed the balls of his thumbs into the sockets of her eyes.

'Wha-what happened . . . what happened to Da-Darryl?'

The man didn't answer her. He did not hear her clearly. But had he heard, he would not have been able to help her. He did not know the answer. More importantly, the manner in which he'd been taught precluded any possibility of pausing to deal with anything the subject said.

That would have been a violation of protocol.

As straightforward and simple as that.

The pain and pressure in her eyes caused her to black out. And then he lifted her gently, almost as one would lift a child, and he carried her through to the small bedroom where her only child had been conceived.

And he laid her on the bed.

He steepled his fingers and popped his joints.

He got to work.

168

*T*he president directs the Company. The Company follows orders.

If you know what the Company is doing, then you know what the president wants done.

We call it plausible deniability; the non-affirmative affirmation, the non-denial denial. We call it that for the sake of the president. Everything we do is one step removed. The president never gives a direct order. He suggests something to someone, and that someone takes it upon themselves to execute an order that was never officially an order. That someone takes the fall, at least in the press, but in truth he is rewarded with a handsome property in Martha's Vineyard, a seat on the board of an international banking corporation, a very generous pension.

Secretary of State Madeleine Albright once explained the passive-aggressive nature of the CIA: 'It has battered child syndrome', she said.

It has been estimated that in excess of forty percent of the CIA's intelligence gathering activities are concentrated within the United States itself, something that is prohibited by law. December 1974, Richard Helms – at the time ambassador to Iran, later to become the director of the CIA – was recalled from the Middle East to brief Gerald Ford on the extent of the nightmare that they faced if the press or the public became aware of the actual working operations of the Company. Ford was told that Robert Kennedy's personal management of the assassination attempts on Castro was merely the tip of a very big iceberg. The iceberg went down for fathoms – unmapped, uncharted, ultimately unknown.

By the latter part of January 1981 I had already begun to believe that we were doing the right thing, at least more than fifty percent of the time. More than fifty percent made everything good. More than fifty percent was more good than harm.

I was also in love with someone who felt the same way.

*End of January 1981 I had started to consider the possibility
that Catherine Sheridan and I could make a difference. I still had
not asked her out. I still had managed no more than three or four
en passant conversations with her.*

*February 1981 we started to learn some of the basics. Photo
interpretation, agent handling, debrief protocol, analysis of military hardware and economic trends, liaison with congressional
oversight committees, the comings and goings of a routine day in
any field office anywhere in the world. Chiefs of station for
Istanbul, Morocco, Tangier, Kabul, Vienna, Warsaw, London,
Paris . . . their lives, their names, their procedures and histories.
We talked about the reality of what we were doing and why.
We talked about national currency fluctuation, the intentional
downsizing of gross national product, the destabilization of a
political ethos by gradual dissemination of counter-intelligence
and propaganda. We talked about Coca-Cola opening the door
for the Company. Later it would be McDonalds and KFC.*

*In the last week of February I volunteered for field work. The
field office I chose was understaffed. I was twenty-one years old,
and I had a big hard-on for the world that Lawrence Matthews
and Don Carvalho had sold me.*

*Three times I was present when Catherine Sheridan spoke of
what was happening in South America, and each time she confirmed my certainty that she was the one who should go with me.*

Fourth day of March I spoke to her.

*We left a meeting together, almost collided at the door, and I
asked her where she was going.*

*She frowned, shook her head. 'Have someone to meet,' she said
coldly. 'Why?'*

*'Wanted to ask you something . . . no, not ask, I wanted to talk
with you about this thing we've been discussing.'*

*Half smiled, shook her head. 'What's there to say? The oppos-
ition is there. We back the rebels, pay for their training and
military support . . . seems to me to make sense, closing the line
between South American communism and Mexico, you know?'*

*I shrugged nonchalantly. My hands were sweating. I carried a
weight of books and I felt them slipping awkwardly. 'On the face
of it yes,' I said. Relaxed, unhurried. Trying to forget that I was
holding her up, preventing her from meeting whoever it was that
she'd arranged to meet. A boyfriend perhaps?*

170

'On the face of it? What are you talking about?' she asked.

I shook my head. 'You're busy,' I said. 'You're going somewhere, meeting someone . . .'

'Not that important,' she replied.

I shifted the weight of books from my right to my left. 'I have to go do something,' I said. 'I just wondered if you'd have time to talk about it . . . I've been looking at the possibility of going out there—'

She laughed suddenly. 'Me too. Jesus . . . well yes, of course I'd like to talk about it. Later. What are you doing later?'

'Tied up now until late tomorrow,' I lied. 'I'll see you at the next meeting . . . we'll sort out a time that's convenient for both of us.' I smiled, but not too much. Maintained that expression of studious detachment. I was interested in her opinion, nothing more than that.

She seemed surprised for just a moment, then she smiled. Bright eyes, dark hair cut long and tied back, wooden barette that held it up on one side; kind of tilted smile – made her look perpetually curious about something unspoken. Catherine Sheridan looked a little like Cybill Shepherd in Bogdanovich's Picture Show movie, but brunette, her features a little more sculpted, a little more aquiline. When she smiled at me it was like being kicked sideways into something beautiful.

Nodded an agreement to speak tomorrow, turned and walked away.

'John?' she called after me, surprised me, because I had not expected her to remember my name.

I turned back.

She opened her mouth to say something; she did that awkward and curious smile again, and then she shook her head and laughed.

'It's okay,' she said. 'It's nothing.'

I shrugged. Inside I smiled. Wondered if she was playing the same cat-and-mouse game as me.

I walked back to my apartment, sat up most of the night figuring out what to say to Catherine Sheridan, and the following day – despite so many hours of concentration – I found that what I had planned to say didn't matter at all.

171

SEVENTEEN

The call came from Lassiter. It was a little after half past four. Miller was brief in his responses, put down the receiver and gathered up his files, other notes and paperwork.

Roth rose from his chair and started toward the door, Miller right behind him.

One flight of stairs, down to the end of the corridor, Lassiter already standing there waiting, hands on his hips. Looked like Bradlee at the *Washington Post*.

'For God's sake,' he started. 'I don't know what the god-damn is going on with you people . . . Jesus, anyone'd think this was some kind of R and R gig.'

Roth and Miller stepped into the room, Lassiter followed them, closed the door.

Miller started to speak but Lassiter raised his hand and silenced him. 'Start from scratch,' he said. 'Everything from the point that the Sheridan woman was found . . . got your report, but fuck, you guys can't type worth shit.'

'The newspaper clipping,' Miller said. 'You got that, right?'

Lassiter waved his hand in a dismissive fashion. 'Doesn't mean anything—'

'Didn't until we found that the name Catherine Sheridan's social security number tracks back to is actually the name of a South American mountain range.'

Lassiter shook his head. 'Tell me what you actually have . . . tell me what you figure this thing is.'

'Serial,' Miller said. 'No question. Sheridan doesn't exist, at least not as Catherine Sheridan. We backtracked and there's questionable aspects about all of them. We get the newspaper clipping, we find this double connection to South America, and then there's the thing with the girl in the projects.'

'The Joyce woman, right?' Lassiter asked.

172

'The Joyce woman. The phone number given to the pizza delivery people is the case number of her now dead boyfriend, Darryl King. We go back to the Sheridan house, we find some pictures under the carpet . . . Sheridan and some guy. We take the pictures to Natasha Joyce and she confirms that the guy in the pictures is the same guy that went down there to speak with Darryl King a couple of weeks before his death in 2001.'

'And you're going where with this?'

'Track down the original arresting officer, name's Michael McCullough. Seems that King was some kind of CI or something, ended up on a warehouse raid and got himself shot. God knows what he was doing there. And then we have the Sheridan woman herself. Things there that don't make sense. Need to find out what this United Trust thing was where her money came from . . .'

'So we have some connection to a retired cop who worked with this girl's boyfriend five years ago, and some social security numbers that don't tie up. That's what we got?'

'And we have photos of a guy we'd be very interested in talking to,' Roth interjected.

'Which are how old?' Lassiter asked.

Miller shook his head. 'Natasha saw the guy five years ago, and she said the pictures were unquestionably him, but when he was younger. I'm gonna have forensics run that program on them where they can make someone look five, ten, fifteen years older . . . give him a beard, a mustache, grey hair, whatever. Get a half dozen images together and put out an APB, see if we can't track him down.'

'Needle and haystack in the same sentence,' Lassiter said matter-of-factly.

'It is what it is,' Miller replied.

'And what it is,' Lassiter said, 'is a fucking nightmare. I have a report session with the chief of police tonight. Everything you do I am required to report to this Killarney guy from the FBI. Every report you file, a copy goes to him. A second copy is going to Judge Thorne for some fucking reason. Goddamned political agendas. That's the way the chief wants this thing, and I don't know what barrel they've got him over but he's got no fucking choice in the matter. I have four dead women over eight months. That ain't such a big deal in our books, but just you see if the press don't jump all over this Ribbon Killer tag. Be selling fucking tee-shirts on the internet before the end of next week. Remember that shit with the sniper for God's sake?' Lassiter shook his head. He breathed deeply. 'I don't know what to say. I don't have anyone else more qualified to head this thing up. They're gonna wanna know what we're doing about it, I'm gonna tell them we're strenuously exercising all lines of enquiry, the usual shit. Hell, what can I do?'

'Give us more people,' Miller said. 'I get these pictures printed up I'm going to need anyone and everyone I can get hold of to ask questions.'

'You've got Metz and Oliver on the previous three women. They are giving it whatever time they can spare. That's the best it's gonna get. On this one you're going to get an APB. That I *can* do. Beyond that I'm stretched every which way I could be. You know the routine as well as I do. Lots of noise in the press, a few questions at the chief's session, the thing dies down for a little while. Happens twice, the noise gets louder, lasts a few days more. Third time, fourth time, now we're in the shit. I gotta have something I can give them. You have to get me some kind of statement, something that makes sense to these people. Dead drug dealers and murdered women who don't have the right social security numbers . . . ? This is not a fucking Christmas present, know what I mean?'

'You know how it is, captain. You did this shit for years,' Miller said.

'Get your pictures done,' was Lassiter's response. 'Use whatever resources we have down here. Get these things printed up and get them out in the squad cars. Do whatever you're doing but do more of it and faster. Call me on my cell if you get anything tonight. Something tonight would be good. I get a call with some forward progress on this thing while I'm meeting with the chief and I'm gonna seem an awful lot smarter than I feel right now.'

Miller glanced at Roth. Roth shook his head; he had nothing to add.

'So go . . . go do your worst,' Lassiter said.

174

Roth and Miller left the room, closed the door, walked ten feet down the corridor before they spoke.

Miller paused at the stairwell, reached for his pager as it started to bleep.

He pressed the button, viewed the message, looked up at his partner and said, 'Oh fuck . . . oh fuck almighty . . .'

*A*nd what she asked me about was my mother and father, and
I didn't want to tell her. I didn't want to have to explain it all
over again. Seemed to me that I'd spent the last eighteen months
explaining my life to everyone I met.

Catherine was different. I didn't want her to be part of the past.
I wanted her to be the present and the future. I lied to her about my
parents, and I did not feel guilty about it.

So there we were – Thursday the 5th of March, 1981. It was all
of twenty-five days before a disc jockey and former Yale student
named John Hinckley III, the twenty-five-year-old son of a Denver
oil executive, would wait patiently outside a Washington hotel
where Ronald Reagan was speaking before a trade union audience.
Reagan took a single .22 caliber bullet in the chest. It lodged in his
left lung, a little less than three inches from his heart. One of the
attending doctors later said that had Hinckley used a .45 it would
have blown Reagan away. Reagan's wife was driven to the hospital, and here Reagan uttered the first of his famous quotes.
Taken from a 1930s film, he said, 'Honey, I forgot to duck.' To
the surgeons inside the hospital, even as he was being anaesthet-
ized, Reagan said, 'I hope you guys are Republicans.'

The assassination attempt did Reagan no harm. The assassination attempt gave the American public the first real view
of George Bush, Reagan's Vice-President and former director of the
CIA. Little did we know then, but he would play an increasingly
significant part in the construction of the new America, the America of the 1980s and '90s, an America that would be inherited by
his own son, George W.

'The fact that Ronald Reagan was shot in the chest with a .22,'
Don Carvalho told me later, 'tells us something about the nature
of politics and political control in this country. Hinckley was given
a small caliber revolver. They could very easily have secured a .45,

176

a .38, something that would actually have done some damage, but no, he took a popgun to the party . . .'

I opened my mouth to say something but Don raised his hand. 'I'll tell you something about the secret service . . . you've seen these guys, yes?'

'On the TV, sure. I don't know any secret service people if that's what you're asking.'

'You should go talk to one. They're robots, man. Like automatons.' He smiled. 'They're colloquially referred to as roaches.'

'Roaches? You mean like a cockroach?'

'Sure, like a cockroach.'

'Why?'

'You know how long a cockroach lives after you've cut its head off?' Don asked.

'A minute, two minutes maybe?'

'Nine days.'

'What?'

'Nine fucking days. Cut a cockroach's head off and it survives for another nine days, and you know what it dies of?'

'No idea.'

'Starvation . . . it dies of fucking starvation because there's no mouth left. Is that fucking unreal or what?'

'That's sick.'

'Well, that's what they call the secret service. They'll take a bullet for the president. They'll shoot themselves in the head if it means protecting the life of the president. It's a special and particular type of individual that can live that kind of life. No relationships. No friendships outside their own unit, and that's more like a working relationship than anything else. It's a different world, John, a different world entirely, but irrespective of what you might think of such people there is something about that kind of thing that means something.'

I raised my eyebrows.

'Believing in something,' Don Carvalho said. 'Believing in something with such commitment and dedication that it becomes a way of life all its own. That is something I can appreciate. Not necessarily something I could do, not to that degree, but it is something I can appreciate.'

'I don't know that I could ever believe in something that much,' I said, and in that moment realized how utterly naïve I sounded.

'Sure you could,' Don replied. 'If nothing else you believe in yourself that much. Everyone does.'

'Maybe.'

'Sure you do, and if you believe in yourself to any degree then you have to have some kind of basic belief in the necessity to maintain the social structure that permits enjoyment of your own lifestyle.'

'Yes, I suppose so.'

'And with the purpose to maintain one's own lifestyle comes a responsibility to contribute in whatever way you can to ensuring that your lifestyle remains unthreatened by external hostilities, even the ones you are not necessarily aware of.'

'Such as?'

'Criminal elements. Influx of drugs into our society. Influx of ideologies and philosophies that challenge the stability of our democracy.'

'You mean Communism, right?'

'Communism, extreme factions of Socialism, the heroin trade, the influence of organized crime in politics and government. The extent to which the darker aspects of humanity can infiltrate ordinary peoples' lives without them ever realizing that their lives are being influenced.'

'And you want me to do what about this?' I asked.

Don shrugged, smiled nonchalantly. 'Think about it,' he said. 'That's all I want you to do. Just think about it.'

Which is what I did, and had actually been doing for the previous three weeks. The conversation that I had with Catherine Sheridan had been a precursor to these things – the rapid shifts of viewpoint that occurred after the attempt on Reagan's life.

What happened on the 30th was instrumental in determining the decision both Catherine Sheridan and I would make. And that decision was something that would govern our lives for the subsequent twenty-five years. Someone once told me that you didn't join the Company, you married it, especially the 'until death do us part' bit. First time Catherine Sheridan and I sat facing each other in that same coffee shop on the outskirts of Richmond where I'd first seen her, first time we actually had a conversation, it went in a direction that surprised me.

After the initial pleasantries, the things we felt obliged to say, as

178

opposed to the things we wanted to say, she asked how I had come to Langley.

'Professor at university,' I told her. 'You?'

'My father was with this right from the start.'

'He was CIA?'

'In his blood,' she replied. She leaned back in the seat, pushed her coffee cup to one side with the edge of her hand. 'He was there in the beginning, came out of the military at the end of the war into the Office of Strategic Services. OSS went back to June of '42 under Roosevelt.' She smiled, fingertipped a stray lock of hair away from her brow. 'You know, at the beginning of World War Two we were the only great political power without an intelligence service?'

'No, I didn't know that.'

'Roosevelt gave an executive order after God knows how long. He resisted the idea violently, but he buckled under pressure. Gave the job of heading up this agency to a man named William Donovan, World War One hero. Lasted three years and then it fell to pieces under Truman. But they had a man out in Switzerland, a guy named Alan Dulles who had a taste for it, the whole intelligence gathering thing, and he was the one who pushed to keep a central intelligence function working.'

'I've heard of Dulles but not so much of Donovan,' I said.

'Donovan was the one who put bases in Britain, Algiers, Turkey, Spain, Sweden . . . even maintained some kind of regular liaison with the NKVD in Moscow. Then, with the disbandment of the OSS, there was nothing there to keep those bases functioning – not until September of '45 when Truman gave his blessing for the CIA. Dulles finally got control in '53, Donovan was made ambassador to Thailand, had a stroke, lost his mind in '57, then died in '59.'

I started to smile, almost to laugh.

'What?' Catherine Sheridan asked me.

'This is like a documentary, right?'

She laughed. She sounded great when she laughed. Sounded like the realest person I'd known. 'You heard the joke about the rabbit?'

I shook my head.

'CIA, FBI and LAPD are arguing about who's best at apprehending criminals. President decides to test them by letting a rabbit loose into a forest—'

I frowned. 'A rabbit into a forest?'

179

She raised her hand. 'It's a joke. Just listen to the joke, okay?'

'Okay,' I said. 'The president sends a rabbit into the forest.'

'The FBI go in. Two weeks, no leads, they burn the forest, kill everything in it and make no apologies. They report to the president that the rabbit had it coming. LAPD goes in—'

'Hang on a minute . . . I thought you said the forest was burned down and the rabbit was dead.'

'For God's sake. No wonder Don Carvalho likes you so fucking much. Will you just listen to the joke?'

'Go ahead. I'm sorry. So the LAPD go in . . .'

'Right. The LAPD go in. Three hours later they drag this bear out. He's badly beaten, hands on his head, he's shouting, "Okay, okay, I'm a rabbit for God's sake . . . I'm a fucking rabbit." President sends the CIA in. They put animal informants throughout the forest. They question all plant and mineral witnesses. Three weeks later, utilisation of eleven hundred operatives and four and a half million dollars in expenses, they file a seven hundred and fifty-five page report with conclusive and incontrovertible evidence that not only did the original rabbit never exist, there never was such a species in the first place.'

I was laughing before she finished, not because it was so funny, but because it was true.

An hour later, two cups of coffee, half a pack of Lucky Strikes, and Catherine Sheridan asked me whether I was going to stay at Langley. She had no idea who I was. I told her what I believed she wanted to hear. I expressed some uncertainty. I let her read into it whatever she wished.

'And you?' I asked.

She didn't hesitate. I recognized that quality. It would stay with her right to the end. Even then, in the moment of her death – knowing what we knew, so much history behind us – she never doubted that we were doing the right thing.

'Yes,' she said. 'Here for the duration.'

EIGHTEEN

For the first few months of his work in Homicide Robert Miller had counted the dead.

He counted thirty-nine, and then he stopped counting. After a while it went into hundreds. Counting seemed to serve no purpose. The victims started to blur at the edges. The men looked like other men, the girls like other girls, even the kids stopped looking so different from one another. The dead people were just dead people – strangers with unknown faces, unknown names: John and Jane Doe, 123 Regular and 5th, No Place Special.

But Robert Miller never really knew any of the dead people. No-one close had died on his watch.

Albert Roth, however, had been seventeen weeks into his homicide deployment when he was assigned to watch a guy named Leonard Frost. Frost was an informant en route to witness protection. Roth looked after him for three days, played cards with him, watched a little TV, talked about nothing in particular for not very long. Shook the guy's hand and wished him well when they parted company. Four hours later Frost was dead. Shot through the head as he entered the Fifteenth Precinct lock-up. Shot by a man posing as a police officer. Roth had been present at something close to three hundred and fifty crime scenes. He had seen more than four hundred dead. Leonard Frost was the only one he'd ever spoken to.

Faced with the beaten corpse of Natasha Joyce, Robert Miller and Albert Roth were both left silent and stunned. They stood there for some time in the doorway of her bedroom. She had been laid on her back on the bed. Her shirt, the tee-shirt beneath, were stained with wide patches of blood. The marks on her face and neck told them that the beating had been brutal and unrelenting. The skin was broken in many places, reddish-purple welts standing out against the dark coffee of her skin. Her eyes were closed with the swelling, and her lips were caked with thick smears of dried blood, as were the neatly plaited corn-rows of her hair.

Al Roth was pale. He was sweating profusely as he took a step towards Natasha Joyce's body. He and Miller stood on either side of the bed. It was like déja vu, something from a movie they'd seen at different times, a moment of recognition as they realized they'd seen the same thing.

Officer Tom Suskind, the first one to attend the crime scene following a call from a neighbor named Maurice Ducatto, had told Miller that the victim's child – Chloe, a nine-year-old girl – had been down the hall with an old woman named Esme Lewis. Esme Lewis had apparently returned to the Joyce woman's apartment with the little girl, had found the door locked, had looked for the building superintendent and, unable to find him, had alerted the neighbor, Maurice Ducatto who – after beating on the door several times and getting no response – had broken in. Ducatto had been the one to find the victim. The old woman and the child had not entered the apartment. Ducatto had directed them to his own apartment where his wife had stayed with them until the police arrived. The girl was even now being dealt with by Child Services.

'And no-one else has been in here?' Miller asked.

Suskind shook his head. 'No-one has been inside except Ducatto himself, and then myself.'

'And where is your partner, Officer Suskind?' Al Roth had asked.

'Sick,' Suskind replied.

'All day?'

'Yesterday as well . . . I've been on my own for two days now.'

'You haven't been assigned a temporary partner?'

'Don't have the manpower,' he replied. 'Especially to cover this area of the city.'

Miller said nothing. In his mind he was talking through the scenario with Frank Lassiter, answering the questions that he knew Lassiter would ask. How well had they known the victim? How many times had they visited her apartment?

Had they been aware of anything, just anything at all, that indicated she might have been targeted? Was there any real doubt in their minds regarding the identity of her killer? That he was the same man who had murdered Mosely, Rayner, Lee and Sheridan? And why no ribbon this time? And if she was another of his victims then what were they going to do about the fact that they were evidently being watched by the perpetrator? Or was this random? Was this someone else's work?

Questions that Miller did not want to be asked, that he did not want to face, that he did not know the answer to.

'Okay,' Miller said to Suskind. 'Stay here a while. Stay downstairs. Keep people out of here, let forensics do what they need to do, but everyone else—'

Suskind nodded. He knew the beat. He left Roth and Miller in the bedroom with Natasha Joyce.

'What about the kid?' Roth asked.

Miller shrugged. 'What about her? Jesus Al, you know this shit as well as me. Child Services will handle it, what can I tell you?'

Roth backed up and sat down at Natasha Joyce's dressing table – a plain deal seventy-five dollar piece of shit with a mismatched stool ahead of it. He looked at her things – the brushes, the dryer, the hair straighteners, the eyebrow pencils and lipsticks, the face creams and anti-ageing lotion, the de-frizz lusterizer serum for flyaway hair. Same shit as his own wife. Same shit, different price bracket. This was all that remained of Natasha Joyce, this and a nine-year-old daughter who would never really understand what had happened to her father, who would now feel the same way about her mom.

Miller took a step back and closed his eyes. Expression on his face like he was trying to absorb something he couldn't see, as if he was attempting to draw something from the atmosphere that would tell him something new.

'He knows, doesn't he?' Roth said.

Miller opened his eyes. 'Has to.'

Roth shook his head. 'He must be watching what we're doing, where we're going, who we're speaking to.' He inhaled, exhaled slowly. 'Jesus . . . it puts an entirely different light on it.'

'This wasn't random,' Miller said. 'This wasn't random and I don't think the Sheridan woman was random, and I don't think the ones before Sheridan were random. I think there's a reason and a sequence and some kind of method in this madness. Everything that's happened here fits together . . . the shit with Darryl King and Natasha, the way that none of these women have straightforward histories . . . all of it fits together somehow. There's a connection that runs right through it all, straight as a fucking ruler, and we're so busy looking at what's around it that we're not seeing what's right in front of us.'

'Why no ribbon this time?' Roth asked.

Miller closed his eyes and shook his head. 'I don't know, Al . . . Jesus, I don't fucking know.'

'We have to find the guy,' Roth said. 'We have to find the guy in the photographs, the one that came down here to talk to Darryl.'

'And we need to speak to this Frances Gray and get whatever we can on Michael McCullough.'

Impulse made Miller want to reach out and touch Natasha Joyce – something compassionate, something that would make her feel that he cared, that he was desperately sorry for what had happened. Because something inside made him feel he had brought this upon her. And though he knew with certainty that this was not the truth, that her involvement – direct or indirect – with the history of this thing was the only reason she was now dead, he couldn't help but feel what he did. It was personal. It had now become personal. Someone had watched him. Someone had seen him visit with Natasha Joyce, had seen him talk to her, ask her questions, and now she was dead.

'You okay?' Roth asked.

'As can be,' Miller replied.

'So what d'you think?'

'We do what you said. We find the guy from the pictures. We go speak to this Gray woman. We find Michael McCullough. That's what we do.'

Sounds downstairs. Forensics people arriving. Miller shook

184

his head as if to clear shadows. He looked at Natasha Joyce once more, and then he walked to the door.

It had only been three days since the death of Catherine Sheridan. Four months between the first and second, a month and three days between the second and third, a gap of ten weeks or so between the third and fourth, and now just seventy-two hours. Catherine Sheridan. Natasha Joyce. The connection between them – tenuous though it might be – was Darryl King, a heroin addict informant killed alongside a retired police sergeant in a warehouse drugs raid five years before.

Miller knew it was all connected. The links in the web were tenuous, perhaps invisible, but they were there. Of this he felt sure.

The ice-skating rink is closed to the public. Some days, after classes are done, I leave Mount Vernon College and I go to the skating rink at Brentwood Park. On Monday and Tuesday evenings, and alternate Saturdays, Sarah is here, working on her routine, on the piece she is preparing for the All States Figure Skating Championship in January of next year. She is twenty-two years old. I know where she lives, her parents' names, the schools she has attended. I know as much as it is possible to know.

I watch her as she skates, as she trains with such commitment and diligence.

She practises her routine, and though I know she sees me back there at the edge of the rink, though she pretends I am not there, I make believe she is skating for me and me alone.

'C'est l'Amour' by Edith Piaf is the piece she has chosen, and even as it starts up – the unaccompanied piano introduction through the speakers above our heads – she crouches down low to the ice, almost pressed into nothing, and then opens up like a flower growing from nowhere . . .

The strings come in behind the piano, and then Piaf's voice:

> C'est l'amour qui fait qu'on aime
> C'est l'amour qui fait rêver
> C'est l'amour qui veut qu'on s'aime
> C'est l'amour qui fait pleurer . . .

A two-foot turn, a toe loop, a half loop, a salchow, and then she executes a Biellman into a broken leg spin.

Each time she sweeps towards the edge of the rink my heart almost stops.

The second verse, a staccato rhythm, gentle yet insistent, the strings almost pizzicato:

> Mais tous ceux qui croient qu'ils s'aiment
> Ceux qui font semblant d'aimer
> Oui, tous ceux qui croient qu'ils s'aiment
> Ne pourront jamais pleurer . . .

A flying entry into a death drop, and then the ballet jump as Sarah faces the outside of the circle while gliding backwards, picking with the left toe and leaping off the right leg . . .

The third verse, the horn section emphasizing Piaf's crescendo of emotion:

> Et ceux qui n'ont pas de larmes
> Ne pourront jamais aimer . . .

And I watch Sarah, and I wonder whether there will ever be a chance that she could understand what happened, and why, and how such a decision had to be made. Because that is why we did it. That is why we did all of this.

Later, an hour perhaps, I sit in a diner on the corner of Franklin NW. I sip my coffee. I crave a cigarette for the first time in years. I feel a sense of impending closure, and I try once again to convince myself that everything I have done was done for the right reasons. I know this is a lie, but it is a lie I must try to believe. If not for me, then for Margaret Mosley, Ann Rayner and Barbara Lee. I have to believe it for Catherine as well, and ultimately for Sarah.

I think of the years Catherine and I spent out there. I think of the lessons we learned, and those we did not. I remember the heat, the madness, the sense of alienation, the knowledge that we were so obviously the outsiders, the unwanted, the despised. What we did out there would never be reported in the press. What we saw would never be discussed in meeting halls and congressional committees, never be broached as the next topic for debate at some United Nations resolution and ratification assembly. What we did was perpetrate crimes against humanity in the name of— In the name of what? Perhaps I have forgotten why. Perhaps the why was never really explained. We were trained, and we did what we were trained to do, and the things I learned at Langley kept me alive.

Another time I will think of these things. Not now. Now I will sit and drink my coffee. I will close my eyes and recall the images of

Sarah as she turns and steps, as she graces the ice with something altogether too close to perfection. I will hear Piaf's voice as it swells with emotion, and I will say a prayer for Catherine Sheridan and hope once again that we were right.

Tomorrow is Wednesday – Wednesday the 15th. Catherine will have been dead four days. Seems like a lifetime since we last spoke. Seems like an eternity. We possessed a life of sorts, but given the time again I would do everything differently, all the way back to my mother, my father – what he did, and how it has haunted me like a ghost for all these years since.

And something else happened. Two days before Catherine's death.

Markus Wolf, one of the Cold War's most legendary figures, died in his sleep. He was eighty-three. The Russians named him Mischa, the 'Paul Newman of espionage'. He orchestrated one of the most successful spy networks that ever existed. He ran more than four thousand agents across the Iron Curtain during his Stasi tenure. The Stasi did what the KGB did. They did what their Nazi forefathers had perfected. They used the gifts of IG Farben and Eli Lilly to assist them in their experiments, and when the Cold War was over, when the wall finally came down, the very best of them came here. Right into the heart of the United States intelligence community. I've seen some of them. Dark-minded, evil-looking bastards. They work for us now. They tell us how to win the hearts and minds of the peoples we invade. And if we can't win their hearts and minds they tell us how to beat them into subjugation.

I know these things because I have been a part of it all: I became what I worked so hard to escape.

A sacred monster.

NINETEEN

Somewhere after eight. Miller stood in front of his desk. Roth sat to the right, Lassiter to the left, his back against the wall. Lassiter had come from his meeting as soon as Miller had called him. He asked them so many questions. What had they seen? Was there anything – anything at all – that had given them the impression that they were being followed or watched? Had Natasha Joyce said anything that could be construed as a fear for her own life?

Miller answered what he could.

'I don't have the people for this,' Lassiter said. 'Who the hell am I supposed to put on this one? Tell me that much at least for God's sake.'

They went over it again, Lassiter concerned that the newspapers would catch the tail of this thing. Detectives visit potential witness. Witness murdered by the very man the detectives were investigating. Perhaps. The newspapers would spell it out the way they wanted the world to read it. Like with Miller and Hemmings. In-house corruption, everyone covering everyone else's backs.

The photographs from the Sheridan house were spread out across the desk. The face of an unknown man, a man suspected of terrible crimes, but also a man who could be guilty of nothing at all.

'So we're placing these pictures around when?' Lassiter asked.

'Five to ten years before he went out to see Darryl King with the Sheridan woman,' Roth said. 'Say 1990, something like that.'

Lassiter rose from the chair to look at each photograph in turn. He scanned them closely once again. 'There's just nothing,' he said. 'Nothing that indicates where they were taken . . . almost as if they were intentionally framed to give no clue as to time or whereabouts.'

'That was my thought,' Miller said.

Lassiter returned to his chair. 'How long before the photo guy gets here?'

Roth glanced at his watch. 'Should be any moment now.'

Lassiter leaned forward, elbows on his knees, hands ahead of him, fingers steepled together as if in prayer. 'You have no idea how much noise is going to follow on the heels of this,' he said quietly. 'Five dead women. Mayoral elections in February—' He turned suddenly at the sound of someone outside the door. 'Come!' he barked.

The door opened and a man stepped into the room. Mid-forties, greying hair, bespectacled. He immediately identified Lassiter as the one in charge, stepped forward with his hand outstretched, and introduced himself as Paul Irving. Lassiter indicated the pictures on the desk.

'You can make up some images of this guy and age him ten, fifteen, twenty years?'

Irving nodded. 'Sure I can.'

'You don't need to look at them?' Lassiter asked.

Irving smiled. 'Can do anything you want with a picture,' he said. He reached out and picked up the image of Catherine Sheridan and the unidentified man. He held it up. 'This guy here,' Irving said. 'I can take his face out and put your face in there so good you'd never be able to tell.'

'I just need him aged,' Lassiter said. 'This one here is apparently from Christmas of '82. Use that as a guideline. I need him aged, his hair grey, also with a mustache, with a full beard, and then one of those that are just on the chin. I need eight or ten different variations of how this guy could look right now, and I need them within an hour or two. You can do this?'

Irving nodded, started to gather up the pictures. 'Sure I can do it. The city's gonna pay my invoice, right?'

'The city's gonna pay,' Lassiter said.

'This is the Ribbon Killer thing?' Irving asked.

Lassiter shook his head. 'What makes you think that?'

'Second Precinct, phone call out of hours, no questions

about how much I'm gonna charge you for doing this . . . I might not be a detective but I'm not stupid.'

'I need you to say nothing,' Lassiter said. 'I was told you were the best for this kind of work, and I assume that such a reputation is based not only upon your technical skill but also your discretion and confidentiality.'

Irving smiled genuinely. 'I am as good as they told you, and as far as confidentiality is concerned, you needn't have any doubts about how seriously I take this.'

Lassiter nodded. 'Okay. You go do whatever you have to. You can be back here by ten?'

'Sure. Earlier if I can,' Irving said.

'Would be appreciated.'

Irving left. Took all but one of the pictures with him.

'Since when did this stuff go out of the precinct?' Miller asked. 'I thought we had internal people on this kind of thing.'

'Funding,' Lassiter said. 'You ever heard of that?'

Miller waved his hand dismissively. 'As long as we get what we need.'

Lassiter backed up, dragged his chair to the desk. The three of them were silent for a moment, and then Miller asked if there could be additional detectives assigned to the task of locating the suspect.

'I can assign who I have, and who I have is Oliver, Metz, Riehl, Feshbach . . . maybe Littman, I don't know yet. They have their own caseloads you understand, but once we have those pictures out with the patrol guys I can have those four assigned to phone duty, follow up some leads perhaps. Whichever way it goes, I don't have enough.'

'Any chance we can get Killarney back here to help?' Miller asked.

'I'll call some people, see what's available, but I'll tell you this – the expectation from the chief and the mayor's office is that we handle this ourselves. I'll make some calls to the Fourth and the Seventh, but don't hold your breath, okay? You're the front line as far as anyone is concerned.'

Al Roth smiled sardonically. 'That's reassuring.'

Lassiter stood up, put the chair back against the wall. 'You have this guy,' he said. 'He evidently knew Catherine

Sheridan. He met with the Joyce woman on at least two occasions. Go with what you have. Push hard and something else will show up.' Lassiter glanced at his watch. 'It's ten after eight. Picture guy should be back before ten. Make sure they're good. If not, send him back to do them again. I've got one of the computer people coming in to scan them and start printing however many hundred we need. See that through and then call it a night. Nine tomorrow morning I want you to brief the patrols before they go out, get the pictures into their hands and make sure they understand how important this is, alright?' Lassiter hesitated for a moment, almost as if there was something else on his mind, and then he shook his head and started towards the door. 'You have my cell,' he said. 'Call me whenever, okay?'

Miller and Roth sat in silence for a moment.

'You wanna call Amanda for me?' Roth asked.

Miller shook his head. 'Do your own dirty work.'

They reported her death on the TV. Natasha Joyce.

They reported it as I sat there in the diner, and had I left moments before I would not have seen it.

But I saw it, and then I walked away from the corner of Franklin NW with the cold and quiet certainty that soon they would find me.

I believe, in some small way, that the relief will be immense.

TWENTY

Irving came back at quarter of ten. He knocked on the door, waited a moment, entered, dropped a heavy envelope on the desk.

Miller opened the envelope, up-ended it, spread the pictures out across the table.

'Okay?' Irving asked.

'Very good,' Miller said. 'Very good indeed.' He signed Irving's receipt, and once Irving had left he and Roth stood side by side, looking down at Catherine Sheridan's unknown companion.

Unmistakably the same man, regardless of the alterations in appearance. One thing was constant however. The man's eyes. Eyes always stayed the same.

Roth gathered up the images, left the room, was gone the better part of twenty minutes. Miller wondered if the APB would come to anything, if anyone in Washington would recognize the man they were looking for. And even if they did, he could be no-one. Simply a friend accompanying Catherine Sheridan on some journey into the projects to speak with Darryl King. Natasha Joyce had not known the reason for the meetings. Darryl King could have told them but he was dead. The only other person aside from the man himself was retired Sergeant Michael McCullough, and that was another job entirely.

Miller needed to sleep. He felt as if his mind had been punished by the intensity of events since the 11th. The frustration was almost physical, a tangible sense of pushing against something that seemed determined not to yield. Roth would work late. He would do the same hours, but always there was something to go home for. His wife, his kids. The house on E Street and Fifth. There was a life beyond the walls of Washington's Second Precinct. A life

194

in which Robert Miller was ever more aware he did not participate.

Miller rose and walked to the window. He looked out across the city, his eyes gritty and dry, the taste in the back of his throat coppery and bitter.

He smiled to himself, his emotions tinged with a sense of philosophical resignation, and then he became aware of where he was standing, the fact that he was nothing more than a silhouette against the light behind him.

A sudden rush of electricity ran through his body. He stepped back instinctively, moved quickly away from the window. His heart skipped a beat and ran on ahead of him. With his left hand he reached up and tugged the cord for the blind, pulled it down rapidly and closed the slats.

He glanced toward the door as he heard footsteps in the corridor.

Roth appeared. 'Under control,' he said. 'We'll have a hundred of each—' He stopped, frowned. 'Jesus, Robert, you look like—'

'I'm okay,' he said abruptly. 'I'm fine. Just tired . . .'

'Okay, so we'll have a hundred of each picture for nine in the morning. Meeting with the patrol guys will be downstairs in the meeting room. Anything else tonight?'

Miller shook his head just as the telephone rang on the desk ahead of him. He picked it up. He listened for a moment, said, 'Sure . . . come on up.'

'Metz,' he told Roth as he set the receiver back in its cradle. 'He has info on the first three for us.'

They waited a few minutes, neither of them speaking, Miller aware of the sweat on his palms and the sense of panic, now diminishing, in his lower gut. Then Metz was in the doorway, looking awkward.

'What you got?' Miller asked.

Metz sat down. 'Not what you want to hear,' he said. 'First two properties, Mosley's and Rayner's, both rentals, now leased to new tenants. Major redecoration jobs. Third place, Barbara Lee, repainted throughout, still empty, but new tenants likely in the next week or so. Cannot find records of any living children, grandchildren, aunts, uncles, cousins, brothers, sisters, parents. Nothing.'

Miller leaned forward. 'You what?'

Metz nodded his head. 'You know what I think? I think they were on a witness program . . .'

'I figured that,' Roth interjected.

'No fucking way,' Miller said. 'You can't be serious . . . absolutely no relatives whatsoever? None of them?'

'Nothing,' Metz replied. 'And their possessions have been handed over to the county probate court. Packed up and shipped off to some storage facility outside of Annapolis. I've applied for inventories but was told that it could be a month before they get to it—'

'Get a warrant,' Miller snapped.

'I've applied already . . . should get word back tomorrow.'

'This is unreal,' Miller said. 'This is just un-fucking-real . . . I can't actually believe that I'm hearing this.'

'It's got to be witness protection,' Metz said. 'It's got to be. Only time I've ever come across anything like this is with people on the program.'

Miller didn't reply.

'Anything else?' Roth asked.

Metz shook his head. 'Just follow up on the warrant application in the morning. Take it from there.'

'Good,' Roth said. 'So go home . . . need you in for a briefing at nine.'

Metz wished them luck and departed.

Miller still didn't speak.

'So?' Roth asked.

Miller shook his head. 'I'm stunned,' he said quietly. 'I'm actually fucking stunned by this entire thing . . .'

'Go home,' Roth said. 'Go get something halfway decent to eat, get some sleep, for God's sake. You can't do anything more about this tonight.'

'I will, I will . . . you go ahead, okay?'

Roth rose to his feet. 'Little one won't go to bed until she's seen me.'

Miller didn't reply.

'I'll be here before nine,' Roth said as he walked to the door. 'Get things set up before everyone arrives.'

'See you then,' Miller replied, and turned back toward the window as he heard the sound of rain against the glass.

Close to midnight, there in the kitchen of his apartment on Church, Robert Miller stood quietly with his back to the edge of the sink. It was still raining. He could hear it against the window behind him. He tried to comprehend the things that were consuming his life. He tried not to think about what might happen. Tried also not to think about what he might become if he failed with this case. It was important. Everything had been important in its own quiet way, but this was perhaps the most important thing of all. He felt as if the eyes of Washington were upon him. Five women were dead, and no-one knew why. No-one even possessed an inkling, could see no rhyme nor reason . . . There were so many things that would have made his task easier to confront. A witness, for example. Just one. One single eyewitness to look at the pictures, to answer questions, to maybe give some kind of idea of whether they were even on the right track. But no, they had nothing at all. Nothing but hope and luck. They were the most valuable commodities an investigator could wish for. Continuing hope, a willingness to persist methodically in the face of all accumulated dead-ends, and a piece of luck. Something that would open this thing up and make it whisper the truth.

He watched the darkness through the window until it was once again light, the memory of how he had felt in his office ever present. Like being watched. The same way Natasha Joyce had been watched.

Miller showered, shaved, dressed, and by seven-fifteen he was back in his kitchen. After a piece of dry toast and half a cup of black coffee, he returned to the Second as if it was his spiritual home.

He collected the pictures for the patrolmen – half a dozen to a set, a hundred sets in all. The patrols would go out in squad cars, and those squad cars would fan out across this sector of the city, and the men in the passenger seats would keep their eyes wide. There would be calls, there would be false alarms, there would be people who knew with absolute certainty the name and address of the man in the picture. And the patrolmen would follow up, and they would find that the man looked nothing at all like the picture, and they would thank everyone for their diligence and apologize for any inconvenience caused, and they would return to the precinct in the certain belief that Catherine Sheridan had visited Darryl King accompanied by a ghost. Such was the way of the world within which Robert Miller existed. It was not *NYPD Blue* or *CSI* or *Law and Order*. It did not begin and end within an episode. Life was not like that. Life was laborious and exhausting, it stretched patience and nerves, and results were obtained through diligence and industry and tireless perseverance. And sometimes, despite all those efforts, they found nothing.

He would brief Oliver and Metz, Riehl and Feshbach. He would tell them to respond to every call as if it was the only one they'd get. He knew there were no guarantees, no foolproof systems that could be employed; knew that there would always be someone who knew something but did not call, or reached the point of dialling the number only to have reservations and hang up, or hated the police and decided that assisting them in their investigation would be a betrayal of their principles. Or they were scared. That more than anything.

Miller went out for coffee. He carried it back and sat in the meeting room until Roth arrived at eight forty-five.

'You been here all night?' Roth asked.

Miller smiled, shook his head. 'You're s'posed to be a detective, right? I have a different color shirt on.'

'You don't look like you went home.'

'I sent my body,' Miller replied. 'I stayed here trying to work this thing out and I sent my body home without me.'

Roth frowned. 'I'm starting to worry about you.'

Miller opened his mouth to retort with a wisecrack, but a knock at the door stopped him.

Carl Oliver and Chris Metz came in.

'We're in here for this briefing, right?' Oliver asked.

'We sure are,' Roth said. 'Take a seat.'

Metz glanced at his watch. 'Time we starting?'

'Nine, officially.'

'Gonna go get a smoke and a cup of coffee before we kick off. You guys want anything?'

Miller shook his head. 'I'm good.'

'Get me a latte,' Roth said.

Metz frowned. 'Sure as fuck I ain't gonna get you anything of the sort. Black or white, that's your choice.'

Roth waved his hand. 'Get whatever.'

Metz turned to leave.

'I'm gonna have a semi-skinny hot wet decaf cappuccino with a hint of almond essence and a parasol on the top,' Oliver said, following after Metz.

'Screw you,' Roth called after them.

'This is what we have,' Miller said. 'This is who's gonna find the Ribbon Killer.'

Roth shook his head. 'Who the fuck comes up with these names, that's what I wanna know. The Ribbon Killer. Jesus, it's all so goddam melodramatic. The Ribbon Killer. Half the problem we have with these things is we create a legend around these people—'

Miller raised his hand to stop him. 'I got a headache, Al. I can't take any more.'

Roth nodded understandingly. 'You need to get laid.'

'I need a lot of things . . . and right now that comes round about fifteenth on my list of priorities. First thing is get this meeting done and get these pictures out. Don't know about you, but I want to get down to the administrations unit and find this Frances Gray woman.'

'Sure,' Roth said, 'and then we check out whoever Natasha spoke to at the Fourth.'

The sound of voices from the corridor, the hubbub and commotion of men gathering.

'Lock an' load,' Roth said. 'We're up.'

The first handful of men came in through the door and started to take seats. Miller stood at the front of the room, to his right a table laden with the photo packs.

Lassiter appeared in the second wave, behind him Oliver and Metz. Everyone quietened down. Lassiter indicated the back of the room with a nod of the head. He was there for added authority, to remind them of the gravity of the situation.

Eight minutes past nine the last of the attendees was seated.

Miller cleared his throat, picked up one of the photo packs, withdrew one of the images.

'This man,' Miller started, 'is someone we need to talk to as a matter of extreme urgency.'

*P*erhaps something preternatural, perhaps merely a figment of my own imagination or paranoia, but I believe they are nearly here.

Wednesday morning. November 15th. I stand before a class of students, and there is a moment of silence. Possibly they imagine I have forgotten what I intended to say. Possibly they do not care. They could never know that within those brief seconds I visualized and remembered a conversation about balance, a conversation that now seems to belong to someone else's life.

'You have balance,' he said, as if of some rare and extraordinary thing. A thing of beauty. A thing to be guarded and preserved.

His name was Dennis Powers. He had a wide face, his lantern-jawline almost caricature, and he smiled with too many teeth. He was a training instructor, and though he stood a good three or four inches taller than me there was something compact and tight and wired about him. There was something about Dennis that frightened me. He made me feel as if I had to be ready for anything, the likelihood being that it would not be good.

'He's a good guy,' Catherine had told me the day before. She had on the hat again, that turquoise beret, and she was on her way somewhere, and she was carrying books under her arm, and the whole scenario could have been something from some East Coast university campus. That's what we were; we were students, but what we were studying would not be found on any Ivy League curriculum. Geopolitics and World Affairs; War Against Communist Infiltration; Subversion, Military Coups, Assassination . . .

It was April of 1981, three months or so before my twenty-second birthday, and I already believed it. It was indoctrination, brainwashing, propaganda – whatever the hell you wanted to call it – but it was subtle, and it worked. By the time Catherine and I really got to know one another we were in deep. By the time they asked us to go into the field we were affiliated and registered, enrolled, signed up, stamped and passed and printed. By July of the same year, even as we boarded the plane together, the belief that we were doing the right thing was in our blood.

'There has to be something inside of you,' someone told me many years later. 'Something inside of you that fundamentally agrees with the crazy fucking shit they do out there to be involved in the first place. The shepherds, the readers, the trainers . . . they all know how to look for it, and they can see it in you like you have a lit-up sign on your goddam forehead.'

Later I would understand, but to this day I cannot tell what it was they saw in me. Perhaps the fundamental disagreement with the way life had been thrown at me. Perhaps the death of my parents – or, more, the circumstances of their deaths – and the indirect way in which I had been involved. Perhaps the fact that what my father did was crazy, but at the same time I understood why he did it, and perhaps it was this that they saw in me because that Sunday, the day I met Dennis Powers for the first time, he looked right at me, dead square in the eye, and he told me I had balance.

'You need balance,' he said, and then he smiled, and I guessed he was somewhere around forty-five or fifty years old, but later he told me how young he was when he went out to Vietnam in 1967 . . .

'I was all of twenty in 1967, younger than you are now.'

Dennis Powers was born in 1947. When I met him in April of 1981 he was thirty-four years old. The fact that he carried so many more years scared me. It looked like three or four lives had been jammed handful-over-handful into his skin.

'I can tell you a little of what I've seen, but I don't wanna tell you,' he said. 'You don't wanna hear about the things I have seen, believe me.'

I looked up, raised an eyebrow.

Dennis smiled. 'Now you're gonna tell me that you do wanna hear some stories, right? You wanna hear about all the horrors I have witnessed, and that will help put everything in perspective. You're gonna tell me that, aren't you?'

He didn't give me time to respond.

'Not gonna tell you that shit,' he said, 'but I will tell you one thing. What I've seen out there—' He nodded his head toward the perimeter of the Langley facility as if everything beyond belonged to some strange and faraway world. 'Out there is fucking madness,' he said quietly. He was relaying universal truths, passing them on generation to generation. 'Out there you have the beginning of a world you wouldn't even wanna be part of. World that's coming is not something that you'd ever want to bring children into. People don't give a fuck about the planet. They don't give a fuck about anything but money and sex and drugs and more money and more sex. People need to wake the fuck up, you know? But with TV, and whatever the hell else they can get to keep their minds shut down, they ain't never gonna open their eyes and see what the hell is going on around them. You understand what I'm saying?'

I nodded.

'The hell you do,' he said.

We were in an annexe to one of the main compound buildings. Out through the window I could see people walking by.

'You're part of it, my friend,' Dennis Powers said. 'Until you've been out there and seen some of the things human beings are capable of doing to one another . . . hell, you haven't even got a clue.'

I stayed silent.

'I give you a gun,' Dennis said. 'I give you a gun and send you all the way back to somewhere in the 1920s, right? You're somewhere in Europe – Austria, Germany maybe – and I point you in the direction of a bar someplace. I tell you there's a man sitting at the bar and you gotta walk right in and take your gun and shoot the motherfucker in the head right where he's sitting drinking his beer.' Dennis paused and looked at me. 'I tell you to do that and you're gonna go and do that for me, right?'

I laughed nervously. 'No,' I said. 'I'm not gonna do that.'

'So I tell you the guy sitting in the bar is Adolf Hitler, and you walk on in there and see him sitting there drinking his beer, and you have a .38 in your pocket . . . what the fuck you gonna do then?'

I smiled, nodded my head. 'I'm gonna walk right up to him and shoot him in the head.'

'No question?'

I shook my head. 'No question at all.'

'Why?'

203

It was obvious. 'Maybe twenty, thirty million people are not gonna die if I kill Adolf Hitler,' I replied.

'You're sure?'

'Absolutely.'

Powers nodded slowly. 'Okay, okay, okay, so now we have a benchmark for this kind of thing. Adolf Hitler, no question, okay?'

'Sure.'

'And Stalin, what about him?'

'Same, no question.'

'Genghis Khan, Caligula, Nero, Kaiser Wilhelm?'

'God knows, yes . . . Jesus, all of them I suppose.'

'And Churchill?'

'Winston Churchill? No, of course not,' I replied.

'In 1914 he was known as "The Butcher of Belfast",' Powers said. 'He put the Third Battle Squadron on station off Ulster. Churchill put warships in the harbor and he resorted to bombing the city . . .'

I shook my head. 'You're taking a number of negative incidents over a considerably greater number of positive incidents.'

'So you're saying that one should view the actions of such people in light of history, then you can evaluate whether they did more good than harm, and if they did more harm—'

I smiled. 'Then it's too late to do anything about it anyway.'

'Right,' Powers said. 'Which raises a question of who makes the decision about such things, and when do they make it.'

'If there are such decisions to be made at all,' I replied.

Powers looked toward the window for a moment, and before he turned back he spoke in a quiet voice. 'There are such decisions,' he said. 'There are indeed such decisions, and there are also the people that make them, and right now those kinds of decisions are being made about three hundred yards from where you're sitting, and once they're made people will be despatched to deal with the consequences of those decisions . . . and I'll tell you something now, John . . .' Powers turned and looked at me directly. 'Those people are very interested in the part you might play in such consequences.'

'The part I might play? What d'you mean?'

'You're not a fool,' Powers said. 'You know what's been happening here over the past few weeks. People you came in with have disappeared, right? You see them one day, the next day they're *gone, they didn't make it. But you've made it through this far, and right now you're faced with me, and I'm gonna be asking you to make a decision, and the way this goes is gonna be the most important decision you ever made. You go one way, and your life is gonna be something worth remembering, and if you go the other way . . . well, if you go the other way your life is gonna be whatever you decide to make of it, but it sure as hell won't be comparable to what it could have been.'*

He paused, and then smiled understandingly. 'That girl you hang around with . . . what's her name?'

I didn't reply.

'Oh come on, man,' Powers said. 'You think there's anything that goes on around here that we don't know about? Her name's Catherine Sheridan.'

'If you knew why'd you ask me?'

Powers laughed. 'You've got to bring some of the walls down, my friend. You've got to learn to trust someone. You trust Lawrence Matthews, right?'

'Sure I do,' I replied.

'And Don?'

'Don Carvalho . . . yes, I trust him. I don't know that I agree with everything he says but—'

'Trust isn't about agreement. This isn't about all of us having the same view about the world. Jesus, what the hell kind of shit would that be, everybody agreeing with everyone else? No, we're not talking about having the same attitude about things, we're talking about having enough of the same attitude to be able to make a decision about something, and then going and doing something about it.'

'Such as?'

'Okay, okay, now we're gonna get somewhere. Such as South America, that's what.'

'South America?'

'Sure, why the fuck not? It's a helluva place. Fucking war zone at the moment, but nice countryside all the same.'

'So what about it?'

'That's where your girlfriend is going in July.'

'She's not my girlfriend.'

'Okay, so that's where Catherine Sheridan who you wish was your fucking girlfriend is going in July.'

'Why?'

'Because we need her to go.'

'For what?'

'To set some things straight. To play her part in the game. To make as much difference as she can. But the basic reason she's going is because she really wants to.'

'And you're telling me this because?'

'Because I think you should go with her.'

'What the fuck would I want to go to South America for?' I asked, challenging him, simply because his tone inspired in me the desire to challenge.

'What would you want to go to South America for?' Dennis Powers smiled knowingly. 'To kill Adolf fucking Hitler, that's what for.'

TWENTY-ONE

'Yesterday afternoon,' Miller said, 'at approximately 4.45 in the afternoon, a young woman named Natasha Joyce was found murdered in her apartment in the projects between Landover Hills and Glenarden. She was twenty-nine years old, had a daughter of nine named Chloe. There was no husband, no known current boyfriend, and the father of her child, a heroin addict named Darryl King, was killed in October 2001.'

Miller looked at the men before him. Weatherworn veterans, without exception inured to such things. Nothing new here. Someone got killed. Black woman in the projects, single mother, dead father, no-one to look out for her, no-one to take care, and more than likely no-one but her daughter to attend the funeral.

Miller cleared his throat. 'And this follows close on the heels of the murder of Catherine Sheridan four days ago. Found dead in her house on Columbia North West. As you already know the papers have given this guy a name, dubbed him the Ribbon Killer. He leaves a ribbon tied around the neck of each victim. He beats them savagely, strangles them, leaves the ribbon. With this last one there was no ribbon, but she was directly connected to the investigation. The fact that we were questioning her may have alerted the killer to her whereabouts.'

A patrolman raised his hand. 'Any known connection between the victims?'

'Something circumstantial, nothing probative. What we have is an unidentified male, age uncertain, at a guess early forties to mid-fifties, apparently seen in the vicinity of the fourth victim five years ago. This man was identified to me and Al Roth by Natasha Joyce as the same man who accompanied Catherine Sheridan on a number of visits to the

207

Glenarden district projects back in September and October of 2001. They went there in an effort to contact Natasha Joyce's boyfriend, Darryl King—'

Same patrolman raised his hand again. 'So there was a connection between the fourth and fifth victims.'

'As I said, little more than circumstantial, but we now have a picture of this man, and he appears to have known both Joyce and Sheridan. We have made up a number of images to give an idea of how he might look now. These are approximations based on an estimate of his age.'

Roth rose from his chair and started distributing the photo packs.

'Take these out with you today,' Miller said. 'Take them out every day. Speak to people, show them around . . . see if anyone recognizes this man.'

Lassiter stood up and walked to the front of the room. 'This is a priority,' he said. 'In between assignments or call-outs I need you to walk these pictures around your areas. Speak to the people you know. Storeowners, people in the markets, go into the bars . . . you know the routine with this kind of thing. I need to know if anyone recognizes this man, and the moment you get anything, just anything at all, I want you to contact either Oliver, Metz, Feshbach or Riehl. They will be acting as a coordination point for Roth and Miller. Everything comes back through here. And I mean everything.'

'And if he's seen?' one of the patrolmen asked.

'If he's seen . . .' Lassiter thought for a moment. 'If he's seen I want him followed until he can be taken without force. He should be considered armed and dangerous. Raise no alarms, contact us immediately. Give as much detail as you can but ensure he is followed. If he runs you go after him. If he fires, fire back. If at all possible we need him alive and answering questions. Any calls coming in you prefix Code Nine, and the desk will be instructed to put you through to whichever of the assigned detectives is available. If there's no questions, out you go.'

The gathered officers and patrolmen began to leave. Lassiter stepped forward. 'You four guys,' he said, indicating Feshbach, Riehl, Metz and Oliver. 'You guys are not relieved of any traffic that comes in as routine, but I need you to deal with the incoming calls on this guy. I've assigned two additional uniforms to handle any overload if you're all out on business, but I would prefer you organize yourselves in such a way that at least one of you can be here all the time. I need someone reliable to coordinate with Despatch if squads need to go out to a possible sighting.'

'Figure we'd do better to work out of the central office if we're on this together,' Metz said.

Lassiter nodded. 'You arrange it the way you figure is best. Anyone gives you any shit tell them I said it was okay. Set yourselves up. We're gonna need all the organization and cooperation we can muster to deal with the traffic that'll come in.' He waved his hand and indicated the photographs on the desk beside him. 'There's gotta be a hundred thousand middle-aged guys in Washington alone who could pass for this character.'

'Overtime?' Riehl asked.

'As and when,' Lassiter replied. 'If there's overtime needed I'll try and get it paid for. But be sensible, okay? If it's late and you're not getting calls I don't need all four of you on double time.'

Metz nodded. Riehl made some comment that Miller didn't catch. The four of them filed out of the room, one after the other.

Lassiter turned to Miller. 'So what's next for you pair?'

'Find out who it was at the Fourth that Natasha Joyce spoke to, and then this Frances Gray at the administrations unit to help us with McCullough.'

'Which precinct was he from?'

'Seventh,' Roth replied.

'And he went out when?'

'2003 . . . March I think.'

Lassiter frowned. '2003 . . . 2003 . . . I think Bill Young was still down at the Seventh in 2003. You run into difficulty on that give me a call. Bill Young retired but I have a number somewhere. He'd remember any of the people down there.'

'That's good to know,' Miller said. 'We'll go check these people out and come back.'

'And go see what they have set up in the central office,' Lassiter said. 'Make sure these guys have whatever they need, enough phones and shit, you know what I mean. And keep me posted on anything that moves with this, okay? I'm getting three or four calls every fucking hour.'

Lassiter left the room.

Miller waited until he could no longer hear the man's footsteps, and then he walked to one of the chairs and sat down heavily. He breathed deeply and closed his eyes. 'I stood over the body,' he said quietly. 'Natasha Joyce. Yesterday I stood in that room and looked down at that girl, and I couldn't help but think of her kid.' He looked up at Roth. 'Nine-year-old kid. Born to a girl like that down in the projects, her father a doper, so deep in all manner of shit he winds up a CI, gets himself shot in a fucking raid . . . someplace he sure as hell shouldn't have been as far as any protocol I'm aware of. So he dies, and this kid is raised by her mom, the whole single parent thing, and then mom gets herself carved up by this guy. Now she has a dead junkie father and a mother who's the victim of a famous serial killer.' Miller opened his eyes, leaned forward. 'What the fuck is that, eh? I mean to say, what the fuck kind of life is that for anyone? Now she's with Child Services. She'll wind up a ward of the state, some juvenile facility, and then from one foster home to the next . . .' He exhaled; it sounded like a sigh of defeat and exhaustion.

Roth leaned forward and gripped Miller's hand for a moment. A gesture of patience, of reassurance. 'Tell you something—' he began.

'What? You gonna tell me I need to get laid more often, right?'

Roth laughed. 'No I'm not . . . well, actually not so far from that if you wanna know the truth. What I was gonna say was that you lack balance—'

Miller frowned.

'I deal with this shit all day, same as you right? I deal with the scumbags and the lowlifes. I see the whackos and the leapers and whatever the fuck else the world decides to throw at us on any given Monday morning, but there's one fundamental difference between you and me.'

'You have a wife and a family. Jesus, I know, man . . . how many times do I have to listen to this stuff?'

Roth raised his hand. 'Weekend before the Sheridan woman was killed, you remember?'

'Sure I remember . . . what was that, the 4th and 5th.'

'The 4th,' Roth said. 'Saturday the 4th.'

'So? What about it?'

'What did you do?'

Miller frowned, shook his head. 'God, I don't know. How the fuck am I supposed to remember what I did two weeks ago on a Saturday?'

Roth smiled knowingly. 'That's my point right there.'

'What? That I got a bad fucking memory?'

'No, for God's sake. That you didn't do anything that was worth remembering.'

'So now you're telling me I don't have a life?'

'Sure I am . . . you know you don't have a freakin' life.'

'Okay, okay, so now we're getting somewhere,' Miller said sarcastically. 'So what the fuck did you do that was so memorable?'

'Saturday morning we went to see Amanda's folks outside of Alexandria Old Town. They'd set up this whole trip for the kids without telling us, a drive out to Shenandoah National Park, a hotel where we stayed overnight, and just the most amazing fucking scenery you ever saw. It was stunning, man, absolutely stunning. Middle of the afternoon we're standing in the foothills of the Blue Ridge Mountains, and Amanda's father has Abi on his shoulders, Amanda's walking alongside Luke, Stacey's back down a while with Amanda's mom, and I stop for a moment and look up towards Bearfence Mountain and the thing just takes my breath clean away. Tell you, man, you see something like that and it kind of kicks everything into perspective for a moment. See something like that and it makes what you've come away from and what you have to come back to a little less overwhelming. Hotel we stayed in was this renovated nineteenth-century—'

Miller raised his hand. 'Enough. We're going to see Frances Gray at the Police Department Administrations Unit. That's what we're going to do.'

'But I haven't finished tell—'

Miller smiled. 'Sure you have, you just think you haven't. Come on, get your coat.' He buttoned his jacket, took his

211

overcoat from where it lay across the corner of the table at the front of the room, and before Roth had even gathered his thoughts he was outside waiting in the corridor.

'Not a normal fucking person,' Roth was murmuring. 'Not anything even close to a normal fucking person.'

'*I* don't understand this,' I said.

Catherine shifted slightly to her right, eased her leg out from beneath her. She sat facing me, there on the sofa in her apartment; I was on the floor, cross-legged, back to the wall, head at an angle so I looked at the ceiling while I spoke.

'What don't you understand?' she asked.

I didn't want to look at her.

'What did he say, John?'

'Dennis? He said that you and I should go out there. Said I should work with someone, get trained on the job.' I shook my head. 'How can he even say that about something like this?'

'What?'

'On-the-job training, for God's sake . . . when he's talking about something that's tantamount to assassination . . . tantamount to murder.'

Catherine smiled, more something I perceived than saw directly. 'It isn't tantamount to assassination or murder. It *is* assassination and murder.'

'And you think this is justified?'

'Unquestionably.' Her tone one of certainty. That was something that could always be said about Catherine – even through the worst of it, even at the very end: Catherine Sheridan was the epitome of certainty.

'Unquestionably?'

'Look at me a minute.'

I lowered my gaze and looked at her.

'Did he show you the films?'

I shook my head. 'Said he was going to show me some films this evening.'

'Go see them. Go see what these people are doing. These people are . . .' She shook her head, and for a moment she looked angry. 'Jesus, I don't even know what to say. See the films, then make a

213

decision about whether you think taking some kind of executive action is warranted.'

'Executive action. Is that what it's called these days?'

'I think that's what it's always been called.'

I didn't speak for a while. Beyond the walls there were people who knew nothing of what was happening. Perhaps the vast majority of the population wanted to believe that such conversations never took place. People did not discuss political assassination and murder. They did not make decisions about other peoples' lives – people they did not know, would never know, would see only once, and then only through the lens of a scope, through the crosshairs of a sight as a trigger was squeezed.

'What?' Catherine asked.

'Just thinking.'

'Weighing up the ethical and moral position, right?'

'Right.'

'You understand the difference between ethics and morals?'

I shrugged.

'Morals are the rules and regulations laid down by the society. Thou shalt not kill. Thou shalt not steal. That kind of thing, yeah?'

'Yeah sure, I understand that.'

'Well ethics is different. Ethics relates to the decisions someone makes when faced with a real life honest-to-God situation. Someone breaks into your house. They have a knife. They grab your child. You have a gun. There's a clean shot, a moment when everything is right there in front of you, and you know with utter certainty that you can shoot the guy in the head and that will be the end of that. What do you do?'

'You shoot him.'

'You're sure?'

'Sure I'm sure . . . self-defense, right?'

Catherine smiled, shook her head. 'No, not self-defense – ethics. Morals say you can't kill him. Ethics says you can. You made an agreement to abide by the morals of society, and the society says you don't kill people. Well, hell, mister, you just went ahead and killed someone.'

'That's different—'

'How so?'

214

'Because the guy was ready to kill your kid. It was necessary to kill him to preserve the lives of people you cared for.'

'And if they were strangers?'

I laughed. 'You're good, you know?' I said. 'You sound so much like Matthews and Carvalho, like Dennis Powers. They really have—'

'Opened my eyes, John. That's what they've done. They've opened my eyes and given me a chance to see something that I haven't seen before. I've seen shit that makes me ashamed to be a human being, for God's sake. I look at this stuff and I feel so utterly fucking useless. Ineffective, so damned ineffective. I want to do something.'

'And now you've seen the light, and Dennis Powers has shown you how you can redress the balance—'

'Don't be so sarcastic. Jesus, listen to yourself. You sound so damn naïve, John. In fact I don't even wanna talk about it any more. You go do whatever you want to do. I've made my decisions. Fuck, they might not even be the right decisions or the best decisions, but at least I have enough of a viewpoint about this shit to make a decision in the first place.'

For a moment I was the child, invited to sit with the grown-ups only to curse and embarrass everyone.

'And yes, I have talked to Carvalho and Dennis Powers,' Catherine went on. 'And yes, I have seen the films, and maybe they are propaganda and bullshit, but I didn't think so when I saw them.' She waved her hand in a dismissive manner. 'Go,' she said. 'Go think about whatever the hell you want to think about, and when you've made up your mind let me know, okay?'

I stayed right where I was.

Catherine moved, set her feet on the floor, and leaned forward. 'This is my apartment, John. I'm asking you to leave. You understand that, or is there something you need me to clarify?'

I was taken aback, evidently looked surprised, and she laughed.

'Now you look about twelve,' she said. 'I'm asking you to go. Is there something you don't understand about that?'

I shook my head resignedly. 'I'm sorry if I—'

Catherine raised her hand, palm towards me: a stop sign. 'Enough,' she said authoritatively. 'Go see the films. You have something different to say afterwards then you come back and talk

215

to me.' Her gaze was unflinching, her expression hard. 'Truth? You wanna know the truth?'

'Sure I wanna know the truth. What do you think I'm here for? You think I dropped out of school and came all the way down here for my fucking health?'

'Truth is that this thing is bigger than both of us, bigger than everyone here. The old saw, right? The whole is bigger than the sum of its parts. You ever read Truman Capote? Well, he wrote a book called Answered Prayers. Title came from an old saying, something about more tears are shed over answered prayers than unanswered ones. You get that?'

I smiled. 'Sure I get that.'

'Here's another one. If God truly hates you he'll grant your deepest wish.'

'That's very cynical.'

'Cynical maybe, but nevertheless very true. Well, you know what? I'm here, John. I got my deepest wish granted. I looked around me and I saw a little of what was going on with the world, and I figured I was just me, just one person. I wanted to do something about it. I really did, you know, but I'm just one girl. Twenty-three years old, a hop, skip and a jump away from small-town America, and someone comes and tells me that I might not be only one person. They tell me I can do something about it, and if there's some questionable morals in the issue it doesn't matter because we got the ethics bang on target. We're not talking about one life out there, one person . . .' She paused for a moment. There was color in her cheeks, her eyes bright as if lit from behind. 'We're talking about a fucking country, a whole nation . . . Jesus, don't you see what's happening here? We're talking about being in a position where we can do something about the injustices that are going on over there—'

'But what about injustices here, for God's sake,' I said. 'There has to be as many injustices here in the States than anywhere else in the goddamn world.'

'Hell yes, America has its problems. We know that. But the problems that America has are far more sophisticated, far more complex. You're talking about illegal immigrants, about corruption in the police department, in the mayor's office, in government. You're talking about miscarriage of justice, this kind of thing.'

'Yes I am, and they're just as important as whatever might be going on over there.'

Catherine smiled. 'You're missing the point, John, missing it so wide it's amazing. You have to have a justice system for there to be a miscarriage of justice. There has to be a police officer there before a police officer can be bribed. We're talking about communism here . . . we're talking about the infiltration of communism up through the South American corridor into Mexico. Say it goes that way, how long will it be before we have communist uprisings in Honduras? And then there's El Salvador and Guatemala, and then it will head south into Costa Rica, and before you know it you have communist control of the Panama Canal . . .'

'So what are you saying, Catherine? You're saying that in order to prevent the communist takeover of the world you and I have to fly out there and learn how to use firearms, learn how to do whatever . . .'

'Some people have to die, John. Tell it how it is, for God's sake. Let's face the truth here. Let's open our eyes and see what's right there in front of us. Some people are out there killing people, and they're killing them wholesale, and they don't give a fuck about human rights or ethics or anything even close to the moral issues we take for granted, and we're in a position where we have the chance to do something about it, and I figured maybe you and I could go out there and make some slight difference—'

I raised both my hands, a gesture that was both placatory and a desire to hear no more. At least for now. 'I'm leaving,' I said, getting up. 'I'll go see Dennis Powers, see what these films are. I'll speak to you some other time.'

I turned and started toward the door of the apartment. I knew she would call after me, that she would make some half-hearted attempt to apologize for being so didactic and overbearing. Or so I believed. I even hesitated in the doorway so she could say something, but she did not.

I did not know Catherine then. Believed I did, but I was fooling myself. Later, I considered that Powers had gone through the whole scenario with her. 'And when he says so-and-so, then what do you say?' I was wrong. No-one had ever told Catherine Sheridan what to say or think. Twenty years before she would have been in Haight-Ashbury, but only for so long as it took her to realize that those guys were all talk and no action. They wanted revolution, but

217

they were too stoned to make molotovs. Catherine wanted to stand for one thing and against something else. She wanted to live a life that would be remembered. She even quoted Martin Luther King at me: 'Injustice anywhere is a threat to justice everywhere.'

After I saw the films that evening I knew without doubt that she was the one.

Twenty-one years of age, and the real world and I were about to collide.

TWENTY-TWO

Corner of A Street NE and Sixth. Bitter wind whipping down the sidewalk, almost knocked Miller off his feet as he came out of the driver's side door and started across the sidewalk. Roth hurried after him, the two of them up the steps and through the double doors at the top.

Miller went to the desk first, smiled at the immaculately dressed man seated behind it; produced his pocketbook, showed his badge, smiled again when the man looked down his nose and raised his eyebrows.

'Yesterday morning,' Miller said. 'A young woman named Natasha Joyce came and made an enquiry here. Understand she was seen by a woman named Frances Gray.'

The man nodded.

'I wondered if we could speak to Ms Gray.'

The man turned to his computer keyboard, the flat-screen monitor ahead of him. 'Yesterday?' he echoed. He tapped on the keyboard. 'Gray with an "a" or an "e"?'

'An A,' Miller said.

The man tapped on the keyboard some more. He paused, scanned data, paused again, smiled and shook his head. 'No-one here of that name,' he said. 'Tried Frances with a "e" and an "i", also Gray with an "a" and an "e". We don't have anyone employed within the unit by the name of Frances Gray.'

'Perhaps she was from another agency?' Miller suggested.

The man shook his head. 'If she was she wouldn't have been seeing anyone here. I don't have any record of anyone named Natasha Joyce coming here, and I can assure you that even if there has been some error in our records and she did attend these offices, then she was not seen by anyone named Frances Gray. Perhaps this young lady made a mistake with the name?'

219

'You have a record of all interviews that were held here yesterday?' Miller asked.

'For what it's worth, yes,' the man replied. He pivoted the screen so Miller could see it. 'Twelve forty-five, a meeting in Office 13. An appeal against disallowance of continued disability pension. Three-thirty, a meeting in Office 8, and that was for the collection of some documents relating to an ongoing firearms tribunal. That's all we had here yesterday.' The man smiled. 'Tuesdays are generally pretty quiet for us.'

'And you're sure there's nothing else?'

'I'm sure.'

'Who was on this desk yesterday?' Roth asked.

'I was.'

Roth took out his notebook. 'And your name is?'

'Lester Jackson.'

Roth made a note of it.

Miller stepped a little closer to the desk. He tried his best to look authoritative without appearing condescending. 'Mr Jackson,' he said. 'A simple question which I kind of know the answer to, but do you consider there might be any possibility in the world that you have forgotten this woman coming here?'

Lester Jackson started to smile in a surprised fashion. He opened his mouth to speak but Miller was there first.

'Things happen,' he said. 'I know how it is . . . I interview someone one day, and then something else happens, and I'm sure that the interview was not yesterday but the day before, and—'

Jackson raised his hand. 'Everyone that comes into this building is logged in and out,' he said quietly. 'Every interview that takes place is registered on the computer system without fail. I would be very lax indeed if I did not ensure—'

Miller stopped him. 'I can assure you, Mr Jackson, that there is not the slightest consideration that there was a failure to abide by department protocol, it's simply that we interviewed this woman yesterday and she said she'd been to this building, to this very department, and she was interviewed by a woman named Frances Gray who represented herself as an official of the Police Department Administrations Unit.'

220

Jackson shook his head. 'It can't possibly have been that way,' he said patiently. 'Believe me, detective, if a young woman named Natasha Joyce came here yesterday I would be able to confirm that she did in fact come, and if there was a member of our staff named Frances Gray then she would be right here on the system. As it is, neither Natasha Joyce's appearance nor this alleged interview have been recorded, and I think the only thing to do is go back and talk to this young lady and see if she hasn't made a mistake—'

'Can't do that,' Miller said.

Jackson frowned.

'Got herself murdered, you see? That's why we're here. She got herself murdered, and as far as we can tell this was one of the last places she went to, and if the information we have is correct and she did in fact come here then that also means that you must have been one of the very last people she saw.'

'You can't possibly be suggesting—'

Miller smiled patiently. 'I'm not suggesting anything, Mr Jackson. I just find it very hard to believe that the young lady was so very specific about where she went and who she spoke to, and now we find ourselves in a situation where these two things appear not to have happened at all.'

'I don't know what to say, detective. I wish there was something I could do to help you.'

Miller smiled. 'You've been very helpful, Mr Jackson, very helpful indeed.' Miller turned, nodded at Roth, and they walked away toward the exit without speaking.

Once outside, the wind battering them as they made their way to the car, Miller looked at Roth and raised his eyebrows.

'He's lying,' Roth said.

'No doubt about it,' Miller replied.

'The question is why.'

'The Fourth,' Miller said. 'Next we go to the Fourth?'

'And find out if Natasha Joyce didn't exist there as well.'

'Gerrity,' Sergeant Richard Atkins said. 'He was on the desk yesterday from noon 'til six in the evening.' Atkins leaned forward, picked up the phone, punched a couple of numbers and waited. The line connected. 'Who's that? Untermeyer?

Hey there, you got Ron Gerrity up there?' Atkins nodded. 'Good enough. Tell him come down here . . . got a couple of suits from the Second wanna speak to him.'

Atkins replaced the receiver and indicated chairs to the right of the reception foyer. 'Take a seat over there, he'll be down in a moment.'

Miller and Roth sat down. Neither spoke for a minute or two, and then Roth said, 'Something about this has to make sense.'

Miller smiled sardonically. 'No it doesn't.'

'Okay, so it doesn't have to make sense as such, but there has to be something about this that is understandable.'

'It feels like it's been arranged this way, you know what I mean?' Miller paused, looked across the foyer, glanced to his left and right. He could not escape the sense of paranoia he'd felt since Natasha's death. A sense of being watched.

A middle-aged police officer approached the reception desk, shared a few words with Atkins, and then turned and looked at Miller and Roth. He walked towards them.

'Sergeant Gerrity,' he said, looking at Roth. 'You're Miller, right?'

Roth shook the man's hand. 'I'm Roth, he's Miller.'

Gerrity fetched a chair from the corner of the foyer and sat down. He looked Miller and Roth over for a moment, and there was that all-too-familiar anxiety. They were as good as IAD, perhaps the deeper end of the gene pool, but still they were some kind of trouble.

'Woman came here yesterday,' Miller started. 'Black woman named Natasha Joyce.'

'What about her?' Gerrity asked.

Miller seemed surprised, hesitated for a moment. 'She came here?' he said.

Gerrity frowned. 'You said that. Black woman named Natasha Joyce.' He looked at Roth. 'I got the name right?'

'We just came from somewhere else,' Roth said. 'We were just told by someone that they hadn't seen her.'

Gerrity shrugged. 'Whatever . . . she came here yesterday, asked a coupla questions, left again. No big deal.'

'What time was it?' Miller asked.

Gerrity rose from the chair. 'I'll go see.'

Miller looked at Roth. Roth was expressionless.

Gerrity checked at the desk, came back and said, 'She came in just after one-forty, here for about five minutes, and then she left.'

'And what did she want to know?' Miller asked.

'Something about a retired police officer. Guy named McCullough.'

'And what did you tell her?' Miller asked.

'Only what I'm permitted to tell anyone. They're looking for an active officer I can give them the precinct, a phone number, if they're on-shift or not. The retireds I can tell them which precinct they last served at, when they left the department, and that's all. We don't keep home addresses on the system for obvious reasons.'

'We're not here in any kind of investigatory capacity,' Miller assured him. 'This isn't IAD, okay? We just went to the PD admin unit, the place Natasha Joyce went to before she came here. They deny all knowledge of her. Fact of the matter is that we're relieved you can confirm that she was even here.'

'Something happen to her?' Gerrity asked, and then he raised his eyebrows suddenly. 'Oh shit, she wasn't that—'

'Yesterday,' Miller said. 'Not an awful long time after she left here. Murdered in her own apartment.'

Gerrity whistled through his teeth. 'Fuck,' he said. 'That's just fucking unreal. God, I don't know what else to tell you. She asked about this McCullough, I told her he was retired . . . from the Seventh, right?'

'The Seventh, yes,' Roth confirmed.

'That was all she wanted to know. Asked me if we had an address, which we didn't, and that was that.'

'And if you had to find him?' Miller asked.

'I'd go back to the PD admin unit,' Gerrity said. 'They're the people who deal with pension records, all that kind of stuff. How many years did he do?'

'Sixteen.'

'Who the fuck retires four years short of a twenty-year pension?'

'We had the same thought,' Roth said.

'And he has something to do with this Ribbon Killer thing?' Gerrity asked.

'We don't know what part he plays in this,' Miller said. 'We don't know that he plays any part at all. We just need to speak with him.'

'As did your woman,' Gerrity said. He hesitated for a moment, waiting perhaps for any further questions, and when he sensed there were none he rose from the chair.

Miller stood up, shook hands with the man, thanked him for his time and help.

'No big deal,' Gerrity said. 'Know where I am if there's anything else I can do.'

'Appreciated,' Miller said.

Gerrity out of earshot, Roth asked Miller if they were heading back to the admin unit.

'Want to see Marilyn Hemmings first,' he said. 'Then back to see our friend who doesn't remember Natasha Joyce.'

Dennis Powers smiled knowingly. There was something in his expression that told me he'd heard everything before.

I had watched the films, sat there in a small room in the Langley complex, a small room fitted out like a movie theater, and on the screen ahead of me Dennis Powers had instructed that several 16mm reels be shown. I watched silently. Powers sat beside me, chain-smoking as always, while decapitations, summary hangings, living burials, disembowelling, rapes and roadside executions were played out before my eyes. Perhaps he expected me to be sick. Perhaps he believed I would look away in horror as people were butchered before my eyes, but I did not. A young man – couldn't have been more than sixteen or seventeen – was dragged from a doorway where he had been hiding. His throat was cut, and then two men proceeded to hook the base of his tongue through the wound in his neck. Blood erupted, running in wide rivulets and drenching the front of his shirt. The body was cast aside, and the men then took it in turns to kick it. A girl of seven or eight was tied into a canvas sack much like a mailbag. Laid on the floor, unable to move within her constraints, she was stamped on repeatedly. Within seconds she had stopped wrestling against the sack, but still they kicked. After a while the bag was nothing more than a map of bloody bootprints.

In a brief pause between the end of one film and the beginning of another, Powers leaned toward me and whispered, 'Collaborators . . . they believe that these children are collaborating with the Americans,' and before I could respond another film had started up, the same monochrome flickering, the same descending numbers from five to one, then images flashing at me, one after the other. Images of headless torsos, of feet hammered to a bloody pulp, of children without their eyes . . . such things as these, over and over, keeping me transfixed, unable to avert my gaze.

And when it was done, and when the lights came up and the

sound of the whirring projector was silenced, Dennis Powers turned his chair to face mine and looked at me without speaking for a very long time.

'From this,' he eventually said, 'we can conclude that there are some places in the world where it's not so good to go.' He lit another cigarette. 'What we have here is a situation of enormous significance about which no-one knows. This is not an important country, but in a way it is of greater significance even than Poland in '39.'

'Poland?' I asked.

'The Allies and the Axis powers in 1939. An agreement was made that Hitler would not invade Poland, but he went ahead and did it. That was what the world saw, what the world was aware of. Before that there had been other attempts to assume right of possession in other territories. Hitler was already at work in '37 and '38. Churchill knew about him as far back as 1931, even earlier when he was First Lord of the Admiralty. He knew what this National Socialist maniac upstart was capable of doing, and yet despite all his protestations, despite everything he said and the number of times he said it, no-one took a damn bit of notice until Hitler moved into Poland in 1939.'

'And how does this relate to—'

'This is not Poland,' Powers said. 'Guatemala would be the equivalent of Poland, right there alongside the Mexican border. If someone came along and invaded Guatemala there would be no question in our minds about what we had to do, but this one is fine. This is three removed from Mexico, and the distance is enough not to concern ourselves.'

'Prevention is better than cure,' I said.

Powers shook his head. 'There is no cure, my friend. There is only prevention. Thirty years of Cold War has proved beyond any question that there is no cure for this thing. You either do something about it before it starts, or you just watch it grow like a cancer. There is nothing that can be done about it once it has got its roots into a culture. It is a disease. Slow, insidious, this thing is amazing to watch. It's like a virus. It ascribes to equality. It ascribes to cultural and social strength. In reality, it is nothing more than an excuse for a select few to remove those they oppose from a society, and to do it in the ways you have witnessed this evening. What you saw on the film is happening about eighteen

226

hundred miles from where we're sitting, and it's happening to people who never agreed for it to happen.' He drew on his cigarette. The ash fell onto his jacket but he ignored it. 'Fact of the matter is that there are very few people who can face such things as this. There are very few people who are strong enough to actually look at this thing and see it for what it is. Catherine saw this. She sat in this room just like you and watched this, and even before the end of the first reel she'd decided to go.' Powers laughed drily. 'Far as I can tell, she'd decided she was going to do something long before she got here; she just didn't have any clear idea of the direction to take.'

Powers expected a hundred questions, all of them important, all of them difficult to ask. I said nothing.

'Why you?' he asked, perhaps voicing a question he saw in my eyes.

I shrugged. 'Tell me.'

'No family to speak of. Very high IQ. No communist background or affiliations. You're a loner. You've never really been involved with any women that have meant anything. Your politics are undecided. You are driven, committed to doing something useful and important with your life, but you don't have the faintest clue what that might be . . . that, and other reasons that are not important.'

'Not important?' I said. 'What reasons could be unimportant?'

He dismissed my question with a wave of his hand. He seemed nonchalant and unperturbed about the films we had seen. He seemed effortlessly at ease all the time. His self-assurance and balance annoyed me greatly.

'So what do you think?' he asked.

'About what?'

'About what you've seen here. About the discussions we've had, the conversations with Catherine. About the idea of doing something about what the hell is happening out there.'

'You're asking me what I think about it in general, or what I think I should do about it?'

'Both.'

'In general? Jesus, I don't know. Something has to be done about it. How is this thing being viewed? Are they looking at this like it might be another Vietnam?'

Powers laughed. 'Who is this "they" you're referring to?'

227

'I don't know, the government—'

'A government by the people and for the people. Isn't that what the Constitution and the Bill of Rights says? Something like that, isn't it?'

'I'm not talking about me, I'm talking about the government, the White House, the president—'

'What they think is unimportant,' Powers said. 'At least it's no more important than what you or I think. Those people are only in Congress and the Senate . . . hell, Reagan is only in the White House because we put him there. You've got to start looking at these things like it has something to do with you. Reason this society is so goddam fucked up is because everyone has got the idea that it has nothing to do with them. They go to work, and they think that the job is always gonna be there. They come home. The wife has cooked supper, the kids are playing in the yard, they watch TV. They just sit there while the world implodes and they think there's someone who's gonna fix it all up, that the government, the White House, the President of the United States has got this thing all figured out. Well, I'll tell you something, John Robey . . . the President does not have it all figured out. He only sees the bigger picture. He sees communist infiltration as a realistic threat—'

'You can't honestly expect me to believe that the President of the United States figures that I can do something about what's going on?'

Powers shook his head. 'President of the United States doesn't even know who you are – and he didn't know any of the people that went to Vietnam either, nor those who went to Korea, or who landed at Normandy. We are the little guys, John, always have been, always will be. We're never going to be generals or admirals or whatever the fuck else, but you know something? It's not the generals or the admirals who win the wars. It's the little guys – hundreds of thousands of them – that win wars. Catherine understands that—'

'Enough about Catherine, okay? What the fuck is the deal with Catherine Sheridan? Jesus, I barely know the girl . . .'

'Well, she figures she knows you, and you were the one she asked to be assigned with, and I know for a fact that she asked for you for a reason.'

'And, don't tell me, that reason would be?'

'Balance.'

I frowned, shook my head, started to laugh. 'That's what you said. That's not what she said.'

Powers smiled. 'She said it first. She was the one who suggested we devote some time and energy to you. She said that of all the people she'd met here you were the one who had the most balance.'

'And what the fuck does that mean?'

'You have a longer perspective than most. You're older than your age. She said you were able to look at something for what it was, not for what you thought it might be—'

'A bit fucking esoteric, don't you think?'

'What do you want from me, John? What the hell is it that you want from me? You're here because of your own willingness to be here. Lawrence Matthews spoke to you, he told you something about what we're doing. This is where it all happens. This is the Central Intelligence Agency. This is the heart of America, where everything you read about in the Constitution and the Bill of Rights has to be maintained as a reality. This is where the people who can't do anything about the situation they're in get something done about it, you understand what I'm saying? And if you don't want any part of it, if you really feel that you've made a serious mistake by agreeing to come here and talk about this stuff—'

'I don't,' I said. I possessed my own resolve. Powers wouldn't understand what had happened until much, much later, and neither would Catherine, but by then the months that we'd spent at Langley would be far behind us. The conversations with Dennis Powers and Lawrence Matthews would be so insignificant they wouldn't even be remembered. 'I came here because I was interested,' I said. 'I came here because Lawrence said that there was more to our discussions than just discussions, that there might be something I could do with my life that counted for something. That's why I came here, Dennis, and that's why I've stayed. The fact that I'm still here despite all this talk of murder and assassination, despite watching films about the horrors that are being perpetrated two thousand miles away . . .' I smiled. 'Well, that tells you everything you need to know.'

There was silence between us for a few moments.

'And you?' I asked.

Powers laughed. 'Me? Why do you want to know about me?'

'I'm interested, Dennis . . . interested in the reasons for your decisions.'

'I feel like I came here hypnotized,' he replied. 'Like I was inside some protective bubble of ignorance. I had a few of my ideals challenged. Some people made me look at things that people don't ordinarily look at, and I felt as though I'd been given a perspective on the truth that is very rare . . .' Powers cleared his throat, for a moment appeared pensive. 'But it never seemed like it was something I'd asked for. I didn't want to have my entire view of the world turned upside down. I didn't ask for that, but I got it, and it seems that once you've seen the truth—' He looked up. 'That thing that Einstein said, that a mind once stretched by an idea can never again regain its former proportions.'

He leaned back and closed his eyes for a moment. 'I knew there were things happening that I didn't fully understand,' he said. 'At the same time I felt like I needed to understand them. I didn't have anyone I could turn to and say "Hey, what do you think about all of this? Is this real or what? Is this what life is all about, or are we in the middle of some god-awful endless practical joke here?" I wanted to know the answer to that question. That's what I wanted, and when I had the answer to that question I figured I'd know what I was willing to do.'

Powers opened his eyes and looked directly at me.

'Unfortunately, in a game like this, it works the other way round. Unfortunately for us we get to do it backwards. We go out there first. We look. We see. We decide first, and then we act. We gain our experience in hindsight.'

'So what are you telling me . . . you want me to make a decision based on nothing but what I have right now?'

'Yeah, that's pretty much it.'

'And I'm supposed to go out there and kill people?'

'We don't want you to go out there and kill people. At least not right away. There's training, you know? We do train people to do this stuff.'

'So until then, what is it you do want me to do?'

'We want you to go with Catherine Sheridan. We have people out there, people who will be working behind the lines, so to speak. We need people who can gather information on things that are happening within the government structure. We need people—'

'Who can tell you who needs to die. That's what you need,

right? That's what you need me and Catherine Sheridan to go out there and do.'

Powers inhaled slowly, exhaled again. 'You can leave if you wish, John. You can pack your things and head back to college, and do whatever you were planning on doing with your life.' He started to rise from his chair. 'Send me a postcard from wherever you wind up. I can't obligate you to do anything, and I'm certainly not going to attempt to force you. This is the way it works. It doesn't work any other way. We need people. We always need people. Where do we get those people from? We recruit them. We have readers all over the country. They keep their eyes and ears open. They figure out who might be in the running for doing something a little more important than a nine-to-five in Pleasant-ville, change the car every three years, vacations in the Rockies, that kind of shit. They're on the lookout for people who don't mind getting a little bit of dirt under their fingernails in the belief that what they're doing might count for something in the grand scheme of things. There are no medals for what we do. We can work all our lives for the greater good and we can't even tell our next-door neighbor what a fucking hero we are. And hell, John, even if we did tell them they wouldn't believe us. We can't have kids. We try not to get married unless it's within the Agency, and even then it's a tough road because one of us might get sent to Colombia while the other one goes to London. It's a fucked-up life, John, a really fucked-up life, but it is a life. That much I can tell you. It really is a life, and there's something about what's happening here that will be remembered by certain people in the years to come as the one thing that really made a difference. You either want to help, or you don't. It's not complicated, John, it really isn't complicated.'

'So what now?'

'What now? Well, you've either made your decision already and you're going to stay and learn something about this business, or you're gonna go take a walk and use some of that objective balance and perspective that Catherine Sheridan believes you have, and you're gonna weigh things up and make your decision, and then tomorrow, maybe the next day, you're gonna come find me and let me know whether you want a bus ticket or a berthing.'

He walked to the door, hand on it ready to leave.

'And if—'

231

'Enough questions, John. All your questions have to be answered by you now.'

Dennis Powers opened the door. He looked up at the ceiling and smiled. 'Don't forget to turn the light out when you leave.'

TWENTY-THREE

Marilyn Hemmings sat down. Miller stood against the wall to the left of the door, Roth perched on the edge of a low filing cabinet. Hemmings did not apologize for the lack of space. As was the case with all visitors, Miller and Roth were transient additions to her day.

'I couldn't say,' she said. 'I said what I said. That was my opinion.' She smiled wryly. 'I watch *CSI* and live the dream, you know?'

'I know it was your opinion,' Miller said. 'There's never been a question about that.'

'The first three were what they were,' Hemmings said. She looked at Miller, at Roth, back to Miller as she spoke. 'The first three were the same guy. This I don't doubt for a moment. The fourth one, Catherine Sheridan . . .' She paused, breathed deeply, slowly shook her head. 'God, I don't know. There were enough similarities, and then there were enough differences. You're asking me to make a decision I can't easily make.'

'And Natasha Joyce?' Miller asked.

'If the Joyce woman had been fourth instead of Sheridan, then there would be no question in my mind. He beat the hell out of her, and then he strangled her. Okay, so there's no ribbon, no lavender, but what the hell? We don't know what happened. Maybe something disturbed him. What can I tell you? The Joyce woman *feels* like the same guy. It really feels like we have one guy . . .' Hemmings didn't finish the sentence. She looked at Miller, her expression one of resignation. 'So what's your take on this?'

'My take?' Miller asked. 'I'm not the forensic pathologist—'

'I'm not the detective,' said Hemmings interjected.

'I think Sheridan was a copycat,' Miller said. 'I *think* it was a copycat. And then our guy read the papers, watched the TV,

233

learned who we were, followed us, saw who we were talking to, and then killed Natasha Joyce.'

'That's Tom Alexander's opinion as well,' Hemmings said, 'but I don't have it. The *one thing*. That's what you call it, right? The signature for this guy? The one thing.'

'I can hope, can't I?' Miller said.

'You can hope. Democratic society, Detective Miller. Hell, you can pretty much do anything you please.'

'As our friend has done,' Roth said.

'He hasn't done what he pleases here, Detective Roth, he's done what he *needed* to do. This kind of thing isn't done for pleasure. Jesus, this shit is about as far from pleasure as you can get for these people. You ever read any books about this stuff?'

'Only the required reading—'

'Up there,' Hemmings said, and indicated a shelf above the filing cabinet.

From where he stood Miller could read the spines of several of the volumes: Geberth, *Practical Homicide: Tactics, Procedures and Forensic Techniques*; Ressler and Shachtmann, *Whoever Fights Monsters*; Turvey, *Criminal Profiling: An Introduction to Behavioral Evidence Analysis*; Ressler, Burgess and Douglas, *Sexual Homicides: Patterns and Motives* and Egger's *The Killer Amongst Us: An Examination of Serial Murder and its Investigation*.

'A little hobby of mine,' Hemmings explained. 'Extra-curricular interest you might say.'

'So the deal with these people—' Roth started.

'The deal,' Hemmings said, 'is that they *have* to do this. This is not a question of predilection or anything else. It isn't like they wake up one day and say, "Hell, shit, of course, I'm gonna be a serial killer. Why in God's name didn't I think of this before?" This is not a matter of choice at all. There's a drive somewhere, a really basic and fundamental impulse, a *compulsion* to do this stuff, and the vast majority of these people spend most of their time trying to hold all this shit inside. They don't *want* to go out and rip people to pieces, they have no decisional concept at all. This, to them, is like putting out the garbage when you're sat watching a ballgame with a couple of beers. You don't want to, but you have to.'

'Interesting analogy,' Miller said. 'And that helps us how?'

'It doesn't, except from the viewpoint that you're looking for someone who needs to do this thing, rather than wants to do it. That's a different angle, a different perspective to look at. I don't know what else to tell you. I'm not a clinical psychologist or anything else. Personally, I don't give a lot of credence to whatever passes itself off as psychiatry. Psychiatry is not a science in the same way as medicine and forensics. You want anything done on this, don't talk to any psychs. These guys'll have you inspecting your own navel and wondering whether or not you might have been the one to do it.'

Miller smiled. 'That's a little harsh isn't it?'

'You don't see the damage that psych drugs do to people.'

'I don't, no,' Miller replied. He stood straight, buttoned his jacket.

'Where to now?' Hemmings asked.

'PD admin unit . . . we have to find a disappeared cop.'

Hemmings smiled, followed Miller to the door. Roth was ahead of them up the corridor and, as Miller started to follow him, Hemmings touched the sleeve of his jacket.

'You dealing with this thing?' she asked.

Miller frowned, smiled quizzically. 'Dealing with what exactly?'

'What's happening here . . . this girl, the one you were questioning, the fact that whoever this guy is knows who you are, knows who you were talking to . . .'

'Are you asking if I feel paranoid?'

She shook her head. 'Hell, all of us feel paranoid every once in a while. I was thinking more along the lines of threatened.'

Miller tried to let nothing show in his face. 'He's after women,' he said. 'He kills women. That's what he does. He doesn't kill police.'

'And Natasha Joyce . . . she had a little girl, right?'

'Chloe,' Miller said. 'Nine years old.'

'She with relatives?'

'Child Services.'

Hemmings looked away for a moment, thoughtful perhaps.

'What?' Miller asked.

'Nothing.'

A moment of something between them. Miller sensed it, and felt awkward.

'What did you want to say?' Hemmings asked.

Miller glanced at Roth. Roth started to walk back towards them but Miller raised his hand and stopped him.

'Sometime—' Miller started.

'Sometime you wondered whether we could go out or something?'

Miller nodded. 'Or something . . . yes, maybe we could go out and have some dinner or something.'

'You always this sure of yourself?'

'This isn't a movie,' Miller said. 'I'm a normal person. I don't have a collection of smart one-liners. I'm not a charming person. I'm a beaten-to-shit police detective.'

'Makes the prospect of going out with you very enticing.'

'You're making fun of me,' Miller said. 'Forget I asked the question.'

'You didn't ask the question. I asked the question for you.'

'You caught me on the back step,' he said. 'I didn't come here to ask you out.'

'Sure you didn't,' Hemmings said. 'You wanna know something?'

Miller raised his eyebrows.

'Couple of times I've been out with policemen . . . and you want to know what I think about them?'

'Go for it.'

Hemmings smiled at Miller's sarcastic edge. 'They spend their whole working lives dealing with all the situations where the police have to be involved, know what I mean?'

Miller frowned.

'They begin to believe that every situation in the world has something to do with the law being violated, with domestic abuse, with death and suicide and drug overdoses—'

'So what're you telling me? That I should stop taking my work home? Jesus, I get enough of that from Roth and his wife.'

'I do the body parts stuff here . . . right here in forensics.

I spend my working day cutting people up and having a look inside. Imagine what would happen if I took my work home.'

'Think that's a little bit different—'

'Physically yes, mentally and emotionally no. You carry all this shit around in your head you're going to—'

'Okay, okay,' Miller interjected. 'Would it be alright if I called you? I don't know when we're going to see the light of day on this thing. I've got my precinct captain, he's got the chief, the chief has got the mayor—'

'I understand, Detective Miller. You know where I am. You call me when you get some breathing space and we'll have this conversation then, okay?'

Miller felt no less awkward.

'One thing on this,' Hemmings said. 'The thing about looking for someone who *has* to do this, not who wants to, right?'

'I got it,' Miller said.

Outside, walking down the steps and back toward the car, Roth said, 'What was the deal there? Looked like she was hitting on you.'

'She was.'

'Okay, okay, okay . . . so now we have something here.'

'Jesus, man, will you leave it out. I spoke to the woman. I might call her. What the fuck is it with you?'

'I have an idea,' Roth said. 'Maybe we could go to a game together, you know? Like me and Amanda, you and Marilyn Hemmings. Hey, that's a good idea. I'm gonna call Amanda and tell her—'

'Tell her nothing,' Miller said. 'You're not gonna call her and you're not gonna tell her anything. Nothing at all is going on here. This is not the way my life works. Right now the only thing going on in my life is a visit to the Police Department Administrations Unit. We're gonna go talk to someone in pensions and they're gonna tell us where to find Michael McCullough. That's my life right now, Al, and I really haven't got time for anything else, okay?'

Roth said nothing.

'Okay?' Miller repeated.

'Okay, okay . . . Jesus, what the fuck shit is this? What the fuck—'

'What the fuck nothing, Al. Get in the fucking car.'

I stood at Catherine Sheridan's apartment door for a long time before I knocked. It was late, a little after ten. Sunday, April 5th, 1981, a day I would remember for the rest of my life. Such days as this ordinarily became important only after the fact. This was different. This was a day I knew would be important from the moment I woke up.

I raised my hand, and then I lowered it. I paced the hallway – back and forth, back and forth – and then I returned to the door and raised my hand again.

She opened it suddenly, unexpectedly.

'What the fuck are you doing?' she said, and started laughing. 'You've been out there walking up and down for a good fifteen minutes. Either you're going to knock on the damn door or you're not.'

I stood speechless for a moment, my eyes wide, my heart missing beats.

'So?'

'I'm going to knock on the door.'

'Okay, right . . . so knock on the damn door will you?'

Catherine paused for a split second. I took a step forward to enter the apartment, but she shut the door hard and firm in my face. I heard her laughing on the other side.

I knocked on the door.

'Who is it?' she called.

'Jesus, Catherine, who the hell do you think it is? Let me in for God's sake.'

She was still laughing when she opened the door. I followed her, closed the door behind me, and once inside the front room I stood there feeling a sense of sympathy for what me and Don Carvalho were putting her through.

'I saw the films,' I said.

Catherine's smile disappeared. 'So you understand why I want to do something about this?'

'I understand.'

She stood there, waiting for me to tell her what I'd decided.

I didn't speak.

'I just don't get what the hell is going on with you, John Robey.'

'Maybe there isn't anything to get.'

Catherine shook her head like a disapproving parent. 'There's always something to get with everyone. You know who Lawrence Matthews is, and Don Carvalho, right? You know who Dennis Powers works for . . .'

'I know who they are,' I replied. 'I know about Langley, about the CIA, about the recruitment program they're running in the campuses . . . I know what they want, Catherine . . . I just don't know whether I can do it.'

'Whether you can do it, or whether you're willing to do it? They're not the same thing.'

'I'm aware of that.'

'So which one is it?'

'I've seen the films. Who in their right mind wouldn't want to do something about what's going on out there?'

She smiled. 'People who aren't in their right mind, that's who.'

I walked to the right of the room and sat down. 'Believe me, Catherine, it's not a question of whether I want to do something, it's simply a question of whether I have what it takes—'

'You have what it takes,' she said matter-of-factly.

'You sound very certain.'

'Believe me, John, if you didn't have what it takes to do this thing you wouldn't be here. There must have been at least twenty-five or thirty people that came in with you. And how many of them are still here? This whole thing . . . it's an Intelligence community. These people are actually very fucking good at what they do. This is a proving ground. This is like college for the CIA. People like Carvalho and Powers know more about you than you know about yourself.'

'You don't think I realize this?' I asked.

'Suspecting and knowing are not the same thing, John. These people see something in you that makes them certain you will do exactly what they want—'

'And that would be what exactly?'

'God, I don't know, John. They want you to gather intelligence. They want you to listen to what people say. Watch people. They want you to evaluate possibilities and report back to Langley.' Catherine looked away for a moment, and when she looked back there was something intense and disquieting in her expression.

'We're all on our own here,' she said quietly. *'None of us has parents. None of us has connections to the world that mean anything at all. We are the invisible ones, the ones who can vanish in a heartbeat. We appear, and then we disappear. We can go anywhere they want to send us. We can be the eyes and ears of the Intelligence community any place in the world, and if we are suddenly lost it doesn't matter. There's no-one to raise a question or file a missing persons report with the police. People like us don't matter at all in the small details of life, but in the grand scheme of things we can actually count for something.'*

'Is that why you're here?' I asked. *'Because you want to count for something?'*

'Isn't that what everyone wants . . . to feel that their life had some kind of meaning?'

I left her question unanswered.

'Christ, John . . . sometimes you sound so definite, so emphatic, passionate even. That's what they see in you. That's why you've made it this far. They recognize that it's people like us who can make some sort of impact on what's happening.'

'And you don't question the way these things are done?'

'Of course I question it. But there's so much more right in this than there is wrong. This is no different from Vietnam, from Korea, Afghanistan . . . a thousand other places where some sort of injustice is being perpetrated on a daily basis. These people don't have the organization to handle it themselves. They have been beaten down so many times they don't have the strength to get back up again. There's an awful lot of history here, John, and you can either be part of it, or you can make it.'

'And the real truth of why we're going out there?'

She looked towards the window – pensive, intense.

'The fact that people have to die . . . ?' I prompted.

'Everyone has to die, John.'

'Sure they do, but they die of cancer and car accidents and strokes and shit like that. It isn't your average citizen who walks down the street and gets shot in the head by a sniper.'

241

'The greater good,' she said.

'The greater good,' I echoed.

'It's not something that has to be questioned by people like us. We do what we do for the greater good.'

'Hitler in a bar in 1929.'

'Precisely.'

'So I agree with you.'

Catherine frowned. *'What?'*

'I agree with everything you say. I came over here to tell you exactly what you've just told me—'

'What the fuck are you talking about?'

'I like to hear you preach,' I said. *'I like to hear you get all wound up and indignant.'*

'Oh fuck off will you.'

'Seriously,' I said. *'It's actually refreshing to listen to someone take a position on something. Out there . . .'* I waved my hand toward the window, the street, the world beyond. *'Out there people are so fucking half-minded. They don't know what they want or need. I see what's happening, and in all honesty I couldn't give a damn, at least not specifically.'*

'What? I thought you just said—'

'Sit down,' I told her.

'I don't want to sit down.'

'Sit down. You're going to need to sit down.'

'I don't need—'

'Catherine, for once in your life will you shut the fuck up and sit down?'

Her eyes wide, her mouth open, she stepped to the left and sat down on the sofa.

'I didn't come here at the same time as you,' I said. *'You thought you were here before me. You were here and then I arrived, right?'*

'Yes, you came after me.'

'I'd been here for three months before you even arrived. I went through the entire routine with Don Carvalho. Dennis Powers came later. He'd been away somewhere. He was told that I knew nothing, that I should be indoctrinated like everyone else, and he was to tell you how I reacted, what I thought, everything I said.'

'You set me up?' Catherine said. *'For God's sake—'*

'No-one set you up, Catherine. I needed to know how certain you

were about what was going on. I decided a long time back that I was going. We needed someone to go with me, preferably a girl. They figured you were the best, but they needed to know that you would go regardless of what you thought of me.'

'And Dennis Powers didn't know that you were already working?'

'Only person who knew was Don Carvalho. He's my coach, if you like. He figured you were the right one, but he had to be sure.'

'So you had already made arrangements?'

'Arrangements were made weeks ago.'

'But you just said that you didn't care what was happening out there.'

'Specifically,' I replied. 'I said I didn't give a damn about what was happening specifically.'

Catherine looked so intense, and yet so confused. I remembered the first time I'd seen her in the damned turquoise beret, how I'd wished that she could be the one.

'What do you mean?' she asked. I could see her assumptions falling apart. She had believed me indecisive and uncertain. Believed it had been her job to convince me of something, and now she saw that it had merely been her own proving ground.

'I mean that there are too many places we could go,' I said. 'Ethiopia, Uganda, Palestine, Israel. There's the attempted Portuguese coup, the Lebanese civil war, the Cuban invasion of Angola. All of this shit and more happening in the last handful of years. This is the tip of the iceberg. This is just the stuff we read about in the newspapers, but it's out there, it's happening and it never fucking stops. So no, I don't care for this any more than I care for any other place, but this is where they want me to go, and they want someone to go with me, and it looks like you're it.'

'And you're an assassin? Is that what you are?'

'Jesus no, I'm not a fucking assassin. Who told you I was an assassin?'

'The conversation we had before . . .'

'The conversations weren't for me, Catherine, they were for you. Everything we discussed, everything you concluded, what you said to Dennis . . . all of it was part of finding out how much you wanted to do this thing, how far you were prepared to go.'

'And you know how far I'm prepared to go?'

'We know enough.'

'So this was all prearranged? Everything that's happened between us was part of my indoctrination into this . . . this . . .'

'Company of wolves?' I suggested.

'So what now? I have to fuck you or what?'

'You're kidding, right?'

She shrugged. 'No, I'm not kidding. Jesus, is this what you thought of me? That I could just be led along day after day, that you could just—'

'Just what?' I said. 'Test you? Test your resolve on these things? What the fuck kind of game do you think this is, Catherine? What the hell kind of thing do you think is going on here? There's a war out there . . . Jesus Christ, even that is one almighty understatement. The movies you saw, they weren't even the rated versions. We're gathering intelligence, that's what we're doing. We're going out into the middle of fucking nowhere to find out what the middle of nowhere actually looks like. There's millions of dollars being spent on trying to defend that scratched-up piece of shit from a complete communist takeover, and the CIA . . . Jesus, I don't even know if this is the CIA. It could be NSA, it could be naval intelligence, it could be some splinter group that answers only to the president himself, but whatever the fuck it is I want to do something about it, and yes I am the same as you. I don't have any parents or anyone else who might be concerned if I don't come home on time. This is not the kind of life . . . hell, I don't even know what kind of life I was planning . . . I only know that this appears to serve a great deal more purpose than anything else I've thought of.'

'And what about me?'

'What about you?'

'You want me to go with you?'

'Yes I do,' I said.

'And I've passed your tests?'

'They were never my tests, Catherine—'

'I'm not talking about Dennis. I'm not talking about late night discussions with Don Carvalho. I'm talking about whatever tests you figured out for me. The things I've said, how I've dealt with everything here . . . you must have had a viewpoint about what you wanted.'

'I've always known what I've wanted.'

'So you want me to come with you?'

244

'Yes I do . . . I want you to come with me.'

'And you think you can trust me?'

'Yes, I think I can trust you.'

'And to work together you think that maybe the trust should be mutual?'

'Of course it should.'

'So tell me something about yourself.'

'What?'

'This whole time you've been pretending to be someone else, pretending to be the new kid on the block, the guy with all the uncertainties and questions. Well, now you tell me that you were here first, that you'd already made up your mind, and you just needed to get me straight enough to go with you—'

'I never said that—'

'But that's what was going on, John. I can see that much.'

I didn't speak.

'So the trust should be reciprocated, and you can only trust someone if you know something about them, and with that some-thing you open the door to something else, and soon you know everything there is to know about them and they have nothing to hide. That's trust – the idea that there isn't anything they can hide from you.'

'I haven't hidden anything from you.'

'You've told me nothing about yourself.'

'Telling you nothing and hiding things from you are not the same thing.'

'That's pedantic.'

'It's not pedantic, it's true.'

'But nevertheless you agree that we should be on the same terms for a relationship to work?'

'Yes.'

'So it can't hurt to tell me something.'

'I don't have anything to tell you, Catherine.'

'Your parents.'

My thoughts stopped dead. 'My parents?'

'Sure . . . tell me what happened to your parents. Tell me why you're all alone in the big, bad world with no-one to call the police if you don't show up for work.'

'I'm not going to tell you about my parents.'

'Then you can go fuck yourself.'

I laughed. 'You're such a tough cookie,' I said. 'You're so full of shit. There's no way after all of this that you would turn this down.'

'Try me.'

There it was again, the intensity in her eyes – the hardness. The thing that had convinced Don Carvalho that Catherine Sheridan was the one. 'You're serious.'

'As can be. You want me to trust you, then you have to trust me. You want me to go two thousand miles into the middle of fucking nowhere with you, then there has to be some kind of give and take—'

'I'll tell you something else,' I said.

'The fuck you will. I want to know the truth about your parents, not the bullshit you told me before.'

'Why? Why on earth do you want to know about my parents?'

'Because it's the one thing you've never mentioned, and when I've mentioned it you close up so fucking tight. Mention your parents and you become someone else entirely. So fucking impregnable. Be different if you were my trainer, if you were my coach, my reader. Be different then. Wouldn't be such a big deal. But you're not those things, John. You're the guy I'm s'posed to trust with my life. You're younger than me, for God's sake. You've probably never had a steady girl. Sometimes you act like you never fucked someone. I wanna know whether this big man on fucking campus is really the CIA hotshot, the golden boy, the whiz-kid prodigy that you probably are, or whether you're just some dumbass wet-behind-the-ears farmhand out of Bohunk, East Jesus, that the CIA thinks they can send over there as cannon fodder.'

'Are you done already?'

She laughed unsympathetically. 'No, as a matter of fact I am not done. What I'm saying means something.'

'I know . . . we know how easy it is for you to get all fired up and—'

'Will you just shut up and stop interrupting me?'

I shut up. It was some performance.

'That's the deal. Right where it stands, that's the fucking deal. Take it or leave it. You tell me what I wanna hear and I'm with you all the way. You clam up and I'm gonna go drink some beers

246

*and find some guy who'll fuck me just to take my mind off what a
dickhead you are.'*

'You want to know about my parents. That's the deal.'

'Yes.'

'I could tell you anything. I don't have to tell you the truth.'

'You could.'

'You wouldn't know if I was telling you the truth or not.'

'But you'd know.'

'So?'

'So you'd know, and you'd feel like an asshole. You'd start to
wonder whether I'd figured you out. You'd read stuff into innocu-
ous comments I might make. You'd have to remember the lines
you told me for next time I asked about your folks. All that
bullshit, right? We don't have the time, and we sure as hell don't
have the attention for that kind of game, my friend . . .'

'So I'll tell you.'

'The truth?'

'Yes, the truth.'

Catherine looked back at me with an expression of such anticipation it was difficult not to start right on in. I cleared my throat. I
looked away towards the window. I glanced at my watch.

'Speak, John Robey, or you're gonna find me in some bar in
Richmond trawling for rough trade.'

'My father,' I said. I looked down at the floor. Already I felt that
subtle twist of tension writhing in my chest. Vagus nerve in my
lower gut was fighting back. Tears in my eyes? I closed them and
willed myself to think of nothing but what I was saying. I wanted
to feel nothing. I wanted to feel nothing at all.

I looked up at Catherine Sheridan.

'My father killed my mother,' I said quietly. 'And I . . . I helped
him do it.'

247

TWENTY-FOUR

Roth drove while Miller thought about Marilyn Hemmings, a woman he'd known for three, perhaps four years. He'd seen her come in as a forensic assistant, and now she had her own lab, dealt with the workload, the administration, the coroner himself, all the lines and legalities that went with such a territory. Yet she held her own, carried a sharp sense of humor like a campaign medal, looked good an awful lot more than she didn't. Several times he'd considered asking her out, but each time he'd backed down and walked away.

'I'm thinking out loud here,' Roth said unexpectedly. 'Just a thought, an idea. This thing about two killers. The guy that killed the first three, the guy that killed Sheridan. That's something we've been considering since the Sheridan autopsy. Maybe McCullough is one of them, and then the guy in the picture . . .'

'The guy in the picture could be no-one.'

'He knew Catherine Sheridan. She was connected to Darryl King . . .'

'Here,' Miller said, indicating the PD admin unit on the other side of the street. Roth slowed up, came to a stop.

Lester Jackson registered a moment of recognition followed by an expression of unwilling responsibility.

'Mr Jackson,' Miller said. 'Good to see you again.'

Jackson smiled with effort. 'And you, detective. How may I help you this time?'

'Pensions Department.'

'Pensions?' Jackson said, and there was a tone of relief in his voice. 'You need to go out of here, turn left, down half a block or so. It's a different building. Like I said, out of here to the left and down half a block. You can't miss it.'

'Thank you very much, Mr Jackson.'

'You're very welcome, detective.'

Reaching the outer door once again Roth said, 'Certainly happy to see the back of us,' he said.

'Lester Jackson we'll speak to some other day,' Miller replied.

Police Pensions Department was a narrow-fronted office block no more than a hundred and fifty yards from the admin unit. Receptionist directed Miller and Roth to a bank of chairs ahead of the front window, asked them to wait there until someone could see them. The someone, when she finally arrived, was a painfully thin woman by the name of Rosalind Harper. She directed them to an upstairs office that overlooked Sixth Street.

Seated behind her desk, a computer in front of her, she asked how she could assist them.

'Forwarding address for a retired police officer,' Miller told her.

'Name?'

'McCullough. Michael McCullough.'

'Precinct?'

'The Seventh.'

'And do you know when he retired?'

'March 2003,' Miller said.

Rosalind tapped keys, scrolled, read, frowned, tapped more keys. She shook her head. 'I have him here in the department from May of 1987 until March of 2003. That's what? Fifteen years and ten months. Seems we didn't make any pension payments to Mr McCullough.'

Miller leaned forward. 'You what?'

Rosalind reached for the edge of the monitor and turned the screen. She pointed to the columns before them. 'See here . . . this records the date he enlisted, here the date he retired. This column is the cumulative months of his employment, the salary he was paid at the time of his retirement . . . and this blank column here should be the continuing payments each month until he dies.'

'But there are none,' Roth said.

Rosalind nodded. 'That's what I told you. It appears we have made no pension payments to Mr McCullough.'

'And his address?' Miller asked.

Rosalind shook her head. 'No payments, no address.'

'Which means that you have no way of locating him?' Roth said.

'We don't, no. Only way we would have an address is if we were sending something there.'

'Like his pension.'

'No, not his pension. Pension payments are made directly into the individual bank accounts. We send quarterly statements to the address we have on file, and then if they move we receive notification and the statements go to the new address . . .' Rosalind paused, tilted her head to one side. 'One thing,' she said. She reached forward and turned the screen back towards herself. She typed more details, and then smiled. 'You have a pen?'

Miller nodded, took out a pen and his notebook.

'Have some bank details here . . . account registered as the receiving account for Michael McCullough's pension back in April 2003. You ready?'

'Sure.'

'Washington American Trust Bank, Vermont Avenue. You know where that is?'

'It's about four blocks or so south of where I live,' Miller said.

'Nothing was paid over to the account like I say, but those were the details given at the time of pension registration.'

'And that's everything you have on this one?' Roth asked.

'That's everything. Of course, if you're planning on going down there and looking at his bank account you're going to need a warrant.'

'That's not going to be a problem,' Roth said.

'Okay,' Rosalind said. 'We're done then.' She showed Miller and Roth back to the front of the building.

'Thank you for your help,' Miller said.

Rosalind Harper smiled. 'Don't mention it. Little bit of excitement around here is always a good thing.'

It is hard to believe that these things took place more than twenty-five years ago. Seems like we were children – though we did not think so at the time. We thought we were nothing less than the kings and queens of the world. We thought we could go somewhere and make a difference. People were dying. We believed the propaganda. We trusted Lawrence Matthews and Don Carvalho and Dennis Powers. And perhaps they were as blind as us. Perhaps, in turn, they also trusted those above them who said that this was the way of the world. We were the United States of America. We were the most important, the most powerful, the most responsible, the most effective. If anyone could handle this, we could. If anyone could walk out into the madness and bring calm and order and peace, then it would be us. There was no-one else.

And that was the thing we missed.

We didn't see the real reason behind it all.

We were blind to the motive.

But that night – sitting in Catherine Sheridan's apartment a handful of miles from Langley, Virginia – the sanctum sanctorum of the most important intelligence agency in the world – my heart in my hands and perhaps being truly honest for the very first time in my life, I imagined that everything I was, everything I wished to become, was somehow tied up with this girl. I could not tell her I loved her. I did not know what love was.

My father knew what love was, otherwise how could he have done what he did?

'A carpenter?' Catherine asked.

'Yes, a carpenter. A cabinet-maker really.'

'And your mother was sick.'

'She got cancer. It was real bad. She couldn't feed herself, couldn't use the john, could hardly speak . . .'

'She didn't have medical care?'

'My mother and father didn't trust people a great deal. I don't

251

know whether it was a contagious distrust, or they were both like that from the start. Anyway, he figured the doctors would take all the money he had and not cure her anyway, so he read everything he could about it. I think he ended up knowing more than many of the experts he spoke to.'

'But when it got so bad that she couldn't speak . . . why didn't he get help then?'

'Far as I can work out I think they made an agreement. I think my mother didn't want to end up in some hospital. I think she wanted to die at home with her husband and her son.'

'And he killed her . . .'

'She was dying, Catherine. She was dying so fast at the end we didn't know whether it would be today or tomorrow or the next day. It broke him to pieces. They'd spent more than twenty years living in each other's pockets, finishing each other's sentences. That was the way they wanted it. Sometimes I even thought that I might have been a mistake.'

'How so?'

'I don't know. Maybe I just imagined it. Sometimes I got the idea that the time they had to spend with me was time they'd rather have spent just with one another. I remember when I went to college. Been there no more than six months, and he called for me, told me that he needed my help. He couldn't cope on his own. I remember how scared I was of her. How she didn't look like my mother anymore. She'd become someone I didn't even recognize.'

'This is when? The fall of '79?' Catherine asked.

I looked at her, in some way surprised. 'God,' I said. 'It's only eighteen months. It feels like so much longer than that.' I said nothing for a while. I was somewhere else, considering how little time had actually passed since their deaths. 'I went back there in the early part of August. Six weeks later she was dead.'

'So what happened when you came back from school?'

I looked at Catherine for a moment, no more, but in that moment I recognized something so close to myself. Perhaps a vague reflection, a memory of her own that was similar.

'Why do you want to know this stuff?' I asked her.

'I didn't want to know this any more than I wanted to know anything else. It's the only thing you've never talked about.' She tried to smile. 'Well, hell, I can't say that it's the only thing you've never talked about, but it's one thing that people normally

252

talk about that you've never mentioned. Parents are one thing people converse about, along with where they've come from, the school they went to . . . but not you.' She looked away, and for a second she seemed hesitant. 'So tell me what happened when you got back from school.'

'He had me help him in the basement . . . his wood shop.'

'What did you do?'

'I sanded and polished small fragments of wood.'

'He—'

'He had me sand and polish pieces of wood. Mahogany, teak, black walnut. All of them different, and different shapes. Every day for a few hours we would sit down there and do this.'

'What on earth for?'

'You know anything about orchids?'

Catherine shook her head.

'My mother loved orchids. She talked about building a green-house and growing orchids . . . and there was one she was fascin-ated by. I can't even remember what it was called, but it looked like the face of a child. My father built a picture of this thing fragment by fragment and it became the centerpiece in the lid of her coffin.'

I looked up at Catherine.

Her smile died a quiet and lonely death. 'He had you help him build her coffin?'

'He sure did. He was a carpenter, he wasn't going to have someone else do it, was he?'

'And you didn't know he was doing this?'

'Not at first . . . at first I figured he was making a door for a cupboard or something, but when the orchid was finished and he set it in the middle of this . . . Jesus, that isn't the half of it, Catherine. He gave me instructions to follow, and while he was upstairs with my mom I worked down in the basement, and the thing that puzzled me was the size of it. It was just so fucking big, and I couldn't figure out what he was doing at first . . .' I felt that tight fist of tension in my chest. A crazy sense of panic had overtaken me and I needed to slow down, to stop for a moment, to gather my emotions and keep some semblance of objectivity about this thing.

'He . . . he was building a coffin for two,' I said quietly.

'What?'

'For two . . . he was building a coffin for two people, and late at night, Thursday September 13th, he went to my mother's room. He took a hypodermic needle and he filled it with morphine, and he injected it into her and then he lay beside her until she was dead. He dressed her in her wedding dress, and then carried her down to the basement and put her in the coffin. He sat there for a couple of hours, and then he put on his wedding suit and got in the coffin beside her. He took an overdose of morphine, pulled the lid of the coffin over himself until it dropped into place, and then he lay beside her and he died . . .'

Catherine – eyes wide, mouth open – looked at me for quite some time, and when she started to speak I knew exactly what she wanted to know.

'No,' I said. 'I didn't figure it out for about five or six hours. I thought he might have taken her somewhere . . . figured he'd finally conceded defeat and driven her to the hospital, but his pickup was outside, and his overcoat, his boots, all his regular clothes, they were right where he left them at night. And then I went down into the basement, and only after a while did I notice that the coffin lid was closed. I started to think about how I'd been working on this thing every day, and every time I'd asked questions he'd say nothing except that I had to help him . . . said that for my mom's sake I had to help him . . .' I closed my eyes and leaned back.

'Jesus,' Catherine Sheridan said, an exclamation. 'That is the worst— No, God, I don't mean worst . . . fuck, John, I don't know what I mean . . .'

I stayed right where I was – head back, eyes closed – and for a long time I wondered whether I would ever be able to exorcise that image of my parents side by side, my father holding my mother's hand, his head turned toward her, this strange, almost beatific smile on his lips; that, and the smell of camphor from his suit, the smell of wood and varnish, of stain and wax . . . I wondered whether I would ever be able to think of my parents and see anything other than the rigored smile they both wore, together at last – no distractions, no-one to invade their privacy, no-one to disturb them . . .

'What did you do?' Catherine asked.

Her voice startled me. I felt the dryness of my eyes where I had resisted the need to cry. I had not cried – not then, not since – and I *did not want to now. I wanted to be matter-of-fact, consider it for what it was. A dying woman. A compassionate husband. A decision. That was all. I could only imagine what my father had gone through, but in hindsight I wondered if the decision he made had not been whether they would make the journey, but how soon they would leave. He kept my mother alive until everything was arranged. And I helped him. I had tried to remember it a different way. Not with grief or disbelief, but with gratitude. Through those weeks, working together in the basement, we had been closer than ever before, and I had come to know my father. I saw that he was a good man, a man of principles and ethics, of stubborn persistence against all odds. I wanted to think that I had inherited some of those qualities. I wanted a little of my father to be left behind.*

'What did you do, John?'

'I waited for a while. I tried to put the thing into some frame of reference. I tried to understand the decision my father had made. And then I went upstairs and called the local doctor. He came with a policeman and the coroner, and they took them away.'

I was quiet for a moment. I could see myself standing there in the hallway, waiting for a little while before I went down to the basement again. It was cramped. Me and the doctor, the policeman and the coroner.

'They had to lift my father out of the coffin to get him upstairs. I remember how my mother's hand rose as they tried to maneuver him out of the coffin. He was holding her hand, you see? Holding it tight, and rigor mortis had set in . . . and when they realized they'd have to pry his grip loose, they asked me to go back upstairs.'

I saw Catherine's expression change as I spoke.

'They thought that the sight of a policeman and a doctor wrestling my mother's hand out of my father's might upset me, but I didn't want to go. I wanted to stay and see them. I knew this would be the last time and I didn't want to turn my back. They prised her hand away, and I stood quiet while they tipped his body up and lifted it from the coffin. The stairwell was narrow. My dad's jacket caught on a nail and it looked like they might drop him . . .'

Catherine leaned forward, an almost intangible gesture that was a desire to reach out, to extend herself towards me.

'They kept it together. They got him upstairs, put him on a

255

stretcher in the upper hallway, and then carried him out to the car. And then they came back for my mom. And she didn't weigh so much, and she wasn't so tall, and they took her upstairs without any difficulty really. I waited down there until I heard the coroner drive away. The doctor came down and said I should go upstairs, but I didn't want to. I wanted to stay down there amongst the wood shavings and pots of varnish, the coffee cans of nails and screws – all the smells and sounds of the basement, the last place I had seen my father alive, the last place I would remember him.'

I paused to breathe. I felt the emotion, the tension, of remembering.

'The doctor tried to be sympathetic, but he couldn't hope to understand what I was feeling. I think he decided not to try. He wished me the best, told me to call if there was anything I needed. There was that thing in his voice, you know, when someone says to call if you need them but they really hope you won't? What could he say? He was just a doctor. He fixed broken bones and delivered babies and signed death certificates. So he told me to call, and he hoped I wouldn't, and I shook his hand and told him I'd be fine, not to worry, everything would be okay.'

'But it wasn't,' Catherine said.

'I don't know . . . it was, it wasn't. I try not to think about it.'

'And then?'

'The funeral. They buried them together in the coffin I helped him build. I put the house up for sale. Someone bought it. I paid off the mortgage and all the creditors; I paid for the funeral and settled up the overdue bills and bank loans, everything my father had managed to keep at arm's length. And when it was all done I put seven and a half thousand dollars in a bank account in Salem Hill and I went back to college.'

'When was that?' Catherine asked.

'March of 1980.'

'And then you met Lawrence Matthews in August?'

'September.'

Catherine was silent.

'So that's what you wanted to know, right? You wanted to know about my parents.'

'Are you sorry you told me?'

'Sorry? Why would I be sorry?'

'I don't know . . . you seemed so reluctant to speak about them. It was—'

'It doesn't matter now,' I said, and I realized that something had gone. A dark weight – small, but dark – was gone. For that I was grateful.

'You okay?' she asked.

'Sure,' I said. *'I'm okay . . . how about we go get something to eat?'*

'Sure, John, I'd like that.'

I rose from my chair and looked around for my jacket, my overcoat, my scarf.

As we left her apartment she took my hand. I did not feel it for a moment, and then I did. It was a good feeling . . . a feeling I had not experienced before.

'Thank you for telling me,' she said when we reached the street.

'Thank you for listening.'

Later I stood silently in the hallway of my apartment. It was not complicated. She pre-empted any reservation I might have had. She reached out her hand toward me. I was impelled, drawn, magnetized almost. She seemed to fold in toward me as if she was without muscle or bone or strength. I pulled her tight, my arms around her shoulders, her head against the side of my neck, and I could hear her breathing, could smell the faint citrus of her perfume, and beneath that the smell of her skin.

We stayed there for perhaps a minute, and then she walked through to the front and sat down. She held my gaze unerringly, and it was the most transfixing and enchanting thing she could have done.

I wanted her to come back; I wanted to hold her again.

'I don't want you to thin—' she started.

I raised my hand and she fell silent.

'Sometimes,' I said, *'it is better to have someone than no-one.'*

'You are a good man, John Robey,' she said, and though her voice was barely more than a whisper I heard every word. Her eyes were brimming with tears. She fingertipped them away.

'I have to go now,' she said, and started to get up.

'I want you to stay . . .'

'I know, but I can't . . . I shouldn't.'

'Shouldn't?'

'You understand exactly what might happen if I stay . . . and I don't want to—'

'You don't want to what?'

'If we . . . if we get involved then there would be another reason to go out there together, and I couldn't do that to you.'

'Isn't that a decision I should make?'

'Whatever you think . . . our lives will be complicated, John. Secrecy doesn't buy happiness, it buys fear and jealousy and possessiveness. I've arrived at the point where if I care for someone, or think I might care for them, I am compassionate enough not to involve them in my life.'

'Seems to me I'm already involved,' I said.

'You are knee-deep in the water, John, walk any further and you might drown.' She started down the hall to the front door.

I followed her.

Catherine opened the door, paused for a second, and when she turned I was right there in front of her.

She raised her hand and touched the side of my face.

I leaned forward to kiss her.

She withdrew, silently, gracefully, and when it was clear to her that I would not push the issue further she touched her fingertip to my lips.

'No,' she whispered. 'I can't.'

I shuddered. A moment of anticipation. I felt the skin tighten across the back of my neck.

'You ever lonely, John?' she asked. 'Really lonely, like there's no-one else in the world but you?'

'Of course I am . . . aren't we all?'

'And how d'you deal with it?'

I watched her profile, the way her hair was tucked behind her ear, the way her ear so smoothly dissolved into the line of her neck, how that line traveled on toward the curve of her shoulder. Michelangelo would have been proud of that line.

'Sometimes I cannot believe what has happened,' she said, 'and sometimes I get to feeling that perhaps I wished it all upon myself. And sometimes I know that can't be the truth, but I can't help it. Like some of us are put here just for other people and we are never meant to live our own individual lives.' She looked away toward the window. 'My father . . .' she started, but her voice trailed into silence.

She closed her eyes, and without speaking another word she took a single step towards me.

I breathed in slowly, breathed out. I felt it coming like a thunderstorm, felt the tension racking up inside me, and even as I stepped forward, even as I felt the warmth of her body against me, I knew that this was perhaps the greatest and most profound mistake of my life.

I felt her fingers against mine. I closed my hand around her wrist. I felt the tension inside her, could feel the pulse in her wrist. I could feel her defenses rising . . .

I could feel her sadness and loss and heartache and loneliness all tightly bound together. I wanted to untie it all, spread it out and see what was there and decide which to keep and which to cast aside.

She pressed her hand against my chest as if resisting this, as if warning herself that this was no solution, but in her eyes I could see exactly what she felt, and what she felt was a mirror image of what I was feeling. And as my lips brushed against her cheek, as my hand touched the side of her face, as my fingers closed around the back of her neck and pulled her tight, I felt as if I was being consumed by something altogether more powerful than both of us combined.

I could hear her hurried breathing, could feel her heart beating in her chest like a frightened bird, and I felt strength in my arms sufficient to crush her into pieces.

'John,' she urged, her tone a plea for something, a plea for forgiveness, for sanctuary, for respite.

I reached up and closed the door. I stepped back, she walked with me, and then she was ahead of me, almost pulling me down the hallway to the bedroom.

Catherine stumbled, almost fell, and then her arms were free and she took off her coat, was tugging at her tee-shirt, pulling it loose from her waistband . . .

She leaned against the edge of the dresser and kicked off her shoes.

I pulled my shirt over my head, walked after her as she crossed the room, and even as she reached the edge of the mattress she was loosening the button on her jeans.

She stood there for a moment in nothing but her underwear, her

259

skin pale and smooth. She held out her arms, received me, pressed every inch of her body against mine.

I felt her fingernails in the skin of my back, felt her tug at my jeans. She pushed me back onto the bed and dragged off my jeans, and then she unhooked her bra and, for a split second, she seemed to hover at the edge of the mattress.

Then Catherine seemed to explode over me, her hands everywhere, out of control, her movements sharp, almost violent, angry and hungered. She punched and tore and grasped and threatened – and I tore back like a man possessed.

And when she came she screamed, and I screamed with her, and it seemed the windows would burst outward and let the world know where we were hiding.

Then later, labored breath, bodies fired like engines, muscles tensed, nerves shredded, sounds of passion, and triphammered hearts like trains, like drowning and dying and being born, and everything was meaningless yet profound, like poetry in war . . .

And then silence for a time.

A vast silence. Chest fit to burst, but holding it all inside until we mustered sufficient stillness to fold into one another like the pattern of a fingerprint.

The feeling of her warm breath on my neck, her fingers turning small concentric circles in the hairs on my chest, the pressure of her breasts against my back, her leg between mine, the tightening of skin as sweat dried and cooled, and the smell of sex and perfume and bodies blessed with rest.

TWENTY-FIVE

Lassiter shook his head. 'A few,' he said. 'Nowhere near as many as I expected, and so far they've come to nothing. We've e-mailed the pictures to Annapolis, Baltimore, Fredericksburg, Chesapeake Bay . . . Metz and the others have fielded about three hundred calls, but the vast majority have been crazies.'

'And how long for the warrant on this bank account?' Miller asked.

Lassiter glanced at his watch. 'Shouldn't be much longer now.' He walked to the window, talking as he went. 'Aside from this picture we have nothing much at all, right?'

Miller looked at Roth. *Say nothing*, his expression said.

'This bank account business, this cop . . . what was his name?'

'McCullough,' Miller replied.

'Like I said, Bill Young was captain down at the Seventh when your man was there. I called for him, found out the son-of-a-bitch had a stroke last May. Bad apparently, real bad, so whatever you manage to find down there . . .' Lassiter shook his head. 'What the hell use is this cop anyway? What do you think he has to do with this?'

'We don't know,' Miller replied. 'He's connected to Darryl King, King is connected to Sheridan, Sheridan is connected to the mystery guy in the photos. Right now McCullough and the photo is all we have.'

Someone knocked at the door.

'Yes!' Lassiter barked.

A department courier came through with a manila envelope.

Lassiter took the envelope, withdrew the warrant, signed for it, returned the envelope to the courier. 'Get the fuck outta here,' he said, handing the warrant to Roth. 'Go see whether McCullough's bank details shed any light on what the fuck is going on here.'

Nine blocks west, on past Carnegie Library and the Convention Center, crossing Massachusetts at Eleventh, Roth making small talk about nothing consequential, Miller driving, keeping his eyes on the road, wondering somewhere in his myriad thoughts what might come of all of this. Thinking of Marilyn Hemmings, how it might be to take her out to dinner, see a movie; trying to remember the last time he did something like that, trying and failing to have any clear image of Marie McArthur, the last girl with whom he'd had a relationship. How had he hooked up with her? Did someone set them up? He couldn't remember. Felt stupid that he couldn't remember. He was supposed to be able to recall details. He was a detective after all. And then back to Marilyn Hemmings. Attractive woman. She was one of the good people. Miller's mother used to say that. *You'll like him*, she'd say, referring to someone she'd met, a neighbor, a friend of a friend. *He's good people.* That's what Miller's mother would have said about Hemmings. *You should take her out, Robert . . . that girl, she's good people.* He smiled at the thought. Wondered if he should call her. But when would he have time to take her out?

Maybe he should just call and say *I am going to call you, you know? I did hear what you said and I really would like to take you out, but right now we have this thing.* He could say *we* because she would understand that. She'd understand that he wasn't trying to put her off. He could say *Right now we have this thing. There's one hell of a lot of heat on it. From Lassiter – he's my precinct captain, you know? – and from the chief, all the way down from the mayor, and right now I don't even have time to piss straight . . .* No, not that. Not that kind of language. *Right now I don't even have time to open my mail, so please don't get the idea that I'm not interested, but you're in the loop on this and you understand where I'm coming from, right?'*

'Robert?'

Miller snapped to, turned and looked at Roth.

'You just drove past the bank.'

*

Miller parked the car half a block down and they walked back the way they'd come. They waited in the foyer while someone spoke to someone who spoke to someone else, and finally – after perhaps fifteen or twenty minutes – the VP for security came down. Pleasant guy, perhaps early forties. Hell of a suit, Miller noticed. Kind of suit you couldn't buy in a store.

'I'm Douglas Lorentzen, Vice-President for Security,' he said. 'I'm sorry to have kept you waiting . . . please, come this way.'

Walked out back of the reception area and down a corridor that ran the length of the building. They reached a door at the end and Lorentzen punched a code into a pad on the wall. Once through it they took a left, Miller ahead of Roth, every once in a while glancing over his shoulder as if he expected Roth to say something.

They went through a door at the end of the second corridor into an ante-room, beyond that a plush office – large, no windows, a bank of security monitors across the right hand wall. Pot plants, a wide mahogany desk, several chairs around a smaller oval table, its surface buffed to a glass-like finish.

'Please sit down,' Lorentzen said. 'I can get you something . . . some coffee, mineral water?'

Miller sat down. 'We're fine,' he said. 'We just need your help on a small matter and then we'll be gone.'

Lorentzen appeared unruffled, as if this was routine – the appearance of two detectives with a warrant, a meeting in a basement office, questions to be asked and answered.

'I understand you have a warrant,' Lorentzen said, pre-empting Miller.

Miller withdrew the warrant from his pocket, slid it across the table.

Lorentzen read through the warrant and looked up. 'Not a problem,' he said. 'Give me a moment.'

Lorentzen lifted the phone and asked for Records and Archives, shared a few words with someone, gave them McCullough's name, the approximate date the account had been opened, asked for all files or documents relating to McCullough's account to be delivered to the security suite.

Lorentzen replaced the receiver. 'So, is there anything you can tell me about what we're dealing with here?' he asked.

'Unfortunately no,' Roth replied. 'It's an ongoing investigation.'

'Some aspect of fraud perhaps?'

'I don't think so, Mr Lorentzen,' Miller answered. 'We're simply trying to gather information regarding the whereabouts of a particular person.'

'And this person, this Michael McCullough, appears to have opened an account here some years ago?'

'Appears so, yes.'

The phone rang.

'Excuse me,' Lorentzen said. He picked up the phone, listened for a moment, acknowledged the person at the other end and instructed them to come right in. Moments later a knock at the door, Lorentzen opened it, took a file from someone, and then closed the door.

He smiled as he walked toward Miller and Roth. He was efficient. He was VP for Security, and within a handful of minutes he had proven his ability to administer the system, to assist the police, to find what they were looking for. The Washington American Trust bank did what it said it could do.

Lorentzen sat down and opened the thin manila file. He leafed through some papers, and then looked up. 'The account was opened in the name of Michael Richard McCullough on Friday, April 11th, 2003. Mr McCullough attended the bank as a new customer that morning, was seen by the assistant manager for new accounts, Keith Beck. Keith, unfortunately, is no longer with us.'

Roth took a notepad from his inside jacket pocket. He wrote *April 11th 2003* and *Keith Beck New Accounts Manager, Wash Am Trust*.

'Mr McCullough made an opening deposit of fifty dollars. That's the minimum deposit required when opening a new account—'

'Cash or check?' Roth asked.

'Cash unfortunately,' Lorentzen replied.

'And the ID he used?' Miller asked.

'His police department identity card, his social security

card, a bill from the telephone company to confirm his address on Corcoran Street.'

Miller glanced at Roth. 'Three blocks from me,' he said, and turned back to Lorentzen. 'We're going to need copies of all of those documents.'

'Unfortunately that will take a little time. Once an account has been opened we return the originals to the account holder. We have copies, but they're scanned into a computer and held on file at our central security unit.'

'Which is where?'

'Here in Washington,' Lorentzen said, 'but—'

'This is a warrant case,' Miller said. 'We really need whatever help you can give us.'

Roth leaned forward. 'This could actually contribute to the resolution of a tremendously important investigation, Mr Lorentzen. We need to get copies of these documents as rapidly as possible.'

Lorentzen understood. He was not over-complicated. One of those rare officials who actually considered it was his job to help, not to hinder with explanations of administrative regulations and bureaucratic protocol.

'You're happy to wait here?' he said.

'No problem,' Miller replied.

'I'll do what I can, okay?'

'That's all we can ask of you.'

Lorentzen left the room, closed the door firmly behind him.

Miller looked at his watch: it was ten after three.

July 20th, 1981 we landed in Managua. We did not leave until December of 1984. The Nicaraguan electorate wanted the Sandinistas back in power. They wanted the Contras, along with their Yankee support and funding, to be nothing more than another piece of their strained and awkward history.

Anastasio Somoza Snr. started it in 1936. He assumed the presidency of Nicaragua. The United States assisted him in any way they could. With the National Guards as his enforcement arm, Somoza brutalized the nation. He countenanced and condoned the rape, torture and murder of the populace. He massacred thousands of peasants; he robbed, extorted, smuggled drugs and terrorized anyone who considered opposing him. His Somozan clans seized land and businesses. Nicaragua was his kingdom until the revolutionary Sandinista Party overthrew the National Guard and the Somozan clans.

The Sandinistas tried to slow the decay. They established a government for the people. Land reform, social justice, the redistribution of wealth. But we, we mighty Americans, didn't want the people of Nicaragua to own their own country, just as we had resisted and opposed similar self-government plans in Chile. It started with Carter – signing authorization to fund opposition to the Sandinistas. The CIA ran anti-government propaganda in the newspaper La Prensa. *Pirate radio stations out of Honduras and Costa Rica told the people of Nicaragua that their new government was nothing more than an atheist puppet of Marxist Russian godfathers hell-bent on destroying the Catholic Church and all that the Nicaraguan people held dear. We put a front organization down there – the American Institute for Free Labor Development. That's where I ended up. And what did we do? We singled out significant individuals in the Sandinista government's health and literacy programs, and then we killed them.*

266

When Reagan took office in January 1981 he stated categorically that the situation in Nicaragua was nothing more than a Marxist Sandinista takeover. He said he deplored what was happening there. Apparently he deplored it so much that he greatly expanded the CIA's guerrilla warfare and sabotage campaigns. In November, ten months into his first term of office, he authorized nineteen million dollars of taxpayers' money to assist the Argentinians train a guerrilla force in Honduras. And who were the backbone of this force? Ex-members of Anastasio Somoza's National Guard, alongside them known war criminals and American mercenaries. It was even rumored that court-martialed and dismissed Special Forces operatives and members of Delta were amongst those stationed in Honduras ready for the push against the Sandinistas.

By the fall of '83 there were somewhere between twelve and sixteen thousand troops. They named themselves the Nicaraguan Democratic Force. They became known as the Contras, and they hid out along the Honduran and Costa Rican borders, repeatedly striking in hit and run raids against rural towns and known Sandinista outposts. The CIA were under no illusions. They knew the Contras would never overthrow the Sandinistas. That was not their purpose. They were there merely to slow down the machine, to damage and halt the progress of all Sandinista development projects – economic, health, educational and political. They blew up bridges, power plants and schools. They burned crops, laid siege to hospitals. They destroyed entire farms, health clinics, grain silos, industrial plants, irrigation systems. A group of concerned Americans calling themselves Witness for Peace gathered intelligence on Contra atrocities from one single year. The rape of young girls, torture of men and women, the maiming of small children, decapitations, dismemberment, cutting out of tongues and eyes, castration, bayoneting pregnant women in the stomach, genital amputation, breaking toes and fingers, pouring acid on faces, scraping off people's skin, summary executions, crucifixions, live burials, setting people on fire.

Reagan named these people 'freedom fighters'. He referred to them as 'the moral equivalent of our founding fathers'.

The Senate Committee initiated the Boland Amendment, and thus 'prohibited the use of tactics for the purpose of overthrowing the government of Nicaragua'.

The CIA gave another twenty-three million dollars to the Contras and we stepped up our activities.

Nicaraguan harbors were mined with three hundred-pound C4 devices. Vessels were arbitrarily destroyed, some of them French and British. Seamen were wounded and killed. Nicaragua's fishing industry lost millions of dollars from delayed and sabotaged shrimp exports.

April of 1984 the World Court declared the U.S. actions illegal.

The Saudi Arabian government secretly arranged with the CIA to fund the Contras at a rate of a million dollars a month. The money was laundered via a bank account in the Cayman Islands, through a Swiss account, and on to the Contras. The accounts were held in the name of Lieutenant Colonel Oliver North, assistant to Rear Admiral John Poindexter, Reagan's national security adviser. It would be the better part of three years before the world knew what had happened, and then they would only be given the bare bones.

Money also came from Israel, South Korea and Taiwan. Reagan's war in Nicaragua had racked up fourteen thousand casualties. Dead children exceeded three thousand, another six thousand orphaned. In November 1984 the Nicaraguan government officially stated that the Contras had assassinated nine hundred and ten state officials. CIA-backed mercenaries had attacked over one hundred civilian communities and displaced one hundred and fifty thousand innocent people.

In October of 1984, two months before I left, the Associated Press disclosed a ninety-page training manual entitled Psychological Operations in Guerrilla Warfare. The manual was authenticated by the House Intelligence Committee as a CIA-produced manual for the Contras. I can guarantee that the manual was indeed authentic. The chapters that dealt with covert assassination and sniper work were written by me.

In Congress, Reagan was asked, 'Is this not, in effect, our own state-sponsored terrorism?'

Congress cut all funding. The Saudis increased their commitment to two million dollars a month.

The deal came to light. Reagan went on TV. He was a trained actor. Lied like a pro.

He went on to circumvent the ban on military funding by giving the Contras thirteen million in intelligence advice and *twenty-seven million in humanitarian aid. Two years after I left Nicaragua, just two years, Congress went ahead and authorized an expenditure of one hundred million for the Contras.*

Ultimately it was the financial devastation of Nicaragua that lost the election for the Sandinistas. In a country where the average annual income had dropped to two hundred dollars a year, the United States proudly handed forty dollars to everyone who voted for the U.S.-favored candidate, Violetta Chamorra. The new American presidential incumbent, George Bush, called the electoral result 'a victory for democracy'.

Even now we are condemned by the World Court of Justice at The Hague for 'the unlawful use of force' employed in Nicaragua.

I read a report from a Pentagon analyst a while back. He stated categorically and unreservedly that the United States policy for Nicaragua was a blueprint for successful intervention in Third World politics. He said, 'It's going right into the textbooks'.

I know what we did out there. I know exactly what we did. I saw it. I lived it. It was my life for three and a half years. Catherine was my controller. She relayed the orders. She ferried the instructions and pushed the buttons. Not just for me, for others too. And how many of us were there? Eventually I lost count. Dozens, perhaps hundreds. We appeared in ones and twos and threes. We seemed to multiply like bacteria, like some invisible virus, and we grew ever more virulent and destructive. What we did became addictive. It became something above and beyond necessity. After a while it was not a job, it was a vocation, a reason to live.

We went out there to Nicaragua, to Afghanistan, to Tangiers, to Colombia . . . We went out there with our hearts and minds in the right place, and we became something that we never imagined we could possibly be.

Like I said before, the journey to such a place was brief, almost unnoticed, but the return seems to last forever.

Perhaps, in that small way, I was so much like my father.

TWENTY-SIX

Eight minutes to four Lorentzen returned. He clutched a handful of papers. On his face he wore an expression of quiet determination.

'I have moved mountains,' he said as he sat down once more. He set the sheaf of papers on the table ahead of him, and then picked up each in turn and handed it to Miller.

'Copy of Mr McCullough's police department ID card, his social security card, and a copy of the address confirmation bill he used from the telephone company. I also have a copy of the original account application form he filled out.'

Miller looked through the papers, passed them in turn to Roth.

'Mr Lorentzen, I am indebted to you,' Miller said. 'You really have done the most remarkable job here. The police department is grateful, very grateful indeed.'

Lorentzen was happy to have solved the problem.

Minutes later he was wishing Miller and Roth the very best in their investigation, standing at one of the front windows, watching them until they disappeared around the corner. He stayed there for a moment longer, and then he turned and went back the way he'd come.

Twenty-five minutes later, out through the worst of the late afternoon traffic, Al Roth and Robert Miller stood on the sidewalk facing a run-down tenement block on Corcoran Street. They had walked both sides of the street for a good ten minutes. Roth had checked the house numbers twice. There was no escaping it. The address that McCullough had given the Washington American Trust, the address that had been confirmed by an AT&T billing, was nothing more than a derelict building, seemingly unoccupied for years.

Miller stood there for some time, hands buried in his

pockets, his expression a combination of disbelief and resignation. An unstoppable sense of inevitability now seemed to pervade everything to do with this case. Names that didn't match social security numbers. Unpaid pensions to vanishing police sergeants with fictitious addresses. Photos beneath carpets, shreds of newspaper under mattresses . . . none of it really connected, and yet all of it felt the same.

'Back to the precinct,' Roth said. 'Need to check on the social security number and see if AT&T ever had such a customer as Michael McCullough.'

Miller didn't reply.

Took them another half an hour to get to the Second. By the time they arrived it was quarter after five. Roth went down to the computer suite in the basement while Miller went upstairs to see Lassiter. Lassiter was gone, some meeting at the Eighth. Had left word that if either Miller or Roth showed up they were to call him on his cell. Miller figured it could wait until they had something to tell him.

Miller checked for progress on the APB. He spoke to Metz briefly, listened to him bitch about the number of time-wasters that called up on something like this. The whole thing was dispiriting. 'Always the way,' he told Miller. 'The lead that looks the most promising is a waste of fucking time, the obvious waste of time turns out to be the thing itself. I tell you, man, this is just so fucking frustrating.'

Miller left Metz in the first floor hallway and went back to his room.

Roth had returned. 'You wanna guess?'

Miller smiled, raised his eyebrows. 'The social security number is bullshit.'

'Nope, the social security number is not bullshit. It really does come up with Michael McCullough, but the Michael McCullough it comes up with died in 1981.'

'You what?'

'That's right. 1981. Our Sergeant McCullough, sixteen years of loyal service and retired from the Washington Police Department in 2003, has actually been dead for the better part of twenty-five years.'

'No,' Miller said. 'No fucking way.' He dropped heavily

into his chair. 'What in God's name is going *on* here? Does none of this actually go back to a real person?'

Roth shook his head. 'I called AT&T as well. They said they have no such address on their system, and as far as a customer named Michael McCullough is concerned, they did have one but he discontinued his service in 1981.'

'Don't tell me. Because he died, right?'

'I can only assume it's the same guy.'

'Jesus Christ . . . so what does this leave us with?'

'Nothing,' Roth said quietly. 'In essence we have nothing, Robert. Fact of the matter is that every lead stops dead. The person doesn't exist. The address is bullshit. The phone bill is fabricated to get an account opened to receive a pension that never comes. None of it makes sense because it's not supposed to make sense, and when it can't make sense it's because someone *intended* for it not to make sense. You get what I'm saying?'

Miller nodded. He took a breath, closed his eyes. He massaged his temples with his fingertips. 'So we're back to square one,' he said. 'Back right where we started.'

'Unless something comes from this picture we have . . . unless someone identifies this guy and he does in fact have something to do with Catherine Sheridan . . . or maybe he can just tell us something about her that opens up another line of investigation.'

'Enough,' Miller said. 'I've really had enough for today. I'm gonna cut out, go get some rest. Can you tell Metz and whoever else that if anything comes up they should call one of us?'

'Sure I can. You think I should stay here?'

'Go home,' Miller said. 'Way this thing is going I don't think either of us are gonna be home long. Lassiter hears we've gone he's gonna call us right back in.'

'I'll go see Metz before I leave,' Roth said.

Miller sat there, head in his hands, for the better part of half an hour, and then he rose, exhaustion like a deadweight on his back, and made his way out of the building and down toward the car. Didn't know what he would do. Didn't want to think about it. Enough was enough for now.

*

By the time he reached Church Street he was having difficulty keeping his eyes open.

Harriet called to him as he made his way through to the stairs.

'I've been up all night,' Miller told her. 'I am so tired, so damned tired.'

'So go sleep,' she said. 'Go sleep, and when you are done sleeping you come down here and eat something and tell me what is going on with your life, okay?'

Miller smiled, reached out and took her hand.

'Go,' she said. 'I will make food for you.'

Upstairs, Miller took his overcoat off and collapsed in a chair in the front room. He did not ask himself where the investigation was going. The sense of foreboding looming over his thoughts was something he tried not to think about. He did not question his own sense of responsibility for the death of Natasha Joyce. He did not ask himself if his own life was in danger. He tried not to picture Marilyn Hemmings' face, the brief personal conversation they had shared. He did not think of Jennifer Ann Irving, the way she had looked when her body had been found. Like Natasha Joyce. Like someone had stamped her to death. The IAD investigation, the endless questions, the unaccepted answers, the sleepless nights, the newspaper reports, the assumptions, the accusations . . .

The sense that life had closed down, and then it had opened up again and presented him with something that was big enough to kill him.

He had been fooling himself. The Irving case, the death of Brandon Thomas – these things were nothing in the face of what was now happening.

It was nineteen minutes past six, evening of Wednesday the 15th of November. Catherine Sheridan had been dead for four days, Natasha Joyce a little more than twenty-six hours.

Robert Miller's cell phone would wake him at quarter after eight, and Al Roth would be on the other end of the line, and Al Roth would tell Miller something that would stop his heart. Just for a second, no more than that, but it would stop his heart.

Two hours of calm before the storm. Just for a little while the world slowed down for Robert Miller, and for this – if nothing else – he was grateful.

My first killing was not significant. Nowhere near as significant as I had believed it would be.

My first killing was a small man in a beige suit. It took place on September 29th – a hot day, somewhere in the nineties – and the small man in the beige suit had dark sweat patches beneath his arms. Sweated so much it went through his shirt, through his jacket, and the smell of him filled the narrow confines of the office where he worked. All I knew was that he was involved with La Allianza, the Alliance, and he had something he should not have had, or he knew something he should not have known, or he planned to say something to someone that he should not say. It didn't really matter.

Managua was a nightmare of its own creation. There were numerous safe houses and hotel rooms scattered across the city, all of which were changed frequently, used perhaps once or twice, everything paid in cash. I did not speak Spanish, but Catherine did. Place names were bastardized into American slang. Batahóla Norte and Batahóla Sur became North and South Butthole respectively. Reparto Jardines de Managua became simply the Gardens, Barrio el Cortijo became the Farmhouse, Barrio Loma Verde was known as Green Hillock, and the street names – Pista les Brisas, Pista Heroes y Martires, Paseo Salvador Allende became Breezes, Martyrs and Salvador. It was easier to remember, and for those who did not speak English it served to confuse them.

Aside from Catherine as my controller, I had a section director. His name was Lewis Cotten. Mid-thirties, family for two or three generations out of OSS, the birth of the CIA, and knew more about the history of the thing than anyone else I'd met.

'Bill Casey is planning to roll back the communist empire single-handedly,' he said, and gave a coarse laugh. 'You know he was OSS, right? And chairman of the SEC? Guy's a hard-headed

ball-breaking son-of-a-bitch. My father used to play golf with him. Said he'd never met anyone so single-minded in his life.'

Lewis Cotten and I founded an awkward relationship. He knew why I was there. I was the proverbial blunt instrument. I later learned that Cotten was no stranger to this element of the game. Though he would supervise and direct the killing of Nicaragua's foreign minister, Miguel d'Escoto in 1983, and then in 1984 the assassination of the nine commandantes of the Sandinista National Directorate, Lewis Cotten had been involved directly in attempts, successful and unsuccessful, on the lives of the chief of Panama Intelligence, General Manuel Noriega; Mobutu Sese Seko, the President of Zaire; Prime Minister Michael Manley of Jamaica; Gaddafi, Khomeini, and the Moroccan Armed Forces commander, General Ahmed Dlimi. In 1985, after I had left Nicaragua for the last time, he was involved in the deaths of a further eighty people when an attempt was made on the life of the Lebanese Shi'ite leader, Sheikh Mohammed Hussein Fadlallah.

Cotten seemed to live solely to see others die. It was his purpose, his motivation, and sometimes when we met for another assignment he would grip my shoulder, grin broadly, and say 'So you wanna know which unsuspecting asshole is going to the gallows today then?' That was his expression – go to the gallows – and though we never hung anyone, though the means of despatch was invariably close-range sidearm or long-range rifle shots, the expression never changed. Between September 1981 and December 1984 – those three years when Catherine Sheridan and I lived out of each other's pockets; three years when we walked from one day to the next and never really knew if we had just survived or just begun the last of them, three years when we drank and smoked and fucked like it was our last chance for anything – during those three years we were responsible for the deaths of ninety-three people. Lewis Cotten got the order, Catherine organized the diary, I attended the meetings. It was a good arrangement. I was shot once. Caught it in the thigh. They had surgeons and doctors on hand. I was out of service for no more than three weeks.

After my leg healed I went back to work. 'Jesus,' Cotten said, when I walked back into the hotel room where he'd set up his office, a hotel on the edge of the Residencial Linda Vista district north of the Laguna de Asososca. 'How fucking long does it take to get over *a fucking superficial gunshot wound? You have any idea the kind of shit I've had to manage while you've been resting your weary little self for the past three fucking weeks? Christ almighty, anyone'd think this was the fucking army. Take a little R 'n' R why don't you? Dammit Robey, you need to get your act together. Get that girlfriend of yours down here and let's talk about what the fuck has been going on while you've been on vacation.'*

But that conversation took place in the middle of 1983, and I have overlooked the first one. A killing that should have been meaningful, should have been life-changing. But it was not. At least not for me. It was only afterwards, late that night, as I sat in the window of a hotel room on Avenida 28a on the east side of Barrio el Cortijo, the Farmhouse, that I realized the significance of what had happened. The important thing was not that I had killed someone. The important thing was that I had killed someone and I had felt a great deal of nothing.

Back at Langley during those weeks of training, we had talked endlessly about the mental and emotional effects, the psychological impact that killing could have on someone. It was all talk. We spent our lives talking it seemed. We were told that some people, despite the training and the mind-modification procedures, despite our certainty that we were doing the right thing . . . well, some people would not be able to go through with it. And then there were some who would go through with it, who would actually line up the sight and look down the barrel and pull the trigger and watch a small red knot bloom in someone's forehead, and associate cause with effect, and understand that they themselves had done this thing – terminated a human existence. Only later would they collide with the sledgehammer of reality, and they would puke, maybe get drunk, maybe sit and sob about what their mother would have thought if she had known what they had done.

One guy shot some asshole in the head, shot him right through the eye, and then he looked down at the body, understood the implications and ramifications of what he had done, turned the gun around, and blew the back of his own head off.

Me, I didn't get so emotional and melodramatic.

I sat in a corridor outside an office. I waited patiently until the small man in a beige suit came down the corridor, and as he passed me I stood up, aimed a handgun at his head, and shot him through the temple. The other side of his face exploded and hit the opposite wall. The color and the suddenness surprised me. I don't know what I'd expected. I stood there for some seconds, looked down at the man on the floor. I could see the dark stains beneath the armpits of his suit. The gun I'd used had been silenced so no-one came running to see what had happened. My pulse was regular, my heart rate had not risen, and I recalled Lewis Cotten's expression as he'd handed me a monochrome photograph of the man and said, 'He's in the way of the Alliance. That's all I've been told, that's all I can tell you, and that's all we need to know – except that your girlfriend knows where he's gonna be tomorrow so you have to be there to shoot him in the fucking head, okay?' Cotten smiled, and then uttered the words he would say before every job. The smile, the wink, the knowing glance, and then, 'Oh, and one more thing, Robey' . . . He'd pause for a heartbeat – great timing, naturally comedic – 'Don't fuck it up, eh?'

So I stood there for a minute or two, a dead man on the floor at my feet, much of the contents of his head on the wall facing me, and wondered if this was now my life, if this is what I would do, the thing I would be remembered for. Hello, my name is John Robey. What do I do? Oh, nothing much . . . you know, kill people for the government, that kind of thing.

And we were so sure we were right. Me and Catherine. Living like we didn't even exist, flitting from one hotel room to the next, to an abandoned apartment on the north side of Reparto Los Arcos, a semi-derelict adobe villa in Barrio Dinamarca. Eating in restaurants, watching the people come and go – Company people – knowing who was who and who was not by the way they dressed, the words they used, the old-timers and veterans, the greenhorns and cannon fodder.

'Out of the landing craft, across the beaches and into the gunfire,' Cotten would say, and then he would grin his foolish grin, and I would wonder and marvel at the madness of the world, and then look at the pictures of who was next.

Took me a year to figure out what was happening out there. Took me a year to get a grasp of what La Allianza was all about, and by that time I began to understand that Nicaragua was not about communism at all. Nicaragua was about something else entirely. By the time we understood what it meant it was too late to go home. We had become what Lawrence Matthews, Don Carvalho and Dennis Powers had wanted us to be right from the *very start. As Matthews used to be so fond of saying, we were the sacred monster. Catherine was the thinker, I was the blunt instrument. Perhaps the bluntest instrument they ever had. But there was an edge. I realized that after a while. And it seemed that everything I did, every assignment I undertook, sharpened that edge. Just as they'd never really concerned themselves with who I might have been before I belonged to them, so they never questioned who I had become.*

It was with the death of a lawyer, a man named Francisco Sotelo in the fall of 1984, that the seams started to come apart. Prophetic it might have been – the things he told me, the things I understood to be the truth, the nature of his personal circumstances – but it didn't stop me killing him. Then, later that night, and the many nights to come, only then beginning to understand the true significance of what we'd done, I spoke to Catherine of what might happen and we realized how perfectly we had been deceived.

It was at that point that it became personal, and where previously I might have been able to leave the dead where they'd fallen, after that night they followed me home.

TWENTY-SEVEN

News came like a bullet. The sound of the phone woke Miller
abruptly. Slurred when he said his own name, and then he
heard Roth's voice, and Roth said something that he didn't
understand. Miller – still fully dressed – sat up, took a deep
breath, tried to focus on something on the other side of the
room.

'What?' Miller asked. 'What did you say?'

'Got an ID,' Roth said. 'A very certain, very real ID. Someone has given our boy a name.'

'You what?'

'We're trying to get some details right now,' Roth said.
'Metz called me. I'm at the precinct. Lassiter's on his way.
Get over here for God's sake.'

'Time is it?'

'Quarter after eight.'

'On the way,' Miller said, and before the last word had left
his lips the line had disconnected. He tried to get up. Blood
rushed to his head. He took a few deep breaths, felt light-
headed, tried to get up again and spent a few moments
steadying himself before he moved. Felt like a hangover.
Maybe not. So long since he'd had a hangover he couldn't
recall how one felt. Felt like he did at his mom's funeral.
Everything vague, everything unreal, everything shifting
awkwardly across his line of vision. Grabbed hold of the
edge of the table as he crossed the room towards the bathroom. Sluiced cold water onto his face, used the john.
Washed his hands, flattened down his hair, took his jacket
from the back of the chair by the front door, and hurried
down the stairs into the diner. Told Harriet he was sorry, he
had to go, no choice, important things . . .

She scowled, she frowned. She said nothing and waved
him away.

280

Miller searched every pocket for his car keys, had to go back inside to get them. Pulled out of the front drive and aimed for the Second, stop-lights green all the way. Like he was meant to get there fast. Like someone was on his side for once.

He reached the Second at eight forty-eight p.m. Asked the desk sergeant if Lassiter had shown, relieved to hear he hadn't. Took the stairs at a run, found Roth, Metz, Riehl and Feshbach in the office.

'Coffee shop,' Metz said. 'Corner of L Street and Massachu-setts. One of the patrol guys went in, gets talking to the girl behind the counter. He shows her the picture. She says she knows the guy. Says he comes in regular. Two, three times a week. Sometimes just orders coffee to go, other times he stays and has a sandwich. Usually lunchtime, sometimes early, like he's en route to work. Wasn't clear on his name. No surname at all, but says he was named John. She was very certain about that . . .'

'And very certain about how he looked,' Roth added. He looked agitated, got up from where he'd been sitting at the desk. 'She was certain that this was our guy, Robert. Looked at all the pictures. Said his hair was longer in the back, grey at the sides, sort of swept back. Said his eyes were unmistakable. She was absolutely sure—'

'So we have some people over at this coffee shop?' Miller asked.

'Two unmarked cars,' Metz said. 'One out front, one at the back. We have the place covered.'

Miller walked to the window and stood there for a moment, hands on his hips. 'Which picture did this waitress say was most like him?' he asked Roth.

'Fourth in the sequence. Full head of hair, clean-shaven, you know the one?'

'Sure,' Miller said. He faced the window.

'Robert?'

Miller looked back at Roth. His heart was racing. Excited, frightened in a way, like it could be everything, it could be nothing. Nothing else came close to this.

'What is it?' Roth asked.

'I want to go over there,' Miller said. 'I want to go see this waitress.'

Streets were as good as empty. Straight run from New York and Fifth past Carnegie Library and up Massachusetts to L Street. Roth drove. Miller glanced back toward the library and remembered the missing hours from Catherine Sheridan's final day. Still hard to believe that only four days had passed. Wondered what had happened to Chloe Joyce. Nine-year-old kid with nothing left from very little at all. Child Services would have her. She'd be some place with other kids whose lives had car-crashed . . .

'It's over there,' Roth said, interrupting Miller's thoughts.

Bright neon window sign – *Lavazza*. Warm yellow lights within made the place seem welcoming, friendly. The name over the awning read Donovan's.

'Which is the unmarked?' Miller asked.

'Other side of the street . . . see the sports goods store?'

Miller saw the sedan parked a little ways beyond it.

'I'm going inside,' Miller said. 'Get a cup of coffee, speak to the waitress.'

The diner was as warm inside as it had appeared from the street. A knot of regulars at the far end of the counter-bar. Four guys, all of them in their late fifties or early sixties. They did not look up as Miller and Roth came through the door, but when Miller took a seat and asked for coffee, when the waitress came over with the jug – smiled at them each in turn, asked if they wanted anything to eat – one of the old guys nodded at Miller and said, 'You guys after the same thing as the others, right?'

Miller smiled. It was the second time in days that someone had identified him as a policeman.

'We should wear signs,' Miller said. 'It's that obvious, right?'

'Way you people act you might as well wear the uniform and be done with it,' the old guy said. He laughed; the others laughed with him.

The waitress – button badge said Audrey – poured them coffee. She set the jug back on the hotplate and returned to where they sat at the counter. She was in her early forties

282

Miller guessed. She looked tired, but undefeated. Perhaps she owned the place. Perhaps there was something more here than just a badly-paid job.

'Take no notice,' she said. 'These old guys are down here 'cause their wives can't stand to have 'em in the house any more.'

'Guys like these I can handle,' Miller said. He looked down the bar once more; the old guys were back talking amongst themselves. 'So you're Audrey.'

'I have it on my badge here case I forget.'

'I'm Detective Miller . . . Robert Miller.'

'You're not a Bob are you?'

'No. Why? You have a thing for names?'

'People,' Audrey said. 'Have a thing for people, but it's amazing how much someone's name can influence who they are. Like your guy for example. No way his name is John.'

Miller shook his head. 'I don't understand.'

Audrey shrugged. 'Isn't difficult. John's the name he gives, but John isn't the name he was given.'

'You know this for sure?'

'No, not for sure, but you get a sense about some people. John is a regular guy's name. Hardworking kind of guy, you know the type. This character here? The one that other detective showed me pictures of?' Audrey shook her head thoughtfully. 'He's not a regular person . . . may look like one to most folks, but I tell you he's seen and done some things, if you know what I mean.'

Roth leaned forward. 'You telling us you can sense this about him?'

Audrey laughed suddenly, abruptly. Her face creased like a paper bag. The lines around her eyes, the yellowing smoker's teeth, the way her lashes were clumped in little groups of three and four with mascara – these things showed her age. 'Like I'm psychic? Shit no.' She glanced at the group of men at the end of the bar. 'Jesus, you'll have these old bastards burning me for a witch. No, I don't sense anything. I just look, and I see what I see. I've been here more than fifteen years.' She tilted her gaze out toward the front of the diner. 'Donovan. That was my husband. Died thirteen years ago

283

and left this behind for me to take care of. I see people come in and out of here in numbers I can't even add up. Get used to talking to people, you know?' She glanced at Miller. 'You're a cop. Cops do the same thing. They talk to people, they look, they listen, they see what they see and they figure out everything they don't. People aren't so hard to read.'

Miller knew what she was talking about.

'So all I'm saying is that you get a feeling for people. You get to know which ones want company. Doesn't matter who it is, they just roll right on in here and open up their wounds for the world. And then there's the others. Spend several hours with a jackhammer and you don't get more than a dozen words. John? He says what he thinks you'd expect him to say, that's all. I mean hell, I could have read him all wrong, but I don't think so. To me he looks like a man with a burden. That's all I can tell you.'

'And there's no question at all that the man you're thinking of is the same man as the one in the pictures you were shown?'

'That was a gallery of whatever,' Audrey said. 'That was one picture with a whole bunch of different hairstyles and whatever. I saw one, and it was very close to how he looks now. That's what he looks like. He's the kind of guy who looks like a million other guys. Then he speaks to you, you look right at him, and you don't mistake him for someone else.'

'Did he scare you?' Miller asked.

'Scare me? Hell no. Takes an awful lot more than a customer to scare me.'

Miller smiled with her as she started laughing once more.

'He just comes on in here, orders coffee to go, very rarely he might order a sandwich, even sit at the counter and spend a few minutes reading the newspaper and making small talk, and then he ups and goes on his way.'

'Which way does he go?' Roth asked.

'Left,' Audrey said. 'Back towards the library and the college.'

'College?' Roth asked.

'Mount Vernon College, out the other side of the square.'

'And that's the way he comes from?' Miller asked.

284

'Sometimes,' Audrey said. 'He comes both ways, sometimes from the library, other times from the Thomas Circle way.'

Miller was silent for a while. He sipped his coffee, turned things over. 'Want someone to come in here and put a button under the counter.'

'A button?' Audrey asked.

'Sure, a button. Like they have in a bank or something. Wire it up so you trigger a silent alarm.'

Audrey opened her mouth to speak, and then she hesitated. 'This guy didn't fail to file a tax return, right? This guy is up for something a little heavier ain't he?'

'He may be able to help us with something.'

'Which means what it says. I know what that means. He's—'

Miller smiled at Audrey, reached out and placed his hand over hers. 'Audrey,' he said. 'What he might or might not have done is really not much of anything unless we speak with him. Right now you're the only person in the entirety of Washington who's had anything useful to tell us about this guy. We've been looking for him for some time, and seems that somewhere in the next couple of days we might actually get to him. That's because of you. I don't want anything to happen to you, and I sure as hell don't want this guy to get wind of something and take off. He could be someone, he could be no-one, but right now he's the only one we've got. I need someone to come in here and put a button back of the counter. City will pay for it, we won't make a mess—'

'Hell, I ain't worried about anyone making a mess.' She glanced at the clock behind the counter. It was nearly eight forty-five. 'I'm closing at ten,' Audrey said. 'You want someone to come down here and do some handiwork then you better call 'em now.'

Roth took out his cell phone, dialled a number. He slid off the bar stool and walked toward the front door of the diner.

Audrey watched him go, then turned back towards Miller. 'So what's the deal with this guy you're after?' Audrey asked.

'Like I said, we don't know what the deal is until we speak with him.'

Audrey smiled knowingly. 'This is like some serious shit

though, isn't it?' She took a cup from beneath the counter, poured herself some coffee. 'You don't send out three, four detectives for a jaywalker.'

'Sorry, Audrey, this isn't something I can discuss with you.'

'Honey, I know that, I'm just angling for something. Word gets out we had some important gangster down here the place'll fill up before I can get the coffee made.'

Roth walked back toward them. 'Someone'll be here by quarter after,' he said. He nodded his head at the door, wanted Miller to step away from the counter for a quiet word.

'Lassiter's in, wants us down at the Second.'

Miller walked back to Audrey. He thanked her, told her the work wouldn't take more than an hour.

'This alarm thing your people are putting in,' she said. 'That's gonna go where?'

'To us at the Second,' Miller said.

'So he comes in here, he orders coffee, I push the button, he takes his coffee and leaves. I don't see that you're gonna have time to get down here before he's gone.'

'We'll have people outside,' Miller said. 'There's some guys out there now. You hit the button, we get it at the precinct, we radio our people and they're all over him in a heartbeat. You're safe, okay?'

'I'm not worried about safe,' Audrey said. 'I just figured that this guy is so important you wouldn't want to miss him for the sake of a couple of minutes.'

'We won't miss him, Audrey,' Miller said, and realized that they had done just that for eight months, even managed to walk him into Natasha Joyce's life, to let him kill her. Missed him so much he'd managed to leave Chloe Joyce an orphan.

'We have to go,' Miller said. 'It was good to meet you . . . maybe I'll come have breakfast here after this thing is done, okay?'

Audrey smiled, waved her hand. 'On the house, sweet-heart, on the house.'

Miller slowed by the door, turned back. 'Time are you open in the morning?' he asked.

'Six-thirty,' Audrey replied. 'I'm here at six, open by six-thirty.'

Miller and Roth walked to the car. The block was quiet. One of the streetlights was broken on the corner. A dark pool of shadows – almost threatening, somehow ominous.

Roth paused at the car, looked back towards the diner. 'You think we have a chance?' he asked.

Miller looked back at the bright lights of the diner. 'Maybe one,' he said, and opened the passenger door.

I stood, waiting silently, in Francisco Sotelo's narrow office on Paseo Salvador Allende, there between the Dinamarca and San Martin districts. I had already cleared the room for weapons; I knew that he did not carry a gun as a routine precaution. Perhaps Francisco Sotelo believed he would never be in a situation where a gun would be required.

I did not kill him as he walked into the office. I had raised my gun, my finger on the trigger, and when he turned toward me, when he looked right at me as if my presence was entirely expected, he smiled with such warmth and sincerity that it gave me pause for thought.

'I would like a drink,' he said, seating himself at his desk. 'I have just come from a very lengthy meeting. I am tired. I think that considering all I have done to assist your people that is the least courtesy you can afford me before we take this matter any further.'

He spoke with such simple intention, and he seemed so utterly unperturbed by the fact that an armed stranger was waiting for him, that he raised my curiosity.

'You will join me?' he asked.

I nodded.

'What is your name?'

I shook my head.

He smiled. 'I think that unfair. You know my name. In fact you possibly know more about me than most of my friends do. You have my home address I'm sure, the name of my wife, my child. You have more than likely studied my photograph a great many times. I imagine you might have even watched me coming back and forth to work to be sure that there was no mistake in identifying me when the time came. I am right, am I not?'

Again I nodded.

'Then the least you can do is tell me your name. Truth of the matter is that I imagine this meeting will conclude with my death.' Sotelo smiled sardonically. 'Thus it will not matter that I knew your name.'

'My name is John.'

'Imaginative,' he said with a half smile.

'That's my real name.'

'Your real name, or the name they gave you.'

'You know who I am?' I asked.

Sotelo nodded. 'Of course I know who you are. You are CIA. You are Uncle Buck, the representative of the almighty United States of America. In fact, I know an awful lot more about why you are here than you do.'

'Why do you think I'm here?' I asked.

'Let us have a drink, make this a little more civilized. Sit down, let's converse for a while. Is that acceptable to you?'

I shrugged.

'Surely you don't have a more pressing appointment – John?'

'I don't.' I liked the man. His seeming lack of concern, his nonchalant manner, even the way he looked – smart, a tailored suit, a clean white shirt.

'There is a bottle of scotch in the drawer of my desk,' he said. 'You want to come and get it for yourself?'

I shook my head. I knew where the bottle was. I had seen it earlier when I'd searched the room. I also knew that there were glasses in the drawer beneath.

Francisco took out the bottle and glasses and set them on the desk. I watched him carefully as he poured our drinks. He slid a glass towards me. I sat down in one of the high-backed ornate chairs, an intricately carved wooden frame with a wrought iron trelliswork back that extended well above the height of my head. Francisco's chair was the same, and for a moment neither of us spoke, as if we were both waiting for something. I crossed my legs, held the gun in my lap with the muzzle pointed directly at Francisco's chest. I could smell the whisky from the glass in my left hand.

'You understand La Allianza?' Francisco asked.

'I understand what I need to understand.'

Francsico smiled. 'You know what the Chinese say about a quiet man?'

I shook my head.

'A quiet man either knows nothing, or he knows so much he needs to say nothing at all.'

'Is that so?'

Francisco paused for a moment, and then leaned forward fractionally. 'Can I ask what they have told you about me?'

I raised my glass and sipped the scotch. 'No.'

'I am a lawyer,' Francisco Sotelo said. 'You know that much, right?'

I did not reply. Francisco was extending his life as much as he could. He was right. I had no other pressing appointment. It was late afternoon. His offices were officially closed and, based on surveillance reports, we knew he often spent the late afternoon and evening working alone. He had never been visited.

'I am a lawyer, and I represent anyone your government tells me to represent. I have information regarding many of the operations your people have been running since the invasion of Nicaragua. I know about Rowan International and the Zapata Corporation. I know about the offshore oil drilling platforms that act as flight stations for the helicopters that carry cocaine back into the United States—'

I set my glass on the table. 'Why are you telling me this, Francisco?' I asked.

He paused, looked around the room, and there was something in his expression that seemed lost, perhaps saddened, by the fact that he knew this was where his life would end.

'There is testimony in this room,' he said quietly. 'Written testimony from former American drug enforcement agents to the effect that the Quintero and Gallardo drug cartels are responsible for bringing four tons of coke a month into the U.S. You know who they are?'

'No.'

'They are Contra supporters in Guadalajara, Mexico. That's who they are, John, and they take four tons a month into your country, and the money that it makes is funnelled back into the war you are supposedly fighting against the communists.' Francisco laughed bitterly. 'This was never about communism, my friend. This war was about something else altogether. I'll tell you something . . . between Noriega in Panama, John Hull in Costa Rica, Felix Rodriguez in El Salvador and Juan Ballesteros in Honduras – every single one of them a known CIA asset and a

*supporter of the Contras – your beautiful and almighty United
States of America gets seventy percent of the cocaine it consumes.
Your CIA has to engage with the criminal element anywhere it
goes. To gain any degree of influence in an area, it has to come to
an arrangement with the criminal authority in that area. That
kind of arrangement is at the heart of every single covert operation
your wonderful government has undertaken. The CIA is everywhere, the demand for narcotics is everywhere . . . tell me that
they don't have to cross one another's territories at some point,
John. Of course they do.'*

'I know nothing about this,' I said.

'You know nothing, or you know everything and choose to say
nothing?'

I inched the gun upwards so the muzzle of the silencer was
aimed at Francisco's throat. 'I know nothing.'

'Which asks the question . . . is it that you choose not to
ask?'

I took another sip of the scotch. It was a good scotch, a clean
taste, and the sensation in the back of my throat was reassuringly
familiar.

'Did you know that Miami International airport is the take-off
site for CIA and NSC planes supplying material to the Contras in
Nicaragua?' Francisco asked.

'No, I did not know that.'

'They bring supplies out to Managua and take cocaine back. The
pilots are known criminals. They have outstanding federal records
in your country. They are buying back their innocence by doing
these things. Their visas are authorized by your very own Department of Defense. They have CIA credentials, and they use those
credentials to ward off customs officials. The arms and supplies
come here to Nicaragua, the coke goes back on the same planes,
the pilots deliver the coke, fly the money to Panama, and that
money is laundered through bank accounts established by Manuel
Noriega.'

I said nothing.

'You know who Manuel Noriega is, don't you?'

'Yes,' I said. 'I know who he is.'

'Well, he's established bank accounts on behalf of your government, and the cocaine money is passed through those accounts
and wired into Costa Rica. And those accounts in Costa Rica . . .*

they are held in the names of known Contra officials. It's organized under the banner of something named Enterprise. Enterprise was created by a man named Oliver North. He's assistant to your President's security advisor. And Enterprise works with the Pentagon, with the CIA, the NSC . . .' Francisco Sotelo laughed quietly. 'Lieutenant Colonel Oliver North, assistant to the U.S. President's security advisor, Admiral John Poindexter, is more than aware of this organization . . . an organization established to support and protect the world's biggest drug dealers.'

Francisco was silent a moment, looked toward the window to his right. 'I read a report some time ago,' he said. 'It was written by a man named Dennis Dayle. He was the former head of an elite DEA enforcement unit, and you know what he said?'

'I don't know that I'm interested, Francisco.'

Francisco laughed. 'Of course you are, John, these are your people. These are your employers, your colleagues, your friends. These are the people who will play golf with you at the exclusive Florida country club when you retire from this dreadful business.' He raised his hand. 'You don't want to know, but I'm going to tell you anyway. Dayle said that in his thirty-year history in the Drug Enforcement Administration and related agencies, the major targets of his investigations almost invariably turned out to be working for the CIA. That's what he said. Are you not impressed and intrigued by such a statement from one of your own?'

'No, Mr Sotelo, I am not. I am not even vaguely interested. All I know is all I need to know. For some reason you have displeased the people that I work for, and in an effort to dissuade your friends from displeasing my employers further I have been sent to deliver a message. The courier does not need to know what's in the package, nor who sent it, nor why it is being sent. He merely needs to deliver it. That is his job. A good courier does not ask these questions, he merely delivers.'

Francisco Sotelo moved awkwardly in his chair. He drained his glass, reached for the bottle to refill it.

'You've had enough,' I said.

His eyes widened. 'One more . . . please,' he said quietly.

I let him half-fill the glass.

'Did you know that there are CIA-protected covert drug smuggling operations in Burma, Venezuela, Peru, Laos, Mexico?' he asked. 'Did you know that the largest overseas station outside the

U.S. for the CIA is in Mexico City? This is also the case for the FBI and the DEA. Did you know that more than ninety percent of all illegal drugs are carried through Mexico into the U.S.? You know how easy it is to get from Nicaragua through Honduras and Guatemala into Mexico? Why do they let this happen, you might ask. Mexico has an external debt of one hundred and fifty billion dollars, most of it owed to U.S. Citibank. It costs them fourteen billion a year to service the interest alone. And where does that money come from? It comes from the very people that they owe the original debt to. Citibank launders millions of dollars for the Salinas brothers and the Mexican cartels. The money pays the interest. Everyone is happy.'

'Enough,' I said.

'It's the truth, John. It is the truth, no doubt about it. As soon as it became evident that drugs were being smuggled back through Honduras and into the U.S. your administration closed the DEA office there and moved the agents to Guatemala. The drugs were not coming through Guatemala, they were coming through Honduras, and the U.S. government knew it. And the moment anyone starts to look too closely at Guatemala that office will move again, more than likely to Costa Rica.' Francisco shook his head. 'There is no question about the timeline, John . . . the moment the United States got involved in Nicaragua the cocaine started flooding into your backyard through Mexico—'

The sound of the glass shattering on the hard wooden floor was louder than the retort of the silenced gunshot. A small rose of color bloomed just above the bridge of Francisco Sotelo's nose, and he stared back at me for what felt like an eternity. Much of the contents of his head passed out as a spray through the wrought-iron trelliswork in the back of the chair. It made a symmetrical pattern on the wall behind him.

I sat there for some considerable time. I refilled my glass twice and savored the whisky. I thought about what Francisco Sotelo had told me, and though he had not told me anything that I was unaware of, nevertheless the details surprised me. I had chosen not to pay attention to the things I had heard. A war has to be funded. Arms have to be bought. Lives are spent in a futile effort to instigate or resist invasions, but once the war is over, what then? Did I want to believe that everything we were doing in South America was being funded by drugs? Hell, no. Did I want to believe that the end product of the advance against communist infiltration was simply greater control over the drug-producing capitals of the world? No, I did not want to believe such a thing.

I searched the room for the documentation, the testimony from DEA operatives that Sotelo had spoken about. I found nothing.

I killed Francisco Sotelo because I had been instructed to kill him. I killed him because he possessed information that was being passed into the hands of the Sandinistas, or so I had been informed by Lewis Cotten.

'The man's an asshole,' he said. 'Francisco Sotelo is a lawyer . . . hell, John, what other possible reason could you need for killing the guy? He's a fucking lawyer for God's sake. Anyway, whatever might or might not be the case, he cannot be trusted. He has information that is finding its way into the hands of the Sandinistas and this channel of information is being used to disable certain operations that are very necessary in the north. It has been established beyond doubt, reasonable or otherwise, that this is the boy that's causing the trouble. You go down there, you fix this thing, and everyone's gonna sleep a whole helluva lot better.'

I fixed the thing.

Whether or not anyone else slept better as a result I had no way of knowing.

I did not sleep better, and that was all that really concerned me.

I left the office unnoticed and crossed the city to Sotelo's house. I went to find the documents that we believed he possessed. That was all I was required to find.

The events that transpired that evening, the effect of what I discovered in that house, became so much more significant than anything that had occurred to date. I realized then that the truth was always so much more powerful and pervasive than the propaganda.

It was the beginning of the end, and I knew – as did Catherine – that we had done a terrible, terrible thing.

TWENTY-EIGHT

'What I have here,' Frank Lassiter said, indicating a half dozen folders stacked on the edge of his desk, 'are the final reports from forensics on each of the cases so far. They reviewed the original findings and cross-referenced them against one another.' He smiled resignedly. 'I say I have something here, but if you read over them very carefully you'll find that we have nothing at all.'

Lassiter walked around the edge of the desk and sat down heavily. He looked as exhausted as Miller felt.

The silence in the room was tangible. It stretched itself out between the three of them as if for the duration.

Miller broke it by saying 'You heard about the diner . . .'

Lassiter nodded. 'I heard about the diner, about this derelict house where McCullough is supposed to have lived. I also understand we have a waitress who thinks she recognized the guy.'

Miller leaned forward in his chair, rested his elbows on his knees, for a moment buried his face in his hands. There was a darkness in his head, like a swollen thing. As if this was a punishment. A penalty for something. He remembered Brandon Thomas's face, the expression as he fell backwards and down the stairs. As if he believed that Miller had intentionally pushed him. Miller looked up at Lassiter. 'We're doing everything—'

'You're doing everything you can,' Lassiter cut across. 'I understand that you're doing everything you can, but everything that *you* can do isn't enough.'

'We need more people—' Roth started.

'You know I don't have more people,' Lassiter replied. 'You know how many murders there are in Washington each year?' He smiled, shook his head. 'I don't need to tell you how many murders there are in Washington every year, do I?

295

These five are just a fraction of what we have to handle here, let alone what goes on in the rest of the city. Thirty-eight precincts, and then you factor in the traffic that we share with Annapolis, Arlington, whoever the hell else considers we have more resources than them . . .' Lassiter's voice trailed away into silence. He swiveled his chair and looked out of the window behind his desk. 'You want to know what my wife said to me this evening?'

Miller opened his mouth to speak but Lassiter continued before he had a chance.

'She said that we were looking too hard to see anything.'

Lassiter turned his chair around suddenly. The smile on his face was one of bemusement. 'My wife is a fucking Buddhist all of a sudden, eh? What the fuck do you think of that? We're looking too hard to see anything. You get that? I mean, I don't even know what that means, but when I have my wife telling me how I should do my job . . .' Lassiter faced the window again.

Miller cleared his throat. 'I believe—'

'I don't need what you believe, Robert,' Lassiter said. 'What I need right now are facts. I need evidence. I need something I can hold up and say "Here gentlemen . . . here we have something that's worth the taxpayer's dollar," and for them to *see* what I've got and say "Yes, Jesus Christ, just look at that will you, that's something right there . . . something we can hang our fucking hats on and go home and tell our wives and daughters to sleep sound because the almighty Second Precinct police have this asshole of a thing under control." That's what I need Robert, and that's *all* I need.'

'And that,' Miller said matter-of-factly, 'is something I can't give you yet.'

'I *know* that, Robert, but that's not what I want to be told. You understand me? I *want* to be told that you have this thing under control, that you're making headway, that come tomorrow you're gonna have this guy in the bullpen and he's gonna be telling you everything you ever wanted to know about what the fuck in God's name happened to the Mosley woman and Barbara Lee and . . .' Lassiter stopped suddenly and started laughing. It was forced and nervous laughter. 'Oh shit, I forgot to tell you. Jesus, how the hell could I have forgotten to tell you this? This is a fucking masterpiece. This is an almighty fucking masterpiece that we couldn't have designed if we'd wanted to. The Rayner woman, Ann Rayner . . . legal secretary, right? Well you'll never guess who the fuck she used to type depositions and summary judgements for?'

Miller shook his head.

'Retired judge, two-term Washington fucking congressman?'

Miller's eyes widened. 'Bill Walford?'

'On the fucking money,' Lassiter said. 'Legal secretary to Judge Walford between June of 1986 and August of '93. Seven years, for God's sake. Seven fucking years. I know guys here who've done two marriages in less time than that.'

Roth was shaking his head. 'Walford?'

Miller glanced at him. 'I'll tell you later.'

Lassiter laughed again. 'You never had the pleasure of dealing with Judge Walford, my friend,' he said to Roth. 'Of all the people one of these women could have worked for it had to be him.'

'He's into this now?' Miller asked.

'Jesus no, the guy's about a hundred years old, but now we have another very good reason to keep it out of the papers. I know that Judge Thorne is very interested, and Judge Thorne happens to be a golfing buddy with the mayor, and Thorne knows Walford . . .' Lassiter paused for a moment. 'So far we've gotten away light, let me tell you. Amount of noise there's been in the newspapers has surprised me. This could have been a lot worse, and when the Natasha Joyce thing happened . . . well, you were very fucking lucky that the papers didn't have anything on this girl. If they'd found out that you were talking to her . . . Jesus, it doesn't even bear thinking about.'

Lassiter stood up, dragged his overcoat from the back of his chair and folded it over his arm. 'Right now I need something on this, some movement somewhere that says we're doing what we're paid to do. Time does the diner open?'

'Officially, six-thirty,' Miller replied.

'Officially?'

'The waitress – she's actually the owner – she's there at six.'

'Five forty-five you're here, both of you,' Lassiter said matter-of-factly. 'The button gets pushed and I need you outside that diner within minutes. I'm leaving Metz and Feshbach on the watch tonight, Riehl and Littman take over at four a.m.' He hesitated, looked at Roth and Miller each in turn, almost as if he was challenging them to say something. 'I'm giving you everything I can on this, you understand?'

'I know Captain, I know—' Miller started.

Lassiter stopped him. 'I don't wanna hear anything now except we have the guy. What I don't want is any more dead women, okay?' Lassiter did not wait for a reply. He stepped out into the corridor and closed the door noisily behind him.

'I'll check on the diner,' Miller said.

Roth didn't argue; didn't challenge Miller. He'd barely seen his family since the first week of the month. This was the life. Amanda knew it, the kids as well, but that didn't change the tone of voice with which they asked the questions. *How long, Dad? When are you gonna come home? Are we gonna see you this weekend?*

Roth put on his coat. As he passed Miller he reached out and gripped his shoulder. 'You're okay?'

Miller smiled resignedly. 'I'm okay,' he said quietly. 'Now will you leave?'

Roth raised his hand. 'I'm gone,' he said.

Miller listened until Roth's footsteps disappeared into silence, then he stood at the window, looked down into the street, pressed his hand against the glass. Glass was cool, and through the spaces between his fingers he watched the lights flicker as cars passed on the highway, as traffic swarmed across the overpass in a constant stream of brilliance. He tried to concentrate on the dark spaces between, but he was drawn back to the colored neons, the streetlights, the arc-sodium, the fluorescents. He wondered if Lassiter's wife was right. Looking too hard to see anything . . .

Fifteen minutes later he called the diner. He spoke to Audrey briefly. Yes, the tech guy had come. Yes, the button was in. Yes, they had tested it and it all worked fine, and now she was going home to sleep, and she'd be back in bright and early, six a.m., coffee ready, should she make him a cup?

Miller told her no, but thanks for the invite. Another time perhaps.

He set the receiver down. He left the room, walked back down to the street and hailed a cab. Took a route north along Fifth, left onto P Street towards Logan Circle. Passed Columbia NW as they went, craning his head back toward it as they drove by Catherine Sheridan's house. Sitting like something quiet and malignant, a dark hollow amidst all the bright lights, and he realized that now, even now, he still had no greater understanding of what had happened there on the 11th.

He closed his eyes, didn't open them until the cab drew to a stop outside his home. Paid the driver, let himself in, took off his jacket. Made some tea and sat in the kitchen. Wondered if the guy would show tomorrow, and if he did . . . well, if he did, would he be able to give them anything at all?

*T*oday is a good day.

Today, above all others, I feel is a good day.

Today is the day I believe something will happen.

I believe that Robert Miller knows what he is doing, at least as well as any of them.

Morning of Thursday, November 16th, I get up and shower. I shave, I comb my hair. Iron a pale blue shirt, choose a suit from the rail in my bedroom. I am not a man who is striking in appearance, but I know how to make the best of my height, my build, my posture. I am forty-seven years old but my students tell me that I look younger, and somehow smarter than most of their fathers, and then they tell me that I am a puzzle, a mystery to them. I smile, and wonder how they would feel if they knew the truth.

I could tell them stories. I could tell them about the training. I could tell them about sand-socks and gilly suits, about AR15s and .223s, about .22 caliber rounds encased in a thin film of plastic so there's no striations, no riflings, no lands and grooves to be found on the shell if recovered. I could tell them about mercury-tamping, about Glaser safety slugs, about wad cutters, flatnoses, long colts, short colts, ballheads and hollow points. I could tell them about the scarlet blooms of blood that grow on the body, about garrotte wires and how to kill someone with a rolled up magazine. About two guys from Puerto Sandino we nicknamed Dexter and Sinister who would kill anyone we asked them to for twenty-five bucks and a bottle of Seagram's. I could tell them about the years it takes to create trust, only to have that trust destroyed in a moment – not by proof, but by suspicion. I could tell them that there's a debt in every favor. Of the means and methods of propaganda manipulation.

What did Cardinal Richelieu say? 'If one would give me six lines written by the hand of the most honest man, I would find

*something in them to have him hanged.' Something like that. I
know all about that shit. All about it.*

If you lie down with the Devil, you'll wake up in Hell.

*Catherine said that to me one time. We were in a bar in
Managua. I had drunk too much. I had drunk too much because
of conscience, because of guilt, because of something I could not
face.*

*Would these kids have the faintest idea what something like
that even meant?*

*And if I told them, what would they think, these rich kids with
their important fathers? Have seen those fathers, all self-appointed
high-powered men with eyes that have seen too much and understood too little. And if I told them what I had done, what would
they think of me then? And would I still warrant the deferential
nod from the vice-principal, the university treasurer? I think not. I
would become a cockroach, a nothing. The worst type of human
being. And they would all talk of me as if I was a disease –
painful, protracted, terminal, but now excised, removed, banished.
And they would tell each other how they knew all along that there
was something different about Professor John Robey; how they
had a feeling, an intuition, and they should trust that intuition
more often, because they'd never been wrong about such things
before . . .*

*The world they have is thanks to people like me. We stood on
the proverbial wall, and we guarded their world against all that
was dark and malign and destructive. We stood on the wall when
no-one else would, and we made it safe. It's fucked. Sure as hell
it's fucked. I know that, you know that . . . hell, we're all grown
up around here, but if it wasn't for people like me it would be an
awful lot worse. Isn't that so?*

*Well, it isn't so. That's the truth, and that's the thing that
cannot be faced. There's the sacred monster, friends and neighbors. There's the thing we all created that we are now trying so
hard to convince ourselves we did not. Well we did, and it is, and
it continues to be.*

Deal with it.

*Thursday morning I stand and look at myself in the mirror. A good
suit – single-breasted wool and cashmere blend – pale blue shirt,
no tie . . . because I don't want to wear a tie today, and if I did*

wear a tie they would only take it away and roll it up and stuff it in a plastic bag and ruin it.

So, no tie today.

Just a suit and a shirt and a pair of brown brogues.

I stand in the hallway for a moment, then I lean down and pick up my briefcase, and I close my eyes, and I take a deep breath, and I pause for another heartbeat or two and then turn toward the door . . .

Outside it is cool and crisp. I walk to the junction and turn right onto Franklin Street. It is four minutes past eight. The bus will arrive between eight and twelve minutes past; I get off at the edge of the Carnegie Library grounds and walk the rest of the way to Massachusetts, get some coffee at Donovan's. I will leave Donovan's by eight thirty-five, walk back the way I came and past the church on the corner of K Street, and there I will sit on a bench for ten or fifteen minutes. At eight fifty-five I will cross the road and walk up the steps of Mount Vernon College. I will say hello and raise my hand to Gus, the college security guard, and then I will walk in through the front entrance, turn right into the hubbub and hustle of a new day, and I will make my way to my classroom. By the time I arrive it will be eight fifty-nine. Class begins at five minutes past nine. I am never late. I do time very well. I was raised on the importance of time. My students understand that also. They rarely need to be late more than once to understand that we do not do late in Professor Robey's class.

I smile at this thought, and with my briefcase in my hand I leave my apartment and walk down the steps to the street.

I am what I appear to be, and what others wish me to be, and above all else I am no longer the man I was.

It is that simple.

I catch the bus. I take the journey south seven blocks, to the edge of the Carnegie Library grounds. Here I alight and walk down Massachusetts. I notice the sedan on the corner, the two men inside. I wonder, just for a moment, if it isn't Miller and his partner. It is not, but they watch me nevertheless, and I sense the tension as they look back over their shoulders once they know I can no longer see them.

I arrive at Donovan's. I am neither late nor early. Even as I approach the counter, even as Audrey turns and smiles and walks towards me, I know.

I wonder what will happen now.

I wonder if she must now do something to alert them to my arrival.

'Usual?' she asks, and her tone is slightly too breezy, slightly too nonchalant. I watch her closely as she makes her way down to the end of the counter to get the coffee jug from the hotplate.

She reaches out her hand toward the edge of the counter. She looks up at me, and in that split second I wonder.

She half-smiles, and then she blinks twice in succession, and I look at her hand on the edge of the counter, and then she's walking toward me again – smiling wide, relaxed, everything's fine, everything's fine, everything's just oh so very fine . . .

'Take out?' she asks.

I smile, I shake my head. 'It's okay, Audrey,' I say quietly. 'I'll wait for them here.'

TWENTY-NINE

Miller had fallen asleep in his clothes. He awoke feeling awkward and nauseous a little before four-thirty a.m. He took a shower, found a clean shirt, was ready by quarter after five. Made some coffee, called Roth on his cell; they shared a few brief words and then Miller left the house. He arrived at the Second at five-forty. It was still dark. A bitter wind made the skin on his face feel tight. Gritty eyes, a sour copper taste in the back of his mouth, a sense of disorientation and vacancy were all-pervasive. Though the city was coming to life around him, he believed he had never felt lonelier. He hesitated at the top of the stairs and looked back towards Fifth. He figured that when this was done he would take a break, a vacation perhaps. He would go someplace he'd never been before and see if life didn't feel somehow different looking back toward home. He knew that he was lying to himself. He smiled inwardly, pushed open the door and crossed the foyer towards the stairs.

Roth arrived within fifteen minutes. He sat down without speaking, merely nodded at Miller.

'Amanda okay?'

Roth smiled. 'Amanda's always okay.'

'She okay with you?'

Roth shrugged. 'She wants a vacation.'

'Don't blame her.'

'I told her maybe . . . maybe when this thing is done we could look at it.'

Miller glanced at his watch: it was four minutes to six. 'She'll be getting in now,' he said. 'Audrey.'

'You want to go down there?'

Miller didn't respond, seemed to be considering the possibility. 'We look how we look,' he said eventually. 'We can't change the way we look. People see us they know we're cops.

304

This guy happens to see us inside he's gonna make a run for it.'

'If he has something to hide he'll make a run for it.'

'I don't want to risk it,' Miller said.

'I agree.'

'You want some coffee?'

'From the machine?' Roth shook his head. 'God no. I could go get some?'

'No, leave it.'

'You hear anything from Littman or Riehl?'

'They're not gonna do anything unless there's something happening,' Miller said.

'So we wait.'

'We wait.'

Roth was silent for a while, seemed elsewhere, and then he looked up at Miller. 'You ever been on something like this before?' he asked.

'A multiple? No. Was on a double murder one time. Hispanic guy killed his wife and her mother. That was a couple of years before I made detective. Messy fucking thing.' Miller closed his eyes, could see the images more vividly so opened them again. Two women – the younger in her early twenties, the mother in her mid-forties. Shotgun killing in the kitchen of their house. Forensics said there wasn't a great deal of either of them left. Husband just stood there reloading, reloading, reloading. Forty-seven shell cases they found. Hispanic mystery meat, the forensics guy said, and then said that most of what evidence they needed was in the treads of his shoes. He smiled like he was out for a ball game. Seemed people were hardened to such things. Miller was not, and though he could walk in on something like Catherine Sheridan or Natasha Joyce without needing to heave, it was never easy.

'You ever get any kind of an understanding of what kind of person does this?' Roth asked. 'You know, beat the living hell out of someone, strangle them, whatever else he did?'

Miller shook his head. 'Makes no fucking sense to me. I don't go with all this abused childhood shit that the psychs keep feeding us. I've met a whole lot of people that had a really rough time, and they sure as shit aren't driving around the place thinking about whose skin they're gonna wear.'

Miller tried to focus. This was now as good as it got. They had something, the first lead of any significance throughout the whole investigation. It was the sense of responsibility that worried at him. If he didn't get it right, someone else might die. If he didn't figure this thing out then someone somewhere would wake up to find a man standing over them, his latex-gloved hands around their throat, his mind already set on doing what he had to do. And did they have a hope? Factually, no. Miller's mind turned to who the next one might be. Where was she now? What was her name? Did she have a job, a family, people who relied on her? How many lives would be affected by her death? Washington was big enough to absorb it. Washington would swallow the magnitude of this thing, and it would become just another part of its history. But individuals? And himself? Miller wondered whether he would survive this thing intact.

He had heard stories. Cops ravaged by the life they'd led, their hearts broken, their minds turned. Left with a handful of difficult years in an apartment somewhere, daily trips to some local bar where they would hang out with other retired cops. Old times, old stories, endless banter about the things they'd seen. The sense of longing, the endless promise of something that would never come close to the rush and buzz and madness of the life they'd lived. And then it all broke down. They came apart at the seams. They cleaned their service revolver, loaded it, drank a glass or two, and ended the dream. No-one spoke of them again.

Was that the future?

What would happen if they never found the guy . . . if the Ribbon Killer was no-one at all? A ghost, a haunting, a thing that was, and then was not.

Robert Miller wished for something better. Perhaps he even invoked a handful of words from some half-forgotten prayer. Let it not be the way I fear it will be. Let it be something else.

It was half past six. Traffic was on the streets. Squad cars were pulling out of the underground car park and heading away from the precinct. He watched one disappear down

New York Avenue toward Mount Vernon Square and Car-
negie Library. Remembering the library reminded him of
Catherine Sheridan's last hours. The unanswered questions:
Where did she go? Who saw her? And Natasha Joyce's visit
to the Police Department Administrations Unit. Was this
Frances Gray a figment of Natasha's paranoid imagination,
or was there something altogether more suspicious? And
Michael McCullough . . . Had he even existed, or was he an
invention, like Isabella Cordillera, a woman named after a
Nicaraguan mountain range?

For a moment Miller felt overwhelmed, as if the weight of
these things was more than sufficient to crush him right
where he stood.

He looked at his watch: six thirty-eight. The diner would
be open. Audrey would have made coffee, put on the hotplate, perhaps started frying bacon and eggs, hash browns.
Regulars would be making their way toward her from various
parts of the neighborhood. People she knew by name, by
face, by breakfast order. Take-outs, eat-ins, coffee to go, triple
shot, half and half, Sweet 'n' Low. Early morning banter,
wisecracks . . . And then *he* would come. Perhaps. He would
come, and she would feel what she felt, and what she felt
might be concern, or worry; and there might be something
in her expression that gave it away. People had been to see
her. Police detectives. Two of them. They had talked to her,
and people had come after them and fitted a buzzer beneath
the edge of the counter, and there might be something in her
eyes – despite her cheery smile, her air of nonchalance – that
he could read as clear as daylight, because there was something about this man that was special, different, peculiar;
something about him that made the cops very nervous about
whether or not they were going to have a chance to speak
with him . . .

She didn't know. Didn't *want* to know. But he would be
able to see right through her, and she would never get a
chance to hit the buzzer, and she would be too afraid to tell
the police that she'd seen him, and he would know that
she'd tried to betray him, and when it suited him he would
come down and—

307

Miller tried not to think of what someone would do to Audrey.

At twenty minutes after seven the phone rang. Roth snatched it from the desk. 'Yes?' he barked, and in his eyes was a spark of something, and then the spark died. 'Oh, for God's sake . . .' he said, and he dropped the receiver into its cradle noisily. 'Wanted the other office,' he said.

Miller decided there were few things worse than waiting. The combination of boredom and anxiety. The two emotions playing one against the other. The eventual belief that whatever might lie behind the door, whatever might lurk inside the warehouse, whatever your imagination could conjure for you *had* to be better than the vague and insubstantial nothingness that waiting had to offer. And then something would happen, and it was like being kick-started, and no-one save those in the emergency services – the firemen, the medics, the ER and triage nurses – would have any comprehension of how it felt when such things happened. Hours of silence, motionlessness, a stagnant nothing of anything at all, and then mayhem breaking loose. Sirens, flashing lights, people running and shouting, ambulances, fire engines, bleeding arteries, people leaping from windows, from bridges, pile-ups on the highway, the smell of burning rubber and the incendiary crump of gas tanks igniting, and the sound of people hollering blue murder as greenstick fractures and splintered bones protruded from open wounds. And not a moment to even think about what might have happened, or what might happen beyond this, because every ounce of adrenaline, every nerve and sinew, every impulse that the brain could generate was driving your body forward against the natural impulse to withdraw, to run, to hide, to pretend to yourself that the world you were seeing and the world you inhabited were not the same thing . . .

Miller looked up at the clock: three minutes after eight. He rose from his chair, paced back and forth between the door and the window. 'So where do we go if we get nothing?' he asked, almost to himself.

'If we get nothing from him, or if he doesn't show?'

'Either which way,' Miller replied. 'He turns up, we speak to him, there's nothing he can tell us, or he doesn't show at all. The whole thing's a dead end and we're back where we started. What the fuck then, eh?'

'Jesus, I don't know. I try not to think about that. This is the only solid lead we have right now.'

'Solid as fucking air.'

'Sure, I know that . . . Jesus Christ, you know what I'm talking about, Robert. This guy could be someone—'

'Or he could be no-one.'

Through the window Miller watched the city go about its business. Traffic filled the streets, people crowded the sidewalks, all of them walking safe in the knowledge that whatever might be happening to someone else was not happening to them. He wondered if there was a time for people to die. If your death possessed a day, an hour, a minute, a second . . . If such things were already pre-ordained then the man standing at the junction up ahead, who might be awaiting news of his pregnant wife's check-up or just learned that he'd gotten a raise or that his father had responded to chemo and was on a fast-track to recovery . . . he might step out into the street and find himself on the receiving end of a pick up driven by a drunk, or an engine on its way to a fire, or an ambulance on the way to his wife who'd just called the hospital to say her waters had broken . . .

Life was like that. Perhaps dying was the same.

Miller stretched his arms above his head. He yawned, and yawned again.

Roth caught the bug and yawned too.

As Miller turned and walked back to the desk, the sound of feet hammering up the stairwell assaulted the silence.

The desk sergeant came charging through the door, stood for a second trying to catch his breath. He glanced at the desk where the receiver was tilted slightly off the cradle.

'God's sake!' he said. 'God all-fucking-mighty, I can't reach you guys. Littman called. The guy's in the diner . . . the guy's in the fucking diner . . .'

He was nearly knocked off his feet as Robert Miller and Albert Roth hurtled out of the office and started down the stairs.

THIRTY

Audrey, whose surname was Forrester, whose husband had died and left her a diner named Donovan's on Massachusetts Avenue, would remember that morning for quite some time to come. The crowd of early-morning regulars, however, would remain oblivious. People like Gary Vogel – tail-end of his third divorce, forty-two years old and still dating the twenty-six-year-old girl he'd been fucking when his wife walked in on him; Lewis Burch, gas system repair technician, fifty-three, whose eldest son had just let everyone know he was gay, living with someone named Simon, and if the family didn't accept it he would never come home for Thanksgiving, Christmas, birthdays, Easter, understand?; Jennifer Mayhew, thirty-seven, first week of a new job, loving every minute of it, couldn't understand why she'd spent so many years afraid of change, and dinner this evening with a great guy – okay, so she'd only met him on the subway, but they'd traveled together so many mornings, and he seemed really genuine, and she felt life really had turned a corner; Maurice Froom, a man who'd somehow survived forty-eight years without becoming Morry, and was a minor celebrity in his own right, responsible for the voice on more than two hundred and thirty radio ads aired during the previous decade . . . These people. Ordinary people. People with wives and husbands and children, with cats and dogs and mortgage payments; people who'd managed to evade the edges that lurked unseen, those edges where others crossed the line and watched helplessly as their lives irretrievably changed for the worse. The dark edges of things that people like Al Roth and Robert Miller dealt with each and every day.

That Thursday morning those dark edges were hidden to all but Audrey Forrester and, at eight twenty-two a.m. –

there, on the corner of Massachusetts Avenue – a man crossed the threshold of Donovan's diner and brought a little darkness with him. He was recognized immediately by Audrey and, recognizing him, she smiled, acknowledged his presence, and then she busied herself along the counter, refilling a coffee cup that was obviously left behind, and the man who had entered smiled to himself like he knew something was happening, perhaps more than anyone else.

His name was John, just as Audrey Forrester had told the detectives who'd come, and John surveyed the people at the counter – Gary Vogel, Lewis Burch, Jennifer Mayhew, Maurice Froom, others whose names he also did not know, would never know, did not care to know.

And looking back at him, these strangers saw nothing but a smartly dressed middle-aged man, late forties perhaps, something about him that made it difficult to place his age exactly. They saw his dark suit, his blue shirt, the brown leather briefcase he carried, the overcoat folded across his arm. They saw his collar-length greying hair, his face – perhaps handsome, perhaps not, but certainly a face of character – the face of a man who had lived a life, a man who carried stories inside him, and all of them the kind of stories that would provoke an emotional reaction. He looked like a successful property developer, maybe. Or he looked like a scriptwriter, a poet, an author of dense and intellectual novels about human relationships that few people would understand, but those that did would consider him a genius, a man of insight, of wisdom and fortitude. Or perhaps he was no-one at all. A person just like them. A normal guy, a regular guy, a nine-to-five, fetch-some-coffee-on-the-way-to-work kind of guy.

He approached the counter. And when Audrey Forrester smiled at him for the second time, he knew. He knew when he saw the brief flash of anxiety in her eyes. He knew when he glanced out through the window, out to the sedan parked against the curb, out to the street where he sensed something was happening . . . merely a perception, an intuitive thing, but it was all there, right there in front of him, and he knew . . .

'Take out?' Audrey asked.

311

John smiled. He shook his head. 'It's okay, Audrey,' he replied quietly. 'I'll wait for them here.'

And it was all Audrey could do to conceal her surprise, the sense of unease it created within her, because she already had a paper cup ready, the plastic snap-on lid with the imprinted message – *The beverage you're about to enjoy is HOT!* – and she was walking toward the jug of coffee on the hotplate . . .

And John said, 'I'll wait for them here', and this caused her a second thought, and she set down the paper cup, and she reached for the regular cups, and she wondered how many seconds it had been since she'd pushed the damn buzzer, and already she felt scared, and the cup seemed to weigh an awful lot in her hand, and when she stood near the coffee jug she looked in the bright shining chrome surround of the espresso machine to her left, and in the chrome fascia she could see John's reflection, and there was something different about him . . .

Was it her imagination?

Did he seem relaxed?

How many seconds since she'd pushed that damn buzzer?

She wondered what the hell was taking these people so long, and then she wondered if maybe the buzzer wasn't working. The thing was wireless, and it worked on the basis of radio waves or some such thing. There was a girl standing at the counter with a cell phone, and perhaps the cell phone was cutting the wavelength or creating some kind of inter- ference, and maybe the buzzer hadn't worked and the police weren't coming . . .

She thought of Robert Miller and his partner. She filled a cup for John and took a small porcelain jug of cream from the refrigerator. She carried the cup and the jug back across to him, and she set them down in front of him, and she said, trying to sound breezy and unimportant and nonchalant, 'Not to go today?' and he said the strangest thing. He smiled at her, right at her, the kind of smile you give someone when you're really pleased to see them, and he kind of half-closed his eyes – reminded her of a lizard sunbathing on a rock in Mexico . . . in a small town she'd visited with her hus- band when they went on their honeymoon, a small town named . . . and for the life of her she couldn't think what

312

that place was named . . . and then it came to her, suddenly, like a bolt from the blue, and she remembered that lizard on a rock right there near the sidewalk, and the town was named Ixtapalapa, whatever the hell that might have meant, and for a second John looked like that sunbathing lizard, and Audrey smiled – not at John, but at the memory of her husband and how in love she'd been with him – and then John said the other thing, and the thing was, 'I'm waiting,' and then he shook his head resignedly, and added 'For someone, you know? I'm waiting for someone.'

And Audrey thought, *who is he waiting for?* Like John was the sort of person who would never wait for anyone. People would wait for him – that's how he seemed. People would wait for John, and he might show, or he might not show, and people would never be pissed off at him because John was the kind of guy people would be fortunate to know, and if he didn't come when he said he was going to then it could only be because there was something an awful lot more important . . .

Audrey looked away from him. Realized she'd been staring even as the thoughts ran through her mind.

'Sugar?' she asked.

John shook his head. 'I don't take sugar, Audrey, you know that.'

And in that second she knew she was done for, and if they didn't come, if the detectives didn't come right now, he was going to leave, and he would know that something was wrong, and he would know that Audrey had somehow betrayed him, and he wouldn't come again, not for a while, and then one night, out back in the yard as she carried the trash bags to the dumpster, she would hear a sound, and she would feel a chill down her spine, and she would turn slowly, fear rising in her chest, and she would see John standing there with that half-smile, eyes kind of closed, lizard sunbathing on a rock in Ixtapalapa, and she would know . . .

'Hey, Audrey, you okay?' John asked.

She felt like she was going to faint. 'Tired,' she said, and even as she said it she knew she'd said it too fast. Hell, what the fuck was this? What did they want from her? She wasn't no actress. This wasn't the kind of thing she'd had to deal

313

with before. Some guy coming in for coffee and the cops are so eager to talk to him they spend a couple of hours in the place, and they even put a buzzer beneath the counter, a goddam buzzer that doesn't work, and they expect you to keep your cool and play-act like everything's fine and dandy . . .

And she's remembering something, something she put to the back of her mind, and she wonders if the man she's looking at has anything at all to do with the women that have been murdered . . .

Her heart missed a beat.

'You should take a day off,' John said, and he said it like he meant it. 'Every day you're in here, for God's sake. You should close the place for a couple of days and have a rest . . .'

'Can't afford it,' Audrey said, and she tried her very best to sound as relaxed as possible. 'Amount of money this place costs me I couldn't afford a vacation. You know how it is.'

'I do,' he said, and he smiled again, and he lifted his cup and sipped his coffee, and even as he looked away Audrey saw the two detectives coming in through the door.

John looked up at her.

He didn't turn around.

He tilted his head to one side, and then he said something that made her feel like her skin would crawl right off of her, something that she would remember for several days to come, like *Here we are. Here it all is. Here's what we expected* . . .

And he said: 'It's them, right? They're here, aren't they?'

Audrey backed up.

Miller and Roth stood behind John.

Miller took his pocketbook out, flipped it open to reveal his badge. 'I'm Detective Miller. I wonder if it would be possible to take a moment or two of your time, sir.'

And John, neither lowering his cup from his lips nor turning around to face them, nodded slowly, closed his eyes, and said, 'Got all the time in the world, Detective Miller . . . all the time in the world.'

THIRTY-ONE

Clearing his throat, Dean Alan Edgewood of Washington's Mount Vernon College leafed through the manila folder before him and found the page he was looking for. He smiled, withdrew the page from the sheaf, and then looked across his vast desk at the detectives facing him. Their names were Riehl and Littman respectively, the former a middle-aged, grey-haired man with a face like a dockyard prize-fighter, the latter somewhat younger, but something around his eyes that spoke of in-built suspicion regarding everything he heard and saw.

They had come to speak about Professor Robey. They wanted to know about Professor Robey's classes, his students, how long he'd worked at the college. They asked where he'd come from, the nature of his employment, the terms of his contract, his salary, his home address; they wanted his social security number, any forms of ID that existed on file, and where they would find his on-campus car parking space. They wanted to know everything. It was already past ten o'clock, they had been there more than an hour, and it seemed they had only just started.

'His resumé, right?' Littman asked.

Edgewood held up the single sheet of paper and nodded. 'Yes,' he said, 'his resumé.'

Riehl crossed his legs and leaned back in his chair. 'Shoot,' he said.

'Well, he was deputy head of the English Language Department, NYSU—'

Littman was making notes. He looked up at Edgewood.

'New York—' Edgewood began.

'State University,' Littman said, and looked down at his notebook and wrote something.

'Yes, like I said, he was deputy head of the English

315

language department at New York State, graduated from Oxford University, England, with an honors degree in European Studies. He holds a Bachelor of Arts degree in Philosophy from Quincy College, Illinois, a Ph.D in Special Sociological and Anthropological Studies . . . He's a National Defense Foreign Language Fellow, and also a member of the team who lectured in the Great Books Program, St. John's College, Santa Fe, New Mexico.' Edgewood smiled. This was something of note, something of significance. Neither Riehl nor Littman reacted at all.

Edgewood looked at the page once more. 'He was resident for three years at La Salle, Philadelphia, he has testified before the U.S. Congress, the legislatures of Massachusetts, Philadelphia and Ohio, and he's also a life patron of the American Academy of Arts and Sciences.'

There was silence in the room but for the rustle of paper as Edgewood returned the resumé to the file.

'And he wrote some books you said?' Littman asked.

'Yes, detective, he wrote some books.'

'Under his own name, or did he use a pseudonym?'

'His own name.' Edgewood rose from his desk and went to the wall of bookshelves. A moment or two scanning the volumes, and then he withdrew a pair of slim hardbacks. He handed the books to Littman.

'*Easier Than Breathing*,' Littman read out.

'And the second one,' Edgewood said, 'is entitled *A Sacred Monster*.'

'And what kind of books are they?' Riehl asked.

'What *kind* of books?' Edgewood asked.

'Sure . . . they're – like – thrillers or horror books, romance stories, you know?'

Edgewood smiled understandingly. 'They're not John Grisham or Dan Brown. Nor are they Nora Roberts. Professor Robey writes challenging literature. The first one was long-listed for the Pulitzer in its year of publication.'

'And the second one?' Riehl asked.

Edgewood shook his head. 'The second one upset a few too many people to be considered for anything at all. Professor Robey wrote some things that certain people did not take too kindly to.'

Littman frowned. 'Such as?'

'Open the book,' Edgewood said. 'Read the first line of the prologue.'

Littman opened the book, leafed through to the first page, read out loud. ' "As far as worldwide organizations are concerned, the Catholic Church is the richest, the CIA the most powerful. The jury's still out on which is the more corrupt." '

Edgewood laughed to himself. 'That, gentlemen, is not the opening line of a Pulitzer Prize-winning book.'

'I get what you mean,' Riehl said. 'So how is he? What's he like?'

'How is he?' Edgewood echoed. 'Far as I can tell he's fine, detective. He very rarely takes time off sick.'

'As a person. How is he as a *person*?' Riehl said. 'I'm sorry, that's what I meant to ask.'

Edgewood frowned. 'I'm a little confused about the reason for your visit, gentlemen. Am I under some sort of legal obligation to answer your questions, or is this merely an appeal to my generosity of nature? You haven't really given me a proper explanation as to why you're here, and right now I have a junior lecturer taking Professor Robey's class, and though the lecturer is a perfectly good teacher he is most definitely not someone who should be taking Professor Robey's class.'

Littman smiled. 'You're not under any legal obligation, Mr Edgewood.'

'Doctor Edgewood.'

'Sorry, Doctor Edgewood. Like I say, you're not under any legal obligation, though I would say that our questions do have a degree of importance.'

'Which implies that Professor Robey is in bad with you boys, does it not?'

Littman looked at Riehl, Riehl looked back at him and then at the dean.

'Answer me straight and I'll help you,' Edgewood said. 'Bullshit me and I'll ask you to leave. Politely of course, like the well-meaning and contributive member of this community that I am, but nevertheless I will ask you to leave.'

'Professor Robey is assisting us with an investigation,' Littman said.

'You have arrested him?' Edgewood asked.

'No, he has not been arrested.'

'And where is he now?'

'He is with one of our detectives,' Littman told him.

'And he's being questioned about something you think he might have done or something he might know about?'

'We can't tell you that,' Riehl said.

Edgewood nodded. He leaned back in his chair and turned slightly towards the window. 'John Robey has been here since May of 1998. We consider ourselves very lucky to have him. He has been a great asset to this college. There are many students here who came simply because John Robey is here. Their parents knew who he was – by name and reputation – and they wanted their budding-writer children schooled in the ways of the writer's world by the man himself.' Edgewood inhaled deeply and sighed. 'John Robey is an enigma to me, gentlemen. He does not assume importance, and yet he knows he is important. He does not deal with things in an intense manner, and yet he is one of the most intense people I have ever met. He is a quiet man . . .' Edgewood paused, looked away for a moment. 'But then the Chinese say that a quiet man either knows nothing, or he knows so much he needs to say nothing at all. If that is true I would place John Robey in the latter category. As far as I can tell he has no vices. He does not drink, nor does he smoke, and as far as women are concerned, he could have the run of any of the faculty wives or girlfriends or mistresses, but he does not. Is he gay? I am sure he isn't. Does he take drugs? God knows, but if he does he disguises it so well I would swear that he does not and never has. What do I think of him as an educator, as a scholar and a lecturer? I hold him in the highest regard, though that does not necessarily mean that I approve of or condone all of his teaching methods.'

'How d'you mean?' Littman asked. 'What don't you approve of?'

Edgewood smiled knowingly. He walked to the window, a leaded light with a centerpiece of red and green diamonds. Through the window the grass verges were a dull mid-brown, the paths swept clean, the flower-beds pruned back for winter.

'I have received a not insignificant number of pupils in tears during John Robey's tenure here. He does not criticize his charges, but he challenges them aggressively. He is a man of passion perhaps . . .' Edgewood clasped his hands behind his back and closed his eyes for a moment. 'The world of the academic is a world all its own, gentlemen,' he said quietly. 'Whereas you might find the car chase and the gunfight reason enough to feel exhilarated, we in the circles of academia find our adrenaline in much more sedate and cerebral things. A new text by Norman Mailer. A collection of previously unknown Emily Dickinson poems.' He smiled. 'I understand that such things may seem desperately unimportant to you, and perhaps they are, but the fact of the matter is that Man has been telling stories for an awful lot longer than he has been breaking into houses and stealing things. John Robey is a man of extremes, you could say. He will not tolerate complacency, unprofessionalism, mediocrity. He would rather you hand in a dreadful piece of prose that you believed in than a great piece of prose that took no effort at all. He does not upset his students about what they do, but about what they do not. He sets exceptionally high standards, and he demands those standards be met as best the student can.'

'You said there were students who had come to you in tears?' Riehl asked.

Edgewood walked away from the window and once more sat at his desk. 'In tears, yes. Because of something they themselves believed they could not do. Professor Robey demands of them ten thousand words a month. For a professional writer such a number of words could be produced in a day or two, but these students are not professional writers. What they are and what they aspire to be are not the same thing. Robey pushes them to run before they have begun to walk, and though this is his method, and though he has produced consistently higher results than any other teacher here, the extent to which he drives them has sometimes upset the board of directors and the parent–student liaison group.'

'And there have been words about his methods?'

'Words? There will always be *words*, detective, but whatever anyone might say they cannot argue with results, with statistics of performance. Regardless of what a parent might say about how upset their son or daughter was, you can see in their eyes a sense of gratitude for someone like Robey. This is not an inexpensive college, detective, and parents are reassured to know that their sons and daughters are being pushed to their limits.'

'You think a great deal of him,' Littman said.

'I think a great deal of him, and I am envious of the man, and other times I am very pleased that I am in no way like him.'

'How so?'

'Because he has no life,' Edgewood replied. 'He has no wife, no children, no interests that he pursues. He appears at the parent-student liaison only because his contract states that he has no choice but to do so. He is brusque with people, he is a loner, his sense of humor is drier than Arizona scrubland. He can look at you in a way that makes you feel like nothing, and then he can say something that makes you feel that he understands you with greater clarity than you have even considered yourself—'

Edgewood stopped mid-flight. For a moment he looked awkward. He frowned, shook his head almost imperceptibly, and then he smiled. 'I'm sorry,' he said. 'I am rambling. You understand that what I'm saying is merely my own personal opinion of Professor Robey . . .' He laughed, a touch nervously. 'I really wouldn't want him to think I'd been talking about him out of school – if you'll excuse the pun.'

Littman smiled reassuringly. 'Not at all, Doctor Edgewood, not at all. This is simply an enquiry about Professor Robey as a person, how he is viewed by the college, what his contemporaries and colleagues might think of him. Obviously, being the dean, you are better qualified than anyone to—'

Edgewood interrupted. 'I would have to disagree with you, detective. I might have employed Professor Robey, but I don't have to work with him day in and day out. The lecturers in his department and his students would be far more qualified to level an accurate opinion about his everyday manner and attitude. I see him in the corridor. We pass, we nod deferentially, but we very rarely speak. I meet with him once a month for a departmental review, and those meetings are relatively brief and one-sided. I tell him the areas where there have been questions, sometimes complaints. He makes notes, he grunts a half dozen acknowledgements, and we . .' Edgewood smiled, tailed off.

'What?' Riehl asked.

'We always seem to end up talking about the book I keep threatening to write.'

'You are writing a book?'

'I am *threatening* to write a book, detective. Professor Robey is my literary conscience, my taskmaster. He urges me to write, but I do not. I rationalize and justify, and he tells me that my excuses are more lame than those on offer from his students. We laugh about it, but I know he means well.'

There was silence in the room for a handful of seconds.

'So is there anything else, gentlemen?' Edgewood asked.

'Is the college open on Saturdays?' Littman asked.

'It is open yes, for extra-curricular studies. The library is in use of course, and there are some tutors who supplement their income by taking additional classes. Why do you ask?'

'Do you keep a record of who takes those classes?'

'Yes we do.'

'And Professor Robey . . . can you tell us whether he was here on Saturday, November the 11th?'

'I know he was not,' Edgewood replied.

'Because?'

'Because the college was closed on the 11th for Veterans Day.'

Littman and Riehl were silent.

'So, gentlemen, is there anything else?' Edgewood asked.

'I don't think so,' Littman replied, 'Except to thank you for your time and your candor.'

Riehl started to rise from his chair.

Edgewood raised his hand. 'One moment,' he said. 'It would be appreciated if you could give me an estimate as to how long you might be in discussion with Professor Robey. If I have to employ substitute lecturers for any length of time . . . well, you have no idea the amount of paperwork, let alone the expense.'

'We have no clear indication at this time—'

'Oh, come on, detective. You sound like Richard Nixon. All I'm asking is for some kind of idea as to what we might be facing here.'

Littman leaned forward, his expression serious, focused. 'Doctor Edgewood. I understand your situation, I really do, but we are in a somewhat unpredictable situation ourselves. There's a possibility that Professor Robey can assist us with our investigation, and if he can he may be some time. If not, then I think we'll know before the end of the day and he'll be back at work in the morning. That, honestly, is pretty much all we can tell you.'

'And this matter he may or may not be able to assist you with?'

'I'm sorry, sir, but I really can't say anything else.'

'Very well then,' Edgewood said, and rose from his chair.

Riehl and Littman followed suit, started toward the door.

Edgewood arrived there first, opened it, showed them out into the hallway. 'Please give my best wishes to Professor Robey,' he said. 'Let him know that we are all behind him.'

'Of course,' Littman said.

Edgewood watched them go, open curiosity in his expression, and perhaps a small sense of guilt for saying so much about Robey. Such forthrightness was perhaps not called for but what was done was done, and if John Robey was the man Edgewood believed him to be – well, then, he was more than capable of taking care of himself. The dean stepped back into his room and closed the door quietly behind him.

THIRTY-TWO

'My name is Detective Robert Miller.'

Robey nodded, said nothing.

'And your name?'

'Robey. I am Professor John Robey.'

'I wanted to ask you some questions, Professor Robey.'

Robey smiled. 'About what?'

'About some people that you might know.'

'I don't know a great many people, detective. We academic types lead solitary lives, you know?'

'I understand, sir, but I think that you might be able to help us nevertheless.'

Robey was silent for a moment. He looked toward the door of the diner, through the window to the right, and then he turned back to Miller. 'If you're planning to delay me then the least you can do is send someone to the college. Tell them to go and see Alan Edgewood. He's the dean. Explain that you have detained me and apologize for me, would you?'

'I can do that,' Miller said.

'That would be appreciated.'

'So will you sit with me for a moment?' Miller indicated the window booth.

Metz and Oliver were in a car against the opposite curb with a clear view of the window. In the facing building, third story, Miller had two SWAT officers. They were not on high alert, but they were there should Robey go postal or try to run.

Robey carried his coffee to the booth and sat down. Miller sat facing him. Roth stayed on a barstool at the counter.

'You look tired, Detective Miller.'

'I have been busy looking for you,' Miller said.

'For me? Why on earth have you been looking for me?'

Miller looked at Robey closely. He placed him in his mid-to-late forties, mid-brown hair greying at the temples, clean-shaven, rugged features. His eyes were an awkward color – neither grey nor green nor blue, but somewhere between all of them – and around them the map of crow's-feet and fine lines that scored his face. His manner was that of a man *arrived*. There was no other way Miller could describe it. Unlike so many people – everything a stepping stone, a way-station en route to something better – Robey seemed settled. He wasn't nervous, had not reacted in any untoward way to Miller's approach, nor his request to answer some questions. His entire demeanor was that of someone who had expected such a meeting, had in fact been anticipating it.

'We have been looking for you because of some photographs,' Miller said.

'Photographs?' Robey raised his cup and sipped his coffee. He glanced toward the car against the curb on the other side of the street, back towards Roth at the counter.

'Your people?' Robey asked.

Miller nodded.

'For me?'

'We're looking at something important, Professor Robey, and we've reached a point where we thought you might be able to help us.'

'You mentioned photographs.'

'I did.'

'Of what?'

'Of whom?' Miller replied. 'Photographs of you and a woman named Catherine Sheridan.'

'Catherine who? Sheraton?'

'Sheridan, Catherine Sheridan.'

Robey nodded understandingly. 'I have lived a life, Detective Miller. I have traveled the world several times over. I have met hundreds, if not thousands of people, and I can't say that I remember someone named Catherine Sheridan. It is not a name that immediately comes to mind.'

'I thought you academic types led solitary lives.'

Robey laughed but did not challenge Miller's comment.

Miller reached into his jacket pocket. He withdrew a copy of one of the pictures that had been found beneath

Catherine Sheridan's carpet and slid it across the table toward Robey. Robey took a pair of glasses from his jacket breast-pocket. He spent a moment cleaning them with a table napkin, and then he put them on, lifted the picture, and stared at it for some moments. He shook his head. He handed the picture back to Miller and removed his glasses.

'I'm sorry,' he said. 'I don't know that I can help you with this, Detective Miller. I cannot recall this woman's face and, as I said, the name means nothing to me.'

'Despite the fact that you have been photographed with her?'

Robey looked toward the car again, and then back at Miller. 'I have been at Mount Vernon for a few years,' he said. 'Before that I travelled extensively, much of it work-related, other trips purely for pleasure. There is insufficient background in your photograph for me to determine where it might have been taken. Perhaps it was someone I met, perhaps the wife of some tourist who insisted he take my picture with her after I had taken their photograph for them. It could have been a lecture tour, a group of us at some university campus or something. Such things happen, you know? You collide with strangers, and for a moment there is something . . . like now perhaps.' Robey gestured at the diner around them. 'Someone would see us here, perhaps even take our picture, and we would appear to know one another. Why else would we be seated at the same table drinking coffee? We must be friends, perhaps work colleagues. But no, we are neither, and we do not know one another, and we have never met before, and the likelihood of us meeting again is slim at best. An apparency, Detective Miller. What one sees and what one assumes to be are very rarely the same thing.'

Miller nodded slowly. 'Have you ever heard of a woman named Natasha Joyce? She has a little girl named Chloe. She lives in the projects out between Landover Hills and Glenarden—'

'Natasha, you say?'

'Natasha Joyce, yes.'

'Oh, sorry, I was thinking of someone else. A student I had

some time ago. I think her name was Natasha, but I don't think Joyce was her surname.'

'You don't know anyone named Natasha Joyce then?'

'I don't think I do, but then here I am in a photograph with someone I don't even remember, so who knows eh? I wonder how many people we've met in our lives, and we hear their names, and as soon as we hear them we forget them. We forget their faces too, I'm sure. You must experience that in your line of work.'

'I am fortunate in that I have an exceptionally good memory for names and faces.'

'Yes, that is fortunate indeed, detective. Good that you're in a line of work where such a faculty can be employed beneficially.'

'Do you know someone named Darryl King?'

Robey appeared thoughtful, turned his mouth down at the corners, and then – once again – slowly shook his head. 'It doesn't ring a bell.' He smiled, sort of half-laughed. 'I really am not being very helpful am I?'

'The reason I ask, Professor Robey—'

'Please, detective, my name is John . . . no-one but my students call me professor.'

'Okay. So the reason I ask – John – is that Natasha Joyce confirmed that you had gone to see her boyfriend, this Darryl King, some years ago. Apparently you went to the projects with this Catherine Sheridan, and you were looking for Darryl King. You were unable to find him, and you spoke with this Natasha Joyce . . .'

'Apparently is the operative word here, detective . . . I may have difficulty remembering some things, but this trip to the projects you talk about, going out there to find someone with this Sheridan woman . . . I really don't know how I could have forgotten something like that. This woman, Catherine Sheridan, she can confirm that these visits took place?'

Miller shook his head. 'Unfortunately she is dead.'

Robey raised an eyebrow. He seemed concerned, almost troubled. 'I am sorry,' he said quietly. 'Well, perhaps this Natasha Joyce could—'

'She is dead as well,' Miller interjected.

326

Robey frowned. 'I don't understand. You think there is some connection between me and two women I have never heard of who are both dead?'

'Yes I do,' Miller said. 'You visit someone, they identify you by your photograph, and you deny it ever occurred.'

'So how is it that you think I might help you?' Robey asked. He glanced at his watch, and with that simple action Miller realized that he had no reason to delay the man, nothing whatsoever.

'Where were you during the late afternoon of Saturday, the 11th of November?'

Robey paused for some time. He closed his eyes for a moment, and then he smiled. 'Yes, of course. Saturday the 11th. I was at the Brentwood Park Ice Rink. Alternate Saturdays I go there and watch the training session.'

'Training session?'

'The ice rink is actually closed for the afternoon, at least between two and five. One of the U.S. Olympic team skaters trains down there. I go and watch her.'

'You know her?'

'Not personally, no. I have spoken to her on a couple of occasions, but I don't *know* her as such.'

'So if the ice rink is actually closed for the afternoon how are you allowed inside?'

'I met her trainer a few years ago. He was a good man. He's dead now, but his assistant has taken over and he knew that we were good friends. He lets me come in and watch the training session.'

'And her name?'

'Her name is Sarah Bishop.'

'And her trainer?'

'The dead one or the current one?'

'The current trainer.'

'His name is Amundsen, Per Amundsen.'

'And they would be able to verify that you were in fact there on Saturday the 11th between two and five in the afternoon?'

'Sure they would,' Robey said. 'Aside from them I am the only person there. I sit right at the back. I don't interrupt them. I watch the training and then I go home.'

'Okay, Professor. We will have to verify your alibi—'

'Alibi?' Surprise was evident in his voice. 'You are considering that I need an alibi for something?'

'Most definitely yes, I do,' Miller replied. He was tired, on edge, and there was something about Robey's nonchalance that grated on him. 'I have two dead women, both of whom were connected to you—'

'You say they were connected, but neither of these women can confirm this.'

'Because they are dead, Professor Robey—'

'John.'

Miller hesitated. 'Whatever,' he said aggressively. 'I have two dead women and a photograph of you with one of them, a statement from the second that you visited her.'

Robey inhaled slowly, and then he leaned forward. 'What you say is unsubstantiated, Detective Miller. This is the word of a dead woman who I do not know against mine, so, if there's nothing else . . .'

Miller felt his fists clenching involuntarily. 'I need your address and phone number.'

'There will be more questions?'

'Most definitely. We have a number of incidents we are investigating, and I am sure there will be further questions.'

Robey smiled. 'You sound like a TV movie.'

Miller laughed suddenly, almost surprising himself. The tension between them had been very real. In that moment it broke – unexpectedly, almost without effort. A simple comment from Robey, *You sound like a TV movie,* and Miller felt something give. It was almost a physiological reaction, the feeling that something wound tight inside him had been released. He looked at the man facing him, this Professor John Robey – a man he'd believed might give him something significant to work with, something that would help him unravel the madness that these killings had brought to bear upon the police department, upon the city itself, and Robey had given him nothing.

'You imagined that I would be able to help you with whatever you are fighting, detective?'

'I considered you might be able to tell us something about this woman, Catherine Sheridan.'

328

'I know how it is. You get a squall, you think it's going to be a storm – but it isn't. I am sorry.'

Miller didn't reply.

'These women were killed by someone?' Robey asked.

'I cannot discuss this with you. You have answered my questions. I appreciate that you have work matters to attend to.'

Robey reached into his jacket. He took out his wallet and from it he produced a business card. On the back he wrote his home address and his cell phone number. He passed the card to Miller and stood up.

'I would ask you not to leave the city, Professor Robey,' Miller said.

Robey smiled. 'I have no intention of leaving the city, detective.' He gathered up his overcoat, his briefcase, and without another word he left the diner. Miller watched as he set off in the direction of Mount Vernon College.

Moments later Metz and Oliver joined Miller and Roth in the diner.

'Professor John Robey,' Miller said. 'Lecturer at Mount Vernon College. Lives locally, up on New Jersey and Q Street. Doesn't know Catherine Sheridan. Says he cannot remember having his photograph taken with her. Does lecture tours, visits university campuses, that sort of thing. Says that such a photograph could have been taken without him necessarily knowing everyone present. Says he's never heard of Natasha Joyce or Darryl King. Ostensibly cooperative, but didn't give me anything.'

'And on Saturday when the Sheridan woman was murdered?' Roth asked.

'Professor Robey was watching someone train at the Brentwood Park Ice Rink between two and five.'

'How does he explain the fact that there were three pictures of him with her?'

'I didn't ask him that, I don't want to show him everything we've got,' Miller explained. 'I need to check his alibi. If he was at the ice rink then we simply need to question him about the pictures. If he wasn't there, or if his alibi cannot be corroborated, then we'll have enough to get a warrant to search his house perhaps, see if there's something that links him to Sheridan. Right now, the way this thing is going, I want to make sure that we keep as much as we can to ourselves. If he thinks we've got nothing more than one picture to connect him to Sheridan, then he won't be so guarded.'

'You think it was wise to let him walk?' Oliver asked.

'We have nothing to hold him for. We get one shot at this,' Miller said. 'We arrest him for what? There's nothing here but three pictures. He says he doesn't remember her. He says he doesn't know Natasha Joyce or Darryl King. We need to get something on him, maybe catch him in a lie. Then we're in a position to act.'

'So we're going to Brentwood Park,' Roth said.

Miller turned to Oliver. 'You guys wait here for Riehl and Littman, then go back to the Second and get them to write up whatever they got from the dean at the college. Wait for me to call you on where we go next, okay?'

Miller and Roth stayed in the window booth. Audrey reappeared, brought them coffee, asked Miller if everything was okay.

'As can be,' he said. 'Thank you for your help. You did a very important thing.'

Audrey hesitated for a moment. 'Is he the guy? He seemed like he was waiting for someone, and I'm really worried . . .'

'We're gonna find out if he's someone to be worried about long before he comes back, okay?'

'You promise me that?'

'I promise, yes. You go on like nothing happened. It's gonna be fine.'

'I'm trusting you people on this one. I helped you out, and I don't want some crazy motherfucker figuring out that I set him up.'

'Audrey. Seriously. It's okay. Right now he's just a lecturer at the college. He hasn't done anything that we know of.'

She laughed. 'I'm sorry. I didn't mean to—'

'It's fine. It's absolutely fine. We're going to make sure whatever happens doesn't come within five blocks of here, alright?'

'Alright. Thank you.' She smiled at Miller, at Roth, and

330

then she went back behind the counter and started preparing for the lunch traffic.

'So?' Roth asked.

'There's something with this one,' Miller said. 'The complete lack of surprise. Like he knew this was coming and he was ready for it.'

'Shit, Robert, that counts for nothing. Lassiter's gonna tear his fucking hair out. I don't think you should have let him go.'

'What would you have me do? Arrest him? For what? What the hell has he done?'

'You could have pressed him further about the pictures. It wasn't just one picture, it was three. One picture yes, okay, fair enough . . . someone could have one picture taken of them with some stranger and not know it. But three?'

'I know what I'm doing, Al. You have to trust me, I know what I'm doing.'

'Would help if *I* knew what the hell you were doing, Robert. Lassiter comes to me and asks why we let the guy walk. Why did we let this character walk? What am I telling him?'

'Tell him to speak to me.'

Al Roth said nothing for a while. He drank his coffee. He seemed to be unwinding himself for a moment, calming himself down, trying to gather his thoughts together and come to terms with what had happened. 'So what's his name?' he asked eventually.

'Robey,' Miller replied. 'John Robey.'

'You're kidding, right?'

Miller frowned, shook his head. 'No, why?'

'That's the name of Cary Grant's character in *To Catch A Thief*.'

Miller took Robey's business card from his pocket and handed it to Roth. 'Here,' he said. 'Professor John Robey, Mount Vernon College.'

'Spelled different,' Roth said. 'The movie guy's name is R-O-B-I-E, but nevertheless it's—'

Miller waved his hand aside nonchalantly 'It's nothing. It's just the guy's name.'

'So we go check out his alibi, and then what?'

'Depends on whether it checks out.'
'And if it does?'
'We jump off that bridge when we get there.'

THIRTY-THREE

It was close to noon by the time they tracked down Sarah Bishop. A health club on Penn Street no more than a quarter mile from the ice rink. Lassiter had called three times. Miller had spoken to him, each time the conversation brief and perfunctory. Lassiter wanted to know if they'd found the Bishop girl. He wanted to know the same things that Roth had predicted. Why had Miller not shown Robey the three pictures? Why had he let him go? He knew the answers already, but this did not preclude his frustration.

Sarah Bishop was in the canteen at the health club. Dressed in a jogging suit, her hair tied back, Miller placed her somewhere around twenty-one or two. She was a pretty girl, dark-haired, almost Mediterranean; sort of girl who would skip the cheerleaders for the tennis team, take languages instead of social studies.

She seemed taken aback by the sudden interest of two Washington police detectives, was curious as to how they found her.

'We spoke to someone at the ice rink,' Miller told her. 'They gave us your trainer's phone number. He said you'd either be home, the library or here. We tried the library, then here. He said he wouldn't give us your home address until we'd checked out the library and the health club.'

'So what's up? Is there something the matter? Has there been an accident or something?'

Miller smiled. 'No,' he said. 'Nothing like that.' He looked around at the few people who populated the canteen. They seemed to be minding their own business. 'Can we sit down?'

'Sure,' Sarah Bishop said. 'Make yourselves at home.'

Roth took a chair from another table.

'We wanted to ask you about someone,' Miller said. 'I

understand that you train at the Brentwood Park Ice Rink on alternate Saturdays.'

Sarah nodded. She unscrewed the cap on a bottle of mineral water and drank some.

'Alternate Saturdays I'm over here seeing my father. He and my mom are doing the trial separation thing, you know? It's all so much horseshit. I mean, Jesus – they've been together for like a hundred and fifty years, they're not going to find anyone better than each other. They're just being so childish about the whole thing.'

'I'm sorry,' Miller said. 'That must be tough.'

Sarah laughed. 'Sometimes I wonder if I didn't come from another planet, you know? We are *so* different, alright? I mean, come *on* . . . A trial separation for God's sake. What the hell is that all about?'

'Okay, so you train there on alternate Saturdays.'

'I do, yes, and most weeks I do Monday and Tuesday evenings as well.'

'And you're on the U.S. Olympic team?'

Sarah laughed, almost choked on a mouthful of water. 'God no, who told you that? Did Per tell you that? God no, I'm not on the Olympic team. I *want* to be on the Olympic team, but do you have *any* idea what it takes to get to that level? Jesus, man, you've gotta be good like you wouldn't believe . . . and besides that, I'm getting a little too old now.'

'Too old?' Miller asked, somewhat incredulous.

'I'm twenty-two,' she said. 'Believe me, as far as Olympic skating is concerned that's getting a little too old. Way it's going right now I'll probably end up a trainer or something, but I'm still on the ice pretty much every day. You have to want it enough to let it run your entire life.'

'I wanted to ask you about the 11th,' Miller said. 'Last Saturday.'

'What about it?'

'About who was at Brentwood while you were training.'

'Last Saturday I wasn't training.'

Miller frowned. 'You weren't training?'

'No, not last Saturday. Last Saturday all three of us had to go to this Veterans Day thing, you know? There was a memorial service over where my mom lives, and we had to

334

go there. My grandfather, my mom's dad, he was killed in Vietnam when my mom was like thirteen or fourteen or something, and every year we have to go do the church thing and spend the day with my gran, and they all sit around and look at pictures of him and stuff. It's like really sad, you know? My grandma, she's real old now, and she never married again, and she spends all her time talking about what her husband was like and whatever. She's kind of a little bit crazy I s'pose. You know what I mean?'

Miller's nostrils had cleared. He could sense Roth beside him. Robey had lied to them. A simple straightforward lie. He had said he was somewhere when he was not. He had reported his whereabouts at the time Catherine Sheridan was being murdered and the report was untrue.

'You're sure of this?' Miller asked.

'Sure of what? That my grandma's crazy?'

Miller was trying to contain himself, trying not to show anything but unhurried ease. 'No, about where you were last Saturday.'

'Course I'm sure. It was Veterans Day, right? That was last Saturday. I spent the whole day with my mom and dad . . . they haven't told my gran – you know, that they're doing this separation thing? They haven't said a word of it because she'd like, you know . . . she'd like probably have a heart attack or something, right? Anyway, we spent the whole day together. Church in the morning, and then over at my gran's place in Manassas. We didn't get back until after eight in the evening. I remember that because there was something I wanted to watch on the tube and it was like half finished by the time I got back home.'

'Okay, Sarah, that's good. Really good. We really appreciate your help with this.'

'So what was the deal with where I was? Why was that so important?'

'We just needed to clarify where you were, that was all.'

Sarah frowned. 'Hey, come on. This isn't fair. You can't just come over here and ask me where I was last Saturday and then walk away. That can't be right. What's going on here? Did someone say I was somewhere or something? Am I in some sort of trouble?'

Miller shook his head. 'No, you're not in trouble. And no, no-one said you were somewhere. Someone said that they saw you at Brentwood, that was all.'

'Was that John?'

Miller stopped in his tracks.

'John Robey, right? Did he say he was at the ice rink last Saturday?'

'Yes . . . as a matter of fact he did.'

'And now he's in the shit, right? Did he do something? Is that what this is all about? Did he say he was over at Brentwood, and I've just ruined his alibi?'

Miller tried to laugh, tried to make light of her comment. She had hit the thing square, head-on, but she couldn't appreciate the importance of what she'd done.

'You know John Robey?' Miller asked.

Sarah shook her head. 'Not as such, no. My trainer, Per Amundsen, well he used to not be my trainer, right? When I was younger there was this other guy, Patrick Sweeney. He was a great guy, a real sweetheart. Tough, you know? Like a coach should be. But he was a real great guy. He died. Per was his assistant, and then Per became my coach. Anyways, John knew Patrick Sweeney. I think they were friends from way back when. They kept in touch. John used to come down to see Patrick, and that's how I got to know him. I say *know* him, but I don't really know him properly. He comes down and sits in the back of the rink. There's seats up there, where like family people can watch their kids while they skate, that kind of thing. Anyway, John comes down on alternate Saturdays and watches me train. He likes to see the Edith Piaf routine.'

'Sorry?'

'There's a routine I do. The music we use is a song by Edith Piaf called *C'est l'Amour*. John says that that's the one I should do when I go for the Olympic elimination trials in February next year.'

'But not last Saturday.'

Sarah Bishop shook her head. 'No, not last Saturday, and if I got him in trouble because I was his alibi and it didn't work out . . . will you tell him sorry for me?'

'It's okay,' Miller said reassuringly. 'It's nothing like that.

You've been really helpful, and we really appreciate your time.'

'So . . . is it like something bad that he might have done?' Sarah asked.

'I can't say anything, Sarah, I really can't. This is what we do. We get a question about something, we have to follow it up. Nine times out of ten it doesn't mean anything.'

'You know he's a real clever guy, right? He's a college professor and he's written books and everything. Per told me about it. John didn't say anything, but then John isn't the kind of guy who would say anything like that.'

'How d'you mean?'

'Well, you know . . . he's like real quiet. He doesn't say a great deal at the best of times, and when he does say something it's always about you.'

Miller frowned.

'You ever met someone like that? Like no matter how important they are you always feel like you're the important one in the conversation. Friend of mine, she once met John Travolta. She said he was, you know, really sweet, a really nice guy, and the whole time they spoke to one another he just asked about her, and what she was doing, and how well she was getting on with her skate training and all that. Just really interested and everything. Like the whole conversation revolved around her and he was, like, nobody. Well, John Robey's like that. I get the idea he's a really important person, but from what he says and how he acts you'd never think it.'

'How long have you known him?'

Sarah shrugged. 'Jeez, I don't know. Patrick died about five years ago . . . yes, it was November 2001, and John used to come down before that. I don't know, maybe for a year or so. I s'pose about six years, something like that. I started training with Patrick when I was twelve so I guess I was about sixteen when I first met John.'

'You didn't mind him coming down and watching you, even after Patrick died?'

'Mind? Hell no, he's no trouble. He just sits right at the back and watches. Most of the time I don't even notice he's there. Sometimes he comes late, like I've already started my

337

work-out, and then I stop for a moment and look up and there he'll be, all the way in back with a bag of donuts or something. He's harmless enough.'

'You never got the impression that there was anything improper about his interest?'

Sarah laughed. 'What's that? The polite way of asking me if I thought he was a kiddy-fiddler?'

'I'm sorry,' Miller said. 'It's not an easy question to ask. I didn't want to upset you.'

'It's okay. Me, I'm bulletproof. Remember, I'm from another planet and I've got parents who figure they'll do better than each other at their age. So did I think he was a pervert? No, not at all. He wasn't like that. It's not difficult to spot when someone looks at you that way. You sort of get a sense for what they're thinking. John's just a friendly guy. He knew Patrick and Patrick died, and maybe he figured he should carry on coming over to see me train so I didn't feel like Patrick was the only reason he ever came. I like him . . .' Sarah paused and looked up. 'And now you're gonna tell me that he is a kiddy-fiddler, right? Or that he's a mass murderer or something really freaked out like that?'

'Nothing like that,' Miller replied. 'Like I said, we're just following up on something. Thank you for your time. I really appreciate it.'

'Whatever,' Sarah said. She rose from the chair, took her bottle of water, the towel she'd been sitting on, and she turned toward the door.

'If I need to get hold of you again . . . ?' Miller asked.

'You've got Per's number. He can reach me.'

'Okay. Thanks again.'

'No problem. Say hi to John for me.'

Miller nodded. 'I will.'

Miller and Roth watched her go.

'Nice kid,' Roth said.

'Who just demolished Robey's alibi for the time of Catherine Sheridan's murder.'

'You'd think he would have checked, right? If he's so smart, as smart as she says he is, then you'd have figured he would've checked that she was training before he gave her as an alibi.'

338

Miller smiled, shook his head. 'That's the point though, isn't it? Guy like that, if he did this thing, then he's nuts. That's the disadvantage, however brilliant they might be. If they do this kind of shit then they're crazy, and crazy doesn't serve you so well when you're trying to avoid being investigated.'

'So we go see him again.'

'Sure as hell we do. I wanna speak to Lassiter, just make sure we do this by the book, use every angle we can, and then we go pick him up. Want Riehl and Littman there, want to hear what they found out from the dean of the college.'

'We can call ahead from the car,' Roth said.

They left the health club, drove west back towards the Second, something at the back of Miller's mind, something that Robey had said during their conversation in the diner. He'd used a strange phrase, and when he'd said it Miller had barely paid attention, but now – thinking back – it seemed out of place, an anomaly.

'What's a squall?' he asked Roth.

'A squaw . . . like an Indian's wife or something?'

'A squall . . . double *l* at the end.'

'A squall. I think that's like a strong wind or something, like a sudden strong wind. Why d'you ask?'

Miller shook his head. 'Something Robey said . . . I don't know. Maybe it's nothing. I'll call Lassiter, get this meeting together.'

Roth nodded, slowed for the lights at the junction of Florida and Eckington, and then the lights were with him, the conversation forgotten. There were more important things ahead; the right way to use their one chance with John Robey and learn what he really knew.

THIRTY-FOUR

Quarter after two. They were all present, everyone except Littman; there in the same second-floor office that overlooked the street. Lassiter, Riehl, Metz, Oliver, Miller and Roth. Littman was still down near the college. He was parked outside and across the street, keeping an eye open for Robey's departure.

Lassiter held court. He asked questions, repeated those questions until he felt he'd drawn everything he could out of the answers. He wanted to know about Dean Edgewood, what the Bishop girl had said, each of them corroborating the other's view that Robey was a loner, a man of few words.

'These characters,' he said. 'They're always the quiet types, always on their own.'

He wanted to know the exact and specific tone of Miller's conversation in the diner. He paused between each answer, he made notes, he asked the same questions in a different way, and after an hour, perhaps longer, he rose from his chair and walked around the room.

'You were right,' Lassiter told Miller. 'We don't arrest him yet. Littman's down at Mount Vernon and will contact us as soon as Robey shows. He took his lunch inside, right?'

Riehl nodded. 'Couple of times I went in there, walked the corridors. The dean was very agitated, didn't like the fact that we were on campus. Robey took his class and, like you said, he didn't leave at lunchtime. They have a canteen in there for the students and the teachers. We assume he ate there.'

'Or doesn't eat lunch,' Metz interjected.

'So we have an alibi for the time of the Sheridan woman's death that is bullshit. That tells us nothing more than he didn't want us to know where he was on Saturday afternoon.'

'Over on Columbia beating the poor bitch to death,' Oliver said. 'He's our guy . . . he's our fucking guy, I tell you. There's something about this motherfucker that I don't like.'

'Funny that,' Roth said, 'because he said the same thing about you.'

'Okay, okay,' Lassiter interjected. 'We're assuming nothing. We're jumping to no conclusions here. Just because the guy doesn't want us to know where he goes on a Saturday afternoon doesn't mean he's Hannibal Lecter.'

'But he likes cute ice-skaters,' Metz said.

'Hey, who the fuck doesn't like cute ice-skaters,' Oliver retorted.

'That's enough with the wisecracks,' Lassiter said. 'We have one shot at this guy. He may be someone, he may be no-one, but we fuck this up and not only do we not get a second chance, we're also up against the D.A.'s office on a harassment thing. We go after him with nothing behind us and we're fucked.' Lassiter paused for a moment. 'The question is this: Miller . . . you figure you can get him to talk to you again? Could you suggest that there's a question regarding his whereabouts that afternoon?'

'I can try, sure.'

'Okay, so we do it this way. Miller and Roth . . . you guys go down and pick him up after college has finished. You take him somewhere social, a coffee shop, whatever. Ask him if he doesn't mind answering another couple of questions. Suggest there has been some difficulty ascertaining the truth of his alibi, that Brentwood was closed on Saturday, and if he bullshits you again tell him that we have more than one picture of him with the Sheridan woman. Gauge his reaction to the alibi thing before you throw the second thing at him. I wanna do this bit by bit. I don't want to show him the whole hand before he makes a play, you know? We arrest him on nothing and he'll have a lawyer get him out in twelve hours, and we'll be up in the D.A.'s office asking ourselves why we've got a pending lawsuit. He seemed willing to speak with you before. If something happens and we have a live one here, then I wanna make his arrest so fucking watertight it'll take Clarence Darrow working overtime to get him out, you get me?'

A murmur of consent from Miller and the others.

'Littman can stay down there at the campus. Miller, Roth . . . go down there and wait for Robey. You guys,' Lassiter nodded at Metz and Oliver. 'You guys go take a look in Homicide, see if there's anything on the Natasha Joyce thing. If there's something you can help with then do so, but don't get caught up in anything that's gonna take you out of the city. I need you on call in case this thing goes anywhere.'

The gathered ensemble rose collectively and made their way out of the room. Lassiter nodded at Miller, asked him to stay back with Roth.

'So what's your take on this guy?' he asked.

Miller sat down. 'I don't have one,' he said. 'And that's the odd thing. This guy . . . he didn't seem anything other than calm the whole time. He took the whole thing in his stride, like he wasn't even concerned that we were after him.'

'Which means?'

'That he has nothing at all to hide, or he has everything to hide and he's very good at hiding it.'

'And which way would you go on it?'

'I don't know, I really don't. Usually you get something, some kind of feeling for someone, whether they're the one or not. Like that thing last year, the thing with the college girl that drowned in the pool. But this guy . . . John Robey—'

'Why the fuck does that name ring a bell with me?' Lassiter asked.

'*To Catch A Thief,*' Roth said. 'The Cary Grant film. His character is named John Robie . . . same name, different spelling.'

Lassiter smiled. 'You're right. That's where it is. I saw that movie with my wife when we first started dating. Anyway, you were saying?'

'Yes. This one I can't tell. First impression I'd say no, he's not the guy. But the more I think about him the more I *want* him to be the guy.'

Lassiter frowned.

'Maybe it's just my frustration. I know how important it is to put a cap on this thing.'

'Which is all the more reason not to fuck it up before it gets off the ground,' Lassiter replied. 'I want a search warrant for the guy's house. I want to start stirring up all manner of shit in his life, but I need something concrete behind our accusation. I don't want some twelve-year-old out of law school shredding us before we even get to ask him the time of day.'

'I'll be real nice with him,' Miller said. 'I'll be so fucking nice to him he'll think it's his birthday.'

Lassiter stood up. 'One other thing . . . I know you guys haven't had any let-up on this. When did you last take some time out?'

'Me?' Miller asked. 'I don't know . . . couple of weeks ago maybe.'

'And you?'

Roth shrugged. 'Saw the kids a couple of nights ago, I think. It's been a while.'

'I understand how it is, believe me. I know you're pissed off at nothing coming back, but you're the best I have for this. I can't send anyone else to speak with the guy, you get me?'

Miller raised his hand. 'It's okay. I wanna see this thing through.'

'When we're done we'll look at getting you a few days off, maybe a week or something.'

'Appreciated,' Roth said. 'I know my wife would love you for that.'

'So go,' Lassiter said. 'Go meet with John Robey and find out why he lied to you on your first date.'

By the time they reached Mount Vernon College it was close to four. John Robey appeared at the front of the main faculty building at twenty after. He carried his briefcase, and in the crook of his left arm he balanced a stack of work books, presumably student assignments to read at home.

Miller approached him, and when Robey looked up and saw him there was an expression on his face that said nothing at all. Once again it seemed that nothing could surprise the man, and Miller thought back to the phrase he'd used, the one about the squall that never became a storm.

John Robey paused on the college steps; he smiled, he

tilted his head to one side, and when Miller was in earshot he said, 'Detective Miller . . . so soon.'

And Robert Miller, taken aback by the man's seemingly effortless composure, didn't know what to say, and so he said nothing.

THIRTY-FIVE

Robey suggested the campus coffee shop, a franchise of one of the bigger chains, and there Miller and Roth found a secluded table near the back of the room. It was decorated to conform with the college atmosphere – wooden paneling, subdued colors, leather armchairs to the right near the window.

Robey insisted on paying for the coffee, and he carried the tray to where they had taken seats.

'So how can I be of assistance now?' Robey asked.

'Just a few more questions, Professor Robey.'

'You can't lose that can you? The professor thing.'

'Seems to me that a man who's earned such a title should get to hear it.'

Robey laughed. 'So ask me your questions, Detective Miller.'

'Just regarding your whereabouts last Saturday.'

'You checked up on me, right?' Robey interjected. 'You went and spoke to whom? Sarah? Per Amundsen?'

'We spoke to both of them.'

'And learned that I was not at the Brentwood Park Ice Rink last Saturday, because neither were they, correct?'

Miller didn't reply.

Robey lowered his head. 'And now I have embarrassed myself by being caught in a simple lie.'

'Perhaps not so simple, Professor Robey. It was important to know where you were last Saturday, and we asked you and you told us. You appeared to be very cooperative, more than happy to answer my questions, but the most important answer you gave me has turned out be incorrect. I am curious as to why you felt it necessary to lie.'

'I wanted to find out how diligent you were. I didn't expect you to come back until tomorrow.'

'I don't understand, professor. You knew we would come back?'

'I certainly hoped you would.'

'I think I'm missing something here—' Miller began.

Robey looked directly at Miller, and the expression he wore was so intense it stopped Miller mid-flight. 'No, detective, you are not missing something, or rather, it would be more accurate to say that you are only missing those things that you are supposed to be missing.'

'I'm not sure that I understand what you mean.'

'There is a very famous quote, Detective Miller. It was made by the Marquis Charles Maurice de Talleyrand-Périgord at the Congress of Vienna in 1814. He was asked what treason was . . . he said it was merely a matter of dates. Do you understand that, Detective Miller?'

'I've heard that before.'

'I didn't ask whether you'd heard it before . . . I asked whether or not you understood it.'

'Sure I do . . . it means that if you support something, a government or whatever, then it can become an act of treason if that government then becomes unpopular.'

'Indeed so.'

'And this has something to do with what we're talking about?'

'It has everything to do with what we're talking about, detective.'

'Enlighten me, Professor Robey, because right now all I have is a false alibi for your whereabouts last Saturday and a lot of other stuff that makes no sense at all.'

'Would you consider yourself a patriotic man, detective?'

'Sure, I s'pose so. As much as anyone else.'

'Your patriotism to the United States of America remains despite the climate within which we now find ourselves?'

'The climate?'

'We are becoming the unpopular aggressors, wouldn't you say? What with Iraq, and goodness knows what else, don't you think the world is finding our arrogance and bullishness a little tiresome?'

'I try not to think about it too much. In my line of work I am far more concerned about what Americans are doing to

346

other Americans, rather than what we might or might not be doing to the rest of the world.'

'Me,' Robey said. 'I am very much the one to take a wider view. I look at things globally, internationally. I look at the long-term not the short-term. I look at the season rather than a single game. You can lose a single game, and as long as you don't lose too many you can still take the Superbowl, right?'

'Right, but I still don't know what this has to do with anything we're talking about, and I definitely don't see what it has to do with where you actually were last Saturday.'

'Where do you think I might have been last Saturday, Detective Miller?'

'Professor Robey, I really don't think it's an appropriate time to be playing games. Me and my partner—'

'My partner and I.'

'What?'

'You said "Me and my partner" . . .'

'Don't even go there, professor. I didn't come over here to get a grammar class. I want to know where you were last Saturday. You told us you were at the Brentwood Park Ice Rink. You told us you were watching someone train there, and we have spoken to this person and confirmed that they were not training last Saturday, in fact they were nowhere near the damned ice rink. So I'm asking you again, real nice and everything . . . where were you last Saturday?'

'And I ask you in return, where do you think I was last Saturday?'

'Why are you doing this, professor?'

'Doing what, detective? You haven't arrested me. You haven't given me any indication as to how you think I might be able to help you with your investigation. You have mentioned the names of two dead women, and I can only guess that you think I might be connected in some fashion. But even now, coming to me twice on the same day, waiting for me outside my place of work, you are still being circumspect and evasive. You tell me where you think I might have been, and I will tell you where I was.'

'Okay, fair enough. I think you were with Catherine Sheridan.'

'Catherine Sheridan . . . one of the dead women.'

'Right, the one that you said you didn't know.'

'I said that, yes.'

'And if you didn't know her, and you're sticking to that, then how come we have found three pictures of you standing right there beside her? One picture I can understand, maybe even two, but three?' Miller turned to Roth. 'What was that thing you told me about conspiracies?'

'Once is happenstance, twice is coincidence, three times you have a conspiracy.'

'A conspiracy?' Robey said. 'I think that's a very apt turn of phrase considering the nature of what you're getting into.'

'What I'm getting into is your alibi, professor.'

'So an explanation of my whereabouts last Saturday has taken on the color of an alibi. For an alibi to exist there is ordinarily a crime. Are you accusing me of being involved in a crime, Detective Miller?'

'I'm not playing games, Professor Robey. This is a conversation I don't want to have with you, and you're beginning to annoy me. Answer the questions please. Where were you last Saturday? Why did you tell us you were somewhere when you evidently were not? Lastly, how come there are three photographs of you with a murder victim named Catherine Sheridan and yet you say you don't know her?'

Robey was silent for an uncomfortably long time. He looked at Al Roth, his gaze unflinching until Roth glanced away, and then he turned his attention to Robert Miller, holding his stare even as he raised his coffee cup, sipped from it, returned it to the table. All of this without looking away, without averting his gaze for a second.

'I am forty-seven years old,' Robey said eventually. 'I work at Mount Vernon College as a lecturer in English and American Literature. I have been there since May of 1998. Before that I was involved in a great many things, most of them of an academic nature, and as a result of my work I came into contact with a great many people. There have been trips to the Far East, to South America, to England, Paris, Prague, Vienna, Poland, and many others I cannot even bother to recall. Some of those trips were to other universities and colleges, some as a guest of the government, other times as an independent observer into foreign education systems. Other people went with me, sometimes people who had been on other trips. Perhaps I had my picture taken. Perhaps I was part of a group, and this woman was beside me or behind me. I'm only guessing, detective, but right now I don't have any better or clearer explanation than you. That's the point here I'm afraid . . . that what occurred and what you think might have occurred are not the same.'

'And last Saturday?'

'Last Saturday I cannot tell you where I was.'

'Because?'

'For no other reason than I choose not to.'

'So it's not that you cannot, it's that you will not?'

Robey nodded in the affirmative.

'You place us in a very awkward position, Professor Robey. We are investigating a matter of great importance and you choose not to cooperate.'

'I consider that an unfair analysis of the situation, detective. You have approached me twice in the same day. You delayed my arrival this morning and then waited outside the college until I finished work, and you are questioning me again. You have offered no cause for your concern about my activities. You have not arrested me. You have not read me any rights. You have not suggested I seek legal counsel, yet because I choose not to answer one question you suggest that I have been uncooperative. I don't see that I could have been any *more* cooperative detective.' Robey rose from his chair. He lifted his cup and drained it. He set it down and reached for his overcoat and briefcase. Miller watched him as he gathered up the armful of assignments and edged out from behind the table.

'So that's the end of this conversation then?' Miller asked.

'I believe it must be, Detective Miller, or I would not be leaving.'

Miller rose. He took a step around the table and faced Robey. The tension in his chest was unbearable. He could feel a thin film of sweat across his shoulders and down his back. For some reason he felt scared. Scared and angry, the way he'd felt at Brandon Thomas's house, the way he'd felt when he saw what had been done to Jennifer Irving.

'I am sorry not to have been of more help—'

'Professor Robey. You seem to have absolutely no understanding of the seriousness of your situation.'

'Quite the contrary, Detective Miller. It seems that you are the one who fails to appreciate the seriousness of *your* situation.'

'Are you threatening me?'

'Good God no, I don't need to threaten you. You are in enough trouble already without any assistance from me.'

'What the hell is that supposed to mean?'

Robey paused. He smiled and nodded his head deferentially. 'We shall meet again I'm sure, though next time I suggest you come a little better prepared.'

'Prepared for what?'

'What you want to know, detective.'

'I believe I have made it very clear what I want to know. Your relationship with the Sheridan woman, and where you were at the time of her death. I don't know that I could have made that any clearer.'

'You are asking about the what and the when, detective, not the why. Good day gentlemen.'

And Robey was away toward the door and gone before Miller could gather his thoughts sufficiently to respond.

Roth rose to his feet. 'Jesus,' he said quietly. 'What the fuck was that?'

Miller couldn't speak for some time. It was there. The feeling he'd had before. The sense of being watched, of being observed, the feeling that there was so little he knew, and so many people who knew more.

THIRTY-SIX

Lassiter shook his head. 'No, just tell her exactly what Robey said.'

Miller looked at the woman facing him – Assistant District Attorney Nanci Cohen. Three times he'd met her, and three times he'd been impressed by the sheer tenacity of the woman. She neither looked nor dressed like a lawyer. Her hair was not pinned back in an austere, almost masculine style; no business suit in navy blue or charcoal chalk stripe with patent leather shoes, no brusque manner or sharp attitude ordinarily embraced by such women. Nanci Cohen dressed like a middle-aged Jewish station wagon-driving mom collecting her kids from after-school Hebrew tutorials. There would be fresh-baked cookies, cold milk, washing hands before homework, other such things. But Nanci Cohen was forty-eight and single. Rumor had it she was fucking a twenty-seven-year-old paralegal from a major city law firm. Rumor had it she'd inherited a fortune from her grandfather's delicatessen business, started when he came out of liberated Germany and made it good in the U.S. Rumor also had it there were other rumors . . . No-one knew what to believe, and very few people ultimately cared. Nanci Cohen did what very few ADAs would do these days – she came down to the precinct when help was needed and answered questions the way they needed to be answered.

'He said that he chose not to answer the question—' Miller started.

'About where he was last Saturday?' Nanci interjected.

'Yes, about where he was. And then just before he left he said that thing about how we were asking the wrong questions, that we were asking about the what and the when, not the why.'

Nanci Cohen was writing as Miller spoke. 'So let me get

this straight. This is the second time you're talking to him, right? You spoke with him this morning at the diner, and then he goes back to school, he does his lessons or whatever, and when he comes out of the college you're waiting for him and he takes you for a cup of coffee.'

'That's right.'

Nanci smiled knowingly. 'And this guy pays for the coffee, right?'

Miller nodded.

'He's a smart boy,' she said matter-of-factly. 'You look at that from an exterior viewpoint. Look at that how a judge is gonna see it. John Robey goes into a diner to get his morning coffee, same as always. There's a bunch of cops there who wanna talk to him about someone. They show him a picture. He says he doesn't remember this person, either by name or from the photograph. The cops mention another couple of names and he says he's none the wiser. The cops let him go. He's very polite. He's not defensive. He makes like he's being real helpful, and then he's on his way. Same cops are waiting for him when he comes out of school in the afternoon. They wanna ask him some more questions. He's Mister freakin' Polite again, he takes them for coffee right there on the campus grounds. He's a good citizen. He doesn't resent the police giving him a little attention. I'm surprised he didn't buy you blueberry muffins as well.'

Miller shook his head. 'There were no muffins.'

'Jesus,' Nanci Cohen said, exasperated. 'I don't know that you could've gotten yourselves into a tighter situation if you'd tried.'

'How so?' Roth asked.

'How so? You're a Jew, right?'

Roth frowned. 'Sure I am. What the fuck's that got to do with anything?'

'Don't say anything else,' Nanci Cohen said. 'You're being an embarrassment to our people, okay? We're s'posed to be the smart ones around here, for God's sake.' She reached down into a cavernous leather bag beside her chair and retrieved a bottle of water. She popped the cap and took a generous swig. 'Okay, okay, okay,' she said quietly, and then she leaned back in the chair and sort of half-closed her eyes.

'So we have nothing except the photographs and the word of a dead girl from the projects, a black girl who fathered a child with a known drug user, possibly a dealer, to say that this guy went down there to see the druggie . . .' Her voice trailed away into silence. Miller glanced at Lassiter. Lassiter shook his head and touched his finger to his lips.

'You have three choices,' she said after a short while. 'Number one, you arrest him on suspicion of attempting to pervert the course of justice. You read him his rights, he gets a lawyer, and then he either answers the questions about where the hell he was last Saturday or he pleads the Fifth. If he pleads then you might have something you can take before a judge for a search warrant on the property. You get inside the property you might find something that ties him to the Sheridan woman or another of the victims. Secondly, you can cite 1989, Lansing versus California State, where a motion to suppress an affidavit from a deceased party was overturned. You could work that in such a way as the black woman's confirmation of Robey's presence with Sheridan gives you reason to believe he's lying. It's slim – you'd need a very open-minded judge – but it could be tried. Thirdly, and this is what I would do . . . you go visit him at home and you talk real nice to him, and I mean *real* nice, and you hope to God he lets you into his house.'

'For what purpose?' Miller asked.

'To keep the monologue going. Jesus, you people are the detectives here. You've got someone who *wants* to talk, for God's sake. He's even challenging you about the damned questions you're asking him. He tells you to come back next time with some smarter questions, right? That's as good an invitation as you're gonna get. You better get a shoeshine and a brush-up, change your freakin' shirt and go down there and talk very pleasantly to him and see what else he's gonna give up.' Nanci Cohen turned and looked at Roth. 'You,' she said. 'You like this guy for these killings?'

Roth shook his head. 'I like him for something. Whether it's these killings or not I don't know, but I like him for something.'

'Seems to me he's all too happy to speak with you, but you're not giving him anything interesting to talk about.

You have to figure out how to ask him what he wants to be asked, and then go see him.'

'And what is it that he wants to be asked, d'you think?' Miller asked.

Nanci Cohen sighed and shook her head. She looked at Lassiter. 'These guys the best you got?'

Lassiter smiled. 'I'm afraid so . . . you know what they say, you just can't get the help these days.'

She turned back to Miller. 'Sweetheart, he's already told you what he wants you to ask him. He wants you to ask him—'

'Why,' Miller said.

'On the freakin' nail,' she replied. 'He wants you to ask him why.'

'What about a wire?' Roth asked.

Nanci Cohen turned and scowled at him. 'Thought I told you not to speak. A wire, for God's sake. Are you serious? This guy has done nothing. You have zero on him, absolutely zero. We take it for granted he's lying. This thing with the pictures doesn't wash with me. I also believe what you say about the black woman down in the projects, but we don't have probable cause, we don't have any testimony that'll stand up to a gentle breeze let alone a judge.' She looked at Miller. 'You,' she said. 'He talks to you more than he talks to your Jewish buddy here, right?'

Miller nodded. 'Sure, yes . . . I s'pose he does.'

'Then you go down there. Go to his home. See if you can talk your way in there. Be concerned. Be interested in what he has to say. Find a way to ask him why *he* thinks these women are being killed. If he's your whacko then he's gonna wanna share his shit with the rest of the freakin' world. These assholes are always the same. All this bullshit about deprived childhoods and God only knows what. So they got a kicking every once in a while . . . Jesus, if everyone that ever got a kicking took it out on a total stranger where the hell would we be, eh? Nevertheless, they're amateurs, and they're theatrical, and a theatrical amateur is the worst kind of pain in the ass.' Nanci Cohen shook her head. She reached down and gathered up her bag. She rose from the chair and straightened her skirt.

'So do whatever,' she said. 'No more bullshit about wires, okay? Don't fuck this up by pulling some stunt that'll get us kicked out on arraignment. Take it easy. Talk to me. Ask questions. Keep me briefed on everything he says and I'll tell you when you have something you can get a warrant for.' She smiled widely at Lassiter. 'Always a blast, captain. Say hi to your wife for me. She's a good lady. She has her head set straight. Gotta go.'

Roth, Miller, Lassiter – each of them said nothing as ADA Nanci Cohen breezed out of the door and started down the corridor.

When her footsteps disappeared Roth looked at Lassiter. 'She's for real, right?'

Lassiter frowned. 'What are you talking for? I thought she told you to keep your mouth shut.'

Miller couldn't catch his breath for laughing.

THIRTY-SEVEN

Miller went home. He did what Nanci Cohen told him to do. He showered, shaved, pressed a clean shirt and put on a tie. He took the best of his four suits and brushed it down. He cleaned his shoes, used mouthwash, combed his hair, and then drove back to the Second to meet Roth. By the time he arrived it was ten after seven. Roth was waiting outside on the sidewalk for him.

'You're good with this?' Roth asked.

'As good as.'

'You scrub up well.'

Miller smiled. 'Take a picture . . . you ain't gonna see this again for a while.'

'He has an apartment on New Jersey and Q over past Chinatown.'

'Did Littman follow him when he left work?'

Roth nodded. 'He went to the Carnegie Library of all places.'

'You're kidding me?'

'No, he was there for about an hour, and then he went straight home. Riehl is there now, says he's inside, hasn't moved.'

Miller was quiet for a moment. Robey at Carnegie Library? Another coincidence? 'And what have we learned about our John Robey?'

Roth shook his head. 'Nothing at all. He's never been arrested, not even a traffic violation. His name appears on social security, the land registry, a couple of membership organizations affiliated to the college, and then if you track back far enough you find stuff on him as an author. He published two books, last one in 2001. Doesn't appear to have given many interviews. Seems to have played the whole thing down. Of course, we don't have his fingerprints so we can't check on AFIS or anything like that, but right now, as far as we can tell, he's clean.'

'So we know no more than we knew this morning,' Miller said.

'Seems that way. He isn't exactly a public figure.'

'Public figure I don't need,' Miller said. 'What I need is something that tells us whether or not he's capable of doing these things.'

'So go there,' Roth said. 'Go there and get him talking.'

'And if he won't?'

Roth shrugged. 'Then we're no further backward than we are now. We do what we can until there's something better, you know what I mean?'

Miller held out his hand. 'Car keys.'

Roth took them from his pocket and tossed them toward Miller. Miller caught them and started towards the underground parking lot.

'Good luck,' Roth called after him.

Miller didn't reply, didn't turn back.

He walked down the incline into the semi-darkness of the Second Precinct car park.

Forty minutes later Robert Miller pulled to the curb a half block from the junction of New Jersey and Q Street. He sat there for a little while, listening to nothing but the sound of the engine cooling, the hum of distant traffic, the intermittent rush as a car passed by on the other side of the street. To his left a small group of young women emerged from the doorway of a bar, laughing together; one of them started running toward the crossing, the others followed her, and then they sort of collided in a huddle at the edge. Miller closed his eyes and listened. He listened to everything. He could hear the sound of his own heart, and it was beating fast.

At four minutes past eight Miller stood at the bottom of the stairwell that led up to Robey's apartment. His hands were sweating. Even as he'd crossed the road he'd questioned the sense of what he was doing. There was nothing illegal, nothing discreditable, nothing underhanded about visiting with Robey. He wanted to talk to the man. Rather, he wanted

357

the man to talk to him. He wanted to know what he'd meant, and ever since he'd left his own apartment, that same question had been playing back and forth in his mind. The expression Robey had used, the one about the squall that never became a storm.

And then it came to him. Almost as if it had been there all along. Almost as if it had been wrapped in a box somewhere in the recesses of his mind, and merely raising the question, merely directing his attention toward it, had caused it to open up. The memory surfaced, and he was standing right back there in Catherine Sheridan's house, and he could see the TV screen, he could see the whole room before him, and from the TV came those words.

'Gotta see Poppa, Uncle Billy.'

'Some other time, George.'

'It's important.'

'There's a squall in there, it's shapin' up into a storm.'

It's A Wonderful Life. The movie that was playing when Catherine Sheridan was killed.

The memory came at him slowly, but when it arrived it arrived with sufficient force to stop him cold. He reached out his hand and steadied himself against the wall.

Too many coincidences. Too many altogether.

Miller took several deep breaths. For a moment he felt light-headed, a little nauseous, and then he put his foot on the first step and started up towards Robey's apartment.

Once again John Robey seemed unsurprised by Miller's appearance.

'Detective Miller,' he stated matter-of-factly when he opened the door.

'Professor Robey,' Miller replied.

There was an awkward silence, and then Robey looked down for a moment. 'You have come with more questions I presume.'

'No, no more questions. I have come with answers.' He smiled as best he could. 'Not exactly answers . . . more like information that doesn't make sense, and I figured that if I explained myself . . .' Miller took a deep breath. He tried to focus, to center himself. He tried to make everything level and solid and quiet.

Robey opened the door wide and stepped back against the wall. 'Come in, Detective Miller.'

Miller took a step forward, then another, and then a third. He passed Robey, and when he heard the door close behind him he knew there was no way out of this.

'Come on through,' Robey said. 'Come and tell me what this thing is really all about.'

Miller let Robey pass, and then he followed him through to a room in the rear of the apartment. A dark carpet, a sofa against the right hand wall, the window on the left over-looking the back of the building. The walls were painted a uniform parchment color, and on the wall facing him were a series of line drawings with stainless steel frames. There were eight of them, each no more than quarto-size.

'You appreciate art, Detective Miller?' Robey asked.

Miller nodded.

'These are prints of course, but very good ones. You've heard of Albrecht Dürer?'

'Yes, I've heard of Dürer.'

'These were preparatory works for *Knight, Death and the Devil, St. Jerome in his Cell, Melancholia I*. The one at the top is from the *Apocalypse* series.'

'They are quite something,' Miller said.

Robey smiled. 'They are more than something,' he said quietly, and though his words should have suggested criti-cism, Miller did not feel criticized.

'Please . . . sit,' Robey said, and he indicated the sofa. 'You would like something to drink perhaps?'

Miller shook his head. 'No, I'm fine, professor.'

Robey took a chair from against the wall and positioned it on the opposite side of a low coffee table.

'You live here alone?' Miller asked.

Robey smiled. 'You know I do, or you're nowhere near the detective I thought you were.'

Miller was struggling to find some point to begin. He believed he was not altogether clear on what he was *trying* to begin.

Robey made it easy for him. 'I checked you out,' he said. 'I went to the library after I left you this afternoon. I looked up newspaper reports, this Sheridan woman you were talking about, and I know who you think I am.'

Miller opened his mouth to speak.

'It's okay,' Robey said. 'I am not offended. I understand what you are doing, and more importantly why it needs to be done. You have a job to do, right?'

'Right,' Miller replied. 'A job to do.'

'And there is something that makes you think I can help you – either because I am the man himself, or I knew this Sheridan woman, thus I might understand why she was chosen?'

Miller leaned forward and looked directly at Robey. 'I have five dead women. The first one died—'

'In March,' Robey interjected. 'The second one in July, another in August. Catherine Sheridan was murdered five days ago, and this woman you mentioned before, Natasha Joyce . . . she was murdered two days ago.'

'I thought you knew nothing of these things.'

'I didn't. Not until you brought them to me, and then, like I said, I went and did a little research.'

'You read newspapers in the library.'

'I did.'

'Which library?'

Robey laughed. 'What on earth does that matter?'

'Humor me, professor.'

'Carnegie Library, you know it?'

'I do. I know it well. And if I went down there tomorrow morning and spoke to—'

'Julia Gibb?' Robey said. 'And asked her if I'd been there today asking for newspaper articles about the recent Ribbon Killer murders, would she confirm that I had in fact been there, and that I had asked for those very same newspaper articles, and would she tell you that this Catherine Sheridan who was murdered actually came into the library the very morning of her death? Would she tell you this? Yes, she would, Detective Miller, she would tell you exactly what I'm telling you now.'

'You know the woman there then?'

360

'Yes, detective, I know the woman there. I am a college lecturer. I visit the library frequently—'

'Did you ever meet Catherine Sheridan there?'

'Not that I am aware of.'

'And how long have you been using the library?'

'All the years I've been at the college.'

'Which is how many?'

'I told you. I've been at Mount Vernon since May of 1998.'

'And before that?'

'I was teaching elsewhere.'

'Another college?'

'It's on my resumé, which I know Alan Edgewood has already shown you.'

Miller was quiet for a moment, and then he leaned back once more and tried to relax. 'Tell me something, professor . . . .what do you think about these murders?'

'What do I think? Probably what most people think.'

'Which is?'

'I don't know. A sense of horror perhaps. A sense of tragedy. I look at it as a man, perhaps because we fundamentally believe that if we were faced with such a person we would give as good as we got. We would be better equipped to fight back. The abiding emotion is one of numbness.'

'Numbness?'

Robey smiled knowingly. 'This stuff doesn't touch my life. This sort of thing doesn't even reach me. Numbness. The incomparable ability we all possess to pretend that such things only ever happen to others, and they more than likely deserve it. We are extraordinarily capable of convincing ourselves that it happens over there, and as long as we don't look over there then we won't have to deal with it.'

'I deal with it.'

Robey nodded. 'As do I.'

'In what way do you deal with such things?' Miller asked.

'I possess an inquisitive nature, Detective Miller. You come to me and ask of my whereabouts. You imply that I know something. You mention the names of women I do not know, and then you walk away. I am not going to leave it be. I want to know what you think; why you would consider that I could be capable of something like this. I want to understand what it is about me that gives you such an idea. I am inquisitive. I look. I listen. I try to understand.'

'And from what you've heard, what you've read in the newspapers, what is your impression of what I am dealing with here?'

'You are dealing with a nightmare.'

Miller laughed suddenly, unexpectedly, an inexplicable reaction. It was just a simple statement of opinion, stated so emphatically, with such certainty, and voicing a thought Miller himself had had so many times, that he reacted.

Robey inhaled slowly, exhaled again. 'If I were you?'

'Yes professor, what would you do if you were me?'

Robey leaned back and crossed his legs. He tilted his head back and looked at the ceiling for quite some time. When he returned his gaze to Miller there was something almost sympathetic in his expression. 'I would find the common denominator, detective.'

'Between?'

'The women.'

'The common denominator.'

'Yes indeed. Five dead women. All of them apparently murdered by the same man. They all live in Washington. Right now that's all that seems to exist as a common thread. A serial killer is killing women who live in Washington, but there must be something else. I know I must be stating the obvious. I can imagine that more time has been spent trying to identify the common thread—'

Miller cut across. 'You want to know what the only thread is? The only thread is you. You say that you *didn't* know Catherine Sheridan, and yet Natasha Joyce saw your picture and confirmed that you went down to the projects a few years ago looking for a man named Darryl King. I could take you over to see Natasha Joyce, but hell, oh shit, she just happens to have gotten herself murdered too.'

'He strangles these women, correct?' Robey asked.

'Yes.'

'No weapon,' Robey said.

'That's right, no weapon.'

'The closer you get the more professional you have to be.'

Miller frowned.

'Killing people. You start with a rifle. You graduate to a handgun, then a knife, then strangulation. The better you are the closer you can get.'

Miller frowned. 'This is something you know because–?'

Robey laughed. 'Because I watch Luc Besson films, no other reason than that.' He shook his head. 'I still don't understand why you're here, Detective Miller. I appreciate that you *think* you have something . . .'

'I have a picture of you with Catherine Sheridan. I have three pictures of you with this woman, and on the back of one of them is written "Christmas '82". Does that mean anything to you?'

Robey was silent for a time, and then he looked up and shook his head. 'No,' he said, 'it means nothing of any significance to me.'

'Where were you in Christmas of 1982?'

'God, that's what? Twenty-four years ago?'

'Right,' Miller said. 'Twenty-four years ago . . . where were you then?'

'Let me think . . . '82, '82 . . . I was still in New York around Christmas of '82. I took a temporary job in New York in the summer of '81, and then it became something more than temporary, and I ended up staying there until the summer of '83.'

'What were you doing?'

'Same thing I'm doing now. I was much younger.' Robey laughed. 'It seems like a different life.'

'You were teaching?'

'Yes, teaching, lecturing. Lecturer's assistant was the job title, but the lecturer was sick much of the time so I ended up taking most of the classes myself.' Robey smiled nostalgically. 'It was a good time in my life. I enjoyed New York, not enough to want to live there, but it was good. I met some good people there, people that helped me find myself so to speak.'

'And you left in the summer of '83?'

'I did, yes . . . what is this? This is becoming something of an interrogation.'

'Hardly an interrogation, professor.'

'So I was in New York when this photograph was taken.

363

Perhaps the picture was taken without my being aware of it. Perhaps this woman was a student there, a fellow teacher. God, I don't know. Like I said before, there could be a hundred reasons for someone winding up in a picture and not remembering it, not even being aware of it.'

Miller nodded. 'You're right, professor. I'm not questioning such a possibility. The thing I'm questioning is that it could have happened three times.'

Robey didn't respond.

'And the fact that I took those pictures down to this woman's house, this Natasha Joyce, and she didn't hesitate for a second in identifying you as the man that came down to the projects with Catherine Sheridan. She looked at your face and she said, "That's him. That's the man", and there wasn't the slightest doubt in her mind about who you were.'

'That is something I can't explain,' Robey said matter-of-factly.

'Nor me, professor. I simply cannot explain how she could have been so certain. There was no maybe in it. And she was not a stupid woman. She was very quick indeed.'

'It seems these killings are becoming more frequent,' Robey said. 'Unfortunately, I believe that we are responsible for creating these things.'

Miller frowned.

'The French have an expression. *Monstre sacré*. It means, literally, the sacred monster. It refers to something created that the creator wishes he had not.'

'Your book,' Miller said.

Robey waved his hand dismissively as if mention of his book was unimportant. 'We have anesthetized ourselves, detective. We have anesthetized our sensibilities to such things. It becomes the norm to expect such atrocities on an almost daily basis. Of course, an element of it is generated by the free press, to give them their chosen title. They are free to exclude the good and promote the bad. They tell us exactly what they want us to hear, and I'm not talking about a single case, detective. I'm talking about confusing and misdirecting an entire nation, even the population of the planet itself.'

'I don't know that I'm that cynical or suspicious, professor.'

'Is that so, detective? You think you're not affected by these things?'

'I'm not saying that I'm not affected by these things, but—'

'But what? Tell me how much of the difficulty you run into in your day-to-day work is influenced by drugs – like this Natasha Joyce woman. You say she had a boyfriend, the father of the little girl? He was into drugs?'

Miller nodded.

'That's what I'm talking about. How much of your day-to-day work is directly or indirectly connected to the illicit drug trade here in Washington?'

'A lot,' Miller said.

'How much? Ten, twenty, thirty percent?'

'More than that. I'd say, God I don't know . . . maybe fifty, sixty percent.'

'Fifty, sixty percent. And the bulk of that is what? Cocaine?'

Miller nodded. 'Sure. Cocaine. Crack cocaine predominantly.'

Robey's eyes lit up. 'Perfect. Absolutely perfect. Crack cocaine. The crack cocaine epidemic which has ravaged Washington, Baltimore, L.A., New York, Miami, right? This is a big deal, yes? This is something that has directly affected the lives of millions of Americans, wouldn't you agree?'

'No question about it.'

For the first time Robey seemed actually alive. His eyes were animated, his hand gestures emphatic. 'So who created the monster?' he asked. 'Who created the crack cocaine epidemic that is now a monster in our midst?'

Miller shook his head. 'I don't know. Most of it comes from Colombia, South America . . . the drug cartels out there. They bring it in and—'

Robey was shaking his head. 'No,' he said quietly. 'We created it ourselves.'

'We created it? I don't understand what you mean.'

'We created it. *We* did. We Americans. The taxpayers, the homeowners, the people with jobs and mortgages, the ones with bank accounts and private schools for their kids. The

365

ones who read the newspapers and watch TV. *We* created the crack epidemic.'

Miller was beginning to feel agitated. He didn't get what Robey was talking about.

'You know where the vast majority of cocaine came from in the '80s? The cocaine that kick-started the crack cocaine business?'

Miller shook his head.

'Nicaragua.'

Miller flinched noticeably.

Robey looked at him. 'What?'

'Nicaragua?' Miller asked.

'Sure, Nicaragua. You seem very surprised.'

'No, it's just that . . . it's just a coincidence, that's all. I was reading something about Nicaragua the other day.'

'The fact that Daniel Ortega has surfaced once more? Now that's a coincidence if ever there was one.'

'How so?'

'Bush is struggling. He loses the mid-terms. He puts Rumsfeld out to pasture, and who do they bring in but Robert M. Gates. You know who he was?'

'Can't say I do.'

'Bush Senior's CIA director. He held the position of deputy director for central intelligence under William Casey in the Iran-Contra affair, and now we go full circle back to Nicaragua. Ortega has gotten himself voted back in, the Sandinistas are in power once more, and we are still blissfully unaware of what happened out there, and how we – in our ignorance and fear – allowed them to do what they did.'

'Allowed who to do what?'

'The select few. The government. Those responsible for the welfare and care of the American people. The Nicaraguan war was supposed to be in the name of protecting the American people from a communist presence in our backyard. Was it, hell. They wanted the supply line all the way from South America kept free of interference. It was a fiasco from day one.'

'I don't understand what you mean. You're telling me that the war in Nicaragua . . . the whole Oliver North thing, right? That war was started because the American government

366

wanted to keep cocaine supply lines from South America uninterrupted?'

'Amongst other things, yes. That was one of the main reasons. Not the only one, but the main one.'

'I find that very hard to believe, professor.'

Robey smiled. 'You know John Kerry, right? Ran against George W. Bush?'

'Sure I know of him.'

'Back in the Spring of '86 there was a guy named John Mattes. He was a public defender from Miami. Kerry was a senator at the time, and Mattes started working with him on an investigation into the Contra drug connection. You know who the Contras were, right?'

'The American-backed rebels . . . they were trying to take out the Sandinista government.'

'Right. Well, Mattes said a very interesting thing. He said that what they investigated and uncovered was the very infrastructure of the CIA operations out there. He said the whole thing had a veil of national security protecting it. People were loading cannons in broad daylight, in public airports, on flights going to Ilopango airport, and then the very same people were bringing narcotics back into the U.S. unimpeded. John Kerry, running an office under the Senate Subcommittee on Terrorism, Narcotics and International Operations, worked for two years and produced a report totalling eleven hundred and sixty-six pages. The three major news networks ignored it. Out of something in the region of half a million words, the stories that ran in the *Washington Post*, the *New York Times* and the *Los Angeles Times* totalled less than two thousand words.'

'And this report? This report said that Americans were out in Nicaragua shipping cocaine back into the United States?'

Robey laughed. 'You sound so shocked, Detective Miller. I find it difficult to believe that something such as this is even a surprise.'

'A surprise? I can't even begin to grasp what it means.'

Robey smiled resignedly. 'This is nothing compared to what really happened out there. United States officials involved in Central America could not even look at the drug issue. Anything that could jeopardize the war effort in

367

Nicaragua had to be curtailed. America's senior policy makers knew that drug money was a perfect solution to the Contras' funding problems. There was another guy, a man named Jack Blum. He was former chief counsel to Kerry's subcommittee. You want to know what he said before the 1996 Senate hearings?' Robey didn't wait for Miller to reply. He got up, crossed the room, and from a drawer in the desk near the window he took a sheaf of papers and started leafing through them.

'Here,' he said, and sat down again. 'Jack Blum, 1996 Senate Hearings for the Senate Subcommittee on Terrorism, Narcotics and International Operations, quote: "We don't need to investigate the CIA's role in Contra drug trafficking. We already know. The evidence is there. Criminal organizations are perfect allies in covert operations. The two go together like love and marriage. The problem is that they then get empowered by the fact that they work with us. There was a judgement call here. We looked the other way. That judgement call erred so far on the wrong side of where judgement should have been that we wound up with a terrible problem."'

Robey looked up and smiled at Miller. 'That's what he said before the Senate. And you know what they did?'

'Nothing?'

'Precisely, detective.'

Robey leafed through more pages. 'Here,' he said. 'An article in the San Jose *Mercury News*, August 18th, 1996 . . .' Robey leaned forward and handed the photocopied headline to Miller:

Roots Of Crack Plague Exist In Nicaraguan War.

'You know what a Memorandum of Understanding is?'

Miller looked up from the newspaper clipping. 'A what?'

'A Memorandum of Understanding.'

'No, I've not heard of that.'

'In 1981 the CIA and the Department of Justice made an agreement. That's what it was called, a Memorandum of Understanding. It specifically stated that the CIA was released from any requirement to report drug-related activities by its agents to representatives or agents of the Department of Justice.'

'You can't be serious,' Miller said.

Robey laughed. 'I'm not serious, no. There's no point in being serious about it. In fact it's probably better to laugh at the sheer idiocy of what we have created here. Jack Blum couldn't have said it better.' Robey turned to his papers again. ' "In the process of fighting a war against the Sandinistas, did people connected with the U.S. government open up channels which allowed drug traffickers to move drugs to the United States, did they know the drug traffickers were doing it, and did they protect them from law enforcement? The answer to all those questions is yes." And he went on to say that he believed a decision was made by those in power at the time. The decision related to the sacrifice, and he actually used the word *sacrifice* . . . he said that the American government made a conscious decision to sacrifice a percentage of the American population in order to raise the money to fight the Sandinistas in Nicaragua. That sacrifice was considered acceptable, because the people who would die as a result of cocaine coming into the U.S. were people that were considered acceptably expendable.'

Miller shook his head slowly and leaned back in his chair.

Robey held up another sheet of paper. 'This is a Senate Committee memorandum. It says, "A number of individuals who supported the Contras and who participated in Contra activity in Texas, Louisiana, California and Florida, have suggested that cocaine is being smuggled into the U.S. through the same infrastructure which is procuring, storing and transporting weapons, explosives, ammunition and military equipment for the Contras from the United States." Another piece here: "Investigation further revealed that the Contras had direct supply lines into black gangs such as the Crips and the Bloods in L.A., and this huge supply of cocaine kick-started the crack cocaine epidemic of the 1980s. Efforts by the Drug Enforcement Administration, U.S. Customs, the L.A. County Sheriff's Department and the California Bureau of Narcotic Enforcement to identify and prosecute the three men believed to be responsible for the huge influx of coke into L.A. have been inhibited and railroaded by the CIA."

Robey smiled again, that same expression that said every-thing and nothing simultaneously. 'That, Detective Miller, is one of the very few monsters we have created. And your killer, your Ribbon Killer . . . well, he's just another product of the same society that allows things like this to go un-checked. It's a slow deterioration of liberties, a gradual war of attrition . . .' Robey smiled. 'You know what Machiavelli said about war?'

'What?'

'He said, "War cannot be avoided. It can only be post-poned to the advantage of your enemy." So that's what we did in Nicaragua. We did not postpone the war and give the Sandinistas the advantage. We took the war to them.'

Miller's head had started to hurt. 'We have gotten off the subject,' he said. 'It's getting late—'

'I am sorry, Detective Miller. Sometimes I get a little heated about such issues.'

'Might I use your bathroom before I go, professor?'

'Of course. Out the door, turn right, end of the hallway.'

Miller left the room, stopped for a moment in the dimly-lit corridor to look back the way he'd come, and for a moment he felt like a thief, an outsider. He was tired, no doubt about it, but he felt as if Robey had battered him with information – things he did not want to know, things that were not relevant to the questions he'd asked. More than an hour he'd been there, and he was leaving none the wiser.

He stepped into the bathroom and closed the door.

Moments later, standing at the washbasin, he was com-pelled to open the mirror-fronted cabinet in front of him. For some reason he shuddered. The fine hairs on the nape of his neck stood to attention. He felt a bead of sweat break free from his hairline and start down his brow. It reached the bridge of his nose and he wiped it away. He felt disembodied, as if he was watching someone else as he hesitated before his own reflection.

He knew he shouldn't, but there was something within, something deep that drove him to open that cabinet and look inside. His fingertips touched the cold surface of the handle. He tugged lightly. The door popped open with an almost indiscernible sound.

With his left hand he inched the door ajar and peered inside.

Anacin. Excedrin. A tube of Ben-Gay. One-A-Day Multiples. A bottle of Formula 44. A pack of Sucrets. Chloraseptic mouthwash. A tube of toothpaste.

And then right at the back, second shelf up, a brown plastic hairbrush. He reached in and gently lifted it out by one of its bristles. He stood there with the brush in his hand. He didn't want to look. Had to look. Felt as if here he was committing the worst sin of all. He rotated the brush by its head, slowly, until the handle was clearly visible beneath the light above him. There was no question. A clear partial, in fact several of them, were right there on the smooth handle of the brush.

Miller's breath caught in his chest. He dropped the brush into the sink and it clattered noisily around the drain and came to rest. He reached out suddenly and flushed the toilet handle. The sudden rush of water startled him. Miller hesitated for a moment, and then he took a handkerchief from his jacket pocket, and once again lifting the brush by its bristles, he wrapped it in the handkerchief and tucked it into his inner pocket. He stood there for a moment, his heart thundering, his nerves like taut wires. A sense of nausea invaded his chest. He believed he might be sick right then and there. He washed his hands, dried them furiously on a towel hanging on the rail beside the sink, and then he opened the door.

'You okay?'

Miller jumped suddenly.

Robey was standing right against the door, almost as if he'd been caught pressing his ear against it and stepped back suddenly for fear of being discovered.

'Yes,' Miller blurted. 'Yes, yes, I'm fine . . . just tired.'

Robey nodded understandingly. He stepped back to allow Miller past, and then walked with him to the front door of the apartment. He opened it, and before he stood aside to allow Miller out, he turned and said, 'Perhaps we will talk again, Detective Miller. I, for one, have enjoyed your company.'

Miller extended his hand and they shook.

371

'I'm sorry I could not have been of more help to you.'

'It was at least interesting,' Miller said. 'Goodnight.' He stepped past Robey and out into the exterior walkway.

'Have a safe journey, detective,' Robey said, and closed the door behind him.

THIRTY-EIGHT

En route to Pierce Street Miller found it hard to concentrate.

He had forgotten to ask Robey how he knew Sarah Bishop's trainer; to question him again regarding the afternoon of Saturday the 11th.

Tomorrow morning he would face Lassiter and Nanci Cohen, and what would he be able to tell them?

That he had stolen a hairbrush from Robey's apartment?

At one point he pulled over to the side of the road. He opened the window and took deep breaths. A rush of nausea left his body damp with sweat.

After ten or fifteen minutes he wound up the window, started the engine, drove on toward Pierce.

Marilyn Hemmings was just leaving. 'A late one?' she asked.

Miller took the handkerchief from his inside jacket pocket and opened it up for her.

'Whose is this?' she asked.

Miller shook his head.

'You don't know or you're not going to tell me?'

'The latter.'

'So you do know?'

'Yes.'

'And do they know you have it?'

'I figure they will soon enough.'

'And what do you want me to do with it?'

'Can you take prints off of it?'

Hemmings looked at Miller, her expression one of concern, and then she took the hairbrush carefully by the bristles and turned the handle toward the light.

'There's some things I can look at here,' she said. 'This is from a suspect we don't have on file, right?'

'We don't know whether he's on file or not. We don't have any prints for AFIS if that's what you mean.'

'But now you're hoping we do.' She hesitated for a moment. 'I do this then I'm an accomplice to whatever it was you did, you understand that?'

Miller nodded.

'So answer me this question . . . what makes you think that I'm gonna do what you want?'

'Nothing. I don't know that you *are* going to do it. I just figured that you might.'

'You ever do something like this before?'

'No, never before.'

'This is on the Ribbon Killer guy?'

'Yes, I think so.'

'This conversation didn't take place, you understand that?'

'I understand.'

'Call me in the morning, maybe ten, eleven o' clock. I'll see what we have.'

'I really appreciate—'

Hemmings did not smile. She shook her head. 'Go,' she said coldly. 'Get out of here. You didn't come here tonight. I didn't see you. Like I said, this conversation never happened.'

'I owe you.'

'For what, Detective Miller? I didn't do anything.'

Miller nodded. He turned and started walking. There was a line somewhere. He'd walked over it. It did not feel good.

An hour later, sitting at his computer, he typed 'CIA Drugs' into a search engine. He was offered thousands of pages to visit. He opened up a site and scanned what was before him:

Operation Snow Cone. Operation Watch Tower. Secret beacons stationed at remote locations between Colombia and Panama to assist CIA drug pilots flying from America to Panama at near-sea level without being detected by U.S. drug interdiction aircraft. Destination was Albrook Army Airfield in Panama. Operation Buy Back, using CIA-front organization Pacific Seafood Company. Drugs are packed into shrimp containers and shipped to various points in the U.S. A joint CIA-DEA operation. Operations Short Field, Burma Road, Morning

Gold, Backlash, Indigo Sky and Triangle. Information provided by CIA and Office of Naval Intelligence operatives Trenton Parker, Gunther Russbacher, Michael Maholy and Robert Hunt. Recommended reading: Rodney Stich's seminal work 'Defrauding America'. Estimated profits from the CIA's combined marijuana and cocaine smuggling operations sits between ten and fifteen billion U.S. dollars.

Miller closed down the files, typed in 'Nicaragua Oliver North Cocaine Smuggling.'

It was as if a different world had opened up before him, a world he had never questioned, never considered. Page after page of testimonials and documents were right there before him. He chose one at random, read through it with ever-increasing unease:

On Feb 10th, 1986, Lt. Colonel Oliver North was informed that a plane being used to run materials to the Contras was previously used to run drugs, and that the CIA had chosen a company whose officials had known criminal records. The company, Vortex Aviation, was run by a man named Michael Palmer, one of the biggest marijuana smugglers in U.S. history, who was under indictment for 10 years of trafficking in Detroit at the same time that he was receiving $300,000 in U.S. funds from a State Department contract to ferry 'humanitarian' aid to the Contras. Simultaneously, DIACSA, a Miami-based company used to launder Oliver North's arranged funding for the Contras, was run by Alfredo Caballero, a business associate of Floyd Carlton, a pilot who flew cocaine for Panama's General Manuel Noriega. Carlton ultimately testified against Noriega at his trial.

And another:

On Nov. 26th, 1996, Eden Pastora, an ex-Contra leader, stated before the Senate Select Intelligence Committee: 'When this whole business of drug trafficking came out in the open in the Contras, the CIA gave a document to Cesar, Popo Chamorro, Marcos Aguado and me . . . they said this is a document holding us harmless, without any responsibility, for having worked in the U.S. security . . .'

Miller closed the files. He shut the computer down. His eyes were gritty, his head pounded. He was hungry but could

375

not consider eating. He did not want to know what had been done. He did not want to see the sacred monster.

Robert Miller just wanted to sleep, but he knew he would not.

THIRTY-NINE

Nanci Cohen looked at her watch for the third time in five minutes. 'You have me only for a matter of minutes,' she said abruptly.

It was a little before ten, morning of Friday the 17th.

Roth sat to Miller's right, Lassiter to the left beside ADA Cohen.

'So he let me in,' Miller said.

'And he told you what?'

'He told me nothing,' Miller said.

Nanci Cohen frowned. She reached into her voluminous bag for a notepad and a pen. 'He told you nothing? How can he have told you nothing?'

'I don't mean that he told me nothing, he just told me a lot of stuff that I haven't figured out the precise relevancy of yet.'

'So?' she asked. 'What did he tell you?'

'About cocaine.'

'Cocaine?'

'About cocaine smuggling in Nicaragua.'

Roth turned suddenly. 'The newspaper clipping beneath her bed.'

'The what?' ADA Cohen asked, and then she nodded her head and smiled. 'Beneath the Sheridan woman's bed, right? He left a newspaper clipping there about the Nicaraguan election.'

'And this guy talked to you about Nicaragua?' Lassiter asked.

Miller nodded.

'He's fucking playing with us, isn't he?' Nanci Cohen said. There was a wry smile in her tone. 'He's playing with us. He's teasing us. I mean, tell me the odds, for God's sake. We find a newspaper clipping about the Nicaraguan election beneath

Catherine Sheridan's bed, and you go over to see the guy and he just happens to end up talking to you about Nicaragua.'

'He was making a point,' Miller said.

'You're telling me that this was a coincidence?' she asked.

'I don't know what it was . . . it left me disturbed to say the least.'

'What did? He did?'

'No, not him. What he said. About coke smuggling in Nicaragua . . .'

'You mean Ollie North and the CIA?' Nanci asked.

'Yes,' Miller replied.

'Old fucking news, amigo. You know Janet Reno?'

'Sure I do.'

'Right . . . well she is one very tough lady. Anyway, the Miami PD discovered that Contras were being trained in Florida, paid for with money from coke trafficking. Filed this huge report, I mean it was fucking huge, and they gave it all to the FBI. Had a stamp on every page that said "Record furnished to George Kosinsky, FBI", the name of the agent they collaborated with. And yet despite this report Janet Reno, Chief Prosecutor for the State of Florida, saw no reason to investigate the matter further. You can't tell me that a tough lady like that would be backed off by some coke dealer somewhere. She was told not to look into it. She was asked politely to turn the other way, you know what I mean? Like I said already, this is old news.'

'Whatever it is, that's what Robey talked about.'

'Jesus,' Lassiter said. 'Who the fuck is this guy?'

Nanci Cohen waved her hand at Lassiter and he fell silent. 'So?' she asked.

'So I don't know how he fits into this,' Miller said, 'but still I can't get away from the identities of these women . . . the fact that we have not been able to establish precise and factual histories for any of them.'

'The black woman?' Cohen asked.

Miller shook his head. 'I don't think she was part of this guy's agenda. She started talking to us. Maybe she knew something, maybe she didn't . . . there's a good possibility we'll never know exactly how she and Darryl King were involved. Anyway, the mere fact that she was talking to us was reason enough for him to kill her. The first four . . . I think they are connected – and I think that Robey knows something. I think he's involved. I have no idea if he's the one who killed these women, but I am convinced he knows something and he's trying to tell us what he knows without implicating himself.'

'And the thing with Nicaragua?' Nanci Cohen asked.

Miller shrugged. 'God knows.'

'We've got two pointers . . . the newspaper clipping and this lecture you got last night, but it still doesn't really give us anything. Not for a search warrant, and certainly nothing to justify an arrest.'

'We have to follow up on these identities,' Miller said.

'Sure you do,' Nanci Cohen said. 'You need to do the work that should have been done back when the first one happened. Someone hit a brick wall and stopped. That was just plain lazy as far as I'm concerned.'

Lassiter opened his mouth to speak.

'Save it, Frank,' Cohen said. 'I get the picture. Not enough good people, not enough funding, overtime caps, the same shit we all run into. It happens, okay? I'm not criticizing anyone. I'm not pointing the finger at anyone. But now we have five dead women and we better get our act together before there's another one.' She looked at her watch. 'I have to go. I don't want to hit traffic.'

At the door she looked back toward Miller. 'You did good to get in there,' she said, 'but right now I've gotta figure out some reason to pull him in, something a little more substantial than wasting police time. Meanwhile, follow up on your IDs. And Frank?'

Lassiter looked up at Nanci Cohen.

'Call me when you have something I can do something with, okay?'

Lassiter raised his hands in a conciliatory manner. He smiled and shook his head. 'What d'you want me to do, Nanci?'

'Hell, I don't know, Frank . . . get something better.'

And with that she was gone.

Roth, Miller and Lassiter said nothing. Lassiter got up

slowly. He walked to the door, and when he reached it he looked back at the two detectives.

'I don't know what to say,' he said quietly. 'Follow the IDs. Get something she can do something with, okay?'

'Can we have more people?' Miller asked. 'Maybe Metz . . . Oliver too?'

'You are the people I have,' Lassiter replied. 'Just you. I've got three other murders, a manslaughter, some gang of ass-hole joy riders terrorizing Gallery Place down in Chinatown. You want to know the truth? Catherine Sheridan was six days ago. She's old news now. And Natasha Joyce? Hell, Natasha Joyce was some black woman down in the projects that no-one except us gives a damn about. I don't know how to tell you this any better, but you are as good as it gets on this thing.'

Lassiter shook his head resignedly and left the room.

'Do me a favor,' Miller said to Roth. 'Get all the files we have, everything on all five victims, and bring them up here. I have to go run an errand. I shouldn't be more than half an hour or so, okay?'

Roth got up from his chair.

Miller watched him go, and then he made his way quickly down the back stairs and out the rear of the building.

FORTY

Miller took an inconspicuous sedan from the car pool, told the pool chief he'd be back within the hour. He drove east toward Pierce, found Hemmings in her office and walked in without knocking.

'I don't know what you did but I don't like it,' Marilyn Hemmings said. 'And I am very, very tempted to ask you precisely where this came from. If it came from where I *think* it came from . . .' She shook her head. 'No, I'm not asking, and I'm not making any assumptions. I already told myself that I wouldn't ask you about this.'

'So what is it?' Miller asked.

'The prints? God, I don't even want to know what this is about, Robert. The prints came back flagged. I can't tell you who they belong to.'

'Flagged?'

'Right. Flagged. You understand what that means?'

'That whoever this is . . . that this person is . . .'

'Is FBI or NSC or Internal Affairs or Department of Justice. God, any number of groups within the intelligence community.'

'DEA?' Miller asked.

'Defense Department, State Department, Department of the Interior, Office of Naval Intelligence . . . any one of them. You know the beat on this kind of thing. Whatever you're looking at stops here, Robert. It stops dead in its tracks. I mean, what the—' She stepped back and took a deep breath. She raised her hands like she was trying to placate Miller. 'I don't want to know where this came from, and I haven't even told you the best bit.'

'The best bit?' Miller could already feel his pulse racing, could feel how his heart had quickened. Marilyn Hemmings looked scared and he felt for her – felt precisely the same thing. He remembered all too easily what Robey had said in the coffee shop, how it was Miller who had failed to appreciate the seriousness of the situation.

'I put the print together from a number of partials, but there was another print on the handle, too little of it to ID. But there were hairs, long hairs, and I got to thinking that maybe the prints and the hairs weren't from the same person. This was just a wild one, Robert, a real wild, out-on-the-edge thing, but I processed one of those hairs and I got DNA from the follicle, and I typed the DNA and made a comparison . . .'

'And it belonged to someone on the system?' Miller asked.

'Catherine Sheridan.'

Miller's mouth opened like he was catching flies. 'You're not serious?'

'As serious as I ever was. I typed it twice just to be sure. The prints are not hers, but the hair is. I even have a physical match to compare it to. I have the woman in my freezer, for God's sake.'

'Jesus Christ,' Miller said. 'Jesus Christ almighty.'

'So who is it, Robert? Tell me you didn't get this hairbrush from someone in the department.'

Miller frowned. 'Jesus no, Marilyn, don't be crazy.'

'It's not someone we know? Someone we work with?'

'God no, of course not. What the fuck do you think this was?'

'I don't know, Robert . . . what was I supposed to think? You bring me this thing on the quiet, I know there's a problem with it . . . You lifted this from somewhere, right?'

Miller shook his head. 'I'm not saying anything, Marilyn. What you don't know—'

'Okay, okay . . . so you lifted this from somewhere and you bring it to me on the quiet, and you ask me to check it out and I find flagged prints, and hair belonging to our murder victim. What the hell am I supposed to think?'

'Where's the hairbrush now?' Miller asked.

'I have it in the evidence room.'

'Get it for me,' Miller said. 'I have to put it back where it came from.'

She laughed nervously. 'You can't be serious . . . no way! You're not going to—'

'What the hell do you expect me to do with it? Of course I'm going to put it back. It's not staying here, and I'm not having it any nearer to you than it needs to be. Get it for me and I'll be gone, okay?'

Marilyn Hemmings paused for a moment or two, and then she hurried out of the room. She was back within moments, in her hand a blue evidence bag containing the brush. Miller rolled it up tight and put it in his jacket pocket.

'So what do you have?' Hemmings asked.

Miller shook his head. 'I have a liar. I have a man who says he knows nothing who evidently knows a hell of a lot more than he's saying . . .'

'Do I have to tell you to be careful?'

Miller's expression didn't change.

'I mean it, Robert. I want you to be careful. I don't know what the hell you've gotten yourself into, but you're too good to waste it all on one case.'

'It's alright,' Miller said. 'It's gonna work out. Trust me.'

Hemmings smiled, started to laugh. 'That sounds like the sort of thing they say in movies just before it all goes to shit.'

'Let's hope not, eh?' Miller said. 'Thanks for your help, okay? I really do mean that.' He wanted to reach out and take her hand. He wanted to put his arms round her. He wanted to tell her that she'd been in his thoughts, but he couldn't say these things. He couldn't do anything but walk to the door and leave quietly. He drove back to the Second and put the hairbrush inside a sneaker in his locker. Twice he checked that the locker was closed up tight before he left the changing area, and when he reached the door he went back and checked it a third time. He felt like crap. He felt afraid, tired, unsettled. He felt like a criminal and a thief and a liar. He tried to convince himself that he was doing the right thing, but it was merely a rationalization. He had broken the law. Plain and simple. The simple fact that he'd broken the law and learned something of use, knowing full well that he would never be able to use that something, only served to make it worse.

*

He took the stairs back up to the second-floor office and found Al Roth amidst the files.

'This is bullshit,' Roth said as Miller appeared. 'This is pretty much the worst administration . . . Jesus, I don't even know where to begin on this stuff.' He tossed a manila file on the desk and stood up. He walked to the window, hands in his pockets, and stood there for a little while. He arched his back and inhaled noisily.

Miller looked through the pile of folders. Margaret Mosley's case sheet was incomplete. Half the page was blank, the other half barely legible. In the Rayner file he found three interview sheets that belonged to Barbara Lee, an autopsy report, no case sheet, and scrawled across the top of the back cover a question from Metz: *Where's the original incident report?* He read the words, but he could not concentrate. All he could see was the brush, the hair tangled through the bristles, the certainty that Robey had lied and lied and lied . . .

'So Catherine Sheridan becomes Isabella Cordillera,' Roth said, interrupting Miller's thoughts. He had a whiteboard from one of the adjacent offices. He had Catherine Sheridan's name on the board. Underneath he had written Isabella Cordillera, underlined it twice. 'And Isabella Cordillera died in a car accident in June 2003. However, the details of this supposed car accident aren't available.'

Miller – forcing himself to focus on what Roth was saying – indicated the right hand side of the whiteboard. 'Write single on there.'

'Single?'

'Sure. Write the word "single" and then write "no known friends."'

Roth did so. 'Then we have Margaret Mosley,' he said. 'No record in June '69 of anyone of that name being born.'

'The same with all of them,' Miller interjected. 'And don't forget Michael McCullough.'

'Criminals,' Roth said. 'Informers, witness protection like we said. At least that would make sense, but how the hell do you find out?'

'I don't think you can,' Miller said. He realized his fists were clenched, his knuckles white. His heart was slowing, the sweat back of his hairline was drying and making his scalp itch. He could not remember a time when he'd been more frightened . . . except after Brandon Thomas. Perhaps then.

Roth didn't reply. He stared at the whiteboard intently.

'*Why* is Robey lying?' Miller suddenly asked, and he realized that he'd uttered something that he was thinking, almost involuntarily.

'Because he killed Sheridan,' Roth said. 'He killed her and he did the others as well. Maybe he's contract. Maybe he's just simply out there to get people on the Program. Maybe that's what he does.'

Miller asked himself what he knew. Robey knew Sheridan. At least knew *of* her. Her hair was in the brush. She had been to his apartment, or perhaps Robey had taken the brush from her house after he'd killed her. A memento? A keepsake? Something that would forever remind him of the special moments they had shared together? Whatever the reason, there was now no question that Robey was in as deep as could be.

He couldn't tell Roth. He sure as hell couldn't tell Lassiter or Nanci Cohen. And when Roth looked over at him, a question in his expression, Miller found himself turning away suddenly.

'We go back to the women,' Miller said. 'Back to the fact that their identities do not tie in with their records.'

'But where?' Miller asked. 'Where the hell do we even begin?'

'Did anyone fingerprint ID them, or were they only ID'd on their records?'

Miller shook his head. 'I don't know . . . I actually don't know.'

'The files,' Roth said, and he got up from his chair and walked to the desk on the other side of the room. Miller joined him, the two of them poring over the documents in each file.

Roth shook his head. 'Not this one, Margaret Mosley,' he said. 'She was ID'd on her driving license and social security number.'

'Same with this one, Ann Rayner,' Miller replied.

'Were they even fingerprinted, d'you think?' Roth asked.

Miller nodded. 'It's standard procedure, surely,' he replied.

'Call Tom Alexander . . . ask him if they have prints on file for them.'

Miller dialled the desk, asked for the coroner's office, waited while they patched him through.

'Tom? Robert Miller. Question . . . you guys have prints on file for all the victims, all the way back to Margaret Mosley?'

Miller paused, glanced at Roth.

'You know if they were ever print ID'd?' Miller frowned. 'No, it's okay. I'll hang on.'

Miller placed his hand over the mouthpiece. 'He doesn't think so. Says they only print ID if there's no physical identification possible . . .' He suddenly turned away. 'Yes, sure . . . you can hold onto those and we'll come over.'

Miller hung up. 'They have them on file but they didn't check the first three, Mosley, Rayner and Lee. They didn't need to because they had positive ID from their personal effects. Let's go see what they have to say for themselves on AFIS.'

Roth pulled on his jacket and followed Miller from the room.

*S*o now I have spoken with Robert Miller.

He came to my house. He talked with me. He let me speak. He listened to what I had to say, and then he went to the bathroom and stole a hairbrush. Whatever he finds he will not be able to use. Something like that will haunt him. He crossed the line. He knew where the line was, right there in front of him, and there must have been a moment – a single, simple moment, perhaps no longer than a breath, a heartbeat – when he made his decision.

Shall I? Shan't I?

Just like me. Just like Catherine Sheridan. Just like Margaret Mosley, Ann Rayner, Barbara Lee, Darryl King, even – in some strange way – Michael McCullough. Thinking of McCullough makes me smile . . . The line was there and they saw it, and there was a moment when they could have made a decision to turn back, to walk the way they'd come . . . but no, they didn't. None of us did. We did what was expected of us, and we did it out of fear, out of some imagined loyalty, some belief that we possessed something worth possessing . . .

Different reasons for different people.

I wonder what Miller's reason is. He is single. He has no wife, no girlfriend. His parents are dead. He has no brothers, no sisters. Robert Miller does not have a family, and perhaps never will. He has his work. Maybe his work is everything. Maybe he tries to convince himself that it is everything, but I know that it isn't. I think he knows that too.

Robert Miller is a star in orbit. A dead star, but a star all the same. There is no light at the end of the day for him. There are no reasons for him to hurry home.

Perhaps he crossed the line because he believed that unravelling the madness of what faces him will give him some sense of purpose, some direction. A reason to be.

387

Perhaps I did what I did for the very same reason. A reason which, in hindsight, seems to be no reason at all.

But now it does not matter. The past is gone; it cannot be recovered or retrieved to live all over again.

And, if I could go backwards, would I . . . Who knows? Who cares?

We will play the game, Detective Robert Miller and I, and we will see what comes to pass.

FORTY-ONE

Marilyn Hemmings was out when Miller and Roth arrived. For this Miller was grateful. He did not want to be reminded of what he'd done.

Tom Alexander met them in the corridor. He seemed tired, the grey shadows beneath his eyes pronounced.

'Overload,' he told Miller. 'Double shift yesterday and the day before. My mom's not well, and the girlfriend . . .' He smiled knowingly.

'So you have these prints?' Roth asked.

'I have them, and then I don't,' Alexander replied. 'Of course I have them, but I put them through AFIS and got nothing. They're running on another database right now, the one we use for screening potential employees, but I doubt anything will come up. The biggest percentage of people is not on any of these systems.'

'What happened when they came in originally?' Miller asked. They had reached the small office at the end of the corridor and Alexander showed them in.

'Standard procedure. When they first come in we deal with immediate spillage issues. You can guess what that is so I won't explain it. Once the cadaver is contained from the viewpoint of contamination, we make an initial exam for any obvious indications of death – head wounds, GSWs, drowning, things like that, you know? These go in a preliminary report. A relatively obvious cause of death doesn't necessarily turn out to be the official cause of death, but we do make our preliminary report based on what we see when the body comes in. Then we do ID. If the body was found at a place of residence there are many things that can serve as ID. Name and address on utility bills, the victim's social security number, driver's license, passport, all that kind of thing. If they all tie up then we don't take it any further. We print the body simply for records purposes, but we don't operate on the assumption that the person isn't who they appear to be. We operate on the basis that this person *is* who they appear to be, and then we're looking for things to confirm the identification, not disprove it. Hence, no necessity to fingerprint the first three. They came in with name and address, positive ID from however many official documents, you know? We see it for what it is. We're dealing with them simply as a dead body. If there's a question about identity it's ordinarily handled by the PD before the body even gets here.'

'So what system is this they're running on now?' Miller asked.

'It's a state employment database. It ties in with AFIS, the DMV records, the Education Board, all that kind of thing. It's something that we use to vet people who apply for jobs in state-funded positions. It was just a thought, you know? When nothing came up on AFIS I figured it wouldn't do any harm.'

'Margaret Mosley was a city employee,' Roth said. 'She worked at one of the libraries, didn't she?'

'She'll be on there then,' Miller said. 'The other two I doubt. Ann Rayner was a secretary for a private legal firm, and the Lee woman was a florist.'

'It should be run through by now,' Alexander said. 'I'll go check if they've appeared.' He squeezed past Miller and left the office.

'So this is another dead end,' Roth said. 'I want to follow up on McCullough. That's the one that sticks in my craw. This pension money that never arrived.'

'You remember the name of the guy at the Seventh that Lassiter said he knew?' Miller asked. 'Was it Young?'

'Yeah, Bill Young. Lassiter said he had a number.'

'We'll call him,' Miller said. He started to say something else, but turned at the sound of Alexander making his way back into the office.

'Ready for some fireworks?' Alexander said.

'You got something?' Roth asked.

'All three of them have been screened.'

'Screened? For what?'

'God knows. All I can tell you is that they've all been

checked out for a government-related position, something like that.'

'It doesn't tell us who screened them?' Roth asked.

'No, just the date it was done. Margaret Mosley in August 1990—'

'Hang fire,' Roth said. He took his notepad from his jacket pocket and started writing.

'So Mosley was done in August of '90,' Alexander repeated. 'Ann Rayner, February 1988. Barbara Lee, September 1999.'

'Where is this database system?' Miller asked.

'In back of the admin office,' Alexander replied. 'Why?'

'Is it connected to the records you have here?'

Alexander nodded.

'Can you check something else for us?'

'What?'

'Can you pull Catherine Sheridan's prints from your records and see if she was screened?'

'Sure I can,' Alexander said. They left the office, made their way down the corridor to the admin department. Roth and Miller watched as Alexander exited one program, started another, typed Catherine Sheridan's name and waited for her file to appear. He did a drop and drag on her fingerprint ID and ran it on the screening database. It took no more than a few moments.

'She was screened,' Alexander said, 'but it was prior to computerization.'

'Which means what?' Roth asked.

'Means it was before 1986.'

'That's all it can tell us?'

'That's right,' Alexander said.

'Can you check someone else?' Miller asked.

'Shoot.'

'Darryl King.'

Alexander frowned.

'Go with it,' Miller said. 'He's on file in the PD database. Has an arrest from August 2001 for cocaine possession.'

It took a few minutes but Tom Alexander found Darryl Eric King, date of birth June 14th, 1974, arrest file from August 9th, 2001. Sergeant Michael McCullough's name appeared larger than life once again.

Tom Alexander pulled King's print and ran it.

'August 1995,' he said quietly.

'Say that again,' Miller said.

'Your friend here was screened in August 1995,' Alexander said.

Roth shook his head. 'So what are we saying here? That all of them were screened for government jobs, every single one of them?'

'That would appear to be the case,' Miller confirmed.

'This gets worse,' Roth said. 'God, this makes less sense than the disappearing police sergeant . . .'

Miller's expression changed suddenly. 'Try that one,' he said. 'Try McCullough. Maybe it will give some detail that will help us find him. Go back to the King file, the record of his arrest from 2001. I want you to run McCullough's name through the system and tell me when he was screened for the PD.'

Alexander had already typed McCullough's name, was watching the screen as it flashed once and then displayed a narrow box in the right hand corner.

'What's that?' Miller said, and then he could read the words within the box. NAME NOT FOUND. CHECK SPELLING.

Alexander frowned, typed the name again.

The screen flashed. The box appeared.

'What the fuck is that supposed to mean?' Miller asked. 'Is that pre-1986 again or what?'

Alexander shook his head. 'Means your man wasn't screened. Even the ones before '86 come up, they just don't tell us when. What this means is that the guy was never put through the system in the first place.'

Miller leaned closer to the computer screen. 'Could there be errors in this system?'

Alexander smiled sardonically. 'Hell, there are errors in everything when it comes to computers. I wouldn't know. I'm in there, Hemmings is in there, you guys are gonna be in there too, but nothing's infallible, detective.'

'You can print off these others for me?' Miller asked.

'Sure I can,' Alexander said.

'And how do we find the date of Catherine Sheridan's screening?'

'I don't know,' Alexander said. 'There would be some paper files somewhere I should think, but I've never needed to look.'

The hard copies ran off the printer. Roth picked them up and the three men left the admin office.

'Thanks for your help on this,' Miller told Alexander.

Roth had already started down the corridor, and once he was out of earshot Miller looked down at the floor, something like a moment of awkwardness there, and then he looked up at Tom Alexander.

'Where's Marilyn Hemmings?' he asked.

'Right now she's waist-deep in a trench full of water trying to get a drowned body out of there without it falling to pieces. You want I should call her?'

'That's a bad attitude you have there, Tom Alexander,' Miller said, and started down the corridor towards Al Roth.

'I'll tell her you asked after her,' Alexander called after him, but Miller, thinking about Bill Young and Michael McCullough, chose not to respond.

Catherine Sheridan is dead.

So are Natasha Joyce and Margaret Mosley, Ann Rayner and Barbara Lee.

My heart is a broken-up thing.

I eat my dinner in a narrow-fronted diner on Marion Street, no more than a couple of blocks from where I live. Chicken-fried steak, a side salad, some fries. I drink 7-Up from the bottle. I dip my fries in mayonnaise and ketchup. It's the way I like them. I want to smoke while I eat but I gave up some time ago and I'm testing my resolve. Catherine always said I had resolve. 'Takes resolve to do what you do,' she said, and I'd smile and nod and say nothing in return.

And now she is dead.

Tomorrow I'll get up like normal. I'll get dressed. I'll wear a suit. I will go to work like any other regular day, and more than likely one of the girls will comment on the suit, and she will say 'Hey, John . . . you got a hot date or what?' and I will smile and nod or wink as if there is something conspiratorial between us, and she will wonder about me. They all do, at least once in a while. They all wonder about the English lecturer in Room 419.

And when it ends, as I know it will, there will be talk in the lecturers' canteen. They will ask each other questions, and they will guess and assume and try their best to figure it all out. But they won't come close. Not even close. And the students will gossip and trade rumors, and wonder how many I killed. Or if I killed any at all.

Why is it, every time you can do something good, the nice people come in and mess it up? Who said that? It was La Guardia wasn't it? Fiorello Henry LaGuardia – 'The Little Flower' – Mayor of New York from '34 to '45. He knew the deal. He knew the kind of people we were. On the face of it we were the good guys, but the shit we did? Jesus, the shit we did you couldn't even keep your head on. And we've been doing this shit for ever. People like me, believing somehow that we were involved in something good, something that would make a difference. Catherine Sheridan and John Robey, all the way out to Managua to make a fucking difference to the world. Well, we made a difference alright, and the difference we made has reverberated right the way through twenty-five years. Right the way into Washington, and all the way into the lives of people who didn't even know what was happening back then. People like Margaret and Ann and Barbara and Natasha. People like Darryl King. And now Robert Miller. Scratched the surface? Hell, this boy doesn't even see the surface, let alone what lies beneath.

Why is it, every time you can do something good, the nice people come in and mess it up?

I'll tell you why. 'Cause there ain't no money in goodness. There's the rub, friends and neighbors. There ain't no money in goodness.

FORTY-TWO

Back in the office at the Second, Roth found his notes from the original meeting with Lorentzen, VP for Security at the Washington American Trust Bank on Vermont Street.

'McCullough opened the account 11th April, 2003,' he said. 'Month or so after he retired from the PD. Deposited fifty dollars. Account manager's name was Keith Beck—'

'Who no longer works for the Washington American Trust Bank,' Miller interjected. He took off his jacket and draped it over the back of a chair near the window. He had Roth's note pad, and from the notes made at the coroner's office he started to write on the whiteboard the dates of security screening for Mosley, Rayner and Lee. He added Darryl King's name at the bottom of the board, wrote 'August 1995' beside it.

'This,' he said quietly,' opens up another avenue entirely.'

'And what avenue do you think that might be?' Roth asked.

'That they were all something other than who they appeared to be. I mean . . . well, we always suspected that was the case with Catherine Sheridan, ever since the Isabella Cordillera thing came to light, but not all of them.'

'You still with this witness protection thing?' Roth asked. 'That would go some way toward explaining why Darryl King might have been cooperating with the police department.'

'Witness protection is primarily federal isn't it?' Miller said. 'Fuck Al, I don't know. Jesus, it looks like one thing and then it looks like something else entirely.'

'Which is probably the way it's supposed to go,' Roth replied.

Miller massaged his temples. It was early afternoon. He had not eaten lunch and somewhere back of his forehead a migraine was gearing itself up for the duration.

'I think you're gonna have to go back to see Robey,' Roth said.

Miller's heart stopped for a second. He thought of the hairbrush – neatly wrapped in a blue evidence bag and tucked inside a sneaker in his locker downstairs. He couldn't believe he'd done it. What had it earned him? It had earned him the certainty that Robey was a liar, that Robey knew Catherine Sheridan or had been to her house, that there was some distinct and definite connection between them, but it had also earned him a sense of futility, of impotence. There was nothing he could do with this information. Even to the point that he'd somehow managed to forget about it while he'd been discussing the case with Roth. And now Roth was telling him to go back and see Robey again. It would give him the opportunity to return the brush, that much at least.

'At this stage I don't think you should speak to him without it being official. We have to coordinate with Nanci Cohen—'

'I don't see that we're going to get anywhere on an official basis. We have nothing of any significance on this guy.' Miller paused, listened to his own words, confronting the possibility his viewpoint would have been different had he not taken the brush. He had compromised not only the investigation, but also his own objectivity. 'We go after McCullough. That's what we were going to do. We go check out McCullough some more, talk to this guy that Lassiter knows from the Seventh, see if he can shed any light on this character.'

'Okay,' Roth said. 'That I can deal with.' He called Lassiter's secretary, learned that Lassiter would be unavailable for much of the day.

'Can you find a current address on a retired captain from the Seventh? Guy named Bill Young?' Roth asked her.

The secretary put him on hold, came back a moment later. 'Have a Bill Young on a personal file here,' she said. 'This is not something I can give you without Captain Lassiter's authority.'

Roth didn't argue, knew he'd accomplish nothing. 'Admin unit,' he said to Miller when he came off the phone. 'They'll have a record of where he is.'

'Just call the Seventh,' Miller said. 'Someone down there is sure to know.'

Fifteen minutes later, much of it on hold while people talked to other people who talked to other people, someone came back with an address. It was four years old, but it was an address. Roth called Information for a number, came back with nothing.

'We go down there,' Miller said, looking at the slip of paper with the address scribbled across it. 'This is no more than fifteen minutes from here.'

Miller asked Roth to get the car, said he'd meet him out front. Once Roth was out of sight he headed down past reception to the locker rooms. He left with the hairbrush tucked down in his inside jacket pocket.

Miller drove, hit the early afternoon traffic. What should have been a fifteen-minute drive took the better part of forty, and when they reached Wisconsin Avenue out near Dumbarton Oaks Park it was close to three. The house they were looking for was on the corner of Whitehaven Parkway and Thirty-seventh, an attractive wooden colonial-style bungalow set back from the road behind a low bank of trees. Miller went up there first, and when a middle-aged woman came to the door Roth stayed back on the sidewalk.

The conversation between Miller and the woman was brief. Roth was too far away to hear anything specific, but after a moment or two the woman pointed back toward Montrose Park and the Oak Hill Cemetery. Roth wondered whether Young had died.

Back in the car Miller said, 'He's in a care home. Bancroft Street, opposite Woodrow Wilson House.'

Bill Young had a crew of nurses who ran interference between him and the world. The Bancroft Care Home was a vast complex of houses on a single plot, presumably an estate that had been modified to accommodate its current purpose. The reception building was a low-rise modern block at the end of a short drive. Security was evident, questions were asked and answered, and by the time Miller and Roth stood before someone who could tell them about Bill Young it was quarter after four.

'He's not so great,' Assistant Facility Director Carol Inchman told Miller. 'Bill has been here a good fourteen months now. Had a massive stroke which paralyzed the left side of his face and much of his body. He's improved considerably with treatment, but he struggles to speak and eat. He tires easily.' Carol Inchman's manner was brusque, yet she somehow also managed to convey some warmth in her tone. She was businesslike, yet compassionate-sounding – precisely the manner that would give potential clients' families the degree of confidence needed to start writing checks.

'Is this matter of great importance?' she asked Miller.

'Very much so,' Miller said. 'Our captain, Frank Lassiter, was a very good friend of Captain Young's, and he felt certain that Captain Young would be able to assist in the resolution of an important aspect of this case we're on.'

Inchman smiled. 'We call him that even now, you know?'

'I'm sorry?' Miller asked.

'Captain. That's what we call him. He appreciates it. I think being a policeman was his entire life, and when he became ill it had a very deteriorative effect on him, mentally as well as physically.'

Miller nodded understandingly. 'So do you think there's a possibility we could see him?'

'I should think so. Perhaps doing something to help might cheer him up. He's been rather down these past few days.'

'That's really appreciated,' Miller said. 'I promise we won't keep him long . . . we'll make it as brief as possible.'

Inchman leaned forward, lifted the receiver and dialled a number. 'Visitors for the Captain,' she told someone. 'Tell him there's some official help required from the police department.' She hung up the phone and rose from her chair. 'Shall we go?' she asked breezily.

Miller and Roth followed Assistant Director Inchman out of her office and down the corridor.

The side of Bill Young's face had all the tension of a damp paper bag. The effect was disquieting, and when he smiled the left side of his mouth merely tightened awkwardly and produced an expression that seemed designed to unsettle. He had lost muscle control around one eye, he blinked with great difficulty, and the pupil had become opaque with cat-aracts. When the nurse showed Miller and Roth into his room, Young appeared to be asleep in a reclining chair, but the sound of the door closing was sufficient to rouse him.

'Captain?' Carol Inchman said gently.

Young turned slowly, and from his semi-prostrate position he looked at all three of his visitors in turn. Recognition seemed to dawn slowly, and Miller realized then that Young was seeing them for what they were: one-time colleagues, fellow police officers, a brief return of something that he'd once been, something that he'd lived for.

His agility surprised Roth. Bill Young was out of the chair and across the room toward them within a moment. The strange grin, the outstretched hand, something that told them that though his body might have suffered a hurricane of trouble, his mind was as present as ever.

'Captain Young,' Miller said as he shook Young's hand.

Young laughed. 'She tell you to call me that?'

'We're from Frank Lassiter's precinct . . . came to see if you could help us with something.'

Young's eyes widened. The right side of his face smiled wider, the left merely tightened a few more degrees.

Carol Inchman backed up a step or two. 'I'll leave you boys to your business,' she said. 'Come see me before you go, detectives.'

She closed the door quietly behind her leaving Roth and Miller standing in the middle of the room, Bill Young look-ing them up and down, waiting with anticipation for what-ever might serve to restore his sense of usefulness.

'We have a case,' Miller started.

'This serial thing, right?' Young said.

'The Ribbon Killer . . . you know of this?'

'Hell, I might be a hopeless case, but I still read the news-papers. You have a wild one there. You said you were from Frank's precinct . . . how the hell's he doing?' Young's voice was strained, but they had no difficulty understanding him.

Miller smiled sardonically. 'Stressed . . . you know the beat, right?'

'Do I know the fucking beat?' He laughed. 'Jesus Mary

Mother of God, do I know the fucking beat. Stressed like the Brooklyn Bridge, right?'

'And then some,' Miller replied. 'We can sit down?'

'Sure, pull up a chair.'

Young returned to his recliner, pulled a lever and came upright to face them.

'I'll give you a brief rundown on what we have and what we don't,' Miller said.

Young raised his hand. 'Back up and go from the start. I ain't got nothing else happening here.'

Miller started in on the case, told Young about the victims, all the way back to Margaret Mosley, told him about Natasha Joyce, Darryl King, the information they'd gleaned, and before he even mentioned McCullough's name Young was smiling like he knew what he was going to be asked.

'You want to know about McCullough,' he said.

Miller and Roth were left speechless.

'Darryl King,' Young said. 'That was the black guy that got killed on the drugs raid, right?'

Miller nodded.

'And McCullough was his keeper. Darryl King was McCullough's CI on that hoe-down.'

'You remember that?' Roth asked.

Young shook his head slowly. 'I don't remember what I had for fucking lunch yesterday, son, but the important stuff, stuff that happened back then . . . shee-it, I remember all of that like it was this morning. I know about McCullough. He came on loan back in . . . Jesus, when the fuck was that? July, maybe August 2001. That gig with the black guy went down a couple of months later as far as I can remember—'

'October 2001,' Miller said.

'That's right. The kid got himself killed. There was an almighty fucking row that broke out and then nothing. Never seen anything like it. All of a sudden it was the most important thing that had ever happened on my watch, and then there was nothing. Like walking out of one thing right into the opposite. McCullough was there for about an hour and then he just disappeared—'

Roth leaned forward, frowning. 'I'm sorry, what did you say?'

'What?'

'He was around for an hour . . . you said something like that?'

'Sure, yes. McCullough was shot too. Not badly, a flesh wound really. He hung around for like two weeks, maybe less, spoke to IAD, spoke to me a couple of times, said nothing of any fucking use to anyone, and then he pulled out of the precinct and vanished.'

'But he retired in March 2003,' Miller said.

'I know when he retired. I had to sign his final release docket. But he wasn't around for a while before that. I'd say a week, maybe ten days at the most after the King shooting, and then he was gone. Raised a few questions about him, where the fuck did he go, but I just got a polite word that suggested I stop asking after him, you know what I mean?'

'From who? Who told you to stop asking?'

'Chief of Police. Figure that's where it came from ultimately, but it came through the lines. Sometimes you just get the message without someone being that fucking direct, you know?'

Miller didn't know what to make of what he was hearing. Assumption right from the start had been that McCullough stayed with the Seventh until he retired. This suggested an entirely different agenda.

'You say he came on loan from somewhere?' Roth said.

'Yes, he was replacement for someone we transferred. Back then we had a more understanding policy. Compassionate relocation, you ever heard of that?'

Roth and Miller shook their heads.

'Meant that if your folks got sick or something, if you got married and your sweetheart wanted to be closer to her family, then you could apply for transfer to another precinct, even another county. Now they're not so sympathetic. Now they tell you to deal with it or fuck off. Anyway, we had a guy we transferred out to Port Orchard as far as I can recall, and the guy we got in his place was McCullough. But even then, McCullough was not the guy we were supposed to get. Can't remember the original guy's name, Polish-sounding maybe, all Zs and Ks, but something happened with him and we got McCullough. Can't remember where he came from. Think it might have been Vice, or Narco maybe. Good record, nothing too outstanding, straightforward kind of guy. Fitted right in, didn't make any waves. Kept his arrest sheet up, made some half-way decent busts, and then he started bringing in some interesting traffic through this CI he'd cultivated.' Young grimaced cheerfully. 'You know the beat on this shit, right? Well, McCullough had a way with this Darryl King feller. Got us the largest coke snatch of the decade in September of that year. I remember it because it came about a week after 9/11, right before the precinct evaluation. Scored us some brownie points with the chief, you know? Everyone's happy. Everyone's dancing around making whoopee about this bust . . . better part of three kilos. Quite something.

'Well, then the shit goes missing out of evidence lock-up. Just takes a walk right out of there, and the thing that surprised everybody was how un-pissed off McCullough was. He seemed to take the whole thing in his stride, said that we shouldn't worry too much about it, that there'd be other busts, you know? IAD got in there, turned the place upside down, and then it just all went quiet again. Second strangest fucking thing I ever saw. Anyway we dropped the thing, didn't ask any more questions, and then McCullough starts to be late. Starts to show up three hours off the schedule. All this kind of shit kicks off, and I'm having to pull him in and tell him what the fuck, you know? Make his life a misery to the degree that he's making everyone else's life a misery. Finally it comes down to business. I'm telling him he's gonna have to shape up or ship out, and that's when he tells me about this warehouse thing, about this crack-house gig he's got set up with his CI. This thing sounds like the biggest thing since the French Connection. I get all excited like I'm gonna lose my cherry, and McCullough has everyone wound up like a clock spring for this bust. Of course, it all went to shit in the end . . .'

Young paused, breathed deeply for a moment. Roth started away from the bed toward him but Young raised his hand and backed him off. He reached down the side of his chair

403

and pulled an oxygen mask up from nowhere. He clamped it over his face and sucked like crazy. He closed his eyes and seemed to settle down somewhat. A few more inhalations, and then he lowered the mask, hawked a mess of spit into the back of his throat and spat it into a pressed-cardboard kidney dish.

'Excuse the melodrama,' he said. His voice was raspy. It caught in the back of his throat. 'Gonna die sooner or later, you know? Figure there's some scenery left so I'm taking the long way round. Never fucking smoked, had a drink maybe five, ten times a year. Did my job, stayed faithful to my wife, raised my kids good, 'cept one of them turned out to be a faggot, for God's sake . . . do everything right ninety percent of the time and this is what I get.' He raised the mask and breathed deeply once more, and then he looked back at Miller and Roth.

'I was a precinct captain . . . I had the politics and proto-col, I had funerals of Killed In Actions, I had overtime budgets and IAD all over the place, all the shit that goes with that neighborhood. I sent a guy out to Port Orchard, I get this McCullough in exchange. He makes some noise, some black CI gets killed, the bust goes to hell, it's all over within a handful of days. Things moved so fast down there, you know? Even when the shit hit the fan there was very little of it that stuck to the blades, know what I mean?'

Miller nodded.

'So what you got?' Young asked.

'We have a lot of questions about a lot of people,' Roth replied. 'Seems every victim was screened as a government employee.'

Young smiled. 'You don't say?'

'We don't have an explanation for that,' Roth said. 'And McCullough doesn't appear on that system, and there's no record of where he went after he resigned, and even his pension goes to a bank account that never received the money.'

'A ghost you have then,' Young replied. 'You think he was federal?'

'We don't know. Line we're looking at is whether or not

the victims were witness protection, and whoever is killing them—'

'That was my thought,' Young cut in. 'Witness protection people are screened through that same system as far as I know. Whatever the fuck anyone tells you about that program, their names and addresses, their pictures, their aliases, all that shit is kept on files which you can access in most police precincts. Witness protection isn't all it's cracked up to be.'

Roth leaned forward. 'And then there's John Robey,' he said quietly, and he glanced at Miller, and the mere fact that Miller didn't look back at him disapprovingly, the fact that Miller kept looking right at Young to gauge his reaction to the name, told Roth that Miller was interested in anything that Young might be able to help them with.

'Who?' Young asked.

'John Robey,' Miller repeated. 'He's a guy we've got floating around the edges of this thing.'

'Tell me,' Young said. 'Tell me who this guy is.'

Miller leaned back in his chair. He started talking – went right back to Natasha Joyce, the fact that someone went to the projects with Catherine Sheridan to see Darryl King, that Robey had been identified from the photographs beneath Sheridan's bed, all the way to the last discussion about Nicaragua in Robey's apartment, the connection to the newspaper clipping beneath the mattress . . .

Young was silent for some time. The only sound in the room was the strain of his breathing. After a few minutes he reached for his oxygen mask again and inhaled deeply. He closed his eyes and leaned back. For a moment Miller thought he might have drifted off.

'Special Forces,' Young said eventually. 'Special Forces or Delta maybe. Ex-military. These guys are all for hire for the best price. Some of them lose it, you know? They become mercenaries, hired guns. Some of the worst messes we ever got into as a country have been started by people like this. The thing with Bush Senior and Noriega. He put that asshole in power back whenever, and as soon as Noriega started unloading too much coke Bush sends in the gunships. They had a crew of ex-Delta and Special Forces in Old Town,

405

hooked them up with the anti-Noriega rebels, and what the fuck happens? The gunships bomb the wrong target, blow the hell out of everyone down there so there's no-one on the ground to back up the incoming troops. Those kind of people do this kind of work.' Young breathed deeply; his eyes rolled backward as if he was truly exhausted.

Eventually he looked up, anemically pale, his eyes clouded over, spittle covering his chin. 'Seems to me you have a bigger mess than I imagined, detectives. Looks like you have someone out there disconnecting people from something. Has to be a link between the victims. Maybe not the black woman, I don't know. Maybe she got herself killed because someone thought it made sense to tidy up the playing field. But these others? All of them have questions about their respective identities. Too many coincidences, but hell, I'm telling you something you already know.'

Miller nodded in affirmation.

'Dangerous fucking ground you're walking on,' Young said. 'Chasing ghosts over thin ice, right?'

'I don't understand what we have—' Miller started.

'Want my advice?' Young asked. 'Hell, for what it's worth, my advice is stick with what you have, not what you don't have. You like this guy Robey for this thing?'

'For something, yes. I don't know that he's the one.'

'Well, he's a name. He's a face. He's someone right there in front of you. The victims . . . well, they're victims, right? They're not gonna tell you anything they haven't already. And McCullough? He's somewhere, God only knows where, but you don't have him right now. You have John Robey. At least he's talking to you. He might not be saying a helluva lot, but at least he's saying something. Work that line, that's my advice to you. Work on Robey and see what he gives you.'

Miller looked away. He wanted to tell Young about the hairbrush, could feel it right there in his jacket pocket, wondered what he'd have done had he been alone with the man. But he could not. He would not have known what to say. The position he had created for himself was untenable, almost unbearable, and he hoped like hell that Robey would let him back into his apartment, if only to give him a chance to return the thing.

Roth glanced at his watch. 'He'll be out of school in a little while,' he said.

Miller rose from his chair. At once he saw something in Young's expression – perhaps some relief that they were leaving, a chance to rest, to recover something of the strength he had expended – but also a feeling of loss.

Miller did not embarrass Young by trying to shake hands, but merely stepped forward and gripped the man's shoulder firmly. 'You have helped us a great deal,' he said. 'I'll come let you know what happens.'

'Before I read it in the funny papers, right?' Young said. He tried a smile, but he was too fatigued.

Before they left the facility they thanked Carol Inchman for her help, told her that Young had been of great assistance.

'Don't think he'll be around for much longer,' she said. 'Hell of a thing, a man like that. He lost his wife a few years ago, and—' She shook her head. 'You don't want to hear this, and I shouldn't really be telling you.'

Miller extended his hand. 'We have to go,' he said, his voice sympathetic. 'We have to catch up with someone before they disappear.'

Carol Inchman shook hands with Miller, with Roth also, and then returned to her office.

Neither detective spoke until they reached the car. Then Miller said, 'Back to the college. See if we can't get there before he leaves for the day.'

Inevitability.

I'll tell you about inevitability.

Death and taxes, right? They're inevitable.

Tell you what else is inevitable. Love, that's what. Inevitable like gravity.

Taxes you can avoid. People cheat death, or at least postpone it. You read that in newspaper headlines. Man Cheats Death *kind of thing, you know?*

But show me someone who's never loved anyone.

I'm not talking about lust. Not talking about wanting to be with someone so bad it hurts. Not talking about fraternal, maternal, paternal, avuncular. Not about adoring someone, or worshipping, or caring for someone more than anyone you've ever cared for before . . .

I'm talking about love.

Love so strong you can't see it, feel it, touch it, taste it; can't hear it, can't speak it, can't define or describe or detail or delineate; cannot explain or rationalize or justify or reason it all out over a glass of bourbon and a pack of Luckies . . .

Love so strong you don't really know how hard it's holding you until you try to move . . . And you find you can't.

You're stuck tight, and you realize that what you're experiencing is something that's as much a part of you as anything you ever believed was your own.

It is you. You are it.

And you're done for.

It's something you feel for so long, and you feel it is so much a part of you, that whatever happens, whatever the person you love might do, you'd consider it inhuman not to go on loving them for ever.

That's love . . . what I felt for Catherine Sheridan.

And something else that's inevitable? That Robert Miller will find me. He'll find me because I want him to. Because we finally concluded that this thing had to end.

I recall Don Carvalho, the question I wanted to ask so many years before. I can see him sitting there in front of me, see the expression on his face, the quizzical light in his eyes.

'You have a question? You want to ask me if there was someone within the United States Intelligence community who organized, orchestrated, paid for, or in some way contributed directly or indirectly to the attempt to kill President Reagan?'

'Yes,' I said. 'You're not going to tell me that that sort of thing really happens, are you?'

Carvalho smiled. 'Kennedy?' he said. 'Both Kennedys, Martin Luther King – even Nixon was assassinated in his own special way.'

I said nothing. I knew, but I did not want to know.

'You heard what Reagan said when his wife came to the hospital?'

'Some line from a movie . . . something about forgetting to duck, right?'

Don Carvalho nodded. 'Honey, I forgot to duck. That's what he said. Why would he say that, John? He forgot? Surely you only forget what you've already been told to do.'

'He was told to duck?' I asked.

'I'm not saying that,' Don said. 'I don't have an opinion about this one way or the other. Specific events mean nothing. Reagan's assassination attempt will be forgotten in five years' time. It's not the attempt to kill him that means something, it's that someone could even get that close that's really the disconcerting fact here.'

'But what about Kennedy?' I asked. 'Kennedy said that anyone could be killed if the killer was prepared to lay down his own life.'

Don laughed. 'Of course he said that. Kennedy said a lot of things. Doesn't mean that they were true. Kennedy was the golden boy, the one to save the nation, and then he became a pain in the ass just like the rest of them. They created him, just as they'd created every single one before him, and when they had him they realized it had been a terrible, terrible mistake.'

'What does Lawrence Matthews call it? The sacred monster?'

Carvalho smiled. 'Better believe it, my friend . . . you better fucking believe it.'

409

FORTY-THREE

Miller and Roth drove to the college campus, learned that Robey had left some minutes before their arrival, and it was at that point that they decided to separate.

'McCullough,' Roth said. 'That's what I want. Young said that he replaced the original guy assigned to the Seventh. Well, he must have come *from* somewhere. He must be in the system—'

'Thing I'm learning on this one is that nothing is what it's supposed to be,' Miller replied.

'Regardless, the guy was a cop. There's the records we found at the Fourth when we spoke to Gerrity . . . at least that's a start.'

'See if you can't find out what the earlier drug bust was all about, the one from September,' Miller said. 'The one where the stuff went missing from evidence.'

'I'll find whatever I can,' Roth said. 'So – Robey's apartment next?'

They reached the corner of Franklin and New Jersey and pulled over. 'Going to walk the last block,' Miller said.

'And if he's not there?'

'I'll find a coffee shop or something. I'll wait half an hour or so and then go back to the apartment.'

'You're sure?'

'We don't have anything concrete. Six days since Catherine Sheridan was murdered, right?' Miller shook his head slowly. 'We haven't even gotten to Natasha's apartment, let alone the other victims' houses for God's sake. Do whatever you can on McCullough, and see if you can't get Metz and Oliver to get some of these records together on the phones and the internet usage.'

He got out of the car. Roth came around the front and got in the driver's side.

Miller buried his hands in his pockets, watched until Roth drove out of sight, and then started walking to Robey's apartment.

'Detective Miller,' John Robey said matter-of-factly when he opened the door.

'Professor Robey. Have some more questions if you don't mind?'

'Well, as a matter of fact I'm rather busy marking some test papers. Could this wait for another day?'

Miller took a deep breath. He felt the weight of the brush in his pocket. 'I'm sorry, no, it really can't wait. I am following numerous lines of investigation relating to these murders, and there's certain questions I have that I think only you will be able to answer for me.'

There was a momentary flash of exasperation in Robey's expression, and then he stepped back, opened the door, asked Miller to come in.

'You want some coffee or something?' Robey asked.

'Yes . . . please, that would be good.'

'How d'you take it?'

'Cream, no sugar,' he said. 'And could I possibly use your bathroom again?'

'Of course,' he said. 'You know where it is.'

Miller made his way down the corridor, entered the bathroom, ensured the door was locked securely behind him, and then carefully withdrew the plastic evidence bag from his jacket pocket. He waited a couple of minutes, and then he depressed the flush lever, used the sound of rushing water to obscure the rustling of the bag as he took out the hairbrush, opened the medicine cabinet above the sink, and replaced it precisely where he'd found it. He folded the bag neatly, tucked it into his pocket, and then turned on the faucet as if washing his hands.

The sense of relief he felt as he stepped back into Robey's front room was immense. He knew how utterly reckless and ill-considered his action had been. He could not bear to think what might have happened had Lassiter or Nanci Cohen learned of what he'd done.

411

'Your coffee,' Robey said, and indicated a cup on the low table centering the room.

They sat in facing chairs, Robey with his back to the window.

'So you have some further questions, detective.'

'I do, yes. Last time we spoke . . . last time I was here, you were talking about Nicaragua. You talked about a lot of things . . . some of them I don't remember too well.'

'You were very tired I think,' Robey said. 'I myself have spent a little time thinking about who you might believe I am . . .'

Miller smiled.

'You find that amusing?'

'Amusing? No, not amusing. People don't just smile when something is funny. They smile when they recognize a truth where it wasn't expected.'

'And what truth did you recognize?'

'That we spend so much of our time concerning ourselves with what others might think of us.'

'My interest wasn't prompted by vanity or egotism, detective. Perhaps self-preservation . . .'

'Self-preservation?'

'Everything we do is driven by self-preservation, and if not self-preservation then the preservation of something that we consider is ours. Your killer here, he does these things because something is threatened perhaps.'

'An individual who does these things must be insane. He must be, or he wouldn't do them.'

'By whose standards?'

'Ours,' Miller said. 'Society's standards. The rules and regulations we have agreed to.'

'And that is the standard against which you can consider someone insane?' Robey asked. 'You forget so easily the discussion we had last time you were here?'

'About what? About Nicaragua? About the cocaine that was smuggled into the U.S.?'

'*Is* being smuggled, detective. This still continues today. Would you not consider that such things were the work of insane men?'

412

'Of course I would . . . certainly by men who believe money has greater worth than human life.'

'You have to look at the bigger picture,' Robey said.

'And that would be?'

'I'm sorry to harp on about Nicaragua,' Robey said, 'but it's a subject that's close to my heart—'

'Why is that, Professor Robey, why is Nicaragua so close to your heart?'

'I lost a friend some years ago. He was a good man, a colleague of mine. He found out that his son was a drug addict. He came to me, he asked me for help, but I knew nothing about such things. The son overdosed before his father could do anything effective to help him, and the loss hit him so hard he never recovered. Four months after the death of his son he committed suicide. He was a truly exceptional scholar, and I can honestly say that I have never felt so impotent in my life.'

'And how does this connect to Nicaragua?'

'That's where he was from. At least that's where his family was from. He managed to get out before Reagan's war really tore the country apart, but his son stayed behind, fought with the Contras for a while, and that's where he first became acquainted with drugs.'

'I am sorry, professor—'

Robey waved his hand nonchalantly. 'Like I said, it was all of twenty years ago. The experience taught me something however. It taught me that pretending not to see such things does not lessen their effect. In fact, it has been said that the less one faces something the greater the chance it has to master you . . . like your little difficulty some months ago.'

Miller was aware of how obviously his eyes widened.

Robey started laughing. 'I checked you out as well,' he said. 'This little situation you had with the pimp and the hooker. Brandon Thomas, right? And Jennifer Irving? That whole fiasco was another beautiful example of something becoming what someone else wanted it to be.'

Miller was still taken aback. 'I don't understand—'

'What? You don't understand *what* exactly? How that situation was made to appear as if it was something else? A simple matter of questioning a potential witness becomes a question of coercion, of vested interest, of whether or not a police detective is corrupt. Were you involved with her? Did the detective fuck the hooker? Was the argument with her pimp because the pimp saw that the hooker had fallen in love with the cop and might leave him behind? Was it jealousy? Was the pimp fucking the hooker, or was he beating on her when the detective came calling? Did they fight, and was it a fair fight, and did the detective defend himself? Or did he pull his gun and walk that pimp out to the stairwell, and then push him down the stairs? What really happened that day?'

Miller opened his mouth to speak but Robey interjected.

'I'm not asking you, detective,' he said. 'It really isn't any of my business whether you killed the pimp or not. To tell you the truth, if you did it would be of no concern to me whatsoever. The issue here is not whether you killed the pimp intentionally. The question is how the newspapers made it a question of race. The hooker was black, the pimp was a mulatto with dreadlocks. He had a rap sheet. He had been arrested four times in the previous year for aggravated assault. He probably deserved to die. Faced with a man like that in their back yard . . . Jesus, any one of those liberal assholes who bleated endlessly about how you should have been hauled before the grand jury would have prayed for someone like you to blow the guy into the neighbor's swimming pool . . .' Robey paused. He was almost breathless.

Miller was watching him intently, the way he emphatically stated everything as if it was so important. The man was driven, somehow compelling.

'This is the world within which we live, Detective Miller, and this is the world we have created for ourselves, and though you might have a hundred thousand questions for me the truth of the matter is that you should not be looking so narrowly at what has taken place.'

'You say these things, Professor Robey,' Miller said. 'You say these things as if you have some idea of what's happening here . . . like you know things that I don't. And I'm listening to what you're saying, and even as the words are coming out of your mouth I'm wondering what the hell it *is* that you know.'

'I know almost nothing, Detective Miller, only what I have read in the newspapers.'

Miller felt angry, infuriated. He wanted to grab Robey by the throat and shake him. He wanted to hold him still and press a gun to his forehead and ask him how, if he knew nothing, if he only knew what he'd read in the papers . . . then how the fuck did Catherine Sheridan's hair wind up in a brush in his bathroom?

But he did not ask this. Robert Miller did not take out his gun, nor did he raise his voice, nor did he grab Professor John Robey by the throat and push him against the wall. Robert Miller leaned back in the chair.

'I believe you are being too patient, detective.'

'Too patient . . . what the hell are you talking about, too patient?'

'All these things I've talked about . . . about Nicaragua, about the cocaine wars that went on back then—'

Miller raised his hand. 'This is somewhere we are not going.'

'Not going? What d'you mean, not going? It is already somewhere we have *been*, detective. This is the sacred monster you are looking for . . . this is the thing you are finding it so hard to face. You are looking for a man, and what you need to be looking for is a monster that men have created.'

'If you have something to tell me then tell me, professor—'

'I believe that there is something *you* have to tell me, detective.'

Miller thought to respond, and then he stopped dead in his tracks. Robey looked at him with such knowing certainty that Miller felt tension crawl along his spine and grip the back of his neck. He thought of the illegal removal of evidence, of soliciting the help of Marilyn Hemmings, of implicating and involving a colleague in a felony, of how the papers would view it, of the photograph in the *Globe*, and how they would run that picture over and over again . . . Assistant Coroner Marilyn Hemmings and Detective Robert Miller, now appearing before an Internal Affairs enquiry, making statements before the Grand Jury regarding whether they had conspired to implicate respected author and Mount Vernon College Professor of Literature, John Robey . . . hell, if they could steal something from such a man's house, then wasn't it possible that they planted the hair of the dead woman? The dead woman was right there in the coroner's freezer. It could not have been easier. Take some of her hair, wind it between the bristles, and suddenly they have incriminating evidence. How convenient. How perfect. People capable of doing such things were evidently more than capable of falsifying autopsy documentation. Did the mulatto pimp fall or was he pushed? The exonerated detective now looks like an altogether different type of man, and his accomplice, the beautiful and dangerous assistant coroner . . . ?

Miller closed his eyes for a moment. He felt something, but for a moment it was difficult to identify it as fear. For so long he had pretended that these events had not touched him, *could* not touch him, but every time he closed his eyes he saw the image of Jennifer Irving, and then beside it, almost as if those images were related, was the image of Natasha Joyce, the way she'd been found lying there on her bed, the sheer brutality inflicted upon her . . .

'Lavender,' Robey said matter-of-factly.

Miller started. 'What?'

'Does he leave the smell of lavender at the scene of the crime?'

Miller couldn't believe what he was hearing. There was no way Robey could have known about the lavender. It had not been reported in the newspapers, it had not been part of any official statement. Miller's mind went back to the conversation with Hemmings and Roth, the hypotheses presented, that the man who had done these things would've had to have access to police files, the autopsy reports . . . Either that, or he was the one who left the lavender in the first place.

'How—'

'How did I guess?' Robey asked.

'You did not guess, Professor Robey. There is no way in the world—'

'But there *is* a way in the world, detective . . . there is most definitely a way in the world that I could have known. I keep telling you things. I keep pointing you in the right direction.

416

I keep dropping hints and leaving signs, and waving flags to get you to look at what is right there before your eyes, and for some reason you are finding it so hard to see it. That's all I'm asking, detective. That you simply look. Just open your eyes wide and look at what's right in front of you. Ask the questions that you really want to ask. Go talk to people who were involved in these things. Find out what they can tell you . . . more importantly, find out what they are *not* willing to tell you, and then you will begin to see the big picture.' Robey spoke patiently, like a teacher, accustomed to explaining things over and over and over again. 'Most importantly perhaps,' he added, 'you will begin to see what I have seen.'

'I don't know that there is anything that makes sense—'

'Lavender,' Robey said. 'He leaves the scent of lavender at the scene of these killings, yes?'

'I cannot tell you that,' Miller said.

'Which means that he does, because if he didn't you would simply deny it.'

'The simple fact that you are so sure of this gives me sufficient justification to make your interrogation official.'

Robey laughed. 'It does not do anything of the sort. What are you going to do? Arrest me? Take me to the Second Precinct and have me questioned?'

'Yes . . . based on the fact that you have demonstrated specific knowledge of a crime scene that was not in any way made public.'

'Who said I did?'

'I did.'

'So it would be your word against mine . . . Me, the reputable and respected Mount Vernon College professor, and you, the cop who was dragged through the newspapers because everyone thought he might have killed a pimp in a fit of jealous rage? You want to play that game, detective . . . is that really the way you want to play this?'

Miller didn't reply.

Robey shook his head. 'I didn't think so . . . and all you have managed to do is confirm that he does in fact leave the scent of lavender at the scene of the crime.' Robey paused. He closed his eyes for a moment, and when he spoke he said, 'And he leaves a ribbon tied around their neck, yes?'

'That much was in the newspaper,' Miller replied.

'And there is a tag . . . a blank tag, rather like the tag you find suspended from the toe of a dead person when they are stored in the morgue.'

'Yes, that's right.' Miller had lost ground he could never take back. Had he not been guilty of stealing potential evidence from this man's apartment he might have been in a more defensible position. But he had taken it, and he had implicated someone else, and if it came down to it would she lie for him? Would the world believe her a second time?

'So why the lavender, and why the name tag, detective? Why does he leave these things behind for you to find?'

'He doesn't leave them for me . . .'

'You don't think so?'

Miller smiled, something almost nervous in his expression. 'No, he doesn't do these things for me . . . of course he doesn't.'

'He did Natasha for you,' Robey said.

'For me? Are you crazy? What the hell are you talking about? He did not kill Natasha Joyce for me . . .'

Robey was nodding his head. 'I'm afraid he did. I'm afraid to tell you that if you and your partner hadn't gone over to her apartment, she would still be alive today and her daughter would not be with Child Services—'

'How in fuck's name do you know—'

Robey waved aside Miller's question. 'Like I said, I did some research. I did a little digging of my own. I read up on these things so I could understand the kind of man you believe me to be—'

'This is just so much horseshit, Robey—'

'Horseshit? Is that what it is? Jesus, detective, what is it that you are so afraid of? Do you have any idea in the world how wide and deep this thing is? Do you have the faintest clue what you're dealing with here? This isn't about the death of some women . . . this is about the murder of a generation—'

'Enough,' Miller interjected. 'Say what you mean to say or say nothing at all.'

'Or what?' Robey asked. 'You will arrest me? What will you arrest me for? Answer me that question if nothing else, detective . . . what on earth could you possibly arrest me for?'

Miller looked back at Robey. The man was not arrogant, merely self-assured. He possessed no air of self-importance, merely the confidence of certainty. His eyes were still and quiet, his gaze unwavering, and when he smiled it was not a smile of conceit or superiority, but an expression of conviction.

'I say what I mean to say,' Robey replied. 'Always.'

'Then I simply don't understand you,' Miller said.

'Understanding is not a quality that can be bought or sold, Detective Miller. Understanding is something that results from observation and personal experience.' Robey rested his elbows on his knees and pressed his hands together palm to palm. 'I have seen things that would make a dog retch. I have seen children running from burning homes with their hair on fire. I have seen a man shoot his own wife to protect her from what he knew would happen to her. I have seen men buried alive, decapitated, hung and butchered . . . I have seen three or four hundred innocent people massacred in a handful of minutes . . . and all of it has been carried out in the name of democracy, unity, solidarity, in the name of the great and wonderful United States of America . . . or perhaps I am crazy. Perhaps these things exist merely in my imagination. Perhaps I am the craziest person you will ever meet.'

'And are you going to tell me how any of this relates to what has happened to these women, Professor Robey?' Miller asked. 'Are you going to give me any idea of how this connects to those five dead women?'

'No, detective, I am not. I am not going to tell you anything. I am going to show you something, and then you can work it out . . . you can go look for yourself. You can make the decision about whether you want to pursue this nightmare or not.'

'Show me something? Show me what?'

'Show you the sacred monster, detective . . . I am going to show you the sacred monster.'

FORTY-FOUR

'None of them owned anything as far as I can tell,' Chris Metz said. He tossed a manila folder across the desk towards Roth.

'Went back as far as we could. All three of them – Margaret Mosley, Barbara Lee, Ann Rayner – all leased their respective houses or apartments. Rent paid on time month in, month out. As I said before, the first two, Mosley's apartment on Bates and the Rayner woman's house on Patterson, have been leased to new tenants. Barbara Lee's place on Morgan has been completely redecorated. And,' Metz continued, 'there was no testament or will in any case and no-one came forward to make claim against any estate. All possessions and records were turned over to the County Probate Court—'

'So we have this stuff?' Roth asked.

'Application in writing, minimum turnaround is a month regardless of who's asking for it.'

'So we get a warrant . . . we get a warrant from whoever and go and get this shit out of Probate Court.'

Metz shook his head. 'Not as easy as it sounds . . .'

'You can't seriously tell me that Probate Court—'

'We spoke to Probate Court,' Metz interjected. 'We spoke to the county registrar, and he said that even if we had a warrant signed by the United States Supreme Court it would still be at least a week before they got through the paper-work. They have hundreds of cases a month, sometimes as many as a thousand. This stuff goes into a vast network of storage facilities, and it can take days to even track where it went.'

'Okay, whatever . . .' Roth said. 'Jesus, I don't believe this shit. So we're gonna leave that the fuck alone and go after McCullough, okay? That's what we do . . . you and me, we go after McCullough. Track this guy down once and for all.'

Metz raised his eyebrows. 'McCullough?'

'Retired sergeant from the Seventh.'

'And what's Miller doing?'

'He's doing a thing.'

Metz frowned, started to smile. 'Doing *a thing* . . . what the fuck is that supposed to mean?'

'Means he's doing something.'

'Like the coroner woman, right?'

'Whatever,' Roth said dismissively. 'Miller is doing something, and it's not the coroner woman. Jesus Christ, you are an animal.'

'Answer me something,' Metz said. 'That thing with the pimp . . . you figure Miller did that? You figure he actually killed the guy for real?'

'He defended himself against an asshole,' Roth said. 'You know how this shit gets turned around by the papers. Last thing he needs is people inside his own precinct—'

'Oh come on, man,' Metz retorted. 'You really think I give a fuck about the moral issues here. Jesus, half the people we deal with deserve to get pushed down the freakin' stairs. I'm not making some kind of accusation here, Al . . . I'm just—'

'Talking about something I don't know anything about. That's what you're doing.'

'Hey, you're the guy's partner . . .'

'Which means what?' Roth replied. 'That I have some kind of inside line on what Miller does when he's on his own?'

'Partners talk, right? That's what partners do. They sit in cars for hours and they talk shit to each other. And what you said there. The fact that he was on his own when he went out to see that chick—'

'Enough already,' Roth said emphatically. 'Miller is a good fucking detective. He happens to be my friend. I don't give a fuck what you might or might not think about him. He did what any of us would have done in the same situation, and that's the end of it.'

'Okay, okay,' Metz replied. 'Hell, man, I didn't mean for you to get so wound up.'

'Then why the fuck d'you keep winding, eh?'

'I've backed down, alright? End of discussion. We go do this thing with the McCullough guy, okay?'

'Yes, we go find McCullough.'

'So what have you got?'

'We have a copy of his ID card.'

'Old or new issue?'

'Old.'

'So no picture then. You haven't been able to pull a picture from archives?'

'Haven't had a chance to take a piss. We need to follow it up.'

'What else?'

'Social security card, the number of which tracks back to a Michael McCullough who died in 1981. We have a fabricated phone bill, an account with the Washington American Trust that McCullough opened with fifty dollars, an account that never received the pension he was supposed to get.'

'And he was in the department how long?'

'Sixteen years . . . apparently.'

Metz shook his head. 'Don't make sense.'

Roth smiled. 'If I had a dollar for every time someone has said that while I've been on this case . . .'

'So what d'you wanna do with this one? All the usual lines exhausted . . .'

'Guy named Bill Young was captain at the Seventh when McCullough came on temporary transfer. He remembers him. He had one fuck of a stroke, but he hasn't lost his memory. Young actually saw the guy, so we know he exists.'

'Or someone who said he was McCullough.'

'Right.'

'So how the fuck do you find someone who's got a false name, a false social security number, and you don't even know what he looks like?'

Roth assumed an expression that was becoming all the more frequent, an expression even Amanda had identified – a sense of quiet disbelief, as if he believed he'd heard every- thing, and then it simply got worse.

'We go back to the Seventh. We find someone who worked with him. We ask questions until we know which division he came from, and then see if there's a picture, anything at all that will help us. We look up this drug bust from 2001 . . .

and the other thing we need is the forensics reports from the Joyce woman's apartment.'

Metz got up and put on his jacket. 'And we leave Miller to his own devices . . .'

Roth nodded, almost expressionless. 'We leave him to his own devices.'

*T*here was no reason to start running. I just started running. Like Forrest Gump.

One Saturday, standing in the yard back of the house, the middle of summer, the blunt bruising heat that made me feel as if I'd been slapped, though there was no recollection of impact. It was a subtle thing, and it drained me and made me dizzy.

I went out front and stood on the road, and then I sort of aimed myself toward Rhode Island Avenue and started running. First day, I found muscles in back of my legs I'd forgotten I owned. I woke on Sunday morning feeling betrayed and abused, dehydrated, a bitter taste in my mouth like salty garbage. That was the day I decided to stop smoking. And I did. Smoked for the better part of twenty years, and then I stopped. Within a week I could run a mile – half a mile out, half a mile back – and feel very little of anything at all. Within a month I got all the way to Rock Creek Park. I cheated. I followed Sixteenth Street, and then turned onto Military Road and cut the park in half. It took another two weeks to get the necessary stamina to run right round the park and home. But I did it. I didn't stop. I didn't puke. I ran slowly, with surety and rhythm, and I kept going until I stood once more on the corner of New Jersey and Q Street.

After a while I stopped thinking about myself, and I started looking.

I ran around the grounds of Shaw Howard University. I looked at young men and women carrying books, carrying bags and satchels, CD players and iPods and MP-3 players, carrying youth and vigor and some sort of trusting self-belief that told them they'd make something of themselves;

I ran the length of Florida Avenue as far as Seventh Street, past the line of cabs at the corner of Fourth, and saw the gang of cabbies leaning against hoods and fenders, smoking, drinking Dr Pepper, laughing at some wisecrack, falling silent one after the *other, their heads turning with no subtlety or finesse as a girl walked past, each of them thinking 'Do her? Man, would I do her . . . Jeez, give me ten minutes in the back of the cab with that one and I'd make her cry for home' . . . but knowing that given such a chance they would feel self-conscious, foolish, naïve even, and awkward and apologetic, and a sense of guilt that would never give them the oomph to get it up;*

I ran to the Constitution Gardens, from one end to the other, past the Federal Reserve Building, past the Veterans' Memorial, along Ohio Drive at the edge of West Potomac Park, right round the tidal basin and along the Fourteenth Street Bridge, and figured that if this were New York I would be running through a Simon and Garfunkel song;

I ran to music; bought a CD player and listened to Sinatra and Shostakovich; I listened to Kelly Joe Phelps and Nina Simone; I listened to Gershwin and Bernstein and Billie Holliday. I listened to a CD that came free with a magazine – Sounds of the Amazon – and I hurled it from the Clara Barton Parkway into the Potomac because it was reminiscent of another time, another place, and it brought tears to my eyes and made me afraid;

I ran past pregnant women and smart-suit officials; past storefronts and massage parlors, past tenement blocks where the sense of loneliness and desolation kind of hung in the air like cheap perfume; past factory complexes and corrugated iron garages where black-faced men, smelling of diesel and paint and oil and sweat, peered out of semi-darkness; past refrigeration units where frozen fish were unloaded by the ton and collapsing in some fluid rush out of the backs of trailers into the street and along the gutter, and were scooped up by men with shovels who knew they would never have to eat them.

And I thought: In your daydreams, your moments of absent thought, there's always one place you return to. And I would think of such things, and remember places I had been, and always she was there – with her smile, with her warmth and humanity, and her passion for oddly colored berets.

What did Kafka say? A cage went in search of a bird.

The cage found me, and it was alluring and seductive, and everything it promised turned out to be a lie.

I ran past memories and emotion: fear and failure and

frustration, and the faltering doubt of what I was doing, which in turn became a doubt about who I was.

I ran past these things, and I left them behind, and I thought: Victory has a hundred fathers, defeat is an orphan, and could not remember who had said it.

Confronting this kind of thing makes everything else in your life seem utterly unimportant.

I ran past faces – those that I shot, those I strangled, those I detonated into the afterlife with homemade incendiary devices, with grenades and letter bombs and gas; past those who looked right at me as I raised a gun and pulled the trigger; those who never saw it coming, but knew something had come when they felt the sudden brutal impact of a bullet in the chest . . . and those who didn't even realize they were dead because the bullet hit them smack-bang in the forehead and dropped them like deadweight to an unforgiving ground.

Through late nights, the strange awkward hours before dawn – always dark, always cold – hearing footsteps somewhere and not knowing whether they were real or a dream, and for a second feeling your heart stop dead in its rhythm, and thinking that maybe, just maybe, one of them was on their way back to get you.

Ran past all of them and out the other side, and kept on going, just kept on going . . . and I was not so naïve to believe that I was running away from something, or to consider that the thing I was running from was myself. Such bullshit! What kind of sanctimonious, self-serving, shallow-minded, pathetic bullshit would that be? No, I was not so ignorant. But one time, just for a moment, I believed there was a possibility I was running toward something. I did not know what it was. Clemency, forgiveness, absolution . . . Peace? But then I reasoned that moving toward something was always a result of moving away from something else. A logical corollary. One could not move away from nothing. Catherine would have laughed and said that a man of my superficiality was not capable of such depth. Homespun philosophy had no place in me, neither in my heart nor in my life. People like us could never afford to be philosophical. We were doing the right thing. We knew that. We knew that so well we didn't need to question the nature of our rightness.

I ran past the ones we bagged and tagged and stacked in rows – and doused with lavender in an effort to hold back the stench as they decayed before our eyes. But the smell got inside you, insidious and unforgiving, and that is a smell I carry in my pores, in my hair, in my nerves and sinews and synapses and muscles, a smell that is embedded in the flesh of my nostrils, and I will always smell it because – in the end – that smell represented everything.

And I know that someone will find me three days after my death, and I will smell the same.

I ran out of the past and into the present, and the dead came with me, and I saw their faces and heard their voices, and realized that I would carry that load for the rest of my life, and if Catherine was right I would carry it into my next life, and the one beyond, and the one beyond that . . .

We allowed ourselves to get played like the fools we were.

We believed in all of it so goddam hard . . . believed in it enough to kill for it.

That's what we did. And when the war was over we believed it would stop – the guns, the drugs, the murder, the wanton greed and corruption and back-stabbing lying deceitful Machiavellian horror of everything we created. But it did not. It did not stop. We left Nicaragua and it came with us.

And what she said to me. What Catherine Sheridan said to me . . .

'I cannot continue to live in a world that is blind and ignorant. Blind to what we have done. Apathy is not a solution I will subscribe to, John. You see what I mean? You agree with me, don't you, John?'

And so we brought the sacred monster home . . . big enough to devour us all.

FORTY-FIVE

'We walk,' Robey said. He stood on the sidewalk and looked at Miller.

'Walk where?' Miller asked.

'This way,' he replied, and turned his back on Miller.

They headed down New Jersey Avenue, Robey moving swiftly, Miller hurrying to keep up with him.

'Where are we going?' Miller asked, aware even as he asked it that the question would not be answered.

'You ever hear of a man named Robert McNamara?'

'McNamara?' Miller asked. 'No, should I have?'

Robey shrugged, buried his hands in the pocket of his overcoat. 'Originally he was NSA, then he was the first CEO of Ford Motors who wasn't actually a member of the Ford family. Secretary of Defense from 1961 to 1968 . . . learned a great deal about covert operations, warfare, all the way through the Vietnam years. Worked under Kennedy until '63, and then LBJ until '68.' Robey glanced back at Miller, still hurrying to keep up with him. 'You know the lesson McNamara learned from those years?'

Miller shook his head.

'Learned that you can't control a foreign country with arms.'

Miller said nothing.

'You know where he went after Nixon took office?'

'No idea.'

'President of the World Bank. Went on a committed program to control the finances of as many Third World countries as possible. Loaned in excess of seven hundred and eighty million dollars each year for the first five years of Nixon's presidency. And he proved to Nixon, and subsequently to Ford and Carter, that there was a sequence in which you did this thing—'

'What thing? What are you talking about?'

'The control of a nation, Detective Miller, the control of a nation. Not by arms. Not by war until war is the last resort. You begin with economic control, and if economic control fails you employ the resources you have from within the intelligence community—'

They passed O Street and the turning for Neal Place.

'You instigate your black ops, your assassination program . . . like they did in Chile and Ecuador. You undermine the acting government, you put your own people in, and then – only then – if these actions do not bring you control of the nation, you commit to war. If you see the United States invade a country then you know that there has been action for a year, perhaps two, and those actions have not resulted in the desired effect.'

'You're talking about Nicaragua again, aren't you?' Miller asked.

'Nicaragua, Guatemala, Cuba, the Congo, Cambodia, Grenada, Libya, El Salvador, Afghanistan, Yugoslavia . . . hell, the list is endless. And those are just the ones we told you about.' Once again Robey smiled like there was some huge practical joke being played out for everyone's benefit. He was smiling because Miller hadn't got it, because he wondered whether Miller would ever get it.

Morgan Street to the left, and then they were bearing right toward the New York Avenue junction.

Miller started to wonder if they were headed towards Robey's workplace.

'The college . . . ?' he started.

'Wait and see.'

At the end of New York Avenue, the commotion of late afternoon traffic that came down from Massachusetts and K Street onto Seventh, the sudden way in which Robey rushed out into the oncoming stream of cars . . .

Miller was caught unawares, already breathless from keeping pace, and he turned away for a second, couldn't have been any more than that, and when he turned back he saw John Robey dodging and weaving through oncoming vehicles, horns blaring, a taxicab driver leaning out of his window and hollering abuse.

'Jesus,' he exhaled, and turned his head as a dark blue Pontiac almost caught Robey broadside.

But Robey was fast, deceptively so, for as Miller watched it seemed that he disappeared through the oncoming rush as if he was walking between stationary objects.

It was a minute, perhaps more, before the traffic was sufficiently sparse for Miller to take the crossing at a run. He charged across to the other side of the street and started running. Robey had turned right past the corner of Mount Vernon Square, on through the trees at the edge of the park.

Then, and only then, did Miller understand where Robey had taken him.

The high façade of Carnegie Library stood before him.

Left and right, back over his shoulder; he craned to see through the stream of cars on the highway, back toward the church on the corner of Massachusetts Avenue, the Post Office behind him on the corner of I Street and Seventh.

Robey was gone. Not because Miller had missed him. Not because Miller had let him go, but because Robey had never questioned his own ability to disappear.

He had simply vanished.

Miller breathed deeply, felt his pulse return to normal.

The library. One of the very last things Catherine Sheridan had done. She'd returned the books. Returned the books . . .

Miller glanced down. He had on the same overcoat he'd been wearing on that Sunday following the Sheridan murder.

From his left outer pocket he retrieved the slip of paper given him by Julia Gibb. He had not considered the possibility that it meant anything at all. Not until now; not until the moment John Robey had returned him to the library.

Why?

To tell him something perhaps.

Miller looked down at the piece of paper, the titles written in Julia Gibb's precise librarian script.

Ravelstein by Saul Bellow, two books by Steinbeck – *Of Mice and Men* and *East of Eden*. *Beasts* by Joyce Carol Oates, and *Yesterdays* by Ella Wheeler Wilcox.

Miller read them through several times. The he started walking, and his walking got faster and became a run.

The books. She returned the books but withdrew none.

Ravelstein. Of Mice and Men. Beasts. East of Eden. Yesterdays.

It was stupid. It was foolishly simple. The titles were his name. R-O-B-E-Y. Robey. The books had something to do with Robey.

Catherine Sheridan had returned the books in order to tell them something about Robey.

Miller pounded up the library steps and caught the door even as Julia Gibb was coming to lock it for the evening.

FORTY-SIX

'McCullough? Sure I remember McCullough.'

Sergeant Stephen Tannahill, assigned representative from the Seventh, was seated in a back office behind the central briefing room, Roth and Metz facing him across an oval table, a window to the right overlooking the junction of Randolph and First. Tannahill carried the same world-weary look as Oliver, Riehl, Feshbach, even Lassiter. Carried something in his eyes that spoke of too many years doing this thing to ever consider doing something different. Such a shadow was not unique to policemen, but they seemed to earn it harder and wear it with greater pride. Metz and Roth had arrived just as Tannahill was leaving, but the alacrity with which he agreed to speak with them suggested that he did not have a great deal to look forward to at home. Perhaps there was no-one. Perhaps there was someone but she did not recognize the man she'd married and communicated it, silently but with everything she possessed. These were awkward and disjointed lives. Roth could see that, ever reminding himself of his own good fortune in having Amanda and the kids waiting for his return. Many of the people he met in the various precincts had a quality of life no better than the vast percentage of those they spent their time investigating, searching for, and arresting. It was a sad commentary, but nevertheless true.

'You spoke to Bill Young, you say?' Tannahill asked. He was a short man, no more than five-six or seven, but he was wide in the shoulder, narrow in the waist. He was not a man who could wear off-the-rack suits and look like anything but a cop, a doorman, a convict released for a funeral.

'We spoke to Bill, yes.'

Tannahill nodded as if quietly remembering something. 'He okay?'

Roth shrugged. 'As can be, you know?'

'Fucking tragedy man, a real fucking tragedy. Guy was a fucking admiral. Fucking beast of a guy. Good fucking cop.'

Roth didn't speak. Tannahill was on a *fucking* monologue and Roth felt it unwise to interrupt him.

Tannahill was elsewhere for a little while longer, and then he turned and smiled at Roth and Metz in turn. 'You guys got this Ribbon bullshit then.'

'We have,' Metz replied.

'Pair of fucking schmucks then, ain'tcha?' He laughed. 'You're after McCullough now?'

'We need to see him yes,' Roth said. 'He was here back in 2001—'

'Very short while,' Tannahill said. 'Some guy was s'posed to come. I was a grunt back then, just your regular cannon fodder. Made sergeant in the middle of 2003. Knew the guy who went out to Port Orchard, guy named Hayes, Danny Hayes. His wife got pregnant, twins. Some problem. Something went awry. She wanted to move out near her folks in Port Orchard and it was fixed up so Danny transferred out there. We were supposed to get some guy from the Ninth, but then we got McCullough instead.'

'You remember where he came from?' Metz asked.

Tannahill shook his head. 'He never said, I never asked. McCullough was not the sort of guy you'd choose to socialize with.'

Roth frowned. 'How d'you mean?'

'I don't know where he came from. Vice maybe. Heard Narcotics. Fucked-up guy. Real fucked up.' Tannahill smiled knowingly. 'You ever see one of these characters, like you think they've maybe lost it, but they can still do the job, can still make the busts?'

Roth nodded.

'McCullough was one of them. Normal world you'd have him put away somewhere quiet so he didn't harm anyone; sugar paper and red crayolas, you know? But he had a good record as far as I know, and when he did that gig in September everyone was all over the place saying what a fucking hero he was. Me? I didn't know what to make of him. Too intense for me altogether.'

'That was the coke?' Metz said.

'Yes. Some high-quality shit that was.'

'And it went out of lock-up?'

'In a heartbeat,' Tannahill said. 'IAD was into everything within seconds. They questioned McCullough, but he could've eaten three or four IAD guys for snacks and still sat down for dinner. It was a real fucking circus. What really happened no-one knew. No-one got busted because there was no-one to bust. Guy on lock-up was as trustworthy as they come, had been doing it for about three hundred years. It was ghost fucking cocaine, I tell you.'

'You think McCullough took it out?' Roth asked.

'Course he did,' Tannahill replied without hesitation. 'Wouldn't surprise me if the guy went into lock-up and hoovered it out the bag right then and there.'

'You figure him for a user?'

'I couldn't figure him for anything. Drugs. Crazy. On the take. Hookers. Running some sort of sideline in stolen goods. God knows, man, I haven't a clue. All I know is that the shit went down with the coke vanishing, IAD came in and out like a wet whirlwind, and then it went quiet until October.'

'The drugs raid,' Roth said.

'Raid?' Tannahill said, and smiled. 'Who called it a raid? Was a fucking fiasco. CI got himself killed, McCullough was wounded. Whoever the fuck they might have been after got clean away—'

'You saying it wasn't a raid?' Metz asked. 'McCullough went out on his own?'

'He sure did.'

'But that's not what the newspaper reports said . . .'

'PR department,' Tannahill said. 'A raid gone wrong looks an awful lot better than a renegade cop and his CI trying to change the world on their own.'

Roth was quiet for a moment, trying to take this in.

'McCullough was on his way out, you see,' Tannahill went on. 'After the September thing he started fucking things up. He was late all the time. He got his ass chewed by Bill Young more times than I care to recall. Far as I know, Young was looking at instigating disciplinary proceedings, and then we get this tip-off that McCullough has another sting going on like the September thing, but this time it's a lot bigger. Everyone's ready for some kind of operation briefing . . . we're all wired up to get this thing going, and then before we know it we hear that McCullough went on his own with some black guy, the black guy got himself killed, and McCullough is once again in the firing line with IAD and God only knows who else.'

'But IAD didn't get a chance to do a full investigation, or so I understood from Bill Young,' Roth said.

'McCullough vanished, just like the coke in September. Disappeared, never to be heard of again.'

Roth was quiet. He looked at Metz. Metz was expressionless.

Tannahill shrugged his shoulders. 'That's as good as it gets really,' he said. 'I don't know that there's anything else I can tell you.'

'One thing,' Roth said. 'We have not been able to find a picture of him. The ID card that he used to open a bank account was the old style without the picture.'

'Fuck, I don't know,' Tannahill said. 'His folder went off with IAD way back when. They don't store records here now. They're all centralized somewhere near the Eleventh. You could go see them . . .' Tannahill stopped for a moment. He paused in thought, and then shook his head. 'Unless . . .'

'What?' Roth asked.

'The evaluation,' Tannahill said. 'We had a precinct evaluation right after the September bust.'

Roth nodded his head, started smiling. 'Evaluation pictures, right. You have them here?'

'Sure we do,' Tannahill said. 'I can go check now if you wanna wait.'

'Definitely,' Roth said. 'Here?'

Tannahill got up from his chair. 'Fuck it, it's only upstairs . . . might as well come and help me look through the files.'

Roth and Metz followed Tannahill out of the office and up to the next floor.

Records was the usual confusion of mismatched filing cabinets circumventing the room and numerous tables in the center, many of them buckling beneath the weight of the folders stacked on their surfaces.

Tannahill smiled wryly. ''Scuse the mess . . . cleaner's on vacation, you know?'

'Where do we begin?' Roth asked.

'Files over there are precinct records,' Tannahill said, indicating the right side of the room. He walked toward the corner, Roth and Metz following. Tannahill tugged open the upper drawer of the cabinet nearest the window. '1988,' he said. ''88 to '90.' He pulled open the upper drawer of the adjacent cabinet. ''93 to '94 here . . . it's gonna be the fourth or fifth one from that end.'

Metz opened drawers, Roth too, and within a moment they had found the cabinet that carried files from 2000 through 2002.

After twenty-five minutes Tannahill resorted to pulling every file out and spreading them on the floor. The three of them went through each one twice, every picture, every document from July 2001 to the end of the year. There was no file for McCullough. No records. No picture.

'Someone must have pulled it,' Tannahill said. 'It happens. You know how this shit happens, right?'

Roth didn't reply; he was at the end of his tether. He knew that if he said anything he would lose it. He was preparing himself for yet another dead-end, another return to the Second with nothing, when Tannahill looked up suddenly and smiled. 'Too fucking obvious,' he said quietly. 'Shit, this is just too fucking obvious.'

'What?' Roth asked.

'The annual pictures, they're downstairs . . . he'll be small, but he'll be there.'

Once again Metz and Roth followed Tannahill as he made his way out of Records, down the stairwell and into the central reception area of the precinct house. Precinct photographs, taken annually, were ordinarily displayed along the corridors, but at the Seventh they had them lining the walls of the canteen and the communal briefing room. Tannahill found 2001 within a moment, stood on a chair to gain sufficient height to bring it down off the wall, and spent a moment scanning the nickel-sized faces of the men pictured there.

'Here you are,' he said, and pointed to a man, second row from the back, three or four from the end of the line.

Roth took the picture, Metz peering over his shoulder. Roth frowned, shook his head, and then he started laughing. It was an awkward sound, abrupt, brief, and then he stopped and shook his head.

'What?' Tannahill asked. 'What is it?'

'I don't fucking believe it,' Metz said.

'What?' Tannahill repeated.

Roth said nothing, but he started to feel the sheer weight of it. He started to get some kind of an idea of what they were dealing with, and it unsettled him deeply.

'You know this guy?' Tannahill asked. 'You know McCullough?'

Roth was shaking his head. 'No, we don't know McCullough,' he said quietly. 'But we know someone who was using his name.'

I think it was Matisse who said that a painter should begin by cutting out his own tongue.

To stop him talking.

To stop him explaining what he meant with each and every brush stroke.

To stop him rationalizing and justifying, analyzing, interpreting what he felt at the time. He just expressed what he felt. The feeling was there, and then it was gone. That was art. That was life. Perhaps it was death.

Perhaps they should have cut our tongues out as well.

I feel for Miller. I feel for what he will find and what it might do to him.

I feel for the edge of things, the line that was drawn, and I see a man walking toward that line without ever realizing it was there.

At Langley, again in Managua, they taught me how to disappear.

I have never forgotten how to do that, and so I do it again.

I am gone . . . like I was never even there.

FORTY-SEVEN

Miller stood at the counter while Julia Gibb gathered together the five books that Catherine Sheridan had returned.
He'd already called the Second from his cell phone, told
Oliver to get to Robey's apartment, to call him if Robey
showed. But Miller knew that Robey would not go back
there. Not yet. Not until something had happened. What
that was Miller had no way of knowing, but he was certain
Robey was now orchestrating every aspect of this, perhaps
had done so from the start.

Miller felt nothing but a sense of impending horror.

He did not understand the significance of these books, but
he had no choice but to secure them, to take them back to
the precinct and pore over them, see if there wasn't some
clue, some message that Catherine Sheridan had left.

But now it was different. Now it appeared that Robey was
leading him toward something that Catherine had wanted
them to know. That could mean that Robey and Sheridan
were in collusion, or she had known he was coming for her,
and if that was the case then it opened up all manner of
possibilities. First and foremost, it indicated that Sheridan
knew she was going to die. She returned the books, and then
she was murdered. Miller did not believe in coincidence. The
pizza number. The Darryl King case records. Visiting Natasha
Joyce. Natasha's murder on Tuesday. Now it was Friday and
still there was no complete forensics report. The photographs
beneath the bed, those unmistakable images of Robey as a
younger man, the pretended alibi, in itself so weak Robey
knew they would expose it effortlessly . . . All these things
were part of something else.

Miller's heart was missing beats. His pulse was erratic. He
felt dehydrated and nauseous.

As Julia Gibb rounded the end of the nearest shelves, her

arms laden with books, Miller's pager went off. He glanced at it. Roth. He silenced it; Roth could wait until he got back to the Second.

'Here we are, detective,' Julia Gibb said. 'Fortunately no-one has taken them out since they were returned.'

Miller thanked her, gathered up the books and started towards the door.

'I presume they will be returned to us,' she called after him.

'As soon as possible,' Miller said.

'I'm not so worried about those four, but the Wilcox isn't in print any more . . . very hard to find, you know?'

'I'll take care of them,' Miller said. 'Bring them back as soon as I can.'

He almost dropped the books as he maneuvered himself sideways through the door, and then he hurried down the steps. He crossed Seventh and started up New York toward the Second Precinct. No more than two blocks and he was already out of breath, hurrying back toward whatever Roth had to tell him, whatever he might find in the books he carried. He thought of the forensics report from Natasha Joyce's apartment, the autopsy results, and with that came thoughts of Marilyn Hemmings, of Jennifer Irving and Brandon Thomas . . . All so distant, so far removed from what he was doing, a part of some other life. Everything had moved so fast. Six days since Catherine Sheridan's death. Less than a week. Reports daily to Lassiter, those reports passed on to Killarney, whoever else might have been interested at the FBI. And what did they have? Proof of Robey's involvement came from the illegal acquisition of evidence, the use of city staff and facilities to determine the incriminating nature of that evidence. Where did that leave him? More importantly, where did it leave Marilyn Hemmings?

Miller's mind reeled at the possibilities and implications.

He reached the Second and went up the steps and through the doors into reception.

'Roth was after you,' the desk Sergeant called over. 'He's up there now.'

Miller took the stairs two at a time, hurried along the corridor and entered the office, using his elbow to lever down the handle and move in backwards with the armful of books.

'Miller,' Lassiter said. 'Jesus, man, where the hell have you been?'

Miller turned, surprised to hear Lassiter's voice, and found Al Roth and Nanci Cohen, Chris Metz, Dan Riehl, Vincent Littman and Jim Feshbach seated in a group on the right side of the room.

Miller dropped the stack of books on the nearest desk and hesitated for a moment.

'Better come take a look at this,' Lassiter said. He rose from his chair, took what appeared to be a monochrome photograph from the desk and held it out for Miller to look at.

'What is it?' Miller asked as he walked toward the assembled group.

'Your friend Sergeant Michael McCullough,' Lassiter said, 'or more accurately, the reason we have not been able to locate Sergeant Michael McCullough.'

Lassiter leaned over, indicated a man standing in the second row from the back, fourth from the end of the line.

Robert Miller's heart stopped beating.

It did not start again for quite some time.

'So what does this mean?' Lassiter asked.

Miller could not speak. He stared at the face before him, the uniformed figure of John Robey, the way the man looked back at him, almost smiling in the bright sunlight. A slight frown as if the brightness bothered him, but he was there, standing alongside fellow officers at the Seventh Precinct.

'So?' Lassiter prompted. 'What the fuck *is* this? We're dealing with a renegade cop here or what?'

Miller shook his head. 'I don't know . . . God, I don't even know what the fuck to say. This is so—'

'You sent Oliver over to Robey's apartment,' Lassiter interjected. 'Apparently Robey is not there.'

'I went to see Robey. He said he wanted to show me something. He walked me back to the Carnegie Library and then he disappeared.'

Lassiter frowned. 'He what?'

'He disappeared. I walked with him all the way to Second

441

Street, and then he just ran right into the traffic and disappeared.'

'And the books?' Lassiter asked.

'They're the books that Catherine Sheridan returned on the morning of her death. He wanted me to get them from the library—'

'What the hell for?'

'I don't know . . . there's five of them . . . the first letter of each book title spells Robey. They spell his name. I think there's something in them . . . a message perhaps, I don't know.'

Nanci Cohen spoke. 'So she knew he was going to kill her?' She stood up, walked toward Miller and picked up one of the books. She opened it, leafed through it, turned it upside down and shook it to see if anything fell out. There was nothing. She did the same with each of them. Roth and Metz joined her, started looking through them also.

'Hang fire here,' Lassiter said. 'Back to something that's a little more pressing right now . . . the fact that this college professor is either a cop, or is someone impersonating a cop. This is just un-fucking-believable.'

Nanci Cohen put down the last of the books. 'Thing that amazes me is that you had him, and then you lost him . . .'

'I didn't *have* him,' Miller replied, something of frustration, exasperation, in his tone. 'You were the one who said we had nothing on him. You were the one who said there was nothing we could do—'

Lassiter raised his hand and silenced Miller. 'Stop,' he said. 'We're not getting into a firefight here.' He turned to ADA Cohen. 'We have sufficient evidence to get a warrant on his apartment?'

She nodded. 'Sure we do. Suspicion of impersonating a police officer is good enough for me.'

Lassiter turned to Metz. 'Get the paperwork sorted out. Get it done now. I want a warrant tonight. We're gonna get into that place and find out whatever we can about this guy in the next two fucking hours, okay?'

Metz started towards the door.

'I'll come with you,' Nanci Cohen said. 'I'll drive it over to Judge Thorne.'

Lassiter turned to Miller. 'Go through these books with Roth and the others. See what you can find. Soon as we have this warrant I want you over at the Robey apartment. Tear the fucking place to pieces. Find out who the fuck this guy is and what he's doing.' Lassiter glanced at his watch. 'I have to go see someone. Be an hour. Call me soon as you have the warrant. If I can I'll meet you there.'

Miller watched him go, hesitated for a moment and then sat down heavily.

It was a few minutes past six. He'd not eaten since breakfast.

Roth sat facing him. Feshbach, Littman and Riehl stood on the other side of the room, uncertain of what was needed.

'One book each,' Miller said, and picked up *Beasts* by Joyce Carol Oates.

FORTY-EIGHT

Detective Carl Oliver sat in an unmarked sedan on the junction facing New Jersey and Q Street. He did not envy Miller. The thing had smelled bad since day one. He was willing to help, for sure, but help had a limit. There were certain cases that assumed possession of your life for the duration, and this was one of them. Miller had been on the radio. The APB guy, this John Robey, now appeared to be Sergeant McCullough. Seemed a cop had killed the Sheridan woman, or something such as this. It didn't matter. Ultimately none of it mattered. It was all politics anyway. Serial killers had been big in the '80s. Serial killers were passé. Now it was simply a matter of closing a case because the chief of police wanted it closed. All he had to do was watch the apartment for a man that would not return. That was easy enough. He could smoke, listen to the radio, whatever he wanted, and watch the street.

Seemed it was money for nothing, until Carl Oliver turned to the right and saw a man fitting John Robey's physical description cross the junction up ahead and start toward the end of the block.

Littman picked it up, the small marks at the bottom of certain pages, like the flick of a pencil above certain numbers. He was holding a copy of *Ravelstein* by Saul Bellow. As soon as he mentioned it, Feshbach picked up on the same thing. Tiny pencil markings to indicate a number, then another, then another. Scrutinizing each page individually, each of the five detectives listed the sequence as it was noted.

'Some kind of code,' Miller said. 'A cipher perhaps . . .'

'Letters also,' Riehl said. 'I've got a coupla letters marked on page one here, and then I get a sequence of six numbers, then I get another coupla letters, then a sequence of five.'

'Just write them down,' Miller said. 'Write them down in the sequence you find them.'

Miller did the same. Page One: 'In the Oceania wing of the Louvre I saw it: the totem.'

A mark above the *a* in Oceania, and then on the seventh line, 'Except the infant was only a head, grotesquely large and round', a mark above the *q*.

Miller noted these, and then found a mark above page numbers: the *1* in *10*, the *2* in *12*, the *5* in *15*, the *9* in *19*, lastly the *8* in *28*.

He wrote them down in sequence: *a q 1 2 5 9 8*.

The sequence started again, this time *g j 6 6 9 9*, and again *b d 7 14 99*.

'Dates,' Miller said. 'They're fucking dates aren't they?' He looked at Roth. 'Got three here . . . December 5th, 1998, then June 6th, 1999, next is July 14th, 1999 . . .'

'And the letters?' Roth asked.

'Initials, what the fuck d'you bet they're initials,' Riehl said.

'Jesus,' Miller exhaled quietly. 'Names and dates. They're goddamned names and dates . . .'

'Don't miss one, for God's sake,' Roth said. 'Miss one and the whole thing goes awry.'

'Everyone complete the book they're on,' Miller said. 'Mark every letter and number in sequence, and then pass the book along. We cross-check to make sure we're right.'

Roth looked at him, raised his eyebrows, slowly shook his head. 'This is just so fucking beyond me . . .' His voice trailed away into silence. He looked down, focused on what he was doing, started writing again.

Carl Oliver called the precinct from his car, told them to get Miller and Roth out to Robey's place. It looked like John Robey was on his way home.

Oliver exited his car and crossed the street. The man he'd seen had passed the junction, turned left, was now approaching the stairwell that led up to Robey's apartment. Oliver stayed close to the façade of the adjacent building. He did not need to try and look inconspicuous. Inconspicuousness was in his nature.

Oliver did not see the man's face. All he knew of Robey was the image from the treated photographs, the basic height and build Miller had told him. Oliver waited for him to reach the stairwell, and then he followed.

'Thirty-six,' Roth said. 'Thirty-six separate sequences . . .' He paused, looked across at Miller. 'You see them, right?'

Miller nodded. A slow-dawning realization had blanched the color from his face.

'What?' Littman asked. 'See what?'

Miller turned the page around and pointed to a sequence of three:

m m 3 6 6
a r 7 1 9 6
b 1 8 2 2 6

'And they mean what?' Littman asked.

'Margaret Mosley, March 6th, 2006, Ann Rayner, July 19th and Barbara Lee on August 2nd . . . the three women this year before Catherine Sheridan.'

Feshbach frowned, leaned forward. 'So what? So you're telling me that there's thirty-six murders here . . . that this woman had information about thirty-six murders? You can't be fucking serious!'

Miller opened his mouth to reply, but was interrupted by the telephone to his left. Roth picked it up, was getting out of his chair even as he acknowledged and hung up. 'Someone at the Robey apartment,' he said.

'Robey?' Miller asked.

Roth shook his head. 'Don't know. Oliver called the desk, said he was checking it out.'

Miller got up, tugged his jacket from the back of his chair, turned to the three seated detectives as he reached the door. 'Put a search through the Washington system for those dates. See if there's missing persons or homicides that match the initials for those dates. Check our newspaper records, anything you can think of, okay?'

And then he was out the door behind Roth, the two of them hurrying down the corridor toward the stairwell. Roth called the car pool from his cell, told them to have a vehicle ready. A siren was the only thing that would get them through the early evening traffic.

Carl Oliver stood on the lowest rung of the stairwell leading to John Robey's apartment. He unholstered his gun, chambered a round, set the safety and returned it to the holster. He held his breath for a moment, reached for the handrail, and then started up the risers.

Miller drove, pulled the car out onto New York Avenue.

'Don't take Fifth,' Roth said. 'Back up there.' He indicated over his shoulder and through the rear window. 'Take Fourth, take a right onto M, and then take New Jersey at the Morgan Street junction . . .'

Miller followed Roth's advice, and within a minute was hitting gridlock at the New York Avenue turning.

'Radio Oliver,' he told Roth. 'Tell him to keep an eye on whoever but not to go up there until we arrive.'

'You think it's Robey?' Roth asked as he reached for the handset.

Miller shook his head. 'No,' he replied. 'I don't think it's—'

'Then who?'

Miller leaned on the horn as a car swerved from the left and cut him up. 'Asshole!' he hissed, and then looked back at Roth. 'Who is it? Jesus, I don't fucking know who it is,' he said. 'Don't even know that I *want* to know.'

Roth pressed the handset button and waited for someone at the Second to pick up.

At the top of the stairwell Oliver paused. This was the shit he didn't like. Some guys got a rush for this stuff, went looking for it, but not him. He had a leaning towards the methodical stuff, the questioning, the interrogations. In-your-face heroics was for other people.

He leaned against the edge of the wall and eased around the corner. The walkway to Robey's apartment door was clear. He stepped back toward the top riser and hesitated before moving again. A moment's consideration of whether he should wait. He didn't want to go into the apartment. Then again, he didn't want to be the guy who was too scared to act. Rock and a hard place. He wondered whether he should take out his gun, hold it down by his side. Knew that if something happened fast he might react, and in reacting he might shoot someone who didn't need to get shot. A sweat had broken out down the middle of his back. He reached up and ran his finger around the inside of his collar. He decided, for no other reason than to end the indecision. What harm could be done by checking it out? He had to check it out. It was a situation without choice. This was police work. You went looking for trouble, you checked things out, you were the other side of the crime scene tape and you knew exactly what had happened.

Carl Oliver took a deep breath, put his hand on the grip of his holstered gun, and started down the walkway to John Robey's apartment.

'Can't reach him,' Roth said. 'He can't be in his car. They're patching through to his radio but he's not answering.'

'Fuck,' Miller said. He swerved around a car as it pulled out, and he flipped the siren. The junction of O Street to their left, P Street up ahead, then Franklin. Miller hammered the heels of his hands on the steering wheel. Every way they turned they'd been stopped. Everything had been an almost-answer, an almost-truth, something that led to something that led to something else. And they were all just small parts of some greater picture, a picture that Miller felt he was beginning to see. He did not want to assume what it might be; he did not want to let his imagination run with it. He felt that it would only serve to complicate something that was already too complicated. He wanted to get to Robey's apartment, find out if anyone was in there or if Oliver had made a mistake. He wanted Cohen and Metz to return with the warrant so they could take a look inside. He wanted the books to give up their ghosts, the things that Catherine Sheridan wanted the world to know, and then he wanted it all to end.

That most of all: he wanted the nightmare to end.

A stream of traffic seemed suddenly to run to their left down Franklin. The road ahead cleared.

'Go!' Roth said, and Miller put his foot down to cover the last two hundred and fifty yards to their destination.

Standing at Robey's apartment door, Carl Oliver closed his eyes for a second and then raised his hand slowly. He knocked once, stepped back, rested the palm of his hand on the butt of his sidearm. No mistaking: his heart was running ahead of itself, his pulse trying to catch up.

He gave it a good thirty seconds. There was nothing. Not a sound from inside.

He raised his hand and knocked again, louder this time, gave it ten seconds and then shouted, 'Police! Open up, Sir!'

This time there was something, definitely a sound from inside the apartment.

Oliver felt his heart stop. Thus far it had been assumption: that someone had returned, that someone had found their way into the apartment, that he would knock on the door and there would be a response. Now it was more than assumption. Now the situation created an entirely different range of emotions and thoughts.

Oliver stepped back a pace, wondered if he should stand to the side of the door. He was not familiar with such scenarios. Movies he had seen yes, and at the academy they went through some brief explanations of how one handled such situations. But no amount of training with other rookies could prepare you for what you felt at such a time. This was something that could not be compared to anything else he'd experienced. He was not a veteran cop or an ex-soldier. He had not done two tours of duty in Iraq. He did not know how to deal with the feelings he was experiencing. He only knew that if he screwed this up another woman could die. Maybe two. Maybe more.

He sensed that whoever was inside was now close to the door, and then Oliver heard the man's voice.

'Who is it?'

'Police, sir. It's the police. I need you to open up the door.'

'Why? What do you want?'

'Is that you, Mr Robey?'

Silence.

'Gonna ask you to identify yourself there, sir. This is the apartment of Mr John Robey. Are you John Robey?'

Again there was silence.

Oliver felt his heart in his throat. This was where it went one way or the other. This was where he'd get a reprimand for not waiting for back-up. This was where the voice command drills only served so much purpose.

'Sir . . . gonna have to ask you one more time to open the door—'

'Okay, okay, okay . . . chill the fuck out for God's sake will you?'

The sound of the lock snapping back. Oliver felt himself tense up inside.

The door handle turned, the door started to open. Oliver took a step to the left. Put himself out of any direct line of fire. He wondered what on earth he believed might happen. There was someone inside. Right now they were cooperating. They would open the door and everything would be fine. It would be someone who was supposed to be there . . . Robey's brother with a spare key come to visit . . . a friend from down the block come to feed the cat at Robey's request. They would identify themselves, and there would be a moment of awkwardness as Oliver realized that some kind of mistake had been made.

Everything was going to be fine. Everything was going to be just fine . . .

The door opened.

The man who looked back at Detective Carl Oliver was not identifiable, because he held a scarf over the lower half of his face.

'John Robey?' Carl Oliver said, and it was the very last thing he would say, because the man took one step back, raised his hand, and with a silenced .22 he put a neat punctuation mark in the middle of Oliver's forehead. With insufficient force to make it through the cranium and out the other side, that .22 would ricochet back and forth inside Oliver's skull for a good eight or nine seconds.

Oliver stood there, his mouth slightly open, a crooked smile on his face as if a joke had been played on him, some kind of prank, and it was registering slowly, dawning on him

450

that he'd been taken for a fool, and even now people were laughing, and he was going to start laughing too, and he was going to be a good sport, he was going to take it well, be one of the crew, and everyone would have forgotten about it by tomorrow . . .

But he didn't start laughing, and nor did the man in the apartment. The man just waited until a thin line of blood oozed like a tear from the corner of Oliver's eye and ran down his cheek, waited a moment more until Carl Oliver dropped like deadweight to the floor, and then he closed the apartment door quietly behind him.

He made his way quickly and quietly toward the back of the apartment, collected a few things that he could manage to carry unaided, and then he went out of the window.

Robert Miller and Al Roth found Carl Oliver four minutes later, and by that time whoever had shot him had disappeared.

Disappeared but good . . . like he was never there.

FORTY-NINE

Within thirty minutes the Robey apartment was a confusion of people. Robert Miller stood for some considerable time in the outer walkway ahead of the front door. He felt the same as he had that night of Catherine Sheridan's murder. He did not know Carl Oliver, not well, not as he knew Al Roth, but the death of a colleague brought an exceptional kind of fear. It was not the man who had been killed, but what it represented. He had been here at the wrong time. That expression had never made sense to Miller. *He was in the wrong place at the wrong time.* No. It was either the right place at the wrong time, or vice versa. It was never both. Both didn't make sense. Robey's apartment. That's where Oliver was supposed to have been. Had he been two hours earlier he wouldn't be dead. Right place, wrong time. That simple.

But Oliver's killing meant a great deal more. His killing meant that whoever was involved in this considered themselves above the law. This was now no longer a matter of a few dead women. This was perhaps a matter of more than thirty killings, persons as yet unknown and unidentified, a matter of connections that went back through John Robey and Catherine Sheridan to something far, far greater. Miller believed this, believed it with everything he possessed, but there was no proof, nothing probative to suggest any connection – except a hairbrush that was ten or twenty feet from where he now stood.

Lassiter appeared, alongside him ADA Cohen and Chris Metz, in his hand the warrant to search the apartment – a warrant that was no longer required. Robey's apartment was a crime scene; Robey's apartment was full of photographers and forensics people, and when the crime scene unit showed up it was as if the Second Precinct had moved to New Jersey and Q Street.

'This is just fucked,' Lassiter kept saying, an edge to his voice that told of all the late night phone calls, the questions he would not be able to answer, the beratings, the criticisms, the threats and innuendoes regarding what would happen to his career if he didn't . . .

Miller could not speak. He watched while pictures were taken of Carl Oliver's body. He watched while he was put on a gurney, as the medics awkwardly maneuvered him down the stairway to the street. Marilyn Hemmings appeared. She raised her hand and smiled at Miller. Miller raised his hand back. He saw her just the once, saw her sign something, and then she went away.

A slick of blood was all that remained. It was small. It had leaked from Oliver's mouth. There had been no visible exit wound to his head. He was thirty-four years old. He liked R.E.M. He smoked cigarettes that he rolled himself.

At one point Miller slid down to his haunches and wrapped his arms around his knees. Al Roth came out of the apartment and stood over him silently. After a minute or two he said, 'When you're ready . . . when you're ready you better come in and take a look at this.' And then he went back inside and left Miller there, in the outer walkway, with his forehead on his knees and his heart in his mouth.

By the time Miller got up it was close to eighty-thirty. He stepped into the apartment and waited patiently for someone he recognized to appear inside. It was Lassiter, and though Lassiter looked beaten to hell, though he didn't really have a great deal of anything to say, Miller could tell from the man's expression that whatever existed within that apartment had changed his mind about what they were dealing with. Changed it completely.

The room where Miller had spoken with Robey was the same. The dark carpet, the sofa against the right hand wall, the window on the left overlooking the back of the building, the parchment walls, the line drawings in their stainless steel frames.

'In back,' Lassiter said. 'You need to come and see what we've found.'

Nanci Cohen was there, Al Roth and Chris Metz. Metz left

when Miller and Lassiter stepped into the room. He looked overwhelmed and exhausted.

Miller didn't say anything for a long time. The window overlooking the street had been boarded over, and beneath it was a wide table. Upon the table were two desktop computers, a police receiver, two laptops, a stack of manila folders, some of which had spilled to the ground. There were leads hanging free from the edge of the table.

'We think there was another laptop,' Roth said. 'There's a window back there in the kitchen. Whoever was here went out that way. There's a fire escape . . .' His voice disappeared as he realized that Miller was paying no attention at all.

The wall was ahead of them.

The wall was what it was all about.

The wall was a good twelve feet wide, maybe eight or nine feet high, and aside from the maps and sketches, aside from the confusion of multi-colored pins that marked streets and junctions and other unspecified locations, it was the pictures that communicated everything that needed to be said. Some of them photographs, some polaroids, some of them clipped from newspapers and magazines.

Miller found Ann Rayner without difficulty. As soon as he found Rayner he found Lee and Mosley. Catherine Sheridan had her own little collection of pictures to the furthest right-hand edge of the wall, her own memorial shrine – a good eight or ten pictures, all of them showing her at different points in her life. In amongst them was an exact duplicate of one of the pictures that had been found beneath Catherine Sheridan's bed.

Miller turned and looked at Lassiter. Lassiter was no more than three or four feet behind him. On his face was an expression of both disbelief and realization.

'Robert,' Roth said.

Miller turned.

Roth raised his hand and indicated one of the photographs pinned to the wall. 'Alan Quinn, December 5th.'

Miller was nodding. He knew who these people were. He knew their names and the dates on each photograph would compare precisely with the initials and numbers marked on the pages of Catherine Sheridan's books. Whatever had happened between these people was bigger than anyone in the police department could have imagined. John Robey and Catherine Sheridan knew something, and whatever they knew went all the way back to however many years ago, and he and Al Roth, Frank Lassiter and Nanci Cohen – they stood there facing a wall of photographs, more than thirty of them, that said everything that needed to be said without any words at all.

There were a lot of dead people. They had been murdered, every single one. They had been murdered for some reason unknown. Perhaps by Robey, perhaps by Robey and Sheridan. Perhaps by someone else entirely, and Robey had merely recorded these events, collected evidence, and then drawn Miller right into its web.

'He knew,' Miller said at some point, turning toward Roth, toward Lassiter and Cohen. 'He knew about all these people . . .'

Roth reached forward, and with his latex-gloved hand he carefully took one of the lower pictures off the wall. He held it for a moment, and then turned it so Miller could see.

'Natasha Joyce,' he said quietly. 'She won't be in the books.'

'Whatever this is, it's gone back I don't know how many years,' Miller said. 'I think they're all the same . . . I think we're gonna find that all of them have been security screened at some point in their life, and then we'll find that their name stops somewhere, or their social security number isn't right, or they'll have a bank account that was supposed to receive some money but the money never arrived . . .'

'I have one man for this,' Lassiter said. 'John Robey. And right now he's the *only* name and face we have for this thing. He goes on the TV.' Lassiter turned and looked at Nanci Cohen. 'We have a state-wide manhunt to organize,' he said. 'We have a dead police officer . . . and thank God that he wasn't married and didn't have kids, that's all I can say. That doesn't change the fact that he's dead, and right now the only one who could have done this thing as far as I'm concerned is John Robey—'

'I don't think it's Robey,' Miller said, matter-of-fact.

'You don't think *what* is Robey?'

'Who killed these people . . . I don't think Robey killed the people on this wall. I don't think he killed Natasha Joyce. I think he knows who killed them and he's trying to help us—'

'You *what*?' Lassiter exploded. 'Are you out of your fucking mind? Everything about this says Robey. Right now we have the most successful serial killer in the history of the human race, or near as goddammit. Jesus, I can't believe you're telling me this—'

'I'm saying it because I believe it,' Miller replied. 'I think he knows the truth, and he's been trying to tell us the truth and we haven't been listening—'

'Well listen to this,' Lassiter interjected. 'We have a suspect on the run, and right now I don't give a fuck what his real name might be or whether or not he's our guy or the Arch-angel fucking Gabriel come down to guide us to the truth. I need him found. I need TV coverage. I need a press conference organized. Whatever the hell we did on the APB before I now need for every patrolman in the state. I need people at the airport, the docks. I need car hire firms, the bus stations, train stations . . . everything goes into finding John Robey. That's what we're doing right now. We're finding this guy. We need to speak to him in relation to the murder of a Washington Police Department detective. That's the line we take. We don't go with the serial killer thing. We take this public. We get them behind us. We might piss them off completely with the parking citations and whatever, but they sure as shit don't like it when people start killing us, know what I mean?'

Miller was silent. He stared at the faces on the wall. Image after image after image. One after the other, seemingly end-less. Who were these people? What were their names? What did they do that prompted their deaths? He had a vague thought in the back of his mind. A vague thought that came out of the things that Robey had told him. Nicaragua. The memory of a long-forgotten war that no-one wanted to re-member. That's what Robey talked to him about. That's what Robey wanted him to understand.

Lassiter looked at Roth. 'You're going with this bullshit too?'

'Give us a minute or two,' Roth said. 'Let us deal with what

456

we have here . . . we'll get the search going. Give us whatever authority we need for this thing and we'll get the search going.'

'I'm getting the whole fucking department going,' Lassiter said. 'Several more departments besides. I'm going to see the chief now. I've got a dead cop, for God's sake—' He turned mid-sentence as a crime scene unit came through the door. Cameras started flashing.

'Jesus, this is a fucking zoo,' Lassiter said. He backed up, Nanci Cohen behind him, Roth and Miller behind her. The four of them made their way into the front room where Miller had first spoken with Robey. Miller remembered how Robey had looked. He remembered what he'd felt when he'd stolen the hairbrush and when he'd returned it. The conversations they'd had – Nicaragua, the cocaine trafficking, the CIA, all of it rushing through his thoughts now as he began to confront what Robey had left behind. Because there was no question in Miller's mind that Robey had created all of it, that he had wanted this apartment searched, that there were things here that he had intended them all to see. John Robey and Catherine Sheridan. Whoever the hell they were, they had created their own world, and now the wider world had been invited to see what they had done.

'You guys stay here,' Lassiter said. 'Make sure everything is done by the book. Soon as I have authority for the statewide and the news I'll call you. You'll need to be there at the press conference.' Lassiter glanced at his watch. 'Ten after nine now . . . expect word by ten, okay?'

Roth nodded in the affirmative.

'Miller!' Lassiter barked.

'I got it, I got it,' Miller said.

They left together, Lassiter and Cohen; Miller and Roth stood in John Robey's front room as the procession went back and forth, people with evidence bags, cameras, with armfuls of files and rolls of paper from the back room.

Miller held his breath for a moment. When he exhaled he seemed to fold in the middle with the pressure of what he was experiencing. He looked back at Roth, opened his mouth to speak, and then a voice called him from the back room.

Miller hadn't even realized it, but Greg Reid was heading up the crime scene unit.

'Have something here,' Reid said. 'Gonna take it away, but I figured you might want to see it before it goes.'

The three of them re-entered the room. A desk-top computer was running, on the monitor a frozen frame – Catherine Sheridan looking back at them as if she was right there in the room.

Reid clicked the mouse and the video started playing.

'Put it down for God's sake,' Catherine Sheridan said. She waved her hand at whoever was filming her. There were trees in the background. She had on a turquoise woollen beret, her hair tucked beneath it. She looked no younger than she had appeared in her autopsy photographs.

'This is recent,' Miller said.

Catherine Sheridan started laughing.

'John, for God's sake,' she said. 'Put the camera away.'

And then it ended. A handful of seconds, nothing more. A fraction of Catherine Sheridan's life.

'It's him, isn't it?' Roth said. 'John Robey . . . he took that footage, didn't he?'

Miller was nodding.

'And he wanted us to see it . . .'

'He wanted us to see what she looked like when she was alive.'

Ten thirty-one p.m, night of Friday, November 17th, 2006, Captain Frank Lassiter appeared on TV screens in bars and pool halls, in airports, in bus and train station waiting rooms, in houses and apartments across the vast expanse of Washington's transmission zone. His words were succinct and clear, and back of him was a large image of John Robey's face, one of the small library of photographs that had been taken when John Robey first appeared at Donovan's diner. This was how John Robey had looked until now. This was how he had looked when Miller had last seen him. There was no guarantee that this was how John Robey would continue to look.

Miller and Roth were present, beside them Assistant District Attorney Nanci Cohen and two staff from her office.

Washington's chief of police was not present: at that moment he was in discussion with the mayor of the city. What they discussed was their own business, the significance of these things in the face of popularity polls and reelection schedules.

Lassiter's statement was brief and concise. A Washington police department detective had been murdered. The man pictured was needed for questioning in connection with this matter. That was all, just questioning. At this time the police could neither confirm nor deny his involvement in the incident, but regardless it was of the utmost importance that he be located. No reference was made to anything else. Not Catherine Sheridan. Not the Ribbon Killer. Nothing.

The news statement lasted approximately one minute and eight seconds, and then the cameras were off, and Miller and Roth stood there, their eyes stunned from the brightness of the TV lights, and Lassiter was walking away from the platform with Nanci Cohen, the two of them deep in conversation.

'At least my wife will know where I am,' Roth said, attempting somehow to make light of the matter.

Miller smiled resignedly.

'So where to now?' Roth asked.

'Back to the Second to see what they've found in the books.'

Roth agreed. There was in fact nowhere else to go.

FIFTY

'Alan Quinn,' Jim Feshbach said. 'Hit and run outside his own home just before Christmas '98. Killed outright.' He held up the sheet of paper with the initials and dates. 'We've only found a few of them . . . girl here, twenty-six years old, Jacqueline Price. Shot in the head with a .22 in Archbold Park. Early evening, no clues . . . no-one ever arrested.'

'Executions,' Miller said quietly.

'What?'

'Executions, that's what they were . . . every single one of them.'

Feshbach, looking puzzled, said, 'I don't understand?'

'Neither do I,' Miller said. 'There won't be any common denominators between them, not as such, not on the surface . . . go a little deeper and I can guarantee that every single one of them was security screened at some point—'

'We found your black guy, the CI,' Vince Littman said.

'Darryl?' Roth asked.

'That's your boy,' Littman replied. 'Darryl King . . . 7th October 2001. Shot dead in the middle of a drugs raid with your friend Sergeant McCullough supposedly guarding his back. What the fuck he was doing taking some regular joe on a drugs raid—'

'He wasn't a regular joe,' Miller said. 'None of them were regular joes.'

'Then who the fuck were they?' Littman asked. 'You said something about witness protection maybe?'

Miller smiled sardonically. It was almost ironic. 'Witness protection? I suppose it was kind of witness protection . . . more like witness removal.'

'You think they knew something?' Roth asked. 'What could they have known? I mean, for God's sake, all of them had different jobs . . . you're talking about killings that go back all of nine or ten years . . .'

'Longer I think,' Miller said. 'I don't think that this is all of them . . . I think this is just the ones that Robey started keeping a record of when he realized what was happening.'

'You've lost me,' Roth said. 'Realized *what* was happening?'

'I don't know yet,' Miller said, 'but all of this has been an effort to get us involved. This is something that I figure he tried to handle himself . . .' Miller shook his head. He leaned forward, rested his elbows on his knees and pressed his palms together. 'I haven't got it,' he said quietly. 'I haven't got what happens here. He knows that people are being murdered. He keeps a record of them. How does he know which ones are related murders, and which are random kill-ings, the work of hit-and-run joy riders, things like that? How does he know this stuff? Because he has records, or because he can access records. He trawls through news-papers, he finds reports of deaths – murders, killings, unex-plained homicides, apparent accidents . . . he crosschecks them somehow. He has computers in his apartment, two or three of them. He has a police receiver. He knew what he was doing, he knew what he was looking for.' Miller turned to Roth. 'When did he start working at Mount Vernon?'

Roth reached for the file, leafed through it. 'May of 1998,' he said.

'And the first date we have is what?' Miller said. 'May 12th, 1998.'

'Which makes me think that he's the one doing the kill-ing,' Feshbach said. 'He arrives in Washington and people start dying. Makes sense, right?'

'Makes sense, but I don't think that's what's happening here,' Miller said.

'So the Ribbon Killer thing . . . where does that take us now?' Riehl asked.

'I'm thinking more than one killer,' Roth said.

'He knew about the lavender,' Miller said.

'He what?'

'Robey, he knew about the lavender—'

'How in fuck's name could he have known that . . . that wasn't even in the papers.'

'Then Robey must be one of them,' Riehl said. 'He *must* have killed these people if he knew about the lavender. And he probably killed Oliver as well.'

Miller got up. 'I don't see it,' he said, pacing the room. 'He knows what's happening, but I don't think he's the one . . .'

'Either he's in on it, or he's accessed confidential case records and found details that weren't made public.'

The desk phone rang. Feshbach picked it up. 'Yes,' he said, held out the receiver towards Roth. 'Lassiter.'

Roth took the phone, listened for a moment, acknowledged and hung up.

'Lassiter's office,' he said to Miller.

Miller and Roth headed upstairs to Lassiter's office.

'Sit down,' Lassiter said as Miller and Roth entered the room.

The captain looked beat-to-shit. ADA Cohen, however, still looked good. She was a tough lady, she endured this shit. Miller respected her greatly.

'We have a major fucking situation here,' Lassiter said. 'Seems we have created a Frankenstein for ourselves . . .' He smiled wearily. 'I got a phone call about fifteen minutes ago from someone named Carol Inchman at the Bancroft Care Home . . .'

'Where Bill Young is,' Miller said.

'Exactly,' Lassiter replied. 'Said that Bill told her to call to let us know that the picture we showed of John Robey was the wrong picture—'

'That it was McCullough, right?' Roth interjected.

Lassiter leaned back in his chair. 'I have some kind of a vague idea of what we have here . . .' He looked at Nanci Cohen as if for some kind of reassurance. None was forthcoming. 'You wanna tell them, or shall I?'

'We have a statement,' ADA Cohen said.

'A statement?' Miller asked.

She nodded. 'A statement.'

'From who?'

'The Justice Department,' she said.

Miller looked at Roth. Roth looked at Lassiter. Lassiter shook his head resignedly.

'The Justice Department?'

Cohen nodded. 'The Justice Department. You know how this works, right?'

'What?'

'The command line on this kind of thing.'

'How d'you mean?' Miller asked.

'You have the president. He's the top of the food chain. You have three bodies beneath him. Legislative, judicial and executive. You'd think that the Justice Department would come under judicial, but it's right there in the executive branch of the government.'

'CIA is in executive, right?' Roth asked.

Cohen nodded. 'CIA, FBI, State Department, National Security Council . . . all of them. Judicial Department is the U.S. Supreme Court and the chief justices . . . ultimately the people I am answerable to as a lawyer, as an assistant district attorney.'

'So we got a statement from the Justice Department, and . . . ?'

'And they are very careful to confirm that—' Nanci Cohen paused as Frank Lassiter handed her a slip of paper. 'Here,' she said. 'Exactly as transcribed from the telephone call we received about fifteen minutes after Frank's broadcast.' She cleared her throat. 'The Justice Department would like to state that at this time there are no clear indications that John Robey was ever employed in any official capacity by any branch or office of the government of the United States, and that there are no extant records of any criminal proceedings that may have been taken against him. However, considering the nature of the investigation that is now being conducted in the capitol, and that an officer of the Washington Police Department has been murdered, it has been concluded by the Secretary of the Justice Department that this investigation will be turned over to the offices of the Federal Bureau of Investigation—'

Miller was up out of his chair. 'You what? What the *fuck*–'

'Sit down!' Lassiter snapped.

Miller dropped into his seat, his eyes wide, his mouth open.

'—Federal Bureau of Investigation, and all ongoing investigatory actions will be coordinated through and by that office. The officers presently responsible for this investigation are acknowledged for their hard work and commitment, but will now be reassigned as determined by their precinct captain.'

Nanci Cohen looked up at Miller and Roth in turn.

Miller was stunned. He felt as if his legs had been cut from beneath him. His breathing was fast and shallow. He felt himself blinking too rapidly, his hands clenching and unclenching involuntarily. 'I don't—' he started, and then he turned and looked at Roth. Roth was looking down at the floor, his eyes closed. Roth looked like he'd been told his kids had died.

Nanci Cohen got up and walked to the window. 'Killarney is on his way,' she said quietly.

'Killarney?' Miller said.

'James Killarney . . . the one who came after the Sheridan murder.'

'I know who he is . . . Jesus, they're sending him over now?'

'Already on his way,' Lassiter said. 'He'll be here before midnight. He'll have people with him. They're going to take everything . . . every record, every file, every shred of paper. Robey's apartment has already been closed off. It now falls within federal jurisdiction.'

'This isn't right,' Miller said. 'This cannot be right. They can't do this . . . for God's sake, how can they even think about doing this?'

'Because they are who they are,' Nanci Cohen said. She had a cigarette in her hand and she put it in her mouth. She raised a lighter, and for a moment her face was half in shadow. 'They made it their business to know what was going on through the reports that were sent to Killarney. Everything that we knew they also knew within a few hours.'

'They were never going to let us complete this thing were they?' Miller asked. 'I mean, for God's sake, who the fuck is this guy Robey?' He shook his head. 'Don't tell me . . . I know who he is . . .'

'They made a point of confirming that he isn't employed in any government office or department,' Roth said.

464

'Point being that they answered a question that we never asked,' Cohen said. 'Which can mean only one thing—'

'That he *is* government,' Miller said. 'But who? FBI? CIA? NSA? Department of Justice?'

Lassiter rose from his desk. 'This conversation isn't happening,' he said quietly.

Miller looked at him; saw Frank Lassiter as he didn't believe he'd ever seen him before. A man scared. A frightened man.

'This conversation isn't happening in this office right now,' he repeated. 'We're going home . . . me and ADA Cohen are going to our respective homes, and you guys are going to wait here for Federal Agent James Killarney and his people to arrive. You're going to give them access to everything that you have on this case, and you're going to let them take it away. You're not going to withhold anything from them, and you're going to accept the fact that this is no longer an active police department investigation. It is now a federal matter, and we're going to leave it to them to handle. When they've gone, you're going to go home too. You're going to spend the weekend with your families or friends . . .' Lassiter paused, took a deep breath, and then sat down again. He gripped the arms of his chair. His knuckles were as white as his face. 'We're going to come back to work on Monday, and we're going to take up some new cases—'

'This is just so much bullshit!' Miller interrupted, his voice insistent, commanding. 'I don't believe you're going to let them do this.'

'*Let* them do this?' Lassiter said, his voice equally loud. '*Let* them do this? What the hell are you talking about? Do you have any fucking idea who you're dealing with here? This is the federal fucking government, Miller. That's where we are right now. Washington, D.C., and the federal government is telling me that a case I am investigating is being turned over to one of their own departments, and . . . God almighty, you think you have any authority over what's happening here? You think *I* do? What do you want me to say? You want to call them back right now . . . oh shit, why didn't I think of that? I'll just give the chief of staff of the justice department a quick call and tell him to go fuck himself. Hell . . . fuck, Jesus fucking Christ—'

'Enough!' Nanci Cohen snapped. 'Wanted to listen to language like this I'd go down the projects. You see what's happening here? You people have to work together on Monday morning. This thing is being taken off of you by the highest authority in the land and they can do whatever the hell they like. No-one has a choice here. You' – she pointed at Miller – 'You have to do what he says because he's your captain. And you,' she added, turning to Lassiter. 'You have to appreciate the frustration these guys are experiencing. You're the only one they can be pissed off at right now, so let them be pissed off. It isn't anyone's *fault*, for God's sake. We took this thing on, we fucked up . . . now I'm even starting to sound like you people.' She gathered up her briefcase, her purse, a PDA and her cell phone from the corner of Lassiter's desk. 'I'm going home,' she said. 'Suggest you do the same.'

Lassiter got up. He walked her to the door, opened it, saw her out. He closed the door and returned to his desk.

'She's right,' Lassiter said. 'We end this thing now, we go home. Monday we talk about it . . . or we don't talk about it. Jesus, I don't know. I can't even think straight right now.' Lassiter looked at Miller, then at Roth, and in his eyes was something that challenged them not only to help him understand what was happening, but also to understand the intractability of his position.

'Monday,' Miller said.

'Monday it is,' Lassiter replied. 'You did good, both of you. You took this thing as far as you could.'

'We took this thing as far as we were allowed—'

Lassiter raised his hand. 'The case has ended, as have the discussions about it.'

'It's not worth our lives, is it?' Miller said. 'I mean, if we pushed on this then they'd find some reason to—'

Lassiter reached out and closed his hand around Miller's forearm. 'Robert,' he said quietly. 'I'll say this once, and then I'll not—'

'I got it,' Miller said. 'I got it completely.'

'So go downstairs. Wait for Killarney. Be polite. In fact,

don't say a thing to the guy . . . just whatever you need to, nothing more. Let them take whatever, okay? Give me your word on this.'

Miller looked down, looked at Roth, looked back to Lassiter. 'You have my word.'

'Good,' Lassiter replied. 'I can't fault what you did. Go home, spend the weekend with your family. Put this thing behind you, okay?'

Lassiter opened the door and watched as Roth and Miller made their way down the hallway to the stairwell.

When they were gone he closed the door quietly, walked back to his desk and sat down. He believed he'd never felt so tired, or so old, in his life.

By the time James Killarney and his six Federal Bureau agents left the Washington Second Precinct building, by the time they drove away in three SUVs carrying everything that Miller and Roth possessed regarding the Ribbon Killer case, it was after two a.m. They left behind an empty office, a room that looked like it had never been occupied. All that remained were trash baskets, ashtrays and blank notepads.

The weekend had already started, and neither Miller nor Roth had had a break since the 11th of November.

'You wanna come over Sunday and have dinner?' Roth asked Miller as they stood outside the precinct house. The night was cold, the sky clear, and Miller could see his own breath in the air.

He shook his head. 'I'm gonna sleep,' he said. 'I'm gonna sleep until Monday morning and then decide whether I want this job any more.'

Roth smiled understandingly. 'You'll want the job,' he said quietly.

'Makes you so sure of that?' Miller asked.

'It's in your blood, my friend . . . this shit is in your blood.'

Less than an hour later Robert Miller stood at his apartment window overlooking Church Street. He stood silently, could barely hear the sound of his own breathing, and then he slowly took a folded piece of paper from his pocket. He turned his back to the window and walked to the coffee table in front of the sofa. He unfolded the paper, pressed the creases out on the hard surface of the table, and looked at the endless rows of letters and numbers that Riehl and Littman and Feshbach had transcribed from Catherine Sheridan's books.

It was the only thing he still possessed from the case. A single sheet of paper scattered with the cryptic representation of more than thirty executions. For that's what they were, of this he felt sure. Executions. For what reason, he did not know. Nor was he sure if John Robey – or Michael McCullough, or any other of the multitude of names he imagined had been used by this man – had been responsible. Regardless, the motive was the important thing, the rationale behind this . . . this nightmare had been created, had been shared by the world, and had now been taken away from him without question or choice or decision.

Quarter after three in the morning, Miller shrugged off his clothes and let them fall to the floor of his bedroom. He lay on the bed and dragged the covers over him. He was asleep within minutes. He did not dream; he had neither the energy nor the will.

FIFTY-ONE

'I said to Zalman, didn't I, Zalman? I said, he has left. Robert has found a girl and he has left. That's what I said.' Harriet poured more coffee. It was nearly one in the afternoon, Saturday the 18th. Miller had slept until noon, had risen, showered, slouched around the apartment for half an hour and then gone downstairs to the diner. He had endured the expected barrage of questions. Where have you been? How come you look so bad? What is this, you can't shave when you get up in the morning? What have you been eating? You've been eating junk food and Coca-Cola again, haven't you? This continued until he put his arms around Harriet Shamir and pulled her close.

'I am a detective of the Washington Police Department,' he whispered in her ear. 'Upstairs I have a gun. If you don't stop with the questions already I will go upstairs and get it . . .'

Harriet wriggled her way out of his arms and hit his shoulder repeatedly with a wooden spoon. She told him to sit down and shut up and mind his manners and wait until some lunch was ready. 'So go – go upstairs and get your gun . . . you hear what he said to me, Zalman?'

'I heard what he said,' Zalman replied.

'What are you going to do about it, eh?'

'Was going to go and get it for him.'

Miller laughed. 'See,' he said. 'We men stick together.'

'Yes, you,' Harriet said. 'Like shit on shoes.'

'Jesus, Harriet, I can't believe you said that.'

'Hey, what's not to believe? I said it. Now shut up – and that means both of you,' she added, raising her voice so Zalman could hear her from the front of the diner.

Harriet brought coffee. She sat for a moment, her hand over Miller's.

'So tell me,' she said. 'This thing you were doing is finished?'

'Basically, yes,' Miller replied.

'Yes is yes, no is no. Basically yes? This I don't understand.'

'The case was transferred to someone else.'

'Because you were not working hard enough? Because you eat badly and don't sleep enough and got lazy, right?'

Miller shook his head. 'No, because I *was* working too hard.'

Harriet smiled in a self-congratulatory way. 'See, there is someone else where you work who has some sense about them. I am telling you this forever, that you work too hard, yes?'

'I don't mean it like that,' Miller said, and then he felt something, a small sense of anxiety, paranoia almost. As if whatever he now said regarding this matter would be known by other people, would be listened to and analyzed. He had slept. He felt better, he needed to eat, sure, but nevertheless he was still thinking with a clearer mind and straighter head than he'd possessed the night before. The Robey case had been spirited away from them. Taken right out of their hands by people he didn't know, would never know. It was not something that Miller even wished to try and understand. He wanted some distance from it. He wanted to spend some time with people who knew nothing about Catherine Sheridan or John Robey or how the government had created its own crack cocaine epidemic in the '80s and '90s. . . .

'So how do you mean it?' Harriet asked.

'It's not something I can talk about.'

'But this thing is finished for you. I know I agreed that I would never ask about your work as long as it was still going on, but if this thing is now finished . . .'

'It's not finished,' Miller said. 'It's been taken over by another department.'

'But not because you didn't work hard enough?'

'Right.'

'So why? Because of something that someone didn't want you to find out?'

Miller flinched. He knew he'd reacted, and that was the last thing he'd wanted to do. Harriet would now be relentless in her questioning if she believed that Miller was hiding something. Usually it related to girls, but this time . . .

'So tell me,' she said.

Miller held her hand, looked right back at her. 'You ever in a situation where you were concerned for your own life?'

'Concerned for my own life?' she said. 'I am seventy-three years old, Robert. I was eight years old when the Germans came and murdered my parents. I survived the concentration camps, you know?'

'I know, Harriet, I know.'

'I've been in a situation where I have held a small crust of bread in my hand and that would have been enough to be executed right where I stood. But I held it, and I didn't let it show on my face, and I took that piece of bread for my sister.'

'I didn't mean to—'

'Hey!'

Miller looked up.

'How long have we been family? Tell me what's happening here. So what's the worst that could happen? If this is so bad then you're already in as much trouble as you can be, and I am seventy-three years old. Sometimes I think to just lie in bed and starve to death, you know? Sometimes I just can't be bothered, but you know what Zalman says?'

Miller shook his head.

'He says get up and go to work or you'll turn out no better than that lazy bastard who lives above the diner.'

Miller looked at her. He frowned for a moment, and then he realized what she'd said.

They started laughing together, loudly, an uproarious noise that brought Zalman through to the back. He stood in the doorway watching them.

'You people better not be laughing about me,' he said.

'You?' Harriet said. 'I wish that you were so funny to make me laugh like this.'

'Ach,' Zalman sneered, and went back to the front to tend to the customers.

'So tell me,' she said when they had settled. 'Tell me what it is that is so bad it pulls your life apart like this.'

Miller did not look at her. He looked at his hands. He opened his mouth to speak, not knowing what he wanted to

471

say, if he really wanted to say anything at all, but he started talking, and though he was careful in what he said, though he gave no names, no specifics, he did tell Harriet Shamir a little of the previous week. And when he was done, when he had told her all he could about dead women and long-ago wars, about drugs and politics, Harriet Shamir patted his hand and said, 'I'll tell you something about the way I see the world, and then you can make your own decision about what to do.'

'Tell me what?'

'There was a pastor, you know? I can't even remember his name, what church he was with . . . it doesn't matter. He was taken to the camps, and he wrote this thing many years later. He said that first they came for the Jews, but he wasn't Jewish so he didn't say anything, you know? He kept his mouth shut. He made himself inconspicuous. Then after the Jews they came for the Poles, and he wasn't Polish so he didn't say anything. Then they came for the scholars and the intellectuals, but he was not a scholar or an intellectual, and so he did nothing. He said nothing. Then they took the artists and the poets, you know, the artistic people. And he wasn't any of these things so he did nothing . . .'

Miller was nodding. 'I've heard this before . . . they finally come to get him, and because there's no-one left then there's no-one to speak out for him.'

'That's what he said.'

'I understand it,' Miller said, 'but I don't see what it has to do with me.'

Harriet smiled. 'I don't care now what they say about Nazi Germany. Nazi Germany was Nazi Germany. There was a long, long history of this sort of persecution going on before then, and there has been a long history of persecution since that time. Look at the Negros, look at the war between Israel and Palestine. Look at Korea, Vietnam, all these things that the Americans have been involved in . . . it's the same war, and it just goes on decade after decade after decade . . .'

Harriet looked up as Zalman appeared in the doorway. 'What have you started now?' he asked Miller. 'You haven't started her on the politics thing have you?'

Miller smiled.

Harriet frowned. 'Away with you,' she said to her husband. 'This is a private conversation.'

Miller could hear Zalman muttering as he went back in front.

'The best kept secrets are the ones that everybody can see,' Harriet said.

Miller raised his eyebrows. 'Whoa, that's a bit deep . . .'

'What are you doing there? You're mocking me?'

'No . . . no, I'm not mocking you.'

'So listen to what I'm saying. You take a look around you. People are afraid to talk about what they see right in front of them.'

'Enough already,' Miller said. 'This is not the conversation I was planning on having today.'

'So why did you tell me about this thing then?'

'God, Harriet, I didn't exactly have a choice.'

'A choice?' Harriet laughed. 'You wear this thing like a coat,' she said. 'You come down here carrying the weight of the world, and all over your face you're saying "Ask me what's wrong. Ask me what's going on . . ." You think I don't see it?'

Miller didn't reply. There was that tension in his lower gut that came from a sense of fear and frustration. He didn't know whether such feelings were attendant to the prospect of what he would find, or the fact that he would risk his career, perhaps even his life, if he looked further into this thing. Regardless, it didn't matter. He knew now there was no other route to take. Already he had his ghosts. He did not want more. Just as it had been with Brandon Thomas and Jennifer Irving, he knew what he knew. It was a small secret, but a secret all the same. Everyone carried demons. John Robey. Catherine Sheridan, whoever was out there doing this work, these executions . . .

They were out there, and Miller knew he had to do something.

'So come eat with us,' Harriet said, 'and then you figure out what you're going to do, okay?'

'Okay,' Miller replied, and they rose from the table together and walked through to the front of the store.

FIFTY-TWO

Miller did not drive to Old Downtown, to Roth's house on E Street and Fifth. He did not call and ask for his viewpoint, for there was no time.

Miller ate with the Shamirs. Afterwards, he went upstairs to shave and get cleaned up, and it was then, sometime before three, that his cell phone rang and without thinking, without even looking at the caller ID, he picked it up from the edge of the dresser near his bed and said, 'Yes?'

'Go to the projects.'

'Who is this?' The voice was familiar.

'Shut up and listen—'

'Robey?' Miller couldn't catch his breath. For a moment he was ready to drop the phone.

'Go to the projects. Find the diplomat.'

'What? Find the diplomat? Who's the diplomat?'

The line went dead.

'Robey? Robey!' Miller shouted into the phone, knowing that it was useless. And then he quickly searched the caller ID function. It said nothing, simply 'Call 1'.

Miller stood there, cell phone in his hand, unable to move. *Go to the projects. Find the diplomat.*

What the fuck did that mean? The projects? Where Natasha Joyce had lived? Those projects? And who was the diplomat? What the hell was that supposed to mean?

Miller dressed quickly, put on a clean shirt, his shoes, a jacket. He took his gun from the drawer beside the bed, his ID, his pager, and left the apartment. He went down the stairwell at the side of the building and walked half a block to where his own car was parked.

It could only be where Natasha Joyce lived. There wouldn't be any other projects . . .

And then Miller stopped. Stopped right there with the key

in the ignition, and for a few moments he considered the significance of the call he'd received. He'd taken a call from John Robey, a man wanted by police and federal authorities, a man who knew more about what had happened than anyone else involved in the investigation, a man who'd just disappeared, gone on the run, subject of an APB across the police network and the TV stations . . .

And the question was simple. Did he really *know* that Robey was not the Ribbon Killer? Was he so sure? Sure enough to do what Robey told him without question, without back-up, without telling anyone?

Miller's hands were sweating profusely. He found the rag he used to clean the inside of the windshield and dried his palms. He lowered the window on the driver's side. He breathed deeply again and again, felt the effort of trying to get his own emotions under control, felt himself trying to focus, to understand what it was that John Robey wanted, why John Robey had chosen him, or whether it had simply been a matter of luck. Luck? Miller smiled to himself. He did not believe in luck. Coincidence, serendipity? Jesus, it couldn't be serendipity. What good could possibly come out of this for him? Right now he was about to continue an unauthorized investigation, to follow an instruction given to him by the very man he was supposed to be looking for. This had been his heartfelt return to the real world, and it had assumed complete possession of his life. Now he had a chance to walk away. Now, for the first time since this nightmare had started, he had a chance to walk away, to do something different, to escape from whatever conspiracy and madness had been created . . .

But he could not.

Harriet Shamir knew that. So did John Robey.

Miller's hand was shaking. He gripped the steering wheel and leaned forward until his forehead touched the back of his knuckles.

'Jesus,' he exhaled.

And despite what he felt, despite the surge of fear that filled his chest, he put the car in gear and pulled out into the street.

*

475

Forty minutes later, again faced with the bleak scenery he'd confronted when he and Roth had visited Natasha Joyce, Miller sat in his car, the engine clicking as it cooled, and looked out across the deserted lot ahead of the project buildings, the same desolate and unrelenting wasteland; and Miller could not help but think of Natasha, of the scene that had faced him when they'd found her body. He thought of Chloe and what would become of her. Thought of those left behind when Margaret Mosley and Barbara Lee and Ann Rayner had died, however many others there might have been . . .

Find the diplomat.

Miller checked his gun and opened the door.

Twenty minutes later, having spoken to three or four people already, he found a gang of teenagers at the corner of a building that looked like something from a war zone.

'Ain't no-one here goes by that name,' the outspoken one said. There was always a self-appointed leader, the one at the front, the one with a voice for all of them. He grinned. Gold teeth alternately. A hell of a smile.

'We got all sorts here, my man, but we ain't got no diplomat.'

One of the kids in the back, couldn't have been no more than fourteen or fifteen, stepped forward and motioned for the leader to come close. The leader backed up, shared a few words with the kid, and then once again grinned at Miller with his five thousand-dollar smile. 'Someone send you down here to find the diplomat?'

Miller nodded. 'That's right.'

'And that's a person there yo' talkin' 'bout?'

'I figure so.'

'So it might not be a person is what I'm sayin'.'

Miller shook his head. 'Don't see how it could be anything but a person.'

'You got fifty dollars?' the leader asked.

Miller frowned.

'You want some help . . . you wan' a little guided tour, then yo' gotta pay the tallyman, yeah?'

'I don't have fifty dollars,' Miller said.

'Bullshee-it! You ain't got fifty dollars?'

Miller laughed. 'I haven't. Seriously. I've got maybe thirty, thirty-five dollars, that's all.'

'Pay it over here, my man.'

'What?'

'Pay over the thirty-fi' dollar and we gon' show you the diplomat.'

'You know who it is?' Miller asked.

The leader turned and gestured toward the younger kid he'd spoken to. 'My boy here knows where the diplomat is at. Pay the thirty-fi' dollar and we gon' take you there.'

Miller went through his pockets, turned them out, collected together everything he had.

'Thirty-six seventy,' he said. He handed the notes and change over to the leader who buried it in his jeans pocket.

'Yo!' the leader snapped at the younger kid. 'Show my man where the diplomat is at.'

The kid grinned, turned, started at a jog within a moment, and then Miller went after him, the six or seven others following on behind. It became an event: shouting kids, Miller up ahead, a single kid ahead of him. It looked like the first kid was being chased, the gang behind Miller trying to catch up with Miller and stop him. They jogged for a good two or three minutes, and then the kid slowed up and looked back at Miller. He went backwards, right arm outstretched, and after another thirty or forty meters he pointed to the right, and Miller was looking for what the kid was showing him.

Miller could see nothing but the shell of a burned-out car, crates and pieces of wood scattered across the ground, an up-ended armchair, the stuffing torn out of the back like it had been ceremoniously gutted. He could see no-one. He could not see whoever the kid was pointing at.

'Where?' Miller said. 'Where are you pointing?'

The kid started laughing. 'There's your diplomat,' he said.

The leader was alongside Miller now, laughing himself, Miller wondering what the hell was going on.

'He's right,' the leader said. 'There's your fuckin' diplomat.'

Miller looked again, could see nothing. 'This is bullshit,'

477

Miller said. 'What the fuck is this . . . there was a deal here . . .'

'And we kept the fuckin' deal,' the leader said. He waved the younger kid over. 'Tell the man,' he said. 'Tell the man what we have here.'

'Dodge,' the kid said. 'Dodge le Baron Diplomat '78,' and he pointed at the burned-out wreck of a car.

'That's a Diplomat?' Miller said.

'Sure the fuck is,' the leader said. 'My boy here knows every goddam car ever been made in the last I don't know how many fuckin' years. Kid's head is like a rolodex for cars, man, a fuckin' rolodex for cars.'

Miller approached the vehicle. The thing was black with fire, the original color long since unidentifiable, the window gone, the tires melted to the ground. The whole thing had been consumed.

Miller turned back to the gang of kids. 'How long's it been here?'

'Two days ago,' the car expert said. 'Was brought out here and burned two days ago.'

'Thursday,' Miller said.

'Thursday,' the kid echoed.

Miller looked in through the holes where the windows had been. He walked around the blackened shell of the thing, the sound of broken glass beneath his shoes, the smell of burned rubber and burned paint and burned metal in his nostrils. Someone had brought this thing out here the day after Natasha Joyce's murder and had set it on fire. Why? What was the significance of it?

The gang of kids came up behind Miller, curious, looking into the car, wondering what the deal was.

'I need to open the trunk,' Miller said.

A couple of kids started searching for something. One of them handed him a tire lever with a twisted end. Miller took it with both hands and drove it repeatedly into the trunk lock until the thing popped through and fell with a clatter into the well beneath. He then used the edge of the lever to prize open the trunk.

The smell was unbearable.

One of the kids started screaming. Another one turned

away and started retching. Miller stood there for a moment trying to gain some semblance of understanding of what he was looking at. He knew what it was. He knew exactly what it was, but it was almost as if his mind was fighting to make it something else.

The man had been bound tightly, his hands and feet behind him, the rope pulled taut so his back was arched. Some sort of covering had been put over his head, but this had charred and degraded with the heat of the fire, and what remained of his face was visible. A rictus expression of the most horrendous pain. His teeth were bared, his lips burned away, much of his nose gone, his ears and hair sort of glued together in a dark matted clump of blood and tissue that had appeared to settle across one side of his head and then dissolve down his cheek. The protection offered by the trunk itself had meant that instead of burning, the man had baked to death within. Nausea rose in Miller's chest and throat.

Many of the kids had run away. The leader of the group stood there, his eyes wide, his mouth open. Two or three times he started to say something and then he just closed his mouth and said nothing at all.

Miller took out his cell phone. He dialled Roth, told him where he was, what he'd found. Roth asked him how he'd known, where the information had come from. Miller said he'd call later. Miller then called the Second, told them to get someone from the coroner's office down there. Lastly he called Marilyn Hemmings directly.

'Detective Miller,' she said.

'Hey there . . . I was gonna call—'

'No you weren't.'

'Sure I was—'

'What do you want, Detective Miller?' Her tone was cool, a little dismissive.

'I need your help, Marilyn . . .'

'Again? What am I? The Detective Robert Miller Appreciation and Support Society?'

'I got a body down here, burned to fuck in the trunk of a car, and I need an autopsy done now.'

'Now? It's getting on for five o' clock on a Saturday evening . . .'

'I know, I know . . . but this is really important.'

'I'm very sure that it is really important, Detective Miller, but where I have agreed to be at seven o'clock this evening is also really important. After forensics have done whatever they need to do out there I wouldn't even get the body until nine or ten o'clock, and that's at the earliest.'

'Can you come later . . . could you come in later? You know . . . after you've done whatever you're doing at seven o'clock, could you come back and do this thing?'

Marilyn Hemmings was silent.

'Marilyn?'

'What the fuck is this, Robert? Who the fuck am I? You think I'm here to attend to your whims as and when you feel like it? This is my job, sure it is . . . but I'm off-shift at five-thirty, and then I'm going out, and when I'm done going out I'm planning on going home, and it'll be late then so I'll have some herbal tea and answer my e-mails and go to bed. That's what I do, Robert . . . at least that's what I'm planning on doing tonight, and no, I don't have any interest in dragging myself back to work at ten or eleven o'clock tonight to look at the burned corpse of some poor bastard who got locked in the trunk of a car . . .'

'Marilyn . . . Marilyn, I really need your help with this—'

'Leave it alone, will you? Have the night shift guys do it. Who's on tonight?' Hemmings turned away from the mouthpiece and shouted for Tom Alexander. 'Tom? Tom? Who's on tonight?'

Miller heard Tom Alexander speaking in the background.

'Urquhart, Kevin Urquhart. He's as good as any of us. He's on all night, Robert, and he can do your party favors for you, okay?'

'Marilyn, seriously. I need this done by someone who knows what's been happening here. This is a big deal to me, a really big deal, and I need your help.'

'And why the fuck should I, Robert? Tell me that. Why the fuck should I go out of my way to help you yet again . . . seems to me you've gotten me into enough trouble already, and I really don't know why—'

'Are you pissed off at me because I didn't call you?'

Marilyn Hemmings laughed – suddenly, abruptly. 'I'm not

having this conversation, okay? I don't want to have this conversation with you.'

'I'll call you later,' Miller said. 'I'll call you when the body's back at the coroner's office.'

'Do whatever you like, Robert . . .'

The line went dead, and as Miller began wondering if he could have possibly managed to handle the situation any worse he was interrupted by the sound of vehicles, the sound of a siren, the flashing of lights as two unmarked cars and a coroners' wagon started down along the road at the edge of the tenement block.

The kids scattered, all of them except the leader, and when Miller looked at him he smiled his five-thousand dollar smile and shook his head.

'Hey,' he said. 'Down here, man . . . hell, we might be fucked up, but least we don't barbecue our people in their fuckin' cars, you know?' and then he turned, and before Miller could speak he too was gone.

FIFTY-THREE

Eight forty-eight p.m. forensics released the body to the coroner's office. Miller had spoken with Roth once more, had told him that it was best he stayed out of it, that if anything came of it he would let him know. He was aware of the relief in Roth's voice. Miller did not call Lassiter, did not relay a message to ADA Cohen. For now he wished for no-one but himself to be aware of the connection between John Robey and a burned-out Dodge Diplomat in the projects. There was also the fact that the forensics report on Natasha Joyce's apartment had never been forwarded. He began to wonder if there had in fact been a forensics examination at all.

It was Greg Reid who called Miller, asked him where he was, what he was doing, whether he could make his way down to the forensics complex. Miller said he could, that he'd be there by quarter after nine.

Reid met him in the annexe corridor, indicated that they should walk down the side of the building and go in through the rear doors. Miller didn't ask, didn't need to ask; he knew that Reid would not have called him unless there was something of significance to relay.

He showed Miller into a laboratory in the furthermost wing, directed him to an examination table, on it some fragments of something, beside them a plastic evidence baggie with something unidentifiable inside.

'This is not good,' Reid said quietly. Even as he spoke he looked nervously toward the door through which they'd come.

Miller didn't reply. His expression was all the prompting that Reid needed.

Reid snapped on a latex glove, and then with a pair of tweezers he lifted one of the small fragments from the examination table. 'This,' he said, 'was found around the neck of the victim . . . as far as I can tell it was originally orange.' Reid lowered the fragment to the desk, set the tweezers aside, and then carefully lifted the baggie. 'In here, this small melted mess of whatever, is a collection of similar multi-colored items—'

He looked up at Miller.

'Ribbons,' Miller said calmly.

Reid nodded.

'Same composition?'

Again Reid nodded in the affirmative.

Miller looked around for a chair.

Reid joined him, the two of them seated beside one another in silence for a good three or four minutes.

'Who knows?' Miller asked.

'You do.'

'When do you file your report?'

'I have a week's backlog already.'

'Anything in the car or on the body that indicated who he might have been?'

'Nothing in the car could have survived. Just luck that those fragments of ribbon weren't ash already.'

'Did you do the Joyce apartment?'

'Another team,' Reid replied.

Miller felt the agitation in his lower gut, the blood in his temples.

'How did you know about the car?' Reid asked.

'I got a call.'

'From?'

'Anonymous.'

'Was it him?'

Miller shook his head. 'I don't know who it was . . . they disguised their voice.' He did not look at Reid; he was not a good liar, and he knew Reid would see right through him.

'So what do you want me to do?' Reid asked.

'Do what you ordinarily do . . . though if you can handle your backlogged reports first it would be appreciated.'

'That won't be a problem,' Reid said. 'I'm supposed to handle the backlog in date sequence anyway.'

'Appreciated.'

483

'So what are you going to do now?'

'Gonna try and get Hemmings to do the autopsy.'

'Keep it in the family, eh?'

'Meaning?'

Reid shook his head. 'As few people as possible that are involved in this the better.'

Miller looked at Reid quizzically. 'Why d'you say that?'

''Cause this is someone else's Watergate isn't it?' he said. 'This really is someone's nightmare coming home, don't you think?'

'I was hoping not,' Miller said. 'With everything, I was hoping it wouldn't be the case.'

'You still working on it?'

'Not officially, no.'

'Unofficially?'

'That's the second question you've asked me that you don't really want to know the answer to.'

'Sure I do,' Reid said, and he smiled sarcastically.

Miller rose to his feet.

'Good luck, eh?'

'Don't believe in luck,' Miller said.

'Maybe you should start.'

Miller called Marilyn Hemmings at ten after eleven.

'I'm at home,' she said.

'Tell me where you live . . . I'll come pick you up.'

'Where are you now?'

'Your office.'

'Is Urquhart there?'

'Yes, he is.'

'So get him to do your autopsy . . . I've been out. I went for a meal and had some drinks. My hands aren't as steady as they should be. Besides, what the hell does that even matter, I'm not at work. It's nearly quarter after eleven. Leave me alone.'

'Marilyn . . . . I *need* you to do this one. I need *you* to do this for several different reasons, and I wish I could tell you what they were but not over the phone. Let me come and get you and bring you over here, okay? I need to know who this guy is—'

'Tomorrow—'

'I might not have tomorrow—'

'Oh come on, don't give me that shit. What kind of melodramatic crap is that, huh?'

Miller was taken aback. 'I don't know what I did, Marilyn—'

'You don't know what you *did*? You're not listening to yourself are you? You don't know what you did? How about theft of evidence or collaboration to withhold evidence . . . how about employing a city official to assist you in the theft of evidence . . . how about that for starters?'

'Look, I know . . . I'm sorry, I'm really sorry. I didn't want to put you in this situation, but right now there are only about three or four people who really have any kind of an idea about what's going on here and I have to keep it that way. I cannot allow this thing to get out, Marilyn. I've had the entire case taken off me by the Feds—'

'You what?'

'You didn't know that the FBI are now running the entire thing?'

'No. God, when the fuck did that happen?'

'Yesterday.'

'So . . . what? So, what you're actually telling me is that you're off this case but you'd like me to come in and do an autopsy anyway, an autopsy on someone who might very well be directly connected to the case that you've just had taken from you by the FBI?'

'As it stands they are not connected, Marilyn—'

'Is that the same way the last favor you asked of me was not connected to this case, or is this some other way it's not connected?'

'Okay,' Miller said. 'We haven't even been out and already we're fighting . . .'

'This isn't a joke, Robert.'

'No, I'm sorry, I didn't mean for it to be a joke. I'm just a little puzzled why you're so upset with me.'

Marilyn Hemmings said nothing for a moment, and then she sighed audibly. 'How bad is this thing?' she asked.

'I don't want to speak on the phone, Marilyn, I really

don't. It's late. I'm sorry for troubling you. I'll get Urquhart to do it.'

'Are you in trouble . . . I'm asking now, seriously, Robert, are you in some kind of trouble?'

'I don't know, Marilyn . . . I really don't know what we've got here.'

'Do you know . . .' She paused. 'Hell, what am I thinking? It's after eleven. God almighty, Robert Miller, the shit you have gotten me into . . . I don't know what the fuck I'm doing. I'll be there in half an hour.'

She hung up before Miller had a chance to reply.

Miller waited for Hemmings in the foyer of the building. Without authorization he was not permitted access to the coroner's laboratory. As she walked down the outer corridor toward him she did not look up. She seemed subdued, and when she took him back of the reception zone there was something amidst the myriad ways she looked at him that told him that she was angry. With the situation yes, but more than that she was angry with him.

'I don't like this,' she said coldly. 'I have done something that I should not have done. Now you're calling me in out of hours. What do I do, Robert? Do I log my hours and then come up with some sort of explanation as to why I'm here at this time of night, or do I say nothing, file the report, and then wait for someone to put two and two together and come and ask me what I was doing here. I saw Urquhart. I told him I'd left something behind. That sounds good, eh? Oh, yes, I left something in my office, so important I came in after eleven. And while I was here I figured I'd do everyone a favor by doing an autopsy while I had a few moments.'

Miller didn't speak.

'Where did you find the car?'

'The projects.'

'Same as the black woman?'

'Yes.'

'Then they're connected.'

'Assume so.'

'And this anonymous call you got . . . it wasn't anony-mous was it?'

Miller shook his head.

'Was it him?'

'Yes.'

'And you're telling me that you've been taken off of the case, the Feds have assumed complete control over it, and you're not reporting this to them.'

'That's right.'

'So where the fuck does that put me?'

'You plead ignorance,' Miller said. 'You do the thing, you plead ignorance.'

'But I'm not ignorant—'

'Doesn't mean you can't say you were.'

'Is that the way it works with you?' she asked, and there was an edge to the question, a pointed edge which arrived exactly as it was intended, right between the ribs. It was a stiletto knife of a question. *Did you push Brandon Thomas down the stairs and kill him? Did you murder that man, and then tell the world that you were innocent, that it was an accident?*

'No,' Miller said.

'But that's what you're asking me to do?'

Miller looked down at the floor. He felt the weight of it all. He felt conscience and responsibility, obligation, the promise he'd made to Natasha Joyce. He felt a sense of loss, the beginning and end of so many things. He felt lonely and tired and sick and confused, and none of it made sense, and he was beginning to wonder if he even wanted it to make sense any more. He wanted to know what right John Robey had to break his life apart and kick the pieces all over.

'What do you want from me?' Marilyn Hemmings asked. 'You want me to break the law? You want me to violate protocol? You want me to do an autopsy on someone and not file a report?'

'I want to know who he is, Marilyn, that's all. I want to know who the guy is. I know how he died. I know what happened to him. I know someone tied a ribbon around his neck and locked him in the trunk of a car, and then they set the car on fire and he burned to death inside . . .'

'He had a ribbon around his neck?'

'According to CSA Greg Reid, yes . . .'

'Oh God, no.'

'Yes. And in the glove box of his car was a collection of ribbons—'

'So who the fuck is this?' she asked.

Miller shook his head. 'I don't know who it is. I need to know who it is, I need to know now, and you're the only person I can trust to do this . . .'

'Trust? Is that what this is about? You think someone's after you?'

Miller didn't reply.

'Oh for God's sake,' she said. 'This is really beginning to scare me now.'

Miller reached out and took her hand. He held it for a moment, looked right at her. For a moment she did not seem to want to look at him.

'Can you just do this?' he asked. 'Can you just see if there is a name to go along with this guy?'

'Where did they put the body?'

'They said Lab Four, is that right?'

Together they walked through the complex to Lab Four. Hemmings told Miller to stay back against the wall and away from the door. The charred remains of the trunk victim were on an examination table. Hemmings switched on the overhead lights and the brights to the left of the table. She took latex gloves from a box on the side, and then she stood quietly for a moment before the blackened and distorted cadaver.

'Definitely male,' she said, almost to herself, but loud enough for Miller to hear her. 'Appears to be late forties, perhaps early fifties. Five-nine or ten. There had been some bruising beneath the skin, the appearance of centimeter-wide lines at the ankles and wrists. Appearance of having been bound tightly by something that has left a plastic-type residue. Nylon rope, perhaps ziplock-ties.'

Miller stepped closer and watched as Hemmings took a sliver of skin from the man's arm, a layer of epithelials which she placed inside a glass receptor. She processed it for DNA sampling, and while the machine did its business she prepared a scalpel.

'Just sting for a second,' she said quietly, and then she inserted the blade of the scalpel into the arch of the foot and scraped away a sample of coagulated blood. She transferred the blood from the blade of the scalpel to a petrie dish and covered it.

'Two alleles,' she said, once she had typed the blood. She concentrated to such an extent that Miller believed she'd forgotten he was there. 'One comes from each parent, and in this man's case one was a dominant A, the other O.'

Miller looked away for a moment. There was tension in the atmosphere, something palpable, as if a shadow was pressing against him from all sides and there was no way to determine how it was being cast. He backed up and sat down for a moment, afraid he would lose his balance. He leaned forward with his elbows on his knees, hands together. 'I don't know why I came here,' he said.

Marilyn Hemmings turned and looked at him. 'I have no prints to work with,' she said. 'His hands are too burned for me to print. There's not enough for me to work with, Robert . . .'

Miller wanted to stand. He wanted to walk towards her. He wanted to leave behind the charred remains of someone found in the trunk of a car and just vanish. Either that or go backward and decline the call to the Sheridan house that night of the 11th. He wished it was someone else's problem, but it was not, and now he had made it Marilyn Hemmings' problem, also Greg Reid's, even Al Roth's to some extent, because if one member of a partnership was drowning then the other would usually go with him.

The machine bleeped. CODIS had come back with nothing. That would have been too rich for words.

'So we have no way of knowing who he was?' Miller asked unnecessarily.

'You knew that before you called me,' she replied. 'You knew that it would be a dead end.'

Miller didn't speak.

'Why?' she asked.

Miller looked up at her. 'God, Marilyn, I don't know . . . because of what happened before. Because you seemed to understand what I was going through when they were trying to crucify me for what happened with Thomas and the hooker.'

Hemmings didn't speak for a moment. She peeled off her gloves and dropped them in a waste bucket. She crossed the corner of the lab and sat beside Miller. She reached out and took his hand, held it for a moment. When Miller turned she was looking directly at him. It made him feel tense, awkward. He knew what she was going to ask him.

'Was she just a hooker?'

Miller lowered his head and closed his eyes.

'Answer the question, Robert . . . was she just a hooker, or was there something else going on?'

'She was just a hooker,' Miller said.

'Did you ever—'

'Did I what? Did I ever sleep with her? Did I fuck her?'

'Don't be angry . . . I'm not the one who's got you into this. Don't vent your—'

'I'm sorry,' Miller replied. 'I'm sorry. The whole thing makes me angry. You're right. It's not you. Jesus, this thing is driving me crazy.' Miller released Hemmings' hand and stood up. He took a couple of steps and then turned to face her.

'I don't know why I got you into this,' he said.

Hemmings smiled sardonically. 'I'm all grown-up now,' she said. 'I'm perfectly capable of saying no . . .'

'Then why didn't you? Why didn't you just say no and stay the fuck out of this? It's not safe. It's dangerous. There's something going on here that has resulted in a whole lot of dead people, and it seems like whoever is behind this has no intention of stopping.'

Hemmings shrugged. 'What d'you want me to say? That I did it for you? That I wasn't interested in the case but I was interested in you? That I thought it might give us a chance to spend some time together . . . because if that's what you think then that's not what happened, Robert. This isn't all about you, you know.'

'I didn't say it was—'

'Let me finish, okay? That much at least.'

Miller nodded.

'This isn't all about you. This is about something that I am having great difficulty understanding. I only know so much about what's happened. And you think I don't feel for you? I

490

don't have any kind of compassion for someone who's in difficulty? I'm human, just like everyone else. You came to me and asked me to help you, and I saw someone who'd been through the mill with IAD and the newspapers. I saw someone trying to do a good job who got himself kicked all over the place by some bullshit about a pimp and her hooker, and I thought that maybe you needed a hand, okay? I figured that you were someone who was trying to make a difference, trying to make things better, and you needed a bit of moral support. That was all there was to it. Nothing more nor less than that. You want to be a magnet for trouble then be a magnet for trouble. Maybe there's something about people like you that makes people like me want to help you. Maybe I just think you're so fucked up that if you don't have someone giving you a hand then you'll wind up dead.'

'That might be exactly what happens,' Miller said, and though he did not intend to imply anything humorous, Marilyn Hemmings smiled and said, 'I'll do your autopsy, okay? I'm the best they've got and I'll make sure it's done by the book.'

'Thank you . . . that's very reassuring to know.'

'So what are you going to do?' she asked. 'You gonna keep pushing at this thing until someone finds out and threatens you with your job?'

'I don't know,' he said.

Hemmings rose to face him. Though she was a good four or five inches shorter than him, she had sufficient presence to make him feel as if he was being looked down on.

'Tomorrow I'll do a full autopsy,' she said. 'I don't know that there's anything I'll be able to tell you about the guy. His DNA isn't on our system. We have no prints. Maybe there was something in the car.'

'There was nothing in the car. I don't know . . . I really don't know. I'll give you a ride home. Do you need a ride home?'

'I have my own car here. I don't think it's a good idea that we speak to one another on anything but a professional basis until this thing is finished. That's what I feel right now, and I don't think I'm going to change my mind.'

'I understand,' Miller said. 'It's not the way I wanted it to be, but I understand.'

'So go,' she said. 'Go the way we came in. Don't speak to anyone. I'll clean up here, put our guest in storage, and then if anything comes of the autopsy tomorrow I'll send you the report, okay?'

'Thank you,' Miller said. He held out his hand. 'I'd hug you but I don't think you want me to,' he said.

Hemmings shook Miller's hand. 'Goodbye, Detective Miller, and good luck.'

'Don't believe in luck,' Miller said.

Hemmings nodded toward the body on the examination table. 'He probably didn't either.'

FIFTY-FOUR

One a.m., morning of Sunday, November 19th. Robert Miller had not even removed his shoes, such was the inertia he felt. He remembered the night he'd walked along Columbia Street, the questions he'd asked, his first inkling that there was something beyond the death of Catherine Sheridan than just her murder. It was not rage or jealousy, neither was it the work of some uncontrollable sociopath. It was premeditated, calculating, decisive and exact. Eight days had passed. Everything had turned upside down. Catherine Sheridan had merely been the precursor to a far greater horror. Catherine Sheridan had been his introduction to an entirely different world.

In his hand he held a single sheet of paper. The initials, the dates, like a roll-call of the dead. Seemed everyone who'd touched this thing was dead.

Roth had called – two missed messages on Miller's cell phone – but Miller had not returned them. Roth did not deserve this. Roth had Amanda and the kids to consider. Roth had a life worth something. What did Miller have? He had a dead hooker, her dead pimp, an assistant coroner who wished to keep everything distant and purely professional. He had two old Jewish people who worried whether he ate too little and worked too much. He had a rented apartment, a piece of paper, a sense of failure.

And he had John Robey, or rather – more accurately – John Robey had him.

We are bound by the secrets we share. That was the thought in his mind. Where it had come from – something he'd read, a line from a movie – he couldn't recall, but it went round and round ceaselessly.

We are bound by the secrets we share.

At one point he considered that Robey must have said it,

493

but then it seemed to make no sense at all. Robey had said everything, but nothing. Robey had given him all that he needed to know, but given it in such a way that it could never be understood.

Miller turned over every single word he could recall, every statement Robey had made, every implied question and inconclusive answer. The man had engineered everything, of this Miller was sure.

And who was the man in the trunk? The Ribbon Killer, or another victim? Had Robey killed him, or was he merely another of the thirty or forty or fifty that had already been murdered? And again he pondered on why were they killed . . . for something they'd done? Surely not. Surely all of them couldn't have been part of one punishable crime.

Miller sat down and worked his shoes off without untying the laces. He kicked them sideways, wished he had a drink – a can of beer, a glass of whiskey, anything at all to close down the rush of thoughts. It was remorseless, all of it. Remorseless, unforgiving, nothing to hold onto, nothing that indicated any way of escape or resolution. If there was an investigation to pursue, he would not be pursuing it. It would be Killarney. The FBI's guest, the serial killer expert, the man who knew everything and yet had come to the party without a gift of his own. What had he told them? He had told them how difficult it would be to find the man who had done these things. He had made it all seem so vague and imprecise and unclear.

What was the thread that linked these victims? Had they all been involved in something that made them a danger to someone? What possible motivation could precipitate the killing of thirty, forty . . . however many people?

Miller reached for the list again, the single sheet of paper that revealed a greater horror than he could have imagined. The initials and dates of murders, dozens of them, and he found it so hard to believe they were all for one reason. But then such things had happened before. The death of sixty-four material witnesses to Jack Kennedy's assassination. Car accidents. Falls. Suicides. Heart attacks. All within eighteen months of the event. This was something of similar magnitude. And what was back of it? Nicaragua. That was the direction that Robey had kept on pushing him. Nicaragua was like Salvador, like Korea, like Vietnam. Periods of America's history considered unsafe to remember, events that people pretended had never occurred.

And then Miller thought of Carl Oliver. Thought of his body there on the walkway outside Robey's apartment. Someone had been inside, someone had opened up that door and shot Oliver right where he stood.

And there had been no autopsy or forensics reports issued on the Natasha Joyce killing.

And there was no thread, and nothing that made any goddamned sense at all . . .

Miller leaned forward, elbows on his knees, head in his hands. He closed his eyes and tried to breathe deep and slow.

He was exhausted, a fatigue so bone-deep he could barely feel his body any more, but these questions would prevent him feeling anything at all but the tension and paranoia of all that he did not understand. He just needed one thing to follow, one thing that would open another door beyond all those that had been closed . . .

In the early hours of the morning he fell asleep fully clothed. Exhaustion swallowed him wholesale, and he did not wake until the early afternoon. By the time he had showered and dressed it was close to four, and for no other reason than to breathe fresh air, to see something other than case files and computer screens, he took a walk from his apartment. He stopped at a restaurant beyond Logan Circle, ate more than he had in the previous forty-eight hours, and realized that somewhere he had to find a balance. If he continued in this manner he would not make it.

He walked home, let himself in the back way, tried to watch some TV, but his mind was elsewhere.

A little after eight it came to him.

Follow the money.

Catherine Sheridan had received money at the end of each month from . . . from where?

Miller got up and started pacing back and forth between the door and the window. He tried to recall when he'd seen the statements. He tried to picture himself standing in the room with Al Roth, leafing through those pages, one after the other after the other . . .

Miller thought to call him, glanced at his watch, decided against it.

He went through to the kitchen and made coffee. He stood there, concentrating, trying to see nothing but the minutes when he'd had those pages in his hands.

It was like the McCullough account. Not the account, but the bank. Washington American Trust. There was something that connected them. Washington? Trust?

Miller suddenly got it. Trust . . . United Trust. Those payments had originated from some entity that called itself United Trust. They had never pursued it. He shook his head, cursed himself. There were so many things they hadn't pursued, but they'd had so little time, and so much had happened . . .

He sat down at the kitchen table. He took an unopened envelope, some piece of junk mail, and scribbled 'United Trust' across the back of it. He went to the internet, ran a search for any such company. There was nothing within the Washington city limits. He checked nationally, found a good dozen companies with 'United Trust' somewhere in their corporate name. The closest was Boston. There hadn't been anything in Catherine Sheridan's house to suggest some line of work – a remote salesperson, an out-of-state representative of some financial institution. Once again, it was the reality defying the appearance. Fact still remained that she'd been receiving an income from some outfit bearing the name United Trust. These things went both ways. If he couldn't find the company directly, he would have to go at it from a different direction. The money she'd received had arrived into an account. Miller had seen the statements in her house. Now it was a matter of remembering the name of the bank that Sheridan had used.

Maybe he could do something, but to do it he had to remember the name of the bank.

Miller smiled when he thought of who would know. John Robey would know. More than likely he knew everything there was to know about Catherine Sheridan. Would Roth remember it? There was no way of telling. There were lines drawn in sand, and Roth would not be willing to cross them. Not because he was afraid, but because he was attuned to his family, a concern for their welfare, the fundamental necessities of survival for which he was responsible.

Miller went back to the internet. There were dozens of banks in the city. Washington Finance, American Union, Corporate Loan & Savings, East Coast Mercantile, Capital, Merchant & Legal – page after page, the names blurring one into the other until Miller couldn't see properly. He leaned back and closed his eyes for a moment. Once more he tried to picture the pages that he held in his hand. He could see a blue and green logo, of this he was sure. A blue and green logo, almost a square, perhaps an oval? He ran the images option, and then typed in 'Washington banks'.

Bottom of the second page he found it. A blue and green logo, an oblong design with rounded corners. He clicked on the image, waited a moment, and the site came up. First Capital Bank. This was it. This was definitely the logo he remembered in the left-hand corner of Catherine Sheridan's statements. Payments from United Trust into the First Capital Bank in the name of Catherine Sheridan.

There was a direction to take. There was something he could do.

Miller took a note of the bank's address. Vermont Avenue, the same as the Washington American Trust where the McCullough account was held.

His feelings of anxiety had increased. He was scared, no doubt about it, but how else should he feel? There was no other appropriate emotion for such a situation. He was planning on doing something that he knew he absolutely should not do. Despite every rational thought he possessed screaming at him to let it go, he could not.

Monday morning he would go see Nanci Cohen. He would ask her for something without directly asking, and then he would visit the First Capital Bank on Vermont Avenue and see what he could learn.

Miller drew the drapes a handful of inches. He looked

through the gap into the late night of Washington. The streetlights, the sound of traffic somewhere on the highway, the sense that everything was out there waiting for morning.

The sense of being watched was suddenly overwhelming. He pulled the drapes together and stepped back. His heart missed a beat. He felt his knees begin to give, and he turned and walked back to the chair by the door.

He looked down at his hands. They were shaking.

He'd never felt like this before. Invaded. Possessed by something. Driven to find something out that he had been instructed to leave alone.

He wondered whether Robey had chosen him all along, and if so . . . if so, for what possible reason?

Catherine Sheridan's death had been reported like any other murder. How could Robey have known that he would get the call-out?

Miller tried to convince himself that Robey could not have known. Robey could not have been *that* much in control, surely . . .

And then Miller tried to stop thinking. He lay down on the bed. He wanted to sleep but could not. He had slept into the early afternoon, and now felt nothing but agitation and restlessness. He put on the TV again, surfed until he found something that caught his attention, lost interest, surfed again, and on it went until he could bear it no longer. Close to midnight he took a drive, listening to the radio, trying to focus on nothing but the road ahead of him.

Back at the apartment by two, he showered again, lay on his bed again. He knew he would not sleep, and it took all his patience to wait until daylight broke through the curtains and told him that Monday had arrived.

When Miller finally went downstairs to the deli there must have been something in his expression, for Harriet took one look at him and nodded understandingly. She did not press him to eat breakfast. She made him fresh coffee, set the cup before him at the table in the back, and then went through to help her husband in the front.

Miller drank his coffee. He looked back at Harriet as he

closed the street door behind him. She did not speak, and Miller himself said nothing.

Perhaps she, of all people, understood more of what he was doing than anyone.

FIFTY-FIVE

Miller called Roth a little before nine, told him he was going to take a drive somewhere, perhaps down to Hampton to look at the Atlantic.

'You okay?' Roth asked.

'As can be.'

'You wanna come over watch some football later?'

'No,' Miller replied. 'I wanna spend some time outside. Get some air. This thing is bullshit. I just want to get away for a few hours.'

'Call me if you need anything,' Roth said.

'It's okay. Say hi to everyone for me.'

'Come over later, say hi yourself.'

'I might do that.'

Miller hung up, pulled away from the back of the Second Precinct and drove west toward Nanci Cohen's offices.

The Assistant District Attorney smiled a lot for someone in her position.

She had one of her people go out and get coffee. She insisted Miller try some kind of macchiato thing. It had a caramel under-taste that he found nauseating.

Nanci Cohen was the kind of woman that Harriet Shamir would recognize. She put herself right up front, right there ahead of everything, and there was no ignoring her.

'You can't,' was Nanci Cohen's response. It was an uncomplicated and unconditional response, and there was something about her directness that made Miller smile.

'What? You think I'm joking?' she asked.

'No, I don't think you're joking.'

'So what are you telling me then? You smile like this is some kind of comedy scene. You don't have a case, detective. You don't have a case. There is nothing. It is all gone.

Someone who has an awful lot bigger balls than Lassiter, even the Chief, has sent his thugs down to take all your shit away. There is nothing left, Detective Miller. Like I say, you have no case. You can't *do* anything.'

'So what? I just let the thing drop—'

'This is the only murder we have in Washington? Of course you let it drop. In fact, you don't even have a question here. The thing has been taken off of you . . . the whole goddam thing. These people have the authority to do anything the hell they want. They've taken the case, they pulled the APB on your guy—'

Miller looked up suddenly. 'They did what?'

'Your guy, Robey . . . they pulled the APB.'

'Why? What the hell would they do that for?'

'He killed a police officer, Detective Miller. John Robey killed a police officer who was in the line of duty. This becomes an entirely different kind of thing now. You know the story on these things. People don't kill family, right?'

'There's no evidence that it was Robey.'

Nanci Cohen smiled knowingly. 'Don't be so naïve, detective. Whether he shot Detective Oliver or not is beside the point. This man is a danger to the public, also to the police. He is . . . hell, you know how this goes better than anyone. The dangerous ones they tell the public about. They stick their faces in the papers and on the tube. The *really* dangerous ones we never hear a word about. Don't matter if they catch them or not, 'cause no-one's any the wiser.'

'So my hands are tied,' Miller said in a flat tone.

'More like they cut your hands off completely. Hell, take a couple of days vacation. You earned it. I saw how you guys worked that thing, but those are the breaks, right?'

Miller, hiding everything he was feeling, trying to control the anger, the frustration, trying to show nothing more than philosophical resignation, rose to his feet and smile at ADA Cohen.

'It's a mess, eh?' he said. 'It really is a fucking mess.'

'Be grateful it isn't your mess any more, detective.'

Cohen rose also, walked him to the door. 'So what're you gonna do?'

'Take a drive down to Hampton, look at the sea.'

'Good for you,' she said.

She had one of her people show Miller out.

Miller stopped at a deli and bought a 7-Up to settle his stomach. He drove north west to Greg Reid's forensics laboratory, had to wait half an hour for Reid to appear, and then asked him for a copy of Catherine Sheridan's death certificate.

Reid seemed unsurprised by the request. He showed Miller through to the admin station, took a seat at one of the computers, typed his request, and within a moment a printer spat out a copy.

Reid walked Miller to the outer doors. There was a moment of awkward silence between them before Miller thanked him once more.

'Good luck,' Reid said.

Miller smiled resignedly. 'That is a rare commodity on this one, believe me.'

He walked away, around the side of the building and back to the car.

By the time he reached Vermont Avenue it was ten-thirty.

Standing in the foyer of the First Capital Bank, Miller realized how quickly the initial investigation into Catherine Sheridan's murder had moved. This was something they had never done. They had never traced back the money she'd been receiving each month. It should have been such a simple and fundamental thing, but somehow – in amidst everything that had occurred – there were so many small details overlooked. Afterwards it always seemed straightforward, uncomplicated – he should have done this or that, he should have pursued such-and-such – but it was impossible to see the outside of something from within.

Miller remembered what Harriet had said: *The best kept secrets are the ones that everybody can see.*

Catherine Sheridan's life, the lives of Margaret Mosley, Barbara Lee, Ann Rayner – even John Robey – all the names in the books that Catherine Sheridan had so patiently and meticulously annotated for his revelation . . . these people had lives that were something other than first presented. They were ghosts, each and every one of them, and behind the face they wore for the world was an entirely different reality, an entirely different explanation for their deaths. These were not accidents, not the result of foolish misadventure. Miller felt sure that the hit-and-runs, the drug overdoses, the heart attacks, even these most recent killings attributed to some specter that the newspapers had dubbed The Ribbon Killer, were in fact nothing other than executions. Lives had been terminated for a reason. By Robey? Had Robey killed all of these people, and if so why? And if not Robey, then who? The identity of the man in the trunk of the car, the ribbons in the glove box, those in his hand . . .

'Detective Miller?'

Miller looked up, a little startled. 'Sorry,' he said. 'Elsewhere for a moment.'

The man extended his hand. 'Richard Forrest,' he said. 'Deputy Manager.'

'Mr Forrest . . . thank you for seeing me,' Miller said. 'I wondered if there was somewhere—'

'A little privacy, of course.' He crossed the foyer and took a left-hand corridor. A little way down on the right he stopped, opened up an office door, and showed Miller inside.

'Some coffee perhaps?' he asked as Miller sat down.

'No, it's fine, Mr Forrest. Thank you.'

Forrest sat down facing Miller. 'So, detective, how can we be of assistance to you?'

'We're closing up some details on a case. Unfortunately it concerns the murder of one of your customers . . .'

'Oh dear,' Forrest said, genuinely alarmed. 'How terrible.'

'A Miss Catherine Sheridan?'

Forrest hesitated for a moment. 'I'm sorry, Detective Miller . . . over two and a half thousand customers . . .'

Miller smiled. He took Catherine Sheridan's death certificate from his pocket. 'As far as we can determine she had no living antecedents or living relatives. We have to act on behalf of the state in such matters and deal with her affairs, at least the basic things such as her bank account. I've just spoken with Doug Lorentzen at the American Trust Bank down the street . . . VP for security?'

'I think I know him . . . yes, that name rings a bell.'

'Insurance and suchlike was held there. We're just going to finish up on those aspects of her affairs today. Her bank account is here, and she received an income from a company named United Trust.'

'And you wish us to inform them that the account is being closed?'

Miller smiled. 'We have a department that can do that. We send them a copy of the death certificate and an official notification.'

'So what can I do for you, detective?'

'Somewhat unusual, and this we have not been able to explain, but amongst Ms Sherdian's effects there are numerous references to a half dozen different offices of United Trust, but it appears she might have been employed by an office outside of Washington. We just need to know which of the offices her salary was originating from.'

Forrest smiled, seemingly pleased that he was being asked for something that he could in fact provide. From experience, Miller was aware of the fact that all usual restrictions imposed by bureaucratic martinets seemed to fall away in the face of murder. Normally unsympathetic and self-important officials demonstrated their ability to be human.

'You can bear with me a little while?' Forrest asked.

'Of course, yes,' Miller replied.

'And you're sure you wouldn't care for some coffee, some mineral water perhaps?'

Miller shook his head.

At the door Forrest paused.

Miller, doing everything he could to maintain his nonchalant air, felt his heart miss a beat.

'For our records, in case there's ever a question . . .'

Miller raised his eyebrows.

'I'm wondering if I could take a photocopy of Ms Sheridan's death certificate?'

'Of course, of course,' Miller said. He rose and stepped toward Forrest, handed him the single sheet of paper.

Forrest took it, said he'd be as quick as possible.

For the few minutes that Miller waited he tried not to think what would happen to his career if his current actions came to light. He was not in good with the chief of police or the PR department. He knew his file would be flagged by Internal Affairs. He knew that his request to Greg Reid would be considered highly irregular. He was barely out of the woods on the Brandon Thomas case, and here he was – sitting in the offices of the First Capital Bank on Vermont Avenue, waiting for the deputy manager to return with the personal details of a murder victim's salary, that victim now part of a case that had been taken off him by the Federal Bureau of Investigation . . .

In and of itself, each violation seemed to be nothing more than the narrow lines so often crossed by a diligent and committed detective pursuing a case. Even Lassiter, even ADA Cohen and the chief of police – they knew all too well that officers sidestepped those lines so many times it was becoming all the harder to see them. They all had their own Memorandum of Understanding, the acceptable truths, the points where the upholding of the law and the provision of justice became more important than the exactitude of statutes. These things were implicitly understood. They were not discussed. But what Miller had done, what Miller was now doing, was a blatant violation of even the most basic tenets of investigation.

It was now a question of whether he could make it out the other side, or whether this thing would kill him. There was no question in his mind regarding the necessity to continue. Not after all he'd been through. And Oliver was dead. That was sufficient to motivate him. And there was something else: the certainty that understanding could be gained. Whatever justification or explanation might have existed for the deaths of these people, there was still the fact that there was a *who*. Someone had caused these deaths. Someone was guilty, and Miller did not believe it was one person. He believed something else entirely, and when he considered the evidence, the small flags that indicated which way he should go, what he should look at, how easily they had all been fooled into thinking that one thing was something else entirely . . . only when he looked at all this did he experience the substance of his fear. This was a matter of life and death, not only of those who had been murdered, but now of his own. He'd been asked to back down, to step away, to let the real professionals handle it. He had already previously suspected that the very same people who were now supposedly investigating this case knew an awful lot more about it than they were communicating. Like Harriet said, the best kept secrets were the ones in plain view . . .

The door opened. Forrest came through, crossed the room and sat down. He returned the original death certificate to Miller, and then handed him a single sheet of paper.

'Unfortunately this is all we have,' he said. 'United Trust Incorporated is the name given, and their address is a post office box here in Washington. Strictly speaking, a post office box should not have been accepted, but—'

Miller nodded. 'These things happen, Mr Forrest, I understand.'

'So that's the best we can do. You're going to have to see the post office. They should have a billing address on record for the rental of the post office box. PO Box number is 19405. Means the rental agreement was taken at Nineteenth Street.'

'And there's nothing else on file regarding this account.'

Forrest shook his head. 'From what I can see the money came into the account, it was withdrawn in cash from ATMs. No checks were written . . .' He looked up at Miller, seemed a little confused. 'Not in all the years that the account was open was there ever a check drawn on it. Ms Sheridan never came to the bank. She never took a loan, never asked for a credit card, never met any of the bank staff.'

'Unusual,' Miller said.

'Very,' Forrest replied. 'But not against the law, eh?'

'No, not against the law.'

'I'm sorry there isn't anything else we can do to help you, Detective Miller.'

Miller rose from his chair, shook hands with Forrest. 'You've done everything you can. I appreciate your help.'

'A terrible thing,' Forrest said. 'Somehow it seems all the more disturbing considering the fact that she had so little contact with us . . .' He shook his head. 'I suppose you must feel that sort of thing all the time in your work . . . the sense that there might have been something you could have done that would have made a difference. Not that that makes any particular sense, but you can't help but feel that . . .' Forrest's voice trailed away. He could not explain what he felt, but Miller knew what he meant.

'Always,' Miller said. 'You can't help feeling that you could have done something.' He thought of Jennifer Irving, of Natasha Joyce. He even thought of Carl Oliver.

'If there's anything else . . .' Forrest added.

'Thank you. I can find my own way back,' he said, and started walking. Didn't want to look back at Forrest, wanted Forrest to remember as little about their meeting as possible, wanted Forrest never to think of mentioning it to anyone at all. Miller knew that that would not be the case. Forrest would mention it at lunchtime, perhaps at an internal meeting. *Did you know that one of our customers was murdered . . .* That wouldn't mean anything. He could tell everyone in the bank, but that didn't mean it would go any further . . .

Miller went out through the front door and couldn't help looking over his shoulder.

The night before. The feeling that he was being watched. Same thing. Same sensation . . .

He made his way back toward the west of the city, headed for the Nineteenth Street post office, trusting in his badge, his official status, the fundamental belief of the vast majority of people that they should cooperate with the police. Sometimes it worked, other times not.

Miller's luck was in. He found a young man who seemed more interested in the manner of Catherine Sheridan's death than whether Miller had the right to obtain post office box details.

'Murdered? Murdered how?' he said. His name was Jay Baxter, had a gold-colored name tag on his shirt.

'You don't wanna know how she was murdered,' Miller said.

Baxter smiled. 'Sure I do. Interesting stuff, man . . . real interesting. How often do you get the chance to actually get an inside line on some of the shit these people do?'

'You're interested in murder?'

Jay Baxter laughed. 'Not so interested to find out first hand,' he said, 'but you know, the whole psychology behind this kind of thing. Read a bunch of books, was gonna major in Psychology, but then I started figuring out what a bunch of horseshit that stuff was. They don't know what makes people do that shit, right?'

507

Miller shook his head. 'No, they don't . . . I think you're right there.'

'So tell me . . . trade-off, right?'

'Cut her head off,' Miller lied.

Baxter's eyes were wide. 'No shit!'

'Clean off,' Miller said. 'We think it was a machete . . . maybe a samurai sword. Clean as anything you've ever seen.'

'And you saw her? Saw her . . . you know . . . like without her head and everything?'

'Sure I did. That's what we do. We go look at the god-awful shit that people do to each other.'

'Fuck it,' Baxter said. 'Fuck it . . . Jesus, you ever like puke or something?'

Miller smiled. 'I puked a few times, yes . . . you deal with it after a couple of times, and then it doesn't bother you any more.'

'And I'm gonna read about this in the papers, right?'

'Sure you are.'

'So the deal with the PO box . . . what's the scene there?'

'A lead,' Miller said. 'You're helping me follow up a lead on this.'

'No shit?'

'No shit.'

'Cool . . . good, yeah sure . . . I mean whatever, you know, whatever help we can give you. Give me the name again.'

'United Trust,' Miller said. 'PO Box 19405.'

Jay Baxter, eyes still wide, wanting to ask Miller more questions perhaps, but feeling like he shouldn't, typed the number into the computer on his desk and paused for a moment.

'United Trust . . . registered to the office of United Trust Incorporated Finance, 1165 E Street, junction of Fourteenth, you know where that is?'

'I can find it.'

'Box taken in the name of Donald Carvalho.' Baxter spelled the name as Miller wrote it down.

'Great help,' Miller said, rising from his chair.

'No problem.'

Miller paused at the door, looked back at the young man. 'Do I need to read you the riot act on confidentiality?'

Baxter smiled, shook his head, made like a zipper on his mouth.

Miller returned the smile. 'Good man,' he said, and closed the door behind him.

It was then, as he was making his way across the reception lobby and toward the main exit, that he saw the raincoat man.

Miller noticed the man merely because the man appeared to notice him. Once again there was the feeling of being watched as Miller walked past him, and at the door he turned for a second and felt the man's eyes on him as he went out, and down the steps to the street.

The man had been leaning against the wall, appeared to be reading something, and he'd stood straight as Miller passed. From Miller's passing glance he estimated he was somewhere in his mid-forties, his hair dark, greying a little, dressed in a black suit, white open-necked shirt and a tan-colored raincoat.

Outside the post office Miller crossed the street and walked down to the junction of Nineteenth and M Street, simply to see if the raincoat man followed him out of the building. He did not. Miller tried not to read any significance into the event. Merely a man attending to his business, a man who'd happened to look up as Miller passed, perhaps had recognized him from a newspaper photograph after the Thomas case, perhaps had mistaken Miller for someone else . . .

Rationalize it as he did, Miller nevertheless felt a growing sense of disquiet.

He hesitated for a few moments more, and then hurried to his car.

FIFTY-SIX

To his right the Willard Hotel, on his left the National Theater. Up ahead was Freedom Plaza, the White House Visitor Center, the Ronald Reagan Building. Two hundred yards and he'd be on Constitution Avenue, two blocks from the FBI Building, the National Archives, the Federal Triangle.

Detective Robert Miller, his heart in his mouth, stood on the sidewalk with the certainty that he was being watched.

He kept thinking back to the moment he'd seen Carl Oliver on the gurney, the medics awkwardly maneuvering him down the stairway to the street. A life and all it stood for extinguished in a second. As simple as that. Marilyn Hemmings' expression – he could remember it too vividly. How she'd raised her hand and smiled at him. A simple smile of recognition, nothing more nor less. He'd seen her for moments, and then she was gone.

He remembered the slick of blood on the floor outside Robey's apartment. Could picture Al Roth's expression, the tone of his voice, the words he'd used: 'When you're ready you better come in and take a look at this.'

All of it.

Up close and personal.

Miller stood in the heart of the intelligence community, up ahead a narrow-fronted building. It was from here that United Trust had paid Catherine Sheridan. And Don Carvalho? Was that another Robey alias, like Michael McCullough? Was this yet another piece of the seemingly infinite puzzle that Robey had created for the world?

Miller crossed the street and entered the front door of the building.

United Trust had a mailbox in the lobby, but the feel of the place was unmistakable. The building smelled musty and forgotten. There was some sort of activity behind a frosted-glass door to his right, the sign silently announcing Amalgamated Federal Workers Union. Up on the third floor he found United Trust's offices. There was no sound from within, no silhouettes against the frosted glass. A narrow corridor ran to left and right, similarly unoccupied offices on each side, and he knew that though Catherine Sheridan's income might have originated here, United Trust was a name, and that was all.

The frustration was almost unbearable. A thread, small though it might have been, but a thread nevertheless, a tension as you pulled, the feeling that this time there would be something at the end, something of substance . . . but suddenly the tension released and the thread came away in your hands.

It had been the same every step of the way, as close to nothing as he could imagine.

Miller wanted to scream. He wanted to kick the door through . . .

He held his breath for a moment.

He stepped away from the door and felt the facing wall against his back.

He took a step forward again and tried the door handle. It was firm, but the door itself was not heavy. A pane of frosted glass in its upper half, the lower half nothing more than a wood panel inset. He would later tell himself that he had known. He would later rationalize it, take it out of the realm of intuition and instinct, and tell himself that Robey had predicted this all along. That's the only explanation he could find, for nothing else made sense. Nothing of this made any sense at all unless John Robey had orchestrated every single step of this thing.

Life wasn't easy on the uncertain, the meek, the quiet. Sometimes things were done because there was nothing else to do.

The sudden sound of splintering wood, a sound that reverberated through the building and brought people from the Amalgamated Federal Workers Union running up the stairs to investigate what was happening – *that* sound never actually occurred. What did occur was a dull tearing noise as Miller kicked a good shoe-sized hole in the panel. He reached his arm through and upward to unlock the door from within. It was a single latch, nothing more, and when Miller felt the latch snap back from the striker plate there was something akin to relief, the feeling that now there was no going back. He had violated the law on two occasions in a single case. The hairbrush from Robey's apartment, and now this. Internal Affairs appeared in his thoughts once more. He was a dirty cop who colluded with corrupt city officials.

Miller stepped back and opened the office door.

A single desk, a plain deal chair. A room no more than forty or fifty square feet in size. The window so dirty he could barely see down into the street, its ledge littered with numerous dead flies. It smelled of dust, the age-old haunt of cigarette smoke perhaps, and beneath that the mold taint from carpets that had lain uncleaned for some interminable time.

On the right-hand side was a single file cabinet, grey metal, three drawers. Miller took a latex glove from his inside jacket pocket, and opened the lowest drawer. That and its neighbor were empty, but in the upper drawer was a single white envelope. He lifted it out carefully, turned it over. It was sealed, but there was something inside.

Miller glanced back toward the corridor, looked to the window, and then he carefully opened the envelope.

It was the same picture. On the back were written the same words. *Christmas '82*. But this time John Robey and Catherine Sheridan were not the only faces that looked back at him. The photograph beneath Sheridan's bed had been cropped from this one. Here there were five faces, and he recognized all but one.

Miller knew who the man to Robey's left was immediately. James Killarney, the Arlington FBI representative. And behind and to the right of Catherine, the unmistakable face of Judge Walter Thorne. They were all younger. But Miller knew who they were, except one. A dark-haired man standing beside Killarney, smiling as if this was summer vacation, a fishing trip . . . .

Miller frowned. Could this be right? What the hell did this mean? What in God's name did Judge Thorne have to do with this?

The FBI and the Justice Department knew the identity of

Catherine Sheridan and John Robey? Killarney had come down to brief them on the Ribbon Killer investigation, and yet he had known Catherine Sheridan personally?

Miller tucked the picture back into the envelope and put it into his pocket. He went through the desk drawers. A couple of pencils, a rusted thumbtack, some more dead flies. He looked beneath the carpet as best he could, behind the file cabinet, ran his fingers along the edge where it met the floor to see if anything was hidden beneath.

There was nothing.

He left quickly, did his best to push the broken panel back into place from the inside, and then returned to the street.

Miller looked back at the building from the opposite sidewalk. There was no movement behind the windows, no indication that he'd been seen or was being watched. But that, as he now understood, meant nothing at all. There were eyes everywhere, and they possessed universal pivots, and they watched ceaselessly, and they saw everything.

He headed back the way he'd come.

It was then that he saw him again. No question.

The raincoat man.

Sure of it. Sure as living and breathing. Passing by the end of the street and turning left at the junction.

Miller went after him, at first a rapid walk and then he was jogging past Freedom Plaza. The man did not look back, did not glance over his shoulder, and when he turned left onto Pennsylvania Avenue Miller speeded up. He knew that by the time he reached the corner the man would be gone, but he was scared, and he did not like what he was feeling, and in that moment he believed it would have been better to face the man than to stay back and do nothing.

Just as he'd predicted, when he turned the corner the raincoat man was nowhere to be seen. He wondered if a car had been waiting for him. He wondered if there were other people, watching him through high-powered binoculars even now; people who knew he had broken into the offices of United Trust Incorporated Finance and stolen a photograph.

Miller stopped to catch his breath. Was he now imagining things? He asked himself how many men in Washington

513

wore dark suits and tan-colored raincoats. Did he see the man already running and assume that he was escaping?

Was he losing his mind?

People passed by; Miller looked at none of them directly, saw them all as one faceless wave of humanity, and then he retraced his steps and made his way to the car.

He drove northeast towards the familiar part of the city, past the FBI Building, Ford's Theater, through Chinatown and onto New York Avenue. He could feel the photograph in his jacket pocket when he turned the steering wheel and his upper arm pressed against his body.

James Killarney was in this. And Thorne. Judge Thorne. Was he supposed to talk to him? What the hell did it mean?

Miller wondered where Judge Thorne would be. In court? In chambers? All judges had an office in Judiciary Square near the Verizon Center. Judiciary Square was no more than three or four blocks away. Miller slowed up and pulled the car over to the side of the road. He looked at the photograph again. The words on the back were printed in block caps. There was no point guessing who might have written them. He had a photograph and a name: Donald Carvalho.

Miller drove down Sixth and took a left onto F Street. He walked the remainder of the way, past the National Building Museum and down to the corner. In the precinct there was a directory of judges' offices for the Square. He had spoken with Judge Thorne on a couple of occasions, the standard arraignments and court appearances. Thorne would be familiar with Miller's recent IAD investigation, the small storm of publicity that it had created. Beyond that, Thorne would know as much as Miller regarding this current investigation. Thorne had received copies of all of their reports. Miller wondered if Thorne was an ally or an enemy. Was he being told to speak to him or investigate him?

There was no way of knowing, aside from going up there and finding the man.

He located the judicial administrative office. He was asked about the nature of his business. He told the receptionist it related to an outstanding warrant, and he waited while the judge was paged. The receptionist told Miller that the judge was in his office but unable to meet with him. Did he wish to make an appointment?

'Could you just check with him if he can answer some questions about United Trust?' Miller said.

The receptionist smiled understandingly. 'He really is very busy,' she said.

'I know,' Miller replied. 'I appreciate that, but if you could just check with him—'

The receptionist called through to Judge Thorne's office, spoke with his assistant, waited a moment while the message was relayed. The receptionist frowned, nodded her head, said, 'Okay, I'll tell him.'

She looked at Miller, the understanding smile gone. 'You're to wait here,' she said. 'Someone is coming down to get you.'

FIFTY-SEVEN

Miller waited, apprehensive, his pulse quickening. A cool sweat broke out on the back of his neck. For a moment he wondered if he shouldn't ask to sit down.

He did not wait long. A middle-aged man appeared, smartly-dressed in a charcoal suit, white shirt, dark blue and white polka dot tie. They all looked the same, these men, eminently forgettable, and when he asked Miller to relinquish his gun, said it would be kept safe for his return, showed Miller toward the outer door without ever introducing himself – without offering an explanation for the sudden availability of Judge Thorne – these things simply contributed further to Miller's anxiety and unease.

'Judge Thorne does not have a great deal of time,' the man told Miller as they walked down to a building at the end of the street. There, he punched a number into the external security box. A buzzer sounded, the door was unlocked; Miller followed the man inside.

The inner hallway smelled like a library, took Miller's thoughts to the Carnegie, the books that Catherine Sheridan had marked; he thought of the day after her murder when he and Roth had gone there to speak with Julia Gibb, the small note she'd made in the hope that it might be helpful. He considered the beginning of this thing, his complete lack of awareness of where this thing would take him: here. Nine days after her murder she had brought him here, to the private offices of Judge Walter Thorne, a highly respected and very intelligent man; a man slated for the United States Supreme Court, perhaps the Senate.

Miller was instructed to stand in the reception area for a moment. He did as he was asked, then, in less than a minute, he was shown into a luxurious office, ceiling-high bookshelves to the right, a pair of French windows to the left, and told that Judge Thorne would be with him shortly.

Miller drew aside the lace drape that obscured the view of the yard. The French windows overlooked a walled, neatly manicured yard prepared for the winter, in its center a small marble urn flanked by a pair of intricate wrought-iron benches. He heard the door close gently behind him.

He turned, and Judge Walter Thorne stood there, smiling.

'When it's warm I sit out there,' he said. 'Also when I don't wish for my conversations to be overheard . . . not that it makes a great deal of difference I'm sure. I imagine that if someone wished to eavesdrop on me they could do it any-place at all.'

Miller estimated that Walter Thorne was in his early sixties. He was around five-foot-nine or ten, but the character and authority in his face gave him the presence of someone much taller. There was something about Thorne that communicated a sense of importance.

'You are lucky to be alive,' was the first thing that Walter Thorne told Robert Miller.

Miller frowned.

'Don't be naïve, Detective Miller . . . don't tell me you didn't realize that the officer who died on Friday evening was supposed to be you?'

'What?' Miller felt his knees start to give. He took a step backwards.

'I credited you with a greater understanding of what was happening here,' Thorne said. He smiled, indicated a chair by the windows. 'Please,' he said. 'Sit down. Let me get you a brandy.'

Miller raised his hand.

'What? No brandy? But you're not on duty, detective . . . my understanding is that you have been liberated from this investigation, free to do with your time as you wish . . .'

'The case was taken off us by the FBI.'

Thorne smiled. 'The case was taken off you by James Killarney. The FBI and James Killarney are not necessarily the same thing.'

Miller opened his mouth to speak, but nothing came to

517

him. He didn't understand what Thorne was saying. He thought of the photograph in his pocket, but felt it better not to reveal his hand before he understood the game.

Thorne busied himself with brandy snifters and a decanter. He turned to face Miller, a glass in each hand. 'This is better than brandy,' he said. 'This is a '29 Armagnac, very good indeed . . .'

Miller took the glass, drank it straight down, felt the rush of it filling his chest.

Thorne raised his eyebrows. 'That, Detective Miller, is not the way you drink a 1929 Armagnac.'

Miller couldn't look at the man. He looked, instead, at his own hands, the way they were visibly shaking.

'You have come a little closer than anyone would have wished,' Thorne said quietly. 'I receive word from the desk that you wish to discuss a warrant. Then I receive word that you want to discuss United Trust.' Thorne looked at him, his expression one of understanding. 'You are a man out of your depth, Detective Miller, and the very best advice I can give you at this point is to leave my office, take your car, drive home, and get some sleep. Go back to work in a couple of days and forget that you ever heard of John Robey or Catherine Sheridan, or any of these other people that may or may not have been connected with this thing.'

'This thing—' Miller began.

'This – thing – is what we called a sacred monster.' Thorne smiled benevolently, looked like he knew exactly what Miller was going through.

Miller's eyes widened. He'd heard the expression before. John Robey had used the self-same phrase.

'*Monstre sacré*,' he said, using the French. 'Our Frankenstein.' He smiled broadly now, as if suddenly realizing the irony of everything. 'One of our *many* Frankensteins,' he added. He held the snifter in his hand and swirled it before raising it to his lips and sipping. 'I would offer you another drink but it is very, very expensive and you don't appreciate it.'

Miller leaned to his right and set the empty glass down on the table. 'I don't understand what is going on here . . .'

'And I don't know that you ever will,' Thorne replied. 'Fact of the matter is that there are so many parts to this, so many different viewpoints and understandings of how this thing has happened, that I don't know that anyone has all the information – except perhaps John Robey. Perhaps out of all of us, John Robey is the one who knows the most.'

'All of us?' Miller asked. 'You're involved in this?'

'I use *us* in the loosest sense. I include myself only because I have been aware of this thing for many, many years. It is not something that anyone wants to face. Many of the people who started this are now dead, and the vast majority of those who got any kind of inkling as to what was going on were summarily dispatched—'

'Dispatched? Or *murdered*? Is that what you mean when you say dispatched? You're talking about all these people who've been murdered, aren't you?'

'People? What people are these?'

'The ones that Catherine Sheridan wrote in the books that she returned to the library.'

Thorne frowned. 'I don't know what you mean, detective . . . what books?'

'Her and John Robey . . . she took some books back to the library on the morning of her death. We have them at the Second Precinct and we've found notations all the way through them . . . initials and dates, you know? We started working through them, trying to find out who all these people were.'

'John Robey,' Thorne said quietly, almost to himself. 'To think that after all this time . . .'

'They are names, aren't they, the initials and dates in the book? We've already started going through them, cross-referencing them against missing persons reports—'

Thorne raised his hand. 'Enough, detective. There is no need for me to be apprised of all the numerous details of your investigation. People have died. This I understand. People have been dying for twenty years over this thing—'

'*What* thing? What are you talking about?'

Thorne was silent for a moment, smiling as if granting indulgence to a whim. He walked to the French windows. For a while he stood with his back to Miller, and then he turned.

'Did you ever see a movie called *A Few Good Men*? Tom Cruise, Jack Nicholson, you remember?'

'Yes, I know the one. I've seen it a couple of times.'

'And what do you feel was the fundamental essence of that story, Detective Miller?'

'I'm sorry . . . I don't understand what this has to do with—'

Thorne stopped him. 'Indulge me, detective.'

'I don't know . . . that authority can corrupt a man . . . that people in positions of power can forget—'

Thorne was shaking his head. 'No, detective, quite the contrary. What the movie was trying to communicate was the complete impossibility of preventing the bigger picture. You really consider that taking one man out of the frame would make any difference at all? For every man that falls, there are three more ready to take his place.'

'You've lost me, Judge Thorne . . . I don't know that you and I are even talking about the same thing.'

'Of course we are, detective . . . we're talking about Nicaragua.'

Miller's eyes widened visibly.

'See?' Thorne said. 'We are talking about the same thing. We're talking about Nicaragua, an illegal war that was funded by drug smuggling and arms dealing. We're talking about forty tons of cocaine a month coming in on CIA-piloted aircraft. We're talking about CIA operatives . . . people who by reason of their jobs actually discovered some of what really happened out there and began to understand that the cocaine and arms, and everything else that happened, was simply too profitable to stop once this imaginary war was over . . .'

Miller rose suddenly. He wanted to leave. He was not ready to hear this. Everything that Robey had talked of was now being confirmed from the lips of a Washington judge.

'Sit down, Detective Miller,' Thorne said.

'No,' Miller said. 'I'm out of here right now. I don't want—'

'What you want is the very least of our concerns,' Thorne interrupted. 'Sit down, or I will call for security and they will take you out of here and drive you to some godforsaken project building and kill you.'

Miller could not believe what he was hearing. 'You're a judge . . .'

'Of course I'm a judge,' Thorne replied. 'And you're a Washington Police Department detective, and the simple truth is that you have walked right round the edge of something without ever really understanding what it was you were looking at. And this John Robey?' Thorne laughed. 'John Robey thinks he can take apart something that we spent thirty years trying to build? He is one man, Detective Miller, one man alone, and if he thinks that there is even the slightest chance of breaking this thing to pieces then he is sorely mistaken.'

Thorne stepped away from the window and returned to the chair facing Miller's. He sat down, made himself comfortable. 'You want to understand what happened here?' he asked.

Miller looked up. 'Understand what? That the U.S. government is still smuggling cocaine out of Nicaragua?'

'Not the government my friend, the CIA.'

'The CIA?'

'You remember Madeleine Albright? Secretary of State?'

'Yes, I do.'

'She said that the CIA behaved as if it had battered-child syndrome.' Thorne laughed. 'I don't know that I understand precisely what battered-child syndrome is, but the sentiment communicates nevertheless, don't you think?'

Miller's heart was running ahead of itself. He felt dizzy and nauseous.

'You find yourself in a very compromising position, Detective Miller. You are nothing but the latest in a long line of people who, intentionally or unintentionally, have jeopardized a spectacularly profitable operation that has been keeping the CIA busy for many, many years.'

Miller was finding it hard to breathe. He looked back at Thorne.

'Robey tried it before, you know, five years ago . . . with a CIA operative named Darryl King. Darryl King was broken in about three weeks. Heroin. Crack cocaine. They could have given him anything.'

'Darryl King was CIA?'

'As were Catherine Sheridan and Ann Rayner . . . Ann I knew. A nice lady, used to work for Bill Walford.'

Miller remembered the conversation in Lassiter's office, the fact that the Rayner woman's connection to Walford was sufficient reason to keep this thing out of the papers.

'They were all CIA . . . the ones who were killed?' Miller asked.

'CIA, family of CIA, cohorts, colleagues, snitches, confidential informants . . . any of their extended family . . .'

'But they can't just kill people like that—'

'What do you mean, they *can't* kill people like that? They *did* kill people like that, Detective Miller. They killed an awful lot of people—'

'For money?'

'For money, yes. For money – and power. For political influence. How the hell do you think the CIA funds its operations? Do you have even the faintest inkling of the cost of some of these projects?' Thorne waved his hand in a dismissive fashion. 'Of course you don't. The cocaine that comes in from Nicaragua pays for arms and for political favors; it pays for the subversion of foreign aggressors and the assassination of political figures. You don't think we just go cap-in-hand to the Treasury Department and ask for three hundred million dollars, do you?'

'I . . . I don't—'

'And then there is the question of national security,' Thorne interjected. 'After the war was over, after we ran out of Nicaragua with our tails between our legs, money was needed to keep people secure. The State Department, Defense, the National Security Council, Foreign Affairs, Intelligence, even the CIA itself. There were people who needed to be protected, people who had made decisions regarding Nicaragua and the security of the United States who would have been in the line of fire if the truth had ever come to light. You're talking about people who were needed to deal with Grenada in '83, Libya in '86, El Salvador, Panama, Iraq, the Sudan – people who are still needed to this day. And we had a duty, a sworn responsibility, to ensure that the decisions they had made for the good of the country were never questioned. The truth would have brought

Reagan's administration to its knees. Even his assassination attempt was an effort to distract peoples' attention.'

Miller opened his mouth to speak.

'Isn't it now obvious, detective? He was supposed to be shot at. But, saying that, Reagan was never the brightest light in the harbor, so I don't know what the hell they expected from him.'

'This is insane . . . who the hell would do that? Who the hell would set up an assassination attempt on a president?'

'The CIA,' Thorne replied. 'This is what they do. They stand on the wall. They stand on the wall and they defend America, and they do what's right, and they do all the things that no-one else has the guts or the balls to do, and then they wonder what these liberal-minded assholes are bleating about in Congress when they talk about violations of civil liberties and the rights of foreigners to their own countries.' Thorne leaned forward, his eyes brighter, as if he was now driven to tell Miller what he knew. 'As far as the CIA is concerned no-one has the right to anything until the CIA confers that right—'

'You can't tell me that Hinckley was set up to kill Reagan—'

'I'm not going to say one way or the other, but we were there to ensure that he could not. Oswald took the rap for Jack Kennedy, just as Sirhan Sirhan did for Bobby in the Ambassador Hotel in 1968. And who created an FBI mouthpiece for Woodward and Bernstein when they wanted Nixon out of the Oval Office? We did. This is what we exist for.'

Thorne leaned forward. 'And shall I tell you why I'm talking to you, Detective Miller? Because you can do nothing about this.'

Miller was visibly taken aback.

'There is no reason for you to be surprised. You want to know what happened to John Hinckley after he tried to kill Reagan? They shipped him off to the puzzle factory, pumped him full of psychiatric drugs, turned his mind to mush . . . probably shocked him into a coma. They told him to think one thing one day and then they contradicted it the next. Over and over and over. They confused him, disoriented him, made him question his own name, his own existence.

They brought him to a state of such complete delirium that even if he'd remembered who'd told him to shoot Reagan he wouldn't have been able to say it. Now he can say what the hell he likes because he looks crazy, he sounds crazier, and who the hell is going to believe a man who tried to assassinate the president of the United States of America?'

Miller felt real anger, the anger that had been building up inside him for days, and finally he was confronted with someone who knew more of what was going on than he did, and this person was taunting him.

'This . . . this is un-fucking-real,' Miller said. 'I'm not crazy. I am a Washington police detective, and there's a great many people who would be very interested to know what I have to say about—'

'About what, detective? About some imagined conspiracy that goes back to the war in Nicaragua, a war that most Americans don't even care to know about? Or John Robey, respected college lecturer, published author, long-listed for the Pulitzer, and how he was really an expert CIA-trained assassin, responsible for dozens and dozens of killings in Nicaragua – and in an endless number of other countries – all at the behest of his government controllers? That story, detective? Is *that* the story you want to tell the world? Or maybe the story of this Ribbon Killer, how some other one-time government-paid mercenary was instructed to clean up a couple of situations here in Washington, and he got creative, decided to use the old-style system of filing we employed out there?' Thorne smiled, the expression of someone remembering some past pleasant moment.

'Filing?' Miller asked. 'What do you mean?'

'Bodies . . . dozens of them. Stacked on a rack of wooden shelves and covered in tarpaulin. Used to douse them in lavender water, gallons of the stuff. Real sick . . . an awful smell, rotting bodies and lavender. Who in hell's idea that was I'll never know. And they used to tie a tag to them, a ribbon around the neck just like a luggage tag, and the tag would state the way in which they were to be disposed of. Some were to be found, others to disappear, and there were cleaning crews who dealt with that stuff once the bodies had been shipped in.'

'And this was what Robey did . . . is that what you're telling me? That Robey did that out in Nicaragua and then brought it back here?'

'No, God almighty, no. Robey would never have done that. Robey was, I should say *is,* a very grounded man. No, the one that you people were dealing with was someone else entirely . . . in fact you know him.'

'What?'

'The body you found in the trunk of the car . . . that, detective, was your so-called Ribbon Killer . . .'

'And who the hell was he?' Miller asked, and even as he asked, he understood that the truth was far worse than anything he might have imagined.

'Who was he? His name was Don Carvalho, but who he was is of no importance at all. He was given instructions to deal with certain matters, he added an embellishment of his own for some reason no-one knows or cares, and he had to be excused from the playing field. The fact that John Robey was the one who dealt with that issue might be interesting to you.'

'Robey killed him?'

'Apparently so . . . but only because he wanted to prevent Carvalho from killing you.'

Miller was hardly able to breathe.

'Don't be so alarmed, detective . . . I should think that by now you would be undisturbed by any further revelations. Robey had a purpose in mind for you. He turned many years ago . . . turned against the company, against his own mentors and colleagues. He and Catherine Sheridan believed that the world had a right to know what happened in Nicaragua, what is still happening now, and for obvious reasons this could not be allowed to occur. The fact that he sent documentation to these people . . . Barbara Lee, Ann Rayner, the first one . . . I'm sorry, I don't recall her name—'

'Mosley. Margaret Mosley.'

'Yes, that was it . . . the fact that after this fiasco with Darryl King five years ago he had the nerve to start this thing over, this bleeding heart liberal bullshit about the rights and wrongs of what happened back then—' Thorne thumped his clenched fist on the arm of his chair and Miller jumped.

'There is no question of rightness or wrongness when it comes to the security of a nation.'

'You're crazy . . . you're fucking crazy—'

Thorne raised his hand. 'I haven't finished . . .' He paused for a moment. 'The public has judged you, Detective Miller, and they found you guilty. Doesn't matter what the coroner's enquiry said. Doesn't matter what testimony your friend Marilyn Hemmings might have presented . . . the public has labelled you a maverick, a rogue cop. They believe without question that the police are more than capable of protecting their own, so it came as no surprise when you were exonerated in the murder of Brandon Thomas. They never expected it to be any other way.'

Miller was incredulous. 'How the fuck do you—'

'Come on, detective, you can't honestly believe that this matter has gone unnoticed. Who the hell did you think James Killarney was? The FBI? You think the FBI was interested in the deaths of five lonely women, one of them black, and from the projects? Somehow I don't think so. Killarney is CIA, as much as Robey ever was. He brought those reports straight to us.'

'What d'you mean, straight to us? Who the hell *are* you people?'

'You people? That's who we are, Detective Miller. We are just "you people". We are the ones who see the grand scale of all of this. We're not down there concerning ourselves about the next paycheck or who our wives might be sleeping with or where we're gonna take the kids on vacation. There is a certain view of the world that is maintained, detective . . . the view of the world that people want to see, the way they want it to remain, and we are the very people who give the world – or most of the world – exactly what it wants. The fact that we use the CIA for these operations, well . . .'

'You believe this?' Miller interjected. 'You actually believe this stuff you're telling me?'

Thorne smiled condescendingly. 'I figured you for a man of some depth, you know? I believed you might have a higher degree of perception than your average blue-collar factory worker. But you have proved me wrong. I am seldom wrong, detective. Being wrong is something that a man in my position cannot afford. The future of the current administration, the administrations that are put in place beyond this one, beyond even the span of my life . . . these are things we decide now. These are the matters that concern people like me, not whether a few people who looked a little too closely at something wound up dead.'

Thorne took a deep breath and rose from his chair. He walked to the French windows once again and stood with his back to the room.

'My advice, Detective Miller, is that you walk away from this. As far as you are concerned you are very lucky to be alive. You should have died in place of Detective Oliver. Do not consider that you have earned yourself a reprieve. I cannot guarantee that you will make it to the end of the day, let alone the end of the week, but if you walk away from this, if you accept the fact that this investigation now belongs to the FBI, then maybe, just maybe, you might disappear quietly from the minds of certain men. Some people are dead. It isn't as though we're talking a great many people. Fifty, a hundred, what does it matter? They should have walked away, just as you should now. But they didn't walk away . . . they wanted to know what was going on, even though instinct and intuition would have told them that it was more trouble than it was worth. When people enrolled with this program they enrolled for life, and then they learned something of the truth of Nicaragua, believed that the authorities, perhaps even worse the public, had a right to know. They reported their findings to their superiors, and their superiors came to us, and we took care of things. They made an agreement, and then they broke that agreement. John Robey, Catherine Sheridan, Darryl King. It didn't do them any good. Sheridan and King are dead, Robey is on the run somewhere, and though he might be one of the best killers the CIA ever trained he is still little more than one man against the might of the United States government and all its associated agencies. And as far as all the others are concerned, they were paid to protect the security of this nation, and they were found wanting . . .' Thorne looked directly at Miller. 'Do you understand what I'm saying?'

Miller felt as if a string was slipping through his fingers, and attached to that string were all the answers he wanted . . .

'There are things you don't understand, Detective Miller. That is something I can appreciate, but we only want one thing from you. We want you to walk away from this, walk away quickly and quietly. Accept the fact that you did a good job, you learned some things, but now it's time to take the advice of Frank Lassiter and Nanci Cohen and find another case to work on.'

'I want to know some things,' Miller said calmly. 'I think I am owed that much . . . owed some answers. There are too many things that don't make sense for me to just turn around and forget everything that's happened.'

'It doesn't matter now, detective . . . doesn't matter how many things might or might not make sense.'

'But you know what's happened here. You can answer the questions for me.'

'And why on earth should I do that?' Thorne asked.

'Because, like you said, it doesn't matter what I know . . . I can't do anything about it. People wouldn't believe me, not only because of the sheer impossibility of believing it, but also because they already believe I am a liar, a dirty cop.'

'Yes. Like I said, you have been judged by the world, Detective Miller, and they have found you wanting.'

'So give me enough of an understanding to be able to walk away and forget about it. What's to lose? That's the thing you see, the thing about Washington police detectives, they're stubborn . . . once they have a hold on something they won't let go.'

Thorne laughed. 'I like you, Detective Miller. I respect the fact that you have managed to stay alive this long . . . Alright, for no other reason than that it will do you no good, I will answer your questions. But I will answer only the questions that I want to answer, and those I do not I will refuse, okay?'

'Who killed the first three women?'

'The first three ever, or the first three you knew about?'

'The ones I know about, Mosley, Rayner and Lee.'

'They were killed by Don Carvalho, your trunk victim – and Ribbon Killer.'

'But he was CIA?'

Thorne nodded.

'And this thing with the ribbons was—'

'Was just some stunt that he pulled . . . and even if Robey hadn't found him and killed him, he wouldn't have lasted the week after he killed the black woman.'

'Natasha Joyce?' Miller asked.

'The one from the projects with the daughter? Yes, she was also killed by Carvalho.'

'And Catherine Sheridan?'

'You will have to ask John Robey about her.'

'Was she also killed by this man Carvalho?'

'Like I said, you'll have to speak to your friend Professor Robey.'

'And they were all killed because they knew about the Nicaraguan situation?'

Thorne laughed suddenly, unexpectedly. 'The Nicaraguan *situation*? Now you're really beginning to sound like Capitol Hill there, Detective Miller. You're beginning to sound like an old hand at this sort of thing.'

'Is that why they died? Because they knew what happened out there?'

'No, of course not. There are many, many people who know what happened out there, detective. If we got rid of everyone who knew what happened out in Nicaragua then most of Congress and all of the Senate . . . hell, you'd have three-quarters of the United States administration being buried at Arlington. The CIA uses some judgement, you know? Some sense of restraint. They make decisions that no-one else is capable of making. They make executive decisions, and once those decisions are made they are passed down through controllers and station chiefs and section chiefs and God only knows who else, and right at the end of the food chain you have people like John Robey and Donald Carvalho. The people you are so concerned about were killed because they found out that drug money was still pouring

529

into the CIA's coffers long after the war in Nicaragua was over.'

'And the CIA sent assassins to murder them,' Miller said matter-of-factly.

'Cleaners, mechanics, hitters, fixers, dispatchers . . . any number of different job descriptions.'

'And how many of these people are there?'

Thorne frowned. 'I have absolutely no idea, and even if I did know, that's not a question I would be willing to answer.'

'And who orders that people should die?'

'No comment. We go back to the wall, don't we, Detective Miller? The wall that has to be guarded by someone . . . by someones I should say.'

'A wall against what? Against some imagined communist infiltration? Hell, it's not the 1950s anymore.'

'And the reason it's not the 1950s, the reason there is no longer a Cold War? I'll tell you why, detective . . . because we did things like El Salvador, Libya . . . things that would never have been paid for had it not been for Nicaragua. Because there were people like me and John Robey and Catherine Sheridan who believed enough in what was right and democratic to go out there and do something about it.'

'You really believe that?' Miller asked. 'That flooding the United States with hundreds of tons of cocaine in order to pay for illegal wars is actually justified?'

'Oh come on, detective, don't be so naïve. These people you're talking about . . . blacks and Hispanics, the Cubans, the Mexicans . . . if they hadn't gotten coke from the Nicaraguan sources, it would have come from any of a dozen other places. Seems to me we did them a favor. We gave them the highest grade coke they'd ever had. These people are animals, they do what they're going to do regardless of what anyone tries to tell them. They take drugs. They've always taken drugs. They're going to take drugs from here on out and there's nothing, not a single thing you or I or anyone else can do about it.'

'You really believe this, don't you? You really believe that this is how the world is and you can just dictate who lives and who dies.'

'You make it sound like I have some sort of God complex,' Thorne said.

'Looks to me that it's not far from the truth.'

'God is a myth. People are born, people die. They have whatever time they have to make a difference or not. We do what we do because we believe that people have a right not to be oppressed by Fascism and Communism. CIA operatives gave their hearts and souls to the Agency. They said they would do the job, they said they would protect the security of the nation, and then they found out something that upset them and they wanted to tell the world. A few dozen people. It was a few dozen people, that's all. You really think that the stability and security of this nation can be jeopardized because a handful of people lost their nerve?'

'You should record yourself and listen back to it . . . you have any fucking idea how insane you sound?'

Thorne waved aside Miller's comment. He put his hands in his pockets and turned towards the windows. 'So we are done?' he asked.

'What are you going to do about Robey?' Miller asked.

'Robey? Robey will show up at some point and someone will kill him.'

'That simple,' Miller said.

'Why on earth would it be any more complicated? There are certain interests that have to be protected, and those interests are an awful lot more important to the wellbeing and security of this nation than the lives of a few dissenters.'

Thorne walked to the desk and lifted the phone. He punched a number. 'Security . . . Detective Miller is ready to leave.'

It was as Thorne put the receiver down and looked at Miller that Miller realized what was going to happen. He realized why Thorne had been so willing to talk – not because no-one would believe Miller, but because he would never have the chance to repeat it.

The man who had collected him had taken Miller's gun; it was even now secure in the reception building, ready for his return.

But Miller would never return.

'John Robey might have assisted you thus far,' Thorne said, 'But John Robey is a man of narrow loyalties.'

'You seem to know an awful lot about him,' Miller said, gauging the distance between himself and door, between himself and the French windows, wondering whether the windows were locked, how high the wall was, what was beyond the wall. The street perhaps? Another part of the same Judiciary Square complex? Were there further security measures on the other side?

His pulse was racing, he felt the blood draining from his face. This was how he'd felt when Brandon Thomas had turned on him, when he realized that Thomas didn't care that he was a cop. Thomas was going to kill him, just as Thorne would now do. But Thorne would not be involved. He would direct one of his people, who would speak to someone else, and that someone else would take Miller and shoot him in the head, or throw him off a high-rise . . .

'I know more about John Robey than John Robey himself,' Thorne said. He moved to the left and stood with his back to the windows, almost as if he had read Miller's mind and intended to prevent any escape. Though Thorne was smaller in height and build, he would slow Miller down long enough for security to reach the office.

'Because?' Miller asked, stalling for time, trying to think of something, anything. The telephone on the desk. The heavy glass decanter from which Thorne had poured the Armagnac. There were any number of things he could use to attack the man, but what then? He knocked him down, he ran from the building. He would be seen. He would be guilty of assault. People would follow him. He had no gun, no means to defend himself, and if all that Thorne had told him was true, if Oliver had been murdered in his place, then such people would have no concern or consideration for the fact that he was a Washington police detective.

'Because?' Thorne echoed. 'Because I trained him, Detective Miller . . . I trained Robey and Sheridan and Carvalho, and dozens more like them.'

'And your name isn't Walter Thorne, is it?'

'Walter Thorne, Frank Rissick, Edward Perna, Lawrence Matthews . . . I am all of them and none of them, detective.

I am whoever I am supposed to be whenever that person is required. The fact that you came across the name Donald Carvalho in connection with United Trust is neither here nor there. You have any idea how many names exist for how many façades and businesses and operations that are simply faces we wear for the world?'

Miller's every sense was alert for the sound of people in the hallway beyond the office. He didn't know which way to go – out to the door? Or try and get through the yard and over the wall beyond . . .

'So if Robey was so much trouble—'

'Why didn't we just dispatch him?' Thorne finished the question for him. 'Because dealing with the John Robeys and Catherine Sheridans of this world is not the same as dealing with Margaret Mosley and Ann Rayner and Barbara Lee and the Joyce woman, Detective Miller. There are certain issues that had to be addressed.'

'What did he do? Did he have evidence about all of this? Did he have evidence that would have gone public in the event of his death?'

'He had evidence, detective, and we had something of his. It was a stand-off, a stalemate . . . and nothing moved for a very long time.'

'You had something of his? What? What did you have on Robey?'

'Not so much a what as a *who*.'

'A who?' Miller asked, and then he nodded his head. 'Catherine Sheridan, right? You threatened him with the death of Catherine Sheridan if he—'

'No, detective . . . John Robey was not so concerned with the welfare of Catherine Sheridan that her death would have stopped him.'

'So who then? What are you talking about?'

'I am talking about—'

The fact that there was no discernible sound as the bullet punctured the upper right pane of the left-hand French window gave the moment a sense of surreal disquiet.

Thorne was speaking. *I am talking about*— And then he was not speaking.

There were words coming from his mouth, and then there was nothing.

He seemed to stand there for quite some time, but it was merely seconds, less than seconds, but those few seconds stretched out eternally, and Miller waited for Thorne to start speaking again . . .

Judge Thorne moved sideways awkwardly, like he'd had a sudden shock, the delivery of some terrible news.

It was then that Miller saw the tiny hole in the window pane.

And once he saw the hole in the window pane, he knew why Judge Thorne was trying to hold himself upright against the bookshelf, why the light in his eyes seemed to have gone flat and black and hollow, why the sound coming from his mouth wasn't speech, but some kind of strangled hiss, like steam escaping a lidded pot . . . and then there was the needle-thin trickle of blood making its way from the corner of his right eye and down his cheek . . .

Miller felt his heart stop, and then start again double-time.

Walter Thorne dropped to his knees, and as he swayed to the left his head collided with the corner of the heavy mahogany desk. He went down like a stone.

Miller lurched forward, immediately and instinctively, a futile effort to catch Thorne, but Thorne rolled sideways as soon as he hit the carpet. Miller was on his knees, trying desperately to turn him over, his hands holding the man's head as blood oozed between his fingers.

Miller leaned back on his haunches, held his hands up, the blood trickling down his wrists towards the cuffs of his shirt.

The swelling lake of blood on the carpet belied the small, nickel-sized wound in Thorne's right temple. There was no exit wound on the left. The bullet was still inside his head.

It was then that Miller reacted. He opened his mouth to say something, to shout, to scream for help – a medic, some-one, anyone that could do *anything* – even though he knew it was far too late . . .

But not a sound emerged from his lips.

He started shaking violently. He tried to stand, but fell sideways. He reached out and grasped the arm of the chair

534

where Thorne had sat, got to his feet, and when he let go he saw the scarlet handprint he'd left behind.

He was overcome with nausea and a sensation of sudden and unrelenting terror. He reached for his gun but came back with nothing.

Miller stepped to the side of the window, and through the gap between the frame and the edge of the drape he looked out into the yard.

What had he expected to see?

The empty yard, almost monochromatic, its stillness juxtaposed now against the madness that was occurring inside Walter Thorne's office . . .

Miller could barely stand. He leaned against the wall, once again leaving a bloody handprint behind.

He had spoken to at least two people. The receptionist had his name, Thorne's assistant had his gun. He was here. He had been alone in the room when Walter Thorne was killed . . .

Miller was in deep, deeper than he had been over Brandon Thomas.

He started hyperventilating, talking to himself. He walked to the window again. He looked down at Thorne's body. He knelt on the ground and touched his fingers to Thorne's neck. There was nothing.

He wanted to kick Thorne. He wanted to beat his fists into the man's face and scream obscenities. He wanted to shout at him, to challenge everything that the man had said. He wanted to tell him what he thought of his view of the world, that people like him were the reason the world was so fucked, that people like Walter Thorne were the reason for drugs and crime and war and . . .

But he said nothing.

Robert Miller felt all the pent-up emotion from the previous weeks back up in his chest like a fist. He felt like he was going to choke, that his heart would seize up from the pressure and fear and pain, that he would collapse across the dead body of Judge Walter Thorne and the two of them would be found in the same room, door locked, a small hole in the window, and no-one would be any the wiser as to what had taken place between Detective Robert Miller and

535

Judge Walter Thorne on the afternoon of Monday the 20th November, 2006.

And no-one would ever *know*.

And John Robey would go back to work at Mount Vernon College, and he would lecture students about literature and poetry, and the students would watch him, hear what he was saying, and never even guess that the man who spoke with them every day had killed more people than they could ever comprehend . . .

Miller did not know; he was so disoriented he did not know what to believe . . .

Except that he was fucked.

That much he knew, and he knew it with certainty.

FIFTY-EIGHT

It was in some brief hiatus between the Judiciary Square security chief arriving, between the call made for an ambulance, that call becoming a request for the coroner . . .

Some brief hiatus when Robert Miller stood in the yard beyond the French windows with the security chief, both men looking for any signs of who might have fired a single shot through the window of Judge Thorne's office . . .

Some brief moment of silence when nothing else was in his mind that the image came back to him.

The image on the screen of the computer in John Robey's apartment.

Catherine Sheridan.

Put it down for God's sake.

The image of Catherine Sheridan as she waved her hand at whoever was filming her. There were trees in the background. She had on a turquoise woollen beret, her hair tucked beneath it.

Catherine Sheridan laughing . . .

John, for God's sake . . . put the camera away.

Unable to stand, he sat on one of the wrought-iron benches in the walled yard behind Judge Walter Thorne's offices in Judiciary Square, and he watched as the security chief tried to maintain some sense of order, and then at some point he heard that Marilyn Hemmings was arriving, and for some reason he did not want to see her . . . not again, not like this with another dead body on the floor, another vague smile of recognition, another moment they would both remember as something traumatic and frightening, as if all their shared moments had to have something ugly to define them – some act of evil, some act of murder, some act of betrayal . . .

Miller spoke with the security chief, a man whose name he

537

never did learn, and told him that he would return to the Second Precinct, that he would write his report, that he would speak with the assistant district attorney immediately and would ensure that whoever was available was assigned to assist in the investigation of the murder of Judge Walter Thorne . . .

The man asked why Miller had been with the judge. He needed to know for his own report. Miller told him it had been something to do with an outstanding warrant, nothing of great significance. The security chief seemed satisfied.

Miller went back to reception. He got a secretary to direct him to where his gun was secured. He signed it out, hurried from the building, reached his car and drove away from Judiciary Square, away from the dead body of Walter Thorne, away from everything that Thorne had told him.

He did not head for the Second Precinct; he headed directly for the Brentwood Park Ice Rink.

Forty-five minutes later Robert Miller stood in silence in the foyer of the Brentwood Park building. The place was officially closed, but the presentation of his ID to a janitor had been sufficient to gain him entry. He walked straight on through to the rink, out along the lower ranks of seats, scanned the tiers one after the other.

John Robey raised his hand and smiled.

Miller said nothing until he'd walked much of the rink's perimeter. He came to a stop in the aisle twenty feet beneath where Robey sat.

'Professor Robey.'

'Detective Miller.'

'I've come to ask you about the murder of Judge Walter Thorne.'

'The murder of Judge Walter Thorne will appear to be something entirely different tomorrow.'

'Meaning?' Miller walked up a few steps. He was alert for any sudden movement on Robey's part. Alert for Robey reaching for a gun.

'Meaning whatever you wish it to mean,' Robey replied. 'How it is and how it will appear are not necessarily the same thing . . . as is always the case in my line of work.'

Miller took another step upwards. 'Enough now,' he said quietly. He could hear the fatigue in his own voice. He sounded like a man whose life had been smashed to pieces. 'I know a great deal about what has happened . . . I just spent a considerable time with Walter Thorne and he told me—'

'What did he tell you? Did he do the speech? The one about the way the world is, how there are certain people who carry a responsibility to protect the nation?' Robey smiled understandingly. 'You don't need to tell me . . . I listened to the whole thing.'

'You what?'

'I've had an ear in Thorne's office for months . . . I've known what was going on for a very long time . . .'

'So you appreciate how much there is that I still don't understand,' Miller said.

'He was not Walter Thorne,' Robey said. 'He has lived with that name for years, but that was bullshit. His real name was Lawrence Matthews, and I met him at Virginia State University a long time ago.'

Miller walked the few remaining steps and took a seat beside Robey. He withdrew the envelope from his pocket, the photograph inside.

'This one . . . I don't know who this is.'

Robey smiled, took the photograph from Miller. 'Patrick Sweeney,' Robey said. 'You ever hear that name?'

Miller looked at Robey. There was something different in his eyes. 'Sweeney? I don't know . . . rings a bell. I've heard that name somewhere.'

'His real name was Don Carvalho. He was Sarah's trainer. That's what he did, believe it or not. He was an ice-skating trainer.'

'I remember . . . before Per Amundsen.' Miller frowned. 'But she told me that Sweeney had died.'

'One thing you learn in this business . . . unless you see the body, you can never be sure who's dead. And even if you see the body it doesn't necessarily prove anything.'

'So what happened to him?'

'He was Don Carvalho for a long time, and then he became Patrick Sweeney. He tried to lead a normal life, but then he was drafted back into duty and he became Don Carvalho once more. He and I worked together in Nicaragua. We came out of there determined to do something about the cocaine that was still coming into the U.S., about the people that were dying. I sent documentation to three separate and individual CIA operatives, people I believed I could trust; documentation that was meant to alert them to what Don and I knew. They reported it to their section chiefs, the section chiefs reported it to their controller, and the controller issued the order to Don that these operatives were to be killed . . .'

'Mosley, Rayner and Lee,' Miller said. 'That's who you sent the information to?'

'Right . . . and that's when Don Carvalho came to me and told me that he'd been ordered to kill all three of them.'

'And you told him not to kill them?'

'No, Robert . . . I told him to kill them. Kill them brutally. Beat them and strangle them and tie ribbons around their necks and cover them in lavender. Do it in such a way as the world would take notice. Give the world something that they could not ignore.'

Miller's eyes were wide in disbelief. 'So Thorne was right,' he said. 'Carvalho was the Ribbon Killer . . .'

'Not everything Walter Thorne told you was untrue. We exist in a fragile state of apparencies. Something that appears one way is almost certainly something else. Patrick Sweeney, Don Carvalho, it doesn't matter what name you use . . . he was a killer. He killed people for the government. That's what he did. That's what he'd been doing for years. Same as me. We decided a long time ago that certain lives were expendable, that certain people could be sacrificed for the common good.' Robey smiled. He seemed to be growing more tired as he spoke. 'I can't hope that you'll understand . . . people never want to understand, and the only analogy I can draw is that of a cure for some terrible disease. Cancer perhaps, you know? And in developing that cure, a cure that will save countless millions of lives, there might be a thousand, even five or ten thousand who have to die while it's being tried and tested and tried once more. Eventually they get it right, and then people don't have to die anymore.'

'So you were out there . . . in Nicaragua.'

'We were all out there.' Robey pointed at the faces in the photo. 'James Killarney. His name was Dennis Powers. Judge Walter Thorne. When I met him he was a lecturer at Virginia State named Lawrence Matthews. Me, Catherine, and then Don Carvalho.'

'This is something that you people really believe, isn't it?'

'*Did* believe. We did believe it . . . once. And then we saw it for what it was.'

'So why did Don Carvalho have to kill Mosley and Rayner and Barbara Lee?'

'Because he had no choice. Because if he hadn't killed them he would have been terminated and someone else would have killed them . . . and he spoke to me and I told him what to do.'

'Which was?'

'Do something that would get your attention. The police, the newspapers . . . we gave them the Ribbon Killer.'

'To make us aware that there was a connection between Mosley, Rayner and Lee?'

'To show you there was a connection, to show the people who employed us that we had a voice, that we weren't unthinking, unfeeling killing machines anymore . . . to try and do something about what was happening.' Robey shifted awkwardly. He massaged his hands together as if they were cold.

'But we fucked it up, right?' Miller said.

Robey laughed; he seemed to be in pain. 'You fucked it up, yes. Never seen such an amazingly inept organization as the Washington Police Department. I was part of it remember, with Darryl King. I got inside the department five years ago. Tried to do something from within . . . wound up getting Darryl killed, getting myself wounded, and all for nothing.'

'So when we missed the connections between the first three victims, someone else had to die . . . someone had to die to remind us that it was still there, that there was still a situation . . .'

Robey nodded.

'And that was Catherine Sheridan.'

'Right.'

'And Don Carvalho didn't kill her, did he?'

541

'He refused.'

'So you had to kill her.'

'I did.'

'Hence the fact that she was different from the others . . . the fact that she was not beaten before she died . . .'

Robey raised his hand. 'Enough . . . you have no idea . . .'

'And you left the pictures of you and her beneath the bed . . .'

'Everything,' Robey said.

'And Don Carvalho killed Natasha Joyce as well?'

'No, that wasn't Don.' Robey lowered his head. He sighed deeply. 'Natasha was killed by the man you know as James Killarney . . .' Robey closed his eyes. 'Killarney was also told to kill you. He would have done had it been you at my apartment instead of Detective Oliver. Anyway, it is not a matter of who killed Natasha Joyce, but the simple fact that they did it. They should not have done that . . . not to a mother with a child, but . . .' Robey looked away towards the other side of the rink, and shook his head resignedly.

'But what?'

'What am I saying? They shouldn't have killed a mother. That's what they do . . . hell, that's what we all did when we were out there, right? Mothers, fathers, even kids . . . if they got in the way they died. That was just the nature of the war. The necessary and expected casualties.' Robey sighed. 'I knew Darryl King. He was a good person. He wanted to help. He loved that woman . . . he really loved that woman, and they fucked him up so bad, made him a junkie . . .'

'Thorne said you killed Don Carvalho and put him in the trunk of the car.'

'No, I didn't kill Don. They had Killarney deal with him. They could not afford to have any other victims with luggage tags, you know? It was too close to home. Too close a reminder. Thorne also told you that Don Carvalho killed Detective Oliver, right? Well, that was Killarney as well – Oliver was supposed to be you.' Robey looked at Miller. There was still a light in his eyes, fierce and unforgiving. 'We three . . . me and Catherine and Don . . . we were kids when we went out there. We swallowed the lie. We did the

542

work we were asked to do. We killed . . . Jesus, we killed so many people . . . we killed so many fucking people . . .'

'And five years ago, with Darryl King. This drugs raid. That was cocaine still coming in from Nicaragua? King was killed because of that?'

'Yes . . . I have been trying to bring this to the attention of the world ever since I left Nicaragua.'

'You came back from Nicaragua and Catherine got pregnant, didn't she?'

Robey smiled weakly.

'Sarah Bishop, right?'

'You are not as dumb as you look, Detective Miller, but you have taken a wrong step there . . .'

'Sarah Bishop is your daughter . . . isn't she?'

Robey shook his head. 'No,' he said, his voice almost a whisper. 'Sarah Bishop was not our daughter. She was our conscience.'

'Your conscience . . . I don't understand? What d'you mean, your conscience?'

'Managua. 1984. I killed a man. His name was Francisco Sotelo. He was a lawyer. I was told he was passing information to the Sandinistas. I was told to kill him and find some documents. I killed him, of course, but when I searched his offices there were no documents. So I went to his house. I broke in, and as I was searching the place his wife surprised me.'

'And you killed her too?'

'Yes . . . I killed her too. But I didn't anticipate one thing . . . I didn't anticipate that there would be a child. A month and a half old, right there in one of the bedrooms, and I had just murdered both parents . . .'

'You took her? You and Catherine took the child?'

Robey smiled. 'We took her, yes. We took the child and we brought her here. We found a family for her.'

Miller began to understand the significance of what they had done. 'So you and Catherine and Don Carvalho decided to tell the world what had happened, but James Killarney and Judge Thorne . . .'

'It is hard for me to think of them as anything other than Dennis Powers and Lawrence Matthews.'

'But they were still working—'

'They were still defending the world from the truth. Sarah was our proof. She was our conscience. She was evidence of what we had done in Nicaragua.'

'It's unbelievable . . . all of this. It's too much. I don't understand how this has changed anything . . . this is a nightmare. It has gone on so long, so many years, and here we are . . . people are dead, Catherine is dead, Natasha Joyce is dead, and what will change? And why didn't they just kill you? They could have killed you and Catherine and Sarah and that would have been the end of it.'

'I was far too dangerous just to dismiss out of hand. Between me and Catherine . . . between us we knew everything. They knew we had information. They knew that the information would find its way into the hands of the newspapers, other government offices, if they just had us killed. With us, it was not merely a matter of making us disappear. We were never that simple.' Robey paused, breathed deeply, tried to smile. 'Have spent all these years using everything they taught me to protect myself. Hell, I even taught school and wrote some books, you know? Some places I was John Robey, other places . . . I can't even remember how many names I've had, how many histories I've created. John Robey and Michael McCullough were the very least of who I was, believe me.' He shifted forward slowly as if something was pushing him. 'But they threatened Catherine after we came back. She wanted out, but it doesn't work that way. They didn't know about Sarah at that point, and we didn't tell anyone. We had to make a decision about the child . . .' Robey leaned back again, looked directly at Miller. 'We had to make a decision to have her cared for by another family. We gave her up. We decided to do that. To protect her. To take away the one thing they could use against us. That was the most important decision of our lives, and then when she reached her teens we asked Don Carvalho to help us. He became very close to her . . . he helped her. He told us what she was like. I came down here and watched her train . . .'

'And she never knew who you were?'

Robey shook his head. 'She never believed herself to be

anyone but Sarah Bishop. She was six weeks old when we brought her to the U.S.'

'And Catherine?'

'Catherine saw her. We would come down here together sometimes. Catherine would hide in the car, watch her leave with her parents. They never spoke. To tell Sarah the truth would have been too risky. Whoever kept an eye on me knew that I came here. To have Catherine seen here with me, or to have Catherine meet with Sarah . . . that would have been too much of a coincidence. They would have figured that out in a second . . .'

'They didn't know she was this lawyer's daughter?'

'They didn't know . . . not as far as we could tell, not for years, and then they figured that there was a connection between me and Sarah, but they didn't know who her real parents were. They may even have believed she was our daughter. Her adoption was unofficial. There were no records. But they knew that I cared for her . . . they knew that threatening her was enough.'

'So what changed? What made you and Don Carvalho decide to do these things?'

'We found out that Catherine was dying . . . that's what changed everything,' Robey said. 'She didn't want to die in some hospice. She didn't want to spend the last few months of her life breathing through tubes and pissing into a bag. She wanted out, you know? She wanted out of this life . . . she wanted to feel as though she had done something to right the wrongs.'

'So she let you kill her?'

Robey's eyes were filled with tears. 'You have any idea what it would be like to kill the woman you love . . . to hold her in your arms and know that you killed her?'

Miller shook his head. 'I have no idea,' he said quietly.

'I do,' Robey said, 'and so did my father. Ironic that the only two women I ever really loved were killed by the people that loved them the most.'

'What? Your father?'

Robey ignored the question. 'Loving someone enough to kill them? Be grateful that you know nothing of how something like that feels,' he said quietly.

'That afternoon . . . the day she died, she was with you.'

Robey, closed his eyes. 'In a hotel. We were in a hotel for some hours. We watched that movie . . . that stupid damned movie that she loved so much. That's what she wanted to do . . . God, she even had it playing in the house . . .'

'And you had to kill her to get us looking again? To try and get us to see the connections?'

'Yes . . . so that someone else could understand what had happened.'

For a while Miller did not speak, and then he looked up at Robey. 'And you know it was Killarney who killed Natasha Joyce?'

'Killarney, yes. He killed Natasha Joyce. She was looking into what happened with Darryl. She spoke to someone at the Police Department Administrations Unit. That file was flagged. Darryl King's. It would have come up on the Agency system. I imagine they had someone there within minutes.'

'They did,' Miller said. 'A woman named Frances Gray.'

'They knew what was happening by then. Those reports you gave to James Killarney were going straight to Walter Thorne and the Washington section chief. Killarney was the one who killed Natasha Joyce. He also killed Don Carvalho and Carl Oliver. He was assigned the task of ensuring that this thing never went public. That was his job, his and his alone . . . and he was the one who requested it.'

'Why?' Miller asked. 'Was there some particular reason?'

'Me and James Killarney go back an awful long time . . . there were things that happened in Nicaragua, things that I did . . . and he never—' Robey coughed sharply and held his hand to his chest.

Miller frowned. He leaned closer to Robey. 'You okay?' he asked.

Robey nodded, closed his eyes for a moment. A single tear made its way down his left cheek.

'There was a history,' Robey said. 'That's all I need to say.'

'Until?'

'Until Don was drafted back into operation . . . until the nightmare started all over again. As soon as he was called back we knew that we couldn't protect Sarah the way we

546

wanted to. Don had been there for her, and once he was active again it became impossible . . .'

'And so you had to figure out a way to make any possible threat on her life unimportant?'

'When Catherine got sick, you know? When she got sick we knew . . .' Robey gripped the arms of the chair. His forehead glistened with sweat. 'If Catherine was dead . . . if Catherine's death led the authorities to investigate what was going on . . .' Robey took a deep breath. He screwed up his eyes as if he was in intense pain, and then he hesitated before speaking. 'With Catherine dead . . . and then if documentation was made available . . . a lot of documentation was made available to a lot of people simultaneously . . .' Robey's breath caught in his lungs and he coughed again.

'What's happening?' Miller said. 'Are you okay?'

'It's alright,' Robey said, his voice weakening. 'And if a lot of documentation was made available to a lot of people at the same time, and if Catherine was already dead, and if they could not get to me, then there would be no reason for them to go after Sarah . . . there would be no threat to hold over us . . . nothing to make anybody afraid of . . .'

Robey coughed again, this time louder, the sound sharp and painful. He withdrew a handkerchief from his pocket and held it to his mouth. He stayed silent for a while, trying to breathe, and when he took his hand away there was blood on the handkerchief.

'What's happening here?' Miller said. 'What's going on? Are you sick or something?'

Robey shook his head. 'This is why I had to have someone else,' he said, his voice barely a whisper. 'Someone else had to see what was happening . . . someone else had to know the truth. I knew they'd get to Don . . . I knew Killarney would get to everyone . . . even you, eh? He even tried to kill you but he killed Oliver instead . . .'

Robey closed his eyes.

Miller gripped the man's shoulder and shook him. 'What's happening with you? What—'

Robey opened his eyes. 'I'm sorry it had to be you,' he said. 'Hell, you know it had to be someone . . . I wanted someone without a family, I really did. I wanted someone without a

547

family who could piece this thing together and understand enough of what happened . . .'

'You said that there's a lot of documentation—'

'Already on its way,' Robey said. 'It's already on its way, Detective Miller . . .' Robey's breathing was shallow. He reached out his hand to take Miller's and he pulled Miller toward him. 'And Walter Thorne . . . there's a rifle in a bag . . . follow the trajectory of the shot back to . . . back to the building across the street . . . in a room there's a bag with a rifle . . . prints on it . . .'

Robey's breathing was labored, painful to hear, painful to watch.

'Do something for me . . .' he said through gritted teeth. 'Do something for me . . .'

Miller looked back at Robey, held his breath, waiting . . .

'Need someone left behind to see she's okay . . . make sure they don't get her. That's the most important reason I needed you . . . with me and Catherine gone there is no reason to threaten her, but they are vindictive, you know? They can be vindictive and unthinking and I need someone to help her.'

Robey seemed incapable of holding his head up straight. He struggled to look at Miller. A thin line of blood and saliva crept from the corner of his mouth and descended slowly to the lapel of his jacket.

'You can do that for me?' he slurred. 'That much you can do for me . . . keep an eye on her . . . make sure they don't kill her out of spite . . .'

'Yes,' Miller said. 'I can do that . . . I can do that much.'

Robey smiled weakly, and from his coat pocket he took a white envelope, and he pressed it into Miller's hand. Miller looked at it, and printed neatly across the front was a single word, the same lettering as the words on the back of the photograph he had found in the United Trust office.

SARAH.

And then there was something in Robey's eyes that said everything was done, and there was little else to say, and what else there might have been didn't matter now because the play was over, the thing had run its course, and there was nothing else to keep him in the theater . . .

John Robey sort of slid sideways in the chair until the weight of his head was resting against Miller's shoulder.

Miller didn't move. He closed his eyes, and then opened them once more when music suddenly filled the auditorium.

The sound of a piano through the speakers above Miller's head, and he watched as Sarah Bishop glided out and across the ice as if from nowhere, and Miller sat motionless as she crouched down low, almost pressed into nothing, and then opened up like a flower growing from nowhere . . .

Strings came in behind the piano, and then a woman's voice:

> *C'est l'amour qui fait qu'on aime*
> *C'est l'amour qui fait rêver*
> *C'est l'amour qui veut qu'on s'aime*
> *C'est l'amour qui fait pleurer . . .*

Each time she swept toward the edge of the rink his heart almost stopped.

And he watched Sarah Bishop, and his eyes filled with tears, and he wondered whether there would ever be a chance that she could understand what had happened . . .

And then she saw them – Detective Robert Miller and John Robey, a new acquaintance and a very old friend, watching from the gods as she practised.

She raised her hand and waved, and Miller waved his hand in response, and she paused for a moment before facing the outside of the rink and gliding backwards, picking with the left toe and leaping off the right leg . . .

The singing once more, a plaintive and heartfelt language that Miller did not understand . . .

> *Et ceux qui n'ont pas de larmes*
> *Ne pourrons jamais aimer*
> *Il faut tant, et tant de larmes*
> *Pour avoir le droit d'aimer . . .*

It was an hour before Miller called the police from his cell phone. He sat with Robey throughout Sarah Bishop's entire training routine. As she skated away toward the exit she waved again. Miller waved in return. They did not speak. There was nothing to say.

The police department came, as did Tom Alexander. They bagged Robey's body and put him on a stretcher. Miller sat and watched as they made their careful and circuitous way along the aisles and between the seats.

After a little while Alexander returned, asked Miller if he was okay, did he need a ride somewhere?

Miller shook his head. 'I'm okay Tom . . . I'm okay . . .'

Alexander smiled. 'Gonna give you a citation for getting this guy, eh? Cop killer, you know?'

'Sure they will . . . sure they will . . .'

'You really don't need a ride somewhere? I can take you back into the city.'

'It's okay, I've got my car. Just want to be alone for a little while.'

Alexander nodded understandingly. 'You take care.'

Miller didn't reply, merely smiled an exhausted smile, watched as Tom Alexander turned and made his way down toward the exit.

Miller closed his eyes.

He breathed deeply.

He thought of the highway, of driving somewhere and not stopping. Highways were all the same. White lights came toward you, red lights went away. Just get on the highway and keep going . . . didn't matter where, anywhere but here . . . horizon ahead, as far as the eye could see, as close to forever as he could imagine . . .

FIFTY-NINE

On the morning of Tuesday, 21st November 2006, ten days after the death of Catherine Sheridan, one week after the murder of Natasha Joyce, a Crime Scene Unit headed by Greg Reid accessed an office on Sixth Street, an office with windows that overlooked Judiciary Square. Beneath the floorboards of the office a canvas bag was found, within it a lightweight AR7 rifle. Ballistics confirmed that the bullet recovered from the cranium of Judge Walter Thorne carried the same land and groove markings as the test shot fired from the AR7 in laboratory conditions.

There were prints on the gun. They were not John Robey's.

Despite the fact that gun oil present in the chamber and along the bolt indicated that the weapon had remained unused for many years, it was nevertheless confirmed that it had been fired the previous day. One shot was fired, from a fourth-floor office. The shot passed through the left-hand section of the French window in Judge Thorne's office, entered his head behind the right ear, ricocheted repeatedly through his brain, and killed him instantly.

They printed the gun and ran those prints through AFIS. There was no match.

At ten-eighteen a.m. a FedEx courier appeared at the offices of the Washington district attorney. The D.A.'s secretary signed for receipt of a package of documents approximately five inches thick. Within the subsequent two hours the same package was delivered to the offices and chambers of the United States Chief Justice, eight associate justices, the chairmen of the House subcommittees on Foreign Affairs, Government Operations and Intelligence, eighteen further Congressman, twelve members of the Senate, the Secretaries of State for Defense and Justice, the head of the National Security Council, and the White House press office. Packages were also delivered to the senior editorial directors of the *Washington Post*, the *International Herald Tribune*, the *Los Angeles Times*, the *New York Times*, and at the personal residences of the Washington section chiefs of Central Intelligence Agency directorates for Overseas Operations, Intelligence Production and Support Activities.

It was said later that the central Washington secure network telephone exchange serving the federal triangle, Congress, the Senate, and much of the intelligence community, collapsed beneath the overload of calls. It was a rumor never reported, left unsubstantiated.

At one-eighteen p.m. the body of an FBI agent named James Killarney was found in the car park overlooking G Place near Union Station. He appeared to have committed suicide: a single shot through the roof of the mouth, an exit wound the size of a fist and much of the contents of his head across the roof of his car. Undergoing standard identity confirmation procedure at the coroner's office, he was found to possess the same fingerprints as those lifted from the AR7 that killed Walter Thorne. There was no powder residue on either of Killarney's hands, nothing to suggest he had held either the .38 handgun that ended his own life, or the rifle that ended Thorne's. Nevertheless, they had probative confirmation that Killarney had fired the gun that killed Walter Thorne. Both Thorne's assassination and Killarney's suicide were pursued no further.

It was Tom Alexander who called Miller. Called him at home.

'Atropine,' he said.

'What?'

'He poisoned himself with atropine.'

'What the fuck is that?'

'Comes from belladonna, you've heard of that?'

'I've heard of it yes.'

'Different variations of the same thing . . . they even give a combination of atropine and something called obidoxime to the military as an antidote to nerve agents.'

'Tell me something, Tom,' Miller said.

Alexander paused, Miller could hear his hesitation in the silence.

'How bad was it?'

'Eh?'

'How bad did he hurt?'

'He took a serious amount, detective . . . a very serious amount. He knew he'd die. There was no coming back from this one. Speeded his heart up . . . that's what it does, speeds the heart up. Basically his heart would have gone at eight, ten times the normal speed and then just collapsed. I can't tell you how much he would've hurt . . . a great deal, I should think, but I don't know for sure.'

Miller didn't reply.

'You know why it's called that?' Alexander asked.

'What?'

'Atropine . . . why it's called that.'

'No,' Miller said. 'I have no idea.'

'Named after Atropos, one of the three Fates. It's Greek mythology. Atropos was the Fate who had the job of deciding how someone would die.'

Miller closed his eyes. He could hear his own breathing.

'I'll see you sometime,' Alexander said. 'Figured you'd wanna know . . . about Robey, you know? That's why I called.'

'Thanks, Tom . . . I appreciate it.'

The line went dead.

Miller hung up the phone.

Late Wednesday afternoon. Washington Second Precinct briefing room. Lassiter was present, as was ADA Cohen. Miller had not seen Al Roth until half an hour before the meeting. They shared few words. There were few words to share. Miller asked after Amanda and the kids. They were good. Happy to have him home.

'John Robey did not exist,' Lassiter said quietly.

Miller looked at Nanci Cohen, then at Roth.

Lassiter shrugged, tried to smile. 'Of course, he did exist . . . he was a real person . . .' He stopped, looked at Cohen.

'That is the official line,' Cohen said. 'He sent some things . . . he sent documents to the entire fucking

553

government. He sent papers to congressmen, senators, news-papers . . .' Cohen paused, glanced at Lassiter. 'And the United States Supreme Court—'

'Don't tell me,' Miller asked. 'The United States Supreme Court has barred the newspapers from reporting on any of this.'

Cohen didn't reply.

'There will be a congressional inquiry—' Lassiter began.

Miller cut in. 'It's okay . . . I don't need any explanations.'

Lassiter and Cohen fell silent.

'I'm going to take a week off,' Miller said. 'I want to take a week's leave if that's okay.'

Lassiter was nodding. 'Sure, sure . . . take a week, two if you want.'

Miller stood up.

Nanci Cohen rose with him. 'The bigger the lie . . .'

Miller smiled. 'The more easily it will be believed.'

'So what are you going to do?' she asked.

'About what? This case? Robey?' Miller shook his head. 'Nothing . . . that's what I'm going to do. Not because I don't want to, but because I don't think it's worth throwing any more lives away for this thing.'

'I'd have to agree with you on that point,' she replied. She reached out, touched Miller's arm. 'You take care, eh?'

'I'll try,' he said. He turned, opened the door and stepped out into the corridor.

SIXTY

'As well as anyone who knew him,' Miller said.

Sarah Bishop shook her head. 'It's so sad,' she said quietly. They were seated at the same table in the same gymnasium canteen where they'd first met.

She looked different to Miller this time. She looked like someone with a past.

'He was so young . . . I mean, he was so . . . he seemed fine, you know?'

'Hereditary I think,' Miller said. 'Weak heart. I don't know what to say. He was a good man . . . and he thought a lot of you.'

Sarah nodded, didn't speak. She looked down at the white envelope on the table, her name printed neatly across the front. The edge of the check protruded from the uppermost corner.

Miller took a card from his pocket. 'Three numbers on there. The precinct, my home, my cell phone. Anything you need, you call me. John asked me to keep an eye on you, make sure you were okay.'

'It doesn't make sense . . . I mean, in all the years I've known him I can't think of ten times we've spoken. Never really had much to say for himself. I don't even know what my parents are going to think.'

'You can tell them he was a generous man with no family who wanted to support your hopes for the Olympics.'

'You really think that's the truth? I mean, I cannot think of any reason he'd want to leave me so much money.'

Miller shrugged. 'I don't know . . . he didn't tell me.'

Sarah picked up the envelope. 'Will you come with me?' she said. 'Will you come and tell my parents what happened? They didn't know him. They are going to . . . like freak out, you know? They're going to freak out completely when they see this.'

Miller reached out and held her hand for a moment.

'Sure,' he said. 'I'll come see your parents.'

She smiled, looked away for a moment, and when she looked back at Miller there was something in her eyes, a moment of understanding perhaps, a moment of recognition.

And then suddenly – like a ghost – it was gone.

SIXTY-ONE

'Hard work,' Harriet said. 'He's hard work . . . but I think he will be worth it.' She smiled, reached out her hand and closed it over Marilyn Hemmings'.

'Tell me a man who isn't,' Marilyn replied. 'They're all long-term investments, doubtful returns.'

'Take Zalman,' she said. 'Fifty-two years we are married and still . . . ach, I don't know what to say. We do what we can, eh?'

Miller appeared in the doorway at the bottom of the stairwell. 'What is this?' he said.

Marilyn Hemmings raised her eyebrows.

'See . . . he cleans up good doesn't he?' Harriet said.

'What's going on here . . . is this some sort of conspiracy . . .'

'Enough already,' Harriet said. She rose to her feet, walked towards Miller.

'She's a good girl this one,' she whispered. 'You have to be very stupid to mess this up.'

Miller frowned disapprovingly.

Marilyn Hemmings got up, straightened her skirt. 'You ready?' she asked.

'He's as ready as he's ever gonna be,' Harriet said. 'So off with you . . . go have a good time, okay? I'll be gone when you come back . . . *if* you come back.'

'Harriet,' Miller said.

Marilyn smiled, held out her hand. 'It was wonderful to meet you.'

Harriet took Marilyn's hand, held it for a moment. 'The feeling's mutual, my dear. Now away and enjoy yourselves . . . I have things to do.'

Miller stepped forward, extended his hand to show Marilyn Hemmings the door, and walked her out to the car.

'Nice people,' she said.

Miller nodded. 'They are.'

'She cares a lot about you.'

Miller smiled, unlocked the passenger door and held it open.

He walked around the front and got inside.

'So where are we going?' Marilyn asked.

'Going to eat, but I want to make a brief stop,' Miller said. 'If you don't mind, there's someone I want to see. It won't take a moment.'

Marilyn nodded. 'Sure, of course.'

They drove in near silence. It didn't concern Marilyn Hemmings that Miller didn't speak. It felt comfortable. That was all she could say. Being around him seemed to be comfortable all of a sudden.

The death of John Robey was behind them, the better part of two weeks back, and things had happened, life-things, and work had continued, and the world had gone on without Miller for a little while, and he was due back soon. Miller had earned breathing space, and she had not called him for fear of intruding.

He had called her that morning, almost perfunctory in his manner, but it was okay.

'Hey.'

'Hey back.'

'How's things?'

'Okay . . . they're okay. You?'

A moment's hesitation. 'I've slept a lot.'

That had made her smile.

'I called . . .'

Silence, but not awkward. Like he'd thought of what to say and then it hadn't sounded right.

'You did,' she prompted.

'Tonight. I wondered, you know?'

'What I'm doing?'

'Sure, what you're doing.'

'Why . . . you wanna go out or something?'

'Yes . . . figured it would be good . . . you know, if you wanted to and everything.'

She smiled again. It was like being asked to a prom.

558

'I'd like that, Robert.'

'You want to come here, or you want me to come get you?'

'I'll meet you . . . give me your address.'

She wrote it down.

'Seven?'

'Give or take.'

'Give or take . . . okay. Later then.'

'Later, Robert.'

The call had ended.

Now he sat beside her, driving the car, going someplace she didn't know. Made a left, another left, three or four blocks and then slowed to a halt outside a large three-storey brownstone walk-up.

'You want to wait here, or you want to come with me?' he asked. 'I won't be long.'

'I'll wait here if that's okay.'

He left the car, keys still in the ignition.

He closed the door and walked toward the steps of the house.

Marilyn turned the key, got power for the radio, switched it on. She found a jazz station. Norah Jones. Someone like that.

She watched as Robert Miller went up to the door. He rang the bell, waited, rang it again.

A light came on back of the frosted pane centering the door.

Words were exchanged before the door was opened. Middle-aged woman, in her arms a small child, couldn't have been more than eighteen months old. The woman seemed puzzled, and then she smiled and nodded, and she turned and seemed to call back into the house.

A child appeared – ten, eleven years old. Black girl, her hair tied back in symmetrical pigtails. She carried a Polly Petal doll. She held out her hand and shook with Miller.

The child disappeared back into the house.

Miller said something else, took an envelope from his pocket and gave it to the woman. The woman said nothing, looked like she didn't know what to say.

Miller reached out and touched the toddler's cheek, a

gentle moment, and then he turned and walked back towards the car.

The woman watched him from the stoop.

Miller got into the car, started the engine, pulled away.

Marilyn Hemmings turned and watched the woman as she stood looking down the street, watching the car until they turned the corner at the end and disappeared from view.

'Who was that?' Marilyn asked.

'She's taking care of someone.'

'You gave her what . . . some money?'

Miller nodded.

'How much?'

Miller smiled, shrugged his shoulders. 'It doesn't matter.'

'Who was the girl . . . the one with the pigtails?'

'Just a girl.'

'Natasha Joyce's kid?'

Miller turned and looked at Marilyn Hemmings. 'Now how would I know where to find Natasha Joyce's kid . . . that's confidential, you know? Child Services an' all that.'

Marilyn Hemmings said nothing in response.

Miller looked back at the road.

'You are a strange man, Robert Miller,' she said after some little while.

'Strange is as strange does,' he said quietly.

'Sure, of course . . . now you sound like Forrest Gump.'

'Life is like a box of chocolates . . .'

She swung her hand sideways, thumped him on the shoulder. 'Don't even start that shit,' she said, but she was laughing, and then he was laughing too, and whatever had happened back there with the little girl and the woman on the doorstep, however much money Miller might have given her, it didn't matter any more.

After a while she asked him, 'You wanna talk about what happened?'

'What?' he said. 'With Robey?'

'Sure, with Robey.'

Miller smiled. His expression was one of philosophical resignation. 'That's the point, Marilyn . . . nothing did happen.'

'But—'

'We'll be there soon,' he said. 'Italian okay with you?'

She hesitated, and then she said, 'Yes, of course. Italian is fine.'

He parked up ahead of a small trattoria with burgundy awnings, and through the wide front window she could see small tables and candlelit booths.

He opened the door for her, and as she came out she looked up at him.

'One day?' she said.

Miller paused for a moment, turned and looked toward the horizon. 'I don't know what to tell you,' he said quietly. 'Somewhere I lost about two weeks of my life . . . and I don't think I'll ever get them back. It all seems so vague and unreal, and I don't even understand everything that happened.' He looked down at the ground, and then he turned back toward her.

'I'm alive,' he said. 'A lot of people died but I'm alive. I don't know what else to say, Marilyn. Something happened, and then it was all over, and a lot of people are very concerned that no-one ever knows what happened. I'm just gonna do what I can to salvage whatever good I can out of it all.'

'And this doesn't worry you? That you know all this . . . what happened with Robey, the people that were killed, and you can say nothing?'

Miller closed his eyes. Took a deep breath.

'Today,' he said quietly. 'Today it doesn't worry me.'

Marilyn Hemmings reached out her hand and touched the side of Miller's face. 'I was right about you,' she said. 'I went with my intuition and I think I was right about you.'

Miller looked at her questioningly.

'Brandon Thomas . . . did he fall or was he pushed?'

Miller looked at her, questioning. 'Did you ever doubt that?'

'Honestly? Yes, I did doubt it.'

'Then you don't know me.'

'But now I'm gonna get a chance, right?'

Miller smiled. 'I hope so, yes.'

'So we go eat.'

Miller smiled. 'We go eat.'

He held the door open for her, paused for a moment looking back toward the skyline.

He did not believe Robey had died for nothing, nor Catherine Sheridan.

Perhaps the world would never know the truth of what had happened, but Miller believed that with the death of James Killarney and Walter Thorne, the intelligence community now silently staggering beneath the weight of what Robey had done, the sacred monster had, at least, been wounded.

Perhaps if wounded again, Miller thought, the sacred monster would give up its secrets and die. But that – in truth – was another war for yet another day.

For now, perhaps for a little while longer, the world would be permitted to believe that Catherine Sheridan's death had been nothing more than a simple act of violence.

PROLOGUE

Sound of gunshots, like bones snapping.

New York: its endless clamor, harsh metallic rhythms and hammering footsteps, staccato and relentless; its subways and shoeshines, gridlocked junctions and yellow cabs; its lovers' quarrels; its history and passion and promise and prayers.

New York swallowed the sound of gunshots effortlessly, as if it were no more significant than the single beat of a lonely heart.

No-one heard it amidst such a quantity of life.

Perhaps because of all these other sounds.

Perhaps because no-one was listening.

Even the dust, caught in a shaft of moonlight through the third-floor hotel window, moved suddenly by the retort of the shots, resumed its errant but progressive path.

Nothing happened, for this was New York, and such lonely and undiscovered fatalities were legion, almost indigenous, briefly remembered, effortlessly forgotten.

The city went on about its business. A new day would soon begin, and nothing so inconsequential as a death possessed the power to delay it.

It was just a life, after all; no more, nor less than that.

I am an exile.

I take a moment to look back across the span of my life, and I try to see it for what it was. Amidst the madness that I encountered, amidst the rush and smash and brutality of the collisions of humanity I have witnessed, there have been moments. Love. Passion. Promise. The hope of something better. All these things. But I am faced with a vision, and wherever I turn now I see this vision. I was Salinger's 'Catcher', standing there on the edge of a shoulder-high field of rye, aware of the sound of unseen children playing among the waves and sways of color, hearing their catch-as-catch-can laughter, their games – their childhood if you will – and watching intently for when they might come too close to the edge of the field. For the field floated free and untethered, as if in space, and were they to reach the edge there would never be time to stop them before they fell. Hence I watched and waited and listened and tried so hard to be there before they went tumbling away into the precipice beyond. For once they fell there would be no recovering them. They were gone. Gone, but not forgotten.

This has been my life.

A life spooled out like thread, strength uncertain, length unknown; whether it will cease abruptly or run out endlessly, binding more lives together as it goes; in one instance no more than cotton, barely sufficient to gather a shirt together at its seams, in another a rope – triple-woven, turk's-head closures, each strand and fiber tarred and twisted to repel water, blood, sweat, tears; a rope to raise a barn, to fashion Portuguese bowlines and bring a near-drowned child from a flooded run-off, to hold a roan mare and break her will, to bind a man to a tree and beat him for his crimes, to hoist a sail, to hang a sinner.

A life to hold, or to see slip through uncaring and inattentive hands, but always a life.

5

And given one, we wish for two, or three, or more, so easily forgetting the one we had was spent unwisely.

Time travels straight as a hopeful fishing line, weeks gathering to months gathering to years; yet, with all this time, a heartbeat of doubt and the prize is gone.

Special moments – sporadic, like knots tied, irregularly spaced as if crows on a telegraph wire – these we remember, and dare not forget, for often they are all that is left to show.

I remember all of them, and more besides, and sometimes wonder if imagination hasn't played a part in designing my life.

For that's what it was, and always will be: a life.

Now it has reached its closing chapter I feel it is time to tell of all that has happened. For that's who I was, who I will always be . . . nothing more than the storyteller, the teller of tales, and if judgement is to be made on who I am or what I have done, then so be it.

At least this will stand as truth – a testament if you will, even a confession.

I sit quietly. I feel the warmth of my own blood on my hands, and I wonder how long I will continue to breathe. I look at the body of a dead man before me, and I know that in some small way justice has been seen to be done.

We go back now, all the way back to the beginning. Walk with me, if you will, for this is all I can ask, and though I have committed so many wrongs I believe that I have done enough right to warrant this much time.

Take a breath. Hold it. Release it. Everything must be silent, for when they come, when they finally come for me, we must be quiet enough to hear them.

ONE

Rumor, hearsay, folklore. Whichever way it laid down to rest or came up for air, rumor had it that a white feather indicated the visitation of an angel.

Morning of Wednesday, July twelfth, 1939, I saw one; long and slender it was, unlike any kind of feather I'd seen before. It skirted the edge of the door as I opened it, almost as if it had waited patiently to enter, and the draft from the hallway carried it into my room. I picked it up, held it carefully, and then showed it to my mother. She said it was from a pillow. I thought about that for quite some time. Made sense that pillows were stuffed with angels' feathers. That's where dreams came from – the memories of angels seeping into your head while you slept. Got me to thinking about such things. Things like God. Things like Jesus dying on the cross for our sins that she told me about so often. Never took to the idea, never was a religious-minded boy. Later, years behind me, I would understand hypocrisy. Seemed that my childhood was littered with folks that said one thing and did another. Even our minister, the circuit rider, Reverend Benedict Rousseau, was a hypocrite, a charlatan, a fraud: one hand indicating the Way of the Scripture, the other lost amidst the boundless pleats of his sister's skirt. Way back then, my time as a child, I never really saw such things. Children, perceptive as they may be, are nevertheless selectively blind. They see everything, no question about it, but they choose to interpret what they see in a manner that suits their sensibilities. And so it was with the feather, nothing much of anything at all, but in some small way an omen, a portent. My angel had come to visit. I believed it, believed it with all my heart, and so the events of that day seemed all the more disparate and incongruous. For this was a day when everything changed.

Death came that day. Workmanlike, methodical, indifferent to fashion and favor; disrespectful of Passover, Christmas, all observance or any tradition. Death came – cold and unfeeling, the collector of life's taxation, the due paid for breathing. And when Death came I was standing in the yard amidst the scrubbed earth and dry topsoil, surrounded by carpetweed and chickweed phlox and wintergreen. He came along the High Road I think, came all the way along the border between my father's land and that of the Krugers'. I believe He walked, because later, when I looked, there were no horse tracks, nor those of a bicycle, and unless Death could move without touching the ground I assumed He came on foot.

Death came to take my father.

My father's name was Earl Theodore Vaughan. Born September twenty-seventh, 1901, in Augusta Falls, Georgia, when Roosevelt was President, hence his middle name. He did the same to me, gave me Coolidge's name in 1927, and there I was – Joseph Calvin Vaughan, son of my father – standing amidst the carpetweed when Death came to visit in the summer of '39. Later, after the tears, after the funeral and the Southern wake, we tied his cotton shirt to a branch of sassafras and set it afire. We watched it burn down to nothing, the smoke representing his soul passing from this mortal earth to a higher, fairer, more equitable plain. Then my mother took me aside, and through her shadowed and swollen eyes she told me that my father had died of a rheumatic heart.

'The fever took him,' she said, her voice cracking with emotion. 'Fever came down here, winter of '29. You were naught but a babe Joseph, and your father was racked with phlegm and spittle sufficient to irrigate an acre of good soil. Once the fever grips your heart, it weakens, it never can recover, and there was a time, maybe a month or more, when we were just biding the hours until he died. But he didn't go then, Joseph. Lord saw fit to leave him be for a handful of years more; maybe the Lord was figuring he should wait until you began your adult years.' She reached into the pocket of her apron and took out a gray rag. She wiped her eyes, the kohl smearing further across her upper cheeks; she possessed the hangdog demeanor of a ruined bareknuckle fighter, spirit-broken and defeated on a Saturday night. 'The fever was in his heart, you see,' she whispered, 'and we were lucky to keep him for the years we did.'

But I knew that the rheum hadn't taken him. Death took him, coming down from the High Road, heading back the same way, leaving nothing but His footprints in the dirt by the fence.

Later my thoughts of my father would be fractured and distended with grief; later, thinking of him as Juan Gallardo perhaps, as brave as that character in *Blood and Sand*, though never inconstant, and never as handsome as Valentino.

He was buried in a broad coffin, plain deal and warped, and the farmers from adjoining tracts, Kruger the German amongst them, drove his body along the country blacktop on a flatbed truck. Later they congregated, dour and suited, in our kitchen, amid the smell of onions fried in chicken fat, the aroma of bundt cake, the scent of lavender water in a pottery jug by the sink. And they spoke of my father, airing their reminiscences, their anecdotes, telling tall tales within wider narratives, each of them embellished and embroidered with facts that were fiction.

My mother sat wordless and watchful, her expression one of artless simplicity, her kohl-limned eyes deeper than wells, dilated pupils as black as pitch.

'One time I watched him all night with the mare,' Kruger said. 'Lay there 'til sunrise feeding the old girl handfuls of crow corn to stop the colic.'

'Tell you a story about Earl Vaughan and Kempner Tzanck,' Reilly Hawkins said. He leaned forward, his red and callused hands like bunches of some dried foreign fruit, eyes going this way and that as if forever searching out something that held a purpose to evade him. Reilly Hawkins farmed a tract south of ours, had been there long before we arrived. He welcomed us like long-lost even on our first day, raised a barn with my father, and took nothing more than a jug of cold milk for his trouble. Life had sculpted him a patina, features crazed with fine wrinkles, eye-whites close to mother-of-pearl, kind of eyes washed clear and clean by

9

tears for fallen friends. Family too, all of them long-gone and near forgotten; some from war, or fire or flood, others from accident and foolish misadventure. Ironic now, how impulsive moments – in and of themselves nothing more than efforts to affirm and grace existence with a rush of vibrant life – resulted in a death. Like Reilly's younger brother, Levin, all of nineteen years old at the Georgia State Fair. There was a half-drunk and garrulous stunt pilot, owned a Stearman or a Curtiss Jenny, crop-dusted in season; out to scare the tops of trees and graze the roofs of barns with his senseless and arrogant tricks, and Reilly had goaded and cajoled Levin into taking a flight with the man. Words went back and forth between the brothers like some *pas-de-deux*, a precision two-step, a tango of dares and provocations, each phrase a step, an arched foot, a bowed back, an aggressive shoulder. Levin didn't want to go, said his head and heart were built for ground-level observation, but Reilly kept at it, worked his fraternal angle despite knowing better, despite the haunt of sourmash around the pilot, despite the closing evening light. Levin conceded, went up on a wing and a prayer for a quarter dollar, and the pilot, a good deal braver than he was adroit, attempted a bunt followed by a hammerhead stall. Engine died its death at the apex. Long breathless silence, a rush of wind, and then a sound like a tractor hitting a wall. Killed the pair of them. The pilot and Levin Hawkins like two helpings of scorched roadkill. Plume of smoke three hundred feet high and still a ghost of it come morning. Pilot's run-gofetch assistant, kid no more than sixteen or seventeen, walked around for some hours with no expression on his face, and then he too disappeared.

Reilly Hawkins' folks died soon after. He tried to keep the small farm together after they passed on, both of them broken-hearted after Levin's death, but even the hogs seemed to look sideways at him like they understood his guilt. Never a word of blame in Reilly's direction, but old man Hawkins, chewing ceaselessly on his Heidsieck champagne tobacco, would watch the older brother, watch him like there was a debt to be repaid and he was waiting for Reilly to offer up. His eyes would twitch back and forth like a quit smoker in a cigar store. Never a word spoken, but the word always present.

Reilly Hawkins had never married, some said because he couldn't give children and had no shame to admit it. I believed that Reilly never married because his heart was broken once, and thought to have it broken a second time would kill him. Rumor said it was a girl from Berrien County, pretty as a Chinese baby. Figured not to risk such a venture as he had other reasons to live. Choice between some wide-mouthed girl from an over-stretched family, girl who wore cotton print dresses, rolled her own cigarettes and drank straight from the bottle – that, or loneliness. Seemed to have chosen the latter, but of this he never spoke directly, and I never directly asked. That was Reilly Hawkins, the little I knew of him at the time, and there was no guessing his purpose or direction, for more often than not he seemed a man of will over sense.

'Earl was a fighter,' Reilly said that day in our kitchen, the day of the funeral. He glanced at my mother. She didn't move much, but her eyes and the way she glanced back was permission for him to continue.

'Earl and Kempner went up beyond Race Pond, over to Hickox in Brantley County. Went up there to see a man called Einhorn if I remember right, a man called Einhorn who had a roan for sale. Stopped in a place on the way just to take a drink, and while they were resting a brute of a character came in and started up hollering like a banshee in a warbonnet. Upsetting folk he was, upsetting them and getting people riled and ornery, and Earl suggested the man take his business outside and into the trees where no-one could hear him.'

Reilly looked once more at my mother, and then at me. I didn't move, wanted to hear what my father had done to calm this brute of a character near Hickox in Brantley County. My mother didn't raise her hand, nor her voice, and Reilly smiled.

'Cut a long story down to size, this brute tried to level Earl with a roundhouse. Earl sidestepped and sent the man flying out through the doorway into the dirt. Went after him, tried to talk some sense into the devil, but the man had a fighting

11

heart and a fighting head and there was no reasoning with him. Kempner went out there just as the man came up again and went for Earl with a plank of wood. Earl was like one of these Barnum & Bailey Chinese acrobats, dancing back and around, fists like pistons, and one of those pistons just connected with the big man's nose, and you could hear the bone break in a dozen places. Blood was like a waterfall, man's shirt was soaked, kneeling there in the dirt and howling like a stuck pig.'

Reilly Hawkins leaned back and smiled. 'Heard that the old boy's nose never did stop bleeding . . . just kept on running 'til he was all emptied out—'

'Reilly Hawkins,' my mother said. 'That was never a true story and you know it.'

Hawkins looked sheepish. 'No disrespect, ma'am,' he said, and bowed his head deferentially. 'I wouldn't want to be upsetting you on such a day.'

'Only thing that ever upsets me is untruths and half-truths and outright lies, Reilly Hawkins. You're here to see my husband away to the Lord, and I'd be obliged if you'd mind your language, your manners, and keep a truthful tongue in your head, especially in front of the boy.' She looked over at me. I sat there wide-eyed and wondering, wanting to know all the more gory details regarding my father: a man who could right-hook a brute's nose and deliver death by exsanguination.

Later I would remember my father's burial. Remember that day in Augusta Falls, Charlton County – some antebellum outgrowth bordering the Okefenokee River – remember an acreage that was more swamp than earth; the way the land just sucked everything into itself, ever-hungry, never satiated. That swollen land inhaled my father, and I watched him go; I all of eleven years old, he no more than thirty-seven, me and my mother standing with a group of uneducated and sympathetic farmers from the four corners of the world, jacket sleeves to their knuckles, rough flannel trousers that evidenced inches of worn-out sock. Rubes perhaps, more often uncouth than mannered, but robust of heart, hale and generous. My mother held my hand tighter than was comfortable, but I said nothing and I did not withdraw. I was her first and only child, because – if stories were true, and I had no reason to doubt them – I had been a difficult child, resistant to ejection, and the strain of my birth had ruined the internal contraptions that would have enabled a larger family.

'Just you and me, Joseph,' she later whispered. The people had gone – Kruger and Reilly Hawkins, others with familiar faces and uncertain names – and we stood side by side looking out from the front door of our house, a house raised by hand from sweat and good timber. 'Just you and me from now on,' she said once more, and then we turned inside and closed the door for the night.

Later, lying in my bed, sleep evading me, I thought of the feather. Perhaps, I thought, there were angels who delivered and angels who took away.

Gunther Kruger, a man who would become more evident in my life as the days went on – he told me that Man came from the earth, that if he didn't return there would be some universal imbalance. Reilly Hawkins said that Gunther was a German, and Germans were incapable of seeing the bigger picture. He said that people were spirits.

'Spirits?' I asked him. 'You mean like ghosts?'

Reilly smiled, shook his head. 'No, Joseph,' he whispered. 'Not like ghosts . . . more like angels.'

'So my father has become an angel?'

For a moment he said nothing, leaning his head to one side with a strange squint in his eye. 'Your father, an angel?' he said, and he smiled awkwardly, like a muscle had tensed in the side of his face and would not so easily release. 'Maybe one day . . . figure he has some work to do, but yes, maybe one day he'll be an angel.'